LITTLE,
BROWN
175
LB
YEARS
LARGE
PRINT

Also by Tom Wolfe

The Kandy-Kolored Tangerine-Flake Streamline Baby
The Pump House Gang
The Electric Kool-Aid Acid Test
Radical Chic & Mau-Mauing the Flak Catchers
The Painted Word
Mauve Gloves & Madmen, Clutter & Vine
The Right Stuff
In Our Time
From Bauhaus to Our House
The Bonfire of the Vanities
A Man in Full
Hooking Up
I Am Charlotte Simmons

BACK TO BLOOD

A Novel

Tom Wolfe

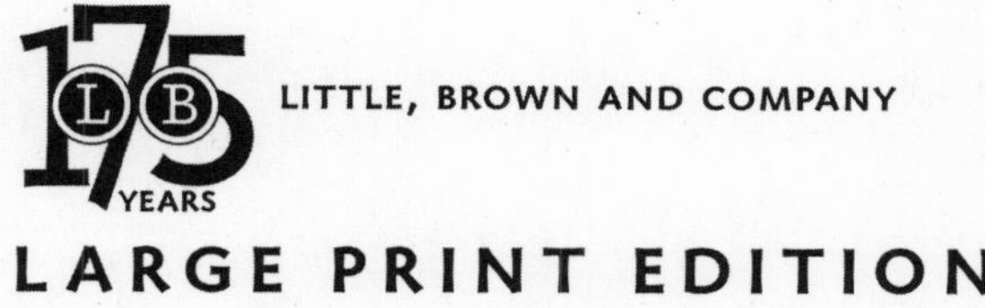

LITTLE, BROWN AND COMPANY

LARGE PRINT EDITION

The characters and events in this book are fictitious. Any similarity to real persons, living or dead, is coincidental and not intended by the author.

Little, Brown and Company
Hachette Book Group
237 Park Avenue, New York, NY 10017
littlebrown.com

First Edition: October 2012

Little, Brown and Company is a division of Hachette Book Group, Inc., and is celebrating its 175th anniversary in 2012. The Little, Brown name and logo are trademarks of Hachette Book Group, Inc.

Library of Congress Cataloging-in-Publication Data
Wolfe, Tom.
Back to blood : a novel / Tom Wolfe. — 1st ed.
p. cm.
ISBN 978-0-316-03631-3 (hc) / 978-0-316-22424-6 (large print) / 978-0-316-22179-5 (international)
1. Emigration and immigration — Fiction. 2. Miami (Fla.) — Fiction. I. Title.
PS3573.O526B33 2012
813'.54 — dc23 2012019545

10 9 8 7 6 5 4 3 2 1

RRD-C

Printed in the United States of America

To

SHEILA

AND TO THE MEMORY OF

ANGEL CALZADILLA

Acknowledgments

The story before you leans heavily upon the generosity of Miami mayor **Manny Diaz,** who introduced the writer to a whole hall full of people on Day One... Chief of Police **John Timoney,** born in Dublin, the consummate Irish Cop in the history of New York, Philadelphia, and Miami, sent him off on a Miami Marine Patrol Safe Boat run right away, then took the covers off an otherwise invisible Miami complete with *aperçus*. *Aperçus* this Irish cop knows. After all, on the night shift he's a Dostoyevsky scholar... **Oscar and Cecile Betancourt Corral,** two hard-charging Miami journalists, gave him the *come-on-down* wave in the first place—then confronted anyone, anywhere, anytime (with the deft assistance of **Mariana Betancourt**)... **Augusto Lopez and Suzanne Stewart** introduced him to the great

Haitian anthropologist **Louis Herns Marcelin**... **Barth Green,** the famous neurosurgeon who devotes much of his time to Haitians in Haiti, led him to Little Haiti in Miami... and to his colleague **Roberto Heros**... **Paul George,** the historian, took him on his much-heralded grand tour... **Katrin Theodoli,** Miami's maker of yachts that look like X-15s and don't so much set sail as lift off, put him on the maiden liftoff of her latest looks-like-a-rocket yacht... **Lee Zara** told him some stories... and they turned out to be true!... Teacher **Maria Goldstein** enabled him to get the inside story of one of the wildest incidents in the history of public education in Miami... **Elizabeth Thompson,** the painter, knew things about the Lives of the Artists in Miami he couldn't have done without... It wasn't part of the job description, but **Christina Verigan** turned out to be a medium, a mind reader, a scholar, and a teacher... Not to mention **Herbert Rosenfeld,** ace Miami social geographer... **Daphne Angulo,** peerless portraitist of Young Miami from high-class to Low-Rent... **Joey and Thea Goldman,** developers and engines of the Wynwood art district, Miami's equivalent of New York's Chelsea... **Ann Louise Bardach,** *the* authority for anything concerning Cuba *fidelista* and the Havana-Miami nexus today... as well as **Peter Smolyanski, Ken Treister, Jim Trotter, Mischa, Cadillac, Bob Adelman,**

Javier Perez, Janet Ney, George Gomez, Robert Gewanter, Larry Pierre, Counselor Eddie Hayes, Alberto Mesa, and Gene Tinney...and one other guardian angel of the new in town. You know who you are.

Contents

BACK TO BLOOD

Prologue

We een Mee-*AH*-mee Now

You...

You...

You... edit my life... You are my wife, my Mac the Knife—the witticism here being that he may edit one of the half-dozen-or-so most important newspapers in the United States, the *Miami Herald,* but she is the one who edits *him. She*... edits... *him.* Last week he totally forgot to call the dean, the one with the rehabilitated harelip, at their son Fiver's boarding school, Hotchkiss, and Mac, his wife, his Mac the Knife, was justifiably put out about it... but then he had sort-of-sung this little rhyme of his to the tune of "You Light Up My Life." *You... edit my life... You are my wife, my Mac the Knife*—and it made her smile in spite of herself, and the smile dissolved the mood, which was *I'm fed up with you and your trifling ways.*

Could it possibly work again—now? Did he dare give it another shot?

At the moment Mac was in command, behind the wheel of her beloved and ludicrously cramped brand-new Mitsubishi Green Elf hybrid, a chic and morally enlightened vehicle just now, trolling the solid rows of cars parked side by side, wing-mirror to wing-mirror, out back of this month's Miami nightspot of the century, Balzac's, just off Mary Brickell Village, vainly hunting for a space. *She* was driving *her* car. She was put out this time—yes, justifiably once more—because this time his trifling ways had made them terribly late leaving for Balzac's, and so she insisted on driving to that coolest of hot spots in her Green Elf. If *he* drove his BMW, they would *never* get there, because he was such a slow and maddeningly cautious driver . . . and he wondered if she really meant timid and unmanly. In any case, she took over the man's role, and the Elf flew to Balzac's like a bat, and here they were, and Mac was not happy.

Ten feet above the restaurant's entrance was a huge Lexan disc, six feet in diameter and eighteen inches thick, embedded with a bust of Honoré de Balzac "appropriated"—as the artists today call artistic theft—from the famous daguerreotype by the one-name photographer Nadar. Balzac's eyes had been turned to look straight into the customer's and his lips had been turned up at the corners to create a big smile, but the "appropriator" was a talented sculptor, and a light from within suffused the enormous slab of Lexan with a golden glow, and *tout le monde* loved it. The light here in the parking lot, however, was miserable. Industrial lamps high up on stanchions created a dim electro-twilight and turned the palm tree fronds pus-color yellow. "Pus-color yellow"—and there you had it. Ed was feeling down, down, down . . . sitting belted into the passenger seat, which he had had to slide all the way back just to get both his long legs inside of this weeny-teeny grassy-greeny Green-proud car of Mac's, the Green Elf. He felt like the doughnut, the toy-sized emergency spare wheel the Elf carried.

Mac, a big girl, had just turned forty. She was a big girl when he met her eighteen years ago at Yale . . . big bones, wide shoulders, tall, five-ten, in fact . . . lean, lithe, strong, an athlete and a half . . . sunny, blond, full of life . . . Stunning! Absolutely gorgeous, this big girl of his! In the cohort of gorgeous girls, however, the big girls are the first to cross that invisible boundary beyond which the best they can hope for is "a very handsome woman" or "quite striking, really." Mac, his wife, his Mac the Knife, had crossed that line.

She sighed a sigh so deep, she ended up expelling air between her teeth. "You'd think they'd have parking valets at a restaurant like this. They *charge* enough."

"That's true," he said. "You're right. Joe's Stone Crab, Azul, Caffe Abbracci—and what's that restaurant at the Setai? They all have valet parking. You're absolutely right." *Your worldview is my Weltanschauung. How about if we talk about restaurants?*

A pause. "I hope you know we're *very late,* Ed. It's eight-twenty. So we're already twenty minutes late and we haven't found a place to park and we've got six people in there waiting for us—"

"Well, I don't know what else—I did call Christian—"

"—and you're supposed to be the host. Do you realize that? Has that registered with you at all?"

"Well, I called Christian and told him they should order some drinks. You can be sure Christian won't object to that, and Marietta won't, either. Marietta and her *cocktails.* I don't even know anybody else who *orders* cocktails." *Or how about a little* obiter dictum *riff on cocktails or Marietta, either one or both?*

"All the same—it's just not *nice,* keeping everybody waiting like this. I mean really—I'm serious, Ed. This is so *trifling,* I just can't stand it."

Now! This was his chance! This was the crack in the wall of words he was waiting for! An opening! It's risky, but—and almost in tune and on key he sing-songs,

"You...

"You...

"*You*... edit my life... *You* are my wife, my Mac the Knife..."

She began shaking her head from side to side. "It doesn't seem to do me much good, does it?"... Never mind! What was that creeping so slyly upon her lips? Was it a *smile,* a small, reluctant smile? Yes! *I'm fed up with you* immediately began to dissolve once more.

They were halfway down the parking lane when two figures appeared in the headlights, walking toward the Elf and Balzac's—two girls, dark haired, chattering away, apparently having just parked their car. They couldn't have been more than nineteen or twenty. The girls and the trolling Elf drew close rapidly. The girls were wearing denim shorts with the belt lines down perilously close to the mons veneris and the pants legs cut off up to... *here*... practically up to the hip socket, and left frayed. Their young legs looked model-girl long, since they also wore gleaming heels at least six inches high. The heels seemed to be made of Lucite or something. They lit up a brilliant translucent gold when light hit them. The two girls' eyes were so heavily mascara'd they appeared to be floating in four black pools.

"Oh, *that's* attractive," Mac muttered.

Ed couldn't take his eyes off them. They were *Latinas*—although he couldn't have explained why he knew that any more than he knew that *Latina* and

Latino were Spanish words that existed only in America. This pair of Latinas—yes, they were trashy, all right, but Mac's irony couldn't alter the truth. Attractive? "Attractive" barely began to describe what he felt! Such nice tender long legs the two girls had! Such short little short-shorts! So short, they could shed them *just like that.* In an instant they could lay bare their juicy little loins and perfect little cupcake bottoms... for *him!* And that was obviously what they wanted! He could feel the tumescence men live for welling up beneath his Jockey tighty-whiteys! Oh, ineffable dirty girls!

As Mac trolled past them, one of the dirty girls pointed at the Green Elf, and both started laughing. Laughing, eh? Apparently they had no appreciation of how upscale Green was... or how hip the Elf was, or how cool. Even less could they conceive of the Elf, fully loaded, as it was, with Green accessories and various esoteric environmental meters, plus ProtexDeer radar—they couldn't conceive of this little elf of a car costing $135,000. He'd give anything to know what they were saying. But here within the Elf's cocoon of Thermo-insulated Lexan glass windows, Fibreglas doors and panels, and evaporation-ambient recyclical air-conditioning, one couldn't begin to hear anything outside. Were they even speaking English? Their lips weren't moving the way lips move when people are speaking English, the great audiovisionary linguist decided. They had to be Latin. Oh, ineffable Latin dirty girls!

"Dear God," said Mac. "Where on earth do you suppose they get those heels that *light up* like that?" An ordinary conversational voice! No longer put out. The spell was broken! "I saw these weird sticks of light all over the place when we drove by Mary Brickell Village," she went on. "I had no idea what they were. The place looked like a *carnival,* all those garish lights in the background and all the little half-naked *party girls* teetering around on their *heels*... Do you suppose it's a Cuban thing?"

"I don't know," said Ed. Only that—because he had his head twisted around as far as it would go, so he could get one last look at them from behind. Perfect little cupcakes! He could just *see* the lubricants and spirochetes oozing into the crotches of their short short-shorts! Short short short-shorts! Sex! Sex! Sex! Sex! There it was, sex in Miami, up on golden Lucite thrones!

"Well," said Mac, "all I can say is that Mary Brickell must be writing a letter to the editor in her grave."

"Hey, I like that, Mac. Did I ever tell you you're pretty witty when you feel like it?"

"No. Probably just slipped your mind."

"Well, you are! 'Writing a letter to the editor in her grave'! I'm telling you. I'd hell of a lot rather get a letter from Mary Brickell from six feet under than from those maniacs I get letters from...walking around foaming at the mouth." He manufactured a laugh. "That's very funny, Mac." *Wit. Good subject! Excellent. Or hey, let's talk about Mary Brickell, Mary Brickell Village, letters to the editor, little sluts on Lucite, any damn thing, so long as it's not* I'm fed up.

As if reading his mind, Mac twisted one side of her mouth into a dubious smile—but a smile, nevertheless, thank God—and said, "But *really,* Ed, being *this* late, making them all wait, it's really *so-o-o-o* bad. It's not nice and it's not *right.* It's so *trifling.* It's—" she paused, "it's—it's—it's downright *shiftless.*"

Oh ho! *Trifling,* is it? Godalmighty, and *shiftless,* too! For the first time on this whole gloomy excursion Ed felt like laughing. These were two of Mac's White Anglo-Saxon Protestant words. In all of Miami-Dade County, all of Greater Miami, very much including Miami Beach, only members of the shrinking and endangered little tribe they both belonged to, the White Anglo-Saxon Protestants, used the terms *trifling* and *shiftless* or had a clue what they actually meant. Yes, he, too, was a member of that dying genus, the White Anglo-Saxon Protestant, but it was Mac who truly embraced the faith. Not the Protestant *religious* faith, needless to say. Nobody on the East or the West Coast of the United States who aspired to even entry-level sophistication was any longer religious, certainly not anyone who had graduated from Yale, the way he and Mac had. No, Mac was an exemplar of the genus WASP in a moral and cultural sense. She was the WASP purist who couldn't abide idleness and indolence, which were stage one of trifling and shiftless. Idleness and indolence didn't represent mere wastefulness or poor judgment. They were immoral. They were sloth. They were a sin against the self. She couldn't stand just lolling about in the sun, for example. At the beach, if there was nothing better to do, she would organize speed walks. Everybody! Get up! Let's go! We're going to walk five miles in one hour on the beach, on the *sand!* Now, that was an accomplishment! In short, if Plato ever persuaded Zeus—Plato professed to believe in Zeus—to reincarnate him so that he might return to earth to find the ideal-typical White Anglo-Saxon Protestant woman, he would come here to Miami and pick Mac.

On paper, Ed was an ideal-typical member of the breed himself. Hotchkiss, Yale... tall, six-three, slender in a gangly way... light-brown hair, thick but shot through with glints of gray... looked like Donegal tweed, his hair did... and of course there was the name, his last name, which was Topping. He himself realized that Edward T. Topping IV was White Anglo-Saxon Protestant to the maximum, to the point of satire. Not even those incomparable nobs of snobbery, the British, went in for all the IIIs, IVs, Vs, and the occasional VI you came across in the United

States. That was why everybody began to call their son, Eddie, "Fiver." His full name was Edward T. Topping V. Five was still pretty rare. *Every* American with III or higher after his name was a White Anglo-Saxon Protestant or had parents who desperately wished he were.

But Jesus Christ, what was some White Anglo-Saxon Protestant, some last lost soul of a dying genus, doing editing the *Miami Herald* with a name like Edward T. Topping IV? He had taken on the job without a clue. When the Loop Syndicate bought the *Herald* from the McClatchy Company and suddenly promoted him from editor of the editorial page at the *Chicago Sun-Times* to editor in chief of the *Herald,* he had only one question. How big a splash would this make in the Yale alumni magazine? That was the only thing that took hold in the left hemisphere of his brain. Oh, they, the Loop Syndicate corporate research department, tried to brief him. They tried. But somehow all the things they tried to tell him about the situation in Miami wafted across his brain's Broca's and Wernicke's areas... and dissipated like a morning mist. Was Miami the only city in the world where more than one half of all citizens were recent immigrants, meaning within the past fifty years?... Hmmmh... Who would have guessed? Did one segment of them, the Cubans, control the city politically—Cuban mayor, Cuban department heads, Cuban cops, Cuban cops, and more Cuban cops, 60 percent of the force Cubans plus 10 percent other Latins, 18 percent American blacks, and only 12 percent Anglos? And didn't the general population break down pretty much the same way?... Hmmmh... interesting, I'm sure... whatever "Anglos" are. And were the Cubans and other Latins so dominant that the *Herald* had to create an entirely separate Spanish edition, *El Nuevo Herald,* with its own Cuban staff or else risk becoming irrelevant?... Hmmmmh... He guessed he already knew that, sort of. And did the American blacks resent the Cuban cops, who might as well have dropped from the sky, they had materialized so suddenly, for the sole purpose of pushing black people around?... Hmmmh... imagine that. And he tried to imagine it... for about five minutes... before that question faded away in light of a query that seemed to indicate that the alumni magazine would be sending its own photographer. And had Haitians been pouring into Miami by the untold tens of thousands, resenting the fact that the American government legalized illegal Cuban immigrants in a snap of the fingers but wouldn't give Haitians a break?... and now Venezuelans, Nicaraguans, Puerto Ricans, Colombians, Russians, Israelis... *Hmmmmh*... really? I'll have to remember that... How does all that go again?...

But the purpose of this briefing, they tried to tell Ed in a subtle way, was not to identify all these tensions and abrasions as potential sources of news in Immigration City. Oh, no. The purpose was to encourage Ed and his staff to "make allowances" and stress Diversity, which was good, even rather noble, and not divisiveness, which we could all do without. The purpose was to indicate to Ed he should be careful not to antagonize any of these factions... He should "maintain an even keel" during this period in which the Syndicate would be going all out to "cyberize" the *Herald* and *El Nuevo Herald,* free them from the gnarled old grip of print and turn them into sleek twenty-first-century online publications. The subtext was: In the meantime, if the mutts start growling, snarling, and disemboweling one another with their teeth—celebrate the Diversity of it all and make sure the teeth get whitened.

That was three years ago. Having never really listened, Ed didn't get it right off the bat. Three months after he was installed as editor, he published part one of an enterprising young reporter's story on the mysterious disappearance of $940,000 the federal government had allotted an anti-Castro organization in Miami in order to initiate unjammable television broadcasts to Cuba. Not a single fact in the story was ever proved wrong or even seriously challenged. But there arose such a howl from "the Cuban community"—whatever that actually consisted of—it rocked Ed clear down to his shoe-shriveled little toes. "The

Cuban community" so overloaded the telephone, e-mail, website, and even fax capacities at the *Herald* and at the Loop Syndicate offices in Chicago, they crashed. Mobs formed outside the *Herald* building for days, shouting, chanting, hooting, bearing placards emblazoned with such sentiments as EXTERMINATE ALL RED RATS... HERALD: FIDEL, SI! PATRIOTISM, NO!... BOYCOTT EL HABANA HERALD... EL MIAMI HEMORROIDES... MIAMI HERALD: CASTRO'S BITCH... An incessant fusillade of insults on Spanish-language radio and television called the *Herald's* new owners, the Loop Syndicate, a virulent "far-Left virus." Under the new commissars the *Herald* itself was now a nest of overtly "radical Left-wing intellectuals," and the new editor, Edward T. Topping IV, was a "Fidelista fellow traveler and dupe." Blogs identified the enterprising young man who wrote the story as "a committed Communist," while handbills and posters went up all over Hialeah and Little Havana providing his picture, home address, and telephone numbers, cell and landlines, under the heading WANTED FOR TREASON. Death threats to him, his wife, and their three children came at him thick as machine-gun fire. The Syndicate's response, if read between the lines, labeled Ed an archaic fool, canceled parts two and three of the series, instructed the fool not to cover the anti-Castro groups at all, so long as the police did not formally charge them with murder, arson, or premeditated armed assault causing significant bodily wounds, and grumbled about the cost of relocating the reporter and his family—*five people*—to a safe house for six weeks and, worse, having to pay for bodyguards.

Thus did Edward T. Topping IV land in the middle of a street brawl on a saucer from Mars.

Meantime, Mac had just trolled the Green Elf to the end of the lane and was heading up the next one. "Oh, *you*—" she exclaimed, stopping short, unsure precisely how to insult the malefactor right in front of her. She found herself on the tail of a big tan Mercedes, that classy European tan, maybe even a Maybach it was, glistening in the diseased electro-twilight . . . trolling the lane looking for a parking place. Obviously, if one came up, the Mercedes would get to it first.

Mac slowed down in order to increase the interval between the two cars. At that very moment they heard a car accelerating insanely fast. By the sound of it, the driver executed the lane-to-lane U-turn so fast, the tires were squealing bloody murder. Now it was coming up behind them at a reckless speed. Its headlights flooded the interior of the Green Elf. "Who are these *idiots?*" said Mac. It was just short of a scream.

She and Ed braced for an impending rear-end crash, but the car braked at the last moment and wound up barely two yards from their back bumper. The driver gunned the engine two or three times for good measure.

"What does this maniac think he's going to do?" said Mac. "There's no room to pass anybody even if I wanted him to!"

Ed twisted around in his seat to get a look at the offender. "Jesus Christ, those lights are bright! All I can make out is it's some kind of convertible. I think the driver is a woman, but I can't really tell."

"Rude *bitch!*" said Mac.

Then—Ed couldn't believe it. Just ahead a pair of red taillights came on in the wall of cars to their right. Then a red diode brake light on the back window! Up so high, the brake light was, the thing must be an Escalade or a Denali, some behemoth of an SUV, in any case. Could it be…someone was actually going to depart those impenetrable walls of sheet metal?

"I don't believe it," said Mac. "I won't believe it until it actually backs out of there. This is a miracle."

She and Ed looked ahead like a single creature to see if the competition, the Mercedes, had spotted the lights and might be backing up to claim the space. Thank God, the Mercedes—no brake lights…just kept on trolling…already near the end of the lane… missed out on the miracle entirely.

Slowly the vehicle was backing out of the wall of cars…a big black thing—huge!…slowly, slowly… It was a monster called the Annihilator. Chrysler had started manufacturing it in 2011 to compete with the Cadillac Escalade.

The harsh light from the car on their tail began to withdraw from the Elf's interior, then subsided sharply. Ed looked back. The driver had put the convertible into reverse and was executing a U-turn. Now Ed could see it more clearly. Yes, the driver was a woman, dark haired, young, by the look of her, and the convertible—godalmighty!—it was a white Ferrari 403!

Ed started pointing toward the rear window and said to Mac, "Your rude bitch is leaving. She's turning around and going back up the lane. And you'll never guess what she's driving . . . a Ferrari 403!"

"Which means . . . ?"

"That's a $275,000 car! It's got close to five hundred horsepower. They race them in Italy. We ran a story about the Ferrari 403."

"Oh, do remind me and I'll be sure to look it up," said Mac. "All I care about the wonder car at this moment is that the rude bitch has gone away in it."

From behind them rose the wonder car's omnivorous growl and then the screaming squeal of the tires as the woman burned rubber in taking off back the way she had come.

Ponderously . . . ponderously . . . the Annihilator backed up. Heavily . . . heftily . . . its gigantic black rear end began to turn toward the Green Elf in order to straighten up before heading down toward the exit. The Annihilator looked like a giant that would eat up

Green Elves like apples or whole-grain protein bars. Evidently sensing precisely that, Mac backed up the Elf to give the giant however much room it needed.

"Did you ever notice," said Ed, "that the people who buy those things never know how to drive them? Everything takes forever. They're not up to handling a truck."

Now, at last, they laid eyes on what had become a very nearly mythical piece of geography... a parking place.

"Okay, big boy," said Mac, referring to the Annihilator, "let's pull ourself together and *move*."

She had no sooner said "move" than the thrashing mechanical roar of a high-speed internal-combustion engine and an angry scream of rubber rose from the exit end of the lane. Godalmighty—it was a vehicle accelerating almost as fast as the Ferrari 403 but coming up the lane the wrong way. With the hulk of the Annihilator blocking their view, Ed and Mac couldn't tell what was going on. In the next split second the acceleration became so loud, the vehicle had to be practically on top of the Annihilator. The Annihilator's horn and brake lights screeeeeam-ing red—shrieeeeeking rubber—the oncoming vehicle veeeeering to keep from hitting the Annihilator head-on—blurrrring white surmounted by tiny blur-rrrring blaaaaack streeeeeaks to Ed's right from in front of the Annihilator—hurtled into the miracle parking slot—laaaaaying down rubber as it braked to a stop right in front of Ed's and Mac's eyes.

Shock, bewilderment—and *bango*—their central nervous systems were flooded with... *humiliation*. The white blur was the Ferrari 403. The small black blur was the hair of the rude bitch. It hit home faster than it would take to say it. The moment she realized a parking spot was opening up, the rude bitch had made a U-turn, sped up the lane the wrong way, swung around the walls of cars, sped down the next lane the wrong way, swung around the rows of cars at the exit end, sped up this lane the wrong way, cut in front of the Annihilator, and shot into the parking place. What else was a Ferrari 403 for? And what was a passive do-gooder like the Green Elf to do other than good works for the desperately wounded Planet Earth and take everything else like a man... or an elf?

The Annihilator gave the rude bitch a couple of angry blasts of the horn before heading down the lane and presumably the exit. But Mac remained. She wasn't heading anywhere. She was furious, livid.

"Why, that *bitch!*" she said. "That brazen little bitch!"

With that she drove the Green Elf forward and stopped immediately behind the Ferrari, which had come to rest on the Elf's right.

"What are you doing?" said Ed.

Mac said, "If she thinks she's going to get away

with that, she's got another thought coming. She wants to play games? Okay, let's play."

"Whattaya mean?" said Ed. Mac had a definitely White Anglo-Saxon Protestant set to her jaws. He knew what that meant. It meant that the rude bitch's transgression was not merely bad manners. It was a sinful act.

Ed could feel his heart kicking into higher gear. He was not by nature one for physical confrontations and public exhibitions of anger. Besides that, he was the editor of the *Herald,* the Loop Syndicate's man in Miami. Whatever he got involved in out in public would be magnified a hundred times.

"Whattaya gonna do?" He was aware that his voice was suddenly terribly hoarse. "I'm not sure she's worth all—" He couldn't figure out how to complete the sentence.

Mac wasn't paying any attention to him anyway. Her eyes were pinned on the rude bitch, who was just getting out of the convertible. They could see only her back. But as soon as she started to turn around, Mac hit the button that opened the passenger-side window and leaned across Ed and lowered her head so she could look the woman squarely in the face.

As soon as the woman turned about fully she took a couple of steps and stopped when she realized the Elf was all but penning her in the wall of cars. And then Mac let her have it:

"YOU SAW ME WAITING FOR THAT SPACE, AND DON'T YOU STAND THERE LYING AND SAYING YOU DIDN'T! WHERE DID YOU—"

Ed had heard Mac yell before but never this loud or with such fury. It frightened him. The way she leaned over toward the window, her face was only inches from his. The Big Girl had gone into the full WASP righteous attack mode, and there would be hell to pay for one and all.

"—LEARN YOUR MANNERS FROM, THE HURRICANE GIRLS?"

The Hurricane Girls were a notorious gang of mostly black girls, formed in a tent city for refugees from Hurricane Fiona, who had gone on a rampage of assaults and robberies two years ago. That was all he needed. "*Herald* Editor's Wife in Racist Rant"—he could write the whole thing himself—and in that same moment he realized the rude bitch hadn't come from a girls' gang or anything close to it. She was a beautiful young woman, and not just beautiful but stylish, chic, and rich, if Ed knew anything about it. She had shiny black hair parted in the middle... miles of it... cascading straight down before going wild in great wavy spumes where it hit her shoulders... and a bit of a fine gold chain about her neck... whose teardrop pendant brought Ed's eyes right down into the cleavage of two young breasts yearning to burst free from the little sleeveless white silk dress that constrained them, up to a point, and then gave up and ended halfway down her thigh and didn't even try to inhibit a pair of perfectly formed, perfectly suntanned legs looking a lubricious mile long atop a pair of white crocodile pumps whose to-the-max heels lifted her heavenly while Venus moaned and sighed. She was carrying a small ostrich leather clutch. Ed couldn't have given any of this stuff a name, but he knew from the magazines that it was all à la mode right now and very expensive.

"—OR HAVE ANY IDEA WHAT A CHEAP LITTLE *THIEF* YOU ARE?"

Ed said, sotto voce, "Come on, Mac. Let's just forget about it. It's not worth the trouble." What he meant was "Somebody might realize who I am." As far as Mac was concerned, however, he wasn't even there. There was only herself and the rude bitch who had wronged her.

Under Mac's onslaught the beautiful rude bitch didn't recoil an inch or show so much as a twitch of intimidation. She stood there with her hips cocked, the knuckles of one hand resting on the higher hip and her cocked elbow flung out as far as it would go, plus a suggestion of a smile on her lips, a condescending stance that as much as said, "Look, I'm in a hurry and you're in my way. Kindly bring your little tsunami in a teacup to an end—now."

"—JUST GIVE ME ONE REASON—"

Far from shrinking from Mac's attack, the beautiful rude bitch came two steps closer to the Green Elf, leaned over to look Mac in the eye, and said, in English without raising her voice, "Why you speet when you talk?"

"WHAT ARE YOU SAYING?"

The rude bitch took yet another step forward. Now she was within three feet of the Elf—and Ed's passenger seat. In a louder voice this time and still drilling her eyes into Mac's, she said, "*¡Mírala!* Granny, you speet when you talk, *como una perra sata rabiosa con la boca llena de espuma,** and it's getting all over *tu pendejocito allí.*† *¡Tremenda pareja que hacen, pendeja!*"‡ Now she was as angry as Mac and beginning to show it.

Mac didn't know a word of Spanish, but even the English part coming out of the rude bitch's sardonic face was utterly insulting.

"DON'T YOU *DARE* TALK TO ME LIKE THAT! WHO DO YOU THINK YOU ARE? A NASTY LITTLE MONKEY IS *WHAT* YOU ARE!"

---

* "Look at her! Granny, you spit when you talk, like a rabid mutt foaming at the mouth."

† "your dumb ass of a man"; literally, "your little pubic hair."

‡ "What a pair you make, you stupid bitch!"

The rude bitch snapped back, *"NO ME JODAS MAS CON TUS GRITICOS! VETE A LA MIERDA, PUTA!"**

The raised voices of the two women, the insults whizzing like bullets past Ed's pale, blanched face from both directions, petrify him. The furious Latina looks past him as if he's nothing but thin air, a nullity. This humiliates him. Obviously he should rouse his manhood and put an end to the whole confrontation. But he doesn't dare say, "Both of you! Stop!" He doesn't dare indicate to Mac that she is in any way in the wrong, behaving like this. He knows that all too well. She would cut him to ribbons for the rest of the night, including right in front of their friends, whom they are about to join inside, and, as usual, he wouldn't know what to say. He'd just take it like a man, so to speak. Nor does he dare remonstrate with the Latin woman. How would that look? The editor of the *Miami Herald* dressing down, thereby insulting, some fashionable Cuban señora! That's half the Spanish he can utter, *"señora."* The other half is *"Sí, cómo no?"* Besides, Latins are quick-tempered, especially Cubans, if she's Cuban. And what Latin woman in Miami could be this obviously rich other than a Cuban? For all he knows, she is about to meet some hotheaded husband or boyfriend in the restaurant,

---

* "Don't fuck with me with your little fits. Go to hell, bitch!"

the sort who would demand satisfaction and thereby humiliate him even more. His thoughts whirl and whirl. The bullets continue to whiz back and forth. His mouth and throat are dry as chalk. Why can't they just stop!

Stop? Ha! Mac starts screaming, "SPEAK ENGLISH, YOU PATHETIC IDIOT! YOU'RE IN AMERICA NOW! SPEAK ENGLISH!"

For a second the rude bitch seems to understand and goes silent. Then, she reverts to her calm, haughty self and with a mocking smile says rather softly, "No, *mía malhablada puta gorda,** we een *Mee-ah-mee* now! *You* een Mee-ah-mee now!"

Mac is stunned. For a few seconds she's unable to speak. Finally she manages to come up with a single strangled hiss: *"Rude bitch!"*—whereupon she gunned the Green Elf and got out of there with such a lurch, the Elf squealed.

Mac's lips were compressed to the point where the flesh above and below them ballooned out. She was shaking her head... not in anger, it seemed to Ed, but something far worse: humiliation. She wouldn't even look at him. Her thoughts were sealed in a capsule of what had just happened. ::::::You win, rude bitch.::::::

---

* "No, my fat, dirty-talking whore..."

* * *

Balzac's was packed. The babble of the place had already risen to the maximum we're-out-at-a-smart-restaurant-and-isn't-it-great level... but Mac insisted on recounting the whole thing *loudly,* loud enough for all six of their friends to hear it, she was so enraged... Christian Cox, Marietta Stillman... Christian's live-in girlfriend, Jill-love-Christian... Marietta's husband, Thatcher... Chauncey and Isabel Johnson... six Anglos, *real* Anglos like themselves, American Protestant Anglos—but *Please, God!* Ed's eyes were darting frantically this way and that. Those could be Cubans there at the next table. God knows they've got the money! Oh, yes! *There!* And the waiters? Look like Latinos, too... *bound* to be Latinos... He's not listening to Mac's rant any longer. A phrase pops into his head from out of nowhere. "Everybody... all of them... it's *back to blood!* Religion is dying... but everybody still has to believe in *something.* It would be intolerable—you couldn't stand it—to finally have to say to yourself, 'Why keep pretending? I'm nothing but a random atom inside a supercollider known as the universe.' But *believing in* by definition means *blindly, irrationally,* doesn't it. So, my people, that leaves only our blood, the bloodlines that course through our very bodies, to unite us. *'La Raza!'* as the

Puerto Ricans cry out. *'The Race!'* cries the whole world. All people, all people everywhere, have but one last thing on their minds—*Back to blood!*" All people, everywhere, you have no choice but—*Back to blood!*

1

The Man on the Mast

SMACK the Safe Boat bounces airborne comes down again *SMACK* on another swell in the bay bounces up again comes down *SMACK* on another swell and *SMACK* bounces airborne with emergency horns police Crazy Lights exploding *SMACK* in a demented sequence on the roof *SMACK* but Officer Nestor Camacho's fellow *SMACK* cops here in the cockpit the two fat *SMACK americanos* they love this stuff love it *love* driving the boat *SMACK* throttle wide open forty-five miles an hour against the wind *SMACK* bouncing *bouncing* its shallow aluminum hull *SMACK* from swell *SMACK* to swell *SMACK* to swell *SMACK* toward the mouth of Biscayne Bay to "see about the man on top of the mast" *SMACK* "up near the Rickenbacker Causeway"—

—*SMACK* the two *americanos* sat at the helm on

seats with built-in shock absorbers so they could take all the *SMACK* bouncing while Nestor, who was twenty-five, with four years as a cop but *SMACK* newly promoted to Marine Patrol, an elite *SMACK* unit, and still on probation, was *SMACK* relegated to the space behind them where he *SMACK* had to steady himself against something called a leaning poleand*SMACK*usehisownlegsastheshockabsorbers—

A *leaning pole!* This boat, the Safe Boat, was the opposite of streamlined. It was *uuuuuuug-lyyy*...a twenty-five-foot-long rubbery foam-filled pancake for a deck with an old tugboat shack stuck on top of it as a cockpit. But its two engines had 1500 horsepower, and the thing went across the water like a shot. It was unsinkable unless you took a cannon and blew twelve-inch-diameter holes, a lot of them, through the foam filling. In tests, nobody had even been able to tip one over, no matter what insane maneuver he tried. It was built for rescues. And this shack of a cockpit he and the *americanos* were in? It was the Ugly Betty of boatbuilding—but soundproof. Outside, at forty-five miles an hour the Safe Boat was kicking up a regular hurricane of air, water, and internal combustion...while here inside the cockpit you didn't even have to raise your voice...to wonder what sort of nutcase you were in for up on top of a mast near the Rickenbacker Causeway.

A sergeant named McCorkle with sandy-colored

hair and blue eyes was at the wheel, and his second-in-command, Officer Kite, with blondish-brown hair and blue eyes, was in the seat next to him. Both of them were real sides of beef with fat on them—and school-of-blond hair!—and blue eyes! *The blond ones!—with blue eyes!*—they made you think *americanos* in spite of yourself.

Kite was *SMACK* on the police radio: "Q,S,M"—Miami Police code for "Repeat"—"Negative?" *SMACK* "*Neg*ative? You saying nobody knows what he's doing up there? Guy's up on top of a" *SMACK* "*mast* and he's *yelling,* and nobody knows what" *SMACK* "he's *yelling?* Q,K,T?"—for "Over."

Staticky crackle staticky crackle Radiocom: "Q,L,Y"—for "Roger"—"That's all we got. Four-three's dispatching a" *SMACK* "unit to the causeway. Q,K,T."

Long stupefied *SMACK* silence... "Q,L,Y... Q,R,U... Q,S,L"—for "Out."

Kite just *SMACK* sat there for a moment, holding the microphone in front of his face and squinting at it as if *SMACK* he never saw one before. "They don't know shit, Sarge."

"Who's on Radiocom?"

"I don't know. Some" *SMACK* "Canadian." He paused—

Canadian?

—"I just hope it ain't another" *SMACK* "illegal,

Sarge. Those dumb fucks are so crazy they'll" *SMACK* "kill you without even meaning to. Forget about negotiating, even if you got somebody who can" *SMACK* "speak the fucking language. Forget about saving their fucking lives, as far as" *SMACK* "that goes! Just get ready for some Ultimate Fighting under water with some" *SMACK* "mook who's a mile high on adrenaline. If you wanna know what I think, that's the nastiest" *SMACK* "high there is, Sarge, adrenaline. Some biker on crank—he's nothing compared to one a these scrawny little" *SMACK* "mooks jacked up on adrenaline."

Mooks?

The two *americanos* didn't look at each other when they spoke. They looked straight ahead, eyes pinned on the prospect of some dumb fuck on top of a mast up by the Rickenbacker Causeway.

Out the windshield—which slanted *forward* instead of back—the *opposite* of streamlined—you could see the wind was up and the bay was rough, but otherwise it was a typical Miami day in early September... still summer...not a cloud anywhere...and *Jesus,* it was hot. The sun turned the whole sky into a single gigantic high-blue-domed heat lamp, blindingly bright, exploding bursts of reflection off every shiny curved surface, even the crests of the swells. They had just sped past the marinas at Coconut Grove. The curiously pinkish skyline of Miami was slowly rising at the horizon, scorched in the sunbursts. In strict point of fact, Nestor couldn't really see all that—the pinkish cast, the glare of the sun, the empty blue of the sky, the sunbursts—he just *knew* it was all there. He couldn't really see it, because naturally he had on a pair of sunglasses, not dark but the *darkest,* magno *darkest,* supremo *darkest,* with an imitation gold bar across the top. That was what every cool Cuban cop in Miami wore... $29.95 at CVS... gold bar, baby! Equally cool was the way he kept his head shaved with just a little flat helicopter pad of hair upstairs. Even cooler was his big neck—cooler and not easy to come by. It was now wider than his head and seemed to merge with his trapezius... way out *here.* Wrestler's bridges, baby, and pumping iron! A head harness with weights attached—that'll do the trick! The big neck made a shaved head look like a Turkish wrestler's. Otherwise a shaved head looked like a doorknob. He had been a skinny five-foot-seven kid when he first thought about the police force. Today he was still five-seven, but... in the mirror... five feet and seven inches' worth of big smooth rock formations, real Gibraltars, traps, delts, lats, pecs, biceps, triceps, obliques, abs, glutes, quads—*dense!*—and you want to know what was even better for the upper body than weights? Climbing the fifty-five-foot-high rope at Rodriguez's "Ññññññooooooooooooo!!! Qué Gym!," as everybody called it, without using your legs. You want *dense* biceps and lats—and even pecs?

Nothing like climbing that twenty-five-feet-high rope at Rodriguez's—*dense!*—and defined by the deep dark crevasses each mass of muscle dropped off into at the edges... in the mirror. Around that big neck he had a fine gold chain with a medallion of the cool Santería saint, Barbara, patron saint of artillery and explosives, that rested on his chest below his shirt... *Shirt*... There you had the problem with the Marine Patrol. On street patrol a Cuban cop like him would make sure he got a short-sleeved uniform one size too small that brought out every bulge of every rock formation... especially, in his case, the triceps, the big muscle on the back of the upper arm. He regarded his as the ultimate geological triumph of the triceps... in the mirror. If you were truly cool and Cuban, you had the seat of the uniform trousers taken in—a lot—until from behind you looked like a man wearing a pair of Speedos with long pants legs. That way, you were suave in the eyes of every *jebita* on the street. That was exactly the way he had met Magdalena—*Magdalena!*

Suave he must have looked when he had to prevent this *jebita* from passing the barricade across 16th Avenue at Calle Ocho and she put up this big argument and the anger in her eyes only made him crazier for her—*¡Dios mío!*—and then he smiled at her in a certain way and said *I'd love to let you by—but I'm not going to* and kept on smiling in that certain way and she told him two nights later that when he started smiling she thought she had charmed him into letting her have her way but then he stood her up rigid with *but I'm not going to*—and it turned her on. But suppose he had been wearing *this* uniform that day! Christ, she wouldn't have noticed anything other than he was in her way. This Marine Patrol uniform—all it was, was a baggy white polo shirt and a pair of baggy dark-blue shorts. If only he could shorten the sleeves—but they'd notice immediately. He would become the object of hideous ridicule... What would they start calling him... "Muscles"?... "Mister Universe"?... or just "Uni"?—pronounced "Yoony," which would be even worse. So he was stuck with this... uniform that made you look like a grossly overgrown retarded toddler in the park. Well, at least it didn't look as bad on him as it did on the two fat *americanos* right in front of him. From here, leaning back against the leaning pole, he got all too close a look at them from the rear... disgusting... the way their flab blubbered out into love handles where the polo shirts tucked into the shorts. It was pathetic—and they were supposed to be fit enough to rescue panicked people in the water. For an instant it occurred to him that maybe he had become a body snob, but it was only that, an instant. Man, it was weird enough just going out on a call with nothing but *americanos* around you. This hadn't happened to him even once during his two years on street patrol. There were so few of them left on the police force. It was double weird being both outnumbered and *outranked* by a couple of minorities like this. He had nothing against minorities... the *americanos*... the blacks... the Haitians... the Nicas, as everybody called Nicaraguans. He felt very broad-minded, a nobly tolerant young man of the times. *Americano* was the name you used with other Cubans. For public consumption, you said Anglo. Curious word, *Anglo.* There was something... *off*... about it. It referred to white people of European ancestry. Was there something a little defensive about it, maybe? It wasn't all that long ago that the... Anglos... divided the world up into four colors, the white, the black, the yellow—and everyone left over was brown. They lumped all Latinos together as brown!—when here in Miami, in any case, most Latinos, or a huge percentage, a lot anyway, were as white as any Anglo, except for the blond hair... That was what Mexicans were thinking about when they used the word *gringo:* the people with the blond hair. Cubans used it for comic effect now and then. A car full of Cuban boys see a pretty blond girl on a sidewalk in Hialeah, and one of them sings out, "*¡Ayyyyy, la gringa!*"

Latino—there was something *off* about that word, too. It existed only in the United States. Also *Hispanic.* Who the hell else called people Hispanics?

Why? But the whole thing began to make his head hurt—

McCorkle's voice! jerked him back into the here and now. The sandy-haired sergeant, McCorkle, was saying something to his blondish second in command, Kite:

"This don't sound like an illegal" *SMACK* "to me. I never heard of an illegal coming in on a boat with a" *SMACK* "mast. You know? They're too slow; they're too obvious... Besides, you take Haiti... or" *SMACK* "Cuba. There ain't no more boats with masts left in places like that." He turned his head to the side and tilted it *SMACK* back to speak over his shoulder. "Right, Nestor?" Nes-*ter.* "They don't even *have*" *SMACK* "masts in Cuba. Right? Say 'Right,' Nestor." Nes-*ter.*

This annoyed Nestor—no, *infuriated* him. His name was Nestor, not Nes-*ter,* the way *americanos* pronounced it. Nes-*ter*... made him sound like he was sitting in a nest with his neck stretched straight up in the air and his mouth wide open waiting for Mommy to fly home and drop a worm down his gullet. These morons obviously never heard of King Nestor, hero of the Trojan War. Yet this idiot sergeant thinks it's funny to treat him like some helpless six-year-old with this *Right? Say "Right," Nestor* crack. At the same time, the crack *assumed* a second-generation Cuban like him, born in the United States, would be so absorbed with Cuba that he might in some stupid way actually *care* about masts or no masts on Cuban boats. It showed what they actually *thought* about Cubans. ::::::They still think we're *aliens.* After all this time they still don't get it, do they. If there's any aliens in Miami now, it's *them.* You blond retards—with your "Nes-*ter!*"::::::

"How would *I* know?" he hears himself saying. "I" *SMACK* "never set *foot* in Cuba. I never laid *eyes* on" *SMACK* "Cuba."

Wait a minute! Bango—right away he knows that came out wrong, knows it before he can sort it out rationally, knows that "How would *I* know?" is hanging in the air like some putrid gas. The way he hit the *"I"*...and the *"foot"* and the *"eyes"!* So dismissive! Such a rebuke! Impudent and a half! Might as well have called him a stupid blond retard straight out! Hadn't even *tried* to hide the anger he felt! If only he had added a "Sarge"! "How would *I* know, *Sarge*" might have given him a fighting chance! McCorkle is a minority, but he's still a sergeant! All he has to do is file one bad report—and Nestor Camacho flunks probation and gets blown out of the water! Quick! Throw in a *Sarge* right now! Make it two—*Sarge* and *Sarge!* But it's hopeless—too late—three or four interminable seconds have gone by. All he can do is brace himself against the leaning pole and hold his breath—

Not a sound from the two blond *americanos*. Nestor becomes terribly conscious of his heart *SMACK* hammering away beneath the polo shirt. Idly idly idly so what so what so what he is aware of the skyline of *SMACK* downtown Miami rising still higher as the Safe Boat speeds closer, coming upon more and more "lulus," as the cops call pleasure boats owned and aimlessly navigated by clueless civilians sunbathing *SMACK* too fat too bare too slathered with thirty-level sunblock *SMACK* ointments, and passes them so fast, the lulus seem to *whip* by them *SMACK* backward—

Jesus Christ! Nestor practically jumps. From here right *SMACK* behind the man's chair he can see Sergeant McCorkle's thumb rising above his shoulder. Now he's *SMACK* motioning it back toward Nestor without moving his head—he keeps looking forward—and saying to Officer Kite, "He wouldn't" *SMACK* "know, Lonnie. He never fucking set foot in Cuba. He never fucking laid eyes on it." *SMACK* "He just... wouldn't... fucking... know."

Lonnie Kite doesn't respond. He's probably like Nestor himself... waiting to see where this is all leading... while downtown Miami rises... rises. There's the *SMACK* Rickenbacker Causeway itself, crossing the bay from the city over to Key Biscayne.

"Okay, Nes-*ter*," McCorkle says, still giving Nestor only the back of his head, "you wouldn't know that. Then" *SMACK* "tell us what you *would* know, Nes-*ter*.

How about that? Enlighten us. You *would*" *SMACK* "know *what?*"

Get the Sarge *in right away!* "Come on, Sarge, I didn't" *SMACK* "mean that the way—"

"Would you know what *day* this is?" *SMACK*

"Day?"

"Yeah, Nes-*ter,* this is a particular day. Which particular day is this? Would you know *that?*" *SMACK*

Nestor knew the big fat blond *americano* was fucking with him—and the big fat blond *americano knew* he knew—but he, Nestor, didn't dare say anything indicating that he *did SMACK* know that, because he also knew the big fat sandy-haired *americano* was daring him to say something else *smart* so he could *really* hang him.

Long pause—until Nestor says as *SMACK* simplemindedly as he can: "*Fri*day?"

"That's all it is—*Fri*day? Would you know if it was maybe more than just" *SMACK* "Friday?"

"Sarge, I—"

Sergeant McCorkle's voice runs right over Nestor's: "This is fucking José Martí's fucking birthday," *SMACK* "is what it is, Camacho! Why wouldn't you know *that?*"

Nestor feels his face scalding with anger and humiliation. ::::::*"Fucking José Martí"* he dares say! José Martí is the most revered figure in Cuban history! Our Liberator, our Savior! *"Fucking birthday"*—

filth on top of filth!—and the *Camacho* to make sure Nes-*ter* gets the filth right in the face! And this is *not* Martí's birthday! His birthday is in January—but I don't dare fight back even with that!::::::

Lonnie Kite says, "How did you know that, Sarge?"

"Know what?"

"Know this is" *SMACK* "José Martí's birthday?"

"I pay attention in class."

"Yeah? What class, Sarge?"

"I been" *SMACK* "going to Miami Dade, nights and weekends. I completed both years. I got my certificate."

"Yeah?"

"Oh, yeah," said Sergeant McCorkle. "Now" *SMACK* "I'm applying to EGU. I wanna get a real degree. I ain't planning on making this a career, you know, being a cop. If I was a Canadian, I'd consider it. But I ain't" *SMACK* "a Canadian."

Canadian?

"Look, I don't wanna discourage you, Sarge," said the blondish-brown-haired Officer Kite, "but what they tell me is" *SMACK* "EGU is more than *half* Canadian *itself,* the student body, anyway. I don't know about the" *SMACK* "professors."

Canadian—Canadian!

"Well, it can't be as bad as the Department—" The Sergeant suddenly broke off that line of thought.

He kept his hands on the controls, lowered his head, and thrust his chin forward. "Holy shit! Look" *SMACK* "up there! There's the causeway, and you see up there up top a the bridge?"

Nestor had no idea what he was talking about. Being this far back in the cockpit, he couldn't begin to see the top of the bridge.

At that instant the staticky voice of Radiocom: "Five, one, six, oh, nine—Five, one, six, oh, nine—what is your" *SMACK* "Q,T,H? Need you soonest. Four-three says they got a bunch a *tontos,* they're out a their cars yelling" *SMACK* "at the man on the mast in a disorderly fashion. Traffic on the causeway's" *SMACK* "stopped in both directions. Q,K,T."

Lonnie Kite Q,L,Y'd that for Five, one, six, oh, nine and said, "Q,T,H. Just" *SMACK* "passed Brickell heading straight to the causeway. See the sails, see something on top a the" *SMACK* "mast, see the commotion on the causeway. Be there in, uhhh, sixty" *SMACK* "seconds. Q,K,T."

"Q,L,Y," said Radiocom. "Four-three wants the man down and out a there A, S, A, P."

Canadians! There was no way Canadians made up more than half the student body at EGU—Everglades Global University—but Cubans *did.* So *that* was their not-very-clever little *americano* game! And they were so stupid, they thought it would take a genius to catch on! He ransacked his brain to try to remember how they had used *Canadians* just a few minutes before. And what about *mooks?* Were *they* supposed to be Cubans, too? Latinos? ::::::How much of an insult is it if an *americano* uses *Canadian* to mean *Cuban*...right in your face? *Boiling, boiling, boiling*—but get hold of yourself!:::::: *Cuban? Canadian? Mook?* What did all that matter? What mattered was that the Sergeant felt so insulted, he was now resorting to sarcasm, by the ton, even to vile stuff like "fucking José Martí." And why? To goad him to the point of outright insubordination—and then have him thrown out of this elite unit, the Marine Patrol, and bucked back down to the bottom—or expelled from the force! *Canned! Kicked out!* All it would take would be for him to start an insubordinate confrontation with his commander at a crucial moment of a run—at the moment when the entire department was waiting for them to get some idiot down off the top of a mast in Biscayne Bay! He'd be finished! *Finished*—and with Magdalena, too! *Magdalena!*—already acting odd, distant, and now he's a piece of garbage, expelled from the police force, terminally humiliated.

The Sergeant was easing back on the throttle. The *SMACKs* became less violent and less frequent as they closed in on the huge white sailboat. They were approaching it from the rear.

Officer Lonnie Kite leaned down over the instrument panel and began looking upward. "Jesus Christ,

Sarge, those masts—I never saw masts that high in my life. They're tall as the fucking bridge, and the fucking bridge has a mean water level clearance of eighty-fucking-two feet!"

Busy easing the Safe Boat in alongside the sailboat, the Sergeant didn't so much as glance up. "That's a schooner, Lonnie. You heard a the 'tall ships'?"

"Yeah... I think so, Sarge. I guess so."

"They built 'em for speed, back in the nineteenth century. That's why they got masts that tall. That way you get more sail area. Back in the day they used to race out to shipwrecks or incoming cargo ships or whatever to get to the booty sooner. I bet those masts are tall as the boat's long."

"How do you know about all that, about schooners, Sarge? I never seen one around here. Not one."

"I pay attention—"

"—in class," said Lonnie Kite. "Oh yeah, I almost forgot, Sarge." He pointed upward. "I'll be damned. There's the guy! The man on the mast! Up on top of the forward mast! I thought it was a clump a dirty laundry or canvas or something. Look at 'im! He's up as high as the *tontos* on the bridge! And, man, looks like they're yelling back and forth..."

Nestor couldn't see any of it, and none of them could hear what was going on, since the Safe Boat cockpit was soundproof.

The Sergeant had the boat throttled way down in order to sidle up against the schooner. They came to a stop just inches away. "Lonnie," said the Sergeant, "you take the wheel."

When he rose from his seat, he looked at Nestor as if he had forgotten he existed. "Okay, Camacho, do something useful. *Open the fucking hatch.*"

Nestor looked at the Sergeant with abject fear. Inside his skull he said a prayer. ::::::*Please, Almighty God, I beseech thee. Don't let me fuck up.*::::::

The "hatch" was a soundproof double-paned sliding door on the side of the shack that opened onto the deck. Nestor's entire universe suddenly contracted into that door and the Olympics-level test of opening it with maximum strength, maximum speed—while maintaining maximum control... *now! Immediately!*... ::::::*Please, Almighty God, I beseech thee*—here goes—::::::

He did it! He did it! With the fluid power of a tiger he did it!... Did what? Slid it! Slid a sliding door open! Without fucking up!

Outside—all was uproar. The noise came crashing into the sacrosoundless cockpit, the noise and the heat. Christ, it was hot out here on the deck! Scorching! Enervating! It beat you down. It took the wind kicking up the bay to make it bearable. The wind was strong enough to create its own whistling sound and *SLAP* the hull of the schooner with swells and *FLAP* the huge sails, two masts' full of them—*FLAP* them until they blew up into clouds of an unnatural white brilliance—Miami summer sun! Nestor glanced up toward that ball of fire—burning itself up—and even with his supreme darkest sunglasses he didn't try that again—looking up into that hellish heat lamp, which was the entire sky. But that was nothing compared to the roiling *SURF* of human voices. Cries! Exhortations! Imprecations! Ululations! Supplications! Boos! A great bellowing and gnashing of teeth a mile from shore out in the middle of Biscayne Bay!

The Sergeant emerged from the shack without the slightest flick of the eye toward Nestor. But as he disembarked, he made a jerking signal with his hand down by his hip indicating that Nestor should follow him. *Follow* him? Nestor followed him like a dog.

Once the Sergeant and his dog boarded the schooner and were up on the deck—a regular rubber room, this deck was! Passengers, if that was what they were, were hanging over the railing and gesturing and jabbering at Nestor and the Sergeant... *americanos,* the whole bunch... light-brown and blondish hair... half of them, girls—all but stark naked! Wild blond hair! Wisps of thong bikini bottoms that didn't even cover the mons pubis!... Tops consisting of two triangles of cloth that hid the nipples but left the rest of the breasts bulging on either side and beckoning, *Want more?* Nestor didn't. At this moment nothing could have interested him less than making moves on *lubricas americanas*. They disintegrated in his prayers, which boiled down to *Please, Almighty God, I beseech thee, don't let me... fuck up!*

The Sergeant walked straight to the forward mast. Nestor walked straight to the forward mast. The Sergeant looked up. Nestor looked up. The Sergeant saw the roost of the mysterious man atop the mast. Nestor saw the roost of the mysterious man—a silhouette against a killer heat lamp dome, a black lump the equivalent of seven or eight stories above the deck. A regular storm of raw-throated voices was caterwauling down from above amid a cacophony of outraged vehicle horns. The Sergeant looked up again. Nestor looked up again. The two policemen had to cock their necks all the way back to see where the commotion was coming from. Sheer murder, looking up like this to the topmost arch of the bridge...An angry crowd was leaning over the railing, two deep, three deep, God knows how many deep. They were so far up, their heads looked the size of eggs. Even Nestor behind his darkest supremos couldn't stare at them for more than a moment. It was like being in the street at the foot of an eight- or nine-story building with a mob unaccountably yelling at you from a roof set afire by the sun. And up *there!*—practically eye level with the mob, at practically the same height above the deck, was the man. The Sergeant was looking at him from directly below. Nestor was looking at him from directly below. By shielding their eyes with their hands they could see he *did* look like a clump of dirty laundry, just as Lonnie Kite had put it . . . no, he looked worse than that . . . he looked like a clump of filthy, sodden laundry. He was soaking wet. His clothes, his skin, even his black hair—what they could see of it—everything about him was now the same sopping slurry gray-brown color, as if he had just crawled out of an unpumped sump. It didn't help that he jerked his head about spastically as he shouted to the crowd on the bridge and appealed to them by reaching out with his hands contorted, palms up, into the shape of a pair of cups. But how could he stay up there without holding on to the mast? Ahhhhh . . . he had found a little bucket seat—but how did he get up there in the first place?

"Officer! Officer!"

A great lubberly lulu, no more than thirty years old, had planted himself in front of Sergeant McCorkle. He kept jabbing his forefinger up at the man on the mast. There was fear on his face, and he was talking so fast, his words seemed to be leapfrogging one another, falling over one another, tumbling, stumbling, ricocheting, scattering hopelessly: "Gotta get no business here him like down from there, Officer, I never don't know him like saw him before that you know mob up what do they he's so angry there want who'll him attack my boat like that mast alone destroy it cost a fortune you know that's all I need—"

The guy was *soft*—look at him!—but in such a *luxurious* way, was Nestor's immediate verdict. He had full jowls but jowls so smooth and buttery they had reached the level of a perfect flan custard. He had a paunch but a paunch that created a perfect parabola from his sternum to his underbelly, the paunch nonpareil of Idle Youth, created, no doubt, by the dearest, tenderest, tastiest chefs in the world. Over the perfect parabolic arch of a gut was stretched an apple-green shirt, of cotton, yes, but a cotton so fine and so right-out-of-the-box, it had a perfect apple-green sheen—in short, a real pussy, this guy was, a pussy whose words kept coming out of his mouth in a tangle of pussy attitude shot through with fear.

"—killer nutball I'm fucked sue *me!* The liable sucker who gets sued's *me!* Raving maniac never saw before picks *me!*—"

The Sergeant brought both hands up to his chest, palms up and out in the *Whoa, back off* mode. "Slow down! This is your boat?"

"Yes! And I'm the one—"

"Just *hold it.* What's your name?"

"Jonathan. The thing is, like, soon as I—"

"You got a, *like,* last name?"

The great lubberly pussy looked at the Sergeant as

if he, the Sergeant, had lost his mind. Then he said, "Krin?" It sounded like half a question. "K, R, I, N?" Being a member of the first generation that used no last names, he found the notion archaic.

"Okay, Jonathan, whyn't you" — the Sergeant gave his palms three little pumps down toward the deck, as if to say, *Calmly, without getting all excited* — "tell me how he got there."

It seemed that this portly, but perfectly portly, young man had invited his mates to come along for a cruise up Biscayne Bay to the house and marina of a friend on a celebrity-heavy waterfront enclave aptly known as Star Island. He saw no reason why he couldn't ease the schooner's seventy-five-foot mainmast underneath the eighty-two-feet-high bridge on the causeway... until they got close to it and it began to look maybe dangerous, what with the wind and the choppy water and swells that were causing the schooner to pitch a bit. So they dropped anchor sixty feet from the bridge, and all eight of them went to the bow to study the situation.

One of them happened to turn around, and he said, "Hey, Jonathan, there's some guy back there on the deck! He just came up the ladder!" Sure enough, there was this thin, stringy, soaking-wet, sodden mess of a little man, breathing heavily... homeless, everybody thought. He had somehow come up the ladder on the stern used for slipping into and out of the water. He now stood still, dripping, on the aft deck, staring at them. He started toward them slowly, warily, gulping for air, until Jonathan, in his capacity as owner and captain, yelled at him, "Hey, hold on, whattaya think you're doing?" The guy stopped, began gesturing with both hands, palms up, and jabbering, between gulps of air, in what they took to be Spanish. Jonathan kept yelling, "Get offa here! Go! Fuck off!" and other unfriendly commands. With that, the bum, as they all took him to be, started running jacklegged, stumbling, careening, not away from them but straight at them. The girls began screaming. The bum looked like a wet rat. Half his hair seemed to be plastered across his face. His eyes were bugged wide open. His mouth was wide open, maybe just because he couldn't get his breath, but you could see his teeth. He looked psychotic. The guys started yelling at him and waving their arms in the sort of crisscross pattern football referees use to indicate that a field goal kick is no good. The bum keeps coming and is only a few yards from them, and the girls are screaming, making a hell of a racket, and the guys are screaming—by now their yells have turned into half-a-screams—and flailing their arms over their heads, and the bum wheels about and dashes to the forward mast and goes up it, to the top.

"Wait a minute," says Sergeant McCorkle. "Back up a second. Okay, so he's on the deck back there, and then he comes all the way from there to up here. Did you try to stop him? Did anybody try to stop him?"

Jonathan averted his eyes and took a deep breath and said, "Well, the thing is... he looked like a psycho. You know? And maybe he had like a weapon—you know?—a revolver, a knife. You couldn't tell."

"I see," said the Sergeant. "He looked like a psycho, and maybe he had a weapon, you couldn't tell, and you didn't try to stop him; nobody tried to stop him." He said it not as a question but as a recitation... in a form of deadpan mockery cops like.

"Uhhh... that's right," said the great Idle Youth.

"How did he climb the mast?" said the Sergeant. "You said he was out of breath."

"There's a rope you can see right here coming down the mast. It's got a pulley at the top, and there's a bucket seat. You get in the seat down here, and you get somebody to hoist you to the top in the bucket seat."

Sergeant McCorkle pointed overhead. "Who hoisted him up?"

"Well, he—you can use the rope and pull *yourself* up, if you have to."

"That must take a while," said the Sergeant. "Did you try to stop him? Did anyone try to stop him?"

"Well, as I said, he looked—"

"—looked like a psycho," said McCorkle, finishing the sentence for him. "And maybe he had a concealed weapon." The Sergeant nodded his head up and down in cop mockery posing as understanding. Then he cut his eyes toward Nestor with a certain lift of the eyebrows that as much as said, "What a bunch a pussies, hnnnnh?"

Ah, Bliss! To Nestor, at that point, that look was the equivalent of the Medal of Honor! The Sergeant had acknowledged him as a member of the courageous brotherhood of cops!—not just a probie in the Marine Patrol adept only at getting in his way.

Radiocom transmission... "Guy claims to be an anti-Fidel dissenter... Bridge full of Cubans demanding that he be given asylum. Right now that don't matter. Right now you gotta get him down from there. We got eight lanes a traffic on the causeway, and nothing's moving. What's your plan? Q,K,T."

That was all it took. For any Miami cop, especially one like Nestor or the Sergeant, that was enough to account for... the man on the mast. Undoubtedly Cuban smugglers had brought him this far, just inside Biscayne Bay, aboard some high-speed craft such as a cigarette boat, which went seventy miles an hour at sea, had dropped him off—or thrown him off—into the water near shore, made a U-turn, and sped back to Cuba. For this service he probably had to come up with something on the order of $5,000... in a country where the average pay for physicians was $300 a month. So now he finds himself floundering in the Bay. He sees the ladder on the rear of the schooner and climbs up, possibly believing it's docked, since it isn't moving, and he can just walk off onto the shore, or else that the boat will take him as far as the bridge. That's all a Cuban has to do: set foot on American soil or any structure extending from American soil, such as the bridge, and he will be granted asylum... Any *Cuban*... No other refugees were granted such a privilege. America's most favored migration status the Cubans enjoyed. If a Cuban refugee set foot on American soil (or structure), he was classified as a "dry foot," and he was safe. But if he was apprehended on or in the water, he would be sent back to Cuba unless he could convince a Coast Guard investigator that he would face "a credible threat," such as Communist persecution, if he had to go back. The man on the mast has made it out of the water—but onto a boat. So when Nestor and the Sergeant arrive he is technically still "in the water" and is classified as a "wet foot." *Wet foots* are out of luck. The Coast Guard takes them to Guantánamo, where they are, in essence, released into the woods, like an unwanted pet.

But at this moment the police high command isn't thinking about any of that. They don't care if he's a wet foot, a dry foot, a Cuban alien, or a lost Mongolian. All they care about is getting him off the mast—

right now—so normal traffic can resume on the causeway.

The Sergeant looked off, and his eyes focused on . . . an imaginary point in the middle distance. He remained in that stance for what seemed like forever. "Okay," he said finally, looking once more at Nestor. "You think you can climb that mast, Camacho? The guy don't speak English. But *you* can talk to him. Tell him we have no interest in arresting him and sending him back to Cuba. We just wanna get him down from there so he don't fall and break his neck . . . or stay up there and break my balls." That much was true. The Department openly instructed cops not to get involved in the whole business of illegal aliens. That was the federal government's problem, the ICE's, the FBI's, and the Coast Guard's. But *this* was Nestor Camacho's problem, or problems: climbing a seventy-foot foremast . . . and talking some poor scrawny panicked Cuban into descending the goddamned mast with him.

"So can you do it, Camacho?"

The *truthful* answers were "No" and "No." But the only *possible* answers were "Yes" and "Yes." How could he possibly stand there and say, "Well, to tell the truth, Sarge, I don't actually speak Spanish—certainly not well enough to talk anybody out of anything." He was like a lot of second-generation Cubans.

He could understand Spanish, because his parents spoke only Spanish at home. But in school, despite all the talk about bilingualism, practically everybody spoke English. There were more Spanish-language television and radio stations than English, but the best shows were in English. The best movies, blogs (and online porn), and video games, the hottest music, the latest thing in iPhones, BlackBerries, Droids, keyboards—all created for use in English. Very soon you felt crippled... *out there*... if you didn't know English and use English and *think* in English, which in turn demanded that you know colloquial American English as well as any Anglo. Before you knew it—and it always occurred to you suddenly one day—you could no longer function in Spanish much above a sixth-grade level. That bit of the honest truth shot through Nestor's mind. But how could he explain all this to these two *americanos?* It would sound so lame—and maybe even craven! Maybe he just didn't have the stomach for an assignment like this. And how could he say, "Gosh, I don't know whether I can climb that mast or not"?

Utterly impossible! The only alternatives he had were... to do it—and succeed... or to do it—and crash and burn. Making things still more muddled was the temper of the mob on the bridge. They were booing him! From the moment Nestor and the sergeant boarded the schooner, they had become steadily louder, uglier, more hostile, more raucous. Every now and then Nestor could make out a discrete cry.

"¡Libertad!"

"¡Traidor!"

"¡Comemierda, hijo de puta!"

As soon as he started up that mast, they would have it in for him—and he was Cuban himself! They'd find that out soon enough, too, wouldn't they! He couldn't win, could he! On the other hand... he went out to lunch for a moment... staring at the man on the mast without any longer seeing him. It came to him like a revelation, the question: "What is guilt?" Guilt is a gas, and gases disperse, but superior officers don't. Once they sink their teeth in, they're tenacious as a dog. Possible disapproval of a mob of his own people wasn't remotely as threatening as the disapproval of this blue-eyed sandy-haired *americano,* Sergeant McCorkle, who was already just one button away from canning him—

—and to whom he turned and said, "Sarge—I can do it."

Now he was in for it, whether he could pull off this stunt or not. He sized up the mast. He tilted his head back and looked straight up. Way... way... way up there—Jesus! The sun was burning up his eyeballs, darkest extremos or no darkest extremos! He had begun to sweat... wind or no wind! *Christ,* it was hot out here, grilling out on the deck of a schooner in the middle of Biscayne Bay. The man on top of the mast looked just about the size and color and shapelessness of one of those turd-brown vinyl garbage bags. He was still twisting and lurching about . . . way up there. Both his arms shot out again, in silhouette, no doubt with the fingers once more crimped up into the supplicant's cup shapes. He must have been rocking pathetically in his bosun's chair, because he kept protruding and then withdrawing, as if he were yelling to the mob. Christ, it was a long way up to the top! Nestor lowered his head to size up the mast itself. Down here where it joined with the deck, the damned thing was almost as big around as his waist. Wrapping his legs around it and shimmying up would take forever . . . inching up, inching up, pathetically hugging a seventy-foot boat mast . . . all too slow and humiliating to think about . . . But wait a minute! The rope, the lanyard the turd-brown boy had used to hoist himself to the top—here it was, rising up along the mast from out of a puddle of slack rope on the deck. On the other end was the illegal himself, smack up against the top of the mast in the bosun's chair. ::::::I've climbed fifty-five feet up a rope without using my legs,:::::: it occurred to him, ::::::and I could have climbed higher, if Rodriguez had a higher ceiling in his "Ññññññooooooooooooo!!! Qué Gym!" But seventy feet . . . Christ! . . . No?—I got no choice.:::::: It was as if not he but his central nervous system took over. Before he could even create a memory of it he leapt and grabbed hold of the rope and started climbing up—*without using his legs.*

A foul cascade of boos and slurs pounded down on him from above. Real slime! The cops were going to arrest a poor refugee on top of a mast and send him back to Castro and they were using a Cuban, a turncoat Cuban, to do the dirtiest work, but none of this quite reached the rational seat of justice in the left hemisphere of Nestor's brain, which was fixated upon an audience of one—Sergeant McCorkle ::::::and please, O Lord, I beseech thee, just don't let me fuck up!:::::: He is aware he has climbed practically halfway up hand over hand—still without using his legs. The very air is noise choked with madness... Jesus, his arms and back, his chest are reaching the edge of exhaustion. Has to pause, has to stop... but no time... He tries to look about. He's engulfed in clouds of white canvas, the schooner's sails... He glances down... he can't believe it... The deck is so *far* below... he must have climbed *more* than halfway up the mast—forty, forty-five feet. The faces on the deck all tilted straight up, toward him... how very small they look. He tries to pick out the Sergeant—is *that* him?... can't tell... their lips aren't moving... might as well be in a trance... *americano* faces *americano* faces... fixed on him. He looks straight up... at the face of the man on the mast... his filthy clump of a body has shifted way over so he can look down...

he knows what's happening, all right—the mob on the bridge...their deluge of slime...directed at Nestor Camacho!...such filth!

"¡Gusano!"

"Dirty *traidor* peeg!"

Oh, the filthy clump of laundry knows. Every time his hunter grabs the rope to pull himself up higher, the filthy clump can feel a little jolt in the bosun's chair...The jib and spinnaker start *FLAP FLAP FLAPPING* in the wind...the clouds of canvas blow aside for a moment...there they are, the mob on the bridge...Christ! They're not far above him anymore...their heads used to be the size of eggs...now more like cantaloupes...a great mangy gallery of contorted human faces...my own people...hating *me!...I'm damned if I do and damned if I don't* flashes through his central nervous system—but bucked back down to patrolman—or worse—if I don't. Oh, shit! What's that setting off sunbursts? A *television camera lens*—and *shit!* There's another—and *shit!* One over *there,* too. *Please, O Lord, I beseech thee...* Fear hits him like a massive shot of adrenaline... Don't let me...He's still climbing up, hand over hand, without using his legs. He looks up. The man on the mast is no more than ten feet above him! He's looking him right in the face!...What an expression...the cornered animal...the doomed rat...

drenched, dirty, exhausted... panting... barely able to utter a cry for miraculous salvation.

::::::*Ay, San Antonio, ayudame. San Lazaro, este conmigo.*::::::

Now Nestor—*has to* stop. He's close enough to the top to hear the man's entreaties above the noise from the bridge. He wraps his legs around the rope and stops still.

"*¡Te suplico! ¡Te suplico!*" "I'm begging you! Begging you! You can't send me back! They'll torture me until I reveal *everybody!* They'll destroy my family. Have mercy! There are Cubans on that bridge! I'm begging you! Is one more such an intolerable burden? I'm begging you, begging you! You don't know what it's like! You won't be destroying just me, you'll be destroying a whole movement! I beg you! I beg you for asylum! I beg you for a chance!"

Nestor knew enough Spanish to get the sense of what he was saying, but he couldn't think of the words that might calm him and coax him down. "Credible threat"... That's it! He'll tell him about "credible threat"... A refugee like him gets a Coast Guard hearing, right there on the deck, and if they believe he was endangered by a credible threat, he would get asylum. The word for "credible"—what's the damned word for credible? maybe the same as English?—cray *dee* blay? But "threat"... threat...

What was the damned word for threat? He knew he once knew it... *There it went!*... Right through his brain, before he could catch it. It had a *z* in it a *z* in it a *z* in it... *Almost had it again!*... but once more it was gone. For that matter, what about an official hearing?... He had to say *something—anything—* and so he ransacked his brain and looked up at the man's face and said, *"La historia—"* He caught himself just in time! What was happening to him? A famous quote from Fidel Castro was what his poor desperate brain had almost blurted out!

Boos, taunts, every known loud expression of vilification rained down from the people packed against the railings of the bridge.

The man looked down at him in an anxious way and said, *"¿Como?"* trying to sort out what Nestor has said.

Maddening was what it was!... climbed sixty feet up a rope without using his legs—but he couldn't make himself understood. He needed to get closer. He started climbing the rope again, hand over hand. He glances up at the poor drowned rat. His face is... aghast. How can he tell him he's not coming up to arrest him? He can't think of the words! So he stops climbing and wraps his legs around the rope to free his right hand to give a reassuring signal. But what signal? All he can think of is the peace sign... He spreads his index finger and his middle finger to form a *V.* The man's face, now no more than four feet above Nestor, changes from aghast... to terrified. He starts to rise from the bosun's chair. Jesus Christ, what does he think he's *doing?* He's up on top of a seventy-foot mast with nothing to support him but a tiny bosun's chair—and he wants to stand. He tries to anchor his feet on the pulley housing. Now he's out of his seat, teetering in a crouched position atop a mast that's pitching on a choppy sea... Nestor can see the worst about to happen. He climbs seventy feet up a rope—hand over hand, without using his legs—only to cause a poor refugee to fall to his death—and whose fault is it? Nestor Camacho's! Who has made the Miami Police Marine Patrol—hell, the entire force—look like the brutal, heedless persecutors and killers of a poor man whose only sin was trying to put one foot on American soil! Who has committed this heartless crime? Nestor Camacho, infamy incarnate!

With two furious hand-over-hand hoists he reaches the bosun's chair and tries to catch the man's leg—or even his foot—too late! The man pitches forward—*to his death!* A ferocious fire erupts inside Nestor's skull... No! The man has pitched forward onto the cable. He's trying to slide down it backward... This poor skinny emaciated gray-brown slurry rat—he'll kill himself! The cable runs at a steep angle from the mast to beyond the bow to the bowsprit... more than a hundred feet. Nestor crouches in the bosun's seat...

For an instant he can see the mob on the bridge. He's level with them now . . . three, four, five deep . . . Sunbursts! Sunbursts! Sunbursts! Sunbursts! They're exploding off cameras! Heads are jumping up to get a better view of the show . . . a sign! One of them has a crude sign—from where? . . . written how? . . . COPS FIDELISTAS TRAIDORES . . . never been hated by so many people. He looks down . . . makes him dizzy . . . like standing on the edge of the roof of a ten-story building. The water's a sheet of blue-grayish steel with sunbursts dancing all over it. Boats! . . . small boats around the schooner . . . from out of nowhere! . . . bloodsucking bugs . . . a boat—a sign. Can it really say what he thinks it says? . . . ¡ASYLUM AHORA!—

—all of this in an instant . . . Guilt! Fear! Horror! . . . but the greatest of these is Guilt! Must not let their hero die before their eyes! He swings down onto the cable . . . no use trying to catch up with him by sliding . . . Instinctively, in the mode they used in training camp, he starts swinging from the cable by his hands, heading down swing by swing, keeping his eyes on his slurry gray-brown quarry . . . His arms, his shoulders, the palms of his hands—agony! He's going to tear apart . . . only two swings away from the guy. The guy's body is still on top of the cable, but it's yawing this way and that . . . so scrawny . . . not strong enough for this . . . lifts his head, looks Nestor right in the face . . . worse than terror—utter hopelessness comes over the poor bastard...he's had it!...the poor devil yaws so sharply he can't stay on top of the cable...feebly hanging by his hands for one final moment. *Now* or oblivion! For the poor bastard! For Nestor Camacho! He reaches the poor bastard with two swings—to do *what?*...Only one thing possible. He wraps his legs around the scrawny rodent's waist and locks them at the ankles...the poor little bastard lets go of the cable and collapses. The dead jolt shocks Nestor...the dead weight! ::::::My arms torn off my body at the shoulder sockets!:::::: Can't believe he's still here—an organism composed of sheer pain from his burning hands to the sartorius muscles of his locked legs...sixty feet above the deck...to support this much weight by one hand while he swings the other to descend the cable...*impossible*...but if he doesn't—*¡Dios mío!*—he'll be fucking up! And not just fucking up...fucking up on *television*...Fucking up before *thousands, hundreds* of thousands, *millions*...might as well be billions...since one is all it would take, one officious *mierda*-mouth *americano* sergeant named—*bango!*

¡Caliente! Caliente baby
Got plenty fuego in yo caja china,
Means you needs a length a Hose put in it,
Ain' no maybe—

It's his iPhone ringing in his pocket! ::::::What a fool! I'm one slip from death, holding a man up with my legs and hauling him down a hundred-foot cable by hand—there's nothing I can turn the goddamn thing off *with!* A goddamn song by Bulldog—not even the real thing, Pitbull!—and I still can't keep the words from penetrating my head—::::::

—'bout it.
Hose knows you burnin' up wit'out it.
Don'tcha try deny it,
'Cause Hose knows you dyin' a try it—

—when he needs every neuron, every dendrite, every synapse, every gemmule in his mind to concentrate on the horrible fix he's gotten himself into. If he falls seventy feet onto a boat deck because his iPhone is singing

Hose knows all!
Knows you out tryin' a buy it,
But Hose only gives it free

—then he damn well better die!...He damn well better not wake up gorked out in an electric-motor-powered hospital bed in some morose intensive-care unit listed as "critical but stable"...the mortifying ignominy of it! But—no choice! He's *got to* do it!

Both hands still grip the cable, his legs grip *what?—maybe 120 pounds?*—of panicked-out little homunculus, and *here goes!* He releases one hand—and *that's it*—no turning back! The downswing—the *centrifugal force*—::::::I'm done for!:::::: One hand! Unbearable, the *centrifugal force* ::::::pulling my rotator cuff apart, pulling my arm out of the socket!—my wrist away from the arm! my hand away from my wrist! nothing left but—

To his fav'rite charity,
Hose' favorite cha-ree-tee, see?
Hose' fav'rite cha-ree-tee,
An' 'at's me.

—one hand clutching a cable! I'll crash on the deck from seven stories up, me and the gnome:::::: but a *miracle!* He grabs the cable with his other hand on the upswing—yes, *a miracle!*—it redistributes the weight! Both shoulders, both wrists, both hands are whole again!—kept intact only by the slimmest steely cord of unbearable agony!—only that cord to save him and the slurry-brown elfin man from falling seven stories and winding up as two shapeless bags of ecchymotic-purple integument full of broken bones! Below, down in the Halusian Gulp, the deck is covered with turned-up faces the size of marbles. From above rain the insults, boos, and disgusting *yaaagggggghs* of the animals on the bridge—but now he knows! has the power to persevere in a state of morbidly horrifying pain!—already into *another swing*—and he makes it—fury from

'At's me, see?
An' 'at's me.

above—gawking by the spectators below—but he thinks of only one soul, the minority Sergeant McCorkle, a mindless *americano* but a *sergeant* all the same—another swing—and he makes it—the damned phone is still ringing. ::::::Idiots! Don't you know

An' 'at's me, see?
An' 'at's me.
Yo yo!

you are pumping toxins and messing up my mind? Oh, the hell with it!:::::: Another swing—he makes it. ::::::*Dios mío querido,* together we look into the web of blood in their eyes, and into the affectless red eyes of the television cameras!:::::: Another swing—he

"—Yo yo!
Mismo! Mismo!"

makes it...another...another...another...*¡Dios mío!*—no more than ten feet above the deck—that sea of eyeballs and open mouths—*what the!!??* The slurry little ecchymotic sack of panic has come to life—he's bucking like a fish in the vise grip of Nestor's legs—a regular forest of hands

"Yo yo yo yo yo."

reaching upward from the bow, but the cable extends beyond them to the bowsprit *beep beep beep beep beep*—a text message!—and the two of them, Nestor and the slurry—brown homunculus—he's free of the leg lock!—not *now* you don't!—too late! he *does!* In the next instant the two bodies, his and the gnome's, hurtling off the end of the bowsprit and into the water. They're under water—and it's just as Lonnie Kite said! The little maniac has broken free of the leg lock and is... *attacking* him! *kicking* him! pulling his hair! *craaaaacking* his nose with his forearm... Kite had it right! Nestor wards off the little man's increasingly feeble blows, moves in, clamps him in a police neck lock, and that does it! The little creature goes limp! Done for! Ultimate Fighting under water!

When they reach the surface, Nestor has his slimy little quarry in a police lifesaver's grip... gnome is coughing up water. Two feet away—the Safe Boat! Lonnie's at the wheel. Nestor has reentered the world from a distant cosmos... Lonnie's pulling the slurry-brown homunculus up onto the rubbery pancake deck... and then Nestor—who the hell *are* these people? Nestor finds himself right by the schooner.

He twists toward the deck... the sun bursts off two big eyes of glass—TV cameras—and right there, leaning over the railing... the sandy-haired Sergeant McCorkle.

Sarge doesn't have to say a word—it's all right there in his face. Nestor Camacho is now... *a cop*... a *real* cop... as real as they make 'em... Nestor Camacho enters Heaven.

Sergeant McCorkle turned the drowned rat over to the Coast Guard right out there in the middle of the bay, and Nestor and the Sergeant and Lonnie Kite took the Safe Boat back to the Marine Patrol marina, which stuck out into the bay on the Miami side. All the way over, the Sergeant and Lonnie Kite lavished praise on Nestor in the accepted cop fashion, as if it weren't praise at all. Lonnie Kite's saying, "Jesus Christ, man"—he's a comradely *man* now!— "the way that little fucker was jerking around at the end there, after you've saved his ass—what was *that* all about? You kick him in the balls to see if he was alive?"

Nestor went coasting, coasting, coasting into euphoria.

The other guys at the marina were excited for Nestor. In the eyes of cops, Cuban and non-Cuban alike, he had pulled off a super-manly feat of strength, above and beyond... way over the top.

Sergeant McCorkle was now his pal—his *pal!* "Look, Nestor, all I told you was to bring the guy down from the fucking mast! I didn't say put on a high-wire act for the whole fucking city of Miami!"

Everybody laughed and laughed, and Nestor laughed with them. His cell phone went *beep beep beep beep,* signaling a text message. Magdalena! He averted his eyes ever so briefly—*Magdalena!*—but it wasn't from Magdalena. It read, "Disobeying unjust commands is the test of character." That was all; that was the whole message. It was signed, "Your teacher once, your friend no matter what, Jaime Bosch." Mr. Bosch taught composition and reading comprehension at the Police Academy. He was everybody's favorite teacher. He had tutored Nestor one-on-one outside school hours, purely as a favor and out of a love of teaching. "Disobeying unjust commands is the test of character"... Nestor couldn't figure it out. It made his head hurt... a lot.

He looked up at the rest of them, trying not to show his dismay. Thank God, they were all still in a merry mood, chuckling and laughing. Umberto Delgado, who had been in Nestor's class at the Police Academy, said, in English: "What was all this scissor grip shit with the legs, Nestorcito? That grip's for immobilizing the fuckers when you're rolling in the dirt—not for hauling 'em down a fucking hundred feet of jib sail cable!"

Everybody laughed and laughed and rollicked and rollicked, and Nestor loved it!... but the three text messages that remained... *had* to read them... came in *while* his life was literally on the line... *while* he held the man on the mast between his legs and was descending hand over hand down the jib line. He began burning with curiosity and an apprehension he avoided giving a name... and a hope—Magdalena! Once more he averted his eyes for an instant. The first one... "y u Nestor y u," it read—and it wasn't from Magdalena. It was from Cecilia Romero. Oddly, she was the girl he had been going out with when he met Magdalena. Wacky... what did she mean "y u Nestor y u"? Baffling... but he didn't show it... he rejoined the exhilarating Marine Patrol tide of manly laughter... but a tiny doubt germinated.

"How'd you like that little creep going into the Ultimate Fighting mode soon's he's under water, Nestor?" said Officer Kite. "Didn' I tell you those little fuckers turn into monsters as soon as they're under water!"

"I should a listened to you, Lonnie!" said Nestor. Thirty minutes ago he would not even have considered addressing Officer Kite by his first name. "That little prick—" he said, feeling very manly, "he's a dead weight all the way down the fucking cable and soon's we're five inches under water, he decides to come to! Before I know what's happening, he's breaking my fucking nose with his bare hands!"

And everybody laughed and laughed, but Nestor—*had* to read the two remaining text messages. Curiosity and anxiety and a last spurt of hope—maybe one *is* from Magdalena!—compelled him. He dared flick his eyes down to the cell phone once more. Dared to—*had* to. The first text was from J. Cortez. He didn't know any J. Cortez. It read, "OK u r a big latingo celebrity. Now what?" What the hell did "latingo" mean? All too quickly he got it. A latingo had to be a Latino who had turned *gringo*. And what was *that* supposed to mean? Mirth reigned in the room, but Nestor couldn't help himself... had to dive to the very bottom. The last text was from Inga La Gringa. It read, "You can hide under my bed anytime, Nestorcito." Inga was the counter girl and waitress right around the corner from the marina. She was sexy, all right, a big Baltic blonde with amazing breasts that she managed to tilt upward like missiles and enjoyed showing. She had grown up in Estonia... sexy accent, too... a real number, Inga was, but she was forty or so, not much younger than his mother. It was almost as if she could tell exactly what he was thinking. Every time he walked into the place, Inga would come on to him in a flirtatious but comic way, making sure he got a good, long look down the crevasse between her breasts . . . or was she really *merely* fooling around? "Nestorcito" she called him, because she had once heard Umberto call him that. So he called her Inga La Gringa. He had given her his cell phone number when she said her brother could help him fix the overhead cam on his Camaro . . . which he did. Inga and Nestor teased each other . . . sure, "teased," but Nestor never took the next step, although he was sorely tempted. But why had she said, "You can *hide* under my bed"? Hide from what? She was just kidding around in her Inga La Gringa lubricious come-nestle-in-my-loamy-crevice way, of course, but why "You can *hide* under my bed"?

Somehow this hit him harder than a crack like "latingo." "Hide," says friendly, flirtatious Inga? . . . He felt his face fall . . . This time the rest of them were *bound* to notice—but the Sergeant stepped in and saved the day, saying, "But you know what gets me? Those kids on the boat were such *pussies.* They were scared shitless because some frightened-out-of-his-mind little guy looking like a drowned rat, maybe a hundred and ten pounds after a Big Mac, shows up on their fucking sailboat. Some a those pussies weighed fucking two hundred pounds, half of it fat, but they're big kids. There's no reason on earth why they had to let that poor little bastard climb their fucking mast and almost get himself killed . . . except they're such fucking *puss-*

ies! Do they have any clue they got no business taking a boat that big out on the fucking water . . . being such pussies? 'Oh dear, we didn't know if he had a gun or a knife or something' . . . Bull-*shit!* That little bastard barely had *clothes* on his back. And so we gotta send Nestor here up a fucking seventy-five-foot mast and play Superman and risk his ass hauling the little bastard down off a bosun's chair about this big and down a goddamned hundred-foot jib cable." The Sergeant shook his head. "You know what? We should a booked all those pussies and sent *them* to Cuba and kept the drowned rat here. We would a come out ahead on that one!"

Hey! Who are *those two,* just joining the cluster of Marine Patrol cops? They sure as hell don't look like cops. It turns out they are a reporter and a photographer from the *Miami Herald*. Nestor had never heard of a reporter coming all the way out here in the bay. The photographer was a swarthy little guy wearing some sort of safari jacket, pockets all over it, wide open. Nestor couldn't tell what he was . . . but there was no doubt about the reporter. He was a classic *americano,* tall, thin, pale, wearing a navy blazer, a light-blue button-down shirt, khaki pants with freshly pressed creases down the front . . . very proper-looking. Over-the-top proper. Who ever heard of a newspaper reporter wearing a jacket in Miami? He was soft-spoken to the point of shy, this reporter. His name was John Smith, apparently. How much more *americano* could you get?!

"I can't believe what you just *did,*" said the classic *americano.* "I can't believe anyone could swing hand over hand down that thing holding another person between his legs. Where'd you get the strength? Do you lift weights—or *what?*"

Nestor had never spoken to a reporter before. Maybe he wasn't supposed to. He looked at Sergeant McCorkle. The Sergeant just smiled and gave him a slight wink, as if to say, "It's okay, go ahead and tell him."

That did it. Modestly enough, Nestor began, "I don't think it takes strength exactly." He *tried* to continue on the modest path—but he just couldn't tell the *americano* enough. He didn't believe in weightlifting for the upper body. It's much better to climb a, say, fifty-five-foot rope without using your legs. Takes care of everything, arms, back, chest—everything.

"Where do you do that?" said this John Smith.

"At Rodriguez's 'Ññññññooooooooooooo!!! Qué Gym!' they call it."

The *americano* laughed. "Como en 'Ññññññooo-ooooooooooo!!! Que barata'?"

::::::This *americano* not only speaks Spanish—he must listen to Spanish radio! That's the only time you can hear the "Ññññññooooooooooooo!!! Que barata!" commercial.::::::

"Es verdad," said Nestor. That was a linguistic hand-

shake for John Smith's speaking Spanish. "But you have to use weights and do squats and everything else for your legs. I don't know what you do for carrying some little guy like that with 'em . . . except try to avoid the whole thing." Light touch of modesty there . . . or self-mockery . . . or whatever. Nestor looked down, as if to check out his uniform. He tried to tell himself that what he was about to do was unconscious—which of course made it self-fraudulence per se.

"*Dios mío,*" he said, "this shirt is soaking wet and fucking filthy! I can *smell* it." He looked at Umberto, as if this had nothing to do with the two guys from the *Herald,* and said, "Where's some dry shirts?"

"Dry shirts?" said Umberto. "I don't know, unless they keep them in . . ."

But Nestor had already stopped listening. He was busy pulling his wet shirt up and off his torso and his arms and his head, which involved lifting his arms almost straight up. He winced as if in pain. "*Awwwguh!* Hurts like a sonofabitch! I must a pulled something in my shoulders."

"That figures," said Umberto.

Just like that John Smith's swarthy little photographer had his camera up to his eyes and was pressing that button over and over.

Sergeant McCorkle stepped in and took Nestor by the elbow and pulled him away. "We got shirts inside, not at the *Miami Herald*. You know what I mean?"

He marched Nestor off at a good clip and pulled him close enough to say in a low voice, "You can talk to the press on the spot like this, as long as you don't talk strategy or policy. But not so you can show off your fucking physique. You know what I mean?"

But he was chuckling about it. This was not a day when he was going to get hard-ass toward Officer Nestor Camacho . . . who remained in Heaven.

2

The Hero's Welcome

Todo el mundo had watched his heroics on television... "*Todo el mundo!*" Nestor told himself at the peak of his euphoria... But of his tens of thousands, if not millions, of *admiradores* there was one whose awe he most longed to have shining 'round about him. He closed his eyes and tried to imagine what she, his Magdalena, his Manena, the nickname he loved, was thinking and feeling as she sat—or perhaps the intensity of it all brought her to her feet—riveted, awestruck, before a TV screen, rapt by the sight of her Nestor climbing up that seventy-foot rope hand over hand, without using his legs... then carrying the man on the mast, *with his legs!*... while going hand over hand down a 100-foot jib line... electrifying the city.

As a matter of fact, his Magdalena was utterly

unaware of this high-wattage hero's triumph. The entire time she had her hands full with . . . the mother of all mother-and-daughters. This one was a real catfight. Magdalena had just announced that she was leaving home.

Her father had a ringside seat, an easy chair beside the couch in the living room of their casita, their little house, in Hialeah, barely two miles from the Camachos' casita. Magdalena was standing up belligerently—her fists on her hips and her elbows winged out—as Mother and Daughter traded hisses and growls and eyetooth glowers. Mother was sitting forward on the couch with *her* elbows winged out—this seemed to be an instinctive stance of both combatants in their mother-and-daughters—and the heels of her hands pressed down on the front edge of the frame, a veritable feline, ready to spring, claw, rip guts out, eat livers whole, and bite heads off by sinking both sets of incisors into the soft centers of the temples. Her father, if Magdalena knew anything about it, was possessed by a fervent desire to evaporate. Too bad he had sunk so far down into the easy chair. He'd have to be an acrobat to slip away unnoticed. Their fights mortified him. They were so vulgar and common. Not that he had any great delusions of gentility. He had been a threshing-machine mechanic in Camagüey when he and his wife met. Both had grown up there. He had been a truck mechanic in Havana for five years when they left Cuba in the Mariel boatlift . . . and he was a truck mechanic in Miami now. Nevertheless he had his standards. He hated these goddamned mother-and-daughters . . . but he had long since given up trying to control his two cats.

Mother was thrusting at Daughter. "Isn't it bad enough I have to tell people you've gone to work for a pornographic doctor? For three years I tell them you work for *real* doctors at a *real* hospital. Now I tell them you work for a *fake* doctor, a pornographic doctor, in some dirty little office? . . . and you moving away from home to go live with God only knows who in South Beach? You *say* it's a blan-*ca.* You sure it's not a blan-*co?*"

Daughter made just a flick of a glance at the five-foot-high baked-clay statue of Saint Lazarus up by the front door before parrying: "He's not a pornographic doctor. He's a psychiatrist, a very well known psychiatrist, and it just so happens that he treats people who are addicted to pornography. Don't keep calling him a pornographic doctor! Don't you know *any*thing?"

"I know one thing," riposted Mother. "I know you don't care if you ruin your family's name. There is only one reason girls move away from home. Everybody knows that."

Magdalena rolled her eyes up into her cranium, extended her neck, leaned her head back, stiffened both arms straight down past her hips, and made an *unngghhhhummmmmmmm* sound in her throat. "Listen, you're not in Camagüey any longer, Estrellita! In this country you don't have to wait until you can marry yourself out of the house." *Gotcha... Gotcha...* twice in the space of eight words. Her mother always told people she was from Havana, because the first thing every Cuban in Miami wanted to know was your family history in Cuba—history, of course, meaning social status. Being from Camagüey was synonymous with being a *guajira,* a hick. So Daughter managed to work Camagüey—*gotcha*—into practically every mother-and-daughter. Likewise, every now and then she liked to call her mother by her first name, Estrellita, instead of Mami—*gotcha*—for the sheer impudence of it. She liked to dwell upon the *y* sound of the double *l. Es-tray-yeeeee-ta. That* made it sound old-fashioned, Camagüey and a half.

"I'm twenty-four years old now, Estrellita, and I have a nursing degree—you were there, as I recall, when I got it—and I have a job and a career and—"

"Since when is nurse work for a pornographic doctor a career?" Mother loved the way that one made Daughter wince. "Who are you with all day?—perverts! You told me that yourself... perverts, perverts, perverts."

"They're not *perverts*—"

"No? They watch pornographic movies all day. What do you call that?"

"They're not *perverts!* They're sick people, and that's who nurses try to help, sick people. There are people with all sorts of unpleasant diseases, like... like... like H,I,V, and nurses have to take care of them."

Uh-ohhh. As soon as "HIV" passed her lips, she wanted to snatch it back from out of the air. *Any* example was better than that one... pneumonia, tuberculosis, Tourette's syndrome, hepatitis, diverticulitis... anything. Well, too late now. Brace yourself—

"Hahh!" Mother barked. "Everything is perverts with you! Now it's *maricones! La cólera de Dios!* Is that why we paid all those tuitions? So you can chill up with dirty people?"

"Chill *up?*" said Daughter. "Chill *up?* You don't say 'chill *up,*' it's 'chill *out,*' or just *chill.*" Magdalena immediately realized that given the totality of her mother's insult, "chill *up*" was the least of it. The only thing to do was to rub it in harder. So she resorted to the E-bomb: English. "Don't try to speak English colloquially, Estrellita. You always get it wrong. You don't get the hang of slang, do you. It always makes you sound clueless."

Her mother went silent for a few beats, her mouth slightly agape. *Gotcha!* Magdalena knew that would get her. Answering her in English almost always did.

Her mother had no idea what *colloquially* meant. Magdalena didn't, either, until not all that many nights ago when Norman used it and explained it to her. Her mother might know *hang* and possibly even *slang,* but *the hang of slang* no doubt baffled her, and the expression *clueless* was guaranteed to make her look the way she did right now, which is to say, clueless. When Magdalena let her have it in English like this, it made her crazy.

Magdalena took advantage of the additional milliseconds the hiatus granted her and cast a real glance at Lazarus. The clay statue, almost life-size—not stone, not bronze, but ceramic—was the first thing you saw when you came into the casita. What a miserable saint to have to confront! He had caved-in cheeks, a scraggly beard, a pained expression, and a purply biblical robe—hanging open, to better exhibit the leprosy sores all over his upper torso—plus two clay dogs at his feet. In the Bible, Lazarus was about as low as they came, socially... a beggar with leprosy sores all over his body... begging for crumbs of bread at the gates of a swell place belonging to a rich man named Dives, who didn't give him the time of day. The two of them, Lazarus and Dives, happened to die at about the same time. To make a point—namely, that in Heaven the last shall be first and the first shall be last—and that it's easier for a camel to go through the eye of a needle than for a rich man to enter the Kingdom of God... Jesus sends this poor devil Lazarus to Heaven, where he dwells in "the bosom of Abraham." He packs Dives off to Hell, where he burns alive eternally.

Magdalena was baptized as a Roman Catholic and had always gone to Mass with her mother, her father, and her two older brothers. But Mother was a real Camagüey country girl. Mother believed in Santería—an African religion that slaves had brought to Cuba... replete with spirits, magic, ecstatic dancing, trances, potions, ground roots, divination, curses, animal sacrifices, and God knows what other hoodoo voodoo. Santerians began to match up their hoodoo gods with Catholic saints. The god of the sick, Babalú Ayé, became Saint Lazarus. Magdalena's mother and father were light skinned, as were many believers by now. No way, however, could Santería ever shake loose of its social origins... slaves and simpleminded country *guajiros*. This had become a handy needle for Magdalena in the mother-and-daughters.

It hadn't been like this when she was a little girl. She was a beautiful, irresistible creature, and her mother was very proud of that. Then, at age fourteen, she became a very beautiful, irresistible virgin. Grown men would sneak looks at her. Magdalena *loved* that... and how far were they going to get with her? Not one inch. Estrellita watched over her with the eyes of an owl. She would have loved to revive the role of the chaperone. It hadn't been all that long since Cuban girls in Miami couldn't go out on a date without Mother coming along as chaperone. It could become a bit . . . *off.* Sometimes the Mother-chaperone was pregnant with Daughter's soon-to-be sibling. Bursting with child herself, she would be superintending Daughter's first prim lesson in how to lead, in due course, with due propriety, young men down the path to the portals of the womb. The swollen belly made it obvious that Mother had been doing precisely what she was on duty to keep Daughter from doing with her young beau of the moment. Not even Estrellita could insist on prior approval of a boy Magdalena was going out with. But she could and did insist that he pick her up here at the casita, so that she could get a good look at him, and insist on asking him some questions if he seemed at all shady, and insist that he bring her home by eleven.

The only "older man" in Magdalena's life was someone who was all of one year older than her and had a touch of glamour, since he was now a police officer with the Marine Patrol, namely, Nestor Camacho. Estrellita knew his mother, Lourdes. His father had his own business. Nestor was a good Hialeah boy.

Mother regained her wits and her voice. "Are you sure your little *blanca* roommate in South Beach isn't called Nestor Camacho?"

Daughter went, "HahhhHHHH!"—so loudly and at such a coloratura soprano pitch, it startled Mother. "That's a laugh! Nestor is such a good, obedient little Hialeah boy. Why don't you call up his mother, and she can have a good laugh, too? Or why don't you settle it right here? Why don't you get your coconut beads and throw them in front of old Lazzy-boy there? He'll tell you! He won't steer you wrong!" She thrust her arm and forefinger at the statue of Lazarus like a spear.

Estrellita was speechless again. Something was happening to her face that went beyond the boundaries of a mother-and-daughter. It was black anger. Estrellita already *got it* when Magdalena made references to Santería. It was an indirect way of calling her an ignorant, socially backward *guajira*. She knew that. But now Magdalena was uttering outright blasphemy. "Lazzy-boy" she dared call Saint Lazarus. She was indulging in mockery of the faith's powers of divination, such as throwing the coconut beads. She was ridiculing her faith and her very life.

With a cold fury that came from deep in her throat, she hissed out, "You want to leave home? Then do it. Do it now. I don't care if you never set foot in this house again."

"Good!" said Magdalena. "Finally we agree!"

But her voice had a tremor in it. The look on her mother's face and the rattlesnake tone of her voice...

Magdalena didn't dare say another word. Now... she'd *have to* get out... and that set off a quake in the pit of her stomach. As of now, no longer would her new life among the *americanos* be the exotic, exciting, naughty adventure of a free spirit... As of now, she would be dependent upon an *americano* for a place to live, her paycheck, her social life, her love life. The only things she'd have going for her would be her good looks... and something that had never failed her... not yet... namely, her nerve.

Euphoria! was the name of the bubble that enclosed Nestor when the shift ended and he drove his aged Camaro north across the Miami line into Hialeah. *Superman!* was the name of the hero within. Superman lit up that bubble like a torch held aloft.

The Chief himself, Chief Booker, had driven all the way to the marina at midnight to give him an attaboy!

Hialeah... at the midnight hour... a silhouette in the dark of row after row after row after row after block after block after block of little one-story houses, the casitas, each nearly identical to the one next door, all of fifteen feet away, each on a 50-by-100-foot lot, each with a driveway going straight back... chain-link fencing fortifying every square inch of everybody's property... front yards of rock-solid concrete adorned with little concrete Venetian fountains. But tonight the Camaro's rolling flow made all of Hialeah luminous. This was not the same Nestor Camacho—you know, Camilo Camacho's son—driving home anonymously from the same old night shift—

Not at all—for *the Chief himself had driven all the way to the marina at midnight to give him an attaboy!*

Nestor has arisen, radiant, from the ranks of Hialeah's 220,000 souls. He is now known throughout Greater Miami, wherever the TV digit-rays have reached... the cop who risked his life to save a poor panicked refugee from the top of a towering schooner mast. Even now, at the midnight hour, the sun shone 'round about him. He entertained the idea of parking the Camaro two or three blocks from home and walking the rest of the way with a calm, measured pace, just to offer the citizens a glimpse of the radiant one... and to watch them nudge one another... "Look! Isn't that *him!*" But the fact was, there were damned few pedestrians to be seen, and Hialeah didn't have a nightlife worthy of the name. Besides, he was so damned tired...

His block was just as dim as the rest of them, but he could spot La Casita de Camacho immediately. A streetlight, weak as it was, was enough to create a reflection in the slick, glossy, almost glassy lettering emblazoned upon the side of his father's big Ford E-150 van parked right out front: CAMACHO FUMIGADORES. His old man was proud of that lettering. He had paid real money to have a real commercial artist do it. The letters had black shading that made them seem to pop out of the side of the van in three dimensions. CAMACHO FUMIGADORES!... Camilo Camacho's own bug-and-vermin-killer company... Strictly speaking, FUMIGADORES, plural, was not accurate. The firm had exactly one fumigator, and one employee, period, and his name was on the side of the van. For three years Camilo had "employed" an assistant, his son Nestor. Nestor couldn't stand it... spraying Malathion into the dark, dank recesses of people's houses... inevitably inhaling some of the shit... and listening to Camilo saying, "It won't kill you!"... smelling Malathion every day in his clothes... smelling it on himself... getting so paranoid, he thought everybody he met could smell it on him... When people wanted to know what he *did,* he would say he had been working for a population adjustment firm but was looking for another job. Thank God he finally got accepted at the Police Academy! His father, on the other hand, was proud to have a firm that adjusted populations in people's homes. He wanted *todo el mundo* to see HIMSELF parked in big letters in front of his house. Nestor had been a Miami cop for only four years but long enough to know there were plenty of neighborhoods... Kendall, Weston, Aventura, the Upper East Side, Brickell... where any man who parked such a vehicle in front of his house would be regarded as a cockroach himself. Likewise, his wife and the set of grandparents who lived with them, and the son who was a cop. The whole nest of them would constitute a regular infestation. There were parts of Coral Gables where it was against the law to park a commercial vehicle like that in front of your house. But in Hialeah it was a point of pride for a man. Hialeah was a city of 220,000 souls, and close to 200,000 must be Cubans, it seemed to Nestor. People were always talking about "Little Havana," a section of Miami along Calle Ocho, where the tourists all stopped at Café Versailles and had a cup of terribly sweet Cuban coffee and then walked a couple of blocks to watch the old men, presumably Cubans, play dominoes in Domino Park, a tiny plot of parkland placed right there on Calle Ocho to lend a rather drab neighborhood a little... authentic, picturesque, *folklórica atmósfera*. That done, they could say they had seen Little Havana. But the real Little Havana was Hialeah, except that it was hard to call it little. The old "Little Havana" was dreary, worn out, full of Nicaraguans and God knew who else, and the next thing to being a slum, in Nestor's opinion. Cubans would never sit still in a slum. Cubans were by nature ambitious. So every man who had a vehicle with commercial lettering on it, proving that he was an entrepreneur, no matter how small, parked it importantly in front of the house. CAMACHO FUMIGADORES!

That plus the Grady-White cruiser in the driveway proved that Camilo Camacho was not a working-class Cuban. One out of maybe every five casita owners in Hialeah had some sort of cruiser—cruiser meaning it was too big to be denigrated as a "motorboat"—elevated up, way up, upon a towing trailer. The prow usually extended out beyond the facade of the casita. The towing rigs were so high, they were like pedestals . . . to the point where the cruisers dwarfed the casitas themselves. Here in the darkness, to Nestor their silhouettes made the boats seem like missiles about to take off above your head. Nestor's old man had paid the same commercial artist to do the same sort of glossy, glassy lettering on the Grady-White cruiser's hull. LAS SOMBRILLAS DE LIBERTAD, it said, "The Umbrellas of Liberty." The name stood for the great life-or-death adventure of the old man's youth. Like Magdalena's family, Camilo and his father, Nestor's grandfather, were country boys from Camagüey. Nestor's grandfather had visions of getting away from a life of cutting cane and mucking out stables and humping plows. City Life he craved. He moved, with his wife and son, to Havana. No longer a *guajiro!* Now a full-fledged proletarian! Free at last, the new *prole* got a job as an inspector in the raw-sewage-filtration section of the Malecón waterworks. "Inspector" meant he had to put on rubber boots and carry a flashlight and hunch over like a gnome and walk through drainage pipes in the darkness while rivers of shit and other vile excrescences flowed and occasionally gushed over his boots. It was not perfumed, either. That wasn't the City Life he had in mind. So he and Camilo stealthily built a crude dinghy in the cellar of their proletarian apartment block in Havana. They stole two big café umbrellas to use as sails... and shields against the sun. Camilo and his parents and Lourdes, Camilo's girlfriend (in due course, his wife and Nestor's mother), set out one night for Florida. They nearly died a hundred times, at least as the old man told the story (many more than a hundred times), from sunstroke, dehydration, starvation, storms, towering waves, currents gone amok, winds gone dead, and God knows what else, before reaching Key West twelve days later, all four at the point of death.

Well, now Nestor had a heroic saga of his own... to relate to *them*. He could hardly wait. He had called home three times from the marina. The phone was busy each time, but maybe it was better this way. They would hear it all from his own lips... with their young hero standing before them, watching their faces go from aglow to agog.

As usual, he parked the Camaro upon the little stretch of driveway between the sidewalk and the boat.

The moment he steps inside the house, his father

is there waiting with his arms crossed over his chest and his I, Camilo Camacho, Lord of This Domain look on his face...his lordly demeanor somewhat compromised by the fact that he's wearing a T-shirt that hangs outside his Relaxed-Fit blue jeans...The crossed arms bear down on his paunch from above, and the belt of his low-cut jeans hoists it up from below, causing it to swell out like a watermelon underneath the T-shirt. Nestor's mother is one step behind I, Camilo. She looks at Nestor as if he, her third child, her last-born baby, were a little flame sizzling down a fuse to—

—*Ka-boom!*—I, Camilo Camacho, *explodes:*

"How could you do that to a man of your own blood? He's eighteen meters from freedom, and you arrest him! You condemn him to torture and death in Fidel's dungeons! How could you do that to the honor of your own family? People have been calling! I've been on the phone all night! Everyone knows! They turn on the radio, and all they hear is '*Traidor! traidor! traidor!* Camacho! Camacho! Camacho!' You drag us through *shit!*" He cuts a glance back at his wife. "It has to be said, Lourdes"—turns back to Nestor—"Through *shit* you drag the House of Camacho!"

Nestor was stunned. It was as if the old man had smashed a baseball bat against the base of his skull. His mouth fell open, but no sounds came out. He turned his palms upward in the eternal gesture of baffled helplessness. He couldn't speak.

"What's the matter?" said his father. "The truth cut your tongue out?"

"What are you *talking* about, Dad?" It came out at least an octave too high.

"I'm talking about what you done! If some cop had done to me and your grandfather"—he nodded in the general direction of Nestor's grandfather and grandmother's, Yeyo and Yeya's, room in the back—"what you just done to one of your own people, your own blood, you wouldn't be here now! You wouldn't be a big cop in Miami! You wouldn't be nothing! You wouldn't *exist!* Not even *exist!*"

"Dad—"

"You know what we had to do so you could even *exist?* Me and your grandfather had to build a boat by ourselves at night, down in a cellar so the block warden wouldn't come nosing around. And we set out to sea at night, too, with Yeya and your mother—and all we had was food and water and a compass and two outdoor café umbrellas we had to steal at night and rig up as sails. Café umbrellas!"

"I know, Dad—"

"Twelve days it took us! Twelve days of burning up all day and freezing all night and getting thrown this way"—he pantomimes the boat pitching up and down—"and that way"—pantomimes the boat rolling—"and this way"—yawing—"and that way"—climbing waves—"day and night—and bailing out water day and night, too. We couldn't sleep. We couldn't hardly eat. It took all four of us bailing out water around the clock just to keep the boat afloat. We coulda died a hundred times"—he snapped his fingers—"just like *that!* For the last four days we had no more food and one bottle of water for the four of us—"

"Dad—"

"We were four skeletons when we finally reached land! We were half out of our minds! Your mother was having hallucinations, and—"

"Dad! I know all that!"

He, Camilo Camacho, went silent. He took in a breath so deep and twisted his face into such a grimace, complete with bared upper teeth and popped veins, he was either going to bite someone or have a stroke—until at the last moment he found his voice and rasped out:

"*All that* you call it? *All that? All that* was life or death! We almost died! Twelve days on the ocean in an open boat! There wouldn't *be* no Officer Nestor Camacho without *all that!* He wouldn't *exist!* If some big cop had arrested us eighteen meters from shore and sent us back, that woulda been the end of all of us! You woulda never been nothin'! And you call it *all that!* Jesus Christ, Nestor, what kind a person are you? Or maybe you not a person! Maybe you got claws and a tail like a *mapache!*"

::::::A *raccoon* he calls me!::::::

"Listen, Dad—"

"No, *you* listen! You don't know what it is to suffer! You arrest a guy eighteen *metros de libertad!* To you it don't matter that the Camachos came to America in a homemade—"

"Dad, *listen* to me!"

Nestor said it so sharply, his father didn't try to finish his sentence.

Nestor said, "This guy didn't have to do"—he started to say "all that" but caught himself just in time—"do anything like what you and Yeyo had to do. This guy paid some smugglers three or four thousand dollars to take him straight to Miami in a cigarette boat. Goes seventy miles an hour on the water, a cigarette boat. Took him what—maybe two hours to get here? Three at the most? In an open boat? No, in a cabin with a roof. Starving? Probably didn't have time to digest the big lunch he had before he left!"

"Well—that don't matter. The principle's the same—"

"What principle, Dad? The Sergeant gave me a direct order! I was carrying out *a direct order!*"

A derisive snort. *"Carrying out a direct order."* Another snort. "So do Fidel's people! They carry out direct orders, too—to beat people and torture people and 'disappear' people and take everything they have. You never heard of honor before? You don't care about your family's honor? I don't wanna hear that pathetic excuse again!... *Carrying out a direct order*..."

"Come on, Dad! The guy's up there screaming to the crowd on the bridge and throwing his arms around like this"—he demonstrates—"Guy's lost it! He's gonna fall and kill himself, and all six lanes of traffic are backed up on the causeway, Friday rush hour, the worst—"

"Oh ho! A *traffic jam*. Why didn't you *say* so?! *Whoa, a traffic jam!* That's *different*... So you're trying to tell me a traffic jam is worse than *torture* and *death* in Fidel's dungeons?"

"Dad, I didn't even know who the guy was! I still don't know! I didn't know what he was yelling about! He was seventy feet up above me!"

In fact, he *had* known, more or less, but this was not the time for fine distinctions. Anything to bring an end to this tirade, this terrible judgment—by his own father!

But nothing was going to stop I, Camilo Camacho, Lord of This Domain. "You said he was gonna fall and kill himself. *You* were the one who nearly made him fall and kill himself! You were the one crazy to *arrest* him, no matter what!"

"Jesus Christ, Dad! I didn't *arrest* him! We don't arrest immig—"

"Everybody *saw* you do it, Nestor! Everybody knew it was a Camacho who did this. We saw you do it with our own eyes!"

It turned out that his father and his mother and his grandparents had been watching the whole thing on American TV with the sound muted and listening to it on WDNR, a Spanish-language radio station that loved to get furious over sins of the *americanos.* Nothing Nestor could say would calm his father down in the slightest. I, Camilo Camacho, threw his hands up in the air as if to say, "No hope... no hope..." and turned and walked away.

His mother stayed put. Once she was sure that I, Camilo, had gone into another room, she threw her arms around Nestor and said, "I don't care what you've done. You're alive and home. That's the main thing."

Don't care what you've done. The implied guilty verdict so depressed Nestor, he said nothing. He couldn't even croak out an insincere *Thanks, Mami.*

He went to his little room exhausted. His whole body ached, his shoulders, his hip joints, the sartorius muscles on the inner sides of his thighs, and his *hands,* which were still raw. His hands! The joints, the knuckles—it was agony if he so much as tried to make a fist. Just taking off his shoes, pants, and shirt and getting up onto the bed—agony... ::::::Sleep, dear God. Knock me unconscious... that's all I ask... sail me away from *esta casita*... into the arms of the Sandman... Take away my thoughts... be my morphine...::::::

But Morpheus failed him. He'd doze off and then—*jerk alert* with his heart beating too fast... doze off—*jerk alert*... doze off—*jerk alert!*... all night, fits and starts... until he *jerked alert* at 6:00 a.m. He felt like a burnt-out husk. He was sore all over, sore as he had ever been in his life. Moving the joints of his hips and legs was so painful, he wondered if they would ever support his weight. But they *had* to. He had to get the hell out of here!... Go *somewhere*... and kill time until his Marine Patrol shift began at four o'clock. He edged his feet off the bed and slowly sat up... sat there groggily for a minute... ::::::I feel too awful... I *can't* get up. So what are you going to do, hang around here waiting for more abuse?:::::: With straining willpower he made himself get *sheer torture!* up. Gingerly, warily, he tiptoed to the living room and stood at one of the two front windows of the little house, watching the women. They were already out hosing down their concrete front yards up and down the block, this being Saturday morning.

No man would be caught dead with one of those hoses in his hands. That was a woman's job. That would be the first thing his mother did when she got up: power-spray their fifty-by-twenty-foot rock-hard sward. Too bad water didn't make concrete grow. By now their front yard would be fifty stories high.

As far back as he could remember, Nestor's picture of Hialeah was of thousands of blocks like this one, endless rows of casitas with little paved front yards... but no trees... studded here and there with vehicles that had writing all over them... but no trees... boats that said *Conspicuous Leisure*... but no trees. Nestor had heard of a time when all over the country the very name Hialeah summoned up a picture of Hialeah Park, the most glamorous and socially swell racetrack in America, set in a landscaper's dream, a lush, green, wholly man-made 250-acre park with a resident flock of pinkest flamingos... now a shut-down, locked-up relic, a great moldering memento of the palmy days when the Anglos ran Miami. Today a bug-gassing van parked out front with your name on it was enough to make La Casita de Camacho socially swell in Hialeah. He had admired his father for it. Every night the old man came home with his clothes giving off whiffs of Malathion. But Nestor took that as a sign of his father's success as a businessman. The same father now turns on him when he most needs his support!

Christ! It was getting on toward 6:30, and he was just standing here letting his thoughts run wild... The whole bunch of them would be up soon... Camilo the Caudillo, the Caudillo's ever-worried, hand-flensing wife, Lourdes, and Yeya and Yeyo—

Yeya!

It had completely slipped his mind! Today was her birthday! There was no way he could finesse Yeya's birthday. There was always a pig roast... a pig big enough for a hundred people or so... all the relatives... *innumerable,* here in Hialeah alone... plus all the neighbors from the wet concrete yards. His parents and Yeya and Yeyo and even he himself knew the neighbors so well, they had come to call them *Tía* and *Tío,* as if they were real aunts and uncles. If he went AWOL from this party, he would *never* be forgiven. Celebrating Grandmother's birthday was a very big thing in the Camacho domain... it was practically a holiday... and the older she got, the more sacred *it* got.

There were grandparents living in the same house as their middle-aged children all over the place in Hialeah. Until his brother and his sister married their way out of the house, this casita was like the YMCA. There was one bathroom for seven people from three generations. Talk about people getting into each other's hair...

Oh, Magdalena! If only she were beside him right now! He would have his arm around her... in front of everybody... right now... and she would be joking about all the concrete front yards and all the put-upon wives of Hialeah. Why didn't everybody get together and water just *one* tree? That was what she'd be saying. She'd bet there weren't a dozen trees in all of Hialeah. Hialeah started out as a dirt prairie, and now it was a concrete prairie. That was the kind of thing she would say, if only she were here... He could *feel* her body leaning against his. She was so *beautiful*—and so *smart!* She had this... *way*... of looking at the world. How lucky he was! He had a girl more gorgeous, quicker, brighter than—than—than a TV star. He could feel her body against his in bed. ::::::Oh, my Manena:::::: His body hadn't touched hers in that way for almost two weeks. If it wasn't the hours he worked, it was the hours *she* worked. He never knew that nurses for psychiatrists had to work so long and so hard. This psychiatrist was a big deal, apparently. He had patients practically stacked up at the hospital, Jackson Memorial, plus the ones who came in to his office all day long, and Manena had to tend to patients at both places. Nestor never knew psychiatrists had so many hospital patients. Oh, but he's very prominent, very much in demand, Manena explained. She was working day and night. Recently it had become so hard, there was no time to see her at all. When he finished his Marine Patrol shift at midnight, she would be in bed asleep, and he didn't dare call her. She had to start work at 7:00 a.m., she had explained, because first she had to go by the hospital for a "pre-check" and then to the office for a full day of patients that ended at 5:00 p.m., but Nestor's shift began at 4:00 p.m. Just to make things worse, they had different days off. The whole thing had become impossible. What was to be done?

He had called her cell phone not all that long after he got back to the marina. No answer. He texted her. She didn't text back... and she *must* have known about it. If his father was right, *everybody* knew about it.

He had to see his Manena!... if only on Facebook. He rushed back to his room, got dressed as fast as he had ever gotten dressed in his life, and sat down at his laptop, which he kept on a table that only barely fit into the room, and went online... *Manena!* There she was... It was a picture he had taken of her... long luxurious dark hair *streaming* down to her shoulders... her dark eyes, her slightly parted, slightly smiling lips—that promised... *ecstasy* didn't even begin to say it! ::::::But stop fantasizing, Nestor! Go to the kitchen and get some coffee... before you're afflicted with company you don't want to have.::::::

* * *

He sat in the kitchen in the dark, drinking a second cup of coffee, trying to wake up...and thinking... thinking...thinking...thinking...He couldn't very well call her this early, 6:45 on a Saturday morning... shouldn't text, either. Even the *beep beep beep* of a text message might wake her up.

A light came on, and he heard a familiar flush and *glug-glug-glug* of a toilet. *Damn!* His parents were getting up...Camilo the Caudillo would be heading right here...*A wisp of hope!*...His father had had a chance to sleep on it and wanted to make peace—

Click—the kitchen light comes on. His father is in the doorway...He has his eyebrows flexed downward, creating a ditch between them. He's wearing his Relaxed-Fits, an XXL T-shirt whose short sleeves droop down below his elbows...yet it's barely big enough to cover his watermelon belly. He hasn't shaved. The undersides of his jowls are grizzly. He still has sleepers in his eyes. He's a real mess.

"Buenos días...?" ventures Nestor. It starts out as a greeting but winds up more of a question than anything else.

His father says, "Whaddaya doing sitting here in the dark?" *Don't you even know how to sit in a kitchen?*

"I...didn't want to wake anybody up."

"Who the hell's this little light gonna wake up?" *Don't you know anything?*

He brushed past Nestor without another word and fixed himself a cup of coffee... Nestor kept his eyes on Him, Camilo the Caudillo, Lord of This Domain. He feared another detonation. I, Camilo Camacho, downed his cup of coffee without lingering over a single sip. Then he marched out of the kitchen like a man with a job to do. He didn't acknowledge Nestor's presence in any way as he left... didn't so much as glance at him out of the corner of his eye...

Nestor turned back to his coffee, but by now it was cool, too black, too bitter... and beside the point. He thought and thought and thought and thought... and still couldn't figure out where he stood...

He asked himself, "Do I exist?"

The next moment... every manner of grunting, moaning, panting, and gasping for breath known to backbreaking labor commences just outside the kitchen.

It's his father—but what the hell is he doing? His body is tilted to the right because he's carrying an enormous thing on his right shoulder. It's long, it's bulky—it's a coffin. His father is wrestling with it and staggering under the thing... It seesaws up and down on the old man's shoulder... lurches sideways against his neck... It's about to flip out of his grip... He wrestles it back on top of his shoulder... One arm battles the lurches... the other one tries to stop the seesawing... He's red in the face... He's gulping for breath... He's making every inarticulate sound known to heavy labor...

"—messh... cinnghh... neetz... guhn arrrgh... *muhfughh* ... nooonmp ... *shit* ... boggghh ... frimp... ssslooosh... gessssuh *hujuh*... neench... arrrgh... eeeeeooomp."

The old man's legs are buckling. It's *not a coffin*—it's the *caja china* they always use to roast the pig—but when did anybody ever try to carry the damn thing by himself? There—the metal slots on the end where you insert handles for carrying it, one man on this end, one on the other... What fool ever tried to carry it over the shoulder? I, Camilo, built it himself years ago... an inch-thick plywood coffin-shaped box lined with roofing metal... must weigh seventy pounds... so long, so big, nobody could get an arm around it and hold it steady—

Nestor cries out, "DAD, LET ME HELP YOU!"

With that, the old man tries to move away from him... you mustn't lay a finger on it, traitor... *"Arggggh"*... That one little move—that does it! Now the *caja china* calls the shots! The damned thing is a huge raging bull riding *on top of* a little rider... Nestor can see it happening... it's like slow motion... but is in fact happening so fast, he's rooted to the floor... inert... the *caja china* is going into a spin. His father goes into a spin to try to keep up with it... his legs get wound around each other... he's keeling over... *"Arrrggh"*... the raging *caja china* is coming down on top of him... *"Errrnafumph"*... one end of it hits the wall—

CRAAASH!

—soundslikeatrainwreckinalittlecasitalikethis—

"Dad!" Nestor is already crouched over the wreck, starting to lift the huge box off his father's chest—

"No!" His father is looking straight up into Nestor's face. "No! No!"... has the full grimace now... eyes aflame... upper teeth bared... "You—no!"

Nestor lifts the *caja china* off his father anyway and puts it down on the floor... To someone with lats, traps, biceps, bracs, and quads like his—pumped up to the max by adrenaline—it's nothing... might as well be a cardboard box.

"Dad! Are you okay!?"

I, Camilo Camacho... lying on his back... glowering at his son, growling at his son, "Keep your hands off that *caja china,*" he says in a low but clear growl.

His dad isn't injured... he's perfectly lucid... the wall absorbed the momentum of the *caja china*... it just toppled over on I, Camilo Camacho... he's not indicating any pain... Oh, no... he only wants to *inflict* it... Something close to despair sweeps through

Nestor's central nervous system . . . He has been helping his father carry the *caja china* out for the pig roasts ever since he was twelve . . . His father lifted it by the handles on one end, and Nestor lifted it by the handles on the other end . . . *since he was twelve!* It had become a little ritual of manhood! Now his father wants no part of him.

I, Camilo Camacho, doesn't even want his son to lift a crash-stricken coffin off his prostrate form. You really know how to hurt a son, don't you, *Caudillo* Camacho . . . But Nestor can't find the words to say that or anything else.

"What happened!? What happened!?"

It's his mother, *running* from the bedroom. "Oh, dear God—Cachi! What happened? Cachi!" That's her loving nickname for the Master. "Are you all right? What was that terrible noise? What fell?"

She dropped to her knees beside him. He looked at her in an expressionless way, then put his tongue in his cheek and gave Nestor a baleful—and with his tongue in his cheek, accusing—stare. He held it like a laser beam . . . causing Nestor's mother to turn to him . . . wide-eyed . . . baffled . . . frightened . . . fearing the worst . . . as much as asking, "Did *you* do this—to your father?"

"Dad, tell her! Tell Mami what happened!"

I, Camilo Camacho, said nothing. He just continued with his sinister beam fixed on Nestor.

Nestor turned to his mother. "Dad tried to carry the *caja china* all by himself, on his shoulder! He lost his balance—and it crashed into the wall!"

Nestor began hyperventilating... He couldn't help himself, even though it cast a doubt upon what he was saying.

"Tell her why," said the Lord of This Domain in his new soft, low, mysterious voice... implying that much remained unsaid.

Mami looked at Nestor. "What *did* happen?" Then at her husband. "Cachi, you must tell me! Are you injured?"

In a voice that rose an octave, a shaky octave, Nestor said, "I swear! Dad was trying to carry that thing by himself! Look how big it is! He lost control, and when I tried to help him, he jumped away, or sort of jumped—and he lost his balance, and the *caja china* crashed and ended up on top of him! Right, Dad? That's exactly what happened—right?"

Down on her knees, Mami began crying. She pressed her hands against both sides of her face and kept saying, "Dear God... Dear God... Dear God... Dear God!..."

I, Camilo Camacho, maintained his stare at his son, pushing his tongue inside his cheek so forcefully, his lips parted on that side, showing teeth.

"Dad—you've *got to tell her!*" Nestor's voice was becoming shrill. "Dad—I know what you're doing!

You're playing Patience on a Monument, Smiling at Grief!"... Magdalena had introduced him to that expression. Somehow she picked up these things. "You're playing Look What You Made Me Do!"

Same low soft voice: "You don't talk to me that way. The Big Cop—but everybody knows what you really are."

Mami broke into sobs, great blubbering sobs.

Nestor's own eyes began to fill with tears. "This is not fair, Dad!" It was all he could do to keep his lips from trembling. "I'll help you up, Dad! I'll take the *caja china* out to the yard for you! But it's not fair—you can't treat me this way! It's not right! You're playing a game! Patience on a Monument, Smiling at Grief!"

He rose up from his crouch... He was getting out of here! Fighting back tears, he made his way into the little passageway that led from the extension to the rooms in the front of the house. A door opened behind him... a light... He knew immediately... Yeya and Yeyo—the last people on earth he needed at this moment, in the middle of all this.

Yeya, coming up behind him, said in Spanish, "What was that noise? Practically knocked us out of bed! What happened?"

Got to think fast... Nestor stopped, turned about, and gave Yeya the biggest, sweetest smile he could come up with. What a pair of *guajiros* stood before him. Keep them away from their son, I, Camilo

Camacho, that was the main thing... Yeya was short and stout, with a sort of flowered muumuu covering her considerable bulk. But mainly there was her hair. It was the blue ball, the Blue Ball of Hialeah for ladies of a certain age. Old ladies didn't dye their white hair in Hialeah, at least not in the usual way... Forty-eight hours ago, getting ready for her big birthday party, she went to the hairdresser. He cut it suitably short... for a woman of a certain age, added some—"blueing" in English—to give the gray a blue cast, and then blow-dried, back-combed, and teased it until it became a gossamer blue ball, a Hialeah crash helmet, as it was called. Hers was flattened a bit on one side from sleeping on it, but re-fluffing and reviving the helmet seemed to be no problem, as long as it hadn't been pulled apart. Just above her brow her hair was wound about a pair of rollers. Yeyo, right behind her, was a tall man. He had once been big and meaty and strong. He still had a tall wide frame, albeit slightly stooped. By now he was more like a wide but bony rack for the old-fashioned pajamas and bathrobe he had on. At this moment he looked like someone who had just arisen unwillingly from a pleasant time with the Sandman. His gray hair was marvelously thick. God must have nailed down every hair upon his head for the duration. He had been a really handsome man, who fairly rippled with confidence and strength—not to mention an overbearing nature...But at this unwilling moment his hair was sticking out every which way, like a broken broom—

All of that Nestor took in instantly...that, and their expressions. This morning they were not his loving *abuelo* and *abuela*. Not at all. If he read those faces correctly, they resented his breathing the same air they were...

How to distract them. That was the idea.

"Hap—*feliz cumpleaños,* Yeya!"

Damn. Kind of blew it there. Almost said "Happy birthday." Things like that truly rubbed Yeya and Yeyo the wrong way—the next generation using English instead of Spanish for something as traditional as *Feliz cumpleaños.* Yeya gave Nestor a look. Was he simple? A booby? Was he firing blanks? She glanced at his intentionally too-small shirt.

"Ahhh, the strongman," she said. "Our TV star. We saw you, Nestorcito. We saw a lot of you." She began nodding her head repeatedly with her lips drawn together and scrunched up beneath her nose like a little pouch with its string pulled tight...Oh, yes, Nestorcito, we saw *all too much* of you...

Before Nestor could say anything, Yeyo said (in Spanish), "Why did you tell them your name?"

"Tell who, Yeyo?"

"The TV."

"I didn't tell them."

"Who did?" said Yeya. "A little bird?"

"I don't know. They just *got* it."

"Do you know it's my name, too?" said Yeyo. "And your father's? Do you know we *care* about our name? Do you know we Camachos go back many generations? Do you know we have a proud history?"

::::::Do I know you added to that proud history by defying the raging shit-flow in the Havana waterworks? Yes, I know that, you overbearing old crock.:::::: Real anger, not mixed with *hurt,* was now rising up Nestor's brain stem. He had to get away from them before the words actually popped out.

His mouth was so dry, and his throat was constricted. "Yes, Yeyo," he managed to say. "I know that. I have to go now."

He had turned around to leave the house when... *clop-groan-squeak* thump... *clop-groan-squeak* thump... *clop-groan-squeak* thump... in the rear of the passageway... Oh, for God's sake... his mother was trying to support his father... I, Camilo's elbow rested on top of Mami's forearm, which was trembling from the weight of the invalid. He was gimping along as if he had hurt his leg... *clop*—he took a step, putting all his weight on his "good" leg, causing the jerry-built wooden floor of the passageway to groan and squeak... then the lighter thump of the "bad" leg gingerly... "painfully"... trying to come along... *What an outrageous faker Patience was!*

Yeya screamed. "Camilito—oh, dear God—what's happened to you?!"

In an instant she was at her Camilito's side, trying to give him more support by jacking her forearms up under his other arm.

"It's all right, Mami," he said. "You don't have to do that. I'm okay." How courageous he sounded! How stoic! thought Nestor. In fact, it couldn't have been very pleasant, having the heels of her hands jacked up into the soft spot of his armpit.

"But Camilito! My Camilito! There was such a crash! Oh, my God!"

"It's nothing, Lourdes." I, Camilo's new soft, husky voice. "Just a little family...disagreement." With that he pinned Nestor again with his ironic, tongue-in-cheek, teeth-baring stare, interrupting it only long enough to say again, *"Just...a...little...family...disagreement..."*

Now all four of them had their eyes pinned on Nestor. Yeya had become hysterical.

"What did you do to your father?! Your own father! It wasn't enough, what you did to that poor boy yesterday? Now you have to turn on your own father?!"

Nestor was bewildered...couldn't get a word out...just stood there with his mouth open. His mother was looking at him in a way she had never looked at him in his whole life! Even Mami!

When he found his voice, he was almost as

hysterical as Yeya. "Tell her the truth, Dad! Tell her what really happened! You're—you're—*twisting it all around!* In the name of God, tell the truth! Dad, you're—you're—"

He didn't help his own cause by breaking it off right there, wheeling about, showing them his back, rushing to his room to pick up his car keys—bolting for the front door without so much as glancing at the rest of his family.

Bang—he slammed the front door of La Casita de Camacho behind him.

3

The Daring Weak Man

Barely two hours later appeared an Edward T. Topping IV no one in the *Miami Herald* city room had ever seen before. Usually straight down the middle of his forehead, from his brow to his nose, ran a crevice . . . a crevice in the flesh of a man worrying about just how many people on the editorial staff, what was left of it, resented him. But this morning he was grinning . . . grinning a grin so broad, it raised his eyebrows as high as they would go . . . popped his eyes wide open . . . made his rosy cheeks well up atop each cheekbone, like Santa Claus's. The ditch had disappeared. The eyes glittered.

"Take a look at it, Stan! Take a look at it, a really *good* look. You know what you're looking at?"

He was standing in the middle of his office, which opened out into the city room. Standing, he was, not sitting halfway hidden within the cocoon of a high-backed Contract Modern swivel chair up against a kidney-shaped Contract Modern desk, the way he usually was. Not only that, he stood with his back to the wall of glass that provided him, as editor in chief, with the View...of all that was glamorous in Miami...the royal palm trees, the Mandarin Oriental Hotel, the royal palm trees, Brickell Avenue, the royal palm trees, Biscayne Bay, Brickell Key, Key Biscayne, the Venetian Isles, Indian Creek, Star Island, Miami Beach, and beyond that the Atlantic Ocean's great parabolic curve at the horizon, 180 degrees' worth of sun-bleached light-blue tropical sky, and the royal palm trees. No, at the moment he only had eyes for this morning's *Herald,* which he held before him the way one might display a painting, full length, top to bottom, showing off the front page.

"Here it is! You're looking at real journalism! *Real* journalism, Stan!"

Stan, namely Stanley Friedman, a thin, bony man in his forties, six feet tall but with atrocious posture that made his chest look concave and him six inches shorter—City Editor Stan watched this performance from an armchair barely four feet away. Stan had a squint-eyed look on his face. Ed Topping took it to be the look of a man in a state of wonder over what he has helped create: *this!*...this morning's *Miami Herald*! If the truth be told, Stanley Friedman had no room in his heart or on his face for Topping's "real journalism." All he wondered about was how long he would still have a job. Two weeks ago the Mob, short for Chicago Mob, as everyone in the city room now referred to the six men the Loop News Corporation had dispatched from Chicago to take over the *Herald,* had fired another 20 percent of the paper's workforce, bringing the total to 40 percent. Like City Editor Stan, everybody who remained felt as if he were hanging on to his job by his fingernails. Morale was—*what* morale? Everybody heeded Edward T. Topping IV's words only to detect signs of impending doom. Impending Doom was what City Editor Stan's eyes were squinting at. In fact, he was in no danger. The Mob had to have a local as city editor, someone whose memory bank was already stuffed with information he knew by heart about the entire metropolitan area, the street layout in detail, all fourteen police jurisdictions and their boundaries—very important, knowing the cops—the players, very much including all policy-making political officeholders, *all* of them, plus the celebrities, particularly the minor ones who felt more comfortable in Miami than in Los Angeles and New York...and...the nationalities and their turfs...Little Havana and Big Hialeah...Little Haiti, Little Caracas, also known as Westonzuela, Mother Russia (Sunny Isles and Hallandale), the Hershey Highway, that being the cops' nickname for the Anglo enclave of South Beach otherwise known as "gay" . . . There was no end to it, and a city editor had to know who hated whom and why—

"Just look at that makeup, Stan!" Ed was saying, eyes still bright as lightbulbs.

He was referring to the front page. An inky black headline ran the width of the paper—ROPE-CLIMB COP IN "MAST"-ERFUL RESCUE. On the far right was a lone column of type. The rest of the top half of the front page consisted of an enormous color picture of a white schooner with two towering masts and clouds and clouds of white sails . . . floating upon the aquamarine vastness of Biscayne Bay . . . beneath the pale-blue dome of the sky . . . and way, way, way up there, the equivalent of six or seven stories above the deck, no bigger than a thumbnail against such gigantic expanses, two tiny living creatures, two men whose lives depended on one man maintaining his one-hand grip on a jib sail cable . . . two specks popping out amid these overwhelming dimensions, two little human beasts *this close* to plunging to their death . . . all captured in a photograph by an old *Herald* photographer named Ludwig Davis, whose talent had spared him the axe. Down below was a two-column picture of a bare-chested young man with muscles on top of muscle, all highly defined, "cut," "ripped" to the point of looking shrinkwrapped. That picture on page one was a veritable male nude in chiaroscuro, school of Michelangelo.

Ed Topping couldn't hold back the sublime joy the big color picture of the schooner gave him. He thumped it with the backs of his fingers. *"There you have it!"* this semaphore said.

"No other medium could have come close to that image, Stan!" the suddenly animated editor in chief was saying. "Newsprint is great for color as long as you have big shapes of uniform value, such as the sky, the bay, the schooner, the hull, those huge sails—all white—and you know what? The poor resolution of the newsprint makes the color blocks more uniform. It's like a nineteenth-century Japanese print, the uniform blocks of color. The defect turns into an advantage!"

Ed opened his eyes wide...and turned them up brighter and brighter and brighter like a rheostat, as if to say, "*Now* you see what I mean, right?"

City Editor Stan stretched his neck upward and twisted his mouth and lower jaw in an odd way.

"No other medium could come close to this," Ed went on, explaining in some detail why television couldn't, why film couldn't, why videotape couldn't, why the internet couldn't...why not even a great print of the original photograph could come close. It would have "too many values in the color blocks."

City Editor Stan once again did that odd twisted contortion with his neck, mouth, and lower jaw.

::::::What inna nameagod is *that* all about?::::::
But Ed was too enchanted by his learned disquisition

on color imagery...nineteenth-century Japanese prints, no less!...to linger upon old Stan's tracheal twisting. In his heart Edward T. Topping IV took credit for this fabulous front page—or page one, as real newspapermen called it. During the tremendous excitement of putting the paper to bed last night—another Real Newspaperman expression, putting the newspaper "to bed"—he had left his office and gone out into the city room and stood by the shoulder of his managing editor, a fellow Chicago Mobster named Archie Pendleton, who was in turn leaning over the shoulder of the makeup editor, a local survivor who needed to be led like a pony on a lead line—all wondering what to do with this remarkable photograph by the old guy, Lud Davis...and Ed had said to Archie, "Go all the way with it, Archie. Make it big. Make it jump out at you on page one."

And it was done. How was one to explain the immense satisfaction it gave him? It was more than being the big man, the editor in chief, the Power. It was being creative, but aggressive, too...daring to let it all out when it was time to let it all out. It was what was meant by the expression "He's a real newspaperman."

Ed turned the newspaper around so that he could look at page one more closely.

"What can you tell me about John Smith, Stan?—the guy who wrote the story."

Stan's whole expression changed. What a relief! What

a relief to get a break from Grim Reaper IV giving a long-winded lecture! What a relief not to have to swallow yawn after yawn whole in strangulating gulps! He dearly hoped his contortions had seemed like nothing more than strenuous hiccups. What a relief to answer a simple question... and score a few status points by providing information you have and he doesn't.

"John's not a quick study," said Stan. "He's a long study. He's one of these twenty-eight-year-old kids—incidentally, he hates nicknames, hates Jack, hates Johnny, Jay, or anything else anybody comes up with. Won't fucking respond to them. Yeah! Refuses to hear them! He's plain John Smith. Anyway, he's one of these kids with blond hair and a baby face who's twenty-eight and looks about eighteen. I don't even know if he shaves or not, but I'll tell you something he does do—he blushes! He blushes all the time! I don't know another grown man who can still do that... *blush*. And polite? These days it'll—" As Stan burbled on, Ed turned to his computer and summoned up John Smith in the *Herald*'s internal directory.

"Keep talking, Stan. I'm just looking up Smith here."

::::::Well, I'll be switched:::::: thought Ed, as soon as it came up on the screen. ::::::John Smith went to St. Paul's and Yale! We're both Yalies... and St. Paul's trumps Hotchkiss!::::::

To Ed this had the power of... revelation.

"—but you can point the kid anywhere," Stan was

saying, "and he'll go there. He'll go right up to anybody you want and ask him anything you want. You know the lead he wrote? The police brass were trying to keep him away from this young cop, Nestor Camacho's his name—the cop who brought the guy down from the mast? They don't like cops giving interviews without prior approval and briefings and so forth, especially in a case like this. But John won't go away. If he could've handcuffed himself to the cop just to keep the interview going, I bet you he'd've done it. He describes that whole scene later on in the story."

Ed read the lead again . . . "By John Smith, with additional reporting by Barbara Goldstein, Daniel Roth, and Edward Wong.

" '*Weight*-lifting? Rope-climbing beats weight-lifting any day!' Miami Marine Patrol Officer Nestor Camacho, adrenaline still pumping, told the *Herald* yesterday—after his acrobatics had saved a man's life more than seventy feet above Biscayne Bay and electrified an entire city watching it live on television.

" 'That's the way I train! I climb this fifty-five-foot rope at Rodriguez's place, the "Ññññññoooooooooooo!!! Qué Gym!," without using my legs!' he said. 'Lats? Delts? Biceps? Pecs? Even pecs! It's the best thing in the world for the upper body, climbing ropes is.'

"And now, who in all of Miami dared dispute the man?

"The twenty-five-year-old cop had just pulled off an astounding feat of strength—a high-wire act that saved a Cuban refugee from a fatal plunge, stopped traffic cold on the six-lane Rickenbacker Causeway for hours, riveted the entire city via live television and radio coverage—and drew the ire of Miami Cuban activists who called the cop a 'traitor.'

"Shortly before three p.m., just south of the causeway's William Powell Bridge—"

Ed stopped reading and looked at Stan, grinning once more. "You know, when this lead first started coming in, I said to myself, 'What the hell is this? Pecs? delts? Ññññño—or whatever it is—Gym? What's this guy think he's writing, a sidebar on bodybuilding in our time?' It took a little bit before it dawned on me that this was the *perfect* lead. We have this constant problem. If there's a big story, everybody's already heard it on the radio or television or read it online. So by the time we come out, everybody's saying, 'What's this? *Yesterday's* newspaper?' But we were the only ones who got to the cop and interviewed him, isn't that right?" ::::::I'll be damned . . . St. Paul's and Yale.::::::

"Yeah," said Stan. "The cops didn't want to let the media near him, because this story cuts two ways. I mean, you remember all that booing, all those characters yelling down from the bridge—all the LIBERTAD signs and TRAIDOR? It turns out the cop is Cuban himself, Nestor Camacho. When he collars the guy, that makes the guy a Wet Foot. He never reached land or anything attached to land, like the bridge. So he can get sent right back to Cuba. Did you see the way *El Nuevo Herald* played it?"

"I've got it here, but I've been waiting to get it translated."

"The headline says '¡DETENIDO!'" said Stan. "You know, with the two exclamation points, before and aft? '¡DETENIDO! ¡A DIECIOCHO METROS DE LIBERTAD!' 'Arrested! Eighteen meters from freedom!'"

"Sixty feet is eighteen meters?"

"Almost exactly. Sounds shorter, right?"

"What do we have for a follow-up?" said Ed.

"The big question now is what happens to the wet foot," said Stan. "Right now he's in the custody of the Coast Guard. The police took him from their Safe Boat and turned him over to a Coast Guard cutter. John mentions that in the story."

"What does the Coast Guard do with him?"

"I've got John working on that right now," said Stan. "He says he has some contacts over at the ICE he can get to talk to him off the record." Stan began chuckling. That made his bony caved-in chest rock in a curious way. "If they send the guy back, there's gonna be a whole lotta busted balls in Miami. I wouldn't wanna be that cop, Officer Nestor Camacho."

::::::ICE, Immigration and Customs Enforcement.:::::: Ed was listening to Stan but at the same time ::::::Well, I'll—be—damned...a Yalie...I wonder if he worked on the *Daily News*:::::: referring to the undergraduate newspaper, the *Yale Daily News*, which Ed had worked on himself. *Blip!*—and he was at Broadway and York Street in New Haven, looking at the campus...all those magnificent gothic piles of stone and stained glass casement windows and massive slate roofs and arches and gargoyles, the sacred tower of the library, Sterling Memorial.

::::::What did Stan just say about the kid and the ICE? Ahh, yes...the kid knows people at the ICE.::::::

"Stan, have him come in here a minute."

"You mean John?"

"Yeah. I'd like to know exactly how he plans to proceed."

Stan shrugged. "Well, okay. But I should tell you ahead of time: He may go into something else, an idea he's breaking my balls with, a story about Sergei Korolyov and the new museum."

In due course, in came a young man who stopped diffidently just inside the door. To Ed he seemed surprisingly tall, six-one or -two. He was also surprisingly handsome...in a tender coming-of-age sort of way. Otherwise he fit Stan's description. He had a baby face, all right, and a head of longish, thatchy blond hair.

"Come on in," Ed said with a big smile, beckoning the young reporter.

"Yes, sir," said the punctilious John Smith.

—he blushed! No two ways about it! His smooth, pale, utterly lineless face turned almost scarlet.

He looked toward City Editor Stan. His expression was a question: "Why?"

"I think Mr. Topping would like to know a little about what we have on the Coast Guard's decision," said Stan.

Another violent blush. "Yes, sir." He directed the *yes* at Stan and the *sir* at Ed Topping.

"Pull up a chair and have a seat," said Ed, gesturing toward an armchair. He gave the kid another editor in chieftain's big smile.

John Smith pulled up the chair and sat down with both feet flat on the floor and a posture so erectly correct, his back never touched the chair's. He wore no necktie, but he did wear a shirt with a collar, in his case a white button-down shirt. That was about the best you could hope for these days, a shirt with a collar. Not only that, he wore a navy blazer—could that be linen?—a pair of khaki pants freshly pressed with a crease (didn't see that every day around this office), and a pair of well-polished dark-brown moccasins. Most of the male employees of the *Herald* had no idea what shoe polish was, evidently.

::::::A very preppy boy I have here, a very preppy Yale man:::::: Ed thought. ::::::St. Paul's preppy, at that.::::::

Ed picked up the paper and displayed it full-length, just as he had for Stan Friedman.

"Well," he said, "you think your story got enough attention?"

John Smith's lips seemed to be on the verge of a smile. Instead, the blood rushed to his cheeks again, and he said, "Yes, sir."

That was his third *yes, sir* in a row and so far he hadn't said another word. The moment went empty with silence. So Ed rushed into the vacuum. "How did you manage to get to the young cop, Camacho? As far as we know, nobody else got near him."

That was Ed's way of giving the kid a big pat on the back. One didn't just blurt out, "Great story, Smith!" That wasn't the real newspaperman's way.

"I knew where they would dock the Safe Boat when they brought Camacho back. Over at Jungle Island. So that's where I went."

"Nobody else figured that out?"

"I guess not, Mr. Topping," said the kid. "There was nobody else there."

Since he had finally gotten a few words out of him besides *yes, sir,* Ed slogged on. "How did you know about it?"

"From covering police, Mr. Topping. I've been on Safe Boat runs a couple of times."

"What about *El Nuevo Herald*? Why wouldn't they figure that out?"

John Smith shrugged. "I don't know, Mr. Topping. I never see anybody from *El Nuevo Herald* out on stories."

Ed leaned back in his swivel chair as far as its universal joint would go, swiveled away from John Smith and City Editor Stan, cocked his head back, and closed his eyes, as if deep in thought. His ebullient grin returned. The rosy balls of fat regrouped upon his cheekbones, and his eyebrows rose way, way up, although his eyes remained closed. He was back at Broadway and York. It was noon, and freshmen were walking in and out of the Old Campus...He was tempted to stay longer.

But he swiveled toward John Smith and City Editor Stan and opened his eyes again. He was still smiling. He was conscious of that. Why he was smiling he wasn't sure...except that if you're smiling, and nobody else gets it, you appear knowing, possibly even sophisticated. He only halfway admitted to himself that this was for the benefit of Yalie John Smith.

"John, I see by your bio"—he nodded toward the computer screen— "that you went to Yale."

"Yes, sir."

"What did you major in?"

"English."

"English..." said Ed in a certain significant way. He broadened his smile, making it seem more inscrutable than ever.

"Was Theory still a big deal in the English department when you were there?"

"There were some professors who taught Theory, I guess," said John Smith, "but I don't think it was a big thing."

Ed maintained his I-have-a-secret smile and said, "I seem to remember—" *Axxxx* he cut that sentence off at the neck. In the next split second, if he hadn't already, Stan would spot this *I seem to remember* talk for what it was: a labored way of letting John Smith know that he, Edward T. Topping IV, was a Yale man, too. *Bango!* He dropped the smile, rigged up a scowl, and started talking in a business tone that implied John Smith had been wasting his, T-4's, time.

"*Now*... Okay, let's get down to cases. Where do we stand with this Coast Guard thing?"

He made a point of staring first at Stan, then at John Smith. John Smith stared at Stan, and Stan stared at John Smith and motioned toward Ed with his chin, and John Smith stared at Ed and said to him:

"Oh, they'll send him back to Cuba, Mr. Topping. They decided last night."

He showed no particular excitement, but Stan and Ed were a different story. Both spoke at once.

Stan: "You didn't—"

Ed: "How do—"

"—tell me that!"

"—you know that?"

John Smith said to Stan, "I didn't have a chance. I'd just gotten off the phone when you said I should come into Mr. Topping's office." He turned to Ed. "There's a... a person at ICE I know very well. I know he wouldn't tell me if he wasn't sure. But I have to run it by Ernie Grimaldi at the Coast Guard to see if they'll corroborate it." He looked at Stan. "I had just called him and left a message when I came in here."

"You say they made the decision last night?" said Ed. "Who makes the decision? How do they do it?"

"It's pretty simple, Mr. Topping, and it can happen very fast. If it's a Cuban, they give *hihh*—the person... a hearing right there on the Coast Guard cutter. They'll have some officer who does these hearings all the time. If they can convince the hearing officer—"

::::::Aw, shit, the kid is PC... the way he almost said "him" and switched it to "person" on the edge of the cliff... and then gave up "person" for "they," so he wouldn't have to deal with gender in the singular, the "hims" and "he's.":::::::

"—that they've fled from Cuba because of a 'credible threat'—that's the term they use, 'a credible threat'—then they're given asylum. This man says his name is Hubert Cienfuegos and he's a member of an underground organization called El Solvente, the Solvent. But I was here until eleven o'clock last night, Mr. Topping, calling everybody I could think of, and nobody had ever heard of Hubert Cienfuegos or El Solvente."

"Do you speak Spanish?"

"Yes, sir, or pretty well, anyway."

"How do they decide about the credible threat and asylum?" said Ed.

"It's all up to the one man, the hearing officer. He either believes them or doesn't believe them. He does it all right there on the deck. That's the entire proceeding, Mr. Topping. It's over in no time."

"How does he decide?"

"I don't know that much about it, Mr. Topping, but I gather two things can disqualify the person. One is, if they're too vague, they can't come up with dates or a timeline, or they can't tell you who exactly is threatening them. The other is, if the story's too, you know—too pat. It sounds rehearsed, or memorized, and they're delivering it by rote? Things like that? The hearing officer can't subpoena witnesses. So it's a judgment call, I guess you'd say."

"Why do they do this on the deck of a ship?" said Ed. "Like this fellow yesterday—Cienfuegos. Why didn't they bring him ashore and have a hearing—I mean, after all that chaos?"

"If the person's Cuban and they bring them into a police station or a holding pen or a jail or anywhere else, then they get asylum automatically. They've set foot on American soil. If they've committed a crime in American waters, they'll be prosecuted, but they can't send them back to Cuba."

"You're kidding."

"No, sir. And if the person has done nothing more than try to get into the country illegally, the only thing that happens is, they're sentenced to a year's probation and they walk away a free person. The Cubans have a sort of most-favored-migration status."

::::::person person person they they they they they them them them them I fucking don't want to believe it was Yale that made my man here mangle the goddamn English language this way, although most-favored migration is a pretty good play on most-favored nation:::::: but all he said was:

"So this guy Cienfuegos's goose is cooked, and he's out of here."

"Yes, sir. But my source told me they may not say anything about it for four or five days or even a week. They want to give all the protestors some time to cool off."

"That would be *great!*" said Stan, who was so excited he actually sat up straight. "If we go with it right away, we'll have the story to ourselves." Stan stood up...straight, too, for him. "Okay, let's get going, John. We got a lotta work to do!"

Stan began heading for the door. John Smith got up, too, but remained standing there and said to Stan, "Would it be okay if I mention the Korolyov story to Mr. Topping?"

Stan turned his eyes upward and exhaled a

wearier-than-plain-weary sigh and looked at Ed. Ed broke into another big smile, the smile of a man who has Fate going his way. "Sure," he said to John Smith, "let's hear it. Korolyov's a real piece of work. Talk about—"

Ed noticed a dubious look, obviously for his benefit only, passing across Stan's face like a shadow. But a happy man doesn't worry about other people's shadows.

"—colorful," he continued. "I happened to be seated practically next to him at that dinner the city and the museum gave in his honor last year. My God, seventy million dollars' worth of paintings he had donated, and they must have had half of them hung in that dining room! What a show that was... all these Russian paintings lining the walls... Kandinskys, Maleviches... *uhhh*..." He couldn't remember any more names.

"Some Larionovs," said John Smith, "Goncharovas, Chagalls, a Pirosmanashvili, and—"

Ed pulled a face. "Piro—*who?*"

"He was sort of a Russian Henri Rousseau," said John Smith. "Died in 1918."

::::::Christ, Pirowhatsavili?:::::: Ed decided to ascend from the level of the details. "Anyway, they're worth at least seventy million dollars, and that's according to the *low* estimates. No, Korolyov is a great subject. But we had a big profile of him not all that long ago. What would your angle be?"

Cloud after cloud was now rolling across Stan's face as he stood behind John Smith.

"Well, sir, for a start, the Kandinskys and Maleviches are fakes."

Ed cocked his head and lifted one eyebrow so high, so high, the eyeball looked big as a doorknob, and lowered the other eyebrow until it completely shut that eye, and said, "The Kandinskys and the Maleviches are fakes." No question mark. "And by 'fakes,' I assume you mean forgeries." Again, no question mark. But the look on his face implicitly, and dubiously, asked, "Did you actually say what I think you just said?"

"Yes, sir," said John Smith. "That's my information."

Ed cocked his head still further and said in a mock-casual way, "All . . . forgeries." Again, no question mark. His contorted eyebrows posed the question more emphatically than words could have: "What have you been smoking? Do you really expect anybody to take that seriously?" Out loud he said, "And I suppose that Korolyov was aware of all this when he gave them to the museum." No question mark—this time it was an undisguised verbal sneer.

"Sir, he was the one who paid to have them done."

Ed was speechless. ::::::What's *with* this kid? He's nobody's picture of an investigative journalist. He's more like a too-tall sixth grader who keeps raising his hand because he's just dying to show the teacher how smart he is.::::::

"And, sir," said John Smith, "I know the two Larionovs are fake."

Ed started sputtering. "So one of the most generous and...and...public-spirited and...and...admired and respected individuals in Miami has swindled the museum." No question mark even remotely necessary. The statement would sink without a bubble under its own absurdity.

"No, sir," said John Smith. "I don't think it's swindling, because the paintings were a gift, and he didn't ask for money or anything else in return, as far as I know. And the recipients can't be called gullible people. They're supposed to be experts in the field."

A very unpleasant sensation, not yet a thought, began spreading through Ed's innards like a gas. He was beginning to resent this skinny, too-tall troublemaker personally and professionally, Yalie or no Yalie. At that dinner last year, no man had sat closer to the guest of honor, Korolyov, than Ed. The woman who sat between them was Mayor Cruz's mousy wife, Carmenita, who was small and painfully shy; in short, a nullity. So Ed was as good as at the very elbow of the illustrious oligarch. In no time they were "Ed" and "Sergei." *The world* was at that dinner, everybody from the Mayor and his City Hall heavies...to the billionaire art collector Maurice Fleischmann, who had his hand in so many things he was known as the Player—rhymed with *mayor*. Fleischmann was about four seats down from Ed there at the head table. Ed could still see the whole scene as if it had happened only last night. Physically, Fleischmann wasn't as big as he looked...which really didn't matter when what you looked like was an angry bear, heavy in the body and hirsute in the face. To make up for his bald pate, he wore the currently trendy "double-stubble," about four weeks' worth of beard running from the temple down over the jaws and the chin and beneath the nose. To keep it neat and even, most men used the Gillette Double-Stubble electric razor. You could adjust it like a lawn mower to maintain whatever level of growth you wanted. This ten o'clock shadow left Fleischmann looking unusually fierce and aggressive. He was by nature a regular bear in business, much feared, much envied, much sought-after. He had made his fortune—*billions*—from a company called American ShowUp in a business nobody had ever heard of: "convenable infrastructure." Several times at least benevolent and knowledgeable souls had tried to explain it to Ed, and he still didn't get it. Yet who was it who sat practically tête-à-tête with the guest of honor, Sergei Korolyov? Not the grizzly bear, but Ed. The point was not lost on the other Miami celebrati there that night. Ed's status got its biggest boost since he had arrived in Miami.

He and the *Herald* had been Korolyov's greatest backers in making him and his huge art donation the keystone of Museum Park. The Park had been dreamed up way back in the late 1990s... as a "cultural destination." Urban planners all over the country were abuzz with this fuzzy idea that every "world-class" city—*world-class* was another au courant term—must have a world-class cultural destination. *Cultural* referred to the arts... in the form of a world-class art museum. Museum Park would also feature a new Miami Museum of Science, but the anchor of the whole project would be the art museum. Times were good in 2005, and the dream began to look believable. The Park would take over the grounds of the old Bicentennial Park—old because the Bicentennial had been almost forty years ago, an eternity in Miami time—twenty-nine acres in downtown Miami with a view and a half. It overlooked Biscayne Bay. The fund-raising began in earnest. The museum alone would cost $220 million, 40 percent in government bonds and 60 percent in private donations. A pair of world-class Swiss architects, Jacques Herzog and Pierre de Meuron, would design the museum, and the world-class New York firm Cooper, Robertson would design the lavish landscaping. But there was a problem in seeking private donations. This world-class cultural destination would lead to a museum full of... next to nothing... the meager, third-rate art collection, several hundred contemporary paintings and objets, from the existing Miami Art Musuem, not founded until 1984, when all "great" art had long since inflated to prices that were out of sight.

But then—a miracle. Four years ago a Russian oligarch nobody had ever heard of arrived in Miami from out of nowhere and offered to give the museum, now called the "New Miami Art Museum," seventy million dollars' worth of paintings by big-name Russian Modernists of the early twentieth century—Kandinskys and Maleviches and the rest. From that moment on, construction began pell-mell. They hadn't quite finished by the time of the dinner last year, but one thing they had completed. After the dessert course, a team of eight union elves rolled a massive object, about fourteen feet high and eight feet wide—*enormous*—and covered by a mauve mantle of velvet, out onto the stage. The president of the now-named New Miami Art Museum said a few purposely vague words and then pulled a velvet rope. The rope was connected to a pulley mechanism, and the velvet mantle flew off, *just like that.* Before *le tout Miami* was a tremendous limestone rectangle incised with huge capital letters reading, THE KOROLYOV MUSEUM OF ART. *Le tout Miami* rose like a single colonial animal in a deafening paroxysm of applause. The board had renamed the museum in his honor. The massive slab of limestone, with incisions so deep the letters disappeared in shadow if you tried to look all the way to the incisions' bottoms. The president of the board announced that the ornamental ten-ton sign would be hung from the girders above the entrance in the middle of a huge hanging garden.

Ed never got over the ecstatic sight of those huge letters carved so deeply—*for all eternity!*—in ten tons of stone tablet. Explicitly they honored Korolyov, those letters that would endure across the ages, but implicitly they honored Korolyov's great herald and champion—I, me, Edward T. Topping IV.

::::::And this too-tall little boy here right in front of me is, in effect, telling me I've let myself be used, duped, gulled, diddled with, in the most humiliating and yokel-headed fashion.:::::: The thought made him furious.

John Smith probably wondered why Ed's voice was seething so when he grimaced and glared at him and snapped. "Okay, fun's over. Anybody can *accuse* anybody of *anything*. It's time to get serious. What makes you think *any*body should believe *any*thing in the tale you've just told me? You're making some"—he started to say "libelous"—"some ugly charges against a highly respected man."

"I got a tip, Mr. Topping. It was about the painter who forged the Kandinskys and the Maleviches. Apparently he can't resist bragging about it to everybody. He's fooled the experts."

"Who's everybody?"

"The hip art crowd, I guess you'd call them, sir, in Wynwood and South Beach."

"The hip art crowd in Wynwood and South Beach..." said Ed. "Who exactly in the *hip art crowd in Wynwood and South Beach* told you about all this?"

"An artist I know who has a studio near the artist who did the forgeries."

"And he has the forger's admissions on tape or in writing, I hope?"

"No, sir, and the forger—his name is Igor Drukovich—he's a Russian, like Korolyov—he hasn't admitted it in so many words, exactly, but he doesn't think of it as an 'admission.' He's *eager* to have people know about it, sir. I gather he has a real drinking problem, and the hints get broader and broader."

"The hints get broader and broader," Ed said as ironically as he could. No question mark.

"Yes, sir."

"Did it ever occur to you that everything you've just told me is hearsay?"

"Yes, sir," said John Smith. "I know I have a lot of work to do. But I trust my sources."

"He trusts his sources," Ed said with maximum sarcasm right to John Smith's face.

He immediately realized he had lost control of himself...but these John Smiths, these goddamned ambitious kids, these self-important children and their visions of "revealing," "uncovering," "exposing" scandals...For what? Civic good? Oh, give me a break! They're self-centered, that's all. Juvenile egotists! If they're so determined to create trouble, to lay bare evil, even if it means libeling people, why can't they stick with the government? With officeholders? With politicians? With government bureaucrats? They can't *sue!* Technically they can—but as a practical matter, they can't. There they are, yours for the kill! Aren't they enough for you, you asinine little brats! You mosquitoes! You who live to sting and suck blood and then fly away and hover and wait for the next poor slob feeding at the public trough to turn his bare ass so you can dive-bomb and sting again and suck some *more* blood! Isn't that enough for you? Do you *have* to choose people like Sergei Korolyov who do selfless public good—and probably have enough lawyers on retainer to tie up and humiliate the *Miami Herald* until it loses all credibility and slinks off into the yellow ooze?

"Now, John," said Ed, struggling to get his composure back. "Have you thought about the . . . the . . . *dimensions* of such a story, should you write it?"

"How do you mean, sir?"

Ed was speechless again. He did know exactly what he meant, but he had no idea how to say it. How could you look a young reporter in the eye and say, "Kid, don't you understand? We don't *want* any such great *stories*. Journalism? Don't you get it? There's journalism, and there's the bottom line. And if you don't mind moving aside for a moment, we have to at least take note of the bottom line here. We're sorry, but you can't be Woodward and Bernstein just now. And, incidentally, kindly note that they went after people who couldn't *sue*. Richard Nixon was the President of the United States, but he couldn't *sue*. They could say he fucked ducks in Rock Creek Park, and he couldn't *sue*."

Struggling, struggling, Ed finally regained the power of speech. "What I mean is, in a case like this, you have to proceed very methodically..." He paused, because he was mainly buying time. He really didn't know *what* he meant now.

"Methodically? How do you mean, sir?" said John Smith.

Ed slogged on. "Well... here you're not dealing with Mayor Cruz or Governor Slate or the Tallahassee Round Ring. You get some leeway with political stories and politicians... politicians..." He studiously avoided the term *sue*. He didn't want John Smith to think of that as an operative word here. "You can speculate about a politician and even if you get it wrong, there aren't likely to be any terrible repercussions, because that's all part of the game in politics, at least in this country. But when you have a private citizen like Korolyov, with no record of anything like this..."

"Sir, as I understand it, Korolyov is like a lot of the so-called oligarchs who come here. He's well educated, he's cultivated, he's charming, he's great looking, he knows English, French, and German, and that's in addition to Russian, of course. He knows art history—I mean, I gather he really knows it—and he knows the art market, but he's a criminal, Mr. Topping. A lot of them are criminals, and they'll get the worst thugs in the world, Russian thugs, to work for them if they have to, and they're just incredibly brutal. I could tell you some stories."

Ed stared at John Smith again. He kept waiting for him to molt into something else entirely, a hawk, a scorpion, a Delta Commando, a stingray. But all this had come out of the mouth of the same face...of a mere boy with perfect manners and perfect posture. And the blush. When he saw the way Ed was staring at him, the boy did it again. He blushed a deep scarlet.

::::::Jesus:::::: Ed Topping said to himself. ::::::This kid is a classic...People have such a colorful picture of newspaper reporters, don't they, all these daring types who "break" stories and "uncover" corruption and put themselves in risky situations to get a "scoop." Robert Redford in *All the President's Men*, Burt Lancaster in *The Sweet Smell of Success*...Yeah—and in real life they're about as colorful as John Smith here. If you ask me, newspaper reporters are created at age six when they first go to school. In the schoolyard boys immediately divide into two types. Immediately! There are those who have the will to be daring and dominate, and those who don't have it. Those who don't, like John Smith here, spend half their early years trying to work out a modus vivendi with those who do . . . and anything short of subservience will be okay. But there are boys from the weaker side of the divide who grow up with the same dreams as the stronger . . . and I'm as sure about this as anything in the world: The boy standing before me, John Smith, is one of them. They, too, dream of power, money, fame, and beautiful lovers. Boys like this kid grow up instinctively realizing that language is an artifact, like a sword or a gun. Used skillfully, it has the power to . . . well, not so much *achieve* things as to tear things down—including people . . . including the boys who came out on the strong side of that sheerly dividing line. Hey, that's what *liberals* are! Ideology? Economics? Social justice? Those are nothing but their prom outfits. Their politics were set for life in the schoolyard at age six. They were the weak, and forever after they resented the strong. That's why so many journalists are liberals! The very same schoolyard events that pushed them toward the written word . . . pushed them toward "liberalism." It's as simple as that! And talk about irony! If you want power through words in journalism, rhetorical genius is not enough. You need content, you need new material, you need . . . *news,* in a word . . . and you have to find it yourself. You, from the weak side, can develop such a craving for new information, you end up doing things that would terrify any strong man from the other side of the divide. You will put yourself in dangerous situations amid dangerous people... *with relish.* You will go alone, without any form of backup... *eagerly!* You—you with your weak manner—end up approaching the vilest of the vile with a demand. "You have some information, and I *need* it. And I *deserve* it! And I *will* have it!"::::::

All this Ed could see in the baby face before him. Maybe these Russian thugs or whatever he was talking about were as brutal as he said. Ed himself had no idea. But he could see John Smith sticking his baby face and blond hair and blue eyes and great slathers of naïveté right in their faces and demanding information about Sergei Korolyov because he needs it, deserves it, and *will* have it.

::::::Well, I *don't* need it, and I don't *deserve* a big, messy, pseudo-righteous, money-hemorrhaging fight staged solely for the greater glory of a kid named John Smith, and I won't *have* it.::::::

But there's something closer to home that you'd rather not think about, isn't there, Ed... If one of these little vipers from the weak side of the playground somehow *did* expose Korolyov and his "seventy million dollars' worth" of early Russian Modernist work as a con artist pulling off a colossal fraud, it would make the entire Miami establishment look like a clusterfuck!... The fools had put $500 million into a world-class cultural destination now worth precisely nothing! They would all become world-class jokes, utterly lamebrained, unbelievably gullible culture strivers! The horse laugh would resound 'round the world!

And who would become the most laughable of all, the most pitiable and pathetic — turning four generations of Toppings, five if you counted Fiver, into a long, drawn-out, scabid dog story?

And he was supposed to help his own minions drown him in shame? . . . ::::::Stand up for yourself, man! Get tough for once in your life! "Real journalism?" Fuck that!::::::

4

Magdalena

Nestor took a deep breath . . . a *free* breath . . . in the open air of a nice clear Saturday morning. He glanced at the watch on his wrist, a big cop-sized watch packed with digital systems to burn. It was 7:00 a.m. exactly . . . unnaturally quiet out here on the street—*good!* . . . nobody stirring except for the women hosing down the concrete . . . a regular two-note concerto of spray hitting a hard surface. ¡SHEEEahHHHH ahHHHHSSHEEEE! He looks about . . . two doors away, Señora Díaz. He's known her ever since the day he moved into this casita. Thank God, a sweet, kind friend from the free world! It makes him happy, just seeing her there with a garden hose in her hand, spraying concrete. Oh so very cheerfully he sings out, "*Buenos días,* Señora Díaz!"

She looked up and started to smile. But only one

side of her mouth moved. The other side stayed put, as if it had gotten snagged by an eyetooth. Her gaze went blank. ¡SHEEEEahHHHH ahHHHHsh-HEEEE! as she mumbled the most mechanical *Buenos días* he had ever heard in his life... *Mumbled* it!... and turned her back, as if she had neglected to hose the concrete... over *there.*

That was all she was going to give him! A mumble and a retractable smile! And a stone-cold back... and he had known her forever! ::::::Got to get out of *here,* too! Off the street I've lived on practically all my life! Got to go—*where,* f'r chrissake?!::::::

He had no idea. Aside from the women hosing down concrete, such as Señora Díaz, Hialeah was in a Saturday-morning coma. ::::::Well... I'm *hungry. ¿No es verdad? Dios mío, I'm hungry.*::::::

He hadn't had anything to eat for almost twenty-four hours, or practically nothing. He had his regular break at about eight o'clock last night, but so many of the guys were there asking him questions about the Man on the Mast thing, all he managed to eat was one hamburger and some french fries. He was counting on having something to eat when he got home. So his dad shoves a shitload of abuse down his throat instead.

He went straight to his aging muscle car, the Camaro... *Muscle* car?... with his big black Cuban cop shades on, jeans tailored until they fit like ballet tights in the seat . . . polo shirt size S, for small, because that made it "too" tight across the chest and shoulders. ::::::Oh, fuck:::: what a stupid mistake! This morning he didn't want to be seen showing off his muscles or in any other fashion calling attention to himself. Ricky's Bakery would be open this early . . . in a shopping strip six blocks away. Six blocks — but he didn't feel like showing his face in his own neighborhood and risking any more surprises like the one Señora Díaz hit him with.

In no time the mighty Camaro was cruising along the strip. The place was still asleep . . . He cruised past the botanica where Magdalena's mother had bought the statue of Saint Lazarus.

Nestor climbed out of the Camaro in front of Ricky's and got a whiff of Ricky's pastelitos, "little pies" of filo dough wrapped around ground beef, spiced ham, guava, or you name it — one whiff of pastelitos baking, and he relaxed . . . *ambrosia* . . . He had loved pastelitos since he was a little boy. Ricky's was a tiny bakery with a big glass counter in the rear running practically the width of the place. In the foreground, on each side, was a small, round, tinny metal café table, painted white — back when — and flanked by a pair of old-fashioned drugstore-style bentwood chairs. A lone customer sat there, his back to Nestor, reading a newspaper and drinking a cup of coffee. He was middle-aged, judging by the way he had gone bald on the crown of his head without his hair turning gray. There were always three girls behind the counter, but the counter was so high, you had to come very close to see much more than the hair on the tops of their heads. ::::::Hey! Is that a blonde back there?:::::: Nestor had never seen a blond waitress at Ricky's before. Maybe he hadn't seen one now, either. His cop shades had engulfed the whole place in a half-dead dusk . . . at 7:00 a.m. So he pushed them up above his eyes.

Big mistake. That also made his own face plain as the moon. The big head at the little white tin-top table turned toward him *¡Dios mío!* It was Mr. Ruiz, the father of Rafael Ruiz, one of Nestor's classmates at Hialeah High School.

"Why, hello, Nestor," said Mr. Ruiz. It wasn't a cheery greeting. It was more like the cat toying with the mouse.

Nestor made a point of smiling at Mr. Ruiz and saying as cheerfully as he could, "Oh . . . Mr. Ruiz! *¡Buenos días!*"

Mr. Ruiz turned away, then gave his head a quarter-turn toward Nestor, without looking at him, and said out the side of his mouth, "I see where you had quite a day for yourself yesterday." No smile . . . none at all. Then he turned back to his newspaper.

"Well, I guess you could call it that, Mr. Ruiz."

The head said, "Or else you could say *te cagaste*."

You blew it. Literally, you shit all over it. Mr. Ruiz turned away completely and showed Nestor his back.

Humiliated!—by this—this—this—Nestor wanted to twist that big head off its skinny neck and—and—and *cagar* down his windpipe—and then he'd—

"Nestor!"

Nestor looked toward the counter. It was the blonde. Somehow she had managed to tiptoe high enough to lift her face above the top surface. He knew her. *Cristy La Gringa!* he wanted to cry out, but Mr. Ruiz's presence inhibited him.

He walked up to the counter. All that marvelous long wild blond hair! *Cristy La Gringa!* "Cristy La Gringa!" He realized that didn't have the poetic wallop of "Inga La Gringa," but it still made him feel like Nestor the Jester... a real wit, *no es verdad?* Cristy had been a year behind him at Hialeah High School, and she'd had a crush on him. Oh, she had made that obvious. He was tempted. She had made his loins stir... *Pastelitos!* Oh yes!

"Cristy!" said Nestor. "I didn't know you were working here! *La bella gringa!*"

She laughed. That was what he used to call her at Hialeah High... when they were supposedly just kidding around.

"I just started here," said Cristy. "Nicky got me the job. You remember Nicky? She was a year *ahead* of you?" She gestured toward the third girl. "And this is Vicky."

Nestor ran his eyes over the three of them. Nicky's and Vicky's hair streamed down into turbulent waves at the shoulders, just like Cristy's, but theirs was dark in the Cuban way. All three were shrink-wrapped in denim. Their jeans hugged their declivities fore and aft, entered every crevice, explored every hill and dale of their lower abdomens, climbed their *montes veneris*—

—but somehow he just *couldn't*...He was too depressed. "Vicky and Cristy and Nicky and Ricky's," he said. They laughed...uncertainly...and that was that.

He went ahead and ordered some pastelitos and coffee...to go. He had come in with a vision of himself sitting at one of the little tables and making a long, leisurely breakfast of it, quietly, on neutral ground, just him and his pastelitos and coffee. Mr. Ruiz had put an end to that. Who knew how many more soreheads with smart mouths would show up here even now, this early on a Saturday morning?

By and by, Cristy brought out a white paper bag—somehow all the little bakeries and diners in Hialeah used only white bags—with the pastelitos and coffee. At the cash register, as she gave him change, he said, "Thanks for everything, Cristy." He meant it in a loving way, but it came out sad and beaten more than anything else.

Cristy had already headed back behind the counter when he noticed a shelf beneath it with two stacks of newspapers.

Whuh! His heart tried to leap out of its thoracic cage. *Himself!*—a photograph of *himself!*—his official Police Department photograph—on the front page of the Spanish-language *El Nuevo Herald*! Next to his, a—a picture of a young man with a twisted face: Nestor knew that face, all right—the man on the mast... above those two head shots, a big photograph of the schooner near the causeway and a mob of people up on the bridge screaming until their teeth showed... and above that, the biggest, blackest print Nestor had ever seen on a newspaper: ¡DETENIDO! 18 METROS DE LIBERTAD—stretching across the entire front page... of *El Nuevo Herald. Shock!*—his heart began speeding. He didn't want to read the story, sincerely didn't *want* to—but his eyes seized upon the first sentence and wouldn't let go.

In Spanish it said, "A Cuban refugee, reportedly a hero of the dissident underground, was arrested yesterday on Biscayne Bay just eighteen meters from the Rickenbacker Causeway—and asylum—by a cop whose own parents had fled Cuba and made it to Miami and freedom in a homemade dinghy."

Nestor felt as if heat were surging up his cerebral cortex and scalding his brain. Now he was a villain, a vile ingrate who would deny his own people the freedom he enjoyed ... in short, the worst sort of *TRAIDOR!*

He didn't want to buy the newspaper ... Its *stain* would spread indelibly upon his hands if he so much as picked it up ... but something—his autonomous nervous system?—overrode his conscious will and ordered him to stoop down and grab one. *Holy shit!* When he stooped down, he got an eyeful of the newspaper atop the other stack. The entire top half of the newspaper's front page was one huge color picture—the blue of the Bay, the enormous white sails of the schooner ... above the picture—English language! The *Miami Herald*!—a headline as big and bold as *El Nuevo Herald's*—ROPE-CLIMB COP IN "MAST"-ERFUL RESCUE ... He turned the newspaper over, to see the lower half of the front page—*¡Santa Barranza!*—a two-column-wide photograph, in color, of a young man with no shirt on ... clad from the waist up in only his own muscles, an entire mountainscape of muscles, huge boulders, sharp cliffs, deep cuts, and iron gorges ... an entire muscle terrain ... ME! So in love fell he—with ME!—that he could barely remove his eyes from the image long enough to scan the story that filled the other four columns ... "amazing feat of strength" ... "risked his own life"—"Ññññññoooooooooooo!!! Qué Gym!" ... rope-climbing ... "rescued a Cuban refugee by locking his legs about him." See that? ... he *rescued* the little bastard ... Rope-Climb Cop hadn't doomed him to torture and death in Fidel's dungeons...Oh, no...He had *saved his life*...It *said* so, in so many words!... Nestor's mood swung so high, so fast, he could feel it in his gizzard. The *Miami Herald* had granted him a reprieve...in English...but *that counted,* didn't it?... The *Herald*-in-English—the oldest newspaper in Florida! But then his spirits sank... *"Yo no creo el Miami Herald."* I don't believe the *Miami Herald.* If Nestor had heard that once he had heard it a thousand times...The *Herald* had opposed Cuban immigration, once Cubans had begun fleeing Castro by the thousands...resented it when there were so many Cubans, they took over politically... *"Yo no creo el Miami Herald!"* Nestor had heard this from his father, his father's brothers, his father's sisters' husbands, his cousins, the whole Hialeah lot of them...from everyone old enough to say the words *"Yo no creo el Miami Herald..."*

Still...this *americano* newspaper was all he had. Somebody in Hialeah must read the damned thing and even believe...some of it. It was just that he had never met that person. Plenty of the people coming to Yeya's party could read English, though...Yes!... They could certainly read those huge letters calling what he had done a "MAST"-ERFUL RESCUE, couldn't they? He ducked out of Ricky's and returned to the Camaro...Ineffable clouds of Ricky's Bakery aroma from the bag next to him took over the entire car... The pastelitos and the *Miami Herald,* which lay next to the bag... two feasts... and "That's him right there, the turncoat cop, stuffing his face with food and reading about his glorified self in the *Yo-no-creo Herald*..." Not cool, not cool... but I'm so *tired*... He took the plastic top off the *cortadito,* indulged himself with a sip and a sip and a sip of the utterly hedonistic sweetness of Cuban coffee... He picked up the *Miami Herald* and consumed some more lip-smacking syllables of the ROPE-CLIMB COP... He reached into the bag from Ricky's—*pastelitos!*—and took out a moon of beef pastelito wrapped in wax paper... *A little bit of Heaven!*... tasted exactly the way he hoped it would... *Pastelitos!* A little flake of the baked filo dough fell... and then another... the very nature of baked filo dough... little flakes of it fell if you picked up a pastelito... little flakes fell on his clothes... upon the Camaro's reupholstered seats... Far from annoying him, the gentle doughfall in the stillness of 7:30 a.m. on a Saturday morning was a little bit of Heaven, too... made Nestor think of home, childhood delights, sunny Hialeah, a cozy casita... soft, fluffy clouds of love and affection... and protection. Gently, gently, the flakes were wafted about by the white-noise zephyrs that blew out from the air conditioner vents... Nestor could feel the terrible tension draining out draining out draining out, and he drank some more coffee... ineffable sweetness—and how warm the cup and the plastic top had kept it!... and he ate some more moons of pastelito, and the flakes fell ever so gently and tumbled about in the zephyrs, and he found himself... lifting the little lever on the side of the seat and letting his own weight take it back to a twenty-degree incline... and the coffee, which was supposed to keep him alert after a sleepless night, sent a wave of perfect warmth up through his body... and his body surrendered itself utterly to the incline of the seat... and his mind surrendered itself utterly to a hypnagogic state, and presently...

He woke up with a start. He looked at the Camaro's keys hanging from the ignition in the ON position and felt the cool breeze of the air conditioner. He had fallen asleep with the motor running... He lowered the windows, to let maximum fresh air in... Christ, that fresh air was hot! The sun was right overhead... it was killer bright... What time was it? He looked at his jumbo watch. It was 10:45! He had been asleep for three hours... stretched out in the Land of the Sandman with the engine running and the air conditioner chundering out electro-breeze.

He retrieved his cell phone from the bucket seat and sighed... Whatever messages its innards contained, they would be toxic. Yet once again he couldn't resist. He punched up the new-messages display. There was one after another after another... until one made him do a double take. The number jumped up at him—a text from Manena!

"coming to yeya party c u later"

He stared at the thing. He tried to detect a sign of love in there...any at all...seven words. He couldn't. Nevertheless, he texted back: "my manena dying to c u"

His spirits turned manic. It would be at least four hours before the party started, but he was going home...*now.* ::::::I'll just ignore you Camagüey *guajiros,* Papa and Yeya and Yeyo. I'll make damn sure I'm right there when Manena arrives.::::::

By now, 11:00 a.m., the streets of Hialeah were walls of parked cars. He had to park the Camaro more than a block away. Halfway down his own block, a couple of casitas ahead, Señor Ramos was walking out of his front door. From behind his big cop shades Nestor could see Señor Ramos staring at him. The next thing he knew, Señor Ramos was turning toward his front door and snapping his fingers in an exaggerated display of having forgotten something—*shoooop*—he's back inside his casita. Señor Ramos is nothing but a baggage handler at Miami Airport. A baggage handler! A little speck of humanity! But this morning, on these streets, he doesn't want to exchange so much as a *buenos días* with Officer Nestor Camacho. But so what? Magdalena is coming.

Wouldn't you know it? From four or five casitas away he can *hear* his own casita...the power spray exacting friction from hot Hialeah concrete. Oh, yeah. There's Mami, wearing a pair of long baggy shorts, a baggier too-big white T-shirt, and flip-flops . . . taming the concrete wilderness for the whateverteenth time this morning . . . and . . . Oh, yeah . . . he gets his first whiff of the pig, which has been roasting for a few hours probably . . . tended by those two macho masters of the big things in life, I, Camilo, and El Pepe Yeyo . . .

As soon as she sees her son coming, Mami turns off the hose and cries out, "Nestorcito! Where did you go? We were worried!"

Nestor wanted to say *::::::Worried? Why? I thought "we" would be happy for me to disappear::::::* But he never spoke sarcastically to his parents and couldn't make himself start now. After all, Magdalena was coming.

"I went out to get breakfast—"

"We had food here, Nestorcito!"

"—to get breakfast, and I ran into some friends from Hialeah High."

"Who?"

"Cristy, Nicky, and Vicky."

"I don't remember them . . . Where?"

"At Ricky's."

Nestor could see the rhymes rickycheting, as it were, in his mother's brain, but she either didn't get it or didn't care to be distracted by it.

"So early in the morning..." his mother said. Then she dropped that subject. "I have some good news for you, Nestor. Magdalena is coming." She gave him the sort of look that gets down on its knees and *begs* for an animated reaction.

He tried, he tried... He arched his eyebrows and dropped his jaw for a couple of beats before saying, "How do you know?"

"I called her and invited her, and she's coming!" said his mother. "I told her to be sure to come before you had to leave for your shift." She hesitated. "I thought she might lift your spirits a little."

"You think they need a lift?" said Nestor. "Well, you're right. When I was out, I could tell... everybody in Hialeah thinks about me the same way as Dad and Yeya and Yeyo. What did I *do,* Mami? There was an emergency, and I was ordered to put an end to it without anybody getting hurt, and that's what I *did!*" He realized his voice was rising, but he couldn't stop himself. "At the Police Academy they kept talking about 'the uncritical willingness to face danger.' That means you're willing to do dangerous things without stopping to analyze everything and decide whether you approve of the risk they want you to take. You can't sit around having a *debate.* That's what 'uncritical' means. You can't sit around *arguing* about everything and... and, I mean, *you* know—"

He forced himself to slow down and lower his

voice. Why lay all this stuff on his mother? All she wanted was peace and harmony. So he stopped talking altogether and gave her a sad smile.

She moved closer, and from her own sad smile he knew what was going to happen. She wanted to put her arms around him and assure him that Mother still loved him. He just couldn't go through that.

He raised his hands up before his chest, palms outward ::::::Hold it:::::: at the same time he gave her a smile and said, "It's okay, Mami. I can handle it. All it takes is a little 'uncritical willingness to face danger.' "

"Your father and Yeya and Yeyo didn't really mean . . . all those things they said, Nestorocito. They were just—"

"Oh, they meant it," said Nestor. He made sure to keep his smile spread across his face.

With that, he went inside and left Mami outside to further chasten the concrete slab with the power spray.

Inside, the casita was overwhelmed by the odors, good and bad, of the pig roasting in the *caja china*. Good—bad—the neighbors wouldn't care either way. They were all Cuban. They all knew what a big thing, what a family ritual, a pig roast was, and besides, most of them had been invited to the party. That was the Cuban way.

Nobody seemed to be in the house. Nestor headed

toward the back. Yeya and Yeyo's door was open, and so he went in there and looked out their back window. Sure enough, the whole macho crew was out in the yard. There was I, Camilo, directing Yeyo, who was bringing a bucket of coals for the *caja china*. There was Yeya, the *muchacha vieja*, pointing this way and that way, directing both of them . . . correcting both of them. Nestor could be sure of that.

So . . . he could either walk right up to the *caja china* clergy and force himself upon them in conversation *::::::Gosh, now that's some pig! How much longer you think it'll take? Dad, you remember the time the pig was so big—::::::* for the ten or twenty seconds it would take the three self-righteous pharisees to start spitting their vile bile all over him again . . . or he could turn his back on the whole scene . . . The birthday girl, Yeya, obviously didn't care whether a nonperson was there or not. It was not a difficult decision.

Back in his room, Nestor lay down to take a nap. The only half-decent sleep he had gotten in the last twenty-four hours were the three hours when the aroma and the flake-fall of pastelitos had put him under as he sat back at a twenty-degree angle in the driver's seat of the Camaro outside of Ricky's with the engine running and the air conditioner on. He couldn't think of any prospect more inviting than *going under* again ::::::here in my own bed where I'm already horizontal:::::: but the phrase "here in my own bed" made him anxious. He didn't know exactly why, but it did. What did "my own bed" mean in a house where three people considered you a traitor and the fourth, kindly enough, said she was willing to forgive you for having sinned against her and the three others and their heritage, and all of Mother Cuba's offspring in Miami and, for that matter, everywhere in the world. So he lay there horizontally in a regular stew of rejection, stigma, and guilt, those three, and the worst of these, as always, was guilt... even though what was he supposed to have done, looked the mere *americano* Sergeant McCorkle in the eye and said, "No, I will not lay one hand on a Cuban patriot!—even though I haven't the faintest idea who the fuck he is," and then just taken his dismissal from the force like a man? *Bubble bubble bubble bubble* went the stew, while the fouler odors of the pig roast wafted over him, the odors and the occasional rude cry, probably of excoriation, from the backyard, and the time passed as slowly as it had ever passed in his life.

After God-only-knows-how-long came the sound of the chosen pig roasters coming back into the casita, bringing their various recriminations with them, although mercifully he couldn't really understand them. It was about 1:15, and Yeya's party was to start at 2:00. They must have come in to get dressed. No one had said a word to him about that or anything else. Why was he even staying? He was nothing but an embarrassment to them all. One of our own, or formerly our own, has turned into a snake...but to bug out on Yeya's party was the equivalent of leaving the family, cutting all ties, and that prospect he couldn't imagine. Besides, in the short run it was another charge they could bring against him, evidence of just how vile he had become. *He was right there in the house, and he couldn't trouble himself enough to come to her party and pay his respects.*

About half an hour later, Nestor heard a high-speed *rat-tat-tat* of Spanish coming up the hallway from the rear of the casita. All at once he was afraid they were starting the party without even telling him. Now it was obvious. He was invisible. He had disappeared so far as they were concerned. Well, there was one way to find out for sure. He got up off the bed. With an impulsive, heedless rush he opened his door. Barely ten feet away and coming toward him—here they were—what an eyeful!

They had changed into their party clothes. From Yeyo's wide but bony shoulders hung, as if from a rack, a white guayabera that was now too big for him. It was so old, the trim that ran up and down both sides of his chest was beginning to yellow. The thing made it look like Yeyo was a sail waiting for wind. As for Yeya, she was a vision . . . of God knew what. She wore a big white shirt, too, a frilly one with voluminous sleeves that ended in narrow cuffs at the wrist. The shirt hung down to her hips, outside of a pair of white pants. The pants—Nestor couldn't keep from staring. They were white jeans . . . tight white jeans that clung to her aged legs . . . but also to her bottom, which was big enough for three women her height . . . clung to her lower belly, which swelled out beneath the shirt—*clung!* But above all there was the perfect blue ball of hair, which enclosed her head, save for her face, in a single puff . . . With that and the jeans and a terribly red gash of lipstick across her mouth and a circle of rouge on each cheekbone . . . she was a real piece of work.

When they saw Nestor, they went silent. They stared at him in the wary way you might stare at a stray dog . . . and he stared at them . . . and his emotions suddenly spun 180 degrees. The sight of these two old people trying to look their very best for a party . . . the one looking like a sail that just blew into Hialeah from off the bay . . . the other one, in the low-slung white flesh-huggers, looking like a jean-ager time-shot fifty or sixty years older *just like that* . . . it was so sad, so pathetic, Nestor was touched by the sight of them. Here they were . . . two old people who didn't want to be here in the first place . . . in this country . . . in this city . . . living at the sufferance of their son and his wife... walled off by a foreign language and maddening alien ways... Once they were young, too—although Nestor couldn't actually picture it—and they must have grown up never having a dream dark enough to imagine their lives would end up like this... How could he have *hated* them the way he did this morning—or come to think of it, thirty seconds ago? Now he felt guilty... His heart was filled with pity... He was young, and he could take setbacks... even the pounding he had taken today... for his life was just beginning... and Magdalena was coming.

He smiled at them. "You know what, Yeya? You look great! I mean like *really* great!"

Yeya gave him an evil eye. "Where did *you* go this morning?"

She was starting in again, wasn't she... By stressing the *you* rather than the *go,* she made it clear it was not really a question... merely another little black mark against his name.

Nestor said, "And I really like your guayabera, Yeyo. You must a had that *made.*"

"You must a *not* had yours—"

Nestor cut him off, although not intentionally. Guilt and pity made him babble on. "You know what? You and Yeya match!"

Yeyo cocked his head and gave Nestor an evil eye

of his own. He was dying to start in again, too, but the kid was busy dousing him with flattery.

Nestor never even thought about it that way. His heart was filled with pity . . . and goodwill. Magdalena was coming.

The guests began arriving a little after two . . . No wonder Mami had ordered a hundred-pound pig . . . My God! They arrived in platoons . . . battalions . . . hordes . . . whole family trees full. Yeya was standing with Mami here in the little living room. The front door opened right into it. Nestor hung back in the rear of the room . . . all of twelve or fourteen feet from the front door. This wasn't going to be fun . . . every single tribesman clucking and fuming and eating up all the delicious gossip . . . *right in our own family!* . . . I can't believe it was Dad's cousin Camilo's *son,* Nestor, who did that! . . . and so forth and so on . . . and on and on . . .

The first to arrive was his uncle Pedrito, Mami's oldest brother, and his family. *Family?* He arrived with a goddamned *population!* . . . There's Uncle Pepe and his wife, Maria Luisa, and Mami's mother and father, Carmita and Orlando Posada, who live with them, and Uncle Pepe's and Maria's three grown sons, Roberto, Eugenio, and Emilio, and their daughter

Angelina, and her second husband, Paco Pimentel, and the five children they have between them, and Eugenio's, Roberto's, Emilio's wives and children and... on and on...

The adults hugged and kissed Yeya and otherwise made a big fuss over her... The children mumbled through it and endured wet smacks from Yeya's scarlet gash of a mouth... and said to themselves, "Urgggh! *I'll* never be a slobbering old mess like *her*"... but mainly they could smell the pig roasting, and they knew what *that* was!... and the moment they were set free, they began racing through the casita toward the backyard, where, no doubt, I, Camilo, would say to them, "Little children, come unto me—and see how a *real man*... roasts a pig."

One of the little boys, one of Aunt Maria Luisa's grandsons or stepgrandsons, God knew which, seven or eight years old, was off like a rabbit with the rest of them when he came to a sudden stop in front of Nestor and looked up at him with his mouth open and just stared.

"Hi!" said Nestor, in the voice one uses for children. "You know what's out back?" He smiled the smile one uses for children. "There's a whole *pig!* It's THIS big!" He held his arms out like wings to show just how colossal it was. "It's bigger than *you* are, and you're a big boy!"

The boy didn't change his expression in any way. He

just kept looking at him, gawking with his mouth open. Then he spoke: "Are you really the one who did it?"

That so unnerved Nestor, he found himself stammering out, "Did *what?—who* said—no, I'm not the one who *did* it."

The boy digested this answer for a minute and then said, "You *are* too!"—and bolted toward the back of the casita.

In came more clans, tribes, hordes, the battalions. Half of them would come in the front door, seek him with their eyes, spot him, whisper to one another—and avert their eyes and never look at him again. But some of the older men, in typical Cuban fashion, deemed it incumbent upon themselves to stick their big noses in and call a spade a spade.

His uncle Andres's cousin-in-law, Hernán Lugo, a real blowhard, came over with a very stern look on his face and said, "Nestor, you might think it's none of my business, but it *is* my business, because I know people who are still trapped in Cuba—know them personally—and I know what they go through, and I've tried to help them, and I *have* helped them, in many different ways, so I've got to ask you something face-to-face: Okay, so technically they had the right to do what they did, but I don't see how you ever—*ever*—let them use *you* as their tool. How *could* you?"

Nestor said, "Look, Señor Lugo, I was sent up that mast to talk the guy down. The guy was up on top—"

"Jesus Christ, Nestor, you don't know enough Spanish to talk anybody down from *any*thing."

Nestor saw red, literally saw a film of red before his eyes. "Then I needed you, didn't I, Señor Lugo. You would have been a big help! You coulda climbed eighty feet of rope, straight up, without using your legs, to get up there faster, and you coulda gotten as close to him as I did and you coulda seen the panic in his face and heard it in his voice and seen the way he was about to slide off a bosun's chair about *this big* and fall eighty feet—and explode on that deck like a pumpkin! And you coulda told me that this guy has gone crazy from panic and he's gonna *die* if he stays up here a minute longer! You could have *seen that face* close up—and *heard the voice,* with your own ears! You ever seen a man who's lost control of himself, I mean really *lost* it? A poor sonofabitch who's opening the lid of his own coffin? If you wanna help Cubans... don't just sit on your big butt in an air-conditioned building! Try the... the... the real world for the first time in your life! Do something, goddamn it! Do something besides run your mouth!"

Señor Lugo looked at Nestor for a single moment more, then lowered his head and slunk away deeper into the casita.

::::::*Shit.* I've really done it now. I'm the one who lost control. That old bastard—he's back there right now telling them all, "Be careful! Don't get near him!

He's a mad dog!" . . . Still—seeing the fear on his face—it was almost worth it.::::::

He'd had it with all these people. ::::::Even if they want to talk, civilly or otherwise, I'm not saying anything and I'm not moving, either. I'm gonna be right here the moment Magdalena comes in.::::::

The platoons, the brigades, the battalions, the clans, the tribesmen, the termites in the family tree who were packed in around him here in the front room . . . drinking beer straight out of the bottles and talking at the top of their lungs. What an ungodly din. Nice atmosphere . . . none of them wanted to talk to him or set eyes on him or in any way be aware of his presence, much less acknowledge it.

::::::All right, if I'm such a non-person that you can't even see me, why would you mind if I force my way straight through you to reach the front door?::::::

With that, he began shouldering through the crowd, cop shades over his face, looking at no one, giving this one a shoulder into his rib cage from behind and that one an elbow in the—"Oooof!"—stomach, muttering, "Coming through, coming through," not pausing for an instant to look back at the tribesmen he had felled, taking delight in their startled objections, the *Hey*s, the *Ouch*es, the *Hey, watch it*s. ::::::So what if they think I'm rude? They already think worse than that of me.::::::

Parading his muscles again gave him a grim pleasure,

self-defeating but satisfying all the same. But the moment he went out the front door—no pleasure remained, grim or otherwise, and no fear. He was empty...

In the instant it took him, cop shades and all, to adjust to Hialeah's eye-frying killer-concrete sun, he was aware of a figure walking across the street here in the middle of the block, but he could make out no details, just a silhouette.

In the next instant a vision—*Magdalena.*

She was walking straight toward him, looking into his face with a certain smile that he had always interpreted as a lure... toward unspeakable delights... the curve of her lips—*pure mischief*... the way her hair flowed in such thick silken waves down to her shoulders... her sleeveless white silk top scalloped so deep in front, he could see the inner curves of her breasts... and *more*... and his loins sent out a bulletin... her perfect lissome legs and thighs and hips, he loved it all, worshipped it, idolized it.

He blurted out, "Manena—I'd given up!"

Magdalena slipped between I, Camilo's FUMIGADORES van and an ancient Taurus parked right in front of it and stepped up onto the sidewalk, and the sun exploded off the shimmers of the white silk barely upon her breasts and the waves of her hair, long enough, thick enough, soft enough to—to—to... She walked up to within three feet of Nestor, still smiling the smile that promised... *all*... and breathing rapidly.

"I'm so sorry, Nestor! I barely got here at all! I was at the hospital. I've never driven so fast—"

"Oh, Manena—" Nestor was shaking his head and fighting back tears.

"—fast in my life! And there was no place to park, and so I just left it over there." With a little swing of her head she indicated somewhere behind her.

"Oh God, Manena, if you hadn't come at all—" More head shaking, more tears pooling on the little edge where his lower eyelids touched the eyeballs—in lieu of the words he didn't know how to say. "Manena, you have no idea what I've been going through—my own family, my own goddamned family!"

He glanced at his watch. "*Shit!* I can't be late for the shift."

He moved toward her. He *must* hold her in his arms. He puts his arms around her, and she put her arms around him ::::::but *shit,* she's got her arms around my *back*. She always puts them around my neck.:::::: He tries to kiss her, but she averts her head and whispers, "Not out here, Nestor—some of them are outside—"

—presumably the crowd at the party. Yes, it's true. Some of them have spilled out of the lawn in the back and onto the driveway. But what *difference* did it make?

He released his sweetheart and looked squarely at his watch.

"*Shit,* Manena! I'm gonna be late for my goddamned shift—and my car's parked four blocks from here!"

"Oh—*I'm* sorry, Nestor," said Magdalena. "I messed up—look, I'll tell you what. Why don't I drive you over to where your car is? That'll save you some time."

As soon as he got in the passenger seat, he poured out his woes in a torrent. For no reason, no reason at all, his whole family—hell, all of Hialeah!—was trying to turn him into a traitor!—a pariah! He let it all out.

As she drove, Magdalena gestured toward the rows of casitas that rolled by on either side. "Oh, Nestor," she sighed without looking at him. "I've told you this before. Hialeah is not America. It's not even Miami. It's a—well, the word isn't *ghetto,* but Hialeah's... Hialeah's a little box, and we grow up here thinking it's a normal part of the world. But it isn't! You're in a little box here! And everybody's poking into your life and poking into everything you try to do and they can't wait to gossip about it and spread stories, *hoping* you'll fail. They *love* it when you fail. As long as you *live* in Hialeah and *think* in the Hialeah way...as long as you assume that the only way you can get out of some wretched casita is to marry your way out—

what kind of life is that? You're just letting them *condition* you so your eyes can't even *see* any life outside of a Hialeah casita. I know who's in your house right now. There's so many people in there who are related to you, part of you, attached to you—they're like one of those parasite plants that has all the *tendrils* that wrap around the trunk and then wrap around the branches, and when there's no more room on the branches, they go after the buds and leaves and twigs, and now the tree lives on in a completely parasitical condition—"

::::::parasitical condition?::::::

"—or it dies. Listen to me, Nestor. I'm very, very fond of you—"

::::::"fond"?::::::

"—and you've got to get out of this trap now. I was talking to a doctor from Argentina yesterday, and he says—"

::::::This is the moment!:::::: They were within a block of his car. He glanced at his watch again. Time was growing short. :::::::*Now!*:::::::

Nestor leaned across the armrest and placed his hand on her shoulder and looked into her eyes close up and in a way so *wet,* you'd have to be pretty dim not to see heavy weather coming.

"*¡Dios mío,* Manena!... oh, my God," said Nestor, "we're thinking the same thing at the same time. I shouldn't be surprised—but it's incredible!"

Magdalena suddenly pulled her head back.

"Sweetheart," Nestor went on, "we're two people with the same—I don't mean just the same feelings but the same—well, we're two people who *understand* things the *same way*. You know what I mean?"

Nothing in her expression indicated she did.

"I've been thinking all day about this. You know how we're always saying, 'It's just not the right time'? You know how we say that? Well, I swear, Manena, I know this *is!* This *is* the right time! This moment!... Manena... let's get married—now—*right* now! Let's just say goodbye to all this!"—he twirled his forefinger in the air, as if to take in Hialeah, Miami, Miami-Dade County—"all of it. Why wait any longer for *the right time?* Let's just *do* it—now! We'll both be gone from... *all this!* Manena! I'm leaving with *you*—right now. How about it? I couldn't love you any more than I do—right now. You and I both know what the right time is... *right now!*"

For a moment Magdalena just looked at him... blankly. Nestor could not read a thing in that expression of hers. Finally she said, "It's not that simple, Nestor."

"Not that simple?" He gave Magdalena the softest, most loving smile possible. "It couldn't be any simpler, Manena. We love each other!"

Magdalena turned her head. She wasn't looking

at him when she said, "We can't just think of ourselves."

"You mean your folks? It's not going to be any sudden shock to them. We've been with each other for three years, and I'm sure they know—well, they know we're not just . . . , just going out on dates."

Now Magdalena looked him squarely in the eye. "It's not just them."

"Whattaya mean?"

She hesitated, but she kept her eyes locked upon his. "I'm seeing someone else . . . also."

Magdalena's car turned into a sealed capsule. Nestor could no longer hear a thing except for a sound that began to fill his head . . . it sounded like the steam that comes out of those big irons at the cleaners.

His voice rose. "Did you just say *also?*"

"Yes." She maintained her laser control.

"And what the fuck is *that* supposed to mean?"

"Don't use that kind of language."

"Okay." He gave her a sardonic smile that showed his upper teeth and turned his forehead into ribbons of wrinkles. "Then just answer the question."

The smile cracked her composure. She began blinking to beat the band. "I mean, just like I see you, I see other people."

Nestor managed to bark out a single rasp of laughter. The steely Magdalena suddenly came back into her eyes. "I don't want to lie to you. I love you too much to do that. I do love you, you know. I finally decided I *had* to tell you about everything. I never *wanted* to keep *anything* from you. I was just waiting for the right time... Now you know everything."

"I know... everything? I know... *everything?* I know you're trying to double-talk me! I know you haven't told me a fucking thing—"

"I told you! Don't use—"

"Why not? Because you're such a fucking lady who fucking *loves* me? Have you ever heard any bigger bullshit?"

"Nestor!"

He could see the disgust, the anger in her eyes. But he could also see she was afraid to say another word.

"DON'T WORRY! I'M LEAVING!" So out of control, he couldn't keep his voice down even when he tried. He opened the door and got out and walked in front of the car and stopped, looking straight through the windshield at her.

"THIS IS YOUR CHANCE! WHY DON'T YOU FUCKING RUN ME OVER AND BE DONE WITH IT!" Out of control and he knew it and was helpless. He walked around to the driver's window, Magdalena's window, and bent over and all but pressed his face against the glass. "YOU MISSED YOUR FUCKING CHANCE... *CONCHA!*" He was vaguely aware of people on the sidewalk across the street stopping to gawk, but he couldn't keep his voice down. He withdrew his head and stood up and screamed at Magdalena from about a foot and a half away. "GO AHEAD! GET OUTTA HERE! GET OUTTA HIALEAH! GET OUTTA MY SIGHT!"

Magdalena didn't have to be told twice. She gunned the engine, the tires squealed, and the car seemed to *spring* away, like an animal. Nestor followed the beast with his eyes every millimeter of the way, watched it screech around the corner on two wheels, for one horrible HORRIBLY GUILTY moment thought it was going to roll over ::::::OH, MY MANENA! MOST PRECIOUS CREATURE IN THE WORLD! MY ONLY LOVE! MY ONLY LIFE—WHAT HAVE I JUST DONE?! I CALLED YOU A *CONCHA* FOR ALL OF HIALEAH TO HEAR! And now I'll *never* have the chance to tell you that I *worship* you... that you *are* my life!:::::: but, thankgod, it righted itself and disappeared.

More people had stopped to gawk. He'd better get outta here himself. He got in the Camaro, but instead of speeding off, he sat back in the seat. Only then did he realize he was breathing rapidly, all but gasping for breath, and his heart was racing within his rib cage, as if it had an urgent desire to be in a better place...

Out the windshield he could see what he had

left…tiny huts all in rows, roasting on an endless arid prairie of concrete…the guilt, the thought of what he had thrown away, the hopelessness; these three, hopelessness, wanton waste, and guilt; but the worst of these was guilt.

5

The Pissing Monkey

Maurice Fleischmann, that big bear of a billionaire, undid his cuff links and shoved his shirtsleeve up as far as it would go, to clear the way for her hypodermic syringe...and as always, tensed his muscles to show Magdalena that underneath all that flesh was bear-like strength and power...And as always, Magdalena said, "Please relax, Mr. Fleischmann," and he always did, apparently oblivious of how often they went through this same overture.

Often he would add a suggestive remark at that point, not egregiously suggestive...just to open the door a crack. This time he said, "Look, you're young and beautiful. Tell me about your adventures since the last time I saw you."

Magdalena always tried to deal with it as if this

were all such witty fun. “Oh, I’m not sure you’d be able to take it, Mr. Fleischmann.”

He laughed. *Oh, the badinage!* “Try me,” he said. “You might be ver-rrry surprised!” Laughter, laughter.

Oh, the badinage! And oh, how queasy-making—since at that point she always stabbed his fat arm with the syringe and pumped a jolt of Deprovan, a “libido inhibitor,” into his bloodstream...to suppress his free-floating lust for every pretty girl and his sexual obsessions...pornography in his case.

It was in fact so unamusing that, as she did at least a half dozen times a day, Magdalena, without even knowing she was doing it, began totaling the pluses and minuses of this new “job” she had. After graduating from EGU, Everglades Global University, in nursing, she had worked for three years at Jackson Memorial Hospital. Last year she had been a nurse in pediatric surgery. But how could she resist when one of the best known physicians in this, one of the biggest and best known hospitals in the South—Dr. Norman Lewis, the famous psychiatrist—had gone out of his way to recruit her for his personal practice? She was bowled over by the glamour of it. He had taken her out of the Hialeah “ghetto,” as she now thought of it, and introduced her to the grandeur and excitement of the real world beyond. In less than half an hour, *60 Minutes*—and not just *60 Minutes* but the program's star, Ike Walsh—would be here to interview him about... the Porn Plague.

No sooner had Maurice Fleischmann departed and the door out to the Lincoln Suites parking lot clicked behind him than Dr. Norman Lewis left his office and walked toward her, beaming the look of a man no longer able to contain his laughter. When he reached her—*the explosion.* He started laughing so hard, he could barely catch his breath long enough to gasp the words out to Magdalena.

"Maurice Fleischmann!" he exclaimed as he put his arm around her waist. "Moe the First!... the lordly Face of Miam*eeee ee ee ee eeaahhahAHHHH hock hock hock hock*"—gasp—"'*ssss*got on an eight-thousand-dollar silk suit lately made on Jermyn Street off Savile Row-*oh-oh-oh-ohhahhhHHHH hock hock hock hock* had to *tell* me that! had to show me the label*lllllahhahha-HAHH hock hock hock hock hock*"—gasp—and with each gasp he tightened his squeeze around Magdalena's waist a little more. "He takes the fucking prize of the week *ahhhHHHH hock hock hock hock*"—gasp—a little tighter he squeezed her—" '*ssssso refined' ahhHHHH hock hock hock hock*"—gasp—and a little *tighter*—"*Hunn*underneath that pretty suit is the biggest mess you ever saw aw aw aw awahhHHHH"—gasp—and tighter—"You gotta admit we got a zo*ooohhh*here *wh wh whuh*"—gasp—squeeze... and squeeze—and he broke into song, "Ohhhhh, we're off to the Hamburg Zoo—to see the elephant and the wild kangarooooo hock *hock hock hock!*" He tried to catch his breath and bring his jollification under control...and failed. "You should see his groin!"—gasp—"His poor penis—it's a little red thing, and it's got so many herpes blisters all over it, it's like looking down at a cluster of balloons! Only it's a blister cluster of ballooning *bliiiiIIIISTERSssssAHHHHH hock hock hock ahhhHHHH!*"—gasping, panting—"What a magnificent specimen of humanity! He do beat all"—gasp—"He do beat all*lllock hock hock hock hock hock* I swear I didn't mean to make a pun...I wasn't trying to be funny."

The eminent Dr. Lewis finally had himself under control, but he kept Magdalena's body pulled tight against his, side to side. "Poor bastard...every time he masturbates, the herpes gets worse, and more blister clusters pop out—and if you think he has the willpower to get up from the internet and stop watching those boys and girls slogging away and sticking this and that and them and those into every orifice in the human body—and stop torturing his poor put-upon little penis, you're dreaming...Wait a minute! I gotta show you! I took some pictures—"

He released her and practically dashed back to his office. Dr. Lewis's laughter—at his own jokes or not—his high spirits, his boyishness, his energy, swelled up into a flash flood that swept Magdalena away helplessly... Should he really be telling her these intimate secrets of his patients' lives? But what were her troublesome little scruples compared to the totality of Dr. Norman Lewis? Any moment—*any moment!*—*60 Minutes* would be here to have Norm give them the last word on the "Porn Plague"—*60 Minutes*!—and Norman was all excited about something else entirely, some pictures of poor Mr. Fleischmann's ravaged loins—as if he couldn't care less about *60 Minutes* and Ike Walsh—*couldn't care less!*

Magdalena was in a panic *for* him—and cried out, "Norman! Show me later! *60 Minutes*'ll be here any minute, like right now!"

Dr. Norman Lewis stopped in the doorway of his office and turned around and said, "Oh, don't worry, sweetheart. It'll take them an hour to set up." He gave Magdalena a smile with a certain cynical twist of the lips. "They're a bunch of unionized elves. Whatever they do, it takes them twice as long as plain elves. Fuck *them*. You've got to see Moe the First *à la noue!*"

"But, Norman! Ike Walsh—"

"Fuck *him,* too. He's a textbook case of the Pissing Monkey syndrome." Whereupon he turned to enter his office.

Fuck *them*...And Them was merely the highest-rated news show on television. And fuck *him*...And Him, Ike Walsh, was merely the biggest star in television news. "The Grand Inquisitor," they called him. Magdalena was fascinated but frightened when she watched Ike Walsh on television. He was a bully. His specialty was going after people until they became flustered and broke down emotionally. ::::::But my Norman writes him off as a poor devil suffering from the "Pissing Monkey syndrome." What in the world is the Pissing Monkey syndrome?:::::: She had never heard him mention that before . . . Pissing Monkey syndrome . . .

She knew he was in a hurry, but she couldn't resist asking. "Norm!" she yelled after him. "What's the Pissing Monkey syndrome?"

Dr. Lewis stopped in the doorway to his office and turned around again. He sighed in a way that said, "I can't believe you don't know what the Pissing Monkey syndrome is." In a tone of put-upon patience, he said, "I assume you know that monkeys make terrible house pets. Okay?"

Magdalena had never heard anyone say *anything* about pet monkeys, but she nodded yes rather than risk exasperating him any further.

"But let's say a man gets one anyway, a small monkey, a cute monkey, like a spider monkey, okay?"

Magdalena obliged with another nod.

"Well, that monkey, if it's a male—as soon as he can get up high enough—and they can climb anything—he'll start urinating on your head. Okay?"

"Urinating on your *head?*" said Magdalena.

"Right. Urinating on the man's head. The *man's* head. He's not interested in women. He'll urinate on the man's head and then he'll grin and go, 'EE EE EE EE EE.'" He's laughing at you, he's mocking you, he's telling you what a pussy you are. He'll piss on your head night and day...while you're in bed fast asleep, when you get up to go to the bathroom, when you're getting dressed to go to work or whatever—*all* the time...And it's no use trying to make friends with the little bastard, no use trying to pet him or coo sweet nothings over him, no use trying to get in his good graces by serving him fabulous monkey feasts, apples and raisins and celery and hazelnuts, Brazil nuts, all that stuff monkeys love. Any way you try to please him is only going to make it worse. He'll play you for a *hopeless* pushover. Okay? The only thing that works is, you grab the little bastard while he's at his bowl gorging himself, and you throw him in the toilet, and while he's flailing about in the water and he's disoriented and he can't get any traction on the toilet bowl, it's so slick, *you* piss on *him*. You deluge him with every ounce you've got. That fucking monkey's going to think he's trapped in a piss monsoon. The whole sky, the whole world is pissing on him. There's no more air to breathe, only piss fumes. At first he'll be going, 'EE EE EE EE'—he's mad as hell—and then the tone will change, and it starts sounding like a cry for mercy...and then it slows down to 'EE...EE...

EE... EE,' and then the decibel level sinks, and nothing's left but a pathetic little whimper, 'ee... ee... ee... ee,' and the next day he'll be curled up on your lap like a little pussycat and practically *begging* you to pet him and coo your sweet nothings. You've shown him who's boss around here. You've shown him *you're* the alpha male, not him. And there's your Ike Walsh of *60 Minutes*... He's a little pissing monkey."

Whereupon he disappeared into his office.

::::::*Ike Walsh is a little pissing monkey!* And he's about to be *interviewed* by Ike Walsh!:::::: Magdalena had never heard Norm say anything quite that contemptuous before, although many times she had heard him refer to TV people in general as suggestible and inflammable children "innocent of any conceptual thinking whatsoever."

Right now the operative word was *inflammable.* The TV news shows were all hot to exploit the results of a National Institutes of Health study showing that an astounding 65 percent of all "hits" on the internet were at pornographic sites. The NIH—the US government!—was warning of a pandemic of pornography addiction. It had risen from naughty to a national health crisis. "They're critically nil," Norman liked to say, referring to the tiny inflamed brains of the TV people. On the other hand, he didn't mind appearing on their shows. "They exploit so-called pornography addiction," he'd say—he always threw in the "so-called"—"and I exploit *them*." He was *great* at it! Magdalena knew she was more than a bit biased, but Norman was wonderful on television . . . so calm, so well-spoken, so all-knowing . . . and yet good-humored . . . and the way he looked—but now he thinks he's going to treat the fiercest man on television as a tiny pissing monkey?

At that moment Norman emerged from his office, beaming, gleaming with enthusiasm. *God,* he was good-looking! Her *americano* prince! Blue eyes . . . wavy brownish hair—she preferred to think of it as blond . . . tall, a little fleshy, maybe, but not really . . . fat. He was forty-two, but he had a strong face, and the energy of a thirty-year-old . . . make that a twenty-five-year-old. Her friends were forever clucking and fuming and warning her that he was almost twice her age . . . but they had no conception of Norman's vigor and strength and joy of living. When the two of them got up in the morning, both of them naked—she had never slept that way with anybody before—she could tell that underneath the good healthy . . . padding . . . he had a really good build. *blip* Nestor was only five-seven and *bulging* with muscles here there everywhere . . . bulging! . . . so *grotesque!* . . . *Norman's hair,* so thick and wavy and blond . . . *blond!* she insisted . . . made all that "jacked," "ripped" stuff Nestor talked about irrelevant. She was living with the *americano* ideal! If there was anyone who was more thoroughly *not Hialeah,* more completely *above*

Hialeah, on a higher, more intellectual plane, she couldn't imagine who. The whole world was opening up to her. Oh sure, people in Hialeah liked to make their *americano* jokes. But in their hearts they knew that outside of Miami, it was the *americanos* who ran things . . . ran *every*thing.

Now Norman stood beside her desk. He put a photograph down in front of her. "Take a look at that, and you'll see what I'm talking about. 'Vengeance is mine, saith the Lord, and I *will* be repaid.' That's the epigraph to *Anna Karenina,* by the way. Anyway, our big bear's sin is onanism, and he *shall* pay for it."

Remarks like that, so offhand and natural to Norman, intimidated Magdalena terribly. She had no idea what an epigraph was. She had a vague notion of Anna Karenina . . . somebody in a book? On *onanism,* she drew a complete blank. A sixth sense told her not to touch *epigraph* and *Anna Karenina*. Anything that had to do with writing, with literature, intimidated her most of all. It hit her sorest point, her lack of education in the books you were supposed to have read, the artists whose paintings you were supposed to be familiar with, the great composers—she knew *nothing*—about *any* composer. She had heard of one name, Mozart, but knew absolutely zero about anything he might have composed . . . So somehow . . . *onanism* was safer.

"Onanism?"

"Masturbation," said Dr. Lewis.

He moved around behind Magdalena, as she sat at the desk, in order to see the photograph from her vantage point. He put his hands on her shoulders, then lowered his head until his chin rested on her shoulder and his cheek was touching hers. She breathed in his cologne, which was called Resolute for Men. Norman's condo in Aventura had a huge bathroom with a vast marble countertop beneath a tremendous wall of mirrors, and when she went to *her* sink in the morning, there would be Norman's stout, manly can of Resolute for Men by *his* sink. The can was designed to resemble a hand grenade... a very masculine device, of course, for spraying sweet perfume on a man's sweet, freshly shaven face and neck *blip* poor Nestor's bathroom in the casita in Hialeah... the poor little windowless hall bathroom he had to share with his parents. It wasn't much more than a closet with a toilet bowl, a tub, and a midget sink squeezed together. Rust had eaten through the enamel around the sink's hot and cold water handles. An unfortunate shade of green paint was peeling off the walls. She and Nestor had been alone in the casita only twice in the three years they had been together, for all of thirty minutes each time. More than once they had scampered half nude or totally nude from his room to that miserable bathroom, terrified that someone might pop into the house suddenly, his mother, his father, a relative, a neighbor, and discover their wickedness. Oh, God, it had been so wicked—and so inexpressibly exciting.

And oh, *God!*—it was so awful what she was doing to Nestor now! She could see his contorted face screaming, "*¡Concha!*" But she couldn't bring herself to even regard it as an insult. It was just the wounded cry of a Latin man with a broken heart. No man, no real Latin man, would just walk away, numb and dumb, after a relationship like theirs. But how could it have been avoided? One way or another she had had to tell him it was over. She was leaving him and Hialeah.

Would she have "stood by him" that day if she had known he was in big trouble for arresting that Cuban underground leader and practically handing him over to the Cuban government? Well, thank God that was a decision she never had to make. She had no idea what was going on with Nestor's "career." For weeks she had been able to think about only one thing: finally making a complete escape from Hialeah and its "big Cuban belly," as she thought of it... which meant, above all, leaving home and leaving Nestor. Thank God she had done both while she still had the nerve!

Hialeah—that little Cuban capsule was Nestor's whole life. Oh, that day, he said he was going to leave Hialeah, too, but all he was, was temporarily hurt. The whole thing would blow over in no time and be forgotten. All he would ever be was a cop serving his twenty years, after which—what? His nice big pension? His life would be over fifteen years from now, and he would only be forty. It was sad... but at least she didn't have to lie to him any longer... and pretend nothing had changed. She really would have to de-Friend him on Facebook. It wouldn't be right if she let him stare at her face every day, every hour, and moon over it and pine away over something he would never have again. That would be cruel...

::::::But come on, Magdalena, be honest with yourself! That isn't what you're really concerned about, is it... One picture of you and Norm wound up on your page, unbeknownst to you, and you were so afraid of upsetting Nestor that you took it off as soon as you knew it was there. From now on let's face facts. You want everybody to know that Dr. Norman Lewis is your boyfriend! Admit it! In fact, you *want* his picture all over the page by the time the *60 Minutes* thing with the famous Ike Walsh is on. Right? You *want* them to know you possess that gorgeous blond, blue-eyed *americano,* that glamorous, famous Older Man!::::: But this happy thought set off another surge of Nestor guilt. The whole thing had been bound to end up the way it had... and better sooner than later. She hadn't been able to think of any way to let him know... not any *painless* way... Better this way, a sudden, clean cut. Oh, Nestor would soon be back in the bosom of Hialeah, as if nothing had ever happened—

"Come on!" said Norman. "You're not even looking at the picture!" And that was true. He slid his hands down from her shoulders over her prim white nurse's uniform. "Well?"

So she looked at the picture, and... *uhnghhh,* it was so *gross!* It was a color photograph of the bare crotch of a man... There were eruptions all over his groin and his penis, which was badly inflamed.

Magdalena said, "That's so"—she wanted to say "disgusting," but Norman seemed to be so proud of his picture for some reason—"that's such a horrible picture."

"That's not so," said Dr. Lewis. "What our very rich and influential Maurice Fleischmann has done to himself may be horrible, but it's not a horrible picture. To my mind it's an important picture, the sort of documentation that's very valuable for our profession."

"That's Mr. Fleischmann?"

"The very one," said Dr. Lewis. "Look at those long skinny legs."

"Where did it come from?"

"I took it myself about half an hour ago and downloaded it onto the computer."

"But why is he naked?" said Magdalena.

Dr. Lewis chuckled. "Because I told him to take his clothes off. I told him we needed to create a 'visible timeline' of his progress. 'A visible timeline,' I told him." He chuckled up to the edge of open laughter.

"I also said I wanted him to take that picture with him and look at it every time he feels like yielding to his so-called addiction. I'm halfway serious about that part. But mainly I took that picture for my monograph."

"Your monograph?" said Magdalena. "What monograph?" She hesitated. She didn't know if she should expose more of her ignorance—but she went ahead anyway. "Norman . . . I don't even know what a monograph is."

"A monograph is a treatise—you know what a treatise is?"

"In a general way," said Magdalena. She didn't have a clue, but Norman had said it in a tone that presumed every literate person knew the word.

"Well, a monograph is what you call a highly detailed, very scholarly treatise that tells you a lot more than you really want to know about a very specific subject, in this case the role of masturbation in so-called pornography addiction. I want this monograph to be so detailed, so dense, so packed . . . in fact, *swollen* . . . with documentation, including photographs like Mr. Miami's crotch, you'll get a migraine just trying to read it. I want this thing to be so . . . *dense* that any scientist who reads the whole thing—any scientist, any physician, any psychiatrist, any medical school academic—I want that sonofabitch to scream with pain from the burden and the meticulous clinical detail, dried and compacted into bricks, that Dr. Norman Lewis has laid on him."

"But why would you want to do *that?*" said Magdalena.

"Because I happen to know these jealous shitheads are starting to call me a 'schlocktor.' "

Magdalena just stared. She didn't want to ask another question that indicated all the things she didn't know.

"*Schlock* is a Yiddish word that means cheap and poorly made," said Norman, "especially shoddy stuff that's being passed off as high-class. So a schlocktor is a doctor who shows what a cheap, shallow, bogus 'expert' he is by appearing on television shows like *60 Minutes* and dumbing down complicated stuff so millions of idiots will think they understand it. It's all jealousy, of course. My righteous colleagues like to think of themselves as bearers of exclusive mysteries up on a peak the idiot-millions can never ascend. Any doctor who goes on television and makes it less mysterious is automatically a cheap apostate"—Magdalena just stared her way through Norman's *apostate*—"trading the mysteries in for some sort of vulgar celebrity. My monograph will hit them like a sandbag. *It*...will be above...*them*. It'll have a title like 'The Role of Masturbation in Pornography Addiction'—'addiction' in quotes—or maybe 'The *Agency* of Masturbation in Pornography Addiction.' *Agency* is a very scholarly affectation among bearers of the mysteries these days. Anyway—masturbation. Many physicians, even many psychiatrists, don't get it. No man gets 'addicted' to pornography without it. Otherwise a poor bastard like our distinguished Mr. Miami would quickly get tired of staring at girls with cocks in their mouths. But if he can keep his hand on his little joystick and keep coming to climax, there's no limit to 'pornography addiction.' A jerk—pardon the pun—like Moe the First may not look like much, but he can ejaculate as many as eighteen times in a single day sitting in front of a computer watching this pathetic garbage online. Eighteen! I bet you never knew a man had that much in him! Well, our Maurice Fleischmann does! And he can't stop, not even when his crotch looks like... *that*."

Magdalena kept staring at the picture, and it *was* a horrible picture, no matter what Norman said—but meantime he was unbuttoning the button-up front of her modest, demure nurse's uniform. She's sitting at her office desk like a professional, a nurse, which makes it all so much more... *wicked*... *60 Minutes* is probably heading for the door—*any moment now!* Her heart rate is climbing—while Norman keeps talking in a perfectly normal voice. "...and he tells his assistant he mustn't be disturbed, no matter who's calling, his wife, one of his daughters—he is *not* to be disturbed. Not even by her, his assistant, and he turns the back of this big, rich swivel chair he has, upholstered in the softest, creamiest leather, and rocks back in it as far as it will go and undoes his belt and his zipper and slides the pants and his boxer shorts down below his knees, and his poor ravaged little bloody cock is sticking up in the air, and so he does the only thing he can do. He grits his teeth and *eats* the pain, raw, and in no time he achieves the little spasm he now lives for—he actually *tells* me all this!... as if I actually *need* all these details in order to treat him—*meeeahhh!*" With that, he broke into another fit of laughter.

Magdalena said, "You sure you should be telling me all this about him?"

Not for a moment did Dr. Norman Lewis stop caressing her breasts. *60 Minutes*! Any second now!

"Ahhahaaaaahh I don't know why not," said Dr. Lewis, trying to fight back his laughter. "Wee wee wee-aahhhhHHH *hock hock* hock weee're both licensed professionals working on his case, aren't we? *Hock hock hock hock hock hock ahhhHHH Hock hock hock hock.*"

He was still bent over behind her chair. Now he moved around the chair until he could look into her eyes. He kissed her and sucked each of her lips very delicately, and continued talking, as if nothing else were taking place in this room aside from an elucidation of the behavioral symptoms in the case of Maurice Fleischmann.

"The moment he achieves climax, the moment any man achieves climax, every last neuron, every last dendrite of the excitement that just a moment ago gorged his generative member with blood... vanishes—*vanishes!*—just like that, all of that monomaniacal *lust* is dissipated. It's as if it never existed. He's incapable even of *desire,* our manly Maurice Fleischmann. He's all business. He pulls his shorts back up and pulls his pants back up and zips them and buckles his belt and stands up and smooths his clothes down against his body...and looks out the window this way and that to see if *anyone* out there could have *possibly* seen him, and then he presses a button, and his assistant, out in the anteroom, picks up, and he tells her she can start putting calls through again, and he's back to work wondering how what just happened...has happened...He's back to work until his system revives, and those intervals are becoming shorter and shorter, and as soon as he revives, he turns the swivel chair's back to the door, and he's riveted to the screen again. It's so simple, turning on the porn. He doesn't need to pay anyone anything or supply his name and e-mail address. All he has to do is go to Google and enter www.onehand.com and hit SEARCH and he's back at Xanadu, and his little blistered Excalibur is vertical and eager again, and he's got a sex menu on the screen, whatever he wants, anal, fellatio, cunnilingus, coprophilia—oh, you bet!—and his entire existence on this earth is a *longing* for *the spasm*. Nothing else is real! And the time between visits to the pleasure dome becomes shorter and shorter, and he isn't getting anything else done, and people start complaining that they can't get an appointment to see our distinguished Mr. Maurice Fleischmann any longer. Of course they can't! He's busy self-destructing!"

Magdalena said, "This is all going on in an *office?*"

"It's *mostly* in the office," said Dr. Lewis. "Home presents all sorts of problems...and obstacles. The wife, the children, the complete lack of solitude. I mean, if our boy Maurice were to create a little room where he could have *complete* privacy, just him and his computer, that would rouse all sorts of suspicions, and you could be sure his wife would find out everything. Believe me, she *would*."

One of Dr. Lewis's hands, still inside her dress, begins descending, sliding this way and that over her lower abdomen. And then two fingers slip under the upper elastic of her bikini panties, which were only barely there to begin with.

"And it's taking up *that much time?*" said Magdalena. Her heart was racing. The words came out in an odd husky whisper.

Dr. Lewis seemed to have no such problem. "Oh, certainly," he said. "Think about it for a moment. His cycle has now reached eighteen times a day, mostly in the office. He has no *time* left for anything else, and he can't *concentrate* on anything else. He only has his intervals while he's building up energy for more spasms. Other things—if he can't take care of them in some kind of routine, rote manner, they don't get done. He's in another world, completely out of control, and that world is called Onanism."

"Onanism." Magdalena could only whisper it... in a husky manner. She was so aroused, she could barely speak.

All at once Dr. Lewis picked up her chair, with her in it, and turned it ninety degrees away from the desk—

"Norman! What are you doing!"

—and didn't put it down until there was room enough for him to move in front of her and step between her legs. He said nothing and she said nothing. He looked down at her, smiling ever so slightly. She looked straight up at him. Dr. Lewis unbuttoned his white cotton I'm-a-doctor coat. His khaki pants bulged in the crotch, no more than six inches from her face. He began to unzip his pants slowly slowly slowly. He beamed a sly sly sly smile at Magdalena, like a grown-up about to give a little girl a present she had always wanted so-o-o-o bad. Slowly slowly slowly slyly the zipper—

A low-pitched burbling ring... It meant someone was pushing the bell at the entrance. You could hear the voices and laughter of men outside.

"Norman! That's *them!* That's *60 Minutes*!"

"*Now*—while they're at the door!" Dr. Lewis's voice was suddenly more constricted and breathless than hers. "Do it *now!*"

"No, Norman! Are you crazy? I've got to let them in—and I'm already half naked! There's no time!"

"This *is* the time—" croaked Dr. Lewis. "While they're—at the—gate—"

He was having a hard time getting his breath. "Be an eternity before a moment like this—ever again! Just *do* it!"

Magdalena recoiled, thrusting the chair backward, and sprang to her feet. Her white nurse's uniform was unbuttoned almost to the bottom. She felt completely naked.

Norman still had both hands on his zipper. He stared at her with a look that implied he was... hurt... baffled... betrayed.

"My God, Norman," said Magdalena. "I think you really *are* crazy."

The interview took place in Norman's office. There were two cameras, one aimed at Norman, the other at the Grand Inquisitor, Ike Walsh. They sat across from each other in the side chairs that patients usually sat in. Already good and paranoid about the savage wiles of the Inquisitor, Magdalena suspected the idea was to keep Norman from sitting behind his big desk, with its aura of authority. She was very worried about what might be about to happen to Norman at the hands of the Inquisitor. After all, Ike Walsh was the pro. He had been through this sort of thing over and over. If he were to humiliate Norman—after all Norman's big talk about the Pissing Monkey, it would be just horrible... Her heart was beating like a bird's.

Ike Walsh was much shorter than he appeared to be on television. But come to think of it, he was always sitting down on *60 Minutes*. He looked even more ominous, however. His perpetually tanned skin, his narrow, steely eyes, his high cheekbones, his wide jaws and low forehead, which was a stony little cliff beneath his mane of thick black hair, very thick inky black—he looked like a *real* savage, barely constrained by civilized clothes, his jacket and tie. Those narrow little robot eyes of his did not blink once, but, then, Norman's didn't, either. He seemed quite comfortable—in his patient's chair. He wore a slight, friendly, hospitable smile. Magdalena's heart raced even faster. Norman's relaxed demeanor only made him look more unwary, more vulnerable, fresher and fatter for the kill.

Some sort of director began counting, "... six, five, four, three, two, one... we're rolling."

Walsh cocked his head to one side, the way he always did when he was setting someone up for the kill. "Now, Dr. Lewis, you say that pornography addiction is not a true physical addiction, like an addiction to alcohol or heroin or cocaine..."

He paused. A red light lit up on the camera trained on Norman...

Norman spoke! "I'm not convinced that addiction to alcohol, heroin, or cocaine is physical in the sense I take it you mean when you say the word *physical.* But please go ahead."

Magdalena clasped her hands together ever so tightly and drew in her breath. Norman had maintained his hospitable smile but altered it, ever so slightly, by parting his lips and moving his lower jaw ever so slightly to one side and... and ever so slightly winking the eye on that side—*winking!*—not blinking—as if to say, "I'm not sure you have the *faintest* idea of what you're talking about, but I'm willing to overlook that. So please plod on, my boy."

Walsh paused a couple of beats longer than Magdalena would have expected. Was he trying to decide whether or not to toss alcohol, heroin, and cocaine into the pot?

With his head still cocked to one side, he said, "But four of the most eminent psychiatrists and neuroscientists in the country—I'm tempted to say the world—couldn't disagree with you more completely." He glanced down at some notes on his lap. "Samuel Gubner of Harvard... Gibson Channing of Stanford...

Murray Tiltenbaum of Johns Hopkins... and Ericson Labro of Washington University—who, as you must know, just won the Nobel Prize—all four have come to the same conclusion. Pornography addiction, looking at pornographic videos on the internet for hours every day, causes a chemical reaction that *hooks* the pornography user in precisely the same way hard drugs *hook* the drug user. It alters the brain in precisely the same way. All four of these eminent authorities agree one hundred percent on that." Now the Grand Inquisitor brought his head up straight, jutted his square jaw forward almost prognathously, narrowed his cold steely eyes even more... and *struck*. "And so *you're* telling me that Dr. Norman Lewis knows better, and those four men—including a Nobel laureate—are wrong. They're all *wrong!* Is that what you're telling me? Isn't that what it boils down to?"

Magdalena's heart skipped a few beats and seemed to slide inside her rib cage. ::::::Oh, poor Norman.::::::

"AahhhuhwaaaAHHHH*Hock hock hock hock!*" Norman cut loose with as loud a burst of laughter as she had ever heard him bellow. He was beaming, as if he couldn't be more delighted. "I know all four gentlemen, and three of them are close personal friends of mine!" He began chuckling, as if this whole train of thought were too rich for words. "As a matter of fact, I had dinner with Rick and Beth Labro a few days ago." He chuckled again and leaned back in his chair and beamed the biggest, happiest grin in the world, as if all the planets were aligned just right.

Magdalena couldn't believe what had come out of Norman's mouth! "A few days ago" was a mob-scene dinner the American Psychiatric Association put on in the Javits Center in New York in honor of "Rick" Labro for his Nobel. Magdalena was with Norman the whole time. His "dinner with Rick and Beth" consisted of him standing about 214th in a receiving line of maybe 400 people waiting to shake hands with "Rick." When Norman finally reached "Rick," he said, "Dr. Labro? Norman Lewis, from Miami. Congratulations." To which "Rick" replied, "Thank you very much." And that was it—"dinner with Rick and Beth"! ::::::Our table was the length of a football field away from "Rick and Beth's."::::::

The Grand Inquisitor shifted into his patented mode of arch irony: "I'm glad you had such a good time, Dr. Lewis, but that wasn't—"

Cruuusssh! "AhhhHAHHHAHAHHH *Hock hock hock hock* 'Good time' doesn't begin to describe it, Ike!"—Norman's laughter, his booming voice, his 250-watt good humor rolled right over Ike Walsh. "It was a *fabulous* time! No one could possibly have a higher opinion of Rick than I do—and for that matter, Sam, Gibbsy, and Murray!" ::::::*Gibbsy?* I don't think he's ever *laid eyes* on Gibson Channing.::::::

"They're pioneers in our fielddahhhHHHH*Hock hock hock* You're a funny guy, Ike! AhhhhHH*Hock hock hock!*"

By the looks of him, Ike found none of this funny. His expression had gone blank. The lights had gone out in his steely eyes. He seemed to be searching for a response. Finally, he said, "All right, so now, I take it, you're admitting that compared to these four authorities, your—"

Craaaaashhhh! Norman's incorrigible exuberance rolled right over Ike Walsh again. "No, you *are* funny, Ike! You're *priceless,* in my book! What I must tell you is that I've been treating pornography *addicts,* so-called, for the past *ten* years, and it *is* a disease, a mental disorder, and a very serious one in this country, even if it has little to do with the conventional notion of addiction. We've just completed the protocols for the largest clinical trial of so-called pornography addicts ever attempted." ::::::What? Since when?:::::: "This will not be in the usual laboratory setting, however. We're sending each patient home with the equivalent of a Holter monitor, and we'll have a steady stream of data in real time as they—shall we say—surrender to their 'addiction' in complete privacy. The results should be monographic within eighteen months."

"Monographic?" said Ike Walsh.

"Yes. A monograph is a treatise—you *are* familiar with *treatise,* aren't you, Ike?"

"Yehhhs..." said the famous Inquisitor. He said it somewhat warily, as if afraid Norman were about to put him on the spot and ask him to *define* this word *treatise,* like a schoolboy.

It went on like that. Norman kept battering the Grand Inquisitor with forty-foot, fifty-foot waves of great good humor, affability, crashing laughter, and mile-high enthusiasm, glistening, flashing waves that rose and fell and masked the riptide, the undertow of condescension that swept Ike Walsh away to he knew not where from below. One of Walsh's specialties was talking right over an interviewee who was taking the conversation down a path he didn't like. But how do you walk right over towering, absolutely overpowering waves? After "You *are* familiar with *treatise,* aren't you, Ike?" Ike Walsh never got control of his own show again.

The Grand Inquisitor spent the rest of the interview curled up in Norman's lap. He got up every now and then to lob a nice fat softball of a question... and Norman hit home run after home run after home run.

What had gone on between Magdalena and Norman earlier, moments before the *60 Minutes* crew arrived, still troubled her. There was something weird about it, something perverse. But my *God,* Norman was quick! He was brilliant! And my *God,* he was strong! He was a real man! He had pissed all over the fiercest, most feared interrogator in all of television... and reduced him to a little pussy.

6

Skin

His office on the French Department floor at the University was a hotel lobby compared to his office here at home, but the one here at home was a little jewel, an Art Deco jewel, to be exact, and Art Deco was French. The floor was only twelve feet by ten feet to begin, and now it looked narrow because someone had built in sets of chest-high amboyna-wood bookshelves—*amboyna!*—absolutely *stunning!*—on either side to within a few feet of the desk long before he bought the place... whose mortgage he was still struggling *struggling!* to pay off... you can't *imagine* how hard the struggle has become! Anyway, his office at home was Lantier's inviolate sanctuary. When he was in his office at home with the door closed, as he was at this moment, *interruptions* of any sort were *absolument interdites.*

He consciously kept this room looking monastic...

no knick-knacks, no memorabilia, no clutter, no pretty little things, and that went for lamps, too... no lamps sitting on the desk, no lamps standing on the floor. The room was lit entirely by downlights in the ceiling... Austere, but this was elegant austerity. It wasn't antibourgeois, it was *haute bourgeois,* streamlined. Behind Lantier's desk was a four-foot-wide window in the form of a pair of... French... doors that swept all the way from the floor to the ceiling cornice ten feet above. The cornice was massive but smooth—streamlined instead of comprising fussy amalgamations of Vitruvian scrolls, rolls, fillets, and billets that spelled ELEGANCE in nineteenth-century *haut bourgeois* design, Art Deco *haute bourgeoise* ELEGANCE substituted the grand gesture: windows as tall as the wall... smooth massive cornices that cried out the Art Deco motto "Elegance through Streamlined Strength!" The only chair besides the one at Lantier's desk was a small white one-piece fiberglass number by a French designer named Jean Calvin. If you insisted on being picky, Calvin was Swiss, but the name, pronounced *Colvanhhh,* told you he was French Swiss, not German, and Lantier chose to regard him as French. After all, even though Lantier was by birth Haitian and had been appointed an associate professor of French (and that damnable Creole) *because* he was Haitian, he had proof that he was in fact a descendant of the prominent de Lantiers of Normandy in France from at least two centuries ago, maybe more. One had only to look at his pale skin, no darker than, say, a *café latte,* to see he was essentially European... *Well,* he *was* honest enough with himself to realize that his eagerness to *feel* French was what had led to his current financial jam. This house wasn't very big or grand in any other way. But it *was* Art Deco!... a genuine Art Deco house from the 1920s!—one of a number built back then in this northeastern section of Miami known as the Upper East Side... not a really high-toned neighborhood but solidly upper-middle-class... lots of Cuban and other Latino business-types... white families here and there... and no *Negs* and no *Haitians!*—except for the Lantiers, and nobody up here ever pegged the Lantiers as Haitian... certainly not the *Lantiers,* an Everglades Global University French professor and his family in an Art Deco house... These Art Deco houses were considered rather special, Art Deco being English shorthand for Arts Décoratifs, the first form of Modern architecture—and it was *French!* He knew paying for it would be a stretch—a $540,000 stretch—but it was *French!*—and very stylishly so. Now, with a $486,000 mortgage on his back, he was paying $3,050 a month—$36,666.96 a year—plus $7,000 in annual property taxes, plus nearly $16,000 in federal income tax, all this on a salary of $86,442—there you had yourself a stretch, all right... he felt like one leg had a toehold on the edge of the cliff back there, and the other leg had a toehold on the other cliff, way out *there,* and in between was the bottomless Canyon of Doom. In any case, the Calvin chair had a nearly straight back and no seat cushion. Lantier didn't want any visitor to get comfortable in here. He didn't want visitors in here. Period. That went for his wife, Louisette, too, before she died two years ago... Why did he continue to think of Louisette at least a dozen times a day?... when every single thought of her caused him to draw in a deep breath and expel it in the form of a long sigh?... and turn his lower eyelids into two tiny ponds of tears?... as they were at this moment—

Twistflimsy clatter!—he himself had tried to fix the old handle on the cheap, damn it, and the door flew open, and there stood his twenty-one-year-old daughter, Ghislaine, *yeux en noir* blindingly bright with excitement, lips trying not to betray the enthusiasm that had lit up those big lovely *sphères*—

—yes, the door of his inviolate sanctuary flew open without so much as a preliminary knock, and there stood Ghislaine... and he didn't even have to say it in his mind as a whole thought because in so many different situations it had come true: Where the happiness of his beautiful, pale-as-the-moon daughter was concerned, his patriarchal rules melted away. He immediately rose up from his chair and embraced her... then sat back on the edge of his desk so they would remain *tête-à-tête.*

In French she said, "Papa! I don't know if I mentioned South Beach Outreach to you, but I'm thinking of joining!"

Lantier had to smile. ::::::*Thinking* of joining... try absolutely *dying* to join!... You're so transparent my dear, sweet, predictable daughter. When you're excited about something, you can't stand taking time to build a nice little sofa of small talk for it first, can you. You have to spill it out *now!* don't you.:::::: That made him smile even more.

Ghislaine apparently took it as one of his ironic smiles, which he had been guilty of in the past, and it was absolutely *not* the way to tell a child what you think. When they figure out you are mocking them, it ignites the bitterest resentment. Ghislaine must have taken it as one of *those* smiles, because she switched to English and spoke rapidly, urgently.

"Oh, I know, you think it'll take up too much time. And it does take up *more* time... You don't just visit the poor and drop off a box of food. You actually spend time with the families and try to learn their real problems, which are a lot more than *hunger*. That's exactly what Nicole *loves* about it! Serena, too! You don't just sit around feeling charitable. You try to help them *organize* their lives. That's the only thing that can possibly *change* their lives! You can give them food and clothes—but only *involvement* can make a real difference!" In a completely different voice, a timid little voice, she said pleadingly, "What do you think?"

What did he think... The next thing he knew, he was bursting out with "What do I think? I think that's *great,* Ghislaine! It's a *wonderful* idea! It's *perfect* for you!"

He caught himself. He was talking with such off-the-leash enthusiasm, he was coming too close to giving the game away. He was dying to ask her a key question. He forced himself to keep quiet enough to calm down... then continued in a matter-of-fact voice, "Is this something Nicole suggested?"

"Nicole and Serena, both! Did you ever meet Serena? Serena Jones?"

"Ummmm..." He compressed his lips and rolled his eyes up and off to one side in the I'm-trying-to-remember mode. It didn't really matter. "Oh, yes... I think I did."

Actually, he knew he hadn't. But he remembered the name Serena Jones from somewhere... could it have been a column in the *Herald?* Swell Anglo families with common names like Jones or Smith or Johnson had a way of giving their children, especially their daughters, romantic or exotic or striking first names like Serena or Cornelia or Bettina, or else Old Family Lineage first names like Bradley or Ainsley or Loxley or Taylor or Templeton. He had a student once named Templeton, Templeton Smith. She was never just mousy little Ms. Smith. She was *Templeton* Smith. His mind was focused on one thing: swell families and families that have a shot at becoming swell. South Beach Outreach was an organization that came up on the social pages of the *Herald* and in *Ocean Drive* magazine's "Parties" section all the time, solely thanks to the social wattage of its members' families. Just take a look at the pictures—Anglos, Anglos, Anglos with a certain social cachet. Ghislaine's friend Nicole, whom she had met at the University, was not a WASP, strictly speaking, or not as Lantier understood what the acronym stood for, namely, White Anglo-Saxon Protestant. But in her case, strictly speaking didn't matter. Her last name was Buitenhuys, which is Dutch, and the Buitenhuyses were old money in New York, *anointed* money in New York. Whether any of them knew that Ghislaine was Haitian, he had no idea. The important thing was, they were accepting her as one of their social milieu. The stated purpose of South Beach Outreach was to go into the slums, such as Overtown and Liberty City—and Little Haiti!—and do good work amongst the poor. So they saw her as a girl as essentially *white* as they were! As white as *he,* her father, saw her! The crowning moment would be his Ghislaine going amidst the people of Little Haiti. The vast majority were black, *really* black, with no qualifiers. Back in Haiti, no family like his, the Lantiers, even *looked* at *really* black

Haitians. Didn't so much as waste a glance on them... couldn't even *see* them unless they were physically in the way. Well-educated people like himself, with his PhD in French literature, were like another species of *Homo sapiens.* Here in Miami they were self-consciously part of *the dyaspora*... the very word denoted high status. How many?—a half?—two-thirds?—of Haitians living in the Miami area were illegal immigrants who didn't *begin* to rate the term. A vast majority had never even heard of any *dyaspora*... and if they had, they had no idea what it meant... and if they knew what it meant, they didn't know how to pronounce it.

Ghislaine—he looked at her again. He *loved* her. She was beautiful, gorgeous! She would soon graduate from the University of Miami in Art History with a 3.8 grade point average. She could easily... pass... He kept that word, *pass,* hidden in his head, beneath a lateral geniculate... He would never utter *pass* out loud in front of Ghislaine... or anybody else, for that matter. But he *had* told her, many times, in fact, that there was nothing to hold her back. He hoped she had gotten the message about... *that,* too. In some ways, she was sophisticated—when she talked about art, for example. It could be the age of Giotto, the age of Watteau, the age of Picasso, or the age of Bouguereau, for that matter—she knew *so much!* In another way she wasn't sophisticated at all. She was never ironic or sarcastic or cynical or nihilistic or contemptuous or any of those things, which are all the signs of the tarantula in smart people, the resentful small deadly creature that never fights... that only waits to *bite* fiercely and maybe kill you *that* way. ::::::I've got too much of that in myself.:::::: They sat down. Ghislaine was in the Jean Calvin chair. He sat at his desk. The desk, with its Art Deco kidney shape, its gallery, its sharkskin writing surface, the delicately tapered shin guards on its legs, its ivory dentils running about the entire rim, its vertical strings of ivory running through the macassar ebony, was school-of-Ruhlmann, and not by the great Émile-Jacques Ruhlmann himself; but it was *very* expensive, all the same, certainly to Lantier's way of thinking. Likewise, the *very* expensive desk chair, with its tapered bands of ivory set into all four shin guards... All *very* expensive... but Lantier had still been in the giddy caution-to-the-winds euphoria of just having bought a house for *madly* more than he could afford. What was an *insanely* high price for his, the *maître*'s, own desk and chair, on top of that?

At this moment Ghislaine sat on that miserable chair with perfect posture... and yet she was relaxed. He looked at her as objectively as he could. He didn't want to deceive himself. He didn't want to expect the impossible from her... She had a nice slim shape and lovely legs. She must have figured that out for herself, because she rarely wore jeans or any other form of pants. She was wearing a tan skirt—he had no idea what material—short but not catastrophically short...a gorgeous long-sleeved silk blouse—or it looked like silk to him—unbuttoned partway, but not irredeemably far down...Ghislaine never used the word *blouse,* but that's what it was to him. From out of the open collar rose her *perfect* slender neck.

And her face—here he found it hard to be objective. He wanted to see her as his daughter.

He himself—he couldn't abide the jeans girls wore to class. They looked *so common.* He got the feeling half of them didn't even *own* anything else to cover themselves up with from the waist down. So there wasn't much he could do about the jeans. But those damned babyish baseball caps boys wore to class—with that infantile fashion he took action. One day, at the beginning of class, he said, "Mr. Ramirez, where do you have to go to find a cap like yours?—fits on sideways like that?...and Mr. Strudmire...yours goes straight down your neck and has that little cutout in front so we can see a little bit of your upper forehead. Do they make them like that, or do you have to get them custom-made?"

But all he got out of Mr. Ramirez and Mr. Strudmire were begrudging half-chuckles, and from the rest of the class, even the girls, nothing at all. They were irony-proof. The next class they and many other boys still had these little-boy baseball caps on. So he said,

"Ladies and gentlemen, from now on no caps or other headgear may be worn in this class unless it's required by religious orthodoxy. Have I made myself clear? Anyone who insists on wearing a cap to class—I'll have to take him to the principal's office." They didn't get that, either. They just looked at one another... puzzled. To himself he said, The *principal*—get it? That's what you have in high school, not in college, and this is college. You're irony-proof, aren't you. You're children! What are you doing here? Look at you... it's not just the baseball caps, it's also the short pants and the flip-flops and the shirts hanging down below the waist, way down, in some cases. You've regressed! You're ten years old again! Well, at least they didn't wear baseball caps to class anymore. Maybe they thought there really *was* a principal at EGU... and I'm supposed to *teach* these borderline idiots...

No, he must not mention any of this to Ghislaine. She would be shocked. She wasn't ready for... snobbery. She was at the age, twenty-one, when a girl's heart is filled to the brim with charity and love for the little people. She was still too young and unsophisticated to be told that her South Beach Outreach pity for the poor was actually a luxury for someone like her. It meant that her family had enough money and standing to be able to afford Good Works. Not that he made much money as an associate professor of French at EGU, Everglades Global University. But he was an intellectual, a scholar . . . and a writer . . . or at least he had managed to publish twenty-four articles in academic journals and one book. The book and the articles gave him enough cachet at least to give Ghislaine a boost up to the level of South Beach Outreach . . . My daughter reaches out to the poor! . . . Everybody had heard of South Beach Outreach. There were even some celebrities, such as Beth Carhart and Jenny Ringer, who were involved with it.

He stared over Ghislaine's shoulder and out the window . . . at nothing . . . with a rueful expression. He was not all that far from being as light-skinned as she was. He could have done what she was now in a position to do, couldn't he . . . but he was *known* as a Haitian. That was why EGU had hired him in the first place. They liked the "diversity" of having a *Haitian* . . . with a PhD from Columbia . . . who could teach French . . . and Creole. Oh yes, Creole . . . they were hot to have a professor who taught Creole . . . "the language of the people" . . . probably 85 percent of his countrymen spoke Creole and only Creole. The rest spoke the official national language, French, and quite a few of the fortunate 15 percent spoke in a casserole of both Creole and French. He made it a rule that here in this house, they spoke only French. To Ghislaine it had become second nature. Her brother, Philippe, on the other hand, although only fifteen, was already contaminated. He could speak French pretty well, so long as the subject didn't go beyond what an eleven- or twelve-year-old was likely to know about. Beyond that he struggled along with something not far above Black English, namely Creole. How had he even picked it up? Not in this house, he hadn't... Creole was a language for primitives! Oh, no two ways about it! The verbs didn't even conjugate. No "I give, I gave, I was giving, I was given, I have given, I had given, I will give, I should give, I should have given." In Creole it was *m ba,* and that was it for that verb... "I give, I give, I give"... You just had to figure out the time and the conditionals from the context. For any university to teach this stupid language was either what Veblen called "conspicuous waste" or one of the endless travesties created by the doctrine of political correctness. It was like instituting courses and hiring faculty to teach the mongrel form of the Mayan language that people up in the mountains of Guatemala spoke—

All this shot through Lantier's thoughts in an instant.

Now he looked directly at Ghislaine. He smiled... to cover up the fact that he was trying... objectively... to assess her face. Her skin was whiter than most white people's. As soon as Ghislaine was old enough to understand words at all, Louisette had started telling her about sunny days. Direct sun wasn't good for your skin. The worst thing of all was to take a sunbath. Even walking in the sun was too much of a risk. She should wear big-brimmed straw hats. Better still, an umbrella. Little girls couldn't very well go around with parasols, however. But if they *had* to walk in the sun, they should at least have straw hats. She must always remember that she had very beautiful but very fair skin that would burn easily, and she should do anything to avoid sunburns. But Ghislaine figured it out very quickly. It had nothing to do with sunburns . . . it had to do with sun-*browning*. In the sun, skin like hers, her beautiful whiter-than-white skin, would darken *just like that!* In no time she could turn *Neg . . . just like that*. Her hair was black as could be, but thank God it didn't have a crinkle in it. It might have been a little softer, but it was straight. Louisette couldn't bring herself to dwell on the lips because Ghislaine's lips didn't tend toward arterial red in the red spectrum but more toward an amber-brown. They were beautiful lips, however. Her nose was perfectly fine. Well . . . that fatty fibrous tissue that covers the alar cartilage and creates those little round mounds on either side of the nose at the nostril—oh, *alar cartilage,* absolutely! He knew as well as any anatomist what he was talking about here. One had better believe that! Hers flared out slightly too widely but not so far that she didn't look white. Her chin could have been a little larger, and her jaw a bit squarer, to balance the little round mounds. Her eyes were black as charcoal but very large and sparkling. Much of the sparkle was from her personality, of course. She was a happy girl. Louisette had given her all the confidence in the world. ::::::Oh, Louisette! I think of you, and I want to cry! There are so many moments like this every day! Is that why I love Ghislaine so much—because I look at her and I see *you?* Well, no, because I loved her this way while you were still with us, too. A man's life doesn't *begin* until he has his first child. You see your soul in another person's eyes, and you love her more than yourself, and that feeling is sublime!:::::: Ghislaine had the sort of confidence a child gets only if her parents spend a lot of time with her—a *lot*. Some would argue that a girl like Ghislaine, who is so close to her family, should go away to college and learn early that she's entering a life in which she is going to find herself in one alien context after another and should figure out strategies on her own. Lantier didn't agree with that. All this business about "contexts" and "life strategies" and *alien* this and *alien* that—it was all a concept with no bottom to it. It was just *faux*-psychological lufts and wafts. The main thing, to him, was that the campus of the University of Miami was only twenty minutes away from their house. Anywhere else she would have been "a Haitian girl." Oh, it would come out, but here she wasn't "that Haitian girl I room with" or any other form of that trap in which "if you say I'm *this,* then obviously I can't be *that*." Here she can be what she is and has become. She's a very nice-looking young woman... Even as those words formed in his mind, he knew he was putting her on a second tier. She wasn't as beautiful as a Northern European blonde, an Estonian or a Lithuanian or a Norwegian or a Russian, and she wouldn't be mistaken for a Latin beauty, either, despite having some features in common with a Latina. No, she was herself. The very sight of Ghislaine sitting there in that little chair with such perfect posture—Louisette!—you made sure Ghislaine and Philippe acquired that while they were too young to question it! He wanted to get up from his anonymous French swivel chair and go over and embrace Ghislaine right now. *South Beach Outreach!* It was almost too good to be true.

Who's that?

Lantier's office door was closed, but he and Ghislaine looked in the direction of the side door, which opened into the kitchen. Two people were coming up the four or five steps that led to the door from outside. Philippe? But Lee de Forest, Philippe's high school, wouldn't let out for more than two hours. The voice sounded like Philippe's—but it was speaking Creole. Creole!

A second voice said, "Eske men papa ou?" (Your father here?)

The first voice said, "No, li inivèsite. Pa di anyen,

okay?" (No, he at the university. Listen, we don't talk to nobody about this, okay?)

The second voice said, "Mwen konnen." (I know.)

The first said, in Creole, "My father, he don't like guys like that, but he don' need know about this thing. Nome sayin', bro?"

"He no like *me,* neither, Philippe."

"How you know that? He don't say nothing to me."

"Oh, he not say nothing to me, neither. He don't need to. I see the way he look at me—or *not* look at me. He look right through me. I'm not there. Nome sayin'?"

Lantier looked at Ghislaine. So it *was* Philippe. ::::::Philippe and his black Haitian buddy, God help us, Antoine.:::::: And Antoine was right. Lantier *didn't* like looking at him or talking to him. Antoine always tried to be cool and speak in perfect Black English, every illiterate, seventy-five-IQ syllable and sound of it. When that was too difficult a linguistic leap, he reverted to Creole. Antoine was one of those black-as-midnight Haitians—and their number was legion—who said *tablo,* Creole for "the table," and hadn't the slightest notion that it might have anything at all to do with *la table,* French for "the table."

Ghislaine had the expression of someone who has taken in a big breath but isn't letting it out. She looked terribly anxious. Lantier guessed it wasn't about what the boys had said, since her knowledge of

Creole was next to nothing. It was the fact that Philippe was jabbering Creole at all *chez* Lantier—and within *Père* Lantier's earshot—and, on top of that, with a very dark Low-Rent Haitian pal her father did not want to set foot in his house . . . and breathe in his air . . . and exhale it . . . thereby contaminating it, turning Franco-*mulat* air into *Neg* air.

Now the Creole boys were in the kitchen opening and closing the refrigerator and this-and-that drawer. Ghislaine got up and went to the door, no doubt to open it and let the boys know that they were not alone in the house. But Lantier motioned for her to sit back down and put his forefinger across his lips. Reluctantly and nervously she sat back down.

In Creole, Antoine said, "You see the look on his face when the cops take him by the elbow?"

Philippe tried to maintain his new deep voice, but it was turning gosling on him. So he gave it up and said in Creole, "They not do nothing with him, you think?"

"Dunno," said Antoine. "Main thing now François. He on probation already. We gotta be there for François. You be with us, right? François, he be counting on you. I see you talk to the cop. What you say, bro?"

"Uhh . . . I say . . . I say François say something in Creole and everybody laugh and Estevez, he get François in a headlock," said Philippe.

"You sure?"

"Uhhh... yeah."

"François do something first?"

"Uhhh... no. I not see him do something first," said Philippe.

"You only say *No,*" said Antoine. "Nome sayin'? Nobody care what you don' see. François say he need you, man. Only his bloods, his crew not enough. He be counting on you, man. Be bad if you not sure. You *see,* man. Nome sayin'? This be the time you show you bro—or you low. Unnerstan'?" He said "bro" and "low" in English.

"I unnerstan'," said Philippe.

"Good. You be good blood, man! *You be good blood!*" Antoine said with what came close to glee. "You know Patrice? André? Jean—fat Jean? Hervé? They good blood, too!" More glee. "They not in the crew, neither. But they know, man! They know what Estevez did to François. They don't 'if I'm correct' and all that shit. They good *blood!*" Glee seemed to turn into laughter aimed at Philippe. "Like *you,* bro!"

Professor Lantier looked at his daughter. She didn't understand what they were talking about, they were speaking Creole so fast. That was a good sign. Creole really *was* a foreign language to her! He and Louisette had steered her right! That was not *une Haitian*—in his mind he pronounced it the French way, "*oon-eye-ee-tee-onnnh*"—sitting so properly in that little chair. She was French. That was what she was by blood, an essentially French young woman of *le monde,* polished, brilliant, beautiful—then why did his eye fix upon those little fatty-fibrous mounds on either side of her nostrils?—poised, elegant, or elegant when she wanted to be.

In a low voice, practically under his breath, he said to his mercifully Creole-free daughter, "Something happened at Lee de Forest today. That's what I get out of it. In some class of his."

The two boys were heading in the direction of his office, with Antoine doing all the talking.

So Lantier himself gets up and opens the door and says cheerily, in French, "Philippe! I thought I heard your voice! You're home early today!"

Philippe looked as if he had just been *caught*... doing something not very nice at all. So did his friend, Antoine. Antoine was a tough-looking boy, heavy but not too fat. Right now he had the tense expression of someone extremely anxious to head in another direction. What a mess the two of them were!... jeans pulled down so low on their hips you couldn't help but see their loud boxer shorts... obviously the lower and louder, the better. The pants of both boys ended in puddles of denim on the floor, all but obscuring their sneakers, which had Day-Glo strips going this way and that... both in too-big, too-loose T-shirts whose sleeves hung down over their elbows and whose tails hung outside the jeans, but not far enough to obscure the hideous boxer shorts... both with bandannas around their foreheads bearing "the colors" of whatever fraternal organization they thought they belonged to. Their appearance—as American *Neg* as it could get—made Lantier's flesh crawl. But he was forced to keep a cheerful demeanor clamped upon his face and said to Antoine, in French, "Well, Antoine... it's been too long since you last paid us a visit. I was just asking Philippe, how is it that you're out of school so early today?"

"Papa!" gasped Ghislaine in a low voice.

Lantier immediately regretted saying that. Ghislaine couldn't believe that her father, whom she admired so much, would do such a thing as toy with this poor clueless fifteen-year-old just to see the baffled expression on his face. Her father knew Antoine didn't understand one word of French, the official language of the country he had grown up in until he was eight. Her father merely wanted to demonstrate to her and Philippe what a Special Needs—the public schools' euphemism—what a Special Needs brain this poor black-as-midnight boy had. After all, it was not as if he ever asked for bad blood. He was born *afflicted* with it. She couldn't believe her father had ended with a question to rub it in a little further. Antoine couldn't very well just stand there nodding. He was obliged to say something; "I don't speak French," at the very least. Instead, the boy was standing there with his mouth hanging open.

The look on Ghislaine's face made Lantier feel guilty. He wanted to make up for it by saying it so Antoine could understand it, and extra-cheerily to show he wasn't trying to make fun of him. So he said it in English. He was damned if he was going to descend into the muck of Creole just to make life pointlessly easy for some fifteen-year-old with bad blood, but he did slather great gouts of cheer over his words and so many exaggerated grins ::::::*Merde!* Am I overdoing it? Is this big lout going to think I'm mocking him?:::::: He finally wound up with—in English—"...just asking Philippe, how come you're out of school so early today?"

Antoine turned toward Philippe for a clue. Philippe moved his head back and forth ever so slowly and unobtrusively. Antoine didn't seem to get any clear message from that semaphore...an awkward silence. He finally said, "They jes say...They jes say... I'unno...They jes say school close early today."

"They didn't say why?"

This time Antoine turned a good ninety degrees, so he could look at Philippe head-on for a sign...any sign to tell him how to answer this one. But semaphores failed Philippe, and Antoine had to fall back on his old standby, "I'unno."

"They didn't tell you?"

He obviously didn't *want* to say why, which interested Lantier...mildly...But quite aside from that, Antoine looked to Lantier like a fifteen-year-old Haitian boy trying to do an imitation of a pseudo-ignorant American *Neg.* Antoine finally muttered, "Naw."

Naw...what a performance!...What a perfect mime he was! He twisted all the way around toward Philippe again. His entire posture, his slumped-over back, his arms hanging slackly down by his hips, was a semaphore for "Help!"

And what is *that?* At the base of his skull Antoine's hair had been buzzed very short...and then carefully shaved down to bare skin, to create the letter *C* and, an inch away, the number 4.

"What does the C4 mean?" said Lantier, still absorbed in his *cheery* act. "I just saw a C and a 4 on the back of your head."

Ghislaine gasped out another *"Papahhh!"*

So Lantier smiled at Antoine in a way meant to project friendly curiosity. It didn't. Now he could hear Ghislaine gasp out an "Ohhhhh, God."

Antoine turned about and gave Lantier a look of live hatred.

"Don't mean nothing. They's jes some us, we in the C4"—duh see-fo'—"at's all."...Gravely humiliated...furious. *And you best not be asking me any more about it.*

Lantier didn't know what to say. Obviously he shouldn't push the C4 button anymore. So he turned to Philippe. "You *are* home pretty early..."

"You, too," said Philippe. It was an uppity snarl,

designed to impress Antoine, no doubt. It impressed Lantier, all right... as unforgivably, irredeemably impudent, an insult too challenging to let slide...

But Ghislaine said, "Ohhhh, Papa..." This time the intonation she gave *Papa* begged him: *Just let it go. Don't dress down Philippe in front of Antoine.*

Lantier stared at the two boys. Antoine was black... in every way. But Philippe still had a chance. He was as light as he himself was... just a shade too dark to pass... but not too dark to keep him from achieving an all-but-white persona. What did that require? Nothing unattainable... verbal skill, a refined accent... a slight French accent was perfect for speaking English or Italian, Spanish, even German, Russian—oh, very much Russian... and it wouldn't hurt if it should happen to recall the Lantiers' ties to the noble de Lantiers of Normandy those several centuries ago. But Philippe was caught in a strong tide going in exactly the opposite direction. When they first arrived from Haiti, Haitian boys like Philippe and Antoine had to run a gauntlet, an actual gauntlet! American black boys spotted them immediately and beat them up on the way to school and on the way home. Beat them up! More than once Philippe had come home with welts on his face, contusions. Lantier was determined to step in and do something about it. Philippe begged him not to—*begged* him! It would only make things worse, Papa. Then he'd *really* get it. So all the

Haitian boys did the same thing. They tried to turn themselves as American black as they could... the clothes, the baggy jeans, the boxer shorts showing... the talk, yo, bro, ho, ain't, ain'no, homey, mo'vucker, ca'zucca. And now look at Philippe. He had black hair as straight as Ghislaine's. Whatever he did with it, it would be better than what he did with it now... which was wear it cut about three inches long all over and frizz it to make it look *Neg.*

With all these things running through his head, Lantier didn't realize how long his eyes were fixed upon his son's face... with disappointment, with the resentful feeling that Philippe was in some way betraying him.

The sudden silence made the moment intense.

Philippe was now staring back into Lantier's face not with mere resentment but with insolence, as Lantier saw it. Antoine no longer looked at him with live hatred, however. He seemed mainly to feel himself backed up in somebody else's toilet. His eyeballs rolled upward for an instant. He seemed to be looking for some white-robed little person with wings who would fly over and wave a wand and make him disappear.

It had turned into a Mexican standoff. Here are the enemies staring daggers at each other without moving a muscle or making a sound. Finally...

"An nou soti la!" Philippe said in Creole to Antoine

with his loudest, deepest baritone or, rather, bari*teen* gang voice ("Let's get outta here").

Both turned their backs upon Lantier without another word and walked across the kitchen doing the pimp roll...and disappeared out the side door.

Lantier was left speechless in the doorway of his little office. He turned back to his desk and stared at Ghislaine. What was to be done? Why on earth would an essentially bright, handsome, light-skinned Haitian, directly related to the de Lantiers of Normandy, like your brother, want to turn himself into an American *Neg?* Those too-big baggy pants, for example...the *Neg* criminals wore them in jail. The jailers weren't about to go to the trouble of *measuring* an inmate before giving him clothes. They just gave them clothes that were obviously big enough, which meant they were always too big. The little *Negs* on the street wore them because they idealized the big *Negs* in jail. They were their heroes. They were *baaaaad.* They were fearless. They terrified the American whites and the Cubans. But if it were just the stupid clothes and the ignorant hip-hop music, and the vile Black English, which be primitive to the max, man, that would be one thing. But Haitian boys like your brother imitated stupid, ignorant *Neg* attitudes, too. That was the *real* problem. The *Negs* thought only "pussies" raised their hands in class during class discussions or studied hard for tests or cared about grades or little things like being courteous to teachers. Haitian boys didn't want to be *pussies,* either, for God's sake!—and so they began treating school like a pussy inconvenience, too. And now Philippe regresses from French to Creole. You heard him!—but you're lucky. You don't speak it, and you don't have to bother understanding it... whereas I'm not so lucky. I *understand* Creole. I have to *teach* the damned language. What is to be done when it's time for your brother to go to college? No college will want him, and he won't want no college. Nome sayin', man?

After about a half hour of this, Lantier realized that he and Ghislaine weren't talking about Philippe—because Ghislaine never got a word in about *any*thing. He was just using her ears as a couple of receptacles into which he could pour his agony and the helplessness he felt... This endless soliloquy of disappointment would not solve anything. It would only depress Ghislaine and make her lose respect for him. An axiom popped into his head: Parents should never confess *any*thing to their children... *zero!* nothing whatsoever!

But he couldn't avoid confessing to himself... in a rising tide of guilt. ::::::What *is* Philippe's problem? It's so obvious, isn't it. His problem is, I let him go to Lee de Forest. My wonderful Art Deco house happens to fall within a school district whose senior high school is Lee de Forest. I knew it had a... a... a not-very-good reputation, "But how bad can it be?" I kept saying to myself. The *truth* is, I don't even *begin* to have the money to send him to a private school. Every dollar I have goes right into the Art Deco maw of this house, so I can *feel* as French as I want to be . . . and *of course* Philippe buckled under the pressure of the Antoines and the François Duboises. He's not a tough boy. *Of course* he feels desperate. *Of course* he grabs at any shield he can find. *Of course* he turns Creole. And I let it happen . . . *of course* . . . Oh, God . . . of course . . . for *me*. Then for God's sake, be a *man!* Sell it for the sake of your son! . . . But it's already too late, isn't it . . . House prices in South Florida have dropped 30 percent. The bank would take every dime I got for it, and I'd *still* owe them money . . . But underneath all that I get a glimpse of the ogre who lives at the bottom: *I can't give up all this!* ::::::

So he said, on the verge of tears, "Ghislaine, I think . . . I have *uhhh* . . . I need to prepare for tomorrow's classes, and I think—"

Ghislaine didn't let him struggle on. "I'm going into the living room to do some reading for class."

Once she left his office, Lantier's eyes misted over. Obviously she had decided that she had better keep him company a while to make sure he got over this rocky state of mind that was pushing him over the edge.

Lantier *did* have a couple of classes to prepare for. One was "The Triumph of the Nineteenth-Century French Novel." This class was not made up of the brightest bulbs in the chandelier. *No* classes at Everglades Global University were.

"Papa, come here! Quick! It's on TV!" Ghislaine yelled from the living room. "Hurry up!"

So Lantier hustled out of his office and into the living room and sat down with Ghislaine on the couch—*Merde!*—the stuffing was coming out the seam of one of the big square pillows he sat on, and he remembered very well how much upholstery cost, and he couldn't spend that kind of money on a damned couch right now...

On the television screen that's the Lee de Forest High School, all right... what a scene... the yowling! the screaming! the chants! A hundred police officers, it looks like, trying to hold back a mob... a mob of dark faces, *Negs* and every shade of brown, *Neg* to tan, and in between... they're yowling and howling, the mob, they're all young—they look like students, except for a group of black students—no, they can't be students—they're more like in their twenties and early thirties, maybe. Scores of squad cars, it seems, with racks of lights on the roofs, flash away in epileptic sequences of red and blue and blinding clear lamps... they're painful! the bursts of clear light! But that doesn't keep Lantier from a sliced second of agony over how small and old-fashioned his TV set is compared to the TV sets other people have—plasma, whatever that is, no big hulking box of tubes or whatever's in there bulging out in back of the screen like an ugly, cheap plastic rump... and everybody else's is forty-eight inches, sixty-four inches, whatever that measures—sliced and diced that mini-moment and on the screen where all is uproar... a hulking *brigade* of policemen, *a battalion*... never saw so many in one place trying to contain a mob of yowling—those *are* students!—all those young *Neg* brown and tan young heads with their mouths wide open howling bloody murder from out of their gullets... squad cars all over the place... more racks of roof lights flashing away... The camera, wherever the camera is, focuses more tightly on the action... you can see the Lexan riot visors the policemen have and the Lexan riot shields... a frontline of *Neg,* brown, *mulat, café au lait* boys, and *une fille saillante comme un boeuf* push back against the shields... they look so small, up against the police officers, these yowling high school goslings—

"Qu'est-ce qui se passe?" (What's going on?), Lantier says to Ghislaine. "Pourquoi ne pas nous dire?"(Why don't they tell us!)

As if on cue, a woman's hyper-voice overrides the yowling—you can't see her—and says, "They apparently want to drive the crowd back far enough—they've got to get the teacher—Estevez, we're told is his name—he teaches civics—they've got to get him out of the building and into a police van and place him in a detention—"

"Estevez!" Lantier said to Ghislaine in French. "Civics class—that's Philippe's teacher!"

"—but won't say where. Their big concern right now is security. The students were dismissed just about an hour ago. Classes are suspended for the day. But this crowd of students—they refuse to leave the school grounds, and this is an old building that was not built thinking about security. Police are afraid students will try to reenter the building, and that's where Estevez is being held."

Lantier said, "Good luck getting him out of there! The police can't hold back a mob of kids like that but so long!"

"Papa," said Ghislaine, "this is a re-broadcast! All this happened five or six hours ago, it must be."

"*Ahhh*... yes," said Lantier. "That's true, that's true..." He stared directly at Ghislaine. "But Philippe didn't say anything about... *any* of this!" Before Ghislaine could respond, the TV voice rose... *"I think they're gonna try to bring him out now. That small door there, at ground level—it's opening!"*

The camera zoomed in... looked like a utility door. As it opened it created a small shadow on the concrete surface... Out came a police officer looking this way and that. Then two more... and two more... and yet two more... then three came squeezing out of the little—no, they were not three policemen but two policemen gripping the upper arms of a burly, balding, light-skinned man with his hands behind his back, apparently handcuffed together. Even though the hair on his pate was getting scarce, he must not have been more than thirty-five. He walked with his chin high but was blinking at a terrific rate. His chest bulged out against a white shirt whose shirttails seemed to be hanging outside his pants.

"That's who it is!" said the TV voice. "That's the teacher, José Estevez! A *civics* teacher at Lee de Forest High School. He's now under arrest for punching a student in front of an entire class and then dragging him to the floor, we're told, and all but paralyzing him with some sort of neck hold. The police have closed in around him in a sort of—uh-uhhh—*phalanx* to protect him until they can get him inside the police van."

—a squall of yowls and howls and gullet-ripping epithets—

"They've figured out that's him, Estevez, the teacher who assaulted one of their schoolmates about two hours ago!"

"What *is* that shirt?" says Lantier, in French.

The teacher and his army of cop bodyguards are pulling nearer and nearer to the camera.

Ghislaine answers in French, "Looks like a guayabera to me. A Cuban shirt."

The TV voice: "They've almost reached the van... you can see right there. The riot police have done an amazing job, holding back this big and very angry crowd of students—"

Lantier looks Ghislaine squarely in the face again and says, "Philippe comes home from school, from the same classroom where all this happens, an army of cops occupies the schoolyard, and there's a mob of his own schoolmates ready to hang his teacher from a tree if they can lay hands on him—and Philippe doesn't want to talk about it, and his *Neg* pal Antoine doesn't want to talk about it? If that had been me, I'd *still* be talking about it after all these years! What's going on with Philippe? Do you have any idea at all?"

Ghislaine shook her head and said, "No, Papa... none at all."

7

The Mattress

::::::Do I exist?... If so, where?... Oh, man, I don't live... *any*where... I don't *belong* anywhere... I'm not even one of "my people" anymore, am I.::::::

Nestor Camacho—remember him?—was evaporating, disintegrating, coming apart—meat from bone, turning into Jell-O with a beating heart, sinking back into the primordial ooze.

Never before could he have possibly imagined himself attached to... nothing. Who could? Not until this moment, just after midnight, as he emerged from the locker room of the Marine Patrol marina and started walking to the parking lot—

Officer Camacho!

... and now he was hearing things. Nobody but cops coming off the shift were out here at the midnight hour, and no cop was going to call him "Officer," unless it was a joke. Himself alone, on a too warm, too sticky, too soupy, too sweaty, too dimly lit dusky September night in Miami... had he ever had the faintest notion of what desolation was? He hadn't tried to kid himself about what was happening to him over the past twenty-four hours.

Exactly twenty-four hours ago he had left this place, the marina, soaring on the applause of his fellow cops, astounded by the realization that the entire city—*the entire city!*—had been watching him—*him!* Nestor Camacho!—on TV as he saved a poor panicked wretch on top of a seventy-foot mast teetering over the edge of the Halusian Gulp. Barely fifteen minutes later he walks into his own house—and finds his father standing right at the door, anger up, paunch out, to dismiss him from the family... and from the Cuban people, while he's at it. Nestor is so upset, he barely sleeps at all and gets up in the morning and learns that the Spanish-language media—which essentially means the Cuban media—has been saying the same thing for the past twelve hours: Nestor Camacho has betrayed his own family and the Cuban people. His father not only considers him a non-person, he acts as if he no longer has a corporeal presence. He acts like he literally can't *see* him. Who? Him? Nestor? He's not here anymore. His neighbors, people he has known practically all his life, turn their backs on him, actually turn around 180 degrees and show him their backsides. His one last hope, his salvation, his one remaining attachment to the life he has lived for the past twenty-five years, namely, all his life, is his girlfriend. He has been seeing her, dating her, which is to say, these days, going to bed with her, and loving her with all his heart. So she shows up just a little over eight hours ago, just before he has to leave for the shift . . . to inform him that she is seeing, dating, and no doubt sharing the sheets with somebody else now, and hasta la vista, my dear Damaged Goods.

To top it all off, the shift starts, and his fellow cops, who were flocking about him like a bunch of cheerleaders twenty-four hours ago, have turned—well, not cold, but distant. None badmouths him. None acts like or insinuates that he has betrayed anybody. None acts as if he wants to take it back, the praise they gave him last night. They're embarrassed, that's all. After twenty-four hours they have this piece of meat beaten black-and-blue by Spanish-language radio, Spanish TV, the Spanish newspaper—*El Nuevo Herald*—and even kindly souls discreetly avert their eyes.

The only one who showed the faintest desire to talk to him about the whole mess was Lonnie Kite, his *americano* Safe Boat mate. He took him aside just before they boarded the Safe Boat to begin the shift and said, "You have to look at it this way, Nestor"—Nest-*ter*. "If that little fucker had been up on top of a mast almost anywhere else, all anybody would be saying is 'This kid Camacho is Tarzan with a pair of stones you could take down a building with.' Your bad luck is that it had to happen in front of a bunch a gawkers on the Rickenbacker Causeway on a Friday afternoon at rush hour. They all get out of their cars and line the bridge, and they got the best seats in the house for a game a Cuban Refugee—he the brave little guy—fighting Dumb Cop. They don't know shit. Without all these clueless assholes, there wouldn' a been nobody with their undies in an uproar."

The *americano* meant to be bucking up his spirits, but he depressed Nestor even more. Even the *americanos* knew! Even the *americanos* knew that Nestor Camacho just got whipped.

He was hoping something would happen on this shift, something so big, like a big boat collision—collisions, mostly involving small boats, happened all the time—that it would absorb his attention entirely. But no, it was the usual... boats adrift and they can't get the engine to turn over... somebody thought they saw swimmers out in a boat lane... some idiot in a cigarette boat is barreling across the water, making extreme turns to rock other boats with his wake... a bunch a drunks are out on the bay, throwing bottles and unidentified trash into the water... that was the night's catch, and none of it was serious enough to distract Nestor from his deep worries... and by the time they returned to the marina, he had begun totaling up totaling up totaling up his miseries…

…and the scene before him captured his tally—desolation—perfectly. He was approaching the marina parking lot. Here in the midnight hour at least a third of it was empty. The parking lot's lighting didn't truly illuminate much of anything. It created the feeblest mechanical dusk imaginable. The palm trees around this perimeter were barely discernible. At best you could see some flat black shapes. As for the cars in the lot, they were not so much shapes as feeble dusky glints of light…off a windshield here, a strip of chrome there…a wing mirror over there…a dub over there…feeble feeble reflections of feeble feeble light… In Nestor's current state of mind it was worse than no light at all…this was light in its junk form…

He was heading for his Camaro…why?…where was he going to spend the night?

He could make out the Camaro only because he knew exactly where he had parked it. He headed toward it out of sheer habit. And then what? He had to drive somewhere and stretch out and log a good solid ten hours of sleep. He couldn't recall ever feeling this tired and empty in his life…burnt out, dried out, drained…and where was that healing sleep going to take place? All evening, every time there was a lull he'd call up friends, asking for a place to crash, anything, even guys he hadn't seen since Hialeah High, and the answers were all like Jesús Gonzalo's, Jesús, his best buddy on the wrestling team, and he says, "*Uhhhh* well, I *ahhhh* guess so, but I mean, how long you wanna stay just tonight, right?—because I told my cousin Ramón—he's from New Jersey—and he said he might be coming to town tomorrow, and I told him—"

His friends! True, for the past three years his friends had been mostly other cops, because only other cops could understand what was on your mind, the things you had to do, the things you worried about. Besides, you had an elite status. You had to face dangers your old friends couldn't imagine. They couldn't imagine what it took to beam the Cop Look and order people around on the street... Anyway, the news of what he had done had obviously seeped like a gas throughout the Cuban community. Okay. He'd ask one of the younger cops on the shift. He had his chance just now in the locker room over the past half hour... had plenty of chances all night... but he couldn't do it! They've inhaled the gas, too!... His own family had thrown him out of his own house... the *humiliation!* Go to a motel? To a Hialeah boy that was not even a thinkable solution. Pay that kind of money just to lay your head down overnight in the dark? Ask Cristy? She was on his side. But could he stop with just a place to sleep? Okay, let's see... there was always the Camaro. He could always conk out in his own car. He tried to picture it... How the hell would you ever get horizontal in a Camaro? You'd have to be a child or a contortionist... a second straight sleepless night... that's all he'd get out of that.

I now live... nowhere... I don't *belong* anywhere. Once more the question popped into his head: Do I exist? The first couple of times it popped into his head, it was with a tinge of self-pity. The next couple of times, it was with a tinge of morbid humor. And now... with a tinge of panic. I'm doing the usual, heading for my car at the end of a shift... and I've got no place to drive it to! He stopped in his tracks. Tell me truthfully now... *Do I exist?*

"Officer Camacho! Hey! Over here! Officer Camacho!"

Over here was somewhere in the parking lot. Nestor peered into the feeble electro-dusk of the place. A tall white man was running toward him along a row of parked cars.

"John! *hunh hunh hunh hunh* Smith! *hunh hunh* from the *Herald*!" he shouted. Not in very good shape, whoever the hell you are *hunh hunh hunh hunh*... panting like that after jogging maybe 150 feet. Nestor didn't recognize the name but "from the *Herald*" sounded okay. Alone in all the media the *Herald* had been at least halfway on his side.

"I'm sorry!" said the man as he drew closer. I *hun-hunhunhunh* couldn't figure out any other way to reach you!"

Once they were face-to-face, Nestor recognized him. He was the reporter who had been waiting with a photographer when he and the Sergeant and Lonnie Kite returned to the marina in the Safe Boat. He couldn't have looked more *americano* if he made a conscious effort . . . tall . . . floppy blond hair, absolutely straight . . . a pointed nose . . . "I'm sorry for intruding *hunh hunh hunh hunh*. Did you read my story this morning?" said John Smith. "Was I fair?" He smiled. He gulped. He opened his eyes like a pair of morning glories.

As far as Nestor was concerned, this John Smith's turning up in this parking lot at midnight might as well have been the sort of apparition that people who don't sleep and don't exist are prey to . . . He still had enough sanity left, however, to take this *americano* at face value. He wanted to ask the *americano* what he was doing here, but he couldn't come up with any diplomatic way to put it. So he merely nodded . . . as if to say, tentatively, "Yes, I read your story and yes, you were fair."

"I know you're probably *hunhunhunhunh* about to go home," said John Smith, "but could you spare just a couple of minutes? There's some things *hunhunhunhunh* I need to ask you."

An eerie form of elation brought Nestor's numb central nervous system back to life. He was reconnecting with . . . *something,* in any case. Someone, even if only some *americano* newspaper reporter he didn't even know, was offering him, if nothing else, an alternative to driving around all night talking to himself. The vagabond in the Camaro! Homeless in the headlines! But all he said was "About what?"

"Well, I'm writing a follow-up story, and I'd hate to have to write it without getting your response."

Nestor just stared at him. ::::::Response? Response to what?:::::: The word set off a nameless sense of dread.

"Why don't we go have a cup of coffee or something and sit down?"

Nestor stared at him some more. Talking to this baby-faced reporter could only get him in trouble unless some lieutenant or captain or deputy chief okayed it. On the other hand, he had talked to this guy twenty-four hours ago, and that was okay... and as long as he talked to the press, he *existed*. Was it not so? As long as he talked to the press, he was... *somewhere*. Wouldn't you say? As long as he appeared in the press he *belonged* in this world... You had to use your imagination... He knew there was not a lieutenant, a captain, or a deputy chief in this world who would understand that, much less swallow it. But maybe they would understand *this:* "Greatgodalmighty, Lieutenant, put yourself in my shoes. I'm all alone. You can't even imagine how alone." It all boiled down to one thing. He needed someone to talk to, not in the sense of talking to a priest or anything like that.

Just someone to *talk* to... just so he could feel like he existed again, after twenty-four hours' terrible toll.

He gave reporter John Smith a very long, blank stare. He once more nodded yes without a trace of satisfaction, never mind enthusiasm...

"How about that place over there?" said the reporter. He was pointing toward Inga La Gringa's bar.

"It's too loud in there," said Nestor. That much was true. What he didn't say was that the noise would be coming from other Marine Patrol cops coming off the shift. "There's a place called the Isle of Capri, over on Brickell, near the causeway. They're open late and you can hear yourself talk, at least. It's a little on the expensive side, though." What he didn't say was that no cop coming off the shift anywhere in Miami would be going to a place that expensive.

"Not a problem," said John Smith. "It's on the paper."

Off they drove to the Isle of Capri, each in his own car. As soon as Nestor turned on the ignition in the Camaro, the air-conditioning blasted him in the face. As soon as he slipped the floor shift into drive and started off, the muffler blew. In concert the air-conditioning and the muffler rupture made him feel trapped inside one of those leaf blowers that are so loud, the seven-dollar-an-hour operators have to wear baffles over their ears... Trapped inside a leaf blower he was... questions were blowing around in his head. :::::Why am I doing this? What's in it for me, besides trouble? What's he want me to respond to? Why would this be "on the paper," as he put it? Why should I trust this *americano?* Just why? I shouldn't, obviously... but I'm bereft of all that matters in this life! I don't even have an ancestry... My goddamned grandfather, the great sluice gate operator for the Malecón waterworks, cut the family tree out from under me... and I don't even know where I'm going to sleep. Christ, I'd rather have a conversation with a *snake* than have nobody to talk to.::::::

Nestor and the reporter sat at the bar and ordered coffee. Very deluxe looking, the bar at the Isle of Capri... Lights from below beamed up through an array of liquor bottles against a vast mirrored wall. The beams lit up the liquor bottles... absolutely glamorous, and the mirrored wall doubled the show. The show dazzled Nestor, even though he knew all these bottles existed for the benefit of middle-aged *americanos* who liked to talk about how "hammered" they got last night, how "wasted," "smashed," "destroyed," "retarded," and even how they "blacked out" and didn't know where the hell they were when they woke up. The *americano* idea of being a Man sure wasn't a Latino's. Nevertheless, the way the bottles here in the Isle of Capri put on their light show made him feel delirious with the luxury of it all. He was also as tired as he had ever been in his life.

The coffee arrived, and John Smith of the *Herald*

got down to business. "As I said, I'm doing a follow-up story to the man on the mast—how you saved the guy—but my sources tell me that far from looking at you as a hero, a lot of Cubans think of you as something close to a traitor"... whereupon he cocked his head and stared at Nestor with an expression that clearly asked what do you say to that.

Nestor didn't know *what* to say... the coffee with the sugar he heaped in it the Cuban way was ambrosial; it made him hungry. He hadn't had enough to eat during the shift. The fact that his existence, if that was what it was, embarrassed other Marine Patrolmen took his appetite away. John Smith was waiting for an answer. Nestor was confused as to whether he should go into all this or not.

"I guess you should ask *them,*" he said.

"Ask who?"

"Ask... I mean... *Cubans,* I guess."

"I've been doing that," said John Smith, "but they're not comfortable with me. To most of them I'm an outsider. They don't want to say much... when I start asking them about ethnic attitudes and nationalities and anything in that area. They're not comfortable with the *Herald,* period, as far as that goes."

Nestor smiled, but not with pleasure. "*That's* for sure."

"Why does that make you smile?"

"Because where I come from, Hialeah, people say,

'The *Miami Herald*' and in the next breath, *'Yo no creo.'* You'd think the full name of the paper was *Yo No Creo el Miami Herald*. You know *'yo no creo'?*"

"Sure. 'I don't believe.' *Yo comprendo*. And they're doing the same thing with you, Nestor."

The reporter hadn't called him by his first name before. It bothered Nestor. He didn't know how to take it. He didn't know whether the man was being congenial or using the first name the way you would somebody beneath you... like a *fumigador*. Many customers called his father Camilo right off the bat. "They're twisting everything around with you, too," the reporter was saying. "They're taking what you did, which I—I think I made it pretty clear in what I wrote—which I consider an act of great courage and strength, and they're twisting it into a cowardly act!"

"Cowardly?" said Nestor. That startled him and hit a nerve. "They can say a lot of things, *traidor* and all that, but I haven't heard anybody say 'cowardly.' I'd like to know how the hell anybody could say 'cowardly'... Jesus Christ... I'd like to see anybody else come close to what I did... 'Cowardly.'" He shook his head. "You heard somebody actually use that word, *cowardly?*"

"Yes. *'Cobarde,'* they said... every time."

"They?" said Nestor. "How do you know that? You said they wouldn't talk to you."

"Some of them talk to me," said John Smith. "But

that wasn't where I heard it. I heard it on the radio, and not just once, either."

"*What* radio? Who said it?"

"The Spanish-language stations," said John Smith. " '*Cobarde.*' In fact, I think it was two or three stations."

"Assholes," muttered Nestor. He could feel his adrenaline kicking. "What's supposed to be *cobarde* about it? How do they figure they can call it *that?*"

"They don't bother with much figuring. Here's their reasoning, if that's what it is. What they say is, it's easy to be a *pez gordo* and go around acting like a *valiente* when you have all the other *peces gordos* behind you, the whole police force, the Coast Guard, the *Miami Herald.*" He chuckled. "I guess they throw in *Yo No Creo el Miami Herald* for good measure. You haven't been listening to the Latino radio?"

"I haven't had time," said Nestor. "If you knew what my last twenty-four hours were like..." He paused. He could feel he was entering some dicey territory now. "...you'd know what I mean."

"Why don't you tell me what happened," said John Smith. Now he was staring straight into Nestor's eyes with an intensity that just wasn't John Smith. Nestor got the feeling that this must be the Reporter Look, the same way cops hit people with the Cop Look. Not that the two were equivalent. He stared off at the liquor bottle light show. Every cop Nestor had ever talked to on that subject considered the press a bunch of pussies. Nestor was willing to bet that the one right beside him at this bar was a pussy, too. There was something about the soft way he talked and all his good manners... He was the kind—if you made the slightest threat physically, he could fold and run away. But the older cops also said that they were like little spiders, like black widows. They could bite and cause you major grief.

That being the case, he now focused on John Smith and said, "I don't know if that's such a good idea."

"Why?"

"Well, I'd probably need approval before I talked about that."

"Whose approval?"

"I don't know exactly, because I've never been through the procedure. But I'd need a zone captain at least."

"I don't get that," said John Smith. "You talked to me after you brought the so-called leader of the underground down from the mast. Whose approval did you have to get before you did that?"

"Nobody's, but that was diff—"

A suddenly aggressive John Smith ran right over Nestor's words with "And who wrote you the most favorable story that came out of the whole thing?... and the most accurate. Did I treat you badly in any way?"

The man bored in with his Reporter Look.

"No," said Nestor, "but—"

The reporter trampled again. "So what makes you think I'd try to make you look bad now? The people who are causing you trouble are *El Nuevo Herald*—I hope you saw what they said"—Nestor averted his eyes and rocked his head forward and back slowly, indicating a very faint yes—"and the Latino radio and Latino TV tried to bury you!" the reporter continued. "And they're not going to stop with yesterday. They'll keep it up today, too. Don't you want anybody on your side? You want to be nothing but a piñata the whole bunch can keep on having fun whacking at? Oh, I can go ahead and write a nice piece analyzing what you did and why it was absolutely necessary and humane. But that would just be an editorial, and not even by an editor. I need some details that only you can provide."

The hell of it was that reporter John Smith was right. The word *cobarde* kept throbbing in Nestor's brain. His sense of honor decreed that such a slur not go unanswered. Revenge is mine, sayeth the Lord—and in the meantime, what happens to your job, big avenger? If he dumps everything out for the reporter's benefit... even if he doesn't criticize the Department in any way... a big newspaper article dwelling upon Himself in a police action this highly publicized—he doesn't need any written-down protocols to know what the Department will think of that. :::::Still, everybody—*everybody*—needs to get one thing straight. No way is Nestor Camacho a *cobarde*... you assholes... but that's not for me to say, is it. That's for the Department to say... and fat chance of them doing it. Oh, they'll defend their decision to bring the guy down off the mast, but they're not going to go into raptures over the cop who went up and did it—::::::

Nestor didn't realize how he must have looked to John Smith. He was staring not at John, but into the mirror behind all the lit-up liquor bottles. He didn't bother looking at himself, even though there he was in the mirror. He was running his right hand over the knuckles of his left hand and then his left hand over the knuckles of his right hand and his right hand over the knuckles of his left hand and his left hand—

Only at this instant did he realize what a picture of indecision he presented. John Smith said, "Okay, Nestor, I'll tell you what. If you'll give me the details, I promise I won't quote you or even indicate I've talked to you."

"Yeah, but there'd be things only I would know about, and then everyone would know it was me."

"Look," said John Smith, "I've run into that problem before, and I know how to handle it. I'll indicate any number of other sources. How do you think the big police stories get in the papers? I'm not talking about straight-out news that a crime has occurred. I'm talking about the inside story on how a big crime was solved, who ratted out who, things like that. It's all cops giving reporters information that makes the reporter look good and reporters writing stories that make the cops look good. Both sides know how to protect the other. It happens all the time, and I mean *all* the time. If you don't have some way to get your story out, other people, like City Hall, for example, will tell your story for you... and believe me, you're not gonna like that. To them you're just this... this... *mosquito* who bites his fellow Cubans. Look, I can get your story out—and make it clear that you *wouldn't* cooperate. I'll say that you failed to return phone calls, which will be true. In fact, it's already true. About nine-thirty I called the Marine Patrol office and asked to speak to you, but they wouldn't put a personal call through to the Safe Boat."

With alarm in his voice, Nestor said, "You mean they already *know* you wanted to talk to me?"

"Of course!" said John Smith. "Listen, I'm going to get a beer. Would you like one?"

A beer? How could the man suddenly start thinking about a beer? It astounded Nestor. He resented it. On the other hand... maybe a beer wouldn't be so bad. Maybe it would calm him down a little, dilute the adrenaline flow. If he had some other kind of drug, he'd no doubt take it right now... and a bottle of beer was pretty mild stuff. "Uhh... yeah," he said. "I'll have one."

John Smith raised his hand to get the bartender's attention. As he ordered the two beers, Nestor's resentment began to build back up. ::::::It's not *his* ass that's on the line, hanging out over the edge.:::::: John Smith turned back to Nestor, acting as if there had been no break in the conversation at all. "Of course!" he said. "If I'm planning to write a story about you—and they'll see that story soon enough—of course I'd try to reach you directly. It would look weird if I didn't. That's just standard operating procedure."

The beers arrived. Nestor didn't wait for John Smith. He just tilted his up and drank... a nice long gulp of it, too... and a wave of warmth rose from his stomach and romped through his brain and flowed throughout his entire central nervous system... and it *did* seem to calm him down.

He started with the end of the shift twenty-four hours ago... and all the other cops going nuts over him and telling him, in a jocular cop way, of course, how he had electrified the entire city... and he had driven home... as if on wings... and he had a big surprise waiting just inside the front door.

"And there's my father. He's been waiting for me, and he's standing there with his legs spread like a wrestler's and his arms crossed like this—"

—all at once he cut himself off and locked on to John the Reporter's gaze with his... and stayed that way for what he hoped would be a suspenseful few seconds... When he resumed speaking, it was in a different tone of voice, one that suited that look precisely.

"Do you remember what you just promised me about how you would use what I'm gonna tell you?"

"Yes..."

"About how you'll cover me with the sources?" He intensified the look.

"Yes..."

"I'm just making sure we understand each other." He skipped a couple of beats... "I'd be really pissed... if we didn't."

With that, he turned that certain look on to the max. Only then did he actually realize it was the Cop Look. Without a word it conveyed a message. On this terrain I rule. I have ultimate power, and I'm quite ready to blow you away if I have to. Oh, so you want to know what it would take to make me "have to"? Well, let's start with *breach of verbal contract*.

The pale *americano* blanched dead white—or so it looked to Officer Camacho. Journalist John Smith's lips parted slightly... but he said nothing. He just nodded yes, dipping his forehead forward ever so diffidently.

The next thing Nestor knew... he was sitting there in the glamorous glow of the Isle of Capri bar's lucent liquor bottles, spilling, as they say, his guts. It *all* came out. He couldn't tell this *americano*—he had seen exactly twice in his life—enough. He had an overwhelming urge... not to confess, for he hadn't sinned...*just one more beer* but to tell somebody, some at least halfway neutral party, of his anguish and humiliation, his rejection by all those closest to him—at once!—in less than twenty-four hours!—and by untold thousands of his own people, *just one more beer* his fellow *cubanos,* who were only too happy to believe what they heard on that most powerful of organs, Spanish-language radio, and even by that old-fashioned medium no one under forty ever looked at anymore, namely, the newspapers...his father standing there in his doorway, which was Nestor's, too, with his wide-legged stance, like a wrestler's, and his arms folded across his chest—like an *infuriated* wrestler's...*just one more beer* and neighbors he had known all his life who turned their backs the moment they saw him coming...and, to top it off, his fellow cops, who had hailed him as a hero twenty-four hours ago *just one more beer*...and had now turned chilly with embarrassment over this tainted man in their midst...*just one more beer—in cervisia veritas*...all of it, *all of it,* right down to his cell phone ringing in his pocket while he's *this close* to falling to his death from seventy feet above a boat deck, trying to go hand over hand down a hundred-foot cable carrying a man *with his legs*...and then the goddamned phone starts *beep-beep-beeping* with text messages, and people—his own people—*cubanos*—are screaming bloody murder at him from the Rickenbacker Causeway bridge... *all of it,* even the cold expression on Magdalena's face when he began shouting *¡CONCHA!* at her—

For three and a half hours Nestor poured out every last drop of his sorrows and his soul... and would have never stopped, had not the Isle of Capri closed up at 4:00 a.m. The two young men were now out in the street. Nestor felt unsteady. His balance was... off. His gait lacked fluidity. Well, no wonder... the stress of the last two days... the lack of sleep... lack of food, too, come to think of it. He never did come to think he might just be close to wasted after downing nine beers in a row, plus a tequila shot, more alcohol than he had ever had in one evening in his life.

But the *americano periodista* must have come to think of it, because he looked at Nestor and said, "You're planning to *drive* home now?"

Nestor barked a bitter little laugh. "Home? I don't have one a those anymore, home."

"Then where are you planning to spend the night?"

"I don't know," said Nestor, except that it came out *I'ownoh.* "I'll sleep inna car if I've to... No! I know... I'll drive overt Rodriguez's and sleep on a mat inna gym."

"What if it's locked?"

Another bitter little laugh. "Locked? Nothing's locked if you know what a cop knows." Even Nestor picked up a whiff of his own cop braggadocio.

"Nestor"—that impudent first-name business again—"I think you're too exhausted to drive anywhere. I've got a pullout in my apartment, and I'm only five minutes away at this hour. How about it?"

Is he kidding? Sleep at some *americano periodista's* place? But that word the *periodista* used... *exhausted.* Just hearing it out loud made him feel even more exhausted... exhausted, not wasted... not wasted, worn out... never felt this worn out. Aloud he said, "Maybe you're right."

Afterward he could barely even remember John Smith's driving him over to his apartment... or passing out on the pullout couch in a cramped little living room... or all the vomiting...

When Nestor woke up, returned to the land of the conscious, it wasn't really as late as he had hoped it would be. Only the dimmest daylight showed through the weave of a length of hopsacking that served as a makeshift curtain over the room's only window. He felt as bad as he had ever felt in his life. If he were to lift his head off this sofa, he would pass out again. That much he knew without even testing it. A pool of pain and nausea had flooded one whole hemisphere of his brain as he lay on that side of his head. He didn't dare tilt that pool so much as one degree or—he could already smell it—*smell* it—the vomitus would gush out projectile-style. He had a bleary recollection of throwing up all over the carpet just before he passed out.

He gave up and closed his eyes again. *Had* to close them, and presently he fell asleep again. It wasn't a good sleep. He kept waking up, fitfully. The main thing was not to open his eyes. That at least gave him a fighting chance of falling asleep again... however troubled sleep might be.

When he finally woke up for good, the hopsacking curtain was all bright points of light. It must have been close to noon. He dared lift his head a few inches. This time it was awful but not impossible. He managed to swing his legs over the side of the couch and sit up... and lowered his head between his legs to bring more blood to his brain. When he brought his head back up, he put his elbows on his knees and covered his eyes with the palms of his hands. He didn't want to have to see any more of this tiny, fetid straw-colored room. He didn't want to do anything, but he could tell he would have to make it to the bathroom one way or another.

He sighed out loud, for no other reason than to hear himself declare how miserable and paralyzed he felt. He sighed some more. The next thing he knew, he could hear the floor creaking with footsteps. What a dump this was... On the other hand, he didn't even have so much as a *dump* to go to.

"Good morning. *Buenos días*. How do you feel?"

There was John Smith... standing in the doorway to the bathroom. Nestor lifted his head just enough to see him head to foot. The *americano* stood there dressed so *americano,* it was annoying... the khaki pants so well pressed you could cut your finger on the crease... the blue button-down shirt, open two buttons' worth at the neck and turned back exactly two cuff lengths' worth on each sleeve... all just so, just so. Had Nestor known and understood the word *preppy,* he would have realized why it got under his skin.

But all he said was "I feel like shit... but I guess I'll survive." He gave John Smith a quizzical look. "I thought you'd be at work."

"Well, since the idea is to write a story about *you,* I guess I *am* at work. I thought I should at least hang around until you woke up."

The idea is to write a story about you. In his fragile state, the thought hit Nestor with a jolt. His heart sank. What had he done? Why had he told the guy all that... crap last night? Was he insane?... all that personal crap? He had an urge to call it off—right now! But then he thought of how weak he would look to John Smith... reneging this morning after dredging his innards up for the *americano* and spreading them out for his inspection... four hours of it, pouring his guts out through his big mouth, and now, hungover, head throbbing... to start whining and begging, "I take it all back! Please, please, I was drunk, that was all! You can't do this to me! Have pity! Have mercy!"—and that, the fear of looking weak and pathetic and frightened, as much as anything else, was what now kept his mouth shut . . . the fear of looking afraid! That by itself was enough to keep any Nestor Camacho from yielding to . . . the Doubts.

"Somebody's got to drive you back to your car," the *americano* was saying. "It's six or seven miles from here, and I'm not sure"—he lowered one eyebrow and twisted his lips up toward it in a mildly mocking smile—"I'm not completely sure you'd remember where it is."

That was true. All that Nestor could recall was a bar where the light show seemed so glamorous . . . the lights from below that filled the liquor bottles with tan and amber and tawny translucent glows and refracted a thousand tiny starbursts off their curved surfaces. He couldn't have said why, but the memory of that glowing tableau began to calm him.

John Smith suggested breakfast. But the thought of swallowing anything solid made Nestor bilious. He settled for a single cup of black instant coffee. Christalmighty, the *americanos* drank weak coffee.

And then they were in John Smith's Volvo, heading for the Isle of Capri restaurant. John Smith was so right. When he woke up during the night and when he first rose from the couch, he had no memory of *where* he had left his car.

They drove over to Jacinto Street and then turned down Latifondo Avenue . . . and the more he thought about it, the more he became convinced that John Smith was a good person. Last night the *americano* had literally taken him in... *off the street!*... and provided him a place to spend the night... and even waited around all morning to let him sleep as long as he wanted and drive him to his car. His fear of what this tall pale *periodista americano* might write began to recede. *Yo no creo el Miami Herald*!... but John Smith was right on about how the powers that be would twist his story... his career... his *life!* any way that suited them best, as long as he had no voice to speak up for him... even if it had to be in the pages of the *Yo No Creo Herald*.

"John," he said—and then he paused, because he had surprised himself. He had never called him by his first name before, or any name, for that matter. "I want to thank you for everything. When I finished the shift last night—I mean, talk about bummed out—I was... I was hard up as I've ever been in my life. I owe you one... no, a shitload. If there's anything I can do for you, just say it."

John Smith didn't say a word. He didn't even look at Nestor at first. He was still looking straight ahead at the road when he finally responded. "As a matter of fact, there *is* something. But I figured this wasn't the right time. You've got enough to think about for one day."

"No, go ahead. If I can do something for you, I'll do it."

Another long pause, and now John Smith turned toward Nestor. "Well . . . I need access to police files"—he glanced at the road and then back toward Nestor—"to see what information they may have on a certain individual, a man who lives in Sunny Isles."

"Who is he? What's his name?" said Nestor.

John Smith said, "Well . . . I haven't mentioned this to anyone except my editors. But if I'm right, it's a big story. His name is Sergei Korolyov. Does that ring a bell?"

"Ummm . . . no."

"You don't remember this Russian oligarch—that was what they kept calling him, a Russian oligarch—this Russian who gave a bunch of valuable paintings to the Miami Museum of Art? It wasn't that long ago . . . a bunch of Chagalls, Kandinskys, and *uhhh* this Russian 'Suprematist,' he called himself . . . his name's gone right out of my head, but he's a famous modern artist. Anyway, the museum figured these paintings were worth close to seventy million dollars—*Malevich!* That was the guy's name!—the one who called himself a Suprematist . . . Kazimir Malevich. This was such a gold mine, the museum changed its name to the Korolyov Museum of Art."

Nestor gave John Smith a long puzzled look. The *americano* had lost him the moment he mentioned Seagulls or whatever the artist's name was . . . and Kadinsky and Malayvitch...and the Korolyov Museum of Art, for that matter.

"The thing is," said John Smith, "I got a very solid tip that they're all forgeries, all those seventy million dollars' worth of paintings."

"No shit!"

"No, my source is a very serious guy. He's not the type who's just full of gossip."

"Did the museum give him any *money* for these paintings?"

"No, and that's the funny thing. These were straight-up donations. All he got out of it was dinner and a lot of flattery."

The fantasy's lights dimmed. *"Mierda,"* said Nestor. "If he didn't get any money out of it, I don't know if it's even a crime. I'd have to ask somebody."

"I don't know, either," said John Smith, "but either way, it's a hell of a story. I mean, there they all were, the mayor, the governor, Maurice Fleischmann, every hotshot in Miami, all trying to outdo each other piling praise on an impostor. It reminds me of Gogol's play *The Inspector General*. Did you ever—anyway, it's a great play."

::::::No, I *didn't* ever—my pale *americano*...::::::
But his resentment evaporated quickly. He was a curiosity, John Smith was. Never had Nestor come across anyone more instinctively unlike himself. The guy

didn't have a Latin bone in his body. He couldn't see him as a cop, either, not for three seconds. There was something bland and weak about him. This kind of guy—it was hard to imagine him being aggressive enough to come up with the Cop Look, even. ::::::Nevertheless, he, an *americano,* is my only hope of keeping the tide of *my own people, my own family!—from sweeping me away.*::::::

When John Smith drove him up to the Isle of Capri, he barely recognized the place. In the noonday sun it looked small and gray and dead. What would have ever seemed glamorous about it? It didn't *glow*... it was a cheap little dump, that was all. He spotted his Camaro, thank God.

He thanked John Smith again and promised to find out what he could about the Russian. As he departed the car, he experienced a strange feeling. In a moment, John Smith would drive off, and he, Nestor Camacho, would be left abandoned. *Abandoned* was the feeling... it began to steal over his central nervous system. Now, that was *strange.* He had an irrational urge to ask the *americano* to stay a little longer... at least until the shift began at the Marine Patrol marina. I'm alone!... more alone than I've ever been in my life! And the patrol shift would only make it worse. By the time the shift had ended last night, at midnight, his "comrades," his "brethren," were looking at him as if they wished they didn't have to. And that was merely the first day after the whole thing with the man on the mast. Tonight they would be wondering why couldn't he do the decent thing... and disintegrate... the way all decent marked men do.

::::::Oh, why don't you just jump into the river and drown, you miserable little *maricón!*:::::: He had always looked with contempt at people who submerged themselves in self-pity. At that point they lost all honor. And here he was, Nestor Camacho, treating himself to the perverse relief of avoiding the struggle—and all the assholes—by giving up and halfway hoping they'll pull him under for the third time. Hey, that'll end the pain, won't it!

In fact, there must be something peaceful about drowning... once you get over the initial shock of never breathing again, never drawing another breath. But he had already gone through the initial shock, hadn't he. What exactly did he have to live for? His family? His friends? His Cuban heritage? His loved ones? The great romantic love of his life? Or maybe for John Smith's approval. That made him laugh... rancidly. John Smith would very much approve of his going under for the third time. That way he could wring one more touching human-interest story out of this shit. Nestor could see the pseudo-sincere look on John Smith's face, as if he were still standing here facing him.

That conniving skinny WASP! Anything to get a story... that's how sincere he is... Other faces began to appear...vividly...vividly...faces for an instant along the railing of the Rickenbacker Causeway bridge. For that instant—a woman in her forties... he had never seen a more hateful face in his life! She spit at him. She raged. She tried to finish him off by beaming death rays from eyes set deep within her contorted face. He could hear the boos coming at him from all directions, including from below, from all the small craft that had come out for no other purpose than to shoot him down. And—who...is... this? ::::::Why, it's Camilo el Caudillo! He's right there before me with his arms crossed smugly atop his paunch...and here's my simpering mother sopping with sympathy, even though she knows el Caudillo's word is Gospel...Yeya and Yeyo—hah!:::::: So every living Camacho generation looks upon him as the Ultimate Traitor...Uncle Andres's cousin-in-law Hernán Lugo, who had taken it upon himself to preach at him at Yeya's birthday party...Ruiz's father, at Ricky's, turning his head about forty-five degrees so he could say out the side of his mouth, *Te cagaste*—"You shit all over it, didn't you, and all over yourself"...and aaahhh, it is Mr. Ruiz who now sits immediately before him with his back turned, snarling out the corner of his mouth beneath his shiny dome. All of them, the whole bunch, would love to see him go under...some, like his own family, to see the stain disappear once and for all...others, like Mr. Ruiz, so they would have such riveting, grossly embellished stories to tell... "He came skulking in wearing dark glasses, thinking I wouldn't recognize him"...and you, Señor Comemierda Ruiz, you'd probably lubricate it with sympathy at the same time... Oh, how you'd love it if I now just went with the current and let the undertow take me all the way to the bottom...well—

I'm damned if I will!

You'd all find it too delicious, and I truly resent that! Sorry, you're not going to have the satisfaction! And if you don't like it, don't blame me. Blame Mr. Ruiz with his *te cagaste* at the break of dawn. And then kindly go fuck yourself!

"You maybe zink thees fonny," said Mr. Yevgeni Uhuhuh—Nestor couldn't catch the last name—"bot I moss say ze kvestion. What you know aboud art?"

Nestor had no idea what to say. He was getting desperate. It was 3:15 p.m. The shift began in forty-five minutes. This was his third Craigslist visit in the past three hours...and he had to have this apartment. By sharing it with the tall bony, somewhat stooped Russian before him he could afford it...and he had to have it! He couldn't survive another night like last night, when he had no choice but to be taken in like a stray—by a reporter from *Yo No Creo el*

Herald! He and this Yevgeni were talking in the pathetically small vestibule between the apartment's two small rooms... Crammed into the vestibule were a tiny filthy kitchen, a tiny filthy bathroom, and the standard clattering aluminum-clad front door you found in Low-Rent apartments like this. Yevgeni, it seemed, was a "graphic artist." He referred to the apartment, which he wanted to share, as his "studio." Nestor didn't know what a graphic artist was, but an artist was an artist, and he lived and worked in his art studio... and now he's asking what does he, Nestor, know about art? Know about art?! His heart sank. ::::::*¡Dios mío!* I wouldn't last two sentences in a conversation about art. There's absolutely no point in pretending otherwise. Damn! Might as well look him in the eye and take it like a man.::::::

"What do I know about art? To tell the truth... nothing."

"Yessss!" exclaimed Yevgeni. He raised his fist to shoulder level and pumped it with his elbow, like an American athlete. "You vant to share zees studio?—eet's yours, my fren!" Noting Nestor's consternation, he said, "Ze graphic art ees now not good, and I haf to share thees studio. Ze last person I vant ees ze person who zinks he knows aboud art, ze person who vants to talk aboud art, and zen zat person vants to gif me adfice!" He put a hand over his eyes and shook his head, and then looked at Nestor again. "Belief me, I cannot zink of any fate vorse. You are a police officer. How much you like it eef zomebody comes een, and he zink he knows about 'ze cops,' or he vants to know about ze cops, and you moss tell him... You crazy in vone veek!"

Besides, he didn't want to live with the Russians up in Sunny Isles and Hallandale. They'd drive him crazy, too. Here, in this studio in Coconut Grove, he felt more at home. It didn't hurt, either, that he liked to work from the afternoon into the night—and Nestor would be away, on his shift.

::::::Perfect:::::: Nestor said to himself. ::::::We're both aliens, you from Russia, me from Hialeah. Maybe we can make it in Miami.:::::: He wrote out a check right away and showed Yevgeni his badge and invited him to write down his badge number. Yevgeni gave him the shrug that said, "Oh, why bother?" He seemed as eager as Nestor to be sharing this place.

This was the sort of thing the Chief never talked about to anybody... *any*body... He wasn't a fool, after all. People would sooner talk about their sex lives—sometimes, among cops, you couldn't shut them up—or their money or their messy marriages or their sins in the eyes of God... about *anything* other than their status in this world... their place in the social order, their prestige or their mortifying lack of it, the respect they get, the respect they don't get, their jealousy and resentment of those who wallow in respect everywhere they set foot...

All this went through the Chief's mind in a single *blip* as his driver, Sergeant Sanchez, pulled up in front of City Hall in the Chief's official Escalade. Miami's city hall was a curiously small white building that stood alone on a half-acre rectangle of landfill sticking out into Biscayne Bay. The Escalade, on the other hand, was a huge brute, all black, with darkened windows and without a single marking to indicate it was a police vehicle... only a low black bar across the roof containing a lineup of spotlight and flasher lenses and a light on the dashboard, no bigger than a quarter, emitting some sort of ominous X-ray-blue radiation. As soon as they stopped, the Chief fairly *sprang* from the passenger seat in front... in front, next to Sergeant Sanchez. The last thing he wanted people to think was that he was an old coot who had to be *chauffeured* around. Like many men in their mid-forties, he wanted to look young, athletic, virile... and so he *sprang,* imagining himself a lion or a tiger or a panther... a vision of lithe strength, in any case. What a sight it was! Or so he was convinced... he couldn't very well *ask* anybody, could he? He wore a darkest-blue military-style shirt, tie, and pants, black shoes, and dark wraparound sunglasses. No jacket; this was Miami... ten o'clock on a September morning, and the cosmic heat lamp was high overhead, and it was already 88 degrees out here. On each side of his neck, which he figured looked thick as a tree trunk, a row of four gold stars ran along each side of his navy blue collar...a galaxy of eight stars in all...and atop that starry tree trunk was his...dark face. There were six feet, four inches and 230 pounds of him, with big wide shoulders, and he was unmistakably African American...and he was the Chief of Police.

Oh yeah, how they *stared,* all those people going in and out of City Hall—and he loved it! The Escalade was in the traffic circle right in front of the entrance. The Chief stepped onto the curb. He stopped for a moment. He lifted his arms out to the side with bent elbows, thrust his shoulders back as far as they would go, and took a deep breath. He looked like he was *strettttching* after being cooped up in the car. In fact, he was forcing his chest to bulge out full-blown. He bet that made him look twice as mighty...but of course he couldn't very well *ask* anybody, could he...

He was still in midstretch, midpreen, when—

"Hey, Chief!" It was a young man, but he had City Hall Lifer written all over him...light skin, probably Cuban...emerging from the entrance and beaming a smile of homage at him and paying his respects with a wave that began at his forehead and turned into half a salute. Had he ever laid eyes on the kid before? Did he work in the Bureau of—what the hell was it? Anyway, he was paying homage... The Chief blessed him with a lordly smile and said,

"Hi, Big Guy!"

He had barely rolled his shoulders forward into a normal position when a middle-aged couple passed him—on their way into City Hall. They looked Cuban, too. The man swung his head around and sang out, "How's it going, Chief!"

Homage. The Chief blessed him with a lordly smile and favored him with a "Hi, Big Guy!"

In rapid succession another "Hey, Chief," a "How ya doin', Chief!" and then a "Hi, Cy!"—short for Cyrus, his first name—and a "Keep 'em flyin', Cy!" and he hadn't even reached the door yet. The citizens seemed to enjoy paying homage with salutations that rhymed with Cy. His last name, Booker, was too much for their poetic powers, which was just as well, the way he looked at it. Otherwise, everything they called him would be mockery or a racial or personal insult... mooker, spooker, kooker, hooker... Yes, it was just as well...

The Chief said, "Hi, Big Guy!"... "Hi, Big Guy!"... "Hi, Big Guy!"... and "Hi, Big Guy!"

Homage! The Chief was in an excellent mood this morning. The Mayor had summoned him here to City Hall for a little... "policy meeting"... concerning this Marine Patrol officer Nestor Camacho and that Man on the Mast business. He broke out into a big smile, for nobody's benefit but his own. It was going to be amusing to watch Old Dionisio squirm. Whenever things were going bad for the Mayor or driving him crazy, the Chief thought of him by his real name, *Dionisio* Cruz. The Mayor had done everything he could to make the whole world think of him as just plain Dio, the way William Jefferson Clinton had become Bill and Robert Dole had become Bob. The Mayor figured Dionisio, the five-syllable name of the Greek god of wine and party boys, was too unusual and too big a bellyful for a politician. He was only five-six and had a very luxurious paunch, but he had enormous energy, the best political antennae in the business, a loud voice, and an egotistical bonhomie that could take over an entire room full of people and swallow them whole. All of that was quite okay with the Chief. He had no illusions concerning the politics of the situation. He was not Miami's first African American police chief, but the fourth. The concern was not the African American vote, which didn't amount to much. The concern was . . . riots.

In 1980 a Cuban cop was accused of murdering an African American businessman, who was already lying on the ground in police custody . . . by bludgeoning his head until it split open and you could see his brains. Two of the Cuban's fellow cops testified against him at his trial, saying they were there and saw him do it. But an all-white jury found him innocent, and he left the courtroom free as a bird. This set off four days of riots and wholesale slaughter in Liberty City, the worst riot in Miami's history and perhaps the country's. A whole string of riots ensued in Miami in the 1980s and beyond. In case after case, you had Cuban cops accused of knocking African Americans' lights out. Liberty City, Overtown, and other African American neighborhoods became lit fuses and the bomb always went off. The latest riot was just two years ago. After that one, Dio Cruz decided to promote Assistant Chief Cyrus Booker to Chief. See? One of your own, not one of ours, runs the entire Police Department.

That was pretty transparent stuff. At the same time, there were five African American assistant chiefs in the Department—and the Mayor had chosen... *me.* Dio Cruz sincerely liked him and admired him, the Chief chose to believe... sincerely.

But this morning, thank God, it was his pal and admirer Dionisio himself who was caught in a bind by his own people. Usually it was *him,* the Chief. Outsiders, usually white people, used to talk to him with the assumption that black folks—"the African American community" was the currently enlightened phrase, and white folks uttered it like they were walking across a bed of exploded lightbulb shards—must be "awfully proud" that "one of their own" now headed the police force. Well, if they were so proud of him, they had a funny way of showing it. Every time a recruiter approached a young African American and suggested that he might make a terrific cop—the Chief had gone on this sort of mission himself—the guy would say, "Why would I want to be a traitor to my own people?" or something close to that. One kid had been so brazen as to look the Chief right in his black face and say, "Tell me why the fuck I wanna help the fucking Cubans beat up on my brothers?" No, if he had any respect on the streets from "the black community," it was only because he was hooked up to the Power... currently. He had the power of the Man... currently. *Unghhh huhhhnh*... You don't be jackin' with the Traitor in Chief, man. He come after you and you be committing "suicide by cop." You be committing suicide by getting a po-lice bullet shot clear through yo' chest, and they be finding a gun on your corpse you didn't even know you had, and they say you pulled this gun-you-never-knew-you-had on a cop, and you be giving them no choice. They got to act in self-defense. You don't know you committing suicide. But that's what you did when you pull this gun-you-don't-know-you-got and aim it at the Suicide Squad. Nome sayin'?—but, hell, you ain't even listening. Oh, I'm sorry, brother. Ain't no *way* you be listening to nothing no more now.

The Cuban Suicide Squads... and so what did that make him? Oh, yeah... the Traitor in Chief. He was happy that this time it was the Mayor who got his dick caught in the door.

As he headed inside for the big "policy meeting," he happened to glance up at the facade of City Hall, and his smile grew big enough for the gawkers to wonder what the Chief of Police thought was so funny. Miami's was the weirdest of all the big-city city halls in the country, if you asked Cy Booker. It was a little two-story white stucco building done in the Art Moderne style, now called Art Deco, fashionable in the 1920s and 1930s. Pan American Airways had built it in 1938 as a terminal for their new fleet of seaplanes, which touched down and took off on Biscayne Bay upon their bulbous pontoon feet. But the seaplane future fizzled, and the city took the building over in 1954 and made it an Art Moderne city hall—and left the Pan American Airways logo on it! Yeah!—and not in just one place either. The logo—a globe of the world, flying aloft with Art Moderne wings on it and launched by the Art Moderne rays of the sun rising beneath it—this typical Art Moderne touch, promising a radiant future lit up by Man's Promethean reach for the stars, was repeated endlessly, creating a frieze that wrapped around the entire building Pan Am Pan Am Pan Am Pan Am Pan Am beneath the cornice. There was something gloriously goofy about it...a big-city city hall proudly displaying a now-defunct airline's seaplane terminal logo!... but this was Miami, and there you had it...

The Mayor's conference room upstairs was not like any other big city's mayoral conference room, either. The ceiling was low, and there was no table, just a random collection of chairs of varying sizes and comfort. It was more like a slightly beat-up little lounge in an aging athletic club. All the rooms up here, including the Mayor's own office, were small and cramped. No doubt they were originally occupied by the work-a-daddies who did the accounting, procurement, and maintenance side of the seaplane operation. Now it was the Mayor's domain. A phrase much resented in city halls across the country popped into the Chief's head: "Good enough for government work."

As he drew closer, he could see through the doorway. The Mayor was already there, along with his communications director, as City Hall PR flacks were now titled, a tall slender man named Efraim Portuondo, who could have been handsome if he weren't so dour...and Rinaldo Bosch, a small pear-shaped man, only forty years old or so but bald as a clerk. He was the city manager, a title that didn't mean much when a man like Dionisio Cruz was Mayor.

As soon as the Chief appeared at the door, the Mayor opened his mouth wide, primed to...swallow him, the gloomy flack, and the little bald man with a single gulp.

"Eyyyy, Chief, come on in! Have a seat! Catch your breath! Get ready! We got some a God's work to do this morning."

"Is that the same as Dio's work?" said the Chief.

Abrupt silence... while the translingual logic of the crack linked up in all three Cubans' heads... God equals Dios equals Dio's...

A short bark of laughter from the communications director and the city manager. They couldn't hold back, but they made it brief. They knew Dio Cruz would not be amused.

The Mayor gave the Chief a cold smile. "Okay, since you're so fluent in Spanish, you'll know what *'A veces, algunos son verdaderos coñazos del culo'* means."

Communications Director Portuondo and City Manager Bosch barked short laughs again and then stared straight at the Chief. From their big expectant eyes, he could tell that old Dionisio had put him in his place, and they were dying to see *you and him* fight. But the Chief figured it would be better *not* to get a translation. So he laughed and said, "Hey, just kidding, Mr. Mayor, just kidding, Dio... Dios... what do I know?"

The "Mr. Mayor" was just some mild irony he couldn't resist tucking in. He never called him "Mr. Mayor." When he was alone with the Mayor, he called him Dio. When other people were around, he never called him anything at all. He just looked at him and spoke. He couldn't have explained exactly why, but he considered it a mistake to ever buckle under old Dionisio at all.

He could see that the Mayor was tired of this exchange anyway. He couldn't stand coming out second best. Old Dionisio took a seat with a this-is-serious scowl on his face. So they all sat down.

"Okay, Chief," said the Mayor. "You know this whole situation is bullshit, and I know it's bullshit. This officer, this kid Camacho, is ordered to bring the guy down from the mast. So he climbs up and he brings the guy down, but first he has to put on some kind a ham-bone high-wire act. The whole thing is on TV, and now we got half the city yelling that we're sitting on our hands while a leader of the anti-Castro underground gets legally lynched. I don't need this."

"But we don't know that's what he is," said the Chief. "The Coast Guard says nobody's ever heard of him, and nobody's ever heard of the underground movement he says he leads, this El Solvente."

"Yeah, but try telling that to all those people we got on our neck now. They'll just tune out. This thing's like some kind of a panic, like a riot or something. People believe it—they think he's a fucking martyr. If we say otherwise...then we're trying to pull off some kind a cheap trick, some kind a cover-up."

"But what else can we do?" said the Chief.

"Where is the guy, the guy on the mast—where is he right now?"

"He's being held on a Coast Guard ship until they decide to announce what they're doing. They'll probably wait awhile and let things blow over. In the meantime, they're not gonna let him say another word. He'll be invisible."

"I say we do the same thing with Officer Camacho. Put him somewhere he'll be invisible."

"Like where?"

"Oh . . . *ummmm* . . . I got it! Put him in that industrial area out toward Doral," said the Mayor. "Nobody goes there except to repair coke furnaces and lubricate earth-moving equipment."

"So what would Camacho do out there?"

"Oh, I don't know . . . They ride around in patrol cars, they protect the citizens."

"But that's a demotion," said the Chief.

"Why?"

"Because that's where he started out. He was a beat cop. The Marine Patrol is one a the special units. He can't be demoted. That's like saying we did the wrong thing and this officer fucked up. He didn't do anything wrong. Everything was done by the book, in the routine way . . . except for one thing."

"Which is . . . ?" said the Mayor.

"Officer Camacho risked his life to save this guy. He did a hell of a thing, when you think about it."

"Yeah," said the Mayor, "but the guy wouldn't a needed saving if the officer hadn't a tried to grab him."

"Even if you believe that, he did a hell of a thing all the same. He locked his legs around the guy seventy feet up in the air and carried him all the way down to the water, swinging hand over hand down the jib sail cable. You know—you won't like this, but we're gonna have to give Officer Camacho a medal of valor."

"What!?"

"Everybody knows he risked his life to save a man. The whole city saw it. His fellow cops all admire him, no matter who they are. They all think of him as really brave, except that they'd never say it—that's taboo. But if he doesn't get the medal, it stinks of politics right away."

"Jesus Christ!" said the Mayor. "Where you gonna do this? In the main auditorium at the Freedom Tower?"

"No... it can be done quietly."

The communications director, Portuondo, spoke up. "The way you do it is, you put out a press release the day after the ceremony with all kinds of announcements, commendations, traffic flow decisions, whatever, and you list Officer Camacho's award about eighth down the line. It's done all the time."

"Okay, but we still gotta make the guy invisible. How do we do that if you can't make him a beat cop?"

"All you can do is give him a lateral transfer," said the Chief, "to another special unit. There's the Marine Patrol, which he's in now, there's the CST—Crime Suppression Team—the SWAT Team, the—"

"Hey!" said the Mayor. "How about the Mounted Police! You never see those guys except in the park. Put him on a goddamned horse!"

"I don't think so," said the Chief. "That's known as a lateral transfer with a *dip*. That would be pretty obvious in a case like this... putting him on a horse in a park."

"You got a better idea?" said the Mayor.

"Yeah," said the Chief. "The SWAT Team. It's the most macho of them all, because you're always marching into a line of fire. You do battle. The guys are mostly young, like Officer Camacho; you gotta be in fantastic shape. The training—at one point you have to jump from the top of a six-story building onto a mattress. I'm not kidding... a mattress. If you can't make yourself do it, you don't make it onto the SWAT Team. You got to be young to do it without getting hurt, but that's only part of it. As you get older, you begin to value your hide a lot more. I've seen it a hundred times in police work. You're older, you've got a higher rank, you're getting higher pay, you've got ambition itching under your skin. Every instinct you got is telling you, 'You're too valuable now, you've worked too hard to get there, your future is so damned bright. How could you possibly risk it all by doing a damn fool thing like that, jumping from six stories up... onto a fucking mattress?' " The Chief could see that he had their rapt attention, Dionisio Cruz's, the flack Portuondo's, and the little bald city manager's. They were staring at him with the nice big unsophisticated eyes of boys. "Yeah... looking down on the mattress from the top of that six-story building—the damn thing looks about the size of a playing card, and that flat, too. If an older man is there on the roof and looking down like that, he starts thinking about some... first things, as they say in church." Oh, yeah! Now he had all three of the Cubans mesmerized. Now for the coup de grâce. "Every year when the SWAT candidates get to that part of the training... I make the jump myself. I want these kids to feel like, 'Jesus Christ, if the Chief does it, and I put my toes on the edge of the roof... and there's no way I can make my legs go into the jump mode... then I'll be branded as a pathetic little pussy the rest of my life.' I want those guys to *refuse* to fail."

For a moment none of the Cubans said a word. But the Mayor couldn't contain his emotions any longer. "Fuckin' A!" he cried. "That's it! If Officer Camacho likes action so goddamned much—take him right up on top of the building and show him the mattress!"

The Chief chuckled somewhere deep inside. ::::::Gotcha.::::::

But all of a sudden ::::::Aw, shit!:::::: he just thought of something, a big something . . . and he had to go and turn the Mayor and the yes-men into bug-eyed little boys with ninety seconds of SWAT Team lore, starring himself . . . He lowered his head and rocked it from this side to that side to this side to that side, slowly, and muttered out loud, "Damn!" Then he looked at the three of them and compressed his lips so tightly the flesh ballooned out above them and below them. "The kid would be perfect for the SWAT Team, but we can't do it. We can't just move somebody onto the SWAT Team for political reasons. They'd spot that right away. Every cop knows who Nestor Camacho is, or they do now. We've got forty-one cops on a waiting list for the SWAT Team right now. They've all volunteered . . . and talk about competition! Nobody can mess around with SWAT Team recruitment, not even the Chief."

"Forty-one cops want to do this?" said the Mayor. "Forty-one cops can't wait to jump from six stories and land on a mattress to qualify to go get shot at?"

The Chief started tapping the side of his forehead in the pantomime that says, "That's using your head." "You answered it yourself, Dio! 'Can't wait to get shot at'! There you have it! There's a certain kind of cop who came to play. You know what I'm saying?"

The Mayor looked away glumly for a moment. "Well . . . I don't care where you put Officer Camacho, as long as you get him off the goddamned water. Okay? But wherever you—what's the word you like?—*lateral transfer?*—wherever you *lateral transfer* this TV acrobat a yours, he's gotta do that thing. That's gotta be one a the conditions."

"*What* thing?" said the Chief.

"That thing with the mattress. If he likes action so goddamned much and has to go around breaking my balls, then you gotta take him right on up to the roof—and show him the mattress!"

The next afternoon Nestor iPhoned John Smith. "John," he said, "you game for a cup of coffee? I got something to show you."

"What?"

"I don't wanna just tell you. I want to show it to you, in person. I wanna see the smile on your face."

"Hey, you're sounding *up* today. When I left yesterday, the look on your face—you should have seen it. You looked like you'd lost your last friend."

Nestor: "You took the words right out of truth. But I got tired of feeling angry, angry at everybody who turned their back on me. One thing about anger is it sort of revs you up and gets the juice flowing. You wanna know what I did yesterday between the time you left and the shift started? I went on Craigslist and found an apartment in Coconut Grove. In three hours on a Sunday afternoon I did that. Anger is a wonderful thing if you get *really* angry."

"That's great, Nestor!"

"Oh, it's a dump, it's too small, and I'm sharing it with a 'graphic artist,' whatever that is, and I get to listen to all the goddamned wacked-out kids who hang around Grand Avenue until about four in the morning. They sound like alley cats. You know that sound, that sort of, I guess, *yowl* cats make when they're outdoors at night... yowling for sex? That's what these kids sound like. You know that sound?"

"Hey, we *are* up today, aren't we!" said John Smith.

"I'm not up—it's like I told you. I'm angry," said Nestor. "Hey, where are you right now?"

"I'm at the paper."

"Well, then, get up off your ass and leave the building and meet me at that restaurant Della Grimalda. It's right near you."

"I don't know. As I say, I'm at the paper—and besides, I wouldn't peg you as the Della Grimalda type."

"I'm not. That's the whole point. Neither is any other cop, and I don't *want* any other cops around when I show you what I got."

Long sigh...Nestor could tell that John Smith was weakening. "Okay, Della Grimalda. But what do you want to get there?"

"Two cups of coffee," said Nestor.

"But Della Grimalda is a real restaurant. You can't just walk in there and take a seat and order two cups of coffee."

"I don't know it for a fact, but I'll bet you a cop can—and he won't have to pay a dime."

When John Smith arrived at Della Grimalda, Nestor was already sitting comfortably at a table for two by a window amid the place's swag and bling—having a cup of coffee. John Smith took a seat, and a very attractive waitress brought him a cup of coffee, too. He looked all around. There were only two other customers in the whole restaurant, about forty feet away, and they were obviously finishing a big meal. Their table gleamed with a regular flotilla of stemware of every sort and squadrons of hotel silver.

"Well," said John Smith, "I have to hand it to you. You did it."

Nestor shrugged and produced a stiff nine-by-twelve envelope from under his chair, handed it to John Smith, and said, "Be my guest."

John Smith opened it and withdrew a piece of cardboard that served as backing for a large photograph, about six by nine inches. Nestor had been looking forward to watching John Smith's expression when it dawned on him what he had his hands on. The pale WASP didn't disappoint. He lifted his wondering eyes from the photograph and stared at Nestor.

"Where the hell did you find *this?*"

It was a remarkably clear digital photograph, in color, of Sergei Korolyov at the wheel of a screaming-red Ferrari Rocket 503 sports car—with Igor Drukovich in the bucket seat beside him. Igor had a waxed mustache that came all the way out to *here* on either side. Korolyov looked like a real star, as usual, but anybody's eye was going to fasten right away upon Igor, Igor and his mustache. The mustache was a real production. It took off from between his nose and his upper lip and flew all the way out to *here*—an astonishing distance—and he had waxed the ends and twirled them into points. He was a big man, probably close to fifty years old. In the I'm-an-artist manner he wore a long-sleeved black shirt open down to his sternum, giving the world a look at his big hairy chest. It was a hirsute triumph almost as grand as the mustache.

"Remember you asked if I could get you access to police files? This picture is from the Miami-Dade Police headquarters. They took it four years ago."

"Why were they interested in Korolyov and Drukovich?"

"They weren't interested in them as individuals. This I bet you don't know, but all the police departments in the area do it. If they see somebody in a car and it looks suspicious or maybe it just looks highly unusual, they'll stop it on some pretext—they were going five or ten miles an hour over the speed limit, or the car's license plate begins with certain digits, or the registration sticker's peeling off—any damned thing—and they check IDs and record them, and they take pictures like this one. Why they stopped Korolyov's car I don't really know, except it's unusual, all right, and it looks like a *lot* of money."

John Smith couldn't take his eyes off it. "I don't believe this!" he kept saying, and then he asked, "How did you actually *get* this? Did you just call up the Miami-Dade Police and ask them what they had on Korolyov and Drukovich, and they just gave it to you?"

Nestor chuckled the happy chuckle of the man who knows secrets and you don't. "No, they didn't just give it to me. I called a cop I used to work with on the Marine Patrol. You'd never get something like this by going through 'channels.' You have to get on the brothernet."

"What's the brothernet?"

"If you know a brother officer and you ask him for a favor, he's gonna do it for you if he possibly can. That's the brothernet. My guy also—"

"God, Nestor," said John Smith, absorbed in the photograph, "that's great. If the time comes and we have to prove that Korolyov knew Igor all along—

here we have him tooling around with him in this half-a-million-dollar toy. What we need now is some more information about Igor's personal life. I'd like to meet him in some—you know—some casual way."

"Well, I was just about to tell you something else my guy passed along. This is not in any file. In fact, it's out-and-out hearsay, but *the word* is—and Igor's pretty hard to *not* notice—the word is that he's a regular at some strip club in Sunny Isles called the Honey Pot. You game for trying to find a mustache in the middle of a herd of whores?"

8

The Columbus Day Regatta

Second week in October—and so what? That great tropical skillet in the sky still boiled your blood, seared your flesh, turned your eyeballs into aching migraine globes if you insisted on staring at anything, even through the midnight-black sunglasses they were both wearing.

In the front seat of Dr. Lewis's convertible the wind blew through Magdalena's hair. But the air was warm as soup. Letting it stream through your hair was like filling your glass from the HOT tap. Norman had the side windows up and the air conditioner on as high as it would go. But all she got out of it was an insipid wisp of cool breeze on her shins every now and then :::::: Forget the maximum air-conditioning, Norman! Just put the top back up, for God's sake!::::::

But she knew better than to say it out loud. Norman

had a thing about . . . *panache* — a white Audi A5 convertible with the top down . . . and the top had to be down . . . had to have hair streaming in the wind . . . his longish light-brown hair and her very long dark hair . . . miles of hair streaming back from the shiny wraparound black shades they both wore . . . had to have the shades — all that, she deduced, must be *panache.*

Norman had given her a little discourse on *panache* two months ago. At the time she hadn't known why. For that matter, she hadn't a clue what *panache* was. But by now she no longer came right out and asked him what new words meant. Now she waited and looked these terms up on Google. Aha . . . *panache* . . . the gist of it seemed to be . . . at this moment . . . that if you weren't driving a Mercedes, a Ferrari, or a Porsche at the very, borderline least . . . you had to compensate for it with *panache.* And if a humble Audi A5, such as he possessed, were to have *panache,* it had to be startlingly white, had to have the top down . . . had to have a really good-looking couple in the front seat wearing big shiny bug-eyed black sunglasses . . . dazzling one and all with youth and glamour. But to have that *panache,* you couldn't leave out any element, and keeping the top down was one of them.

Right now *panache* was a killer out here on the MacArthur Causeway. Magdalena was burning up. Just before the causeway reached Miami Beach, a sign said FISHER ISLAND. Over the past two days Norman must have told her a dozen times that he docked his boat at the Fisher Island Marina and that they would be stopping off at Fisher Island Fisher Island Fisher Island to board it for today's cruise way out to Elliott Key for the Columbus Day Regatta. Obviously the significance was supposed to register on her...so obviously that she didn't dare admit her ignorance of Fisher Island, either.

Norman turned off the causeway and headed down a ramp that led to a ferry slip. The great white hulk of a ferryboat, at least three stories high, already docked, dwarfed everything else. In the immediate foreground three lines of cars were forming for inspection, apparently by guards at booths just ahead. Why was Norman pulling up at the rear of the longest line? Should she ask him—or would that merely betray some spatial dimension of her ignorance?

She needn't have worried. Norman couldn't wait to tell her himself. "See that line over there?" He extended his arm and his forefinger as far as they would go, as if the line were a mile away rather than fifteen feet or so. The mammoth midnight shades obscured the upper half of his face, but Magdalena could see a small smile forming.

"They're the servants," he said.

"The servants?" said Magdalena. "Servants all have to take that lane? I've never heard of anything like that."

"Servants and masseuses and personal trainers,

and hairdressers, I guess. The island is private property. It belongs to the people who own real estate on it. They can make any rules they want. This is the same as a gated community, except that it's an entire island, and the ferryboat is the gate."

"Well, I never heard of a gated community that had a lane for the lower class," said Magdalena. She didn't know why the whole thing riled her so much. "How about a nurse? Suppose I was assigned to a case on Fisher Island?"

"You, too," said Dr. Lewis, smiling even more broadly. He seemed to be enjoying all this... especially the fact that he had gotten her goat.

"Then I wouldn't do it," said Magdalena, a bit haughtily. "I wouldn't take the case. I'm not going to be treated like 'the help.' I'm just not. I'm a professional. I've worked too hard to be treated that way."

This caused Norman's smile to move up to the chuckle stage. "But you'd be breaking your vow as a nurse."

"All right," said Magdalena, "then what about you? If you had to make a house call on Fisher Island, would you get in that line?"

"I never heard of a psychiatrist making a house call," said Norman, "but it's not totally improbable."

"And you'd get in that line?"

"Technically," he said. "But of course I'd drive right to the head of the line and say, 'This is an emergency.' I've never heard of anybody yet with the guts to tell a doctor he has to abide by the protocol when he says it's an emergency. All you have to do is act like you're God. That's what doctors are when it's an emergency."

"The problem is, you actually believe that," said Magdalena rather crossly.

"HahhhHHHockhockhock hock hock! You're funny, Magdalena. You know that? But you don't have to worry. Every time you come to Fisher Island you'll be with meeeeuhuhhuhock hock hock hock!"

"Haha," said Magdalena, "I'm having a convulsion, I'm laughing so hard."

That made Norman even merrier. "I've got you going, haven't I, babe..." She hated that. He was mocking her.

"If you want to know the honest truth," he said, "I don't have to play God in the servant's line. You see that little medallion up there?" It was a round thing, about the size of a quarter but not as thick, stuck to the inside of the windshield on the upper left. "That's an equity owner's medallion. This line is for equity owners only. You're in the upper class now, kid."

Magdalena grew still more irritated. Suddenly she didn't care anymore whether Norman thought she was uneducated or not.

"So what's *equity owner* supposed to mean?"

Norman was grinning right in her face. "It's

supposed to mean, and in fact it *does* mean, you own real estate or real property on the island."

Magdalena grew aggravated on top of irritated. He was mocking her—and at the same time he was burying her in words she didn't know. What the hell was a medallion? What the hell did *real property* mean? Was that different from *real estate?* What the hell did *equity* mean? And if she didn't know that, how was she supposed to know what *equity owner* meant?

She couldn't keep Resentment on its polite behavior any longer. "So I bet now you're gonna tell me you have a *place* on Fisher Island. You just forgot to tell me, right?"

The good doctor's antennae seemed to sense real anger this time. "No, I'm not gonna say that. All I'm saying is I have a medallion, and I have an equity owner's ID card." He pulled a small card out of the breast pocket of his shirt, showed it to her so briefly, and put it back in the pocket.

"Okay, then, if you don't own a place, then how come you have all this stuff... these IDs... and you're so 'upper class,' as you call it?"

The convertible advanced a few feet, then stopped again. Norman turned toward her and gave a sly smile... and a wink with a glittering eye. It was the sort of smile that intimates, *Now I'm going to let you in on a little secret.*

"Let's just say I made certain arrangements."

"What kind?"

"Oh . . . I did someone a very big favor. It's a quid pro quo situation. Let's just say this"—he gestured toward the medallion—"this is the *quid* for the *quo*."

He was very pleased with himself . . . *quid pro quo* . . . Magdalena vaguely remembered hearing the term, but she had no idea what it meant. It was reaching the point where every new term he sprang on her inflamed her resentment. The hell of it was, he didn't think he was *springing* anything on her. He seemed to assume she knew them because every educated person *did* know these things. Somehow that made it even worse. That really *rubbed it in.*

"All right, Mr. Upper Class," she said. "Might as well hear it all. What's this line right next to us?"

He apparently thought she was now making light of things. He smiled knowingly and said, "That's what you might call the haute bourgeoisie."

That really rankled her. He was starting in again. She more or less knew what *bourgeoisie* meant, but what the hell was *oat* supposed to mean? The hell with it! Why not blurt it right out?!

"What the hell is—"

"These people are renters and hotel guests and visitors"—Norman's exuberance, his *joie de* Fisher Island codified status rankings, ran right over her voice. He had never heard her say a profane word before, not even a "what the hell," and he didn't hear it this time, either. "If any of them can't produce an ID card—let's say they're just arriving to go to the hotel—they won't let them through until they call ahead to the hotel to see if they're expected."

"Norman, do you have any idea how—"

Rolls right over her: "They'll take his picture and a picture of his license plate, even if the guy has an ID from the hotel. And I'll tell you something else. No guest of the hotel can pay cash or use a credit card. Nobody on the island can. You can only charge things... to your ID card. The whole island's one great big private club."

Magdalena made an exaggerated angry panoramic gesture, taking in the entire scene, and that so surprised Norman that he paused long enough for her to get a word in.

"Well, isn't this nice," she said. "We've got upper class, middle class, and lower class... *bim, bim, bim*... and people like me would be in lower class."

Norman chuckled, mistaking the irony for joking around. "*Nahhhhh*... not *really* lower class. More like lower middle. If you're *really* lower class, like a repairman, a construction worker, a gardener, let's say, or anybody with a truck or one of those vehicles with lettering on it—I don't know... pizza, carpets, a plumber, whatever—you can't get on this ferry at all. They have one that comes in over at the other end of the island." He motioned vaguely to the west. "It leaves from Miami itself. I've never seen it, but I gather it's kind of a big old open barge."

"Norman...I just don't...know...about your Fisher Island—"

They were moving again. This time they arrived at a booth. A black-and-white arm blocked the way. A uniformed guard with a *revolver!*—no, it was a scanner—stood in front of the Audi and aimed it at the license plate and then at the medallion. When he saw Norman behind the wheel, he broke into a big smile and said, "Hey-ey-ey-ey, Doc!" He came over to the driver's side. "I saw you on TV! Yeah! That was great! What was that show?"

"Probably *60 Minutes,*" said Dr. Lewis.

"That's right!" said the guard. "Something about—I don't remember. But I saw you, and I said to my wife, 'Hey, that's Dr. Lewis!'"

The good doctor put on a serious face and said, "Now let me ask you, Buck—I hope you called Dr. Lloyd, like I suggested."

"Oh, I did! It cleared right up! I can't remember what he gave me."

"Probably endomycin."

"Hey, that's what it *was,* endomycin!"

"Well, I'm glad it worked out, Buck. Dr. Lloyd is tops."

Norman produced his equity owner's ID card from his shirt pocket, but his pal Buck scarcely glanced at it. He waved them through the checkpoint and sang out, "Have a good one!"

Dr. Lewis slipped on what Magdalena by now recognized as his smile of self-satisfaction. "You'll notice Buck didn't even look inside the booth. He's supposed to look at a screen in there. It's supposed to show the picture of the owner that's in the system side-by-side with the picture he takes with the scanner. Likewise the number on the medallion and the one in the system. You'll also notice that our line is boarding the boat first, which means we'll be the first ones off on the other side."

He glanced at her as if waiting for a commendation. She could think of no fitting response. What earthly difference did it make? This ferryboat ride to the island of his dreams would take a little over seven minutes.

"Buck and I are buddies," said Norman. "You know it doesn't hurt to learn these people's names and talk to them a little. They interpret it as respect, and a little respect goes a long way in this world."

But Buck meant something else to Magdalena. No Latino was ever named Buck. It was *americano* through and through.

On the ferry they were parked near the head of one of the equity owners lines. To Norman, this was exhilarating stuff. "If you lean out and look past that car ahead of us, you can see the island."

Magdalena, by now, couldn't have cared less about the damned island. For a reason she couldn't have put a name to, the whole subject was rousing her hostility. Fisher Island... if it suddenly sank to the bottom of Biscayne Bay, it wouldn't bother her a bit. But she leaned out anyway. Mainly she could see the fender of the black Mercedes in front of them and the fender of the tan one at the head of the line next to them. Between the two fenders she could see... something. She took it to be Fisher Island... what little she could make out... It didn't strike her as anything remarkable.

She pulled her head back in and said, "I gather Fisher Island is very"—she was dying to come up with some more cutting word, just to shake up Norman's status bliss, but she constrained herself and said—"very Anglo."

"Oh, I don't know..." said Norman. "I guess I don't think of things in those terms." ::::::The hell you don't.:::::: "I hope you don't, either.

"It's not as if we're in some place where you have to go around *counting* Anglos and Latinos to see if there's diversity. Latinos run all of South Florida. They run it politically, and they've got the most successful businesses, too. It doesn't bother *me*."

"Of course not," said Magdalena. "Because you people run the whole rest of the country. You think South Florida is a tiny version of... of... of... Mexico or Colombia or someplace."

"Oh ho!" said Norman. He flashed another big smile. "So now I'm 'you people'!? Have I ever acted 'you people' to you?"

Magdalena realized she had gone out of control. She was chagrined. In the sweetest voice she could come up with at the moment: "Of course not, Norman." She nestled her head against his shoulder and caressed his upper arm with both her hands. "I'm sorry. You know I didn't mean it that way. I'm so lucky just to be... be with you... Will you forgive me? I'm really sorry."

"There's nothing to forgive," said Norman "We're not taking any heavy baggage along on this trip. It's a lovely day. We're heading off to something that's going to amuse and amaze you beyond anything you've ever seen."

"Which is what?" She quickly added, "Darling."

"We're off across the waters... to the Columbus Day Regatta!"

"What am I gonna see?"

"I'm not going to tell you! This is something you have to experience."

Sure enough, their line, the anointed equity owners line, disembarked first on the other side, onto the legendary Fisher Island. Norman couldn't help calling it, the anointment, to her attention again.

::::::Well, that's all right. I'm not going to make an issue of it. He has a little boy's excitement over these things, these social things. And on *60 Minutes* he looked so self-confident. On national television!::::::

From the ferry slip they headed east on an avenue called Fisher Island Drive. Norman enjoyed explaining that this was, in fact, the only street on Fisher Island. Yeah! The only one! It went all the way around the island in a great loop. Oh, a lot of roads led off of it, as she could see, but these were all private roads leading to private property.

The scenery was not the lush tropical show she thought it would be. There were plenty of palm trees... and plenty of sea views... but where were all the estates she had pictured? There were a handful of small houses, which Norman had said were called "casitas"—*casitas!* She had to come to exclusive Fisher Island to see *casitas!?*... although she had to admit they were a bit more elegant, if a casita can ever be called elegant, than the ones in Hialeah.

They came upon a few large houses with nice green lawns and big banks of shrubbery and gorgeous flowers—bougainvilleas?—but the island really seemed like a big compound of apartments. There were a couple of boring modern apartment towers glass glass glass glass sheer facade sheer facade sheer streaked facade, but there were also lots of lower apartment buildings that looked older and more elegant... painted white... lots of wood... You could imagine them to be part of a tropical paradise, but it would take some doing. Then—

Wow! Now, *there* was an *estate!* A huge manor house—wasn't that the term, *manor house?*—at the top of a hill, with landscaping too grand and too glorious to take in from a moving car like this... huge banyan trees, the ones that looked absolutely prehistoric, with their twisted multiple trunks and immense limbs reaching up higher than any tree's she had ever seen—

Norman clearly enjoyed knowing it all. The place had been a "Vanderbilt estate," but today it was the Fisher Island Hotel and Resort. Norman motioned toward it as if it were his. The pleasure he took in this stuff got underneath Magdalena's skin. It was all part of... *something*... she couldn't stand.

Not far beyond the hotel they arrived at the Fisher Island Marina. Now, this place *was* impressive. More than a hundred boats, many of them real yachts, were docked in slips—Norman called them slips—many close to a hundred feet long, and some much bigger. The whole scene radiated... money... even though Magdalena couldn't have begun to break it down into categories. There were so many employees going onboard the boats and coming off and walking along the wooden... *wharfways?*... between the slips. There were so many flags, so many playful names lettered toward the front of the gleaming, grand white hulls,

Honey Bear, Gone with the Wind, Bel Ami, so many plump, smooth, buttery, bejowled owners—or that's what she took them to be—whom Norman greeted ever so casually, ever so amiably, with his *Hi Billy*s and *Hi Chuck*s and *Hi Harry*s and *Hi Cleeve*s, *Hi Claibornes*, *Hi Clayton*s, *Hi Shelby*s, *Hi Talbot*s, *Hi Govans*— ::::::but they're all Bucks and Chucks, aren't they—*americanos!* The whole lot of them!::::::

At that moment Norman said, "Hi, Chuck!" *Another Chuck! Chuck and Buck!* A big, meaty, red-faced man came over...clad in a work shirt, sleeves rolled up, and a baseball cap, both bearing the legend FISHER ISLAND MARINA.

"Hi ya, Dr. Lewis! How you hangin'? Oh, I'm sorry, ma'm." He had just noticed Magdalena, who was standing behind Norman. "Didn't mean that like it sounded." *Didn' mean 'at lack it sayundid.*

His big face turned even redder. Magdalena had no idea what he was talking about.

"Chuck?" said Norman, gesturing toward her. "This is Magdalena, Miss Otero. And Magdalena?... Chuck. Chuck's the dockmaster."

"Real pleased to meet you, Miss Otero," said Chuck.

Magdalena smiled faintly. This Chuck was not just a plain *americano.* He was a thoroughbred. He was a real cracker. Her hostile feelings rose again.

Chuck said to Norman: "You goin' out?" *Ayot?*

"Thought I'd give Magdalena her first cigarette

boat ride," said Norman. "Come to think of it, the tank may be low. We're going a *long* way."

"No problem, Dr. Lewis. Just take her on over there by Harvey on your way out." *Jes taker on ovair by Harvey on ya way ayot.* His voice got on Magdalena's nerves.

::::::There has never been a Latino named Harvey, either.::::::

Chuck turned about and shouted, "Hey...Harvey!"

Norman chuckled and puffed out his cheeks and brought his arms out to the sides and rounded them at the elbows and made two fists and said to Magdalena, "Chuck's a monster, isn't he?...and about the nicest guy in the world."

When Magdalena saw Norman in that monster pose, it gave her a queasy feeling. ::::::Yes, and you're brothers, aren't you?:::::: She wondered whether the two of them, so different in many ways, realized they were members of the same tribe...yes, a queasy feeling. She just wanted to get away from Fisher Island.

Norman led her out onto a narrow wooden dockway and pointed at a boat in one of the slips. "Well, that's it...It's not the biggest boat in the marina, but I can guarantee you one thing. It's the fastest. You'll see."

It appeared small next to all the other boats, but it was sleek, modern, very streamlined. It *looked* like speed. It reminded her of a convertible. It had no top. And the cockpit was small, like a convertible interior.

Up front were two bucket seats. What did they call the driver? She didn't really know. The pilot, maybe? The captain? Behind the driver there were two rows of tan leather seats with white and dark-red piping. Or would they put actual leather in an open boat like that? It looked like leather, anyway. The small cockpit made the hull seem much longer than it was. The hull was white with a six-or-eight-inch tan streamlined stripe outlined in red sweeping from front to back on both sides. Up near the front, within the tan stripe, some bold but no more than three-to-four-inch-high white letters, outlined in the same red, said, HYPOMANIC. The letters were slanted sharply toward the front.

"That's the name of the ship—the boat—*Hypomanic*?"

"That's a kind of an inside joke," said Norman. "You've heard of manic depression, right?"

Tersely: "Yes." That really ticked her off. ::::::I'm a registered nurse, and he wonders if I know what manic depression is.::::::

"Well," he said, "I've had lots of patients with manic depression, bipolar disorder, and to a man—there've been some women, too—they'll tell you that when they're in the hypomanic stage—*hypo* means lower" ::::::Oh, thank you so much for letting me know what *hypo* means:::::: "when they're in the stage before they start doing and saying crazy things, they say it's absolute ecstasy. Every feeling is magnified. Anybody says anything remotely funny, they're off into gales of laughter. A little sex? One little orgasm, and they think they've experienced the *kairos,* the all-in-one, ultimate bliss. They feel like they can do anything and walk right over anyone who tries to give them grief. They'll work twenty hours a day and think they're achieving wonders. They reign in traffic, and the guy behind them starts blowing his horn, and they'll jump out of the car and shake their fists at the guy and yell, 'Why don't you stick that horn up your ass and play "Jingle Bells," you faggot!' One of my patients told me he did exactly that, and the guy didn't dare confront him, because he thought he was dealing with a maniac—which of course he *was!* The same patient told me that if you could bottle hypomania and sell it, you'd be the richest man on earth overnight." He gestured toward the lettering on the boat. "And there you have my 'cigarette boat'... *Hypomanic.*"

"Cigarette?"

"They've been around a long time. There are all these stories about how they used to use them to smuggle cigarettes because they're so fast. But I don't know what idiot would go to the trouble of smuggling cigarettes."

"How fast?"

Norman gave her *that smile.* He was pleased with himself. "I'm not going to tell you—I'm going to *show* you. But you see how far the hull extends beyond the cockpit? That houses two Rolls-Royce engines, and each one has a thousand horsepower, for thousands of pounds of thrust."

Long pause—

::::::But that's like two thousand pounds, and two thousand pounds is a ton...I wonder if that boat even *weighs* a ton...and there's something about Norman that's...not very stable. Why am I letting myself get into this? But how to ask him...::::::

—finally: "But doesn't that make it hard for the...driver?—is that the word?—to handle all that—I mean, so much power?"

Norman gave her the sort of twisted-lip smile that says, "I already know the bottom line. You don't have to go through a whole lot of indirect questions."

"Don't worry, kid," he said. "I know what I'm doing. If it'll make you feel any better, I have a captain's license. I couldn't give you a number, but I've been out on the bay in this boat *lots* of times, *scores* of times. I'll make a deal with you. We'll go out, but the moment it doesn't feel right, we can turn right around and come back."

She wasn't reassured, but like most people, she didn't have the courage to say she lacked the courage. She smiled in a sickly manner. "No, no, no. It's just that I've never heard of such a powerful...speedboat?" ::::::Is *speedboat* too puny a word? Will that annoy him?::::::

"Don't worry," he said again. "Just hop in. We'll take it easy."

Norman hopped in first, with a single vault over the railing, into his hypomanic vessel, then gallantly supported her as she climbed over the edge. He took the wheel, just behind the windshield, and she sat next to him. Sure *felt* like leather...

He turned on the ignition, and the engines came to life with a terrifying roar before he throttled them back. It reminded her of boys with motorcycles in Hialeah. The *roars* seemed to be what they lived for.

Norman slowly backed the boat out of the slip. The engines made a low growling sound. Now Magdalena thought of a woman who lived near her in Hialeah. She used to take a pit bull out on a leash. The dog seemed to be as heavy as she was. It reminded Magdalena of a shark. It had no brain at all—just a pair of eyes, a pair of jaws, and a sense of smell for blood flowing in human beings' arteries. It eventually killed a five-year-old girl by ripping one arm clear out of the rotator cuff and gnashing half her head off, starting with a cheek, an eye, and an ear, and proceeding to drive its teeth through her skull. Afterward, many neighbors confessed that they were just as terrified of the mindless beast as Magdalena was. But no one, including her, had the courage to come forward and say she was deathly afraid of the brainless pit bull.

And so it was again with Magdalena as the motors of the brainless *Hypomanic* growled a low growl a low growl a low growl a low growl a low growl on a leash on a leash on a leash . . . and the *Hypomanic* slowly headed toward the marina's exit and Harvey the cracker Harvey the cracker Harvey the cracker . . .

So Harvey the cracker pumped fuel into the cigarette boat. Even just listening to the engines idle, Magdalena could tell they must consume gasoline at some astounding rate. She shuddered. The beast was brainless. Harvey the cracker was brainless. The licensed captain of the vessel, Dr. Norman Lewis, was not brainless. He was unstable. She had sensed that in his behavior before the *60 Minutes* interview—but he proceeded to be a rock on the show itself and a brilliant tactician. But now fear had dismantled his record in her eyes. If he did something unstable in this ridiculous overpowered rowboat, he would not be able to *talk* his way out of it.

The mouth of the marina, leading out into Biscayne Bay, was actually a space between two walls built of rock that rose up six feet out of the water and stretched across the entire marina. As they passed through it, ever so slowly, Norman turned toward Magdalena, pointed at the walls, and said, "Anti-surge!"

It was close to a shout. Even at this speed the noise of the engines, plus the noise of the boat traffic on the bay, plus the wind, even though it wasn't much, meant Norman had to raise his voice pretty high to be heard. Magdalena hadn't the foggiest notion of what *anti-surge* might mean. She just nodded. By now the blank spots in her vocabulary were no longer very high on the worry ladder. She had no fear of venturing out on the bay. Her father owned one of the motor craft that were mounted so proudly upon boat trailers all over Hialeah. She gazed out over the water through her dark glasses. It was the usual great sunny-day Biscayne Bay waterscape, with tiny glints of dazzling sun dancing ever so lightly across the surface in swarms . . . and yet her spirits were sinking sinking sinking . . . She was at the mercy of a . . . *hypomaniac!* That was what he was—*at the very least!* He thought he was invincible! That was how he had demolished the Grand Inquisitor! But the sea was no place to feel invincible. And she had *let this happen!* Pure weakness! She had been embarrassed to say, "I'm afraid—and I don't want to go."

At that very moment Norman, both hands on the wheel, gave her a devilish look and cried out, "Okay, kid—HANG ON TIGHT!"

With that the growling engines broke into an explosive roar. The roar wasn't a sound—it was a force. The force went through her body, rattled her rib cage, and shook her from the inside out. No other sense could register. She had the feeling that if she cried out, the cry would never be able to leave her mouth. The nose of the boat began to rise. It came up so high, she couldn't see where they were headed. Could Norman, at the wheel? Would it do any earthly good if he could? She knew what was going on, even though she had never been on a boat like this before. This was supposed to be the... *great moment.* The entire boat was riding on its tail. Well, whoopee. This was supposed to be exhilarating. Girls were supposed to scream from the thrill. Magdalena felt the way she had in her early teens when boys insisted on showing how daring they were at the wheel of a car. She had never felt anything but nervous because of the drivers' blank and empty youth and the pointlessness of their goals as hell drivers. Norman was forty-two, but she felt exactly that way. Oh, blank and empty middle age! Oh, pointless goals! When would this be over? Didn't Nestor's Marine Patrol go after fools like this? But the thought of Nestor left her empty, too.

Finally, Norman let up and the nose came back down. He yelled to Magdalena, "How about that?! Seventy-two miles an hour on the water! Seventy-two!"

Magdalena didn't even try to say anything. She just smiled. She wondered if her expression looked as feigned as it felt. The main thing was not to show so much as a hint of exhilaration. One little hint—and he was *bound* to try it again. The nose was back down, but the *Hypomanic* didn't cut through the water the way other boats out here did... It didn't glide the way the sailboats did... Look at *that* one! So big! Could it be a... yacht? In Magdalena's imagination, a yacht could only be a very big boat with huge sails... On this dazzling day, all sailboats were flashes of white cloth upon a bay... a-dazzle with sun explosions off every little chop on the surface from here to the horizon... not that she could dwell upon any particular part of it for long... Norman's idea of cruising in his cigarette boat was to go fifty-five miles an hour instead of seventy... still so fast, the boat twitches and skips... and skips along... hypomaniacally bounces... and bounces... The hypomaniac at the wheel skips and bounces over the surface of the water... *whips* past every craft Magdalena got a glimpse of. A smile of self-awe took over Norman's face. He kept both hands on the wheel... He loved turning the boat *this* way and *that* way... *this* way to pass oncoming boats... *that* way to pass the boats he kept overtaking.

Nobody they went past in any direction seemed as exhilarated by the *Hypomanic*'s wild rush as Norman was. His passenger wasn't, either. Only Norman... only Norman... People on other boats squinted, glowered, shook their heads, gave the hypomaniac the finger, the forearm, up, up, the thumbs-down, and shouted angrily, judging by the expressions on their faces. The crew of the *Hypomanic* could not hear a word they said, of course. Certainly not Norman, there at the helm of his cigarette boat. He leaned forward in his upholstered pilot's seat, living out a happy fantasy.

Then he could resist no longer. Two more times he turned toward Magdalena and shouted, "HANG ON!" . . . grinning as if to say, "Want more thrills? You're with the right man!" Two more times he let the throttle out as far as it would go. Two more times the nose went up and the sudden forces drove Magdalena back and deeper down into her seat and made her feel like a fool for getting into this in the first place. Two more times the boat shot forward with hypomanic lust for superiority and showboating. Two more times they shot past anchoring boats with speed blurs. The second time, the speedometer hit eighty miles per hour, and Norman thrust a fist of triumph into the air and shot a quick glance toward Magdalena. Quick, because not even the hypomaniac dared keep his eye off where he was going any longer than that.

When he finally throttled down and put the nose back on the water, Magdalena said to herself, ::::::Please don't turn toward me and break into your big grin and say, "Guess what speed we hit!" and then make a face that begs for an awed reaction.::::::

He turned toward her with his self-awed grin and said, "I can't believe it myself!" He motioned toward the gauges in front of him. "Did you see that?! Am I kidding myself?! *Eighty miles an hour!* I swear, I never even *heard* of a cigarette boat reaching that speed! I could *feel* it! I bet you could, too!" He beamed another awed-reaction opportunity her way. ::::::Give him *anything* but that, or he'll do it again. He's feverish with Pride.:::::: So she gave him a compulsory stillborn smile, the kind that would freeze any normal man. To Norman it was nothing more than a cool breeze.

The cigarette boat covered the twenty miles to Elliott Key *just like that.* They knew they were there, not because they could see the key... but because they couldn't. The key itself was obscured by a promiscuous congestion of boats, reaching out at least a half mile... appeared to be thousands of them—*thousands*—some of them anchored, some of them somehow lashed together side by side, as many as ten in a row. Little dinghies motored about amid the bigger boats... What was *that?* It turned out to be a kayak, with one boy standing at the prow, paddling. A boy and a girl reclined behind him, each holding a plastic cup.

Music from God knows how many amped-up speakers rolled across the water—rap, rock, running rock, disco, metro-billy, reggae, salsa, rumba, mambo, monback—and collided above a loud and ceaseless undertone of two thousand, four thousand, eight thousand, sixteen thousand lungs crying out, shouting, shrieking, caterwauling, laughing, above all *laughing laughing laughing laughing laughing* laughing the stilted laugh of those proclaiming that *this* is where things are happening, and we are in the heat of it...

There were motorized boats with two and three levels of decks, enormous boats, and you could see, far and near, the forms of people hopping up and down and flailing this way and that—dancing—and—

Norman had now steered the cigarette boat deep into the regatta's helter-skelter and was trolling slowly, ever so slowly, with the thousand-horsepower engines growling growling growling growling ever so lowly lowly lowly . . . around this boat . . . between those two . . . along the lineups of boats tethered together side by side, closely, ever so closely . . . looking up at the people . . . who were dancing and drinking and squealing and laughing laughing laughing laughing—we're here we're here where things are happening! happening! happening! happening! to the beat—always the beat—of octophonic speakers electro-thunging out beats, beats, repro-beats, and the singers, always girls, became nothing more than beats themselves . . . no melody . . . only repro-beats . . . stringed bass, drums, beat-girls . . .

The closer they got to the key—they still hadn't laid eyes on it—the more boats they found lashed together, side by side, at the widest part of the hulls. It turned the boats into one big deck party, despite the different levels. A girl in a G-string bikini—so much blond hair!—teeters upon the narrow juncture where two boats are joined together and squeals with—she *squeals* with what? fear? coquetry? flirtation? the sheer exuberance of being *where things are happening?*—as guys hurry over and reach up to steady her. Another girl in a G-string bikini leaps over the juncture and lands on the other deck. The boys cheer with slightly ironic gusto, and one keeps yelling, "I would! I would!" . . . and the speakers boom boom boom with a *beat* a *beat* a *beat* a *beat*.

::::::and what does Norman think he's doing?::::::
In front of the lashed-together lineups Norman would unleash a sudden burst of fuel, and the thousand-HP engines would ROAR and everybody on the decks would peer down and cheer drunkenly and ironically. There were many small boats also weaving in and out of the boat mob . . . dinghies, motorboats, and every so often the kayak—that same kayak!—the paddler in the front now drunkenly singing . . . something . . . and the guy and the girl in the back drunkenly extending one leg and then the other . . . and Magdalena can look over and see the girl, lying on her side . . . and her bare bottom has the woven stringlike thong of a G-string bikini in the cleft and the boy, wearing baggy board shorts, has one arm under her head with the hand grasping her shoulder. It looked damned uncomfortable, trying to lie down in the bottom of a kayak . . . Half the girls dancing on the decks, all the decks, had on thongs . . . cleaving their buttocks into pairs of perfect melons just ripe enough for the picking . . . and that girl right there, not ten feet away, climbing out of the water up the ladder of that two-

deck motor launch—her buttocks, her backside, her... her... her *ass*—no other word comes right out and says it—her ass has swallowed her sling-low red thong so completely, Magdalena can hardly see that it exists at all... The water has furled the girl's hair into a wet mass that hangs down her back far below her shoulder blades, and the water makes it dark, but Magdalena would bet anything that it's actually blond—*las gringas!*—so many of them on those decks! Their blond hair bounces when they dance. It flashes when they throw their heads about to squeal... to flirt... to laugh laugh laugh laugh on the decks where things are happening... at Elliott Key... at this sexual regatta she finds herself enclosed in, making her want, despite sane thinking, to show them all—all those *gringas!*—what she's got. She makes herself sit up very erectly in her cigarette boat chair and pulls her abdominals in and flexes her shoulders back to make her breasts stand up perfectly, and she wants all *esos gringos y gringas* to stare at her and she *wants* to catch them staring... that one!... *that* one?... that one over there?—

Norman feeds another gulp of fuel to the engines, and they really ROAR this time, and he starts smiling a comradely smile and pointing at nobody in particular and waving at—empty spaces, so far as she can tell, and gunning the big engines with a bigger louder roar than ever, then cutting back as quietly.

Magdalena said, "Norman—what...are...you... *do*ing?"

A knowing smile: "*You'll* see. You just keep looking luscious, the way you do right now." He thrust his own chest out in an admiring pantomime of hers. Magdalena was pleased in spite of herself.

They were trolling ::::::for what?:::::: along the biggest lineup yet. Magdalena counted thirteen boats—or was it fourteen?—all of them on the large side, and at one end, two sailboats, one of them a schooner with enormous sails. This huge lineup excited Norman. He began going all out with the sound-offs, from growl to ROAR...the broad confident grins...the waving at imaginary people...

They were halfway down the lineup when a boy up on a deck shouted, "Hey, man! Didn't I just see you on TV?"

Norman put on a big congenial smile and said, "Could be!"

The boy shouted, "*60 Minutes,* right?"

Now Magdalena could see which boy. "You were on fire, man! You really had that little fucker...you had him like I mean all fucked up!"

From what Magdalena could tell from down here, he was a good-looking boy—early twenties?—with a head of long, thick hair brushed back into great sun-bleached brown leonine locks like Tarzan's and a perfect tan that made his long white teeth light up every time he smiled. He smiled a lot. He was tickled pink to have a noted TV schloctor doctor looking up at him . . . whatever his name might be.

"I got it!" shouted the boy. "Dr. . . . Lewis!"

"Norman Lewis!" shouted Norman. "I'm Norman . . . and this is Magdalena!"

"I would!" said the boy. He sounded drunk. He had a jumbo container in one hand.

"Me, too!" said another boy.

Magdalena didn't go for that. It came across as mockery.

Ironic whistles . . . Quite a little cluster of people had gathered at the railing. The suntanned boy with the teeth shouted down, "Hey, Dr. Lewis—Norman—why don't you and Madelaine—"

"Magdalena!" said Norman.

"I would!" said the boy. Obviously he was very proud of this rhetorical leap of vaguely sexual logic.

"Me, too!" said the other boy, and all the kids laughed. There was a real throng of them up there on the deck.

"Why don't you and Magdalena—"

"I would!" two of the boys at the railing shouted in unison, and others took up the cry, *"I definitely would!"*

"—come up and have a drink!" the first boy continued.

"Well . . ." Norman paused, as if such an invitation had never occurred to him . . . "Okay! Great! Thanks!"

The suntanned boy told him to just turn about and swing around the end of the row and double back to the stern of *First Draw,* where there was a ladder.

"Great!" said Norman. He turned the cigarette boat about and started off with a big ROAR of the engines, quickly cut back to a growl growl growl growl. "As long as they saw you on TV, you've got an aura," said Norman. He was very happy with Dr. Norman Lewis. "Memory tends to decay rapidly, but I knew I'd have a little mojo left—and I was right." He paused a moment. "Of course, it didn't hurt to have the mighty *Hypomanic.* They love cigarette boats, all these kids. Cigarette boats have... water cred! I knew revving up those thousand horses would get their attention. And you, kid"—he stuck out his lips as if he were about to give her a big comic kiss—"you didn't hurt, either! Did you see them? They were eating you up alive with their eyes! Didn't you love that *I would* business? *I would! I would! I would!* There's nobody on that boat who's even in your league. Face it. You're gorgeous, kid."

With that he put his hand on the inside of her thigh.

"Norman!" At the same time, she didn't object to his interpretation of the catcalls.

His other hand was on the wheel. Intently he stared straight ahead, as if there were nothing on his mind other than steering this growling cigarette boat around the bend.

"Norman! *Stop* it!"

So he removed his hand from her thigh—by sliding it up toward her hip . . . and then walking his fingers down her lower abdomen and under the band of her bikini bottom.

"Stop it, Norman! Are you *insane?!*" She grabbed his wrist and jerked his hand up. "Damn it, Norman—"

She suddenly fell silent. His fingers creeping under her pants, in plain view of everyone—*so gross!* And so *juvenile!* Such a plunge into *naughty-boy* exhibitionism! All that, on top of his open admission that he, Dr. Norman Lewis, nationally known psychiatrist, had trolled a whole line of boats in a humiliating, self-debasing way calculated to achieve such a small, retarded goal . . . crashing the deck party of a bunch of kids—*a bunch of kids!* A bunch of boys still speaking in teenage slang, a bunch of girls scampering naked over boat decks with *thongs* cutting their bottoms into two fresh melons and disappearing into God knew what—and yet it *excited* her. She could *feel* . . . the onset of a heedless bacchanal starring her own *gorgeous* body. A stirring in her loins . . . until she *regretted* not wearing a thong. Was this black bikini where Norman went exploring *small enough* to consummate the concupiscent urge to . . . *abandon* . . . every conscious thought that held her back? But Conscious Thought was tougher than she imagined. It hoisted her up erect. ::::::*Stop it . . . and now!*::::::

"Stop it, Norman!" she said. "Everyone can see us!"

But she had allowed his hand to remain there for a beat too long, and her *Stop it* had no moral strength, merely social decorum. By the way Norman was eyeing her, with a little smile playing on parted lips, she knew that he had detected every neuron of her conflicted feelings and realized what a weak and vulnerable state she was in.

When the *Hypomanic* reached the stern of the *First Draw,* there was quite a contingent of gawkers waiting at the top of the ladder. Magdalena climbed up first, to another chorus of "*I* would!" "*I* would!" "*I* would!" "*I* would!" She could feel their eyes cupping her breasts and massaging her lower abdomen, which was bare all the way down to her mons pubis and swelled out ever so slightly, just enough to give it a little curve. They couldn't take their eyes off her!

"*I* would!"

"*I* would!"

"*I* would!"

It was hard to hear even that much. Here on the boat itself the BEAT the BEAT the BEAT came POUNDING POUNDING POUNDING POUNDING out of the speakers. She could see girls on the deck up front, dancing with one another... next thing to naked. A whole flock of G-string girls!... with thongs disappearing into their buttocks' clefts... They rode their pelvic saddles bareback, they jerked their heads and sent their blond manes flying—blond *americanas!*—suddenly she felt trapped... in a vulgar horde of aliens...

Now young guys in bathing trunks... their skin that looked like custard, like flan... Latin guys had muscles you could see—but she realized she was thinking about Nestor—so she dropped that subject. A guy, maybe what?—twenty-five years old?—a guy with skin of flan was standing right in front of her, and he said, "Hey, you with *him?*"

She knew he meant Norman, who was coming up the ladder behind her.

Norman took Magdalena by the hand and went straight to the guy who had invited them aboard in the first place. He turned out to be a tall, slender man, in his early twenties, probably.

He was wearing a pair of the *au courant* extralong board shorts. They had a go-to-hell Hawaiian print all over them. Nevertheless, up this close he seemed to rate promotion from boy to young man, in nomenclature at least.

When he saw Norman, his mouth fell open, his eyes popped open, and he said, "Dr. Lewis! This is so *cooool!* I just saw you on *60 Minutes*—and here you are... on *my boat!* It's *soooooo coooooool!*"

The awe seemed to be genuine—and Magdalena saw genuine gratitude spread over Norman's face in the form of a smile that said, "That's more like it." He put out his hand, and the young man shook it and felt compelled to say, "Actually, this isn't really *my* boat, it's my father's."

Norman said in the friendliest possible way, "Please tell me your name!"

"I'm Cary!" That was it—Cary. He was part of this, the first generation to have no last names. Using a last name was considered pompous... or else too much of a tip-off as to your background... ethnic, racial, sometimes social. Nobody used a last name until he was forced to fill out a form.

Norman said, "And this is Magdalena, Cary."

Cary flashed those incomparable teeth of his and said, "*I* would! Honest, that's a compliment!"

Laughter and "*I* woulds" broke out among the crowd that had gathered around them to see the supposedly famous Dr. Lewis, whoever he might be.

"*I* would!" Laughter.

"*I* would!" Laughter.

"*I* would!" Laughter.

"*I* would!" More laughter.

"I *definitely* would!" Whoops of laughter over that one.

"That's a *big* compliment," said Cary. "Honest truth!"

A wave of embarrassment... and bliss... Cuban girls were no different from *americana* girls in most things. They spent half of every day asking themselves... or their girlfriends... "Did he notice me? Do you *think* he did? What kind of look was that, would you say?"

Magdalena couldn't dream up a single reply that wouldn't . . . kill the bliss of it. If she openly took it as a compliment, she would sound like an unsophisticated little Latina, and if she tried some becomingly cool and witty piece of self-deprecation, she would come off as an awkward creature who had a fear of being envied. Wisely, she did the only safe thing. She stood there blushing and fighting off the smile . . . and what bliss it was!

The sun had sunk a bit, but it couldn't have been later than 5:30 when Magdalena heard a chorus of those ironic *whooooops* that young men seem to enjoy . . . They were on the deck of the next boat over . . . and there she was . . . a blond girl who had just removed the top of her bikini. She had her back arched and her arms out wide . . . with the bra dangling from one hand . . . and her breasts popped out in a way that said, "No more hide-and-peek. Now we . . . *live!*"

"Come on!" said Norman . . . with a lewdly happy face. "This you've got to see!" He took her hand and hurried her over to the railing to get a better look. "Now it begins!"

The blonde with the breasts did a few mild shimmies with her hips, showing her chorus of admirers how taut her pectoral glories were... how they stuck out, defying gravity...

"*What* begins?" she said.

"The regatta is essentially an orgy," said Norman. "That's what I want you to see. You have to see something like this *once* anyway." But he wasn't looking at Magdalena when he said it. Like every other male on the boat, he only had eyes for the sprung-free naked breasts. *She* was casting glances this way and that, vamping, like a comedienne playing the coquette, urgently trying to convey the message: "Oh, I'm just having fun... just using sex as irony... you can't take this seriously"... as she switched her hips *this* way and *that*... comically, of course, because this was not serious... but enough for everyone to see her body in her tan thong, very nearly the color of her skin.

The girl suddenly stopped her little performance, crossed her arms over her breasts, and doubled over laughing and then rose erect, still laughing, dabbing her eyes with the backs of her hands, as if it had all been so funny. But then she straightened up and shook her breasts... but without the shimmies... and now smiled broadly as she approached three of her *americana* girlfriends who were laughing their heads off. One of them kept thrusting both arms up in the air the way football referees did when a team scored. The blonde no longer tried to cover her breasts with her arms. She posed with her hands on her hips and kept smiling as she talked to the three girls—didn't want anybody to think she was embarrassed by what she had done.

The girl's success did not lead to a wave of breast baring. It started off randomly. Magdalena and Norman kept touring from boat to boat . . . deck to deck . . . thirteen different decks . . . some *this* high off the water, and some *that* high, and some not even *that* high, and a few not much higher off the water than Norman's cigarette boat. Norman kept stopping to yakyakyakyakyakyakyakhockhockhock with fans—not exactly fans . . . more like people who had just been told he was important—and Magdalena would stand there with a smile of interest and involvement on her face but then become so bored that she would look about, and . . . see that some girl over here or over there . . . or over *there*—five or six hundred yards away, even, on some deck on another tethered row of boats—had taken off her bikini top . . . without benefit of *whoops whooooops* and woo-ooOOOs . . . and the sun would sink a little further . . . and the boys would get a little drunker . . . so drunk or so inflamed with lust that they worked up the courage to join the girls dancing on the deck. ::::::And there's that kayak.:::::: It was still coursing among the boats, reappeared below. The oarsman stood up in the front with a paddle, as if this were a gondola. The couple still lay together in back. The girl had removed her string bikini top and lay on her back, flaunting her big breasts. She had opened up her legs. A wisp of G-string bikini cloth barely covered her. The boy, who still had his board shorts on, lay on his side with both legs around the lower half of one of her legs. *Todo el mundo* seemed to be staring down to see if he was aroused. Magdalena, for her part, couldn't tell . . . and then they were gone . . . in order to present their *exhibición* to other boats. Here on deck . . . ripe melons . . . ripe . . . By now, late afternoon, all the decks were filthy . . . littered with every imaginable form of trash and garbage plus, here and there, pools of vomit, some of it still wet, some of it sun-dried vomitus . . . and everywhere discarded beer cans and beer bottles and big plastic beer cups . . . iconic Solo cups . . . favorite at keggers and tailgaters . . . hundreds of them discarded on every deck . . . Solo cups . . . in their traditional tool-and-dye-works red . . . and in every other imaginable color . . . pale pink, corn yellow, royal blue, navy blue, aqua blue, viridian green, puce, fuchsia, cellar-floor gray, garbage-bag brown, every color short of black . . . strewn, crushed, split, or lying sideways, intact . . . and every time a boat rocked, usually thanks to the rolling wakes of speedboats, the bottles and the beer cans would roll across the deck . . . the beer cans with a cheap junky aluminum rattle . . . the bottles with a cheap junky hollow moan . . . rolled rolled rolled over the flat garbage, the stamped-out cigarettes, the cheap plastic beads, the spilt-beer slicks, the used condoms, the puke fritters... canted canted canted over a pair of glasses with a ruptured temple hinge, an abandoned flip-flop... collided collided collided with the plasticized cups, and soon the decks were GRINDING and HUMPING and the sound systems were getting louder and the BEAT thung BEAT thung BEAT thung BEAT thung BEAT thung BEAT thung and more girls were taking off their tops and were left only with little thongs disappearing into the crevices of their only *just now! at just this very taut swollen labial moment ripe melons... ripe melons*... and they got down to it... no more steps, no more Lindys and twists such as the girls did with one another... no, *get down to it*... to GRINDING...

She looks up at Norman. He is transfixed by the sight... absorbed, consumed... leaning forward... His smile curls from amusement to hunger... *Hungry* he is! He *wants* some—

"Oh, shit!" It sounded like something he meant to say under his breath... It was an *Oh, shit* of excitement. Excitement had so overcome him, this choked croak had become an exclamation forced through a husk of a throat. He certainly was not talking to *her*... His smile had turned into a pulse... amusement arousal amusement arousal amusement arousal... His eyes were pinned on a couple barely three feet from them—this *americano,* tall, sandy haired, with an athletic build—this *americano* was behind a girl BEAT thung BEAT thung BEAT thung THRUST hump THRUST hump THRUST hump hump humping BEHIND her HUMP thung THRUST the turgid crotch of his trunks in her buttocks RUT rut rut rut... so hard, the front of his trunks all but disappeared into that ripe gulley... She was leaning forward to make the gulley wider, causing her bare breasts to hang down... with each THRUST they swung forward THRUST hump THRUST thong thong thong thong they lurched forward and swung back—

The americanos! Not that Cuban boys are so—but the *americanos* are... dogs in the park! The thought of a whole deck full of young men and women doing what was so close to the real thing BEAT thung BEAT thung BEAT thung BEAT thung THRUST hump THRUST hump THRUST hump THRUST hump dogs in the park THRUST hump THRUST *grind grind grind* grinding their distended cocks albeit held down by their trunks into the girls' crotches GRIND GRIND GRIND... these *gringas* might as well have been totally naked!... bikinis? Breasts rampant GRINDING. All you can see is the band of the thong bottom BEAT thung BEAT thung BEAT thung barely visible at the hips... otherwise naked girls with guys thrusting humping GRINDING them BEAT thong BEAT thong...

Getting darker... but light still glowed on the edges of the western horizon—a band of purple backlit by a fading gold. She could barely see any light to the north where Miami was... somewhere... or east and the ocean beyond... but still enough light to make Magdalena think this motley corona of—what?—a thousand boats?—was *in the world*... enough to make her believe Miami actually was... up there... and the ocean *was* actually out there... and they really *were* near a known piece of geography, Elliott Key... even though there was such a jam-up of boats. She had only barely laid eyes on it by looking between boats... and this *was* Biscayne Bay they were on... She was still able to gaze out over the bay, although the light was getting dimmer and dimmer. There was a party on every boat...

Great whoops. People were hurrying. People dancing suddenly began hurrying to the rear deck.

Norman pulled her in that direction.

"What's going on?" By now you had to shout to be heard even at close range.

"I don't know!" shouted Norman. "But we've gotta go see!"

Magdalena found herself stumbling behind Norman, who held tight to her hand and pulled her along.

Much excitement on the aft deck. Cell phones were going off. Two of them were programmed with LMFAO's "I'm Sexy and I Know It" and Pitbull's

"Hey Baby." The *beep beep be-beeps* of incoming text messages were going off all over the place.

A young *americano* cried out above the general hubbub, "You won't be*lieve* this!"

BEAT thung BEAT thung BEAT thung BEAT thung—yet now Magdalena could hear it... From down that way, cheers, shouts, two-fingers-in-the-mouth whistles, whoops and *woo-woo-wooooos*—always mockery, the woo-woo-wooo, but this time so very loud. The ruckus was heading toward them like a tide... finally so close, it beat back the sound system... the ruckus and the sound of the speedboats... bearing down—

The crowd against the rail was so thick, Magdalena couldn't see a thing. Without a word, Norman clamped his hands on either side of her waist, just below her rib cage, and lifted her straight up until she could put her legs around his neck and dangle them down over his chest like a child... Grumbling from behind, "Hey, you're *rumble rumble rumble rumble!*" Norman ignored it. In the next instant—

—the speedboats... Behind the first, three water-skiers on long towlines... three girls... three girls towed at a furious rate by one speedboat... all three *stark naked*... three girls without a stitch on, two blondes, one brunette... tall *americana* bodies! Starved to near perfection!... Reaching the lineup of thirteen tethered boats turned them on... All three took one hand off the towline, turned their upper bodies almost forty-five degrees, and threw their free arms up in the air in a gesture of abandon . . . tremendous cheering and laughing from every boat in the line . . . mocking *woo-woo-woooooos*—but even the mockery was exultant—and deliriously happy— Another speedboat. This one towing—

—Christ Jesus!—a young man naked as the day he was born—presenting the Columbus Day Regatta . . . *a huge erection* . . . so gorged with blood, it curved upward at a fifteen-degree angle . . . three naked maidens, with tits rampant! . . . the god Priapus, *the gorged cock of Youth rampant!* . . . all of it lit by the brief domed glow of dusk.

The cheering from the tethered boats rose up in a primal scream not from the heart but from the groin, feral *whoooops, woo-woo-woooooos, hoot hoot hoooooots, arrrrghs, ah haaahhs arrrghhHHHock hock hock*— that last rut rut roar unmistakably Norman's . . .

"Did you see that? Did you see it, kid? That guy broke every known rule of the central nervous system! No man can endure the taxation water-skiing weighs on his legs, the quadriceps, the hamstrings, the latissimi dorsi, the brachialis—and maintain an erection like that . . . it can't happen—but it just did!"

::::::Ah, the scientist, the scholarly research analyst, keeps his eyes fixed upon the very outer boundaries of the human animal's existence.:::::: Magdalena wondered if Norman himself was aware of how often he tried to hide his own sexual excitement behind these thick walls of theory... while even now he scans the bay for one last receding glimpse of the nice young cloven bottoms of the water-ski girls in the sexual water show.

The show was over, but the *americanos,* like Norman, were inflamed by lust. Their hands trembled and they had serious trouble trying to text on their smart phones' tiny keys. Their phones were ringing in a dysphony of "Hips Don't Lie," "On the Floor," "Wild Ones," Rihanna, Madonna, Shakira, Flo Rida, recorded laughing jags, whistled Brazilian salsas, all of them riddled by the abrupt *beep beep beep*s and *alert alert alert*s of incoming TEXTS thung TEXTS thung BEAT thung HUMP thung THRUST thung BEAT thung DANCING thung AGAIN thung the DECK thung DECK thung INFLAMED thung LUST thung LUST WHOOP WHOOP! WOO-WOO!—and all at once *todo el mundo* is mad to reach another deck... down *that* way! Norman grabs Magdalena by the forearm and is pulling her, dragging her, into the stampede. Such commotion—

"*Norman!* What's—"

He didn't wait for her to complete the question. "I don't know! Let's find out!"

"What earthly good—"

"We have to *see!*" said Norman. He said it as if

that were the only rational choice, given the surge of the crowd.

"No, Norman—you're crazy!"

She tries to pull back and go the other way, turns—*¡ALAVAO!* A horde of them are climbing and vaulting over the railing onto this deck and *WHOOP WHOOP! WOO-WOOOO!* charging past her and clambering from this boat to the next and from the *next* to the next—going *that* way, HORDES of them! Magdalena gave up and rushed with the rest and ravenous Norman, struggling up over railings and dropping onto the next deck and struggling up and dropping down and stampeding across deck after deck until at last they could see a crowd in slices that was gathering, sliced and diced by lights streaming over them, in the very last boat in the row, the only sailboat, the schooner with the two towering masts. But why?

Magdalena didn't want to think of Nestor, but Nestor intruded. ::::::God, that first mast is so tall... the height of an office building... and Nestor climbed to the top hand over hand.::::::

"I think I know what this is all abouuuut hock hock hock!" said Norman. In a very jolly way, too. So jolly, he just naturally put his arm around Magdalena's shoulders and drew her close to him. "Ohhohoho, yes, I think... I... do... know," he said. Obviously, he wanted her to say, "What?—my all-knowing one." But she wasn't going to give him the satisfaction. *She* hadn't forgotten their swelling contretemps before they boarded the boat.

Some mock cheering broke out among the boys and girls crowded onto the schooner's foredeck. The boat's huge mainsail had suddenly lit up like a lamp shade—no, like a screen. The sail had been swung about ninety degrees until it was like a screen facing the people on the foredeck, and the lights, Magdalena now realized, came from a beam projected from the prow. An image appeared on the sail—a slice of part of a person?—but a little gust of wind rippled across, and Magdalena couldn't make it out. In the next instant, the wind calmed down, and a huge image appeared—an erect penis six or seven feet long on the huge schooner sail and nearly two feet thick. But where was the end, the glans penis? It had disappeared into a cave—but that couldn't be the entrance to a cave, because it kept expanding and contracting around the glans and moving down and up and down and up...*¡Dios mío!* It was a woman's lips! Projected onto the mainsail! Her head was twelve feet from brow to chin.

Magdalena's heart took a nosedive...porn!...a porn movie projected at gigantic scale onto a gigantic sail...turning these hundreds of *americanos* into pigs, stampeding pigs squealing *eeeee uh eeeee uh* thanks to what? Porn.

And one of those *americano* pigs was Dr. Norman Lewis. He was right beside her, on this mobbed deck . . . trying to resist the drooling adoration that wants to creep across his face . . . eyes pinned on a schooner sail that reaches from here . . . to *way up there* . . . as porcine body parts pop up, drift, and invade one another, oozing and sliding and drooling and sucking and lapping . . . a woman's legs the size of office towers, spread open . . . wide open . . . the labia majorae are three times as big as the entrance to the Miami Convention Center . . . the porn doctor Lewis is transfixed . . . he wants to *enter* that portal or is it he wants his *eyes* to enter . . . transfixed by the alternate galaxy of pornography?

"I don't know about you, Norman, but I've had enough!"

He doesn't even hear her. He's drooling in his own world.

She grabs his elbow and shakes it . . . hard. Norman is startled . . . but more than that, bewildered. "How could anybody—"

"Let's go, Norman."

"Go . . ."

"Back. I wanna go back to Miami."

Bewildered. "Back? When?"

"Right now, Norman."

"Why?"

"Why?" says Magdalena. "Because you look like a

drooling three-year-old standing here... a slobbering porn addict—"

"Slobbering *porn* addict"—but he's not really absorbing the words. He's so far gone, his eyes wander back to the sail... the twelve-foot-high head of a woman trying to nibble the foot-long clitoris of another woman with her yard-wide lips.

"Norman!"

"Uhhh, what?"

"We're *going!* And *that's that!"*

"*Going?* The night is just beginning! This is part of the experience!"

"They"—Magdalena swung her head about to indicate the rest of the crowd—"are going to have this awesome—pathetic—experience... without you. You're leaving!"

"And going where?"—but he obviously had no real comprehension of what the two of them were saying... His eyes floated back to the *sail*—

"WE'RE LEAVING, NORMAN, AND I *MEAN* IT!"

Norman's expression granted her marginally more attention, but not a lot. "We can't," he said. "We can't take the boat back in the dark. It's too dangerous."

Magdalena stood there with an *I can't believe this* expression, staring at Norman. Norman's eyes were already back on the magnified body parts. An immense... cleft buttocks... was on the screen. A giant's hands were spreading the cheeks apart. The anus itself filled the vast screen. It was deep as a gorge in the mountains of Peru.

"Norman, if you want me," she said in a tense, clipped voice, "I'll be in the boat, trying to get some sleep."

"Sleep?" said Norman in the voice that said, "How can you even *think* of such a thing?" Nevertheless, he was at last focusing upon her. He spoke sternly. "Now, listen to me. Tonight is an obligatory all-nighter. All night is what this experience is all about! If you keep your eyes open, you will witness things you never thought possible. You will have a picture of mankind with all the rules removed. You will see Man's behavior at the level of bonobos and baboons. And that's where Man is headed! You will see the future out here in the middle of nowhere! You will have an extraordinary preview of the looming *un*-human, thoroughly animal, fate of Man! Believe me, treating porn addicts is not a narrow psychiatric specialty. It's essential to *any* society's bulwark against degeneracy and self-destruction. And to me, it's not enough to gather data by listening to patients describe their lives. These people are weak and not very analytical. Otherwise they wouldn't let these things happen to themselves. We have to *see* with *our own eyes*. And that's why I'm willing to stay up all night—to get to know these wretched souls from the inside out."

Jesu Cristo... this was the thickest wall of theory she had ever heard Norman concoct! An impenetrable fort!... and an inimitable pulling the rug out from under any critic.

She gave up. What use was it to argue with him? There was nothing to be done about it.

But giving up on the war brought her no peace. In the darkness she looked in every direction. Before the sun went down... Miami had been up there, to the north, even though all you saw on the horizon from here was something the size of a scrap of your little fingernail. You couldn't see Key Biscayne from here, but you knew where it was in the northeast. Florida City was way over there to the west... and all around, the immense sea was black as night... no, *blacker*... *invisible*... the most famous expanse of ocean in the country... vanished. She hadn't the faintest idea where north was, where west was, no sense at all of where *she* was. There *was* no rest of the world—only this flotilla of depraved lunatics. And she was a prisoner here, forced to watch the rot, the pustular oozing of complete freedom. Even the sky consisted of complete darkness and a single beam of light on an immense stretch of canvas upon which filthy body parts oozed and slithered... all that was left of life on Earth, boiled down. Magdalena felt more than depressed. Something about it made her afraid.

9

South Beach Outreach

Nestor was nine years old all over again when he used these German binoculars the Crime Suppression Unit provided, the JenaStrahls. Oh, the childlike wonder this great gadget engendered! The *comemierdas* he had under surveillance at this moment were on the porch of an Overtown ghetto hovel a good two blocks away. With the JenaStrahls he could count the rhinestones on the rims of their ears all the way from here. The smaller one, the one with the lighter skin, the one sitting down on an old wooden chair, had one . . . two . . . three . . . four . . . five . . . six . . . *seven* rhinestones on one ear . . . so close to one another, they touched . . . two inches of ear pierced seven times . . . a perforated tear-here line on one tiny ear, it looked like. The other man, a real bull, 250 pounds at least, maybe a lot more, was leaning back against the front wall next to a set of bars over a window...arms folded, making his entwined forearms look the size of a pig in a Hialeah pig roast...he had three rhinestones on the rim of each ear. Both men wore fitted baseball caps—no any-size belt buckles in back!—with the brims still flat as the day they bought them and still bearing the New Era stickers they came with on top. Both wore virgin-white NuKill sneakers untouched by so much as a speck of grime or slime from the streets of Miami. Both the hats and the shoes cried out to all who knew of and would envy such details, "Brand-new! I'm cool!—and I can *afford New*—every day!"

Hmmmmm...wonder if those little twinkly stones could be the real thing, diamonds...*Nahhhhh*... This didn't look even close to being that big an operation. All that jewelry riveted into the flaps of their ears. They might as well have had signs around their necks reading: YO, COPS! STOP AND FRISK ME! This surveillance was the result of a tip from a lowlife informer who was fingering every dope dealer in Overtown he had ever heard of in a desperate bid to avoid his third conviction as a dealer himself, which could send him to prison for twenty years.

Without removing his eyes from the two men on the porch, Nestor said, "Sarge, did you notice all the blingbling they got stuck in their ears?"

"Oh, sure," said the Sergeant. "I was reading about

that once. All natives love that shit. It don't matter if it's Uganda, Yoruba, Ubangi, or Overtown. What they can tattoo, they tattoo. What they can't tattoo, they stick all that glitter shit on it."

Nestor winced . . . for the Sergeant's sake. The Sergeant wouldn't dare say anything like that to anybody but another Cuban cop. The Department had a whole campaign going, *insusurro,* aimed at improving relations with American blacks. In slums like this one, Overtown, and Liberty City, black people looked upon Cuban cops as foreign invaders who one day dropped from the sky like paratroopers and took over the Police Department and started shoving black people around . . . black people who had lived in Miami forever. They spoke a foreign language, these invaders. They would do anything to avoid paperwork, since the forms were printed in English. Instead of going to all that trouble, they would just take a black suspect out back of the building and beat him in the kidneys until he was urinating blood and admitting to whatever the invaders wanted him to admit to. Or thus spake Overtown street lore.

Nestor and the Sergeant were parked in an unmarked car, a three-year-old Ford Assist. It was hard to come up with an ugly design for a two-door car, but Ford had pulled it off. The Sergeant, Jorge Hernandez, was behind the wheel, and Nestor was in the passenger seat. The Sergeant was only six or seven years older than Nestor. He knew all about the man on the mast episode and thought Nestor had done great. So Nestor felt at ease with him. He could even joke with him a little. It was nothing like dealing with the *americano* sergeant, who had to remind you every other second that you were Cuban—and so alien to him he had a cute word, namely *Canadian,* he could use to talk to other rednecks about you people with impunity.

The side and rear windows of the Assist were tinted black. That wasn't good enough cover, however, if you were watching suspects through the windshield with binoculars. So they had put one of those big silvery sun reflectors across the entire windshield. They would pull the reflector down ever so slightly where it met the headliner and stick the binocular lenses through the gap.

Both of them were in plainclothes. There was *plainclothes,* and there was *undercover,* and in the Crime Suppression Unit—called CST and not CSU, and only God knew why—you usually went on runs in one or the other. Nestor liked that. It made you a detective, although you didn't really have that rank. In undercover you tried to look like your quarry, which usually meant looking like a *comemierda* roach with eight days' worth of stubble, especially from under the chin, back to the neck, and above all a head of hair you hadn't washed for at least a week. If you went around with clean hair, they'd spot you immediately. Compared to that, plainclothes was formal. Nestor and the Sergeant were wearing jeans, clean ones, with leather belts and blue T-shirts, tucked in... *Tucked in!*—these days, how much more formal could a young man get? Naturally, Nestor loved the T-shirts. Needless to say, he wore a size too small. On your belt, in the CST, you wore a holster with an evil-looking automatic revolver in it. In plainclothes, CST officers wore fine twisted-steel necklaces from which their golden badges hung down on the T-shirts squarely in the middle of the chest. You couldn't miss them. The advantage of plainclothes was that you could call in an entire platoon of cops to a particular location in unmarked cars without setting off alarms all over the neighborhood. CST was a special unit, all right, an elite unit, and Nestor was investing his whole life in it. What other life did he have? He had been depressed for months now. His father and his whole family had declared him a non-person... well, not everybody... his mother still called him on the telephone from time to time and probably never even comprehended how profoundly irritated he was by her consolations. In her mind, sweet and tender consolation consisted of saying, in effect, "I know you have committed a terrible sin against your own people, my son, but I forgive you and will never forget you . . . even though nobody else in Hialeah can forget you fast enough."

"What are they doing now?" asked the Sergeant.

"Nothing much, Sarge," said Nestor, eyes still up against the binoculars. "Same old same old. The little guy is rocking on the back legs on his chair. The big guy is standing beside the door, and every now and then the little guy says something, and the big guy goes inside for maybe a minute and comes back out."

"And you can see their hands?"

"Sure can, Sarge. You know the JenaStrahls"— pronounced YaynaStrahls. Somewhere along the way some learned member of the CST had pointed out that the German *J* was pronounced *Y* and the *E* was pronounced *A*.

Just saying the name made Nestor acutely aware of how tiring it was to stare steadily through these triumphs of optical engineering. The image you got was so enlarged and at the same time so refined that moving the thing just a quarter of an inch made it feel as if the apparatus were ripping your eyeballs out. The Sergeant couldn't take it for more than fifteen minutes at a time, and neither could he. They should have had some kind of tripod you could attach to the dashboard.

Nestor always had a lot of new ideas about police work, and Magdalena used to like to listen to them . . .

to his ideas and to his tales of the sea or Biscayne Bay at least, when he was in Marine Patrol. Or she acted like she did... which probably meant she actually *did*. One of the things he had always admired about her was that she was one girl who didn't try to hide her feelings. Flattery was something she really hated. She treated it as the Eighth Deadly Sin. ::::::Oh, Manena! To this day you probably don't realize what you did to me! You didn't come to Yeya's birthday party that day to *see* me. You weren't even curious about what I had gone through. You came to throw me under the bus, and you gave me no warning. You had been a little distant for a couple of weeks, but I eagerly explained that away, didn't I. ... Did I ever tell you how I felt when I lay next to you? I didn't want to just *enter* your body... I wanted to enter you so completely that my hide would wrap around yours, and they would become one... my rib cage would contain your rib cage... my pelvis would be conjoined with your pelvis... forever... my lungs would breathe your every breath... Manena! You and I were a universe! That other universe out there revolved about *us*... We were the sun! It's pretty stupid of me not to be able to get you out of my mind. I'm sure I'm long gone from yours... me and Hialeah... *I'm seeing someone else*... From the moment you said that, I knew it was some *americano*. I'm still convinced of that... We all fooled ourselves in Hialeah, didn't we—everyone but you. Hialeah *is* Cuba. It's surrounded by *more* Cuba... all of Miami is ours, all of Greater Miami is ours. We occupy it. We're Singapore or Taiwan or Hong Kong... But somewhere in our hearts we all know we're really nothing but a sort of Cuban free port. All the real power, all the real money, all the real excitement, all the glamour, is the *americanos'*... and now I realize that you've always wanted in on that... with all that, what was to keep you from—::::::

He was jerked alert by the appearance of a new figure in the eye-ripping JenaStrahl magnification of the world two blocks away.

"Here comes somebody else," Nestor said in a low voice, as if he were talking to himself. His eyes were pressed against the binoculars. "He's just come from behind the house, Sarge. He's heading for the guy in the chair." Oh, Nestor had learned his lesson that day of the man on the mast. Never again! Never again would he go more than one sentence without throwing in a "Sarge" or a "Lieutenant" or whatever was required. He was one of the great "Sarge"-droppers on the entire force now. "It's a... Christ, I can't even tell you what color he is, Sarge, he's such a mess"... never removing his eyes from the JenaStrahls.

"Can you see his hands?" said the Sergeant in a rather urgent tone.

"Sarge, I can see his hands... Guy looks like a real

crackhead . . . he's hunched over like he's eighty years old . . . Hair looks like he combed it with glue and then slept on it . . . Christ, it's filthy . . . itches all the way from here just looking at it . . . Guy looks like somebody hocked him up against the wall like a lunger, Sarge, and he's just oozing down it . . ."

"Never mind all that," said the Sergeant. "Just keep your eye on his hands." It was the Sergeant's conviction that dope dealers didn't have minds, especially the ones here in Overtown and the other big black slum, Liberty City. They just had hands. They sold dope, stashed dope, cached dope, smoked dope, snorted dope, fried dope on a sheet of Reynolds wrap so they could inhale the fumes . . . all with their hands, all with their hands.

"Okay," said Nestor, "he's talking to the little guy on the chair."

The Sergeant was leaning so far toward him from the driver's seat, Nestor could tell he was dying to take over the JenaStrahls himself. But he also knew he wouldn't do it. During the handover they might miss something with the dirtbags' hands.

"He's reaching in his pocket, Sarge. He's pulling out . . . a . . . that's *a five-dollar bill,* Sarge."

"You *sure?*"

"I can see Abraham Lincoln's eyebrows, Sarge. I'm not kidding! Guy's got one hell of a set of eyebrows . . . Okay, now he's handing it to the skinny guy . . . The skinny guy's got it balled up in his fist... The big guy's coming over from the door... he's a big mean-looking sonofabitch... he's giving the crackhead the evil eye... Now he's bending over behind the skinny guy's chair. The skinny guy's putting both hands behind his back... and now I can't see their hands at all."

"Pick up their goddamned hands, Nestor! Pick 'em up!"

How the fuck's he supposed to do that? Thank God, the skinny guy brings both hands around in front of him. "He's handing the guy something, Sarge—"

"Handing him *what?!* Handing him *what?!*"

"He's handing him this little cube thing, Sarge, wrapped in a little piece a Bounty paper towel. Looks like a rock to *me*."

"You sure? What makes you think it's Bounty?"

"I'm sure, Sarge. It's the JenaStrahls. I *know* Bounty. How the hell did *americanos* ever get along in America before Bounty?"

"Fuck Bounty, Nestor! Where's the goddamned little thing now?"

"The head's stuffing it down into his pants pocket... He's starting to walk away, Sarge. He's heading back to the rear of the lot. You should see him. He's got some *baaaad* locomotor problems."

"So it's a *buy*— right? The whole thing."

"I saw Abraham Lincoln's bushy eyebrows, Sarge."

"All right," said the Sergeant. "We're gonna need three cars."

The Sergeant got on the Department radio and called their CST captain and asked him to dispatch three cars, unmarked, two officers per car, same setup as the Sergeant and Nestor's in the Ford Assist. One unit would drive by the dope house and park in a driveway between two houses nearby, and more than likely use a sun reflector disguise the same way the Sergeant and Nestor had been doing it. A second unit would drive into the alley behind the house to cover the rear—and see if they could spot the head who walked like he had a stroke and just made a buy at the house. A third unit would pull up on the other side—right behind the Sergeant and Nestor. The Sergeant and Nestor would be leading the raid. They would arrive right in front of the house as near to the porch and the two rhinestone-studded *cucarachas* as possible. All eight cops would hop out of the cars with the badges gleaming on their chests and the holsters fully visible on their belts in a show of force calculated to dissuade anyone with armed resistance on his mind.

At this point, the *cucarachas* with the body piercings and jacklegged gaits became less amusing... Nestor would have sworn he could actually *feel* the adrenaline rising from above his kidneys and revving his heart up into the racing mode. If CST undercovers had spent a few days making buys at the place and scoping it out, a SWAT team would have probably been called in. But this looked like too rinky-dink a dope store to have to crank things up that high. That wasn't precisely how Nestor looked at it, however, and probably not the Sergeant, either. After all, the Sergeant was no fool. Where there was dope, there was a good chance there were guns... and the two of them would be going in first... At this very moment, Nestor couldn't help remembering something an astronaut had said in a documentary on TV: "Before every mission I told myself, 'I'm gonna die doing this. I'm gonna die *this time*. But I'm dying for something bigger than myself. I'm about to die for my country, for my people, and for a righteous God.' I always believed—and I still believe—that there is a righteous God and that we, we in America, are part of his righteous plan for the world. And so I, who am about to die, am determined to die honorably, fearing only one thing: not living up to, not dying for, the purpose for which God put me on this earth." Nestor loved those lines and believed in their wisdom and remembered them in every moment of police work that involved danger... Did you do that before the ever-judging eyes of a righteous God... or was it the eyes of an *americano* sergeant? Now, be honest.

Nestor still had the binoculars focused on the two black guys with the rhinestone ears. What was it—

this place where dirt-bags like them lived? Overtown... trash everywhere. The buildings were small, and many were missing... burned down, demolished, or maybe they just fell down from lack of upkeep... wouldn't be a surprise. And everywhere there was a vacant lot you had... trash... not *piles* of trash... after all, *piles* of trash might suggest that someone was coming back to haul it away... no, these were spills of trash. It looked like some unimaginably big giant had accidentally spilled some unimaginably big bucket of rubbish across Overtown and surveyed the unimaginably big mess and walked away muttering oh the hell with it. The trash was littered, strewn, whither and wherever. Trash accumulated against the fences, and the fences were... everywhere. If there was any honest money to be made in Overtown, it had to be in the cyclone fence business. Owners who had the money enclosed every square inch of their property in cyclone fencing. You had the feeling that if you took a tape measure and actually measured it, there would be a mile of it on every block. All over the place you'd see a bush growing sideways out from under a cyclone fence or through it... not a couple of bushes, not a clump, not a stand, but *one* bush, some stray left over from a long-gone era of what people used to call shrubbery... now just part of the rubbish strewn against the fences. When you saw rubbish actually stowed in those turd-brown vinyl garbage bags, likely as not they somehow ended up dumped out on the street. The raccoons ripped half of them open. Even here in the car Nestor got whiffs of the stench. Outside, boiling in a tropical sun, it was breathtaking. There were the fences—and there were the iron bars. In Overtown you didn't see a ground-floor window without bars over it. Nestor could see them right now on the black guys' hovel. There was trash strewn under the porch and up against the one side of it. After a while, the hovels began to seem like littered rubbish themselves. They were even smaller than casitas and in terrible condition. Almost all were painted white, and the white was by now grimy, cracked, chipped, peeling away.

The Sergeant must have been thinking along the same lines, as they waited for the other units to arrive and get into position, because apropos of nothing, he said, "You know, the problem in Overtown is . . . Overtown. The fucking people here—they just don't *do right*."

::::::Oh, Sarge, oh, Sarge! You got nothing to worry about with me, but one day . . . one day . . . you're gonna forget where you are and get yourself thrown off the force.::::::

The radio came alive. The three other units were in the immediate area. The Sergeant gave them their instructions. Nestor could feel his entire nervous system revving up again, revving up revving up revving up.

The Sergeant flipped up his sun visor, which held the big sun reflector in place on his side. "Okay, Nestor, take it off and throw it in the back." Nestor flipped up the visor on his side and seized the big screen, compressed it into its accordion folds, and put it behind his seat.

The Sergeant looked in his side mirror. "Okay, Nuñez and García are in the car behind us." Nestor could feel his nervous system revving revving revving revving up to be ready to attack other human beings without hesitation. That wasn't something you could *decide* to do when the moment came. You had to be—*already* decided... He couldn't have explained that to a living soul.

The Sergeant radioed to Command. Not even thirty seconds passed before Command responded with a Q, L, R. "Off we go, Nestor," the Sergeant said matter-of-factly, "and we're out fast. When we get there, the big guy is yours. Me and the little guy don't exist. All you got to do is immobilize that big cózzucca."

Sergeant Hernandez drove the Assist slowly and quietly the two blocks to the dope den and the two black crack retailers. He stopped right in front of them, opened the car door suddenly and furiously, and vaulted the dope den's cyclone fence and landed on his feet in front of the porch and the two black men—did it all so fast, Nestor had the impression that it was a gymnastic stunt he had practiced. ::::::What can *I* do?! He's a foot taller than I am! But I *must!*:::::: There was no decision to make. Decision? Coming out of the passenger door and heading around the front of the car...three and a half, four steps to the fence. He took off the way you would in a sprint, leaped for the top bar—*got it*—Rodriguez's gym!—*vaulted* his five-foot-seven self over the fence—*made it.* He landed awkwardly but thank God he didn't fall. Presence was *everything* in these confrontations. He gave the two black men the Cop Look. The Cop Look had a simple message: *I rule*... me and the golden badge gleaming against the dark blue of my T-shirt and the revolver in the holster on my belt...check it out...This is our style, the style of *we who rule*...all the while using the Cop Look like a ray.

The two black men reacted the way small-timers at this, the bottom-most link in the drug chain, the neighborhood retailer, always reacted: *If we move, they'll think we've got something to hide. All we have to do is be cool.* The skinny one slumped back slightly in his wooden chair, staring all the while at the Sergeant, who was right in front of him, no more than three feet away. The bigger one was still leaning back against the front wall. There was a barred window between him and the front door.

The Sergeant was already talking to the one in the chair: "Whatta you guys doing out here?"

Silence... Then the small man narrowed his eyes in what was no doubt intended as a cool expression in the face of a threat, and said, "Nothing."

"Nothing?" said the Sergeant. "You got a job?"

Silence... narrowed eyes... "I got laid off."

"Laid off from what?"

Silence... still more of a slump back into the chair... narrowed eyes... *very* cool... "From where I was working."

The Sergeant cocked his head slightly, stuck his tongue into his cheek for a moment, and indulged in a favorite form of cop mockery, namely, repeating some evasive roach's own words, deadpan: "You got laid off from working... where you were working." Now the Sergeant just stared at him with his head still cocked. Then he said, "We received some complaints..." He motioned with his head in a slight arc, as if to suggest the complaints came from the neighborhood. "They say you're doing some work... *here.*"

Nestor saw the big one edging ever so slowly toward the barred window, which also meant toward the door, which remained slightly ajar. The Sergeant must have noticed it, too, out of the corner of his eye, because he turned his head slightly toward Nestor and said out of the side of his mouth, *"Manténla abierta."*

Those two words instantly lit up an entire network of deductions . . . and Nestor was expected to comprehend it all instantly. First, every Cuban cop knew that speaking Spanish to each other in front of black people in Overtown or Liberty City made them paranoid . . . followed by infuriated. In the *insusurro* campaign, all Latin cops, and especially Cuban, were told not to do it unless it was absolutely necessary. So the Sergeant's very choice of language was an alarm. *Manténla abierta* meant keep it open. What was it that was open? Only one thing of any obvious importance: the front door—toward which the big man was edging. And why was that important? Not merely to make it easier to enter the house and search it—but also to make it legal. They had no search warrant. They could enter legally only if one of two situations arose. One was, if they were invited in. This occurred surprisingly often. If a cop said, "Mind if we look around?" the amateur sinner was likely to say to himself, "If I say 'Yes, I do mind,' they'll take that as a sign of guilt." So the sinner says, "No, I don't mind," even when he knows the evidence the cops are looking for is right out in the open. The other legal way was "in hot pursuit." If a suspect ran through a door into his house to elude the cops, the cops could follow him through the door into the house . . . in hot pursuit—but only if the door was open. If it was closed, the cops couldn't force it open, couldn't break in—without a warrant. *"Manténla abierta"*—two words only. "Nestor, don't let that big cózzucca close that front door." *Cózzucca* was the way many Latins, even those fluent in English, pronounced "cocksucker." *Cózzucca* was the way the Sergeant himself pronounced it. Nestor heard him. He had said it aloud two minutes ago. *Cózzucca* lit up in the great chain of cop logic.

"So why don't you tell me what kind of work you do here."

Silence. All that turned on in the one second before the skinny one said, "I 'unno. Ain't no work. I'm just sitting here."

"Just sitting here?" asked the Sergeant. "What if I told you some cózzucca just gave you five dollars for a little package." He put his forefinger near his thumb to show how small it was. "Whattaya call that? You don't call that work?"

The moment the big man saw the Sergeant's finger charade of the drug sale, he began moving crabwise in front of the bars on the window, toward the door. Nestor moved with him from three feet away. The moment the Sergeant said the words "call that work," the big man bolted for the door. Nestor sprang onto the porch after him, yelling, "STOP!" *¡Manténla abierta!* The big man reached the door before Nestor could stop him. But he was so big, he had to open the door another two feet just to get through it. Nestor lunges for the doorjamb . . . manages to get his foot between the frame and the door just as the big man tries to slam it shut. Hurts like hell! . . . not wearing good cop shoes with a leather sole but CST sneakers. The big man kicks at Nestor's toe, then tries to stomp on it. An adrenal wave sweeps through Nestor's body. Nestor has the willpower the willpower the willpower the willpower, and he gains about three inches—just enough to use his lungs to yell, "Miami Police! Show me your hands! Show me your hands!" All at once the resistance on the other side of the door—no longer exists! Nestor finds himself hurtling forward—the *eyes!*—he sees all these *eyes!*—in the dark and tubercular blue glow of a TV set in the millisecond before he lands sprawling on the floor. ::::::Where's the big guy? I'm inside the house, completely vulnerable. In the time it takes me to get back on my feet, if the big guy has a gun—what is this?—can't see a goddamn thing! . . . It's these $29.95 CVS Cuban cop supremo darkest shades with the gold bar . . . plunged from the sun outside to here in the dark—they've covered the windows so nobody can see in—damned Cuban cop shades! I'm *in* and I still can't see; I'm practically blind.:::::: He starts scrambling to his feet . . . The moment lengthens lengthens l e n g t h e n s for an eternity, but his motor responses are paralyzed paralyzed p a r a l y z e d . . . all he can see are eyes eyes eyes e y e s . . . and the tubercular glow! He's on his feet—the eyes—what the hell is *that?* Jesus Christ! It's a *white* face! Not just a light-skinned black woman but pure *white!* . . . holding a black child she is . . . ::::::what the hell *is* this place?::::::

—and all of that rushed through his head in the less than two seconds since he came hurtling through the contested doorway—and he *still* can't find that black hulk he was after—::::::I'm nothing but a big fat target now . . . no shield but my authority . . . *I am a cop*:::::: starts bellowing, "MIAMI POLICE! SHOW ME YOUR HANDS! SHOW ME"

—four seconds—

"YOUR HANDS!" . . . Babies start crying—Jesus Christ! *Babies!* . . . Off to one side, four or five feet away: a tan-faced boy and girl, six or seven years old ::::::I can't *see* them:::::: scared to death, holding the palms of their hands up before him . . . obediently! WE SHOW YOU OUR HANDS! . . . Babies crying! Almost directly ahead a big momma holding a bawling baby . . . a momma?—a bawling baby?—in a dope den? Look at her!—sitting down holding the baby, but that doesn't obscure her bulging belly . . . too much for the too-tight jeans she should have never even looked at . . . gray hair frizzed out in some kind of wannabe-young 'do . . . big jowls, deep lines in her face . . . belligerent: "Whatchoo trying to do to my son? *You people*—he ain't done nothing! He ain't never spent a day in jail, and you—"

—six seconds—

"come in here—" She begins shaking her head in disgust . . . Jesus Christ, this ain't a dope den, it's a goddamned nursery! A small room it is, a hovel of a room, filthy . . . no light . . . the windows are blocked . . . two plates on the floor, bits of food left on them, abandoned . . . a girl about ten squatting over another plate . . . Jesus, they eat on the floor . . . got next to no furniture . . . one small couch against the back wall with a fat boy cowering on it with wide eyes . . . an old wooden table in the back and a TV set somewhere over *here* glowing like it's radioactive . . . Shit! Nestor hears a low voice saying, "Fuck the cops . . . ram the bastards . . . your call,"

—eight seconds—

"dude . . . He whack you . . . or you whack him, the motherfucker" . . . followed by the squeal of tires and a loud crash . . . broken glass tinkling on the pavement . . . "Take that, pigs" . . . all the words in a low voice, however . . . Nestor swings his head toward that part of the room . . . the tubercular blue glare of a television set . . . two boys, eleven or twelve years old, maybe thirteen or fourteen . . . Nestor advances toward them... "MIAMI POLICE! SHOW ME YOUR HANDS!"... Wait a minute, brickhead! The two black kids aren't even intimidated... the blue glow of the TV screen lights up their young faces in the sickliest conceivable way... The low voice again, like somebody having a conversation in the background... "Up yours, you"

—eleven seconds—

"fatass cops! Gon' come out through your fucking nose!" Nestor gets a look at the screen... a title comes up: "Grand Theft Auto Overtown"... "Grand Theft Auto *Overtown?*"... heard of Grand Theft Auto, video game... but what the fuck? This *is* Overtown!... There is this fucking world in which Overtown has heroes!—brave hell-driving men who don't give a shit about you cops and all your so-called authority! Fuck *you,* Officer! Up *yours,* Officer! And these two children—they're ready! Some Cuban cop comes in with a badge hanging around his neck and his supremo darkest shades and a holster on his belt, screaming, "Miami Police! Show me your hands!" and so what are *they* supposed to do—cringe?—grovel?—beg for mercy? Hell, no. They're going right back to Grand Theft Auto Overtown. Some people recognize Overtown for what it is... a place where dudes got heart... and tell the fucking foreign invaders to go fuck themselves. Whoever made this game knew that much. They say right there on the screen when we show we got heart, you fucking Spanishit motherfuckers! Grand Theft Auto Overtown!

—fourteen seconds—

Another momma! She's sitting on the floor with a terrified little girl... looks too old to still be sucking her thumb, but she's sucking it for all she's worth... This momma's not fat at all. She looks broad-shouldered and rangy... gray hair pulled back on the sides... but she *hates* the occupying forces... What *is* this place?... Who the fuck ever raided a drug den that's all women and children?... and crying babies!... and resentful children so contemptuous of you and your *authority,* they're playing Grand Theft Auto Overtown Fuck the Cops right in your face... eyes and eyes and eyes—and over *there*—the pure white face again—a young woman—afraid—

—eighteen seconds—

Voice behind him back at the door yelling, "MIAMI POLICE! SHOW ME YOUR HANDS!" It's Sergeant Hernandez, charging into the hovel behind him as backup... Must have turned the skinny light-skinned kid over to Nuñez... Sergeant Hernandez shouts, "Nestor, *¿tienes el grueso? ¿Localizaste al grueso?*" (Did you find the heavyset one?)

"*¡No!*" said Nestor. "*¡Mira a detrás de la casa,*

Sargento!" (Keep an eye on the back of the house, Sergeant!)

"Speak English, damn you!" It's the big momma. She's on her feet, still holding the baby, which is bawling its head off. She's built like an oil burner, the big woman. She's had enough. She's not gonna put up with your army of occupation any longer. "You don't come in my house jabbering like a bunch a baboons!"

"This is your house?" roared the Sergeant.

"Yeah, it's *my* house—and it's—"

"What's your name?"

"—these people's house." She swung her hand about as if to include everybody in the room. "It's the co-mmunity's—"

—thirty seconds—

"What's your *name?*" said the Sergeant. He was boring his most intensive Cop Look squarely between her eyes.

But the big momma played it tough. "What business 'at s'pose be a yo's?"

"S'pose a be you and yo' big mouth, Momma, are under arrest! Everybody in this room is under arrest! You're selling drugs outta here!"

"Selling *druuuuuugs,*" said the big momma with ultimate mockery. "This is a co-mmunity center, man"—and the baby in her arms went off on another wailing jag.

From behind: "MIAMI POLICE! NOBODY MOVES!" and *"Miami Police! Nobody moves!"* sounded out in a curious atonal harmony. It was Nuñez and García, coming in through the front door. Two more babies started wailing, making three in all. It was damned disorienting. Here was stern Sergeant Jorge Hernandez's big baritone voice saying, "You're under arrest! You're selling drugs!" And a choral response of wailing babies, sometimes three, sometimes two . . . when one of the trio goes into a terrifying paroxysmal silence—seconds go by—will she ever come out of it or will her little lungs burst? . . . and then she comes out of it—fully recharged—screaming bloody infanticide . . . How do you deal with an opera like this? How do you snap everybody to cop-style attention in a dark little room full of bigmouth mommas cradling tiny howling tantrums in their arms?

Whuhhh—Nestor sees the table in the back of the room rising up four or five inches on one side . . . *ping a ping a ping ping,* knives and forks and spoons, sliding off onto the floor . . . The Sergeant sees it, too . . . springs toward it . . . Nestor springs toward it from the other side . . . Bursting out from underneath it—it's that big sonofabitch rising up like a monster . . . "Police! FREEZE, YOU PIECE A SHIT!" bellows the Sergeant . . . The hulk hesitates an instant to size up the threat . . . he's seeing red . . . makes a move toward the

Sergeant... to squeeze him like a bug... the Sergeant unsnaps the flap over his holster with his forefinger—*No, Sarge!*—too late! The giant's on top of him, going for his throat... the gun—*useless*—the Sergeant's clawing with both hands trying to pry loose the huge fingers around his neck. Nestor hurls himself *WHOMP* onto the giant's back. The man is *huge,* he's powerful, he outweighs Nestor by close to a hundred pounds... Nestor wraps his legs around the giant's abdomen and locks his ankles together... He must feel like a little amok monkey to the giant, who lifts his arms to reach behind his shoulders and swat this nuisance away... frees the Sergeant from being throttled just long enough to begin drawing the gun from the holster... "*No, Sarge!*" says Nestor—thrusts both his arms under the brute's armpits and clasps his hands together at the base of his skull... Oh, Nestor remembers very well!... in high school wrestling this was known as a "full nelson"... *illegal* because if you pressed down on the base of the skull, you might break your opponent's neck... Oh, does he remember!... the leg lock was known as a "figure four"... the nelson and the figure four—*ride* him!—ride that sonofabitch until he can't move anymore!... force the bastard's head and neck down until he wants to beg for mercy—but can't get words out because of his constricted throat... "Unnnngggggh... unnnngggghh"... trying desperately to pry Nestor's hands off the back of his head...getting nowhere...Nestor and his Rodriguez's Gym rope-climbing arms. The giant can't stand the pain...*Unnnngggghhhheeeee!*... *Unnnnnngggggghhhhhheeeeeee!*...Nestor feels himself going over backward...the giant's propelling himself backward to bodyslam his little tormentor... crush him by making him hit the floor under all that weight...they're both keeling over...Nestor uses his leg lock to torque the giant's body...they crash to the floor...not the big one on top of the little one but side by side. The giant rolls over, trying to flatten Nestor with his great weight *crackle* but every time he rolls over *crackle* Nestor still has a leg lock on him. The giant rolls and rolls *crackle crackle,* he *crackles* every time he rolls facedown on his abdomen...rolls over onto his belly *crackle* with the little monkey on top, the little monkey stays locked upon his back and 'bout like to break his neck—"Sarge, no!" Sergeant Hernandez is free and on his feet, gun drawn, trying to get a clean shot at the giant...too much rolling and writhing. ::::::Which one is he gonna end up hitting?:::::: "No, Sarge, don't! I've got him!"...The full nelson has the giant's head keeled over toward his chest...His moans are escalating into screams *uuunnngohohohohOGHOHHHH!*...one last strangled scream and all at once he's just a great sack of fat—he's struggling...the giant is gasping...trying to suck air...starts thrashing his legs...tries to launch his great thighs, as if that's going to break the grip of Nestor's figure four leg lock. Big mistake... used up every last pocket of air in his lungs... rasping sounds, rasping sounds... pathetic heaves and whimpers... struggling for oxygen... Nestor's able to force the great bull's skull down as far as his own arms will go... The giant's eyes are glassy, his mouth is wide open... he sounds like a huge dying creature... Good! "Let's roll, motherfucker!" he shouts into the brute's ear and presses down even harder on his neck... the bull attempts to roll once more to get some kind of relief... Nestor lets him roll *crackle* until his already bloody face is mashed once more into the floor... and he gives up all hope—*slummmp*—all muscular contraction is gone from his body. He goes slack... he's finished... he can't do anything but lie on the floor with his lungs forcing dying sounds up from his gullet in their struggle for air.

"Okay, you *uhhh* stu-pid *uhhh uhhh uhhh,*" says Nestor, who is out of breath himself. Oh, how ardently he wanted to say *pussy!*—to announce to the entire room his male elation over turning a 250-pound man into a helpless pussy!... He stops himself on the very edge of the cliff—but then takes the plunge: "You stupid *pussy!* If I *uhhh* let you *uhhh* up *uhhh* you gon' be *uhhh* good *uhhh uhhh uhhh*—good boy?"

The giant grunts. He can no longer make a sound.

Nestor releases his clasped hands from behind the man's skull and looks about for the first time. The Sergeant is standing over him, smiling... but with a smile that says, "That's great—and I think maybe you've lost your mind." That was how Nestor read it. He struggled to sound calm and speak in a low, slow voice. "Sarge... *unhh*... tell Hector to get me some *uhhh* wrist ties... I *uhhh*... I don't *uhh* believe *uhh* this *uhhh uhhh uhhh uhhh* bastard will keep his word."

Hector Nuñez came in with the wrist ties, and they bound the giant's wrists together behind his back... He just lay there... He didn't move at all, aside from his chest heaving as his lungs struggled to replenish their oxygen supply... Nestor was now on his feet. He, Nuñez, and the Sergeant stood over their great beached whale.

"Sarge, let's roll him over," said Nestor. "Did you hear that kind of *crackling* sound every time he rolled?" He hadn't. "I heard it every time we rolled over and he was on the bottom, Sarge. It was like he had something on his belly or chest and it made this crackling noise."

So they rolled the man over until he was on his back. The guy was so massive and at the same time so out of it, it took all three of them to do it. It was like trying to roll a 300-pound sack of cement over. His eyes opened once, and he looked at them blearily. His face was absolutely expressionless. The only part of it that worked was his mouth. He kept it open under orders from his lungs. He made a sawing sound somewhere deep in his throat.

"You see something weird?" said the Sergeant.

"What, Sarge?"

"He's got his T-shirt tucked in. Look at him. That's the first dirtbag I've seen in Overtown with his shirt tucked in in five years, maybe ten."

"There's something under it," said Nuñez. "It's like sort of... lumps or something."

Nuñez and Nestor leaned over the man and began pulling the T-shirt out of his pants. His belly was so big and his chest was heaving so much, and his T-shirt was tucked so far down his pants—pulling it out was a job and a half. The man was finally coming around. His breathing had calmed down from mortal panic to mere frantic fear.

"Muhhfuggghh," he kept saying, "you muhhfugghh." He looked up at Nestor out of the corner of his eye. With that one cocked eye he fired some death rays and began muttering. "One day caughtchoo... oughta... slaughter... torture..." was the way Nestor heard it. Nestor felt himself consumed by something he had never felt before... the urge to kill... *kill*... He sank to his knees by the brute's head and looked into his red-mad eyes and said in a low voice, "Say *what,* bitch? Say *what?*" With that, he pressed his forearm and elbow down on the brute's jawbone and kept increasing the pressure until he felt the brute's teeth cutting into the cheek that enclosed them. "Say *what,* you filthy little bitch? Gon' do *what?*"—bearing down until the man began to contort his face in pain—

A hand shook his shoulder. "Nestor! For Christ's sake, that's enough!" It was the Sergeant.

A wave of guilt... Nestor realized for the first time that he could find exhilaration in inflicting pain. No such feeling had ever possessed him before.

When they finally got the shirt out, they saw fragments of something. Nestor's immediate thought was that the brute had a cheap piece of yellowish chinaware under his T-shirt... and it had shattered and crumbled... but why innanameagod would he have hidden *that?* On closer inspection, it looked more like a big sheet of peanut brittle that had begun to crack and crumble.

"I'll be damned," said the Sergeant. He gave a weary chuckle. "I never saw anybody try to hide it on his belly. You guys know what that is?" Nestor and Nuñez looked at the crumbling whatever it was and then at the Sergeant. "That's a sheet of crack... yeah... The supplier mixes the shit into some kind of a, like, batter... and rolls it into a sheet like that and bakes it, kind of like pastry or something. They sell it to meatheads like the ones we got here. They cut them into rocks they call 'em, and sell 'em for ten dollars apiece. So that big dipshit's got maybe thirty thousand dollars' worth a crack lying there on his belly. They could sell all those bits and pieces where it broke, too. Hell, they could sell those little crumbs. By the time a crackhead needs another rock, he ain't very discriminating."

"But why would he stash it on his belly, Sarge, under a T-shirt?"

"Don't you see what happened?" said the Sergeant. "He's out on the porch, and all of a sudden here come the cops. So he makes a run for it. He wants to grab that sheet a crack and hide it or just get rid of it. It was probably lying right out in the open on that table back there, the one we saw moving. He's grabbed the sheet a crack and hidden under the table and stuck the crack under the T-shirt and stuffed the front of the T-shirt down his jeans. The first chance he has, he's gonna make a run for it out the back door and get rid a the crack any way he can, so even if he gets caught he won't get caught with the stuff on him. But he's a hothead, this jigaboo is, and he's a big dick who ain't gonna take no shit off nobody. So when I call him a piece a shit, the big dick in him's bigger than his common sense, assuming he has any, and all he wants to do is tear my arms off and shove 'em up my ass. I was on the way to ventilating him when Nestor here jumped on his back."

"How the hell did you do that?" said Nuñez. "This side a beef is twice your size."

Music *music* MUSIC to Nestor's ears! "I didn't do *any*thing," said this paragon of masculinity with becoming nonchalance. "All I had to do was, you know, *neutralize* him for thirty seconds, and he'd do the rest himself."

The heaving, sawing noise was still coming out of his throat . . . Bloody murder was oozing out of his eyeballs . . . His hatred of the Cuban invaders was now cold-cast forever in concrete. His mind would never change on that score. He had been humiliated by a Cuban cop half his size . . . and then this Cuban cop and another one rub it in by calling him a *piece of shit* and variations of a *piece of shit*.

"Where's the other fucker, Sarge, the skinny one with the mustache?" said Nestor.

The Sergeant looked back at the door from the porch, the door they had all come in. "García's got him. He's right back there in the doorway, him and Ramirez. Ramirez caught the piece a shit who made the buy, the crackhead."

"He did? Where?"

"Found him lying in the alley, wriggling around in the trash trying to dig the rock out of his pocket."

Nestor could now see that six CST cops were here inside the hovel, making sure all witnesses and possible perpetrators stayed put. The three babies were still wailing away... *The white face*... Nestor sought her out in the dimness of the room... and found her with his eyes... her white face and the black baby in her arms... squalling away... He couldn't see her very well, but he could make out her big, wide-open—frightened?—eyes set in a white face that didn't belong here... in a trash-littered bottom-dog dope den in Overtown... It was a dope den, all right, a retail outlet for the crack cocaine trade. It was hard to take that seriously, with all the women and children and bawling babies, but maybe his great victory, demolishing the monster, looked just as unreal and lightweight to them, to her, the one with the white face...

Now began the usual procedure... talking to the prisoners and the witnesses... by themselves, one-on-one, beyond the hearing of the others. A lucky, or canny, CST officer could get good, usable information that way. But you were also looking for inconsistencies in their stories... Why are you here? Where did you come here from? How did you get here? Do you know anybody else in the room? Do you know the two guys in the white baseball caps? No? Well, do you know what they do here? No? Then whose house do you think this is? No idea? Is that so? You mean you just like to drop in on houses-you-don't-know-who-the-owner-is, you don't know what goes on there, you don't know any of the other visitors there? Then Heaven sent you? Or you heard voices? An unseen hand guided you? It's all genetic?...and so forth.

Two cops positioned themselves outside, one in front and one in back, in case some upset denizen of the dope den managed to slip out of the hovel and make a run for it.

Then the questioning began. The Sergeant and Nuñez removed the sheet of crack and its fragments from the giant's belly. His full weight was on his arms, which were bound together at the wrists. He started to complain, and the Sergeant said to him, "Shut your filthy mouth, pussy. You're nothing. You're my pussy. You wanted to *kill* me, pussy? You wanted to choke me to death? We gonna see about who chokes who. Let's shove shit up yo' ass until it's coming outcho mouth. You pussy faggot. He wants to kill a cop—and he's a three-hundred-pound sack a shit-filled faggot."

With groans of exertion, Nuñez and the Sergeant lifted the huge man up into a sitting position. "I didn't know sacks a shit weighed this much," said the Sergeant. "Okay, what's your name?"

The man looked the Sergeant in the eye with molten hatred for a half a second, then lowered his head and said nothing.

"Look, I know you got shit for brains. You were born stupid. Face it. You were going *ooonga ooonga*

ooonga!" The Sergeant lifted his shoulders and curled his fingers up under his armpits in a semaphore for an ape. "But you learned a thing or two since then, ain'tcha? By now you've grown up into a real sub-moron. That's a big improvement, but you're so god-damned dumb, you wouldn't know what a moron is, let alone a *sub*-moron. Right?" The giant had his eyes closed and his chin hung down over his collarbone. "From now on, every time you get up in the morning, I want you to go to the mirror—you know what a mirror is? Or do you have mirrors in the jungle?—I want you to go to the mirror and say, 'Good morning, Shit-Faced Asshole.' You know what *morning* means? You got any fucking idea—about *anything?*—any fucking thing at all, dumb ass? You know what *dumb* means? You *look* at me, stupid! I'm asking you a question! What's your fucking *name?* Do you *have* a name? Or are you so dumb, dummy, that you can't fucking remember? You're in deep shit, shitfabrains. We found enough crack on your big fat belly to put you away for three consecutive life terms. You're gonna spend the rest of your fucking life with subhumans as dumb as you are. Some'um got no brains at all. But I think you got one, or half a one. Count to ten for me." The prisoner remained as dejected and slumped over as before. "Okay, I'll give you a hint. It starts with *one.* Okay, then, count to three. You know about *three,* don't you? It comes after *one* and *two.* Now count to three for me. You don' wanna cooperate? Then rot, you fucking animal!"

"Sarge," said Nuñez. "Let me talk to him, okay? Take a break, Sarge. Go chill. Okay?"

The Sergeant shook his head wearily. "Okay. But remember one thing. This asshole tried to kill me." Then he walked away.

Nestor headed straight for the white girl... *¡Coño!*—it was dark in this room, with all the windows blocked the way they were. But the girl's face was so white, she stood out in the gloom like an angel. He was absolutely intrigued—which made him conscious of how sopping wet with sweat he was. He tried to clear the sweat from his face with his hand. All that did was give him a sweat-wet palm, too. The worst of it was his T-shirt. It was drenched...and being too tight to begin with, it clung to his skin and made his whole torso look wet, which, in fact, it was. Could the girl stand being close enough to him to converse?—a concern that had next to nothing to do with the interrogation he was supposed to carry out. As he drew closer—that pure white face! She was as beautiful as Magdalena but in an entirely different way. Around men, Magdalena wore an expression that as much as said, "I know *exactly* what you're thinking. So let's start from there, okay?" This girl looked absolutely innocent and guileless, a clueless white madonna come to Overtown. She still had the black child—a girl, as it turned out—in her arms. The child was staring at Nestor with what?—wariness?—simple curiosity? At least she wasn't crying. She was a pretty thing—even while sucking on the nipple of a pacifier with a *swee-oooop glug swee-oooop glug* earnestness. Nestor gave her a smile that was supposed to say, "Suffer the little children to come unto me and forbid them not, for I am here on a friendly mission."

"I'm Officer Camacho," he said to the white-white madonna. "Sorry to be so..." He couldn't think of an acceptable adjective to indicate he *knew* what a sweaty mess he must look like. Even "wet" would sound... like, crude. So he lifted his hands chest high and turned his fingers inward toward his torso and added a helpless shrug. "...but we have to ask everyone who saw what happened a few questions. Why don't we go out on the porch?"

The girl began blinking a lot but said nothing. She nodded a tepid *yes* and followed Nestor out to the front porch, still holding the child.

Out here on the porch he saw her in the light for the first time. ::::::*¡Dios mío!* She's so *exótica!*:::::: He couldn't stop staring. He looked her up and down far faster than it takes to say so. Her skin was as white and smooth as a china plate—but her hair was black as black could be...well, straight, thick, shimmering, streaming down to her shoulders as luxuriantly as any *cubana*'s but black as black could be . . . and her eyes . . . staring at him wide-open with fright—and all the more gorgeous for that—and black as black could be . . . but in a china-white face. Her lips were delicate and curved in a certain mysterious way that Nestor thought of—for no good reason—as "French"—French perhaps but not red, more of an aubergine . . . no lipstick . . . she's totally innocent of makeup—but hold on! That's not really true, is it! He has just noticed the eye shadow. ::::::She's got the rims of her lower lids coated with it!—really makes her big eyes pop out! And don't tell me she's not aware of that . . . and hey, don't tell me she's not aware of how short her skirt is—or does it just *happen* to show off her lovely long legs, the kind they call lissome . . . what other white *americana* would *dare* turn up at a raggedy dope den in Overtown showing off a pair of lissomely alluring legs like that?:::::: . . . She doesn't look very daring at this moment, however. She keeps blinking blinking blinking blinking . . . She keeps her lips parted, because she's breathing fast . . . and with that her breasts rise and fall. They're beneath a shirt, Oxford cloth, which has a coarse weave, button-down, only the top button open on the shirtfront, which amounts to not even *trying* to be sensual—even hidden this well they look to Nestor like perfection, those breasts . . . and somehow, her obvious fear really moves the heart of Nestor . . . Nestor the Protector . . . He immediately felt toward her the way he had felt toward Magdalena the day he first met her on Calle Ocho. He was a cop and she was a damsel. He was a *chivalrous* cop—but still 100 percent cop in his core. Not that Magdalena had looked frightened for a second. Nevertheless, the feeling of being the strong chivalrous warrior overseeing the damsel was the same.

"What's your name?" he said.

"Ghislaine."

"*Jee-len*... how you spell that?"

"G, h, i, s, l, a, i, n, e."

"G, *H?*"

Ghislaine, with an *H,* nodded yes, and Nestor cast his eyes down, as if looking at the notes he had just taken, screwed his lips up, and shook his head in an ancient cop mannerism that says, "Life is hard already. So why do you *tontos* go to so much trouble to make it harder?"

At this point, to some punk he would have said, "You got a last name?" But in her case, the exotic Ghislaine's, he just said, "What's your last name?"

"Lon-te-ay," she said, or that was the way it sounded to him. She shielded her face from the sun with her hand.

"How do you spell that?"

Sweee-ooooop glug sweee-ooooop glug—rubber-suckled the child in her arms.

"L, a, n, t, i, e, r. It's French, like Bouvier."

::::::What's a bouvier? With my luck it'll be something *todo el mundo* was supposed to know about.::::::

But before he could ask that or anything else, this Ghislaine with the snow-white face said, "Am I... under arrest?" Her voice broke when she got to the "under arrest." Her lips trembled. She looked as if she might start crying.

Ahhh, the warrior felt very chivalrous now... a bit noble, even. "No, not at all," he said rather grandly. "It all depends on why you're here. That's what I need you to tell me. And let me tell *you* one thing: It's going to be better for you if you tell me the complete truth."

She looked up into his eyes with her big eyes and said, "I'm from South Beach Outreach."

South Beach Outreach... "What's South Beach Outreach?" he said.

"We're volunteers," she said. "We work with Children's Services. We try to help families in poor neighborhoods, especially children."

"*Fam*ilies?" said Nestor, in a tone of cop street wisdom. "This is a crack house. I see a lot a crackheads"—even as the words left his lips, he knew it was a gross exaggeration, said solely to impress this snow-white young thing—"and crackheads don't have families. They have habits, and they don't even *think* beyond that. *Fam*ilies?"

"Well, sir, you know more about this than I do,

but I think—this isn't the first time I've been here, and I know they have children, some of them, and they do care about them."

Nestor never got as far as the "than I do." He didn't hear a thing after "sir." *Sir?* He didn't want her calling him a *sir*. *Sir* meant she thought of him as remote and unapproachable and stuffy, the same way she would if he were a lot older than she was. But he couldn't very well tell her to call him Nestor, could he..."Officer" would be better than "sir," but how did you instruct her—or anybody—on that score without sounding like a protocol nut.

So he had to settle for "If that's a family, where's the mother?"

Tremulously: "Her mother's been in a drug-treatment facility at Easter Rock ever since she"—she looked down at the baby—"was born. You know Easter Rock?"

"Oh, yes," said Nestor. He knew it, and he was surprised. Easter Rock was an upscale rehab facility for upscale people. "How did she rate Easter Rock?"

"We—South Beach Outreach, I mean—intervened. They were getting ready to put her in a correctional facility for addicts."

"Whattaya mean, 'intervened'?"

"Mainly it was our president, Isabella de la Cruz. She knows a lot of people, I guess."

Even Nestor had heard of Isabella de la Cruz. Her husband, Paolo, had a big shipping business. Isabella de la Cruz was always popping up in the newspaper in those group pictures where everybody is lined up in a row grinning for what reason nobody knows.

"So where do you fit into all this?" said Nestor.

"I'm a volunteer," said Ghislaine Lantier. "We're assigned to . . . sort of . . . watch over children from *uhhh* . . . troubled families. I hate the word *dysfunctional.* A lot of the times the child, as in this case"—she glanced down at her little ward again—"is staying with a relative, usually a grandmother, but it could also be a foster home. She's with her grandmother, whom you've already met."

"You don't mean the big woman who kept telling the Sergeant he could shove—kept giving him a hard time . . ."

Ghislaine's tremulous lips wavered into half a smile. "I'm afraid so."

Nestor glanced into the dim dope den. There she was, about ten feet inside the door, the bigmouthed momma. In that gloom Nestor picked her out first by her Big Momma bulk. García was interrogating her . . . supposedly. You could tell she was doing all the talking. ::::::What's that thing she has in her hands? A fucking iPhone! This is supposed to be the most impoverished part of Miami—but everybody's got an iPhone.:::::: He turned back again.

"But Ghislaine, *you're* the one holding her, not the grandmomma with the mouth."

"Oh, I was just giving her a break. She also has two children of one of her daughters to look after. That makes five in all. My job is to check up a couple of times a week to make sure they're being taken care of, in different ways—supervision, attention, affection, compassion . . . *you* know . . ."

No, he didn't know. Nestor was intimidated by this Ghislaine's command of language. She could reel off words like *supervision, attention,* and whatever the rest of it was as if it were the most natural thing in the world. Magdalena was smart, but she couldn't talk like that. This girl also had little mannerisms in talking that intimidated Nestor because they sounded more *proper* than the way he would have said the same thing. She said "the child, *as in this case,*" instead of "like this one here." Or she said "whom." Who the hell said "whom" in Overtown? "With her grandmother, *whom you've already met,*" she said, instead of "who you met."

"Okay, you're a volunteer for South Beach Outreach. Do you live in South Beach?"

"I just happened to hear about it. I live in a dorm at the University of Miami."

"You're a student there?"

"Yes."

"Well, I'm going to need an actual address and a phone number, in case we have to get hold of you."

"Hold of me?" She looked as frightened as she had at first.

"This is a serious case," said Nestor. "We've already got three dirtbags under arrest in there." He motioned toward the interior of the hovel.

Ghislaine just stared at him . . . long pause . . . then, very timidly, "They're young. Maybe there's hope."

"You know what they were doing in there?"

Now she compressed her lips so hard you could no longer see them. All of her body language indicated that, yes, she had known what they were doing. So did the long pause . . . "We don't inquire about anything other than the children's needs and conditions. We don't pass judgment about anything else. If we did, we'd never—"

"*Needs* and *conditions?!*" said Nestor. He shot out a stiff arm and pointed to the interior of the hovel. "That's a *crack* house, for chrissake!"

"At least this way they're with their own flesh and blood. I think that's so important!" For the first time she had allowed her voice to rise. "Her grandmother"—she glanced down again at the child in her arms—"is in there, bad as the environment may be. Half brothers of hers are in there. Her *father* is in there, even though I'll admit he doesn't want to have anything to do with her."

"Her *father?*"

Ghislaine looked more frightened than ever. Once

more tremulously: "Yes... You just had a... a fight with him."

Nestor was speechless. "You—that piece a—flesh and blood?—you think—these—not a drop of morals in his body!—'totally lacking in affect,' as the DAs say—he's a goddamned *crack* dealer, Ghislaine! He'd just as soon yank her head off for the fun of it"—Nestor flicked a glance at the child—"as look at her! He's an *animal!* Holy Christ!"

Ghislaine lowered her head and began staring at the floor of the porch. She started swallowing her words and half-muttering. "I know... He's horrible... He's proud to be the progenitor of children, but he won't have anything to do with them... That's what women—he's so gross—he's a big huge—" She looked up at Nestor and said, "I couldn't believe it when you beat him—and so fast."

Music... did Nestor hear a strum of music?... the thrum of an overture? "These idiots may be 'huge,' but they're sub-morons," he said, quoting the Sergeant without attribution. "Only a sub-moron tries to roll in the dirt with a Miami cop," he said, modestly sprinkling praise over the entire force, not hogging it for himself. "We don't beat them. We let them beat themselves."

"Still—he must be twice your size."

Nestor studied her face. She was apparently utterly sincere. And she made music... she made music...

Here is what he'd say! *Sometime, when this is all over, I'd like to sit down with you and talk about this whole Children's Services business.* Take a chance! Don't hold back your emotions! *I can't believe anybody would let a big dirtbag like that anywhere near a child...*

...He'd say, *Why don't we go get a cup of coffee?* And she'd say, *That's a good idea...At South Beach Outreach we never have a chance to look at things from the Police Department's point of view. I've learned something important today. Criminology is one thing. But actually confronting crime where the rubber meets the road is very different. Subduing a man as big and strong as the one you just subdued—all the criminology in the world doesn't help at that point. At that point you either have it or you don't!*

Or something like that...and the music would build slowly, like an organ's to that chord at the crescendo that makes your rib cage vibrate.

10

The Super Bowl of the Art World

It was December, which in Miami Beach had only the most boring meteorological significance. Imagine a picture book with the same photograph on every page... every page... high noon beneath a flawless, cloudless bright blue sky... on every page... a tropical sun that turns those rare old birds, pedestrians, into stumpy, abstract black shadows on the sidewalk... on every page... unending views of the Atlantic Ocean, *unending* meaning that every couple of blocks, if you squint at a certain angle between the gleaming pinkish butter-colored condominium towers that wall off the shining sea from clueless gawkers who come to Miami Beach thinking they can just drive down to the shore and see the beaches and the indolent recliner & umbrella people and the lapping waves and the ocean sparkling and glistening and stretching out to the horizon in a perfect 180-degree arc... if you squint *just right,* every couple of blocks you can get a skinny, thin-as-a-ballpoint-refill, vertical glimpse of the ocean—*blip*—and it's gone... on every page... glimpse—*blip*—and it's gone... on every page... on every page...

However, at high noon, or 11:45 a.m., to be exact, on this particular December day, Magdalena and Norman were indoors... in the distinguished, if *itching-scratching,* company of Maurice Fleischmann, along with Marilynn Carr, his "A.A.," as he called her... short for art adviser. In fact, he had begun using that as her nickname... "Hey, A.A., come take a look at this"... or whatever. With dignity, insofar as that was possible, the four of them sought to keep their place in a line, more or less, less a line, in fact, and more like a scrimmage at an Iranian airline counter. Two hundred or so restless souls, most of them middle-aged men, eleven of whom had been pointed out to Magdalena as billionaires—*billionaires*—twelve, if you counted Maurice himself, were squirming like maggots over the prospect of what lay on the other side of an inch-thick glass wall just inside a small portal, Entrance D of the Miami Convention Center. The convention center took up an entire city block on Miami Beach. An ordinary person could walk past Entrance D every day for years and never be conscious of its existence. That was the whole point. Ordinary people *didn't* know and *musn't* know that billionaires and countless nine-digit millionaires were in there squirming like maggots... fifteen minutes before Miami Art Basel's moment of money and male combat. They all had an *urge.*

The maggots!... Once, when she was six or seven, Magdalena had come upon a little dead dog, a mutt, on a sidewalk in Hialeah. A regular hive of bugs was burrowing into a big gash in the dog's haunch—only these weren't exactly bugs. They looked more like worms, short, soft, deathly pale worms; and they were not in anything so orderly as a hive. They were a wriggling, slithering, writhing, squiggling, raveling, wrestling swarm of maggots rooting over and under one another in a heedless, literally headless, frenzy to get at the dead meat. She learned later that they were decephalized larvae. They *had* no heads. The frenzy was all they had. They didn't have five senses, they had one, the *urge,* and the *urge* was all they felt. They were utterly blind.

Just take a look at them!... the billionaires! They look like shoppers mobbed outside Macy's at midnight for the 40-percent–off After Christmas Sale. No, they don't look that good. They look older and grubbier and more washed out... the whole bunch are *americanos,* after all. They're wearing prewashed baggy-in-the-seat jeans, too-big T-shirts, too-big polo shirts hanging out at the bottom to make room for their bellies, too-tight khakis, ug-*lee* rumpled woolen ankle-high socks of rubber-mat black, paint-job green, and slop-mop maroon... and sneakers. Magdalena had never seen this many old men—practically all were middle-aged or older—wearing sneakers. Just look—*there* and *there* and over *there*—not just sneakers but real basketball shoes. And for what? They probably think all these teen togs make them look younger. Are they kidding? They just make their slumping backs and sloping shoulders and fat-sloppy bellies... and scoliotic spines and slanted-forward necks and low-slung jowls and stringy wattles... more obvious.

To tell the truth, Magdalena didn't particularly care about all that. She thought it was funny. Mainly, she was envious of A.A. This *americana* was pretty and young and, it almost went without saying, blond. Her clothes were sophisticated yet very simple... and very sexy... a perfectly plain, sensible, businesslike sleeveless black dress... but short... ended a foot above her knees and showed plenty of her fine fair thighs... made it seem like you were looking at *all* of her fine fair body. Oh, Magdalena didn't doubt for a second that she was sexier than this girl, had better breasts, better lips, better hair... long, full, lustrous dark hair as opposed to this *americana*'s sexless blond bob, copied from that English girl—what was her name?—Posh Spice... She just wished she had worn a minidress, too, to show off *her* bare legs... as opposed to these slim white pants that mainly showed off the deep cleft of her perfect little butt. But this "A.A." girl had something else, too. She was *in the know.* Advising rich people, like Fleischmann, about what very expensive art to buy was her business, and she knew all about this "fair." If somebody called it "Miami Art Basel," thinking that was the full name, she would inform him in some mostly polite way that it was officially Art Basel Miami Beach... and that those in the know didn't call it "Miami Art Basel" for short. No, they called it "Miami Basel." She could fire off sixty *in the know* cracks a minute.

At this very moment, A.A. was saying, "So I ask her—I ask her what she's interested in, and she says to me, 'I'm looking for something cutting-edge... like a Cy Twombly.' I'm thinking, 'A *Cy Twombly?*' Cy Twombly was cutting-edge in the nineteen *fifties!* He died a couple of years ago, I think it was, and most of his contemporaries are gone or on the way. You're not cutting-edge if your whole generation is dead or dying. You may be great. You may be iconic, the way Cy Twombly is, but you're *not cutting-edge.*"

She didn't address any of this to Magdalena. She never *looked* at her. Why waste attention, much less words, on some little nobody who probably didn't know anything anyway? The worst part of it was that she was right. Magdalena had never heard of Cy Twombly. She didn't know what *cutting-edge* meant, either, although she could sort of guess from the way A.A. used it. And what did *iconic* mean? She hadn't the faintest idea. She bet Norman didn't know, either, didn't understand the first thing Miss All-Business sexy A.A. had just said, but Norman created the sort of presence that made people think he knew *every*thing about *any*thing any*body* had to say.

Iconic was a word that was beginning to pop up all around them, now that there were just minutes to go before the magic hour, noon. The maggots were rooting amongst one another more anxiously.

Somewhere very nearby, a man with a high voice was saying, "Okay, maybe it isn't *iconic* Giacometti, but it's *great* Giacometti all the same, but no-o-o-o—" Magdalena recognized that voice. A hedge fund billionaire from Greenwich?—Stamford?—someplace in Connecticut, anyway. She remembered him from the BesJet party two nights ago.

And some woman was saying, "Koons'd *die* at auction right now!"

"—Hirst, if you ask me. He's high as a dead fish after fifteen minutes in the sun."

"—what you just said? Prince is the one who's tanked."

"—the fish that's up there at Stevie's, rotting its forty-million-dollar guts out?"

"—iconic, my ass."

"—svear, 'de-skilt' vas vot she said!" ("—swear, 'de-skilled' was what she said.") Magdalena knew that voice very well, from last night at the dinner party Michael du Glasse and his wife, Caroline Peyton-Soames, gave at Casa Tua. She even remembered his name, Heinrich von Hasse. He had made billions manufacturing... something about industrial robots?... was that what they said? Whatever else he did, he had spent so many millions buying art at Art Basel in Switzerland six months ago, people were talking about him at practically every party she and Norman and Maurice had been to.

"—about to see it! A measles outbreak, baby!"

"—and no time to kick the tires!"

"See it—like it—*buy* it! That's all you—"

"Art Basel in Basel?" That was A.A. piping up again. "Have you ever *been* to Basel? The only place worse is Helsinki. There's no place to eat! The food is not anywhere *near* as good as the food here. The fish tastes like it arrived in the backseat of a Honda, and the price—"

"—keep his hands off my adviser, for Christsake."

"—think you've got a fifteen-minute reserve, but five minutes later—"

"—the price is twice what it is here. And Basel's so-called historic hotels? I'll tell you what's historic—

the basins in the bathrooms! Aaaagh! They're that old kind. You know what I mean? You could have somebody scrub them day and night for a week, and they'd still look gray like somebody's old bedridden grandmother with bad breath. No shelf space and these old gray metal cups screwed into the wall they expect you to put your toothbrush in? You just—"

"I'm *what?*"

"—what I said. You're rude. Gimme your mother's phone number! I'm gonna tell her on you!"

"Whattaya gonna do—get Putin to slip an isotope into my cappuccino?"

As covertly as possible, Fleischmann lowered his hand to the crotch of his pants and tried to scratch the itch of his herpes pustules. He could never do it covertly enough to fool Magdalena, however. Every two minutes at least, Fleischmann shot one of his sixty-three-year-old *looks* at her...pregnant with meaning...and lust. Norman's diagnosis was that they were one and the same. The meaning *was*...lust. The very sight of a gorgeous girl like her was live pornography for a porn addict like Fleischmann...better than a strip club. Gross as they might be, Magdalena *loved* those looks. Those pregnant lustful looks she commanded from every sort of man—she *loved* it, *loved* it, *loved* it. First they looked at her face—Norman said her *knowing* lips insinuated ecstasy, even when she didn't have the faintest smile. Then they looked at her breasts—her somehow *perfect* breasts. She was aware of it *all the time!* Then she would see them searching her crotch... expecting to find *what,* in God's name?

All the old men in this wriggling infestation of maggots... if she cared to walk up and down and cock her hips before them... their riches... they'd *melt!* They dreamed of... depositing them into... *her.*

It was as if one of those storybook fairies children love so much had waved her wand over Miami... and—*Wanderflash!*—turned it into Miami Basel... The spell lasted no more than one week, one magical week every December... when the Miami Basel "art fair" went up in the Miami Convention Center... and swells from all over the United States, England, Europe, Japan, even Malaysia, even China, Hong Kong, and Taiwan, even South Africa, *todo el mundo,* came down from the sky in swarms of private planes... to buy expensive contemporary art... or to *see* the swells buying it... to immerse themselves in their mental atmosphere of art and money... to breathe the same air they did... in short, to be *where things are happening*... until the fairy waved her wand again a week later and—*Wanderflash!*—they disappeared... the art from all over the world, the private planes from all over the world, the swell people who had descended from the sky from all over the world, and—*poof!*—every trace of sophistication and worldliness was gone.

At this very moment, however, all these creatures remained under the fairy's spell.

Miami Basel wouldn't open to the public until the day after tomorrow...but to those *in the know,* those *on the inside,* Miami Basel had already been a riot of cocktail receptions, dinner parties, after-parties, covert cocaine huddles, inflamed catting around for going-on three days. Almost anywhere they were likely to enjoy a nice little status boost from the presence of celebrities—movie, music, TV, fashion, even sports celebrities—who knew nothing about art and didn't have time to care. All they wanted was to be... *where things were happening.* For them and for the insiders, Miami Basel would be over the moment the first foot of the first clueless member of the general public touched the premises.

Magdalena would have remained clueless herself without Maurice Fleischmann. She had never even heard of Miami Basel until Maurice invited her, along with Norman, to the fair...at Norman's prodding. Socializing with a patient was very much frowned upon in psychiatric practice. The psychiatrist's effectiveness depended in no small part upon his assuming a godly stance far above the patient's place in the world, no matter what it might be. The patient must be dependent upon his paid god, not the other way around. But Norman had Maurice mesmerized. He thought his "recovery" from his "disease" depended entirely upon Norman, in spite of the fact—or maybe because of the fact—that Norman kept telling him that he was not suffering from a disease but a weakness. For his part, Maurice felt rather special taking Norman around, because Norman was on television a lot and was seen by so many people in Miami as a celebrity. Nobody would suspect that Fleischmann was Norman's patient. They were two well-known men who traveled in the same circles, at the same altitude. What could be remarkable about that?

Every day Fleischmann and his driver, a little Ecuadorian named Felipe, had picked up Norman and Magdalena from the Lincoln Suites, after Norman's last appointment, in a big black Escalade SUV with dark-tinted windows. The first stop, the first day, was the insiders' opening event—a cocktail party known as Toffs at Twilight. A man named Roy Duroy staged that party every year at the hotel he owned, The Random, on Collins Avenue, not all that far south of the Lincoln Suites. The Random was a typical hotel of the much-touted South Beach Retro boom. A clever developer like Duroy would buy a small, crabbed hotel, eighty years old or more usually, give it a lick of paint and some in-room computer outlets, change the name from the Lido or the Surfside to something hip and flip like The Random, and pronounce it an Art Deco architectural gem. Now you had a small, crabbed *gem*. The rear of the property was its saving grace. It overlooked an inlet from the ocean. Duroy had put a lot of big umbrellas with magenta, white, and apple-green stripes out there. Very colorful, these umbrellas, and Toffs at Twilight was already going strong when Maurice, Norman, and Magdalena arrived. A hundred, two hundred Miami Basel insiders were crammed around tables under the umbrellas, drinking, or milling about between the umbrellas, drinking. Everybody was drinking and kicking up a noisy surf of big talk and *haw haw haw haw haws!* and *scream scream scream screams!*

What bowled Magdalena over was the stir Maurice's very presence created. Roy Duroy himself immediately rushed up and gave him a big bear hug. His flattery fluttered down on Maurice like rose petals. A big real estate developer named Burt Thornton—even Magdalena had seen him on TV and in the newspapers—rushed over and all but licked Maurice's alligator-hide moccasins. So many people came rushing over to Maurice, he stood there for an hour without moving six inches from where he first came upon the colorful umbrella-scape. Magdalena had always known that Maurice was a billionaire who had "influence." Nevertheless, what she had never been able to get out of her mind was Norman's photograph of Maurice's crotch rotting with herpes pustules. But now, at Toffs at Twilight, she was looking at a Maurice *el Grande*.

Meantime, Norman was sulking a bit. Nobody had recognized him so far. He had even given up his laughter*rrahHAHock hock hock* strategy for attracting attention. He groused to Magdalena that all Roy Duroy wanted was Maurice's backing for some out-to-lunch dream of turning The Random into a chain operation, and Burt Thornton just wanted Maurice to intervene to keep North Tryon Street Global from foreclosing on him for an enormous loan for a development that hadn't panned out.

The three of them got back into the big black Escalade and headed off to the High Hotel, also in South Beach, where BesJet, which leased private planes to corporations and the mighty rich, was having a cocktail reception...even louder this time, the roaring surf...the big talk, the *haw haw haw haws!* the *shriek shriek shriek shrieks!*...Magdalena was stunned. Across the room she spotted two movie stars, Leon Decapito and Kanyu Reade. No question about it! *Leon Decapito and Kanyu Reade!*—in the flesh! ::::::Leon Decapito and Kanyu Reade...and *me*... we're guests at the same cocktail party.::::::...But not even stars like them could have commanded more attention than BesJet gave Maurice. The president of BesJet rushed over to him, flashing every tooth he could squeeze into his grin. When they shook hands, the president clasped his left hand over their mingled fingers, as if sealing a vow. Five times he must have told Maurice that tomorrow the 170th BesJet flight heading specifically to Miami Basel would be landing. He no doubt knew Maurice had his own plane. He just wanted him to have the word, because in Miami, among all the nobs who could afford private flights, Maurice's seemed to be *the* word. Norman was growing positively glum. They went from the BesJet party to a swell, expensive restaurant called Casa Tua for a big dinner given by *Status,* the new magazine that had become very hot by ranking people in every area of life you could imagine.

No step over a threshold and through a door had ever given Magdalena such a status boost before... and no sooner did she step into the dining room, amid a hundred or more people, than she spotted the celebrated faces of Tara Heccuba Barker!...Luna Thermal!...Rad Packman!...She couldn't get over it. She was breathing the same air they were! But the *Status* people couldn't have made a bigger to-do over any of them than they did over Maurice. In his remarks, the editor in chief of *Status* mentioned Maurice *twice*...

Finally, after dinner, Norman got a break. A big moonfaced woman recognized him and brought over a couple of others, and soon Norman was the star of a big conversation cluster eager to hear the eminent Dr. Lewis go on about porn*nnahhHAHAHock hock hock* addiction. In no time eight or nine people were gathered around him.

Magdalena, standing next to Maurice, found herself engulfed, by default, in a conversation cluster consisting of Maurice and three of his courtiers, all middle-aged men. The only one Magdalena recognized was Burt Thornton, who popped up on TV a lot...some real estate fiasco...or something like that...The other two were Somebody Herman and Somebody Kershner. Maurice was holding forth on the pitfalls of "pyramided mortgage payments," which she gathered was Mr. Thornton's problem. She had never felt more out of place. She would have been afraid to utter a peep, even if she had known what on earth they were talking about. But she was even more afraid of leaving this cluster and trying her luck in a room full of old people now on their feet and getting ready to depart for one *what's happening* après-party party or another. A group of them stopped when they reached the Maurice Fleischmann cluster, and some man stepped up—"Maurice!"—and embraced him in the manly version of women's air kisses among social equals. They separated, and ::::::*¡Dios mío!* I've never seen such a gorgeous man in my life!:::::: Maurice began some rapid introductions. "Sergei, this is Burt Thornton...Burt, this is Sergei Korolyov."

"Ees my pleasure, Mr. Zornton."

"Oh, it's *my honor!*" said Burt Thornton.

Sergei Korolyov's European accent—was it Russian?—only made him more gorgeous to Magdalena.

He looked young, at least for this crowd—midthirties? He was as tall as a girl could ever hope for, and *built.* Men didn't come any handsomer, either. A square jaw, amazing blue eyes—and his hair was a thick light brown with some blond streaks, combed back in long waves. It was *romantic.* And so charming, the way he smiled and the tone of his voice as he greeted "Mr. Zornton" and made those three words, "Ees my pleasure," sound as if he actually meant it. Just before Maurice introduced him to Mr. Herman ::::::he glanced at me—and it didn't just *happen,* either!:::::: Just as he was introduced to Mr. Kershner ::::::he did it again! Now I *know* he means it!::::::

Maurice must have noticed it, too, because he said, "Oh, and Sergei, this is Magdalena Otero." The gorgeous man turned to Magdalena. He smiled the same politely charming smile. He reached out as if to shake hands—and bowed and lifted her hand and air-kissed the back of it and said, "Miss Otero." But when he stood up, he had added a slight insinuation to the smile, and he poured his eyes into hers for far too long—then left with his party. ::::::*¡Dios mío, mío, mío!*::::::

Magdalena whispered to Maurice, "Who *is* that?"

Maurice chuckled. "Someone who'd like to make friends with you, I gather." Then he filled her in.

Norman was happy, too. Now at last they realized who he was. What a lift! Such a lift that Norman was ready to roll to an after-party given by something called the Museum of the Instant, in the Design District, where a performance artist named Heidi Schlossel would be performing a piece of art called *De-fucked.* Everybody at the *Status* dinner was talking about it. Magdalena had never heard of the Museum of the Instant, the Design District, performance art, or performance artists, let alone one named Heidi Schlossel. Norman was only marginally better informed; he had heard of the Design District, although he didn't know where it was. Maurice, now a certified big shot at Miami Basel, was dying to go.

Magdalena took Norman aside. "This performance art thing—it's called *De-fucked.* We don't know what it is. Do you really want to risk taking"—she pointed behind her toward Maurice—"to something like that?"

"It's a museum," said Norman. "How bad could it be?"

Back into the Escalade...and off to the Design District, which seemed to be in an area of abandoned warehouses and small factories. The Instant Museum was a mess...and too small for all the Miami Basel insiders who flocked there...The only halfway-decent-sized gallery in the place had hundreds of worn-out black tires piled up against one wall. A jacklegged, unpainted wooden stanchion bore a sign:

NATIVE TRASH OF THE DAY

—Collection of the Instant Museum

A recorded rhythm track boomed out over a speaker system, *BOOMchilla BOOMchilla BOOMchilla BOOMchilla*... From behind a mound of filthy black tires steps a tall figure in black. She has chalky white skin... and long black hair that comes cascading down upon the puffed and pleated shoulders of the academic robe she has on, the kind you graduate in. But this one is voluminous. It sweeps down to the floor. She isn't smiling.

She stands there motionless, without a peep, for about thirty seconds. Presumably, this is Heidi Schlossel.

She brings her hands to her neck and undoes some sort of clasp. The robe falls from her shoulders suddenly, completely, *clump*. It must have weighed a ton.

Now she stood stark naked in front of a big puddle of heavy black cloth... rigid, erect. Her face was a blank... She looked like one of the undead in a horror movie... without a stitch on.

Magdalena whispered to Norman, "Let's leave— now!" She nodded toward Maurice. Norman just shook his head... No.

The stark naked woman appeared to be fifteen years too old and fifteen pounds too heavy to play this role, whatever it was. She began speaking in the dead voice of the undead. "Men have fucked me...they have fucked me, fucked me, fucked me over, over-fucked me—"...on and on with this I Was a Fucking Zombie poem—until all at once she inserted a thumb and two fingers into her vagina and pulled out a length of sausage and came alive, as it were, and cried out, "De-fucked!"—and out came another sausage linked to the first—"De-fucked!"—and another and another—"De-fucked!" and "De-fucked!" and "De-fucked!" and "De-fucked!" Magdalena couldn't believe how many link sausages the woman had managed to stuff inside her vaginal cavity!

Maurice had his hand clasped over his crotch. But instead of stroking it with his hand, he was rocking his body back and forth beneath his hand...so as not to be detected.

Magdalena nudged Norman and whispered on the loud side, "Maurice!" Norman ignored her. His eyes were fixed on Ms. Schlossel. So this time Magdalena didn't bother hiding it behind a whisper. "Norman! Look at Maurice!"

Norman glowered at her...but did look at Maurice. He just stared at first...calculating...calculating...then he let out a deep, self-denying sigh and put his arm around Maurice's shoulders...tenderly...and leaned close to him and said...in a voice you would use on a child..."We have to go now, Maurice."

Like an obedient child who knows he has disappointed his parents, Maurice let himself be led out of the Museum of the Instant.

Maurice was silent... and penitent... but Norman acted cross. He kept shaking his head from side to side, without looking at either one of them.

"What's wrong, Norman?" said Magdalena.

"There's supposed to be a great after-party at some gallery near here, the Linger, in Wynwood, wherever that is." He kept shaking his head. "But I guess that's out."

Later on, Magdalena asked around and was told that the Linger, a large gallery, wanted to show its "private collection" of photorealistic pornographic paintings, whatever *photorealistic* meant, and sculptures of homosexual orgies.

Why was there so much pornography in this so-called cutting-edge art? Magdalena wondered. For what earthly reason? How in God's name did they justify it?... And just who was more upset about not being able to see it all, the patient... or the doctor?

But by last night it was as if nothing had happened. Here were the three of them, Maurice, Norman, and herself, plunging into another round of parties and receptions before dinner... and dinner was really something last night. Michael du Glasse and his wife, Caroline Peyton-Soames, were the hosts. *Michael du Glasse* and *Caroline Peyton-Soames!*... the most glamorous couple in Hollywood, if you asked Magdalena... a dinner for a hundred people at the Ritz-Carlton... and Magdalena Otero, lately of Hialeah, was their guest... and for one sublime and unforgettable moment she had touched their right hands with hers.

In five minutes, presumably, a pair of doors in the glass wall would open, and these old men, these old maggots, would have first crack at the treasures that lay on the other side... Miami Basel!... For two hours these maggots, and these alone, would have the exclusive run of the whole place... whatever in the name of God "the whole place" was...

"—fuck *off*? *You* fuck off, you fat—"

"AhhggghHAHAHHHHock *hock hock hockdjou* see that big ox trying to slip between those two people? Got stuck between them*mmmaaagghHAHHHHock hock hock hock!* Couldn't get his belly through*ahhHock hock hock!*"

Maurice Fleischmann looked at Norman blankly. Then he looked around among his fellow squirming maggots to figure out what had made Norman erupt*ttock hock hock* like that. He couldn't. He was nonplussed. But Magdalena now understood. Norman cackled when he felt insecure, especially in the presence of people who made him feel defensive or inferior—Fleischmann, for one. It was a way of taking over from them in conversation. Anybody, even a real swell like Fleischmann, had to have a heart of stone not to manufacture a smile and a few chuckles and play along with a bighearted guy who's being swept away, convulsed, paralyzed by laughter over... God knows what. Why even bother with Fleischmann's conversation—when he already controlled Fleischmann's poor porn-mad mind? Why?—it all dawned on Magdalena. It was *very* important to Norman to keep his boat at a place like the Fisher Island Marina—but he didn't own any property there. Maurice Fleischmann made it happen. Or Norman's presence amidst the most important VIPs of *all* the VIPs of Miami Basel, the richest of the rich, the likeliest of the likely big spenders, the deepest of the plungers—all of them slithering over and underneath one another to get first crack at the wonders of ninety thousand square feet of art for sale. What was Norman doing here? Maurice Fleischmann made it happen.

Some sort of dustup at the very head of the line... the big ox *yakking* away, angrily, by the looks of him... a stack of tires—of fat—forming on the back of his neck every time his chin bobs up. ::::::Look at what he's wearing!... an ordinary white T-shirt, the kind that's meant to be underwear. Just look at him!... it's stretched over his swollen belly... making him look like one of those big plastic gym balls... it's hanging outside his jeans, a really gross pair of Big Boy BodiBilt jeans.::::::

Magdalena tapped Norman on the arm. "Norman—"

"Yeah, that's him," said Norman. "But wait a minute... This guy is too muuuuch*HahhhHAHAHock hock hock!*"

By the time he got to his cackle, Magdalena couldn't help but notice, he was no longer aiming his little performance in her direction, but Fleischmann's.

"A second ago the guy was trying to crash the line four or five places from the front... and *nowwwah-HHHHock hock hock* he *is* the front!"...

Fleischmann looks put out. He doesn't even feign a smile over Norman's cackle. He's worried. He sidles over and takes a look.

"Hey, A.A.," says Fleischmann, "come over here. Isn't that Flebetnikov?"

"Oh, yes," she says, "the very one." Fleischmann leaned close to A.A. and lowered his voice: "That bloated bastard. He knows I'm interested in the Doggses—and look at him. He's literally shoved people aside with his big sumo gut, and now he's right up against the door."

A.A. lowered her voice: "And therefore he's going after the Doggses himself? Don't you think—"

"He's got billions of dollars, and he's a Putin thug,

and 'Therefore, I'm gonna grab anything *you* want, just to show *you* you don't have a chance against me.' "

"Who is he?" said Norman.

Fleischmann clearly resented Norman's interrupting a confidential conversation. "Perhaps you've heard of Russian oligarchs." Then he turned back to A.A. and was saying, "Now, the only thing—"

It was the "perhaps" that got Norman. Was Fleischmann by any chance adopting the patient peevish tone one uses with dimwits? Norman wasn't going to put up with that for a moment.

"Heard *of* them?" he said. "Try heard *from* them *ahaaahhhHAHAHAHock hock hock!* Three different psychiatrists have brought me in as consultant with these characters. Have I *heard* of them*mmeeaaahHAAAHock hock hock!*"

Magdalena *knew* that was a lie.

"Well, I seriously doubt you ever consulted for one that obnoxious," Fleischmann said curtly, probably wondering how he had lost control of the conversation.

Without another word, Fleischmann walked away from Norman, over to a wall of the entryway, and took a cell phone out of an inside pocket of his jacket. He looked back to make sure that nobody could overhear him. He spoke to somebody for four or five minutes. When he returned to the group, he was in a better mood.

"Who'd you call, Maurice?" said Magdalena.

Fleischmann gave her a coy boy's flirtatious smile. "Wouldn't *you* like to know!"

At that moment the entire mob of maggots grew quiet. From out of nowhere a woman had appeared on the other side of the glass wall, a blond, bony, gristly *americana* trying to look young in a pair of Art World Black stovepipe pants and an Art World Black T-shirt with a deep V-neck. Thank God a Miami Basel STAFF ID was hanging from her neck. Mercifully, it covered part of the sternum bonescape where her cleavage was supposed to be. She unlocked the glass doors, put on a brittle smile, and gestured down the hall. The maggots remained silent, eerily so, as they began the big push through the doorway.

Flebetnikov *popped* through like an immense cork. He lost his footing for a moment in the hallway beyond and had to do a little hop to regain his balance. His great T-shirt-swathed belly pitched and yawed. He led the pack... with both elbows jutting out, as if to make sure no one passed him. Magdalena noticed for the first time that he was wearing what looked like basketball shoes. She looked down at Fleischmann's feet. He had on sneakers, too!... tan sneakers practically the same color as his poplin pants... not so obtrusive as the Russian's, but sneakers nonetheless... On! Into the Art World! Faster!

Now all four of them, Magdalena, Fleischmann, Norman, and A.A., squeezed through the door. The gristly woman in Art Black had wisely stepped back, out of the way of the pumped-up old men. It wasn't a stampede exactly... not some utter loss of control such as pushing... but Magdalena could feel the pressure... One man was so close behind her, she could hear him breathing stertorously near her ear. She was being swept along in a tide of old bones dying to get *in there,* whatever *there* was.

A little hallway opened up into the main exhibition hall. The place must have been the size of a city block all by itself... the ceiling was—what?—three stories high?—four stories?—all in darkness. The lights were below, like the lights of a city—the lights of incredibly long rows, streets, avenues, of booths—of galleries from all over Europe and Asia as well as the United States... must be hundreds of them! Art for sale! A gigantic bazaar... just lying there, spread out before these, the most important maggots... All theirs!... *See* it! *Like* it! *Buy* it!

The clump of frenzied old men began to break apart... they began to regain their voices, but all were drowned out by a bellowing voice just inside the entrance.

"Gedouda my vay, imbecile! I cromble you and your biece a baper!"

It was Flebetnikov, trying to maneuver his big belly past a security guard who stood between him and all the irresistible treasures beyond... The guard was in a dark blue-gray uniform with all sorts of cop-look-alike insignia on it, including a shiny badge. Magdalena knew the type at a glance... Not just any security guard, but a classic Florida redneck... thick buzz cut of reddish-blond hair... meaty, fleshy... huge forearms stuck out of his short-sleeved shirt like a pair of hams... In one hand he held an official-looking document up before Flebetnikov's face.

Flebetnikov swatted it aside and stuck his face directly into the redneck's and roared in his deepest voice, spraying spittle, "Now you gon' ged ouda my vay! You onderstond?" With that, he placed the heel of his hand against the redneck's chest, as if to say, "—and I mean it! You either get out of my way or I'll throw you out of my way!"

Big mistake. Faster than Magdalena would have thought he could move, the redneck bent the arm of the hand that touched him into some sort of hold that locked Flebetnikov up, his voice, his body, his soul. Not a peep out of him. He seemed to know instinctively that here was a good old country boy who would happily beat a fat Russian senseless and feed him to the hogs.

Magdalena turned toward Fleischmann and Norman—but they were no longer beside her. They were three or four feet ahead. Fleischmann nudged Norman in the ribs with his elbow, and they looked at each other and grinned. A.A. was ahead of them, walking at a terrific pace, heading presumably toward the Jeb Doggses to nail down the advantage, now that the security guard had terrified Flebetnikov and stopped him in his tracks.

Maggots were rooting and slithering all over the place with their advisers, scurrying toward the booths of their dreams. Over there!—a shoving match!... Looked like the two hedge fund managers—from someplace in Connecticut?—Fleischmann had pointed out... Even farther ahead of Magdalena now a *HahaHHHHock hock hock hock* cackle, and Norman's looking back at the two chubby little pugilists... but not Fleischmann. He and his A.A., Miss Carr, are all business, about to head into a booth. A big, hearty maggot—Magdalena remembered him from the line—comes up from the side, smiles, and says, "How's it going, Marilynn?" A.A. looks at him for a split second with a wary look that asks not *who* but *what* is this... creature?... attacking, assaulting her attention at a crucial moment like this? She ignores him.

Norman follows them into the booth and stands beside them... them, and a tall man with gray hair, although he doesn't look all that old, and eerie pale-gray eyes like the slanted eyes of a husky or whatever those dogs that pull sleds through the snow up near the Arctic Circle are called.

A.A. says, "You must know Harry Goshen, don't you, Maurice?"

"No, I'm afraid not," says Fleischmann. He turns to the man with the eerie eyes and gives him a chilly little smile, and they shake hands.

So pale, those eyes... they look ghostly and sinister... He wore a pale-gray suit, too, and a light-blue tie... the only man in a coat and tie Magdalena had seen all day... black shoes so highly polished, the crease between the toes and the arch of the foot shimmered. He had to be the owner of the gallery... or a salesman at the very least... Rich collectors, she had just seen, dressed in rags and sneakers.

Fleischmann and A.A. and Arctic-eyed Harry Goshen stood before a row of stout maple boxes, each three or so inches high and anywhere from nine to twenty-four inches long, unpainted, unstained, but lacquered with so many coats of clear lacquer, they screamed at you. This man Harry Goshen opened the lid of a big one... completely lined, lid and all, with chocolate-colored suede... and lifted out a big, round slab of transparent frosted glass, maybe two inches thick... you could tell by the strain on Harry Goshen's hands and arms and posture, the damned thing was heavy. He turned it at about a forty-five-degree angle... the translucent glass flooded with light and there, somehow carved deep into the glass... exquisitely carved, in the smoothest detail—

"Sort of, you know, Art Deco," A.A. said to Fleischmann.

—in bas-relief, a young woman with long curving locks—

A.A. was holding up some photograph. "Pretty much like him, don't you think?"

—and a young man with short curving locks... were fucking... and you could "see everything," as the saying goes, and "everything" was flooded with translucent light.

Norman was so excited, a foolish grin spread over his face, and he leaned way over to get the closest possible look at "everything." Fleischmann looked totally baffled. He kept switching his eyes from the pornographic carving to A.A.'s face and back to the glass and once more to A.A.'s face... *What am I* supposed *to think, A.A.?*

Pale-gray-eyed Goshen takes a round slab from another lacquered box... turns it until... *there!*... it becomes a man and woman... fornicating in a different way... another slab... anally... another... three figures, two women and one man, fornicating in an anatomically improbable combination... another... two women and two men... fornicating... fingers, tongues, mouths, whole forearms, disappearing into filthy places... Fleischmann now frantically looking from the light-flooded glass to Marilynn Carr... back and forth... Time is of the essence... *others* will be here any moment... Flebetnikov, to be specific... Magdalena moves closer... Fleischmann looks at his

A.A.... pleading... She turns her head ever so slightly, meaning no... Magdalena can hear her saying... in the lowest of voices, "Not iconic Doggs"... Another... fornicating... Fleischmann looking frantically at Marilynn Carr. Without a word she nods her head up and down ever so slowly... meaning yes!... Fleischmann immediately turns to the ghostly husky, who says in a ghostly low voice, "Three." Fleischmann turns to Marilynn Carr, looks at her desperately... She nods her head up and down slowly again... Desperately Fleischmann turns to the ghostly Goshen and mutters from deep in his throat, "Yes"... and Goshen pastes a red dot on the lacquered box containing the slab... Now looking back and forth so rapidly... whispering, giving signals desperately... Goshen says, "Two and a half." Fleischmann, hoarsely, "Yes"... another red dot on another lacquered box... Barely forty-five seconds have elapsed.

A bellow! A roar! Here he comes. Flebetnikov's T-shirt-upholstered hulk must have gotten loose. He's heading this way. He's furious; he's roaring in Russian, for somebody's benefit... then roars in English, "Anodder hole in his nose he vants, dad son ma bitch!"... Goshen acts as if he doesn't hear it or just doesn't care... No raging Russian is going to interrupt *this* streak! Flebetnikov growls and roars and vows to put yet *anodder* hole in the son ma bitch's nose. He's coming closer. Fleischmann seems calmer, but he still accelerates his mission . . . another red dot ("three and a half") . . . another red dot ("one") . . . red dots red dots red dots ("two," "four" for the orgy scene, dear God! . . . then "nine one seven"—) . . . all these red dots. ::::::That must be what they mean when they talk about the "measles.":::::::

If those numbers meant what Magdalena was beginning to believe they meant, Fleischmann had just spent 17 million dollars, or $17 million minus $83,000, assuming 917 meant $917,000, in less than fifteen minutes. And if Marilynn Carr, with her fair white thighs and English bob, got 10 percent from the seller, the ghostly husky, and 10 percent from the buyer, Fleischmann, she had just made $3,400,000 for herself, assuming Norman had explained the commissions accurately.

Flebetnikov's Russian roar was drawing closer and closer.

A.A. said to Fleischmann, "Why don't we get out of here? I *know* Flebetnikov. He's not a rational person."

For the first time since this whole thing began, Fleischmann smiled. "And miss all the fun?"

Fleischmann insisted on waiting for Flebetnikov. He stood right outside the entrance to the booth. A.A. looked very nervous. Fleischmann was suddenly the picture of happiness.

Flebetnikov arrived, roaring in Russian. A tall, dark, anxious-looking man was by his side.

"That's Lushnikin," A.A. whispered to Fleischmann. "He's the art adviser for most of the oligarchs."

Flebetnikov was growling like a bear. He roared at Lushnikin in Russian . . . something ending with "Goshen." For the first time he noticed Fleischmann. He appeared startled; also wary. Perhaps guilty?

"Comrade Flebetnikov!" boomed Fleischmann. "You interested in Doggs?" With his thumb he indicated the booth behind him. "I was, too. But all the good stuff is already gone. At Miami Basel you got to be fast. *See* it, *like* it, *buy* it."

From Flebetnikov's expression you couldn't tell whether he detected the sarcasm or not. He blinked. He looked bewildered. Without another word he turned and entered the booth, yelling, "Lushnikin! Lushnikin!"

Fleischmann departed, chuckling to himself, no doubt envisioning the red-dot desolation and defeat awaiting the Comrade inside the booth. Norman was practically on Maurice's heels, Norman and A.A. Norman had a hazy smile on his face, an interior smile so to speak. He was thinking of himself transformed into a rich man by just being there when it all happened, if Magdalena knew anything about it. He didn't even look to see where she was, he was so deep into his imaginary world. He had walked thirty or forty feet down the row before her existence occurred to him. He didn't want to get separated from his glorious friends, but he hesitated long enough to swivel his head this way and that. When he spotted her, he beckoned her with a big sweeping motion of his arm . . . without waiting for her, however. He wheeled about on one heel and continued in Fleischmann's glorious wake.

Not knowing what else to do, Magdalena began walking after him. On either side, within the booths near the entrance . . . red dots. It was astonishing. So many pieces had been sold so fast . . . Red dots, red dots, red dots . . . "The measles outbreak" . . . but of course—that was what they had been talking about! All the red dots . . . 17 million dollars' worth in Fleischmann's case. Who knew how many more millions all those other red dots represented?! Then it began to make her sick. Think of how shallow and wantonly wasteful these people were! These *americanos!* Think of Fleischmann spending almost 17 million dollars on seven obscene pieces of glass . . . $17 million in thirteen or fourteen minutes, for fear a fat Russian might lay hands on this idiotic stuff first . . . all for show! . . . a 17-million-dollar personal exhibition . . . Norman didn't see that . . . He was absorbed by it. A little Cuban girl named Magdalena no longer existed, did she. Norman had put her out of his mind. Her resentment rose up like flames. *Arson* it became. She took grim satisfaction in feeding the fire. That *bastard*. ::::::Norman, you're a disgusting suck-up to money. No display of money strikes you as trashy, does it. *Insulted me!* Why should I put up with him any longer?::::::

Involuntarily, unbidden, four things popped into the Wernicke's area of her brain: her BMW . . . registered in the name of Dr. Norman Lewis, since he, in strict point of fact, owned it; her pay . . . which she received in the form of a check signed by Dr. Norman N. Lewis; her apartment—her home, as she now thought of it—property of Dr. Norman Lewis; the extra money she needed in a clutch to keep up the payments on her student loan . . . providentially provided by Dr. Norman N. Lewis . . . The rebel streak in her was fading fast.

She shucked off her pride and trooped on toward the VIP lounge. A row of four-foot-high modular partitions had been assembled to compel all who would breathe the same air as very important people to pass through an opening at one end manned by a security guard. Another big redneck. Suppose he wouldn't let her in? He was like a caricature of the breed. What if he gave her a hard time?

The man took a cursory glance at the laminated VIP ID around her neck and waved her in. This one had Couldn't Care Less written all over him.

* * *

The only symbol of one's exalted status in the FIZ (Fuggerzberuf Industriellbank of Zurich) VIP room was the mere fact that one had been allowed in at all. Otherwise, the place was nothing but a sea of what is known in commercial real estate as "Contract furniture," simple modern chairs and small tables made of as much plastic as possible. The very important people therein could sit down, take a load off, go get a drink, and tell war stories of the Miami Basel battles for hot items, which is to say, exchange very important gossip.

Way out in the sea, Magdalena sat at a table with Fleischmann, A.A., and Norman, whom she was now pointedly ignoring. She figured she owed herself at least that much self-respect. Madame Carr was suddenly the life of the party. Magdalena wondered if Norman or even Fleischmann had any idea, out of 3.4 million possible answers why. At the moment, she was answering a question from Norman . . . Norman, who had once told Magdalena, "Be careful asking questions. Asking questions is the surest way of revealing your ignorance." Be that as it may, Norman had asked a question, and Marilynn Carr was saying, "How did Doggs learn how to work in glass? He doesn't work in glass or anything else. Don't you know about No Hands art and De-skilled art?"

"Oh, I guess I've heard about it—but no, not really," Norman said lamely, or lamely for Norman.

A.A. said, "No cutting-edge artist touches materials anymore, or instruments."

"What do you mean, *instruments,* A.A.?" said Fleischmann.

"Oh, you know," she said, "paintbrushes, clay, shaping knives, chisels . . . all that's from the Manual Age. Remember painting? That seems so 1950s now. Remember Schnabel and Fischl and Salle and all that bunch? They all seem so 1950s now, even though their fifteen minutes came in the 1970s. The new artists, like Doggs, look at all those people like they're from another century, which they were, when you get right down to it. They were still using their hands to do little visual tricks on canvas that were either pretty and pleasant and pleased people or ugly and baffling and 'challenged' people. *Challenged* . . . Ohmygod—" She broke into a smile and shook her head, as if to say, "Can you *believe* the way it used to be?!"

"Then how *does* Doggs do it?" said Fleischmann. "I guess I never really asked."

"It's actually fascinating," said A.A. "He got hold of, Doggs did, this call girl, Daphne Deauville, the one who cost the governor of New Jersey his job?—and on the strength of that she gets a job as a columnist for the New York *City Light*? I couldn't *believe* it! So anyway,

Doggs gets a photographer to take some pictures of him... well, *fucking* her brains out"—lately it had become daringly chic for women to use *fucking* in conversation—"and doing this and that... and sent the photographs off to Dalique, and Dalique got their elves to reproduce the photographs in three dimensions in Dalique glass, but Doggs never touched the pieces—never. He had no hand at all in making them. And if he touched the photographs, it was just to put them in an envelope and FedEx them to Dalique, although I'm sure he has an assistant to do things like that. No Hands—that's an important concept now. It's not some artist using his so-called skills to deceive people. It's not a sleight of hand. It's no hands at all. That makes it *conceptual,* of course. That way he turns what a manual artist would use to create... an *effect*... into something that compels you to think about it in a deeper way. It's almost as if he has invented a fourth dimension. And there you've got the very best, the most contemporary work of the whole rising generation. Most of Doggs's work in this show is iconic. Everyone who sees one of yours, Maurice, will say, 'My God! That's Doggs at the outset of his classic period,' because I'm convinced that's what his work is. It's cutting-edge, and at the same time it's classic. That kind of work isn't available every day! Believe me!... Maurice... you have... really... *scored* this time."

Really *scored*... Fleischmann looked very pleased,

but his smile was the baffled smile of someone who can't explain his own good fortune. Obviously he hadn't understood a word of A.A.'s explanation. That made Magdalena feel better, because she hadn't understood a word of it, either.

Rather than just sit there looking like 17 million dollars' worth of bafflement, Fleischmann stood up and excused himself to A.A. and said he'd be right back. Fleischmann was hemmed in by other tables, and so Magdalena stood up and moved her chair to give him room. She happened to look about. Her heart jumped inside her rib cage. There *he* was, about four tables behind her chair—the Russian she had met so briefly, so *profoundly!* after dinner last night—and he was *staring straight at her.* She was so startled and excited, she couldn't think of what to do. Wave? Run over to his table? Get a waiter to take a note? A flower? A handkerchief? Her tiny heart-on-a-string necklace? Before her mind stopped spinning, he had turned back to the six or seven people at his table. But she was *sure.* He had stared *right at her.*

What? Now it was Norman. He stood up and asked A.A. if she by any chance knew where there was a men's room. ::::::Maybe he doesn't want to just sit there while I beam black rays at him.:::::: A.A. pointed way off in *that* direction, the direction Fleischmann had headed in. "It's over in the BesJet lounge," she said. "This lounge doesn't have one."

Without so much as a glance at Magdalena, he headed off *that* way, too. Now there were just the two women, A.A. and Magdalena, on opposite sides of the table, clueless as to what to say to each other.

A lightbulb went on over Magdalena's head. This was her chance! When she sat down, her back was to the Russian. But A.A. was facing him. Up to this point, A.A. had not said a single word to her. She hadn't so much as looked at her. Now Magdalena stood up and beamed a terribly big smile at A.A. Was it a grin? In any case, she was determined to hold it on tight. She headed around the table toward A.A., holding the smile, the grin, so tightly above and below her teeth, it began to feel like a grimace. A.A. looked nonplussed. No, it was more than that. She was wary. Magdalena's approach was so contrary to what A.A. expected. This clueless little girl who had turned up with the famous porn doctor... Magdalena had read all that in her face, that and her wish that the clueless little girl would do the appropriate thing—kindly stop grinning at her and keep away from her... and evaporate. Oh, Magdalena could read all that and *more* within that frame of bobbed blond hair, parted on one side and swept right across her brow and eye to the other... but there was no turning back now, was there... not after so much bolted-in-place grinning... and so she pulled up a chair, the one Fleischmann had been sitting in, right up next to A.A.'s... until their heads were barely twenty-four inches apart...But what was she going to say? *No Hands* popped into her head—

"—Miss Carr—Marilynn—may I call you Marilynn?"

"Certainly"—with a standoffish glare that said, "Call me anything you want and then fall through a hole in the floor. Okay?"

"Marilynn"—Magdalena was aware that her voice had acquired a sound she had never heard inside her skull before—"what you said about No Hands art, that was *so-o-o-o* fascinating! What makes it important?"

Just being turned to for her expertise took some of the chill off A.A.'s countenance. But then she expelled a big sigh, the sigh of someone who knows she's about to undertake something laborious...and useless. "Well," said A.A., "are you familiar with the expression 'All great art is about art'?"

"No-o-o-o..." Magdalena maintained the congenial smile and wide-eyed fixation of someone who has a great thirst for knowledge and has found the fountain.

Another tedium-loaded sigh. "It means it's not enough to create an effect in the viewer. It has to reflect, consciously, upon the art—" She stopped abruptly. She leaned toward Magdalena in an intimate, confidential way. "Actually, do you mind if I ask *you* something? What's your relationship—how do you know your friend Dr. Lewis? Somebody was saying he's a prominent psychiatrist...pornography addiction or something?"

Magdalena didn't know what to say. She was his girlfriend? They were just friends? She worked for him? At this moment, it didn't matter. The main thing was, she was directly in the line of vision of the Russian, Sergei Korolyov. Should he suspend his interest in his own tablemates long enough to look at her, she wanted him to see a young woman who was happy...to the point of merriment...engaged in a confidential conversation at her table, obviously a part of her crowd, whoever they were, perfectly comfortable in the mental atmosphere of VIP lounges...and the inner circles of the Art Basels of the world—in short, a beautiful creature who *belongs,* who is at home *where things happen*.

"Oh, I work for him," she told A.A. "I'm a psychiatric nurse." Sounded better than plain *nurse*.

"And so he just invited you to Miami Basel for the VIP opening?" said A.A. "Nice boss." She looked into Magdalena's eyes with an insincere, insinuating smile.

::::::Bitch! What do I say to *that?!*:::::: Her brain digigoogled for an answer and simultaneously wondered if she looked as flustered as she felt. After too long a pause: "I think Mr. Fleischmann got the VIP passes. He's so-o-o-o generous!"

"Yes, he is," said A.A. "So anyway, Dr. Lewis—"

"And he really *trusts your judgment,*" said Magdalena.

"Who does?"

"Mr. Fleischmann. Anybody could tell *that!*" Magdalena was willing to try anything to steer the conversation away from Norman. And *thankgod!* flattery brought a *sincere* smile to this woman's English-bobbed face.

"I *hope* so!" said A.A. "You know, he really did very well today."

"I wish I knew *half* as much as you know about art, Marilynn. A *tenth* as much. A *hundredth* as much. I have to admit, I'd never heard of Jed Doggs before today."

"Jeb," said A.A.

"Jeb?"

"You said 'Jed.' It's *Jeb* Doggs. He's beyond 'emerging artist' now, and I think he's beyond 'rising star,' too. He's made it. He has real traction. I'm very happy for Maurice... and *he's* going to be very happy when he sees what an upward trajectory Jeb Doggs is on."

::::::I've done it! I've pushed this vain bitch off of me 'n' Norman and onto herself.::::::

Out of the corner of her eye, she could see Korolyov turning away from the others at his table to look ::::::not at me:::::: at something over *there.* As he turned back, his head stopped in mid-arc.

::::::He's staring straight at *me*...he's still staring... *still* staring!::::::

Magdalena couldn't play it cool any longer. She broke eye contact with A.A., even though AA's lips were still moving. She looked straight at him. A.A. was looking straight at *her*. ::::::But I have to take the chance!:::::: She put on a smile that was meant to say, "Yes, this *is* me, the girl whose hand you held too long!...and yes, you are welcome to do it again!"

Korolyov smiled back in a way that said to Magdalena, "Oh, don't worry. I will." And he kept that smile on his face for several beats too long. Magdalena compressed her lips in a way meant to say, "I'm bursting with emotion and anticipation! Please hurry!"

Korolyov turned back to his tablemates...and A.A. said, "Friend of yours? Sergei Korolyov? Don't take this the wrong way, but I can't think of any other nurse who knows so many heavy hitters. I'm not implying anything, but I notice you and Fleischmann are Magdalena and Maurice"...another insinuating smile.

::::::I'm so *stupid!* Why did I have to tell her I was Norman's nurse? Why did I even have to say "*nurse*" at all? Why didn't I just say, "Oh, we're friends"... and let her take that any way she wanted? Now I'm going to have to say, "Well, I *do* work for Norman—but we also *date*." Date! These days *date* is a euphemism for *fuck*. Stupid! Stupid! But that's the only way out! A.A. has her face stuck right into mine. Now she's got this—this *poisonous* look on her face, and she's arching her eyebrows in a way that says, "Okay, why are you taking so long? I asked you a simple question. What are you trying to hide?" *Damn!* and *Damn!* again! Well . . . here goes.::::::

"Uhh . . . the thing is, I work for Dr. Lewis—Norman—like I said. But we're also dating—"

—A whispery "Ahhhhh . . ." came out of A.A.'s mouth. She couldn't hold it in . . . an irresistible *ahhhhhh* <<<I've landed a big fish!>>>—

"—and Norman and—" Magdalena paused for one beat. ::::::"Mr. Fleischmann" or "Maurice"? *Uhhh* . . . Maurice.:::::: "Norman and Maurice are good friends, and so I've gotten to know him, too."

A.A. gave Magdalena a super-toxic smile . . . *Gotcha now, don't I!* . . . Oh, Magdalena knew what was going through *her* mind. <<<Aha! So the great sexpert's fucking his own nurse's brains out! I can dine out on *this* one!>>>

Just then . . . *thank God.* Here came Norman and Maurice, returning, weaving their way between the tables. They looked very jolly, very pleased about something. A moment ago, she wanted them to stay away long enough for the handsome Russian to make a move. Now—be thankful for small things! The two men were back and that was bound to change the subject, the subject being <<<The good doctor fucks his naughty nurse.>>>

"You'll never guess who I ran into over at the BesJet VIP room!" Maurice was pumped up with pleasure. He was grinning and his eyes went back and forth from A.A. to Magdalena and Magdalena to A.A., twinkling—no, more than that . . . sparkling, shining, beaming. "Flebetnikov! Was *he* pissed! He was growling! He was roaring! You should have heard him! Some damned martinet—that was the word he used, *martinet*—how does he know *martinet?* He's so bad at English—some damned martinet of a security guard held him back. 'Some damn stupid *redneck*'—I don't know where he picked up *redneck,* either—on and on about 'some damn stupid redneck.' He was lucky some damn stupid redneck didn't come over and empty his big fat tub for him. By the time he finally shakes the redneck, he's telling me, all the best stuff was gone. 'All da bes'toff vas gon!' "

"So what did you say?" said A.A.

Norman chimed in. "*AahhhHAHHHock hock hock* you should've heard*ddahhhock hock hock,* Mauric*eeeegghehehehahhhHAHAaghhhock hock hock!* He tells the guy—he says, 'Gosh, that's terrible! I'm going to try to find someone who is on the board*ahhhHAHHHhock hock hock!* 'Whose work were you interested in?' he's asking the guy. 'Dosunt matter. Is all gon!' " Norman has to show he can do a Russian accent just as well as Maurice, of course. "And get this *ss-s-s-s-s-sAHHHH hock hock hock!* Then Maurice puts his arm around the guy's shoulders and says, 'That's awful! I'm so sor*RRAHAHAHAHAhh*ry!' He's so sor*RRAHahahAAAHhhhry!* I thought you were gonna shed some *tears* for him*aahhhHAHAHA-HAHHock hock hock hock!*"

"Whatever," said Fleischmann. "But he had it coming. He's the kind of guy who just keeps pushing, keeps pushing, keeps pushing—the same way he pushed everybody aside until he was the first one through that door."

Magdalena found herself feeling sorry for the fat man. Maurice Fleischmann, who had connections everywhere, he had the power to get some big redneck to take care of this big bear of a Russian billionaire with one telephone call. She lowered her eyes while she pondered. She didn't notice the tall figure coming up behind Fleischmann until he had almost reached the table. Yes, it was him, finally, the Russian, Sergei Korolyov. She could actually feel a surge of adrenaline trigger her heart into a split second of fibrillation. ::::::Damn! Why has he waited so long? *Now* he makes up his mind...after Maurice and Norman have come back! Now there'll be nothing but the usual when men with high opinions of themselves run into each other. They'll spend the whole time trying to think of not totally obvious ways of showing off. *Women's rights?* That's a laugh. Women don't exist when men like these meet...unless they happen to be stars of some kind themselves . . . We're just here. We just fill up space.::::::

"Maurice!" Korolyov said in the heartiest possible manner. "I might have known I'd see you here!" ("I my-taf knohhhwn I'd zee you here!") With this, he gave Maurice the sort of manly hug European men give each other—if they are on roughly the same social plateau. Then he gestured in the general direction of the exhibition. "See anything you liked?"

"Oh, a couple of things," Maurice said with a knowing smile in order to make it blatantly clear that *Oh, a couple of things* was meant as a choice piece of understatement. "But first let me introduce you to my dear A.A., Marilynn Carr, my art adviser. If you want to know *anything* about contemporary American art . . . *any*thing . . . you have to talk to Marilynn. She's been a tremendous help today. She *saved* the day! A.A. . . . Sergei Korolyov."

"Oh, I know!" said A.A., standing up and taking Korolyov's extended hand into both of hers. "This is such an honor! You've given us—Miami—our first art destination!"

Korolyov chuckled and said, "Thank you. You're much too kind."

"No, I mean it!" said A.A. "I was at the dinner that night at the museum. I hope you know how much you've done for art in Miami—those gorgeous, gorgeous Chagalls!" ::::::Gushing all over the man, monopolizing his attention, showing off... *Oh, those gorgeous Chagalls!*... and I don't even know what a Chagall is.::::::

A sudden dreadful thought ::::::Maybe it's A.A. he has come over to meet in the first place. Look at her! She has his hand in hers—*both* of her hands—and she won't let go!::::::

Magdalena studies his face for clues. ::::::Thank God! He's giving A.A. nothing but room-temperature formal politeness.::::::

Meanwhile, Maurice is rigid with impatience, both elbows locking his arms into right angles at waist level... frustrated by this interruption in his obligatory round of introductions. Finally he cuts off A.A.'s gusher by saying in a loud voice, "—and Sergei, this is Dr. Norman Lewis. You'll remember Norman from the other night at Casa Tua?"

"Oh, yes!" said Korolyov. "Someone at our table said that she had just seen you on television. You were talking about—I'm not sure what she said."

"Hello again, Mr. Korolyov!" Norman was very cheery. "I'm not sure which show she was talking about, but probably addiction. That's usually the subject." ::::::*Usually*... *which show*... *probably!*... Have to get across the fact that you're *always* on television, don't you, Norman!:::::: "I have the hopeless obligation to tell people there's no such thing as addiction, medically. They don't want to believe that! They'd much rather believe*aahhhHAHAHAHock hock hock hock*—believe they're sick*kahHAHock hock hock hock!*"

Maurice didn't want to linger on that subject. He hastened to direct Korolyov's attention to Magdalena.

"And you'll remember Magdalena, Sergei."

"Of course!" said Korolyov. "I remember very well." He extended his hand; and she hers. He held her hand for far too long without saying another word. He gave the same look he had given her from his table, the same message, except that this time he poured great gouts of it into her eyes . . . before saying, "It's very nice to see you again" in a perfectly uninflected, polite way.

Then he turned back to Maurice and reached into an inside jacket pocket. "Please, let me give you my card. I don't know anything about contemporary American art. I just read about it . . . Jeb Doggs and so on . . ." ::::::Does he already know about Maurice's "triumph" somehow?:::::: ". . . but I do know a bit about nineteenth-century Russian art, and early twentieth century. So if there's anything I can possibly help you with . . . and let's keep in touch in any case."

He extended a card toward Maurice, and Maurice took it. He extended one toward A.A. and she took it . . . *Oh, thank you so much gush much gush gush much.* Korolyov extended one toward Norman, and Norman chuckled, stopped short of a *hock hock hock hock* outright laugh, and took it. Then Korolyov extended one toward Magdalena and she reached up, and he slipped the card down past her fingers and placed it upon her palm and pressed it into her hand with his fingertips, anchoring them with his thumb on the back of her hand, and poured gouts and gouts and gouts of himself into her eyes ::::::for far too long!:::::: before turning away.

And that bit with the card ::::::Now I *know*... That didn't *just happen!*:::::: the serotonin was flooding her bloodstream, with no chance of uptake anytime soon. From that moment on she began to plot plot plot plot concoct concoct concoct concoct some way to see him again.

Norman hadn't noticed anything unusual. But Maurice's lust antennae must have quivered, because about ten minutes later he said, "Have you met Korolyov before?"

"Only the other night," she said, straining to keep the tone offhand, "when you introduced me."

Sergei Korolyov—*he was so gorgeous!*

11

Ghislaine

Finding a long-sleeved shirt to cover up those famous—they were literally in the news today—those famous Nestor Camacho muscles of his took some doing. But it had to be done. Then he remembered a checked flannel shirt he had stuck away on the shelf in the closet he and Yevgeni shared. Obviously a long-sleeved shirt made of flannel with a dark check design was not not not the ideal choice on a hot hot hot Miami halogen-heat-lamp day like this... but it was the best he could do. It was pretty ugly, actually, and he wore it hanging outside the pants to make himself look like a feed sack full of modesty... all this, because he knew the story in the *Herald* this morning would be the Godzilla in the room anywhere his CSTeammates laid eyes on him. The thing was on the front page, with a smaller version of the picture of him with his shirt off after the Mast incident.

Sure enough, Nestor, Hernandez, Nuñez, and Flores, another cop in the unit, had just settled into a booth at Kermit's, the little short-order joint just down the block from the big CVS—come to think of it, every joint in Miami seemed to be just down the block from one big CVS or another—anyway, they had just sat down in the booth when Hernandez said, "Who is this John Smith, Nestor? What's it cost to hire a PR man, anyway?"

Oooof! That one nailed Nestor right between the eyes. But he managed to lie coolly, in a put-on tone, "As far as I know, Sarge, he's just a guy who recognizes real talent when he sees it."

Good one. Nuñez and Flores laughed appreciatively. Sergeant Hernandez didn't. "Yeah, but he didn't see it. He wasn't there. But you'd never know it from this—" Hernandez picked up a copy of the *Yo No Creo el Herald* as if it were a toxic object and began reading out loud. "'The rope-climbing cop, twenty-five-year-old Nestor Camacho, Police Department medal-of-valor winner a couple of months ago for carrying a panicked Cuban refugee down, bodily, from atop a seventy-foot-high schooner mast, yesterday left fellow cops—and a pair of Overtown crack house suspects—agog'—what the hell's a *gog?*"—appreciative chuckles from Nuñez and

Flores—" 'with yet another feat of strength. Camacho and his partner, Sergeant Jorge Hernandez,' unfortunately not a legend in his own time himself—" More chuckles from Flores and Nuñez, and Hernandezswelledupwithhisnewlyfoundgiftforwit—

Nestor broke in. "Hey, come on, Sarge, it doesn't say that!"

"Gee, maybe I misread it," said Hernandez. He continued reading, "Camacho and his partner, Sergeant Jorge Hernandez, still a virgin in the Land of the Legends—were trying—"

Nestor rolled his eyes up into his skull and moaned, "Give me—a—break..."

"—'trying to arrest TyShawn Edwards, twenty-six,'" Hernandez went on, " 'and Herbert Cantrell, twenty-nine, both of Overtown, on drug charges when things turned deadly. According to police, Edwards, six-five and 275 pounds, had both hands around Hernandez's neck, choking him, when Camacho, five-seven and 160 pounds, jumped on Edwards's back and clamped him in a wrestling hold called "a figure four with a full nelson" and rode him rodeo-style until Edwards collapsed, gasping for breath. Nuñez tied Edwards's hands behind his back and completed the arrest. Camacho credits an unorthodox training regimen'—"

Nestor broke in: "Okay Sarge—SARGE! We *got* it, we *got*, it!" Nestor's cheeks were burning with embarrassment.

"Sure, *you* got it," said Hernandez. "But what about Nuñez here and Flores and the rest of the unit? Most a them don't read the *Yo No Creo el Herald*. You wanna *deprive* them?"

He continued reading the article aloud...hugely enjoying Nestor's discomfort. Nestor's cheeks were burning so, he figured his face must be one blazing ball of red. Then Nuñez and Flores really got into the spirit of it. They began hooting..."Wooop! Wooooop!"...as the details of Nestor's triumph began to accumulate.

"Hey, Sarge!" said Flores. "What happened to you? Last I heard, some big *negro* had his hands around your neck, and then we don't hear no more. Did you get offed or something?" Laughs all around for Nuñez, Flores, and the Sergeant.

Flores said to Hernandez, "Where do you suppose the guy got all those details? You know, like giving the big mook a 'rodeo ride' and all that."

Hernandez looked at Nestor and said, "Well...?"

Mierda...Nestor didn't know whether the *Well...?* was laden with accusation or not.

"Don't look at *me*," he said. "They told me to go ahead and answer some questions right after that mast thing. Captain Castillo was standing right there. But nobody's said go ahead and answer questions about this thing. Where do these guys get those details in those crime stories? They're always talking about 'according to police' or 'police said' or 'according to a police spokesman'... I mean, who's a 'police spokesman'... and who's saying it when it says, 'police said'? Is it Public Affairs?—and how do *they* get the details? Call the officers on the case? I mean, they got to go ask *some*body. Know what I mean?"

::::::None of that's an actual lie, is it... but what if Hernandez or Nuñez or Flores asks me straight out? Can I just keep double-talking these guys? Probably none a them even reads the *Herald*. But suppose they add it up... John Smith plus John Smith plus John Smith.:::::: Quite aside from feeling paranoid, he felt guilty.

Just then came a vibration from the left breast pocket of his checked flannel shirt: Nestor fishes his cell phone out of his pocket and says, "Camacho."

A girl's voice on the other end: "Is this Officer Camacho?"

"Yes, this is Officer Camacho." He used the "Officer Camacho" to show the Sergeant, Nuñez, and Flores that this was a line-of-duty call.

"Officer Camacho, this is Ghislaine Lantier. We were talking yesterday?"

"Uhhh... of course." The sound of her voice gave him a lift he couldn't have explained to himself. It just did.

"I probably shouldn't be calling you, because this isn't your responsibility, but I... I need some advice."

"About what?" He could see her as if she were standing right in front of him . . . the pale, pale skin, the dark hair, the big, wide, innocent . . . anxious eyes . . . and her legs. Her legs popped into his head, too.

"It doesn't have anything to do with what happened yesterday. It's sort of complicated, and I couldn't think of anybody else to call, and then I saw that big story about you in the *Herald* this morning, and I thought I'd try. I still have your card. Until I read the paper this morning, I had no idea you were the same officer I'd seen on television carrying that refugee down from on top of a mast."

And the angel sang! Nestor said, "Hold on a second." He covered the cell phone with his other hand and said to his mates, "I gotta take this call. I'll be right back."

With that, he got up from the booth and stepped out the door and onto the sidewalk and said into the cell phone, "I'm just going someplace a little quieter. There was too much noise in there."

Someplace was the big CVS down the block. There was a heavy pair of automated plate glass sliding doors at the entrance. About six feet inside was another pair, creating a vestibule of sorts. Nestor leaned against a side wall and said to Ghislaine Lantier, "I'm sorry to keep you waiting, but this is a lot better."

"Better" had nothing to do with noise, however. "Better" referred to the way this girl's call had extracted him from Hernandez's inquest into his relationship with John Smith. No use trying some flagrant lie, such as I don't even know the man. Who knew who may have seen him with John Smith the night they went to the Isle of Capri restaurant and he crashed at John Smith's apartment? Suddenly he had a dark vision: a departmental investigation of the collusion of a cop and a *periodista.* Come on! A twenty-five-year-old bottom-rank cop feeding information to the press without any authorization from above? *¡Dios mío!* Grimmer and grimmer fates began to slither through his thoughts. He hung on for dear life to this conversation with Ghislaine Lantier... inside a CVS air lock.

"Now, you say you need some advice," he said to her, "but it's not about yesterday. Do I have that straight?"

"Yes... it's about—I'm taking such a chance even bringing this up with you, with a police officer! But somehow I know I can trust you. I wish I could tell my father... I mean, I'll *tell* him, but I can't just, you know, throw it in his lap and say, 'Here!' Am I making any sense?"

"Uhhhh... no," said Nestor with a laugh. "You haven't even told me what this is about. Can't you tell me *some*thing?"

"I don't think I can explain this over the telephone. Is there someplace I could see you? When we were talking after you had that fight—I can't explain it, but I knew you might be sympathetic. I knew you weren't there just to arrest people. It was a *feeling* I had—"

Nestor interrupted. "All right, why don't we meet for coffee somewhere, and you can relax and tell me all about it. Okay?" Good idea, but mainly he wanted to get her off the character analysis. She was beginning to make him feel like... he didn't know what—all this business about how nice he'd been... "I can't do it today. My shift is about to begin. What about tomorrow?"

"Let's see... I have classes until one o'clock."

"Classes?"

"Here at U. Miami. That's where I am right now."

"Oh yeah, you mentioned that. Okay, I'll meet you over there at one-fifteen. Where will you be? My shift starts at four, but that ought to give you enough time..."

Nestor was consciously stringing all this planning out. He had one eye on his watch. He wanted to stay here in this CVS air lock until he knew the others would have to get out of Kermit's to make the shift. One of them would have to eat his check, probably Hernandez. But it was only for one coffee... and hell, he'd pay him back. The main thing was not to have to sink back into that damned discussion.

The girl continued to chatter on about where they could meet on the campus... and Oh God, she hoped she wasn't making a terrible mistake, because after all, he *was* a police officer. It wasn't like seeing a lawyer, but she couldn't afford to go see a lawyer . . . and the words kept popping out of her bundle of nerves, and pretty soon Nestor was only halfway listening. Instead he kept seeing her legs . . . her legs and her alabaster skin. He barely made the shift on time.

Shortly before 1:00 p.m. the next afternoon, Nestor had just entered the University of Miami campus in his Camaro for his rendezvous, or whatever it was, with Ghislaine Lantier. ::::::¡Santa Barranza!:::::: He had no history of deriving aesthetic pleasure from landscaping and horticulture, but now not even he could fail to notice ::::::This place is a real piece of work!::::::

A lush green lawn covered every inch of the campus and rolled on forever over vast distances, it looked like to Nestor from the driver's seat of the Camaro. It was all so luxuriously green and uniform, you'd think God must have laid it out like Astroturf. Rank after soldier-like rank of royal palms with smooth palest-gray trunks created super-sized colonnades on either side of pathways in godly allées. They ran through God's own greensward up to the entrance of every major building. Those grand entryways made the most ordinary white Modern and clay-tile-roof Colonial buildings look magnificent. Yet the allées were merely the most striking part of this arboreal show. There seemed to be hundreds—thousands?—of low shade trees, creating lush green frondose umbrellas fifteen or more feet in diameter...and they were everywhere...they were shades for shady terraces and sun filters for exotic and floriferous beds of tropical flowers. *Lush* was the word, all right. You would think Coral Gables had an annual rainfall equal of Oregon's.

It was lunchtime, and students were coming out of the buildings and heading here and going there.

::::::They look like nice kids having a happy time...in their T-shirts and shorts and jeans and flip-flops. They're smart, them or their parents. They're on the road to running things. These kids walking around the campus right now—right *there*—they may not look like much, but they're all in the game! They'll end up with the degrees you *got to* have, the BAs and BSs and all that. Even in the Police Department these days you gotta have a degree from a four-year college if you want to get anywhere. To rise as high as captain, you got to have that degree, and it's a huge, *huge* plus in the competition for lieutenant. Without those letters after your name, you can't even *hope* to rise any higher than sergeant.::::::

Nestor stepped on the gas, and the Camaro's souped-up engine made a great thrashing sound protesting the unfairness of life, and sped up San Amaro Drive toward Richter Library, the biggest library on campus, and his appointment, his police inquiry, his whatever, his rendezvous, with Ghislaine.

He might have known Richter would have a colonnade of palms. Thank God. It kept the building, which was wide-spread but only three stories high, from looking like a warehouse. He was ten minutes early. Ghislaine had said she would meet him out front. So he parked immediately at the street end of the colonnade and just watched people walk into and come out of the building. Occasionally an older-looking person showed up. He kept wondering just what this . . . appointment . . . was really all about.

Barely a minute before 1:15 a girl comes out of the library—a vision!—wearing only a straw hat with a black ribbon and a brim wide as a parasol, a demure long-sleeved shirt—and *nothing else!* Ghislaine! ::::::You're *seeing things,* you idiot. Fool, you're seeing only what you *want* to see.:::::: Now the fool realizes that a pair of white shorts covers the unspeakable delights that have set off such a tremor in his loins . . . Like those of half the girls he has seen since he got here, her shorts are *short.* They end barely an inch below her crotch. ::::::All those lubricious delights within. But her fair white legs, perfect, smooth as alabaster, are real, and the currents streaming through— ¡for godsake cut it out, Camacho!::::::

Now she's walking toward him through the colonnade. Only when she draws very close to the Camaro does she realize *that* is *Nestor* at the wheel. She smiles . . . faintly . . . more from nervousness than anything else, if he's any judge.

"Hi!" said Nestor. "Hop in."

She glanced at the car's dubs, "dubs" being what car nuts like Nestor called the bespoke Baroque spokes the Camaro's rims boasted. Their fantastic designs had been chrome plated so that when the car was rolling, every revolution of the wheels lit up the lives of onlookers with a thousand flashes from a thousand gleaming surfaces—or else stigmatized the driver as a gaudy Low-Rent lowlife. To tell the truth, Ghislaine's life did not appear lit up by the sight. She looked at those flashy dubs—literally *flashy*—as if dubs, like tattoos, gave off whiffs of criminality.

When she first slipped into the passenger seat, she had to jackknife her legs before she could sit up straight, and the shorts were pushed up high enough to reveal the flesh of her hip—::::::Oh, come on, Nestor! You're acting like some thirteen-year-old who has just felt the first churning of all that stuff in his pelvic saddle. They're nothing but a pair of legs—okay?—and you're a cop.::::::

Aloud he said, "Feeling a little better today?" A cheery tone he adopted, the tone that implies *Of course you do, now that you've had time to think about it.*

"Not really," she said. "Except I'm grateful to you

for coming over here." What open, innocent, frightened eyes she had!

"Where would you like to go for coffee?" said Nestor. "There's supposed to be a 'food court' or something here."

"There is..." But she said it very tentatively.

"Well, you pick a place. It doesn't make any difference to me."

"Starbucks?"—as if she were making a plea he was likely to reject.

"Okay, that's fine," said Nestor. "I've never been to a Starbucks before. This is my big chance."

The Starbucks turned out to be on the ground level, in an arcade that ran through the library, front to back. It was the only commercial enterprise anywhere near the place. *The legendary Starbucks!*

Inside...what a letdown...There was nothing fancy about it. It wasn't all that different from Ricky's—cheap chairs and tables, just like Ricky's... sugar granules left unswept on the tabletops, just like Ricky's...plasticized paper cups, paper napkins, wrappers, the little sticks to stir coffee with, just like Ricky's...a counter the height of the girls working behind it, just like Ricky's...But two things were different...One, no pastelitos and therefore no ambrosial aroma...Two, the place was packed with people, but amidst all the babbling and gabbling he wasn't hearing any Spanish at all.

Nestor and Ghislaine were stuck in a real pileup of people waiting to place orders at a counter. Nestor happened to look at the big glass case he was beside—and what the hell was *that?* Those shelves didn't just have pastries and cookies, they had wrapped-up foods… things like chicken lettuce wraps, sesame noodles with tofu, tarragon chicken salad on eight-grain bread, Mallorca sweet bread. When they finally made it to the order counter, Nestor insisted, grandly, on paying for both cups. He handed over a five-dollar bill—and got *wiped out!* A dollar and twenty cents he got back. This grand gesture had cost him $3.80! One ninety for one cup of coffee! You could get a cup of Cuban coffee, probably a hell of a lot better than this stuff, on Calle Ocho for seventy-five cents! No one could be more bitterly shocked by the price of a cup of coffee than a cop. He led the way to a little round table with a light-colored top…and sugar granules on it. Fuming, he got up and brought back a paper napkin and ostentatiously swept the sugar off. Wide-eyed, innocent Ghislaine didn't know what to make of him. All at once Nestor realized he had become his own father…Patience on a Monument. He calmed down and settled into the table with Ghislaine. But he remained so bitter about the cost of coffee in this place, he looked at Ghislaine as if *she* set the goddamned prices here. In an abrupt I'm-all-business-and-I-haven't-got-all-day tone, he practically growled it out, "Okay, tell me what's up. What's going on?"

Ghislaine was taken aback by the transformation of her sympathetic knight into a plain standard-issue, foul-tempered, officious cop. Nestor could see it in her face immediately. Her eyes were now wide with fear. She seemed to be struggling to keep control of her lips—and Nestor experienced a deep rush of guilt. Patience on a Monument, smiling at Grief—in the form of... an overpriced cup of coffee!

Timorously, oh so timorously, Ghislaine said, "It's my brother I'm worried about. He's fifteen, and he goes to the Lee de Forest High School."

"*SsswEEEEEEer,*" Nestor exhaled through his teeth, creating a soft whistling noise. ::::::*Dios mío*... a nice polite fifteen-year-old white boy from a good family, going to de Forest. I hate to think what that poor kid's been through. I don't know which of them's worse, the *negro* gangs or the Haitian gangs.::::::

"You know de Forest?" she said.

"Every cop in Miami knows Lee de Forest High School." He made a point of saying it with a sympathetic smile.

"Then you know about the gangs," said Ghislaine.

"I know about the gangs." Another faceful of sympathy and kindness.

"Well, my brother—his name is Philippe. He's always been a nice boy... you know, quiet and polite and studious—and he played sports last year in junior high." ::::::Those big innocent eyes of hers!

The very look on her face makes me ashamed of myself. A cup of coffee was all it took.:::::: "If you saw him today," she continued, "you'd think he belonged to some African American gang. He doesn't, I don't think, but his entire demeanor says he does... the baggy pants worn so low, it makes you think, 'One more inch and they'll *fall* off'... and the bandanna around his head with 'the colors'? And he swaggers in a certain way the gang members walk." She rocked from side to side in her chair in pantomime. "And the way he *talks!* Every sentence begins with 'man.' It's *Man* this and *Man* that. And everything is *cool* or it's not *cool.* He's always saying things like, 'Okay, man, I'm cool with that.' Any *one* of those things would drive my father crazy. My father's a teacher, a professor of French literature at EGU. Oh, and I forgot the worst thing of all—my brother's started talking in Creole with his new 'friends'! They consider that very cool, because they can insult a teacher right in his face! The teachers have no idea what they're saying. That's what started all the trouble at de Forest in the first place! My father won't allow us to speak Creole in the house. Philippe's been picking it up from other students at Lee de Forest."

"Wait a minute," said Nestor. "Creole is Haitian, right?" Ghislaine nodded yes... very slowly. "So you're saying... your *brother* is *Haitian?*"

Ghislaine expelled a deep sigh. "I had a feeling"—

she stopped and sighed. "I guess I might as well explain everything now, because it's all part of it. Yes, my brother is Haitian, and my father is Haitian, and my mother was Haitian, and I'm Haitian. We're all Haitians."

"You're... *Haitian?*" said Nestor, not knowing any better way to put it.

"I'm so light skinned," said Ghislaine. "Isn't that what you're thinking?"

Yes, it was... but Nestor couldn't think of any tactful way to talk about it.

"There are a lot of light-skinned Haitians," said Ghislaine. "Well... not a *lot*... but a fair number. People don't notice us for that very reason. Our family, the Lantiers, are descended from a General Lantier, one of the leaders of the French forces that first occupied Haiti in 1802. My father did a lot of research into it. He's told my brother and me not to bring up the subject... about being Haitian, I mean. It's not that he's ashamed of being Haitian, not at all. It's just that in this country if you say you're Haitian, people pigeonhole you right away. 'Oh, so that's what you are, a Haitian.' That means you can't possibly be *this*... or *this*... or capable of *that* or some other thing. And if you tell people you're French, they're just not going to believe you, because they can't imagine anybody born and raised in Haiti being French. But that's what the Lantiers are."

Nestor was bowled over. He didn't know what to think. He had been ready for her to turn out to be some rare bird of paradise, from the way she looked... *Haitian?*—and she claims she's French?

She smiled at Nestor for the very first time. "Stop staring at me like that! Now you see why my father told us not to bring up the subject? As soon as you do, people say, 'Oh, you're Haitian... one of *those*... and we can't count on you for whatever-it-is.' Come on, admit it. I'm right, aren't I."

That made Nestor smile at her, partly because smiling was easier than trying to come up with some appropriate comment... and partly because that smile of hers really lit up her face. She became a different person ::::::*radiant*... is the word, but she's vulnerable at the same time... she needs a protector's arms around her... and what a pair of legs!:::::: but he hated himself for even thinking about that! Hers was the *pure* kind of loveliness... and there was something else, too... She was so *smart*. He didn't say that to himself in so many words at first. The things she knew, the vocabulary she used... it all built up gradually as she spoke. Nobody he knew would ever say, "He swaggers in a certain manner"... They might say "swagger"... maybe... but none of them would ever use the expression "in a certain manner" or a little thing like "he doesn't." He didn't have a single friend who ever said "he doesn't." They all said "he don't."

On the rare occasion he heard "he doesn't," it touched off a visceral reaction that made him sense "alien" or "affected," even though he knew, if he thought about it, that "he doesn't" was plain correct grammar.

"Anyway," said Ghislaine, "I had to tell you, because it gets down to the heart of what happened at de Forest. My brother was in that class."

"He *was?*—when the teacher knocked that boy to the floor?"

"When he was *supposed* to have knocked 'that boy' to the floor. 'That boy' is a big, tough Haitian kid named François Dubois. He's the leader of some gang or other. All the boys are terrified of him...and I'm afraid 'all' includes my brother. I'm sure it happened the other way around. The teacher, Mr. Estevez, is a big man, but I'm sure this Dubois kid knocked *him* to the floor...and to cover it up, Dubois starts pressuring boys to tell the police it all started when the teacher, Mr. Estevez, knocked *him* down. And my poor brother let himself be used that way. Philippe is so desperate to be liked by the tough guys...Now this Dubois has Philippe and four other boys enlisted to back him up when the police come. The rest of the class says they don't know what happened, they didn't see it. That was the way they weaseled out of it. That way they didn't have to lie to the police, and at the same time they didn't have to incur the wrath of Dubois and his gang." *Incur the wrath.* "A teacher hitting a student—that's a very serious thing right now. Not a single student, not one, says that Dubois hit Mr. Estevez. So Mr. Estevez doesn't have *one* witness to support him, and Dubois has four or five. The next thing you know, the police come out of the school with Mr. Estevez. They've got his hands handcuffed behind his back."

"Well, what did Philippe say happened?"

"He wouldn't talk about it to me or my father. He said he never saw what happened, and he didn't want to talk about it. I knew right away that something was up. I mean, most kids—if something sensational like that happens at school—or even if it's *not* sensational—you can't keep them quiet. All we got out of him was that the whole thing began with this Dubois kid saying something to Mr. Estevez in Creole, and all the Haitians in the class start laughing. Mr. Estevez—"

"Wait a minute," said Nestor. "He won't talk about it—then how do you know he's being set up to lie for this kid Dubois, him and the four other boys?"

"My father and I overheard him talking in Creole with a boy from the class named Antoine, one of Dubois's *posse,* I think they call it. They didn't know anybody else was home. I don't know Creole, but my father does, and they mentioned the four other boys."

"Who were they?"

"I don't know," said Ghislaine. "Just other boys in

the class. I'd never heard of any of them. They only said the first names..."

"Do you remember them, the first names?"

"I remember one, because they called him 'Fat Louis.' They said it in English... 'Fat Louis.'"

"What about the other three?"

"The other three? I think—I do remember one was named Patrice. That stuck in my mind...and the other two...both names started with an *H*...I remember that much...hmmm...Hervé and Honoré!...That was it, Hervé and Honoré."

Nestor took a small spiral notebook and ballpoint pen out of his breast pocket and began jotting down the names.

"What are you doing?"

"I don't know exactly," said Nestor. "I have an idea."

Ghislaine looked down and twisted one hand around the fingers of the other. "You see why I hesitated to talk to a police officer about this? For all I know, you're obliged to give all this information to—well, whoever you report to, and maybe that's enough to get Philippe in trouble already."

Nestor began laughing. "Your brother is in no danger right now, even if I turned out to be a *real tough* cop. First of all, what you've told me so far doesn't even reach the level of hearsay. I'd have nothing to go on other than his sister's imagination. Besides, our department has no jurisdiction in anything that goes on inside Lee de Forest or any other public school in Miami."

"Why not?"

"The school system has its own police force. It's been out of our hands from the beginning."

"I didn't know that. They've got their *own police force?* Why?"

"You wanna hear some hearsay of my own?" said Nestor. "Officially they're there to maintain order. But mainly, if you ask me, they're there for damage control. They're supposed to bottle up bad news before it gets out. They didn't have any choice with this one. The thing had turned into a riot, and there was no way to keep it in the bottle."

Ghislaine said nothing. She just looked at Nestor—but her stare became a plea. Finally, looking deeply into his eyes, she said, "Please help me, Nestor." *Nestor!* No more Officer Camacho. "You're my only hope—his life is about to be ruined... before it's even begun."

At that moment she was radiant again, radiant as any angel Nestor could possibly imagine. He wanted to put his arms around her and be her protector. He had no idea what to tell her. He only wanted to hold her and assure her that he was by her side.

With as reassuring an expression as he could contrive, he stood up and looked at his watch and said,

"It's time for me to go. But you have my number. You can call me any time, and I mean *any* time."

They walked out of Starbucks side by side. They were about the same height. He turned his face close to hers. "I have a couple of ideas, but I need to do some research."

He put his arm around her shoulder and pulled her closer as they walked. It was supposed to seem like an avuncular hug, the semaphore for "Buck up, girl. Don't be so worried." He gave his eyebrows a mysterious arch. "If worse comes to worse, there are always... *things*... we can do." He made *we* carry the weight of the entire police force.

She gave him a look you could anoint a hero of the people with. He thought of her legs, to tell the truth, and looked down to get a seemingly random look at them next to his. So long, firm, and bare... He quickly and resolutely chastened his thoughts.

"Look," he said, "Is there some way I can talk to Philippe, without making it look like I'm a police officer asking him questions about some case?"

Ghislaine started twisting her fingers again. "I suppose maybe one afternoon you could just happen to be there, I mean at our house, when he comes home from school—something like that?"

"Approaching destination on the right," said that woman from somewhere up in the GPS cloud. Okay, it was all computerized, that woman's voice, but still— ::::::how do it do it?:::::: Like that time up in Broward when he spun out on a slick pavement and wound up rolling backward into a creek. And he's sitting there with the water up over the Camaro's bumpers, wondering how to get out of this, and that woman says in the calmest voice imaginable, "Recalculating," and in no time she's back, and she tells him to drive three-tenths of a mile upstream on the creek bed and turn left where the remains of an old paved country road stick down into the water—and he drives exactly three-tenths of a mile in the middle of a creek and turns left—and it works! She had it right! He was outta there! ::::::But how do it do it?::::::

Now he slowed down on her say-so, and the houses began drifting by, the kinds of houses they used to build way back in the twentieth century...all that white stucco and clay-colored rounded roof tiles, and so forth. The lots were narrow, and only a few of the houses were any more than twenty-five feet wide... but there were plenty of tall shade trees, indicating it was an old section...With the sun almost directly overhead, the trees cast blotchy shadows upon the stucco and on the front lawns. The houses were pretty close to the street. Nevertheless, the lawns were a lush green, and they had shrubs and brilliant flowers, fuchsia cockatoos, lavender and yellow irises, bright scarlet petunias...Nice neighborhood! This was up in northeastern Miami, the so-called Upper East Side... plenty of upscale Latinos and Anglos up here—and lots of Latins and Anglo gaybos, for that matter... Immediately to the west on the other side of Biscayne Boulevard were Little Haiti, Liberty City, Little River, Buena Vista, Brownsville... Nestor could imagine the Latins and the Anglos up here thanking God every day for Biscayne Boulevard, which fenced them off from the badlands.

"You have arrived," said the unseen Queen of the magical GP Sphere.

Nestor pulled over to the curb and looked to his right. ::::::What's *that?* Ghislaine lives... *there?!*:::::: He had never seen such a house... It had a flat roof you could only see the edge of... walls of white stucco with two narrow bands of black paint about a foot below the roof, running all the way around the house... a couple of dozen tall narrow windows installed next to one another to create an enormous curve that began on one side of the house and swept around until it took up close to half the front. He just stood there gawking until a front door opened and her voice rang out:

"Nestor! Hi! Come in!"

The way Ghislaine smiled! Her sheer unconcealed joy as she hurried toward him! He wanted to stand there with his chest inflated like the prince's in *Snow White* and have her rush into his arms! There she was! Ghislaine!—in her long-sleeved shirt and her shorter-than-short shorts, lovely long legs bare! Only at the last moment did he manage to restrain himself. ::::::This is police work, damn it, not a hookup. Nobody authorized this police work, but—but what *is* this all about?::::::

Now she was right in front of him, looking into his eyes and saying, "You're ten minutes early!"—as if that were the most loving tribute a man had ever paid to a woman. He was speechless.

To his amazement, she took his hand—not to hold, however, just to tug on and said, "Come on! Let's go inside! Wouldn't you like some iced tea?"—all the while beaming a smile of the purest, most defenseless love, or so it seemed to Nestor.

Inside, she took him into the living room, which was flooded with light pouring in through the immense array of windows. The other walls consisted, top to bottom, of shelves of books interrupted only by a door and spaces for three jumbo posters featuring men with hats, European posters, judging by the hats they advertised: "ChapeauxMossant," "Manolo Dandy," "Princeps S.A. Cervo Italia"...

"Have a look around!" said Ghislaine. Her tone was one of inexplicable excitement. "I'll get us some iced tea!"

When she returned with the iced tea, she said, "Well, what do you think?"

Nestor said, "I... I don't know what to say. This is

the most... amazing house I've ever seen." He had started to say "unusual."

"Well, it's all Daddy," said Ghislaine. She rolled her eyes in a rather jocular *what-can-you-do* way. "It's all Art Deco, inside and out. Do you know Art Deco?"

Nestor said, "No." He shook his head slightly. Here was another of those things that made him feel so—*ummmm*not so much ignorant as uncultivated, around Ghislaine.

"Well, it's a French style from the 1920s. In French it's *'Les Arts Décoratifs.'* That means a lot to Daddy, its being French. I'm sure that's why Daddy bought this house in the first place. It's not very big, and it's not all that grand, but it's an original Art Deco house. These easy chairs and the coffee table, they're authentic pieces of Art Deco furniture." She gestured toward one of the chairs and said, "Here, why don't we sit down?"

So they both sat down in the Art Deco easy chairs. She sipped some tea and said, "These chairs all by themselves cost Daddy a *fortune*. The thing is, Daddy doesn't" ::::::*doesn't*:::::: "want Philippe and me to forget that our origins are French. We're only allowed to speak French at home. I mean, Creole—Daddy loathes" ::::::*loathes*:::::: "Creole, even though he has to teach Creole at EGU. He says it's *so-oh-oh-oh-oh* primitive, he can't stand it. That's why when Philippe came home from school speaking Creole with a kid like this boy Antoine, who grew up without ever knowing anything *but* Creole... and Philippe obviously wanted to be accepted by this, I'm sorry... *imbecile*—it just *killed* Daddy. And then when Philippe talked back to Daddy in Creole to impress this moron... that's when Daddy really went up in smoke. I mean, I *love* Daddy, and you will, too, once you get to know him" ::::::"once I get to know him," meaning...?:::::: "but I think Daddy has just a *tiny* bit"—she put a thumb and forefinger out in front of her until they were *this close* to touching—"a tiny bit of snobbery. For example, I could tell Daddy didn't want to let on how excited he was about my joining South Beach Outreach." ::::::*my* joining, not *me* joining:::::: "I honestly think he was more excited—"

"What's Philippe think about his French *origins* and everything?" said Nestor. He hadn't meant to cut her off, but he had no patience with Daddy's snobbery and South Beach Outreach and the rest of this social stuff.

"Philippe's only fifteen," said Ghislaine. "I doubt that he thinks anything about it at all, not consciously. Right now he wants to be a *Neg,* a black Haitian, like Antoine and this Dubois, and *they* want to be like American black gangbangers, and I don't know *what* American black gangbangers want to be like."

So they talked about Philippe's troubles and schools and gangs.

"This city is so broken up into nationalities and races and ethnic groups," Ghislaine was saying, "and you can try to explain all that to somebody fifteen, like Philippe, but he won't listen. And you know what? Even if he understands, it's not going to make—"

Ghislaine suddenly *shhhhhh*ut her lips with her forefinger and turned toward the rear of the house... listening... Barely above a whisper to Nestor: "I think that's him, Philippe. He always comes in through the kitchen door."

Nestor looked in that direction. He could hear somebody, presumably Philippe, plunking something heavy down on the kitchen table... and opening a refrigerator door.

Ghislaine leaned over, and in the same whispery voice, she said: "He always gets something cold to drink as soon as he gets home from school. If he thinks Daddy might be here, he gets a glass of orange juice. If he knows Daddy won't be here, like today, he'll get a Coke."

Thunk. The refrigerator door closed. Ghislaine looked that way warily before turning back to Nestor. "Daddy doesn't try to keep Coke out of the house, but every time he sees Philippe drinking one he'll say, 'Just like drinking a liquid candy bar, isn't it.' Or something like that, and it drives Philippe crazy. He can't stand it. When Daddy says things that are supposed to be funny, Philippe doesn't dare laugh... because half the time Daddy's slipped in some sort of... some sort of *subtle sarcasm* he's got to deal with. He's only fifteen. Sometimes I think I should say something to Daddy about it." She looked rather searchingly at Nestor, as if he might have some wise counsel to offer.

Nestor smiled at her with as much warmth as he could put into a smile... smiled a couple of beats too long, actually. "Depends on your father," he said. *Depends on your father?* What was *that* supposed to mean?... It meant that he was distracted... He loved the completely vulnerable, unguarded look on Ghislaine's face... a look that seemed to say, "I surrender my judgment to yours." When she leaned forward like that, her face was barely eighteen inches from the knees of her crossed legs. Her shorts were pretty short. Her beautiful legs were vulnerable, unguarded innocence in its carnal manifestation. He wanted to embrace— ::::::Cut it out, you idiot! Isn't it bad enough that you've decided to stick your nose into a School Police case? All you need to do now—:::::: He forced this business of conceivable carnal attractions out of his head. But his smile and his stare never changed. Neither did hers... until she began to compress her lips slightly... Nestor interpreted it as meaning "We can't say everything that's on our minds, can we."

Pop! That swelling bubble vanished the moment she heard her brother coming out of the kitchen. She stood up from the chair and said, "Philippe, is that you?"

"Yeah." You could tell the boy was trying to force his fifteen-year-old voice down into a manly baritone.

"Come here a minute," said Ghislaine. "There's somebody I want you to meet!"

A pause... then, "Okay." Somehow he managed to push his voice down still deeper in search of the sludge of put-upon boredom at the very bottom.

Ghislaine arched her eyebrows and rolled her eyes upward. *I'm sorry, but we just have to put up with this.*

Philippe, a tall but terribly skinny boy, came walking into the living room with a slow rocking gait that Nestor recognized immediately as the Pimp Roll. The crotch of his jeans hung down practically to his knees... the waistline went around his hips... revealing about nine inches of a pair of luridly patterned boxer shorts. On top, a black T-shirt featuring some flashy yellow script saying, UZ MUVVUZ, a *Neg* so-called rasta-rap group Nestor was vaguely aware of. A cartoonish picture below the UZ MUVVUZ took you into an alligator's gaping maw, teeth rampant, and right down the beast's dark gullet. The boy, Philippe, topped that off with a bandanna around his forehead in loud shades of green, yellow, and red, shot through with white... all this rather dated black Street Dude haberdashery adorning a body the color of café au lait... and a gang bandanna crowning a babyish teenage head! The boy had a delicate face, or delicate for a Haitian, in Nestor's eyes... almost Anglo lips... but slightly too wide a nose... It was a sweet face... even now as he surveyed the room with his eyebrows folded over on his nose at eye level and his jawbones swung off-center in an attempt at a fuck-you scowl... it was *still* a sweet face.

Ghislaine stood up and said, "Philippe, I want you to meet Officer Camacho. You remember my telling you about Officer Camacho, don't you?... and that big article in the paper—the thing that happened in Overtown while I was there with South Beach Outreach? Officer Camacho's here about that."

By now Nestor was on his feet, and Philippe was looking straight at him. The boy's expression had completely changed. But what exactly was on his mind all of a sudden? He was... wary?... or just surprised?... or baffled?... or maybe startled by the extraordinary musclescape in navy chiaroscuro that now stood before him? As they shook hands, Nestor said, "Hi, Philippe!" with all the Cop Charm he could muster. Cop Charm was the other side of the coin of the Cop Look. The Cop Look worked because the cop had the confidence of someone who knows he has the Power and the official go-ahead to use it—and *you* don't. Cop Charm worked for the same reason. I have the Power—and *you* don't—but my intention right now is solely to be warm and friendly, because so far I approve of you. Radiating Cop Charm tended to strike a mere civilian as a present, a gift from a man who has the sanction to be violent. Nestor could see the boy's entire attitude change with a completely unconscious gratitude.

At first Philippe just stared at Nestor, wonder-struck... all at once not a *basso profundo*... but a timid teenage tenor struggling to work up enough courage to say, "Gosh... I saw you online last night!"

Nestor kept radiating Cop Charm. "Really?" he said.

"There was a picture of you and a picture of this big guy you fought. He was *really* big! How do you fight somebody like that?"

"Aw, that's not really fighting," said Nestor. "You're not trying to hurt the guy. You're just rolling in the dirt, so you can arrest him."

"Rolling in the *dirt?*"

"That's what they call it," said Nestor. " 'Rolling in the dirt.' It could be on the floor, the way I was, or on a sidewalk or out in the middle of the street—that happens plenty of times—and plenty of times it really is in the dirt, but it's all called 'rolling in the dirt.' "

"But that guy was so *big!*" said the boy.

"That can make it easier," said Nestor. "A lot of the really big guys let themselves get fat, because that makes them even bigger. And they don't know what training is. They just wanna look *big*."

"Training?"

"They don't keep fit," said Nestor. "They don't run. Most of the time they don't even lift. This big guy was like that. All you have to do is keep hold of a guy like him and let him wear himself out. The guy's not in shape, and he's jerking that big tub of his this way and that, trying to get loose, and he's running out of breath, and he's sucking air, and pretty soon he's done for. All you have to do is hang on, and the guy does all the work for you."

"But how do you hang on? That guy was *really* big."

"Different cops use different holds, but me, I find a plain old figure four plus a full nelson is all you need in most cases," said Nestor as nonchalantly as he could. Then he explained the figure four and the full nelson to Philippe.

By now Philippe had dropped his *Neg* gangbanger pose completely. He was just a fifteen-year-old boy fascinated by real-life tales of derring-do. Ghislaine said why didn't they sit down. This Philippe did quite willingly...he who had made it clear, through his manner and tone of voice, that coming here to the living room where *There's somebody I want you to meet*— some adult, no doubt—was about the last thing he wanted to do. Nestor gestured toward the easy chair, where he had been sitting, and Philippe sat down there, and Nestor took a seat on the couch. He didn't even try to sit back in it. He sat on the front edge of the seat cushion and leaned toward Philippe.

They began chatting away, mostly about things in police work Philippe had always wondered about, and Nestor started asking Philippe about himself and his interests and remarked upon how tall Philippe was... and wondered if he ever played any sports. Philippe allowed as how he had thought about trying out for the basketball team at his high school but decided against it for this and that reason, and Nestor asked, "What high school do you go to?"

"De Forest," said Philippe. He said it tonelessly.

"No kidding," said Nestor. "De Forest?"

Ghislaine spoke up. "As a matter of fact, Philippe was in that class where that incident occurred, when the teacher assaulted a student, and there were demonstrations, and they arrested the teacher. Philippe was right there when it happened."

Nestor looked at Philippe. Philippe appeared frozen. His face was a blank wall. Obviously his interest in expanding upon the subject didn't exist.

"Oh, I remember that," said Nestor. "Every cop remembers that. The teacher—what's his name?—Estevez?—is charged with felony assault," said Nestor. "That's a *lot* more serious than simple misdemeanor assault. He could go away for a *long* time."

Philippe...still a block of ice.

"As I remember, our department responded when the call came in, and so did Miami-Dade, Hialeah, and Doral. It must have been quite a scene, all these cops from all over... sirens, stagger lights, bullhorns—that must have been crazy. I guess they all take it very seriously, this business of teachers assaulting students. Anyway, the School Police ended up handling the whole thing. It's completely out of our hands, but I remember wondering about it. How did it start, Philippe? You were there. What set the whole thing off?"

Philippe just stared at Nestor—stared absolutely blankly—and when he finally responded, he sounded like a zombie: "Mr. Estevez called François, his name is, up to the front of the class and François said something in Creole, and everybody started laughing, and Mr. Estevez got mad and choked François like this"—he pantomimed a headlock—"and threw him down on the floor."

"And you saw all this?" said Nestor.

Philippe's mouth fell open slightly and now he looked frightened. He had no idea what to say. You could practically see the calculations, the odds, the chances, the lies, churning inside his head. He couldn't make himself say a word. He finally nodded his head up and down slowly and slightly, apparently to say yes without saying yes.

Nestor said, "The reason I'm asking is—do you

know some students in your class ::::::time to go for broke:::::: named Patrice Légère, Louis Tremille—Fat Louis, they call him—Honoré Buteau, and Hervé Condorcet?"

Now Philippe's expression went beyond frozen to sheer fear. This cop's visit, supposedly in connection with his sister's innocent presence in a crack house, was suddenly veering eerily straight toward *him.* Once more he wasn't comfortable saying yes or no. He hit upon another answer that cast immediate doubt upon itself:

"*Uhhh*...yes?" he said.

"The reason I'm asking," said Nestor, "is that I was talking to a detective I know in the School Police, and he told me that one of those boys has recanted his story and they think the other three will, too. All four had originally said the teacher, Estevez, had attacked—what did you say his name was? François?—Estevez had attacked this François, but now they were saying it was the other way around. Estevez had only clamped a headlock on the boy—François?—in self-defense, after the boy attacked *him.* If that's true, then these four kids have spared themselves a lot of very serious grief... You know?... They could already be prosecuted for lying to police officers about this thing. But they won't be, not if they tell the truth now. You have any idea what would've happened if they'd stuck to their original story and been sworn in as witnesses at a trial? *¡Dios mío!* They'd be guilty of perjury *and* lying to police officers! They're all sixteen or seventeen. They could be prosecuted as adults, and now you're talking about serious jail time. And think about the teacher, Estevez! God knows what jail would do to him! He'd be locked up for years with a bunch of gangbangers totally lacking in affect."

He paused and gave Philippe a hard look, waiting for him to ask what "lacking in affect" meant. But Philippe was too petrified to say anything at all. So Nestor just went ahead and told him.

"Half the lowlifes in prison are lacking in affect. That not only means they don't know right from wrong and couldn't care less—they also have no sympathy for other people whatsoever. They don't feel guilt, they don't feel pity, they don't feel sorrow—unless you deprive them of something they want. And four boys from de Forest?—teenagers?—they'll rip a kid-like-that's pants off and—Christalmighty! Well, no use getting into the details, but I'm telling you, you have no idea how lucky these boys are, telling the truth this early. If they got caught later, *Whoahhhh!*" Nestor shook his head and said with a morose chuckle, "They wouldn't even *have* a life after that. They'd just be breathing in and out!" Another morose chuckle... "Oh, and by the way, what do you think of the teacher, Mr. Estevez?"

Philippe's fifteen-year-old mouth fell open . . . and no words came out . . . *agony* . . . He took a couple of deep breaths . . . and finally said in a soft, high-pitched fifteen-year-old voice,

"I guess . . . he was . . . okay."

"Philippe!" said Ghislaine. "You told me you really *liked* him!"

"What did Patrice, Fat Louis, Honoré and Hervé think of him?" said Nestor.

"I . . . I don't know."

Nestor could see Philippe bracing himself for every question. Maybe he had already pushed him too far. "I was just trying to picture them sitting twenty feet from their teacher, Mr. Estevez, in a courtroom and sending him off to prison. I'd sure hate to be in that position myself." He looked downward and shook his head and wound up with a mirthless *I guess that's life* smile twisted on his lips.

"I gotta go now," said Philippe. He was no longer a budding baritone. He was just a frightened boy with an overwhelming urge to turn into thin air. No one can see air.

He looked at his sister as if to ask was it okay if he got up from the couch and departed. Ghislaine gave him no cue one way or the other. Nestor decided to do it himself. He stood up and radiated a high dose of Cop Charm at Philippe, who took that cue right away and all but sprang from the couch to his feet. Nestor offered his hand...like a present, radiating...I have the Power—and *you* don't—but my intention right now is solely to be warm and friendly, because so far I approve of you...as they shook hands. Nestor said, "Nice to meet you, Philippe!"...and added a little extra pressure...Philippe wilted like a peony. He gave Ghislaine the kind of panicked glance that says, "Help me out!"—then headed back to the kitchen. No Pimp Roll this time.

They heard the kitchen door leading outside open and close. Ghislaine followed to make sure Philippe had left...before going back to the living room for the postmortem.

"How did you get the last names of those four boys?" said Ghislaine, "Patrice, Louis Jean—what were the other two?"

"Hervé and Honoré."

"Did you see the look on Philippe's face? He must have thought the police already know everything about this case! Seriously, how did you get their last names?"

"It wasn't all that hard," said Nestor. "I have a friend on the School Police. We used to be in the Marine Patrol together. I noticed that really shook your brother up."

"Well...what about Philippe's involvement?"

"He's scared," said Nestor. "He didn't want to say a word about the whole thing. My guess is he's afraid of the kid involved, this Dubois. My friend told me he's a bad kid, got a juvenile record this long. That's why I wanted to let them all know they've got something much worse than this kid to worry about."

"Let them *all* know?" said Ghislaine.

"Well, you know yourself that the first thing your brother's gonna do is get hold of those four boys and tell them the cops are talking about them, and not just cops from the School Police, either, and that one of them recanted. Each boy will say that it wasn't *him,* of course, but they'll...you know...they'll start wondering who the traitor is. If I'm right, everybody will start mistrusting everybody else, and they'll be thinking, 'Hey, is that what could happen to me if I lie to protect Dubois? It's gonna be worse than what Dubois could do to me.' I also think it'll help if they start talking about this teacher, Estevez, and what's gonna happen to *him*. They can't all be lacking in affect! I can tell Philippe's not that way."

"I *know* he's not," said Ghislaine. She paused...composed...deep in thought...then exploded with "He lacks something worse, Nestor! He lacks courage! He's a baby! He *fawns* over—worthless *delinquents* like Dubois! He fears them more than death itself—and therefore he's drawn to their gross toughness and wants them to *like* him!...I'm sure they laugh at him the moment he's gone, but he grovels before their every opinion. Does he worry about being arrested for perjury? Does he worry about the horrible things that could happen to him in jail? Does he know how guilty he will feel if he helps put Mr. Estevez in jail? *Yes!*—he knows all of that. But none of that is *anything* compared to his fear of the tough guys, this Dubois and all the rest of them. He idolizes them for being tougher and more violent than he is! And right now he's trembling at the thought of the unspeakable horrors of what they will do to him if he betrays them. It's worse than unspeakable—it's unimaginable! In his mind it's the ultimate horror!...! He's just a poor little baby, Nestor, a poor little boy!"

Her lips began compressing and turning down at the corners...her chin trembled upward until it looked like a wriggling fig...her eyes began leaking...

::::::Yes? No? Perfectly okay if I put my arm around her to console her—right? Right...to console her.:::::: So he did.

They were standing side by side as his arm went across her back. Her head was down, but then she tilted it upward until she was looking him right in the face from no more than six inches away. Nestor turned the arm he had around her from a now-now-buck-up gesture to a genuine squeeze. That brought her face even closer to his. Her expression was a primordial plea for help.

"Don't worry. If I have to take care of this Dubois,

I'll do that, too," Nestor said in a hushed voice but quite grandly.

Her eyes still fixed upon his face, Ghislaine spoke a single word barely above a whisper: "Nestor..." Her lips parted slightly.

The lips hypnotized him. ::::::Cut it out, Nestor! This is a police investigation, for God's sake! But she's giving me an open invitation! More than anything else, she needs comfort and protection. Right?... right. It's just a way of restoring her composure. Right?... right!:::::: He brought his lips so close to hers that now she had only one eye, in the center of her forehead, practically on top of her nose—

Sound of a key in the lock on the front door, barely eight feet from where they stood. *Whoops!* Their heads snapped apart. Nestor's incriminating arm retracted from her side back to—*slap!*—his.

The door opened. A tall, slender man, a fifty-year-old Philippe, he looked like... stood before them... startled and embarrassed... Nestor felt the same way, startled and embarrassed... All three of them froze for a fraction of a second... *appalling* embarrassment! The man wore a light-blue shirt open at the collar, but on top of that, a navy blazer. In the blazer he embodied the mortal terror of every young man: Dignity!

Ghislaine tiptoed on the ice:

"Daddy, this is Officer Nestor Camacho! Officer

Camacho is here—but you just missed Philippe! He left just a few minutes ago!"

::::::What's *that* all about? 'Yes, we're alone now, but we haven't been alone for long—Christalmighty! is that what she's trying to say?:::::

Pell-mell romped randy clues in Lantier's head.:::::My God, *that* Officer Camacho! We have a celebrity in our home! He's famous! Why is he standing so close to my daughter—within *inches* of her? And why are their faces so red? Why do they seem embarrassed? What should I do? Rush to shake his hand? Philippe was here?...So what? Welcome him to the house? Thank the famous Officer Camacho... *for what?*...Has he put his hand on my daughter? Is the bastard here to fool around? Why didn't anyone inform me he was coming? Look at him...the bodybuilder build bulging in the highlights of his polo shirt. He won a medal! They keep writing articles about him in the paper and showing him on television proclaiming his heroics. He's *important!* What right does that give him to fool around with Ghislaine? She's a child! He's a goddamned Cuban cop! A Cuban *cop!* What is he doing here? A *Cuban cop!* Why is she standing so close to him?—a *Cuban cop! Qu'est-ce que c'est? Quel projet fait-il? Quelle bêtise?* What's going on?!::::::

12

Jujitsu Justice

Just about 6:30 p.m. Magdalena unlocked the door to her cover story, her beard—which is to say, the apartment she officially shared with Amélia—took one step inside and *UHHhhhnnnngggghhhhhsss*sighed a lot louder and longer than she meant to. She heard a man talking in the living room: "Now, let's just hold on a minute...I am not even *suggesting* that there's anything unlawful about it—although I—" A second man broke in: "But that's almost beside the point, isn't it. A mistake—a *blunder,* to use your word—of this—" Actually, as soon as she heard the querulous, stentorian tone in which the first man said, "I am not even *suggesting,*" Magdalena realized it was only Amélia watching some sort of evening news show on that big plasma TV of hers.

The voices suddenly sank to a barely audible

aububblyblumbling mumble mumble mumble and a single wumble *wonk wonk wonk wonk* of laughter and more mumblemumblemumblemumble, and Amélia appeared in the doorway in her T-shirt, jeans, and ballet slippers with her head tilted to one side and her lips twisted upward on the other side, until they practically closed her eye, that being her way of signaling, "Mockery coming"—and said,

"What was *that?*"

"What was *what?*" said Magdalena.

"That *groan* I heard. *¡Dios mío!*"

"Oh, that wasn't a *real* groan," said Magdalena, "it was a sigh-groan."

"A *sigh*-groan..." said Amélia. "I see... Does that mean it came from the heart?"

Magdalena rolled her eyes upward in the end-of-my-rope mode and said rather bitterly, "Yeah, from the heart or somewhere down there. I can think of several places."

She walked right past Amélia and into the living room and practically *launched* her body bottom-first onto the couch and sigh-groaned again, "Ahh-hunnnggghhhh." She looked up at Amélia, who had come in right behind her. "It's Norman... I don't know how much more of Dr. Wonderful I can take," whereupon she began a detailed recounting of Norman's behavior at Art Basel, "practically shoving Maurice Fleischmann's nose into porn to make sure he can keep him on his string and use him for his own pathetic social climbing, and it's so unethical—I mean, it's *worse* than unethical... it's *cruel,* what he's doing to Maurice—"

Sure enough, on the TV screen were three of exactly the sort of dead-serious know-it-alls she figured they were when she heard them from the hallway... the inevitable dark suits and various amplitudes of scarce hair on their domes, domes determined to paralyze you with solemn opinions on politics and public policy. The TV had such a big screen, their arms, legs, and lips, which never stopped moving, appeared big enough to be right here in the room with you, radiating a tedium Magdalena got only the faintest drone of, thank God, as she explained that "Norman's love of Norman would be embarrassing even if he was subtle about it, and Subtle About It is not Norman in the first place. Sometimes I just want to throw up."

She was only peripherally aware of it when the suits vanished and a commercial came on. A fortyish man in a golf outfit is bouncing on the floor of a living room as if he's a basketball *thubba thubba thubba thubba,* while a woman, slightly younger, and two children point fingers at him and weep with laughter *thubba thubba thubba thubba*. The bouncing man vanished, an event Magdalena noticed only because the screen became much brighter. She was deep into the Columbus Day Regatta—"Norman was just *aching* to be recognized as the great porn doctor and get himself invited up onto one of those boats." She flicked only the quickest glance at what had lit up the screen, namely, a second commercial, an animated cartoon of thirty or forty pigs with wings flying in a military formation beneath a radiant blue sky and then peeling off one by one and diving like dive-bombers, whereupon a single name takes over the screen: ANASOL, and Magdalena was telling Amélia how "the girls were pulling the thongs out of the cracks of their asses and the boys were taking their shorts off and fucking them doggie-style right there on the deck in front of everybody, and Norman's trying to get me to take off my bikini top, and I knew he wouldn't stop there." She was only momentarily aware of it when a news anchorman appears on the screen. A TV news reporter is in some sort of run-down gymnasium holding a microphone up to a tall man about thirty-five with a lot of muscles. Magdalena was vaguely aware of some guys, late teens, early twenties, milling about behind them... Couldn't have been less interesting... All she was interested in was telling Amélia about how Norman was "sitting there on the deck, and he's like crammed in with about forty or fifty other people, mostly men who look like they're gonna need some porn-addiction therapy themselves—and I mean like need it very soon—and here's the noted porn psychiatrist sitting there with them—and I couldn't believe it. It was scary. They're projecting porn movies onto the *huge* sails of a boat—*huge*—and *¡Dios mío!* Norman's the worst of them all! He's got this tent pole underneath his bathing trunks, and it's so obvious! Talk about a porn addict! He's enchanted—I mean like on those huge sails all those erections looked gigantic, and when the girls spread their legs, it looked like a man could walk in standing up. I couldn't believe it!" Magdalena had such a compulsion to impart every detail to Amélia, she didn't even notice it when the same sort of boat, a schooner with very high masts and voluminous sails, appears on the screen, and way up on the highest mast two little figures are struggling, and the bigger one locks his legs around the waist of the smaller one, who's about to fall to his death, and starts swinging hand over hand down the jib sail cable, carrying him down toward the deck and toward the camera, and now you can see the savior's face—

"Magdalena!" said Amélia. "Isn't that your boyfriend?"

Magdalena looked squarely at the TV for the first time "*¡Dios mío!* Nestor!"

The sight took her breath away... She hadn't seen this on TV at the time. She had been too consumed that day with working up the nerve to tell her mother off and kiss Hialeah goodbye... and now she wasn't in the mood for one second of Nestor's great triumph...

yet curiosity got the better of her: "Amélia, turn that up, will you?"

Amélia's instinct exactly; she was already remoting the sound up. On the screen Nestor's face is heading straight for the two of them, his face and the boos, catcalls, imprecations pouring down from the causeway up above, a regular squall of Spanish and English and God knows what other tongues. ::::::Good! His own people hate him! So what does it matter that he gets so much publicity—right?... *right!*... That old Hialeah stuff—you either get rid of it or you get all tangled up in it until it suffocates you completely... and Nestor was part of it, wasn't he, a *big* part... How *dare* these *americanos* prop up his reputation and try to make some kind of hero out of him? How *dare* they insinuate that maybe I've made the wrong choice and given up a... *celebrity?*::::::

"*¡Caramba!*" Amélia said. "He's really cute, that Hialeah boyfriend of yours!"

Magdalena grew quiet, testy, and abrupt. "He's *not* my 'boyfriend,' Hialeah or otherwise."

Amélia had her goat and couldn't resist playing with it. "Okay, he's *not* your Hialeah boyfriend. But you have to admit he is really hot!" On the screen is that newspaper picture of Nestor with his shirt off. "He could pose for one of those statues of a Greek god or something." Amélia's face was fairly sparkling with teasing good humor. "Sure you don't want to reconsider, Magdalena? Or maybe you could fix me and him up."

Magdalena's mouth fell open, but she was speechless. She couldn't think of a single riposte. She was aware that her face had become immobile, and she couldn't do anything about it. ::::::Thanks a lot, Amélia! Thanks a *whole* lot... So sweet of you to put into words everything I'm feeling... Oh, thanks for shoving it all in my face.:::::

An airmada of animated-cartoon pigs with wings is flying at an incredible speed... so fast, white puffs of cloud rocket past against a sunny bright blue sky... all this to the martial music of Wagner's "Ride of the Valkyries"... One by one, the flying pigs begin to peel off and dive like dive-bombers toward an unseen target below. A deep baritone voice-over says, "Smooth... powerful... fast-working, and *always on target*... That's the promise of... ANASOL"... Simultaneously the name ANASOL fills the screen.

"Anasol..." said Yevgeni. "What is the Anasol?"

"Believe me, you don't want to know," said Nestor. "It's a sort of a cream." He and Yevgeni were sitting in front of the TV in Yevgeni's studio. It was about thirty minutes after midnight, and Nestor had just come off the Crime Suppression Unit's four-to-midnight shift. They were watching the local news, broadcast first at 6:00 p.m. and again now at the midnight hour.

Blip the so-called news team has returned, three men and a woman sitting at a maybe fifteen-foot-wide curving TV-Modernistic desk, where they read the news off teleprompters... all four chuckling and making faces to show what a witty, collegial time they had for themselves during the commercial break... and signaling that the lighter-sided, human-interesting, end-of-the-show segment is now on. The anchorman says, "Well, Tony, I gather the business news in Miami has taken a somewhat loopy twist, or is it a knot?"

Business newscaster Tony shakes his head side to side, "Come on, Bart, did you already know this story is about ropes and the business side of rope-climbing, or am I just a really lucky guy?"

He sockets his eyes into the teleprompter and continues: "Rope-climbing, using your arms only, not your legs, was a popular sport in Europe and America for at least a thousand years, until about fifty years ago, up until the Olympics dropped it in 1932, and schools and colleges soon followed suit. It seemed dead and gone for good... That was until one man here in Miami has just brought it back to life... and thrown South Florida's thriving fitness-center industry into turmoil. The turmoil has only boiled hotter since then."

Nestor's heart sped up on red alert. ::::::*¡Dios mío!*

This story can't possibly be heading where it seems to be heading, can it?!::::::

Oh, but it can! Onto the screen comes video footage of a young man climbing hand over hand up a rope alongside the seventy-foot foremast of a schooner. Upturned faces on the deck and in small motorcraft and downturned faces from a nearby bridge look on with great excitement and concern, cheering, booing, screaming God knows what. A telescopic lens closes in on the climber. He's wearing the shapeless shorts and short-sleeved shirt of a Miami Marine Patrol officer, but there's plenty of shape, massive shape, to his shoulders and upper arms. The telescopic camera makes his face unmistakably clear—

Nestor's brain and his entire central nervous system have become numb with something far more powerful than excitement, namely, fateful suspense. ::::::That's me, all right, but *¡Dios mío!*—Fate is sweeping me toward... *What?*::::::

Business newscaster Tony provides the voice-over: "And this is a Miami Marine Patrol officer named Nestor Camacho in action climbing a pulley cable of the seventy-foot-high foremast of a pleasure schooner on Biscayne Bay—that's the Rickenbacker Causeway you see there—to *rescue,* some call it—or *arrest, deport, and send to his doom,* many of Camacho's Cuban compatriots call it—the small figure you can just make out sitting in a little bucket seat up on the very top of the mast."

In a short, highly edited sequence, the video footage shows ::::::*me!*:::::: and ::::::*my*:::::: exploits seizing ::::::*my*:::::: quarry and hauling him down the cable to safety.

Peripheral vision alerted Nestor to Yevgeni staring at ::::::me:::::: with intensity to the max. He didn't dare return the gaze, however. He was having a hard enough time controlling the tremor of elation sweeping through his nervous system.

The voice-over man, Tony, is saying, "Every bodybuilder in South Florida—and their number is legion—has seen only one thing in this 'rescue'...or 'arrest'...call it what you will...and that's this young Miami cop's physique and sheer strength." The *Herald's* original photograph of Nestor's bare upper body appears briefly.

"Since then," business newscaster Tony continues, "awe has turned into a frenzy in the fitness industry. Four days ago, the same young officer, Nestor Camacho, performed another amazing feat of strength when he overpowered and arrested this six-foot-five, 275-pound accused drug dealer who was in the process of choking a brother officer to death in Overtown." On-screen is a newspaper photograph of a hulking, beaten, bleary-eyed, head-down, handcuffed-behind-the-back TyShawn Edwards as he is led into custody by three Miami cops whom he dwarfs in size. "The rush to ropes among fitness devotees began the moment the young cop climbed to the top of the mast—but they can't find any ropes to rush to and climb. In all of Miami's metropolitan region there seems to be only one proper rope-climber's rope—and it's at the gym where Nestor Camacho has been working out for the past four years. It's in Hialeah, and it's called—are you ready for this?—'Rodriguez's Ñññññoooooooooo-ooo!!! Qué Gym'... That's right, 'Rodriguez's Ñññññooooooooooooo!!! Qué Gym.' Channel Twenty-One's Earl Mungo is standing by in Hialeah now with Mr. Jaime Rodriguez in the gym."

Blip. On the screen there he is, Rodriguez, standing next to the TV reporter, Earl Mungo. The suddenly newsworthy rope, one and a half inches in diameter, is hanging—prominently—maybe eight feet back. Magnetized by the presence of a TV crew, a crowd of mostly muscular bodybuilders, Rodriguez's clients, has gathered around, three deep. Rodriguez is wearing a black sleeveless T-shirt so tight, it looks like it's been painted on.

Earl Mungo says, "Jaime, do you have any idea what a ruckus this rope here has kicked up in the South Florida fitness-center business?"

"Oh, man, tell me about it. It's gotten wild! We getting run over by every gym rat in South Florida!" Laughter. "And I'm telling you, ever since Nestor took out that giant the other day, it's gone crazy. So many people want to join this gym, I've had to hire all these girls for the office just to keep track of things, and never mind the new trainers. I'm telling you, sometime I think I got a madhouse on my hands." Appreciative laughter and whistles from the boys. One yells out, "Yo! You go, Madhouse!" More laughter.

"What is it, exactly, that makes rope-climbing such a great exercise?"

"You'd have to combine five or six weight exercises to get the results you can get from rope-climbing, and even then you won't get them all. You're using your biceps—I guess that's obvious—but it also gives a helluva workout to a big muscle a lot of people never heard of because you can't see it. It's called the brachialis, and it's underneath the biceps. If you exercise it right, you'll *really* be able to make a muscle." He lifts his arm and makes a muscle that looks like a big steep rock. "It's very hard to develop the brachs if you're just using weights, but in rope-climbing you're giving it a workout all the way up. Nestor has been working out here on this rope for four years solid, and man, I'm telling you, it's some kinda *paying off!*"

Earl Mungo, beaming, says into the camera, "Well, Tony, Bart, there you have it—rope-climbing is *some kinda paying off!* To bodybuilders it's like the introduction of the iPhone. Everybody jes' gotta *have* it. And it all began where I'm standing right now—in Hialeah, in Rodriguez's—I'm sorry, guys, but I gotta try it once anyway: Rodriguez's Ññññññoooooooooooooo!!! Qué Gym!"

The anchorman was still reciting his segue to whatever was coming next—when Yevgeni said in a reverent, astounded, hushed voice: "Nestor, I have *no* idea—all this time I have no idea you are... who you are... the policeman who is bring that man down from the mast. I saw you myself on television and then you come live here, and still I have no idea it is you! You're famous! My roommate—my *roommate?*—I live with a famous person!"

Nestor said, "I'm not famous, Yevgeni. I'm just a cop."

"No—"

"I just did what I was ordered to do, and if that turns out the right way, the cop is a 'hero'... for about ten minutes. He's not famous. 'Famous' is something else."

"No, no, no, no, Nestor! You just saw it! Famous is causing the crazy time in a whole industry! Famous is being the icon for a whole lot of people!"

"Well, thanks... I guess," said Nestor, who had only a vague idea what *icon* meant. He directed a single dismissive flip of his hand toward the TV screen, that and a sneer, then turned away from it entirely. "They gotta hype everything, that bunch a monkeys." ::::::To lie in behalf of modesty is not really lying, is it . . . There's something generous . . . and thoughtful . . . about it . . . but what if those monkeys have just spoken Truth? . . . Can I prove from the evidence that they just made that up? . . . An *icon?* I gotta google that.::::::

As soon as he was alone, he did. He thought about it and thought about it. It was a quarter to 2:00 a.m. by the time he went to bed.

He fell asleep at once, and his dreams sailed along on a great tide of serotonin.

¡Caliente! Caliente baby . . . Got plenty fuego in yo' caja china . . . Means you needs a length a Hose put in it . . . Ain' no maybe 'bout it . . . Hose knows you burnin' up wit'out it . . . Don'tcha—Bulldog was halfway through the song by the time Nestor managed to ascend from deep, deep down in a hypnopompic fog and realize *try deny it* that masculine voice was his iPhone on the floor beside the mattress—

—What *time* is it? *'Cause Hose knows you tryin' a buy it* The radiation hands on the little clock said 4:45 a.m. *But Hose only gives it free* and for about the fiftieth time he castigated himself for ever programming the phone with a song *To his fav'rite char-ree-tee.* Who would be calling at 4:45 a.m.?! Why?! *Hose' fav'rite cha-ree-tee.* He managed to prop himself up on one elbow *'At's me* and find the right *'At's me, see?* and find the right *An' 'at's me* button *Yo yo!* and *Yo yo! Mismo!* push—

"Camacho." That was the way he always answered. Why waste time with all the rest of it?

"Nestor..." It was a Latin voice. It didn't say "Nes-*ter*." "This is Jorge Hernandez—Sergeant Hernandez."

"Sarge..."

"I know it's early," said the Sergeant, "and I probably woke you up, but you'll want to know about this."

That snapped Nestor fully awake. He racked his brain, trying to figure out what innanameagod he might want to know about in the dead of the night. He was speechless.

The Sergeant continued. "You gotta get up and get online. Go to YouTube!"

"YouTube?"

"You know Mano Perez, in Homicide? He calls me about a minute ago, and he's gotten hold of this newspaper that's coming out today—and he says, 'You're on YouTube! You and Camacho!' I about fell out of the goddamned *bed!* So I go to YouTube—and it's true! The goddamned thing's about *me!*... and *you,* Nestor."

Nestor felt volts going through his brainpan. "You're kidding!" In the hypnopompic fog he felt stupid immediately. Sergeant Hernandez calling him at 4:45 a.m. to kid around? . . . couldn't happen. "You and me, Sarge? What about us?"

"Its about that big *comemierda negro* we arrested at that *comemierda* crack house in Overtown. Well, some asshole there had a cell phone and took some fucking video. You can tell it's a cell phone because it's all jumpy and kinda blurry. But you can see me and you all right, the fuckers! It's got a guy's voice goes along with it, to make sure you get our names and what a coupla mean Cuban bastards we are, torturing this poor *negro* who's lying on the floor with his face all twisted up in pain and me and you, we've hog-tied this jungle bunny so he can't move a muscle—"

::::::Jesus Christ, Sarge, I hope to hell they don't have you on video saying "jungle bunny."::::::

"—I mean he's just lying there and they got you yelling into the fucking guy's ear, 'Say *what,* bitch? Say *what?* Say *what*, you filthy little bitch?' Then they got me saying, 'Nestor, for Christ's sake, that's enough!' They make it sound like you're torturing him and I'm keeping you from killing him. Then they go on about women and children being in this 'supposed crack house' when really it's a day care center. I mean, *shit*—and you never see the fucker who's saying all this."

Guilt . . . a wave of guilt swept over Nestor. Remembering that moment—*feeling* . . . the terrible emotion—the desire to kill—the *madness! Kill!*...He couldn't think of the circumstances in any rational way...only the *guilt*...

"—and then they got me saying," the Sergeant continued, "they got me saying, 'He's a hothead, and he's a big dick jigaboo who ain't gonna take *no* shit off *no*body, no*way*, no*how*.' The pussy fuck calls that a 'crude and slanderous' attempt to mimic a black accent—*crude and slanderous!*—and I'm implying that black people are ignorant primitives. Jesus! That's the least of it! The big bastard just tried to *kill* me! He had both hands around my fucking neck and was trying to crush my windpipe. I already had my gun out when you jumped him. That's supposed to mean I was ready to kill him in cold blood when you distracted me—*distracted* me!—plus, I'd called him a jigaboo. What's the big deal? I was talking to you, not him, and there's no way he could've heard me. And jigaboo means—I don't know what the fuck it means. It's just a word. It wasn't like I was cursing at him and calling him a shitball, which is what he is."

::::::Sarge, you *still* don't get it, do you. You've got to knock it all off—shitballs, macaques, and every other name you have for *los negros*. Don't even think about it!—much less say it out loud, even to me.:::::: But what Nestor said was "The guy tried to strangle you, Sarge! Whatta they say about all that?"

"They don't show *any* a that! They don't even say

like maybe there's some *reason* this huge black bull wound up flat on his back like that in the custody of two cops, except that the two cops are Cubans. You're supposed to figure the only *reason* is Cubans are cruel bastards who live for pushing *los negros* around and abusing them and dissing them and calling them monkeys and pieces a shit and then treating them like monkeys and pieces a shit. And there's no use trying to tell people they have to put themselves in our shoes because they can't even *begin* to imagine what it's like rolling in the dirt with one a these huge gorillas. I'm telling you, Nestor, we're gonna be knee-deep in this shit by daybreak and waist-high by noon . . ."

"Sarge, you gotta stop talking that way, even to me, because later on it comes popping outta your mouth and you're in deep shit. *We're* in deep shit."

"I know. You're right. It's like fucking gargling with cyanide . . . but right now we gotta think a something. We need a PR man. How the fuck do you even *find* a PR man? . . . even if you can *pay* a PR man, which I can't. I don't know about you."

"Whyn't we go straight to the Chief?" said Nestor.

"That's not funny, Nestor."

"I'm not trying to be funny, Sarge. He's not a bad guy; I spent maybe half an hour with him when they transferred me from Marine Patrol to CST."

"I don't care if he's Saint Francis himself. What's he gonna do? He's *un negro,* Nestor! Why do you think they made him chief? . . . So the brothers could say, 'Yo, we got the muh-fuckin' Chief a *Po*-lice now, baby. Now he be on *our* side! He be lookin' out for *us!*' "

::::::Jesus! All this shit Sarge is saying! Talk about *dissolving* . . . He's determined to dissolve himself!:::::: Out loud he said, "Whyn't we just go undercover, Sarge?"

"What the fuck are you talking about, Camacho?!"

"That way they won't see us, Sarge. That way we dissolve *ourselves.*"

"Don't you get—"

"I'm just kidding, Sarge, I'm just kidding. Where you want to meet?"

"Uhhh . . ." Long pause . . . "Shit . . . come on down to headquarters, as usual, and we'll talk in the car. And look behind you. Nobody's got your back on this one. You won't feel like kidding around, after the sun comes up."

Nestor thumbed the END button and remained propped up on one elbow on the mattress. He felt catatonic. His eyes focused on a nonexistent point in thin air. ::::::I'm slipping through a crack . . . into a parallel universe! Oh, come off it, Nestor.:::::: *Parallel universe* was a phrase he had heard on one of those heavy Dread Purple Dimension spook dramas on television. Parallel me no dread purple dimensions, Camacho. He was shocked and afraid, to tell the simple truth.

YouTube YouTube YouTube YouTube . . . the frightened part of him didn't even want to look at the goddamn thing . . . but the rest of him yanked him up off the mattress and dragged him three feet across the floor through the dirty clothes and dirty towels and miscellaneous empty boxes and dust and hairballs . . . to his laptop. He sat down on the floor and propped his back up against the wall . . . and my God, right on the home page . . . there he is, in the crack house. He's spellbound by the sight of himself on that little screen . . . Nestor victorious!! The big brute's hulk is lying facedown on the floor. ::::::Look at that! The brute is twice my size, but I'm the victor! I'm straddling his back . . . *Look!* I've got him locked in the full nelson and the figure four. My hands are interlaced behind his neck, and I'm mashing his face into the floor with all my might. My God!::::::

His muscles had already been pumped up, gorged with blood, from wrestling the brute. Now, right there on that little laptop screen, he's marshaling every last ounce of strength he has to driving the brute's head into the floor, mashing his face flat for him. ::::::I'm . . . *pumped!*:::::: The enormous pressure of the full nelson has bent the brute's neck forward to the point where he,

Nestor, could have broken it, if he really wanted to. You can tell that even on this little laptop screen; the brute's face is twisted beyond recognition—from *the pain!* His mouth is open. He wants to scream. But he wants oxygen more. The only sound that escapes his terrified 275-pound body is "Urrrrrrrunhhh... urrrrrrruhun-hhh... urrrrrrrrunhhh!" Sounds like a dying duck. Yeah! A duck croaking. Another thirty seconds of maximum pressure—that's all it would have taken! Stone-cold dead, O black brute! Nestor is mesmerized, watching his triumph on that little screen. Awesome! Nestor hadn't been aware of the expression on his own face when it was actually happening. ::::::My God! Did I really bare my teeth like that? Did I really put on such a hideous, malevolent grin?::::::

Positively enchanted, Nestor can't take his eyes off himself on the screen. He watches—and hears—Nestor Camacho remonstrating *uhhh uhhh uhhh.* He's out of breath himself *uhhh uhhh uhhh* humiliating the giant as loudly as he can: "Okay, you *uhhh unhhh* stu-pid *uhhh uhhh uhhh pussy!*" He remembers wanting the whole room to know that he had utterly crushed the brute. He watches himself lean over until he's two or three inches from the beast's ear and shouts directly into it, "Say *what,* bitch? Say *what?*"

With that, Nestor's morale sinks. He wants to click the window closed... From now on it only gets worse, doesn't it!... What has he done?... He knows what's next... and here it comes... The epithets, his own, the Sergeant's, start piling on top of the bone heap at a furious red-mad rate—and the heap catches fire. Into the charnel pyre Nestor throws "Say *what,* you filthy little bitch?"

Only then, looking at the laptop screen, does Nestor fully get it. Only then does he comprehend, in so many words, how bad this all is... this YouTube introduction of Nestor Camacho to the world!

And what does the world see in this video? Where does the YouTube story begin? The world sees a black prisoner lying facedown, inert, helpless, racked with pain, struggling just to take the next breath, moaning in a way *urrrrrrrunh* no human being ever moaned before, under arrest at the mercy of two Cuban cops. One of them is mounted on the prisoner's back, flashing a cruel thirty-two-tooth grin as he delights in the prospect of breaking his prisoner's very neck with a full nelson. The other one is crouched barely two feet from him, ready to blow his brains out with a .44-caliber revolver. Both of them are humiliating their black prisoner, mocking his manhood, calling him a subhuman moron. Is there no limit to how abusive these two Cuban cops are willing to be toward a black man who, so far as the viewer knows, has done nothing?... And that is the way the YouTube version *begins*... and, very likely, ends.

No indication whatsoever of the life-or-death crisis that precipitated this vile "abuse," not so much as a hint that this put-upon black man is in fact a powerful 250-pound young crack house thug, nothing to make it at all credible that he might have touched off the whole thing by wrapping his huge hands around the Sergeant's neck, that he was within one second of murdering him by crushing his windpipe, that his life was saved only by the immediate reaction of Officer Camacho, who threw himself onto the brute's back and, weighing only 160 pounds, clamped a couple of wrestling holds onto 275 pounds of crack house thug and rolled in the dirt and the dirtballs with him until the brute became utterly depleted in breath, power, willpower, heart, and manhood...and gave up...like a pussy. How could any man pretend not to realize that, faced with death, even a cop experiences an adrenal rush immensely more powerful than all chains of polite conversation and immediately seeks to smother his would-be killer with whatever vile revulsion comes surging up his brain stem from the deepest, darkest, most twisted bowels of hatred? How could any man, even the mildest and most sedentary, fail to understand?!

But nothing on YouTube could possibly let that man know the first half of the story, the *crucial* half... *Nothing!* And without that first half, the second half becomes fiction! A lie!

I'm telling you, Nestor, we're gonna be knee-deep in

this shit by daybreak and waist-high by noon. For it is already rising, and it is still dark outside.

And it was *still* dark outside at 6:00 a.m., when the Chief, an early riser, took a call on his personal line from Jorge Guba, one of Dio's boy Fridays, saying the Mayor wanted him at City Hall in an hour and a half for a meeting. *Seven-thirty?* Yes. Had the Chief seen YouTube yet?

So the Chief took a look at YouTube. In fact, he watched it three times. Then he shut his eyes and lowered his head and massaged his temples with one hand... his thumb pressing one temple and his middle and ring fingers the other. Then he said aloud, under his breath:

"Like I really need this, don't I."

Grumpily he roused his driver, Sanchez, and told him to have the car ready. When they entered the circular drive in front of the little Pan Am–leftover City Hall at 7:20—one look, and he immediately grew grumpier. Waiting for him, and whomever else, in front of the City Hall entrance, was a platoon of the so-called media, about a dozen of them, dressed like the homeless but lent gravity by all the microphones and notepads in their hands and, above all, by two trucks with telescoping satellite transmitters extended a full twenty feet up in the air for live broadcast. The Chief was not so jolly this time as he got out of the big black Escalade. Hell, he wasn't even able to take a deep breath and expand his massive black chief chest to the max before the so-called media were swarming over him like mosquitoes. *Police abuse* and *racist slurs* were the two terms they kept biting him with in their whining mosquito buzz as he bulled his way through them, without a word, and into City Hall.

Like he really needed this, didn't he.

The Mayor's men's-gym lounge of a conference room was heavily populated with more of his boys Friday: his flack, Portuondo, and his city manager, Bosch, as before . . . plus Hector Carbonell, the district attorney ::::::district attorney?:::::: and his two gray eminences, Alfredo Cabrillo and Jacque Díaz, both lawyers Dio had known since law school and frequently called upon when confronted by big decisions ::::::big decisions?:::::: And the Mayor made six. The whole platoon was Cuban.

Dio was his usual exuberant self as the Chief entered the room. Big smile and "Aaaaay. Chief! Come in! Have a seat!" He pointed at an easy chair. "I think you know everybody in the room . . . Right?" The other five Cubans gave the chief little thirty-three-degree smiles. When they all sat down in the room's jumble of easy chairs and armchairs, the Chief had an odd feeling. Then he realized the Mayor and the boys Friday were arranged in a horseshoe pattern . . . a sloppy horseshoe, but a horseshoe . . . and he was seated midway between the horseshoe's prongs . . . with a big space between him and the nearest seat on either side. The Mayor was directly opposite him in a straight-back armchair at the crest of the horseshoe's curve. The Chief's chair must have been suffering from spring failure, because his bottom sank down so far, he could barely see over his kneecaps. Dio, in his armchair, appeared to be looking down at him. The choir had some chilly looks on their mugs . . . no smiles at all. The Chief had the sensation of being in a sunken dock, facing the grim visages of a jury.

"I think everybody knows why we're here?" . . . The Mayor scanned his platoon . . . lots of *yes* nods . . . then looked straight at the Chief.

"What is it with your boy Camacho?" he said. "The kid's a one-man race riot." He was not joking. "Who's he got left to shit on? The Haitians, maybe? And it's not as if he's a deputy chief or even a captain. He's just a cop, for Christ's sake, a twenty-five-year-old cop with a proven ability to piss people off in gross numbers."

The Chief knew what was coming next. Dio was going to demand that he can him. The Chief didn't have this feeling often . . . of not being sure of himself . . . On his good days his confidence and charisma kept Dio and his whole Cuban gang off-balance. He had been in gun battles, real shootouts. He had risked his life to save cops under his command, including Cuban cops, God knows. He had two medals for valor. He had presence. In this room it would take two Cubans standing side by side to have shoulders as wide as his... three of them to come up with a neck as wide as his... forty of them, or maybe four hundred, to have his willingness to risk his own hide for what was right... He really did jump off that six-story roof onto a mattress that looked the size of a playing card from up there. Not to put too fine a point on it, but he was a man... and nobody else in this room was. His confidence, his vitality, that certain *look* he had in his eyes. In this arena it didn't matter what color he was. He radiated that rarest and most radiant of all auras... no one could help but *behold... the Man!* At this moment that wasn't the way they regarded him, however... He could tell. At this moment they saw only *un negro*... and that damned *negro* was on the spot, because if that *negro* weren't *un negro, nuestro negro, our* negro, doing what we tell him to do, he wouldn't even rate being in this room... None of Dio's boys had dared so much as twitch an eyebrow... even Dio... but he knew what they thought they were now looking at... just another black hambone in a costume.

That got the Chief's back up. "*What is it* with Camacho?" he said, giving the Mayor a 300-watt stare in the eyeballs. "Since you've asked" — in the choir many eyebrows now twitched; they had never heard the Chief speak sarcastically to the Mayor before—"the short answer and the long answer and the in-between answer is, he's a damned good cop."

The room went silent. Then the Mayor said, "Okay, Cy, he's a damned good cop. I guess we have to take your word for that. After all, you're the top cop in this town; you're the commander in chief. So what's the problem here? We've got your damned good cop, and he and another cop are caught on YouTube abusing a citizen of our African American community, calling him an animal and a jigaboo and a subhuman moron with shit for brains—"

"He's a drug dealer, Dio!" The Chief's voice rose and hit a couple of not very commanding notes.

"And that makes it okay for Camacho to address this suspect—this African American *suspect*—as if he's a member of a race of subhumans, a bunch of animals? I hope that isn't what you're telling me, Cy."

"But you have to consider the *context,* Dio, the whole—"

"The context is, your goddamned good cop is shitting all over our African American community! If that's a good context, then we got a *bigger* problem. And that problem is leadership. What else could it be?"

That brought the Chief up short—so short, he couldn't get a word out. What the hell was happening all of a sudden? He was putting his job on the line, his whole career, on behalf of some twenty-five-year-old Cuban cop named Nestor Camacho? And that was being *manly?* After fifteen years of working hard, going the extra mile, risking your life, stepping right over racism as if it were a speed bump on the road to glory, becoming a leader of men, you risk it all...on some Cuban kid? But how could he get out of this... without showing that with a single sentence Dio had delivered such a rocket to the crotch, it had turned the supposed *Ultimate Man* into a pussy?

And Dionisio knew the fight was over, with that one punch, didn't he...for he now dropped the sarcasm and spoke in a soothing, healing tone. "Look, Cy, when I appointed you chief, I had total faith in your abilities, your courage, and a lot of other things that would make you a natural leader, and I still do. You've never done anything that's made me feel like I made the wrong decision...and one of those other things was my hope that with you as our chief, we could overcome many mistakes that had been made in the past. For example, I hoped to show our African American community that yes, they may have gotten the short end before, but now they were going to have not just somebody to stand up for their interests... they would have the Man himself. That's a good thing, and it's also a powerful symbol. Now, when that Man on the Mast thing happened, I told you to put Camacho on ice for a while. So what did you do? You gave him a medal and a 'lateral transfer,' and not to a horse in the park, because the only ones he could annoy there would be the goddamned rats and squirrels. No, that would be a lateral transfer with a 'dip,' I think you said." The Mayor was heating up again, and slipping the leash off his sarcastic attack dog. He seemed to know that the Chief was down for the count. "In a situation like this one, no one person is the issue. You know what I mean? You want to stand up for one of your men, and that's commendable. But right now, you and me, we got the obligation to stand up for hundreds, thousands, tens of thousands of people who can't follow the fine points. You know what I mean?"

The Chief found himself nodding *yes* . . . and immediately realized that he had done the same thing, meekly nodded *yes,* a moment ago . . . They must be marveling at their leader's jujitsu powers of persuasion . . . *Just like that* he reduces Black Superman to about the omnipotence of a smoked oyster—*they* being the boys Friday. They're all staring. They're not glowering. No, they're fascinated, like little boys. They've got the best seats in the house . . . for watching the Incredible Shrinking Chief . . . shrink. You can't put anything past our Dionisio Cruz, can you! All of five-feet-six, but he can handle any six-foot-four Super*negro* who gets in his way. That's why he's . . . the *caudillo.*

He doesn't accuse *el negro* of anything, he doesn't threaten *el negro* with anything... or not in any form you could introduce as evidence... he just lays out his net, and in no time... *Gotcha!*... *el negro*'s inside the net, struggling... punching thin air... trapped in a net of words.

"All they know," the Mayor continued, "is that here's this young cop, this kid—what?—four years on the force?—and everywhere he goes, the Four Horsemen follow... Racism, Chauvinism, Ethnic Slurs, and... *uhhh*..." He had been going great until that point. Now he was stuck. He couldn't come up with a fourth mounted equestrian scourge. "... *uhhh*... and all the rest of it," he finished off with, lamely. "You know what I mean?"

What bullshit! He couldn't sit here and nod *yes* to stuff like that! So he said, "No, I don't, Dio." But it came out just as lamely as little Dionisio's *uhhh... and all the rest of it.* It came out just as faint as his own *yes* nods. He put no *heart* into it... It was very noble, defending one of his men, a lowly one, too... but was it really noble if it put in jeopardy all the things you could do for your real brothers?

::::::It was as if Dio was *reading* my e-mail.::::::

"Look, Cy, the issue is not whether Camacho is a bad cop or a good cop. I'm willing to grant you that point. Okay? But he's become something bigger than himself. He's become a symbol of something that cuts everybody in this town to the quick. Your loyalty, which I admire, doesn't alter the situation. I'm sure the kid never even thought about it at the time. But the facts are the facts. Twice in the last few months he's made whole communities see red . . . He's gotten their bowels in an uproar . . . He's treated them like dirt; don't you think your department could possibly get on with its work without this twenty-five-year-old kid's services?"

::::::I wondered when he was finally going to get to this point. And when he did, I was going to draw a line in the sand and dig in.::::::

"Yeah, I do know what you mean," he found himself saying. But he said it with a sigh, like a man yielding—unwillingly, of course—to destiny. "And I don't like it." That part came out as not much more than a mutter.

At that point the Mayor's expression and his tone turned fatherly. "Cy, I want to tell you a couple of things about this city. These are things you probably already know, but sometimes it helps to hear them out loud. I know it helps *me* . . . Miami is the only city in the world, as far as I can tell—in the *world*—whose population is more than fifty percent recent immigrants . . . *recent* immigrants, immigrants from over the past fifty years . . . and that's a hell of a thing, when you think about it. So what does that give you? It gives you—I was talking to a woman about this the other day, a Haitian lady, and she says to me, 'Dio, if you really want to understand Miami, you got to realize one thing first of all. In Miami, everybody hates everybody.' "

The flack Portuondo chuckled as if the Boss were having his little joke. Dio shot him a reproving glance and continued: "But we can't leave it at that. We have a responsibility, you and me. We got to make Miami—not a melting pot, because that's not gonna happen, not in our lifetimes. We can't melt 'em down... but we can weld 'em down... *weld* 'em down... What do I *mean* by that? I mean we can't *mix* them together, but we *can* forge a secure place for each nationality, each ethnic group, each race, and make sure they're all on the same level plane. You know what I mean?"

The Chief hadn't a clue. He wanted to say he had never heard such bullshit in all his born days, but he couldn't bring himself to do it. What's happened to Old Chief? He knew, but he didn't want to put it into words, not even inside his own head. What happened... happened the moment Dio said, "... then we got a bigger problem. And that problem is leadership." The rest of the plot played out in a flash in the Chief's head. All Dio had to do was to fire Chief Booker and say, "We put him in a position of leadership and he couldn't even look out for his own people. A real leader would create an atmosphere in which this kind of thing wouldn't happen, couldn't happen. So I'm going to appoint a new chief, someone strong enough to change the mental atmosphere around here, a real leader... and he will *also* be from our African American community."

African American community, my ass. The Chief wondered if he or any of the rest of the Cubans in here staring at him so as not to miss a delicious moment of this masterful lip-lashing—he wondered if *anybody* had ever heard Dionisio, Paragon of Democracy, utter the term *African American* before... except in the presence of a TV camera or some sentinel of the press. The Chief had begun to resent the term every time it came slithering out of the mouth of white hypocrites like Dio. *White?* Every Cuban in this room thought of himself as white. But that wasn't the way real white people thought of them. They ought to hang around Pine Crest a little bit or the Coral Beach Yacht Club or some meeting of the Villagers of Coral Gables. That would curl their hair for them! To the real white boys they were all brown people, colored folks, just a shade or two lighter than he was.

You know what I mean? The Chief wasn't nodding a little yes this time. This time he was shaking his head back and forth. It was a *no,* his yawing head was, but it was a yawning yaw and a pallid *no,* so insignificant that old Dio took no notice of it whatsoever. "So that brings us to the question of what we do with Officer Camacho," said the Mayor. "He's a mote in the eye for half of Miami. You know what a mote is? It's from the Bible. A mote is like a speck of dust that gets in the eye. It's just a speck of dust, but it's irritating. It's really irritating. In the Bible people seem to spend half their time removing motes. A mote's not gonna kill you, but it'll put you in a very bad mood. You know what I'm saying?"

::::::No:::::: but this time the Chief didn't bother to make any response, not in any fashion. He was acutely aware of how he must have looked to the other Cubans in the room. He had let himself gradually slouch back into the depths of the chair. So he straightened up and slowly thrust his shoulders back in a half-hearted attempt to show these Cuban brownies that he still had a massive chest. It was a pretty halfhearted thrust, however. How much longer could he afford to let the Mayor fuck with him like this before it came down to either losing all claim to manhood—or else getting up, walking the six or seven feet to where the Mayor was sitting, and *yanking* him up out of his seat by his head of hair with one hand and slapping him across his fucking brown face with the palm of his hand and then the back of his hand the palm and then the back the palm the back the palm the back palm back palm back palm back palmbackpalmback until that brown face turns red as a rare meatball and he's sobbing because he's been totally humiliated by a Man—

::::::—oh sure, Superman...Tell me who, in fact, is just sitting here with his speechless mouth hanging open.::::::

"So how do we remove this pair, Camacho and the sergeant, Hernandez, from the public's eye? I've done more of this, canning sinners, no matter what the circumstances, than you have. And I can tell you there's no gentle way to do it. You have to come right out and say it: 'These two have revealed themselves as racists, and we can't have people like that in our Department.' That's the way you have to do it. *Pow! Pow!* It's painful but it's quick. One sentence—no, two sentences—and it's over." He began slapping palms up and down so that they grazed each other in the *well, we've cleaned that up, haven't we, and it's over and done with* manner. Then he compressed his lips and gave the Chief a little wink, as if to say, "Aren't you glad we got that worked out?"

It was the wink that did it...that little wink... with that wink Dionisio had made too deep an incursion into the Chief's manhood. Every one of Dionisio's boys Friday was blank faced and enjoying this humiliation intensely. Old Dionisio is a piece of work, isn't he? *Snicker snacker snicker snacker snicker snacker* he's got the scissors out and he's cut *el blowhard negro* up into little insignificant pieces in no time.

That little wink—those smug blank Cuban faces—the Chief felt like he had left his own body through astral projection and was beholding another creature when he snapped out, "We can't do that, Mayor Cruz."

It wasn't an exclamation. It came out with a seething sound. The "Mayor Cruz," as opposed to Dio or Dionisio, said it was time to get serious.

"Why not?" said the Mayor.

"It would jeopardize the morale of the whole Department." The Chief knew that was a big exaggeration, but it was out on the table now, and the Chief pressed on. "Every cop who's ever had to fight one a these crackhead slimeballs and go rolling in the dirt with him or had to pull a gun, every one a them puts himself inside the hide of Camacho and Hernandez the moment he hears about it. Every one a them can feel the adrenaline pumping. Every one a them knows the feeling of fighting for his life, because he don't know who he's tangling with, and every one a them knows he's not himself when it's over. Every one a them knows the feeling of fear turning into pure hate. There's nothing in between. If you videotape everything cops say to these scumbags when they finally got 'em restrained and have enough breath to say anything at all, that tape would scorch the hair off every head in Miami. That's just the nature of the beast, because don't kid yourself, at that point you're an animal."

The room went silent. The Chief's vehemence and impudence were a shock. After a few beats the Mayor came back to life. "So what these two cops said about African Americans doesn't bother you... as the highest-ranking African American in this city?"

"Yeah, the *words* bother me," said the Chief. "I've had to listen to that shit ever since I was four or five years old, and I know what the urge to kill is. But I've also been in the shoes of cops like Camacho and Hernandez—many times. And I know that every vile thought you've ever had in your head—the animal in you is likely to say it out loud. Look, Dio, this thing happened in a crack house. You *got* to be afraid when you enter one a them, because with dope comes guns. As it was, the biggest guy in the house tries to choke Sergeant Hernandez. Hernandez pulled his gun and would have shot the guy, except that Camacho jumped on the guy's back, and Hernandez was afraid he might shoot Camacho, too. Camacho clamps some kind of wrestling hold on the guy and rides him until he's out of gas and gives up. If he'd been able to get Camacho off his back, he woulda killed him and yanked his head off for good measure. None a that comes out when you just read from a tape of what they said."

"Okay. Okay," said the Mayor. "I get your point. But my point is we've got a big African American population here, and they've been here a long time. A thing like this could set off another riot. They always riot over the same thing, the criminal justice system. That's not gonna happen on my watch. Your Camacho and Hernandez . . . they *go,* Cy . . . for the good of the city."

The Chief started swinging his head from side to side, all the while staring the Mayor right in the eyes. "Can't do it," he said. "Can't do it." He was seething again.

"You're not leaving me a hell of a lot of room here . . . Chief Booker . . ." The Mayor's sudden formality was more portentous than the Chief's. He had more to back it up with. "*Some*body's got to go."

Sonofabitch! This one knocked the chief off his feet . . . down for the count . . . He could feel his defiance fading . . . This job was the biggest thing in his whole life . . . his family included. *Chief of Police of Miami*—he had never dreamed of such a thing when he became a young cop fifteen years ago . . . a young *black* cop . . . and now he ran the police department in a major American city . . . thanks to that man right there, Dio . . . and now he was putting Dio in the position of having to throw him off that eminent peak, and it was a long way down . . . for the *ex*-Chief, him and his salary of $104,000 and his house in Kendall . . . which cost $680,000 . . . which he never could have swung if the UBT Bank hadn't set him up with a $650,000 mortgage at the near-prime rate of 1.2%... which they never would have done, *never,* were it not important for them to do favors for Mayor Cruz... which they would foreclose faster than you could say *subprime borrower*... reducing him *just like that* from being the Man, though Black, to being another subprime deadbeat black man... He'd have to take the kids out of the Lorimer School... all that, in addition to getting himself stigmatized, big-time, as a traitor to his own people. Oh, Dionisio would see to that. He's no genius, Dio, as the world defines genius, but he sure is a genius looking out for his own hide... and a cutthroat genius, if he has to be—

—and in that microsecond of awareness, all these thoughts hit him, in a single flash of many neurons, and *zzzzzaaaapped* his vows and his courage all at once—

—but not his accursed vanity. Oh no, not for a second. His new vow was not to come up looking like just a run-of-the-mill weakling in front of Dio's Cuban choir, these brownies, these potted palms... his jury. Oh, they would love to see the Big Man, the Chief, the *gran negro* crawling in front of old Dionisio the way *they* crawled. They'd *love* it.

His mind began racing... and then he got it... or he got something. "Well," he said, "let me just give you one piece of advice." ::::::See, I've given in without having to put it that way! *I'm* the one handing out the advice to *him!*:::::: Out loud he said, "Camacho and Hernandez...fired over this?—discharged outright? The union's gonna go apeshit, and the union's run by two real loudmouths, and both a them's Cuban. They'll keep this thing going for a month, they'll turn it into a real inferno, they'll have black folks" ::::::I'm damned if I'm going to say "African American" and sound like I'm walking on broken glass the way they do:::::: "seeing a whole regiment of Cuban cops giving them the finger. You know what I mean?" ::::::Christ, did I really just say *you know what I mean?*:::::: "What we find works better is, we do what we call 'relieve 'm from duty.' The cop has to give up his gun and get relegated to a desk job, and we announce it very loud—once. And everybody gets it right away—everybody. Everybody realizes that taking a cop's gun and badge away from him is like a public castration. After that nobody knows and nobody cares if he still exists. He vanishes. He's the living dead." He stares into the Mayor's eyes some more. He tries to look as sincere as any man who ever lived.

The Mayor looks at the city manager and at Portuondo, the flack. They're trying, but the boys Friday can't pick up any cue as to what they now think. They just stare back at him like five mugs on a shelf.

Finally the Mayor turns back to the Chief. "Okay. But they damn well better vanish. You know what I mean?...If I hear so much as a hiccup out of either one of them, somebody else is gonna vanish. And you . . . *know* . . . what I mean."

Two hours later, which is to say about 10:30 a.m., in Dr. Norman Lewis's office, nothing could have been further from Magdalena's thoughts than YouTube or her old Hialeah beau, Nestor Camacho. To her, all her juvenile days had receded into a dim and dimmer, outworn, outcast, outclassed past. This morning she was obsessed with the brilliant dawn of . . . *him* in her life. *He* had invited her and Norman to dinner on Friday, just a few days from now, at Chez Toi. Restaurants in Miami didn't come any grander than Chez Toi, or so Norman informed her. She had never heard of it before. Chez Toi!! Norman went on about it in tones of socially religious awe. Oh, he was excited, too, Norman was, but not even remotely the way *she* was.

Sometimes her heart literally, *literally,* beat faster just thinking about it . . . which is to say, about *Sergei.* She could actually feel it speed up beneath her breastbone from fear of failure in *his* eyes . . . What should she wear? She didn't possess one thread of clothing that could possibly impress these Chez Toi people . . . or *him.* She'd just have to go *à la cubana* . . . flash plenty of *cubana* cleavage . . . turn her eye sockets into nightclub-black pools with two gleaming orbs floating in them . . . have her long hair cascading down to her shoulders as full-bodied as she and Fructis shampoo, conditioner, and a Conair hair dryer could possibly manage . . . turn her dress, any dress, into nothing but a sheet of Cling Wrap around her breasts, her waist, her hips, her "butt," and her upper thighs . . . only the *upper* thighs . . . at least eighteen inches above the knee . . . She'll lift this whole production up close to six inches on stiletto heels. Sexy—that was the idea. Turn it on . . . the Body! Let sex override all the sophistication she didn't have.

Or would she just look cheap and trashy? Her spirits plummeted. Who *was* she anyway? Who was she supposed to be at this high-class dinner, just an employee of Dr. Lewis, the generous Dr. Lewis who took employees to events like this? Or should she go in the other direction and intimate that there *was* a lot more than that and thereby let Sergei and the world know that a celebrity like Norman Lewis was mad for her, nurse or otherwise?

Plummmmet, went her confidence again. Maybe she was only deluding herself about the whole thing . . . Sergei hadn't said a single *word* to signal any actual interest, not one *spoken word* . . . He had merely poured *a certain look* into her eyes and surreptitiously pressed his fingers into her palm . . . Maybe that was just the way he was around women, a chronic flirt . . . Yes, but pressing a girl's palm with his fingers like that—was so strange that it had to mean something...and he had poured *that certain look* into her eyes not once, but three times...and her heart beat on, beat on, beat on, beneath her breastbone, beat so loudly that—what if Norman could actually hear it? She had reached the point of paranoia...She mustn't let it be known in any way that she was even looking forward to the evening. Whenever Norman mentioned it, she had gone to great lengths to appear indifferent.

She had a magazine from the waiting room open on her desk but had barely glanced at it; so lost was she in a fairyland—that consisted solely of Friday night, Sergei Korolyov, and Magdalena Otero—she didn't notice that Norman had come out of the swami room and was within six feet of her desk.

"Must be a great magazine," he said.

Magdalena looked up, flustered, as if she had been caught out. "Oh, no," she said. "I was sitting here thinking—about something else." She quickly dropped that subject and opened her daybook and said, "Your next appointment is fifteen minutes from now, at eleven, with a new patient, Stanley Roth. I made the appointment myself, but I've got no idea what he does."

"He's a trader for some new hedge fund called Vacuum," said Norman. He smiled. He found "Vacuum" amusing. "I talked to him on the phone."

"Vacuum?" said Magdalena. "Like a vacuum cleaner?"

"Oh, yeah," Norman said with a chortle. "A bunch of young guys. You're gonna laugh when I tell you Mr. Roth's little problem—" He broke off that thought. "What *is* that magazine?"

"It's called—" She had to give it a close inspection herself. "*La Hom*? . . . *Loam*?"

Norman picked it up and inspected it. "It's *Lom,*" he said, pointing at the name at the bottom of a page, *L'Homme*. "It's French. 'The Man.' Take a look at these guys," he said, holding up one of the pages. "All the male models these days are like these two. They're all skinny. They look like they have a serious protein deficiency. They have these sunken cheeks and a six-or-seven-day growth of beard and this gloomy, hangdog look, as if they've just been released after five years of hard time, during which they contracted AIDS from getting buggered so much by other prisoners. I don't get it. This is going to make young men want to buy the clothes these lulus are modeling? Or maybe these days looking like a gay AIDS blade is fashhh-ionable*ahhHHHHock hock hock hock* . . . They look like these emaciated young men Egon Schiele used to paint. They have this look like they're all so weak and sickly, they're going to pass out and collapse and die in a pile of bones right in your face."

Magdalena said, "Who? Did you say Sheila?"

"It's German," said Norman, "S-c-h-i-e-l-e. Egon Schiele. He was from Austria."

"And he's famous?" said Magdalena...glumly... All this art stuff the *americanos* thought was so important...

"Oh, sure," said Norman. "I mean I guess he's famous if you're into early-twentieth-century Austrian art, the way I am. I really consider—" He abruptly broke off whatever he was about to say and averted his eyes. His face fell. He looked sad in a way Magdalena had never seen before.

"Yeah," he said, "I'm 'into' early-twentieth-century Austrian art, all right. I'm 'into' it in those seventy-five-dollar picture books, that's how far I'm 'into' it. It was twenty years ago when I first discovered Schiele and Gustav Klimt and, oh, Richard Gerstl and Oskar Kokoschka and that whole bunch. I could have bought this terrific Schiele for twenty-five thousand at auction. But I was in medical school, and I didn't even come *close* to having twenty-five thousand dollars to spend on some 'artwork.' I was living practically hand-to-mouth. Same thing for another eight years as an intern and a resident. Finally I open my own practice and start making some money and I come up for air, and those Austrians—I look up, and they're in earth orbit! A couple of years ago, that same painting sold for twenty-five *million*. It had increased in price a *thousand times* while I wasn't looking."

He paused . . . He looked at Magdalena in a wary, tentative way that seemed to say *I don't know whether I should be getting into all this stuff with you or not.* He must have decided, *Oh, what the hell,* because he proceeded to get into it.

"You know," he said, "people used to think doctors were rich. If you lived out where the doctors lived, you knew you were in the best neighborhood in town. That's not true anymore. You can't make any real money if you're working for fees. Doctors, lawyers—we get fees for the time we spend on a case, so much per hour. So do violin teachers and carpenters. You go on vacation, you go hunting, you go to sleep—you get no fee. Now, just compare that with someone like Maurice. It doesn't matter if he's asleep, daydreaming, playing tennis, off on a cruise, or, for that matter, doing what he usually does, trying to find a way to wrap at least one finger and his thumb around his erect phallus without pressing upon any of his herpes blisters. Even while he's doing the worst thing he can do in his condition, he's got this company, American ShowUp, out there working for him day and night. They bring in the exhibition cubicles, the revolving platforms, the stages, the tents, the frameworks for everything you can think of from automobile shows and medical conferences to ordinary conventions. Believe me, if you have eighty percent of that business in the United States, the way

Maurice does, that adds up to billions. That's why you have to have a *product*. That's why I go on all these TV shows. It's not just the publicity. You have to admit I'm not bad on television. I could see myself getting a network show like this Dr. Phil. He makes a killing doing that show. That gives him something to sell. The more TV stations take the show, the more money he makes. He's not working for fees anymore. Now he's a franchise. He goes to sleep, he goes to Istanbul on vacation, and the franchise is still doing business while he's not looking. I can see some good spin-offs, too, like e-books, even paper books—you know... like, printed."

Magdalena was astonished, shocked. "What are you saying, Norman! You have a... a... calling—you have something that's so much... so much finer than what they have... these Dr. Phils, turning themselves into *characters* on television. Doctors—nurses, too—I remember the day I raised my right hand—doctors and nurses, we take an oath to devote our lives to the sick. I remember that day because I'm proud of it. TV doctors turn their backs on the Hippocratic Oath. They're devoting themselves to making money and being celebrities. When I think of 'Dr. Phil'... I wonder what he tells his children he's doing?... assuming he has children."

Norman seemed chastened. Perhaps he even felt guilty, which was not his way. Oh, no—not at all.

Quietly—for Norman—he said, "Oh, I'm sure he tells them he can help so many more people this way, people all over the country, people all over the world—or maybe he goes all the way and says 'heal,' not just help the whole world but heal it. If my parents had told me something like that when I was six or seven, I would have chosen to believe them... In any case, you're right, Magdalena." He didn't say that very often, either. Maybe he *did* feel guilty. "Even if you go on television now and then, the way I do, your peers, other doctors, hold it against you. I used to think it was pure jealousy. Now I'm not so sure. I guess it is partly about that honor—but they're jealous bastards, all the same."

"But don't you see?" said Magdalena. "It *is* about honor. We don't do this for money, you and me. We do it for honor. Somebody like Maurice comes in, and he has an addiction that's gradually eating up his life. Here he is, a billionaire—and does that make him feel secure? He's a wreck! Last week at Art Basel I must have seen him trying to scratch his crotch without anybody noticing a hundred times. He's pathetic... and he's totally dependent on you. What's worth more, all his money or your ability to heal people? He's down here"—she lowered one hand and made the palm parallel with the floor and raised the other hand three feet above it—"and you're up here. It doesn't matter how much money *you* have. You're

Dr. Norman Lewis. You have a *gift*. Can't you see that?"

Norman nodded a faint *yes,* looked down at the floor, and didn't say a word. Was this modesty in light of the high place in the life of Man that she had just ascribed to him? But she had never seen him overcome by modesty before. Now he had his eyes aimed down . . . at what? The wall-to-wall carpet apparently. It was perfectly good, practical, with a forest-green background and a fine-line white windowpane plaid. Not bad . . . and maybe worth five seconds of study.

"What are you thinking about, Norman?"

"Oh . . . nothing . . ." He still wasn't looking at her, and she had never heard his voice die like this.

A vile thought insinuated itself into her head. It was so vile, she resolved not to think about it at all. Maurice had been coming to see Norman three times a week, meaning close to $3,000 per week in fees. As far as she could tell, Maurice hadn't improved in the slightest, and in some ways he had gotten worse. His leper-blistered groin was a disaster. But the whole thing was so vile, she just wasn't going to think about it. Why try to out-analyze Norman? Norman was perhaps as well known as any psychiatrist in the country. How could she presume to second-guess him . . . and even wonder if Norman didn't find it to his advantage to have Maurice undergo such endless therapy? But that was the vile part! How could she let her imagination run wild like that? She wasn't going to. The next thing she knew, she would start wondering who was getting the most out of this doctor-patient relationship. How had Norman managed to get a slip for his cigarette boat in the famous marina at Fisher Island?... Maurice... How had he managed to be among the very first in line for the mad rush on the opening day of Art Basel? Maurice. How had he managed to be invited to dinner at Chez Toi by one of the leading figures in the Miami art world, Sergei Korolyov?... Because Sergei had seen him in Maurice's entourage at Art Basel... Anyone who didn't realize that Norman was a shameless climber would have to be blind.

She thought of a way to get Norman on that subject without being too obvious. There was nothing out of place for her to ask—and so she did: "Norman," she said, "you think Maurice will be there Friday night?"

It was as if she had pushed the switch that turned Norman back on. "Oh, yes! He's already talked to me about it. He thinks this Korolyov might be an important new friend. And he *loves* Chez Toi. *Yowza yowza.* It has the kind of cachet Maurice thinks is very important. I've been there and I know how much it impresses somebody like Maurice."

"Cashay?" said Magdalena.

"You know, it's like... a reputation or a certain social level."

"Cashay," said Magdalena in a dead tone of voice.

"They have a black membership card, and if you have that, you can go to the cocktail lounge upstairs. Otherwise, you can't go up there."

"Do you have a membership card?"

Norman paused. "Well... actually... no. But I've been in the lounge."

Magdalena said, "You've been there a lot?"

"Up to a point." Norman paused again, and his expression became tentative, which was not like him. "Come to think of it... twice, I guess."

"Who did you go with?"

Long pause... a frown... finally: "With Maurice."

"Both times?"

Longer pause... deflated scowl: "Yes." Norman gave her a sharp look. Somehow Magdalena had become an interrogator and had found him out, not in a lie... but in the sin of omission... omission of anything that might reveal his dependence on Maurice—his patient. He changed course and brightened again. "But I know Maurice much better than most people, maybe better than *anyone* else. Everybody in Miami wants to be next to Maurice, the art collectors, the art dealers—*art* dealers! I mean, you better believe it*ttahHHHHock hock hock hock!*—the museum directors, the politicians, every type of businessman you can think of—very much including our new friend, Korolyov. You remember the way Korolyov came hustling over to Maurice at

Art Basel? He practically kissed his shoes, like a little Russian serf. I mean, Maurice has the most influential network in South Florida." He smiled broadly, then looked into Magdalena's eyes with great earnestness. "That's why we—you *and* me—we've got to do everything in our power to get Maurice out from under this terrible weakness, this addictive weakness. Weakness shouldn't become addictive, but it does. You put it correctly, Magdalena; it's *wrecking* him. We can't let that happen. He's not just a rich and powerful man. He's also a decent man, who is dedicated to doing good in the whole community. We have to get our job done, Magdalena! That's why I try to stay with him even beyond our sessions. I felt it was *important* for me to be with him at Art Basel, even though most psychiatrists would never do that. So many exciting things in this town are like Art Basel. At their core they're utterly amoral. The people there are comfortable with pornography, so long as it has a 'cultivated' provenance."

::::::provenance?::::::

"Maurice could have sunk into that quicksand and we'd never find him again. But we didn't let that happen, Magdalena. We stayed there with him to the end."

The odd thing... maybe the *happy* thing is... he believes every word of that, thought Magdalena. He's being utterly sincere. Dutifully, she warded off every countervailing interpretation.

13

A La Moda Cubana

It was about five minutes before noon when the Sergeant and Nestor walked three blocks from the Starbucks and arrived at the main police headquarters at 400 East Second Avenue N.W. They kept their cop shades on, even though the shades plunged the lobby, the waiting area, into the last dim dying moments of dusk... but not so dark that they couldn't see all the cops looking at them and checking them out.

The Sergeant said, "The first one a these suckers tries to get smart with me, I'm gonna bite his fucking nose off for him."

The force was spared any impending proboscission when the hot *cubana* named Cat Posada—unh huhhh, *Cat*—appeared from out of nowhere—or nowhere to two men leading a twilight life behind their cop shades, and gave them a perfect Girl from

Ipanema smile—goes *ahhhhhh*—and said they should come with her. Apparently, the Chief was smart enough to know that nothing cools off a young male's rankles faster than a hot girl's charms.

On the elevator up, Nestor practiced the look he wanted to show the Chief: *I'm a real cop*... shoulders back, military-style, correct posture to burn, head back, chin down. He wasn't so sure about the chin down... it did something funny to his lips—and at that very moment the Sergeant glanced over and said, "What's the matter with *you?*" Nestor decided he would only lose points with lovely Cat Posada if he opened that subject up in front of her... Why did he even care? He just *did*. Why did he care about how he looked in front of guys in the video game arcade he'd never see again?... the girl at the cash register at Starbucks?... two young black guys walking toward him on the street yesterday, minding their own business? Did he try to look so tough, they wouldn't even *think* of fucking with him? Half your life you spent wondering how you looked to this total stranger and that one...

When they reached the third floor, lovely Cat led Nestor and the Sergeant down a long, too narrow, too gloomy hallway lined with small offices, doors open... revealing the little bureaucratic cogs, many of whom really would recognize them as the two racist cops from YouTube... He took every glance to be an accusing stare. *Un negro* employee looked his way—nothing more than that—looked his way. He felt terribly embarrassed and falsely condemned. He wanted to stop and *explain…it wasn't like that at all!—not in* my *case!*…They reached an office way down at the corner, and gorgeous Cat—men are terrible! Even under pressure of something serious, something he feared, Nestor kept thinking of her as lovely, gorgeous Cat—and maybe she'd like to go have some coffee later? The sublime Cat motioned for them to wait a moment while she went inside, and they heard her say, "Chief, Sergeant Hernandez and Officer Camacho are here." When the radiant Cat came out, she smiled at them, the irresistible Cat did, and indicated that they should go in. She walked the other way without looking back *pop* went the fantasy.

Nestor was unnerved by the Chief's expression. He was sitting at his desk and barely even looked up when Nestor and the Sergeant walked in. Now he *did* look up and aimed his forefinger like a revolver at a couple of straight-back chairs side by side directly in front of his desk.

"Have a seat," he said in a not particularly hospitable way.

Straight-back chairs…the office was on a corner and had big windows with a view of…not much of anything. It was a lot smaller and less imposing than Nestor had pictured it in his mind.

The Chief leaned back in his big swivel chair and just gazed at them without any expression for a moment, and that moment stretched out s t r e t c h e d o u t... Nestor became acutely aware of just how big the man was... and how dark his face... and that plus the Chief's dark-navy uniform made Nestor hyperaware of the whites of his eyes. He looked powerful enough to be a whole other order of *Homo sapiens*. A cop's Heaven of gold stars, four on each side, ran along each side of his collar, making the Chief's mighty neck official.

Finally the Chief spoke. "You two have any idea what's been going on with your little YouTube performance over the past six hours or so?"

He hadn't even gotten the "or so" out of his mouth before the Sergeant, eyes ablaze, broke in, "I'm sorry, Chief, but that wasn't any 'little performance!' That was the performance of my duties! And some... *bastard*... tries to do me in by posting a... a... a *tampered* version of that *uh uh uh illegal* video on YouTube!"

Nestor was stunned. ::::::For God's sake, Sarge, you're crazy! You're a two-legged case of insubordination.::::::

The Chief was stunned, too. What kind of impudent—whereupon he leaned across the desk and roared in the Sergeant's face, "You're telling me the thing is a fake? That it isn't even you? Or somebody put words in your mouth? Or some *bastard's* trying to do you in? And somehow he can fake your voice and have you ranting like some goddamn Ku Klux Cuban cracker? Who *is* this fiendish *bastard,* Sergeant? I'd really like to know!"

"Look, Chief, I'm not saying what I'm saying. That thing on YouTube's not what I was saying... you know? I'm saying the bastard posts what I'm saying but he don't say he's cut out the part that made me say what I'm saying!"

Roaring: "Shut up, Hernandez! Nobody gives a good fuck about what you're saying you said. What you said is on the fucking world wide web, and you made yourself very clear, and you got any idea at all what that racist YouTube segment a yours has blown up into? Do you know how many other sites, blogs, and news outlets have picked up the fucking video?"

"It's not any segment a *mine,* Chief—"

"What's the matter with you, Hernandez? You deaf? You dense? You don't know what *shut up* means?"

The "Hernandez" is a left hook to the ribs. Jorge Hernandez is no longer "Sergeant." That gets his attention, more than the scolding. He's sitting straight up, rigid in the straight-back chair with his mouth open, while the Chief says:

"I've been getting calls and e-mails, texts, and fucking tweets, ever since six o'clock this morning, and the goddamned thing hadn't been out for more than a couple of hours at that point—and these e-mails and tweets are not just coming from Overtown and Liberty City and Little Haiti. They're coming from all over the goddamned world! I get shit from France like 'You, with all your pious talk about human rights and freedom and the rest of it—and now we see what American criminal justice is really like'—that's the kind of *shit* I'm getting, Hernandez, and what *I'm* getting—"

Hernandez—the guy is too much! He tries to break back in! "Look, Chief, they can't say that, because—"

He never completes the sentence. He's paralyzed by the look on the Chief's face. The Chief doesn't say a word. He gives an ominous smile, the sort of me-beating-the-shit-out-of-you smile that says, *"You little faggot! Any time you want to take this off the official level, just say the word, and we'll step outside and I'll wrap your ascending colon around your head like a turban for you."* Chastened, the Sergeant shut up.

In a softer, calmer tone, the Chief said, "And what I'm getting is nothing compared to what the Mayor's getting. It's a goddamned shit flood over there. This thing has gone viral. This isn't some picture from thirty-something feet away of police officers who look like they're standing over some poor bastard on the ground and just whaling away at him with their billy clubs and you don't know why and you don't know what they're saying. This time the camera was up close and right on top of the two of you, and it picked up every word you said, and not only the words but the expressions on your faces when you said them, and your faces said it all, louder than your words."

The Chief paused in a... significant manner. He stared, not very pleasantly, at the Sergeant and then the same way at Nestor. "Either of you two ever been in a play? You know... onstage?"

Neither of them said a word. Finally the Sergeant shook his head *no,* and Nestor did the same thing.

"I didn't think so," said the Chief. "So it wasn't some great job of acting. The two a you put on a genuine exhibition of racial bigotry for the whole fucking world, didn't you, a nice sincere exhibition."

The Chief was glowering at them, but now it was Nestor who was desperate to break in. ::::::But this is totally unfair! You didn't pay attention to what I actually said! You can't just lump me together with the Sergeant! Don't you have any idea of what started this whole thing? You're not some clueless work-a-daddy who looks at the thing and thinks it all began with two Cuban cops throwing that big black hulk flat out on the floor and then calling him this and that just for the fun of it?!:::::: And then Nestor's rope broke:

"That's not fair, Chief"—his voice started rising on the way to a scream—"because all I said—"

"You, too, Camacho! Shut up! Both a you *listen*

and listen carefully to every word I say." The Chief paused. He seemed to be debating whether or not to let Nestor really have it. He must have decided no. When he resumed, his voice took on a tone of blunt reasoning. "Look, I know the video cut everything that explains what drove you to that point. I know the urge to kill some punk who's just tried to kill me, because I've been there a hell of a lot more than you have. I know what it is to wanna bury the motherfucker with every jab you can get out of your mouth. I've been there, too. But you two had to ring the fucking gong, didn't you. You had to come up with the worst brand of bigotry in America today. You had to come up with a goddamn *thesaurus* of the insults guaranteed to hurt black folks' feelings the most. And I've been there, too. Me, I don't *take* any a that shit anymore, and I'll break every bone in the body of any fool who directs it at me, from the humerus to the hip socket to the hyoid. I guarantee I will fuck up *any* cracker who tries to put that shit over on me."

Nestor was dying—*dying*—to cry out. ::::::But it wasn't *me!* I didn't say anything wrong!:::::: Two things held him back... One, he had a live fear of the Chief and what he might do. And two, if he started trying to pin the blame on the Sergeant... he'd be ostracized—by these guys, the brotherhood, the police force, Hernandez, Ruiz, even *americanos* like Kite and McCorkle from the Marine Patrol, and yeah, even the Chief. ::::::I won't take this kind of abuse from my dad, my *papi,* anymore, but I'll take it from this big black man at that desk. Cops are my whole life, the only people I have now. And what if sixty seconds from now it turns out that the Chief's bone-crushing anger is just the build-up to canning us, me and the Sergeant, firing us, dumping us like a couple of dead fish gone high?::::::

The next words out of the Chief's mouth were "Don't worry, I'm not gonna fire you, I'm not gonna demote you. I think I know you two guys. You're two cops..." He paused, as if to let that sink in. "Whatever else you are—and you're probably a stone-cold irredeemable racist, Hernandez—you both have medals for valor, and they don't just get handed out to improve morale. But what we've gotta do in the short run, it's not so understanding and forgiving of human frailty."

He smiled slightly when he said "human frailty." It was his first affable smile since he began this lecture. Okay, thought Nestor, ::::::but what is supposed to be amusing about "human frailty," unless the Chief wants to show that he knows he was using a bullshit expression? And who was "we"—or was it just another one of these bullshit words politicians like to use by way of saying, "You're not just looking at one man here, you're in the presence of the Power"?::::::

"We're going to have to relieve you from duty," the

Chief said. "As I said, this is what we gotta do in the short run. It's not a permanent thing. You'll be paid as usual."

Nestor looked at the Sergeant. The Sergeant had his lips compressed and kept clenching his jaw muscles. He seemed to have some knowledge about just what "relieved from duty" meant that Nestor didn't have. Nestor worked up enough courage to ask, "Chief... could you tell me what that means exactly? We come in and do desk work?"

"No," said the Chief. "If you're relieved from duty, you don't do any work at all." The Chief's face was a stone once more.

"You don't do *any* work?" By the time he finished the question, Nestor found himself no longer looking at the Chief but at the Sergeant. Somehow he had the feeling—only that, a feeling—that the Sergeant would give him a straighter answer.

The Sergeant was looking at the Chief with an almost impudent little smile.

"No, you won't be doing any work," said the Chief. Same stony expression. "And you won't be coming in. You'll have to be available for calls at home from eight a.m. to six p.m. every day."

"Calls to do..." Nestor couldn't pull himself together long enough to complete the question.

"Not to do anything," said the Chief. "You just have to be available for the calls."

Nestor looked at him blankly, catatonically.

"And you surrender your badge and your service revolver."

::::::Surrender? . . . my badge and my service revolver? . . . and do nothing?::::::

"You might as well hand them over to me . . . now."

Nestor looked at the Sergeant, who was looking at the Chief with a resigned twist to his lips. He had known all along, hadn't he? Nestor was worse than stunned. He was frightened all over again.

Barely an hour after Camacho and Hernandez had left his office, Cat Posada brought the Chief a hand-delivered letter and arched her eyebrows in a way that says, "Oh ho! What do we have here?!"

The Chief had the same reaction, but he didn't show it until she had left the room. ::::::God, she is some kinda *hot,* Miss Cat Posada—and I'm not gonna take one step down *that* road.:::::: He looked at the letter again and shook his head and sighed. The return address was in the upper left-hand corner written in ballpoint pen, and the name was Nestor Camacho. He had never seen an officer relieved of duty begin his appeal barely one hour later. ::::::Bad move, Camacho. There's nothing you can say that won't make it worse.::::::

He sliced open the envelope and read,

Dear Chief Booker,

Respectfully, can an officer relieved of duty give information he got before he was relieved of duty? Hoping that he can, please respectfully accept the following in the case of the teacher José Estevez who was arrested after an altercation at Lee de Forest Senior High School.

::::::The kid's respectfulling me half-to-death, and he's totally offing English grammar.:::::: But as the kid blundered on, he began to make sense. He was saying that the student whom Estevez had supposedly attacked, François Dubois, was the leader of a gang and that he and the gang had intimidated at least four students into giving false information to the investigating officers. He gave their names and said, "Two of them are sixteen years old, and two of them are seventeen years old. They are not 'tough guys,' they are not gang members"—he put *tough guys* in quotes, because he couldn't come up with a more dignified term, no doubt—"they are only 'boys.' They are already afraid they are getting into serious trouble by false testimony. Our Department will get them to tell the truth quickly." The grammar was getting bloodier and bloodier, but the potential of this information the Chief liked... a lot.

He didn't even bother to summon Cat Posada over

the intercom. He just yelled out the door, "Miss Posada! Get me Lieutenant Verjillo!"

Thank God he had Camacho figured wrong. He wasn't making an appeal. He was just being a cop.

Magdalena kept her dressy clothes at her official address, the little apartment she rented with Amélia Lopez on Drexel Avenue. Her declarations about turning her back on Hialeah and the Hialeah Cuban life had been many and open . . . and *loud* anytime she could shove them in her mother's face. Yet there was still enough Catholic upbringing in her to want to keep up appearances. Suppose some old friend or relative . . . or her mother or father, although they wouldn't dare . . . happened to use some outrageous sob story to prevail upon Amélia to let her into the apartment. She wanted it to look like she actually lived there. At Norman's she mainly kept her white I'm-a-nurse dresses and some weekend-type clothes, jeans, matelot shirts, bikinis, tank tops, shorts, sundresses, cotton cardigan sweaters, and the like.

It so happened that on Friday she was inside her bedroom closet—*inside* her closet in the moral apartment—trying to get dressed in a furiously great hurry, clad so far in nothing but a thong, thrashing, thrashing, thrashing, panic-driven, among two closet rods' worth of hanging garments, muttering louder and louder . . . "Oh, my God . . . I don't believe this . . . it was hanging right next to *that*." *Thrash thrash thrash* "Oh, *shit* . . . not even one . . . Chez Toi . . . What's my—"

"*Dios mío, qué pasa,* Magdalena?" And there was Amélia in the doorway, in her T-shirt and jeans. Magdalena didn't even look up. Neither of them was shy about seeing the other stark naked or as near to it as Magdalena was now.

"I can't find anything to wear. *Lo es qué pasa*."

Amélia chuckled. "Who *can*? Where you going?"

Amélia was a pretty girl from Peru, although not as pretty as *she* was . . . she had a round face with big dark eyes and miles of glistening dark hair. She was about Magdalena's size but ever so slightly thick in the ankles. One thing about her Magdalena truly envied, however: Amélia was sophisticated, at least compared to any other nurse she knew. Amélia was twenty-six. She had graduated with a BA from EGU before even thinking about nursing school. Somehow she just *knew* things . . . she caught on to references . . . She was a real adult, at least in Magdalena's eyes . . . a real adult a real adult a real adult—and Magdalena responded: "Some place called Chez Toi."

"*Some place called Chez Toi,*" said Amélia. "You don't fool around when it comes to *some place,* do you!"

"Have you ever been there?"

"Me? I wouldn't even try. It's impossible to get a reservation, and the prices are insane. Who's taking you? Let me guess...your friend Dr. Lewis."

"Yep." Magdalena felt strangely glum about the admission and didn't know exactly why. For whatever reason, she was becoming weary and embarrassed by this sexual bond with her employer. "You got it...but help me anyway, will you? I can't find anything that's gonna look right at a place like that. I just don't own any fancy dresses."

Amélia went into the closet herself while Magdalena stood outside with her arms folded beneath her breasts. She began pulling back hangers rapidly, one after the other, at a machine-like pace *clack...clack...clack...clack.* Then she stopped and looked at Magdalena from deep in the closet.

"You know what?" she said. "You're right. You don't have anything. If I were you, I'd go in another direction."

"What other direction?" said Magdalena. "Norman's going to be here any minute."

"I've got an idea," said Amélia. She emerged from the closet with a hanger bearing a short black skirt.

"*That?* That's just a plain cotton skirt. I got it at Forever 21. Only comes down to *here.*" She placed the edge of her hand barely halfway down her thigh.

"Wait a sec, and I'll show you. You're gonna look

amazing!" She laughed in a slightly mischievous way. "You're gonna love it!" She practically ran to her room, yelling over her shoulder, "And forget putting on a bra!"

In no time she was back with a big smile on, holding what looked to Magdalena like a corset, but a corset made of black silk with two black silk cups at the top. Beneath each cup three rows of what looked like zippers ran to the bottom of the thing.

"What is *that?*" said Magdalena. "It looks like a corset."

"It *is* like a corset, when you get right down to it," said Amélia. "It's a *bustier.*"

"A *bus-te-ay?* Oh, yeah, I've heard of bustiers, but I guess I never saw anybody wear one."

"You just put that on with your black skirt—and you'll look hot as shit!"

"Are you *serious?*" Magdalena stared at the thing. "I don't know, Amélia. They'll think I'm a *hooker.*"

"Bustiers are in right now. I could show you a dozen magazines."

"What do I wear over it?"

"Nothing! That's the whole point! At first it looks like some kind of lingerie. See all these little lines of fake zippers? But then you see it's made of silk, and it covers you from the waist up just as well as a ball gown—*more,* if you've noticed what all the models are wearing these days."

Magdalena looked highly dubious. "I don't know..."

"Look, Magdalena, what do you *want* to look like, some *cubana* wannabe *americana* wearing a proper dress from the tag sale at the discount mall?"

That brought Magdalena up short. She was speechless... running all the possibilities through her mind like a number cruncher. "I don't know... I just don't know..." She turned her hands into tight little frustrated fists. "And Norman's gonna be here any second, and this Chez Toi is such a big deal."

"You gotta be the best *you,*" Amélia went on, "and that's *a la moda cubana!* Just a couple more things. You got a gold necklace? You know, nothing showy."

"I've got *one*."

Magdalena turned and opened a bureau drawer. She produced a necklace with a small gold cross hanging from it.

"A cross!" said Amélia. "That's *perfect!* In fact, you don't know how perfect that is. This won't take a second," said Amélia. "Just get into the skirt and get into the *bustier,* and you're *ready!* I'll zip it up in back."

Magdalena let loose with a big sigh of despair but did it anyway, and Amélia zipped up the back, which was cut so low it left her bare down to about six inches above the waist.

"Now put on the necklace." Magdalena put on the necklace.

"Perfect!" said Amélia. "Now come look at yourself in the mirror."

Magdalena was shocked by what she saw. The bustier had pushed her breasts up so high, it created a very visible cleavage and rounded them slightly on top.

"Oh, my God," said Magdalena. "They look so big."

"'Big' is what we're after," said Amélia. "You look *great*. And that little cross? Didn't I tell you? *Perfection*."

The cross lay upon her bosom right where the cleavage began.

"You're like a virgin on a hill overlooking the Devil's playground, Magdalena! Just have the confidence. Tonight is all yours, Magdalena, *yours!* Smile a lot. Smile at empty spaces on the walls, if you have to. All of Chez Toi will be coming to you, not you to Chez Toi. You know what your secret will be? You'll make your entrance *a la moda cubana*. You won't have to *act*... like *anything!* You'll be the most comfortable, most confident person in the house!"

The whistler began whistling atop Magdalena's bureau, and Amélia practically jumped out of her skin... Magdalena's cell phone ring, it was... Nestor had rigged it up for her—the sound of a man whistling a tune, but nobody knew what tune. He loved playing around with things like that. His own phone rang with some hip-hop song. What was it, now? Oh, yes. "¡Caliente! Caliente baby... Got plenty fuego in yo' caja china"—but that gave Magdalena no twinge of nostalgia at all. It merely made her think about what *babies* they had been...furtively doing the *in and out, in and out, in and out* always looking for some friend's empty bed nobody would stumble upon...She couldn't believe what children they had both been...living for the *in and out, in and out, in and out*—"Hello?"

"Magdalena, I thought you were going to be waiting downstairs!" Norman, of course. "There's no place to park." Norman, resentful and cross.

"Be right down!" Magdalena wheeled about to study herself in the mirror again. She started shaking her head. "I just don't *know* about this, Amélia..."

"I *do* know!" said Amélia. "Chez Toi *needs* you. They *need* a little sex, and it'll be arriving looking very sweet! There's a cross between your boobs!"

Magdalena was still staring at the creature in the mirror, still transfixed by herself. "*Oh, Dios mío,* Amélia!" There was a little tremor in her voice. "You better be right! There's no time to change, anyway. Norman will kill me!"

"You're a vision, Magdalena, a *vision*. Just remember two things. You've been revirginated. You're a virgin with a cross over your heart! You're younger, prettier, and purer than any other woman at Chez Toi. Remember that—and be confident. You're *better* than they are...the snobs..."

By the time she came down the elevator and went out to Norman's car, her spirits, which had been lifted by no more than a thread in the first place, had collapsed. What was she *doing?* Some *virgin*...yeah, some virgin trying her best to look like a slut...in a bustier. What a *fool* she was!

But as soon as she opened the door of Norman's Audi, he broke into a big lascivious smile and said, "Heyyyy, look at *you!* The hell with Chez Toi! Let's go straight to my place!"

Magdalena slid into the passenger seat. "You sure this isn't too much?"

"*You're* too much, Magdalena!" He kept leering at her. Norman wasn't the best judge in the world. ::::::He is half crazed when it comes to sex, my eminent porn-addiction psychiatrist.:::::: Still, it was encouraging. At least her getup wasn't a total obvious disaster. ::::::Be confident! Well, not yet. But maybe I have a fighting chance.::::::

As they drove down Lincoln Road, Norman said, "Have you seen this thing on YouTube?"

"What thing?"

"You've got to see it! There's a video of these two Miami cops on top of a black guy—they're white—they've got this black prisoner lying on the floor with his hands tied behind his back, and they're on top of him, giving him elbows to the head and calling him everything short of *you nigger* you can imagine! You've *got* to see it."

Got to see something? In fact, Magdalena was barely paying attention to what he was saying. The only question was, what will *he* think of it. Will *he* think I look like a little tramp . . . or did Norman have a believable reaction? She looked down at her bosom. Nothing had changed. You could see . . . *everything*.

They arrived at Chez Toi and turned the Audi over to the valet. Magdalena said, "This is it? A hedge?"

"This is it," said Norman. "It's behind the hedge." They were just a few steps from a privet hedge that must have been ten or eleven feet high. An *enormous* privet hedge. The thing had been trimmed meticulously, absolutely evenly, on top. A portal had been cut through it . . . a rectangle well over seven feet high and four feet wide and at least a yard deep . . . a rectangle perfect down to the last trimmed tiny privet leaf. Darkness was closing in rapidly, and in the twilight one could easily mistake the hedge for a battlement, a forbidding wall of solid masonry.

"I don't even see a sign."

"There aren't any signs," said Norman in the tone of somebody who *knows these things*.

Magdalena's heart began racing. All over again she thought of something more basic. All over again she was plunged into despair. What if she were completely deceiving herself! What had Sergei said to her last week? *Nothing!*—not one personal word! Merely the polite, meaningless things proper people are supposed to say when they're introduced to you. She had built this whole thing up out of looks and smiles and gestures that might or might not have revealed any feeling at all on his part. He had poured his long, searching, insinuating looks into her eyes... *three times*. But suppose they weren't *searching* for anything, and they weren't *insinuating* anything? Suppose they were merely long by *her* clock? Too late to figure it out *now!* Here she was, and there he was, presumably, somewhere on the other side of that hedge... and she was still aboard an insane flight, diving, soaring, diving, soaring soaring soaring until the next little what-if sends her into a fatal dive and the next faint hope pulls her out of it... and this had been going on every waking moment for seven days—

"But how does anybody know it's there?" said Magdalena.

"Anybodies don't know," said Norman. "It's open to the public, but it's like a private club. Unless they know you or someone has put in a word for you, it's very hard to make a reservation. Having no signs is... you know... part of the aura of the place."

Magdalena had no idea what an *aura* was... but this wasn't the time to ask for definitions. They were right at the improbable portal, a rectangle cut through a three-foot-thick privet hedge with a precision that would cause a mere stonemason to swoon with envy. Two couples were honking away in English with their amusement turned up to the max. Then she and Norman walked through this precisely, prissily clipped formal hedgeway and—there was Chez Toi, Your House, right in front of them. Magdalena knew the restaurant was literally in a house, but her imagination had built a mansion. This was no mansion. That much was obvious even as the darkness closed in. By Miami standards, it was an old, old house, one of the few remaining examples of a style that had been fashionable a hundred years ago, Mediterranean Revival. Almost the entire front yard was now a terrace and a vista of soft candle lights on the tables of people dining outside. There was more candlelight above, in the old-fashioned lamps that hung from the branches of spreading blackthorn trees. The candlelight did wonders for the white faces of the Anglos... who were everywhere... They seemed to occupy every last seat out here. Their voices created a buzz and a babble... none of it raucous.

It was lovely out here, but *¡Dios mío!* it was *¡hot!*

They found themselves in the entry gallery of what looked like somebody's old house, comfortable but by no means luxurious... near, but not on, the ocean... and certainly not what Magdalena expected to see in the most eminent of all restaurants in Miami. Straight ahead was a set of stairs, but with no grand curving sweep of banisters and balustrades. On either side was an arched doorway... arched, but with arches no one would remember ten seconds later... and yet out from under one of them was pouring the noisy buzz and burble, the shrieks and bassos profundissimos of laughter, the irrational rapture of mortals who know they have arrived *where things are happening.* Anyone who had heard it before, the way Magdalena had at Art Basel, would recognize that sound forever after.

Over to one side, at a console, a maître d' was conferring with six customers, four men and two women. The servitor, i.e., the maître d', was instantly recognizable. He was the one dressed like a gentleman. That was the way it seemed to be these days. He wore a cream-colored tropical worsted suit and a necktie of darkest aubergine. The other four males, being the customers, wore no jackets. In the contemporary fashion, even among older men like them, they wore shirts with open necks, the better to reveal the way the deep lines beside their noses descended into their wattles, their jowls, and that overture to old age, a pair of harp-string-size tendons on either side of the Adam's apple. The maître d' showed them all to the terrace, then hurried over to Norman and Magdalena with a pleasant smile and "Bonsoir, monsieur, madame." That was it for French, unless you counted the restaurant's name. "Welcome to Chez Toi." He had a pleasant smile—and didn't have what a little girl from Hialeah instinctively feared in a fancy place like this, namely, an attitude of *maître de votre destin,* your destiny. Norman mentioned Korolyov and his party, and the maître d' said they were having drinks in the library, as he called it. He led them to the arched doorway of the rapturous noise.

Mr. Korolyov... Magdalena put her hands together and could actually feel them trembling. Now she and Norman were inside the rapturous room. Men and women were gesticulating this way and that for emphasis and rolling their eyes as if *I had never heard of such a thing* or else *My God, how could such a thing be?*... and, above all, laughing so much, the world could tell that each and every one of them was an integral part of this exalted convening of the demigods. Magdalena had walked into Chez Toi swearing to Venus, Goddess of Seduction, that she would remain cool, even aloof, as if she could take the men in this room or leave them. Instead, she found herself caught up in the overwhelming status delirium of the place. Her eyes were *darting about darting about darting about*... looking for... *him*. The library, as the maître d' had referred to it, had shelves of books, real books, on the wall, giving the restaurant still more of the *chez-toi,* your-house, mental atmosphere, but seemed to be used mainly as a small dining room. The tables had been pulled back toward the walls to allow

Mr. Korolyov and his party more room to mingle, linger, tingle, blingle over drinks at this, the cocktail hour... but where is *he?* Suppose he's *not* here, and this whole—

—all at once Norman was leaving her side and heading into the madding crowd.

"Norman!"

Norman stopped for an instant and turned about with a guilty smile on his face and held up his forefinger in the pantomime that says, "*Don't worry, I'll only be a second.*"

Magdalena was shocked... and then she panicked... What was she supposed to do, a twenty-four-year-old girl standing here among all these old people—they're all so old!—and so white!—and she is a little Cuban girl, a nurse named Magdalena Otero, corseted into a bustier shoving her all-but-bare breasts into their faces like two big servings of flan!

And then she was furious. When Norman lifted his forefinger, he wasn't saying I'll be back in a moment... oh, no... consciously or not, he was saying I'm Number One and I've spotted somebody immensely more important than you and, sorry, but I must lay my Famous Dr. Porn charm on him while I have him in my sights!

What was she supposed to do now? Stand here like a tart on call? Already people were cutting glances at her... or was it just at the bustier and her breasts?

::::::*Goddamn you, Norman!*:::::: She remembered what Amélia had said. Always look confident...if you have no one to talk to, put on a confident smile. She put on a confident smile...but somehow standing here alone with a confident smile was no vast improvement upon standing here alone with a long face...*Ahh!* She spotted a painting on the wall nearest her, a big one...must have been four feet by three feet...She'd go look busy studying it...She stood before it...two half-round shapes, one a simple black and the other one a simple white, painted on a beigey-gray background. The two shapes were separated from each other and cocked at cockeyed angles... ::::::*Ayúdame, Jesús*...You'd have to be a cretin to stand here actually studying this *mierda*...Not even the old fools who pay millions for this idiotic nonsense at Miami Basel are so retarded that they actually *look* at it.:::::: She gave up and turned about to face once again this room *where* things were happening. Frantic laughter still reigned...*shriek! shriek! shriek! shriek!* went the women *haw! haw! haw! haw! haw!* went the men...but just then, from across the room, came a laugh that toppled them all "aahaaAAAHock hock hock hock"...and Magdalena stared that way, lasering through all the rapture laughter until she spotted Norman's big head bobbing up and down for the benefit of a woman, a very striking woman—thirty?—but who knew any longer?—fair skin, oh, so fair...thick dark hair parted down the middle and swept back dramatically from her forehead...high cheekbones, lean square jaws, lips as red as rubies, eyes as brilliant and hypnotically blue as the bluest diamondsss*uhhhhHAG-GHH-HOCKhock hock hock hock*...She had made up the rubies and diamonds just to feel sorrier for herself and angrier at Norman, but the laugh*hhfoghhhHH-Hock hock hock hock* was real, all too real, you heartless insensitive sonofabitch! *Back in a second*—sure, you'll be back in a second, as soon as you make your first move on some *americana* with hair as dark as midnight and skin as white as snow! We don't *have* snow, we Cubans, as you, in your wisdom, perhaps know—

"Miss Otero!"

It was a voice from behind, a voice with an accent. She turned about, and it was *him*—*the* him...as handsome and Prince-charming and a lot of other things she had been dreaming of for a solid week. In a *blip* of unbelievable speed Sergei's eyes turned down, inspected her breasts, which were threatening to pop out of the bustier—and blipped back up.

Magdalena caught that...and liked that...and in that instant Norman and the anger he had engendered in her vanished. *Just like that. ¡Mirabile visa!* as one of the nuns, Sister Clota, used to say. *¡A miracle to see! ¡Sublimity itself!* But in the next instant, wide awake in the dreamless real world, the love bombardier from

Hialeah and her sublime self plummeted and crashed and burned, as they had all week from obsessing over the figure before her. Why had he approached her at this moment?...when all there was to see was a poor thing, a social misfit, all alone and trying to cover it up by "studying" an extremely stupid painting on a wall. Oh, it was obvious. He ever so kindly wanted to rescue her from social failure. What a horrid form of rendezvous this was! Who was she in his eyes?...Some silly simpleton who needed his pity! It was humiliating—*humiliating!*—so humiliating, it vaporized every role she might have chosen to morph into...flirt, vamp, disciple of Aesculapius, the god of medicine, merciful mother to the heavy-laden crushed by lust, groupie of great oligarchic Russian philanthropic art collectors. So without meaning to, she reacted with complete honesty...her jaws went slack, causing her mouth to fall open and her lips to part...

Sergei proceeded to pour his charm all over her, as if that were going to help. "I'm so happy to see you here, Magdalena!"

Already another guest was at his shoulder, smile cocked to bag his attention the moment his lips stopped moving.

Sergei leaned in closer to Magdalena and said in a low voice, "I barely had a chance to talk to you at Miami Basel." Once more he *blipped* the quickest, slickest of eye-flicks at her bustier bosom.

By now, from sheer nerves, Magdalena was nibbling the fingernail of her little finger. The intimate way he lowered his voice brought red blood and its bodyguard, guile, back into her system. She could literally feel it. Slowly she removed the little fingernail from her nervous nibblers and let the hand drop down upon the cloven center of her bustiered bust and got her lips to smile in a certain, ever-so-amused way... and said ever so softly and smokily, "Oh, I remember..."

Now three people were huddled about Sergei, their glittering eyes anxious to lock onto his. One of them, a little weasel of a man with one side of his shirt collar collapsed upon his neck because it was designed to go with a necktie, was so gauche as to tap him on the shoulder. Sergei did a hopeless roll of his eyes for Magdalena's benefit and said out loud, "To be continued—" and let his courtiers go ahead and swamp him. His eyes awarded themselves one last little hurried high-speed helping of her bosom.

Magdalena was alone again, but this time she didn't care. It didn't bother her at all. There was only one other person in all of Chez Toi, and now she knew he was interested...

By and by Norman returned from across the room. When she saw him, he did that tight-lipped, head-stuttering thing men do before they say, "I swear, honey, I did the best I could."

"Listen, I'm sorry. I saw somebody I'd been trying to get hold of and I wasn't sure I'd have another chance to talk to him, and I never thought—" His voice slowed down when he saw that Magdalena was giving him a pleasant, friendly smile.

"So you caught up with him?"

"*Uhhh,* yes."

She just smiled at this little white gender lie. What earthly difference did it make? She said, "I'm so glad, darling."

He looked at her in a funny way, as if his radar detected irony. The "darling" probably did it. Somehow Norman wasn't the kind who drew pet names up from Magdalena's heart. He studied her face. If he was a good student, he saw that she was genuinely happy. Under the circumstances, that might have confused him, too.

Presently, the maître d' in the cream-colored tropical suit appeared in the library doorway and said in a loud and eminently cheery voice, "Dinner is served!"

Sergei was in the doorway, too, right next to him. He smiled at his flock and swung his chin up in a great arc that seemed to say, *Follow me!* That they did, and the buzz and the burble and the shrieks and hawhaws increased, if anything. They trooped across the foyer toward . . . the other room.

Norman was tremendously impressed. He leaned toward Magdalena and said, "You know what? He's taken over this whole floor, and there are only two floors!"

"I think you're right," said Magdalena, who was too happy to think much of anything about anything anybody else had to say at this point.

She looked down at her own glorious bosom. And to think she had *feared* what the bustier was going to do to her place in Society and the world!

Now the flock squeezed through the doorway in an energized mass, eager for every drop of social anointment that awaited in the other room. She had never seen a dining room like this. In keeping with the Chez Toi motif, there was nothing grand about it. But it was spectacular... in its own casual way. The wall opposite the entrance wasn't a wall at all. It was a counter almost the length of the room, and beyond the counter you found yourself looking straight into the fabled Chez Toi kitchen. It was huge. Twenty feet of gleaming—*gleaming*—brass... pots, pans, kitchen utensils of every sort, hung in a row from hooks in the kitchen but came down low enough to dazzle the diners. The cooks and the sous-cooks and the rest of an army in white with toques blanches on their heads marched about the kitchen taking care of this and inspecting that... and pushing buttons, Magdalena noticed. Pushing buttons? Oh, yes. Computers ran the roasting ovens, the baking ovens, the grills... even the open skillets, the refrigerators, the shelf rotation in the stock cabinets... Not very Old House–like, but everybody appeared willing to avert his eyes from this intrusion of twenty-first-century American digitalization into the old wood-burning analogical skillet stove top. The brass art show and the march of the toques blanches served as backdrop enough.

A table made of a solid, simple slab of chestnut wood dominated the room. No, it *filled* the room. It was about twenty feet long and four feet wide and ran all the way from *here*... to *there*. It was the kind of behemoth that was good to have on a farm during the threshing season when all the workmen came inside in their bib overalls hungry for all the pancakes with maple syrup they could eat and all the coffee and not-yet-fermented apple cider they could drink before they headed out again. The surface of this table didn't recall any scene like that. It was a stage for a company, a congeries, a prodigious, heavenly constellation of glass stemware great and small arranged in clusters, fairy platoons, clouds, sparkling see-through bubbles, before every place at the table, glasses so fine, so transparent, beaming and gleaming with reflections of light, swelling out with such sublime attainments of the glass-blowing arts that even to a twenty-four-year-old girl lately of Hialeah it seemed that if you tapped one with the tiniest tine of a fork, it would sing out *"Crystal!"* in a very high note,

E-sharp above high C. Flanking each angelic array of glasses were parades of silverware, such stupendous regiments of utensils that Magdalena couldn't imagine what they were all used for. At every place was a place card obviously done by hand by a professional calligrapher. Now ensued an interlude in which the guests hopped about and bent way down, still chirping away, in search of their appointed seats... much milling about... Sergei introducing as many people to one another as fast as he can... taking care to smile at Magdalena in a special way when he introduces her to people... all old people, or old in her eyes. The whole thing is bewildering... the names become nothing but syllables whistling in through one ear and out the other. When it was all over, Magdalena found herself placed four seats from Sergei, who was at the head of the table. To his immediate right was an Anglo woman, probably in her forties, who struck Magdalena as very pretty but affected. To Sergei's left was—*Oh, Dios mío!*—a famous Cuban singer—famous among Cubans anyway—Carmen Carranza. She sat with a regal posture, but she was no longer young. Nor was she an apt model for the dress she had on. It plunged all the way down to the sternum, arousing not the satyrs but the health nuts. Where had all the collagen gone—the collagen in the inner curves of her barely there breasts? Why had she put body makeup on the bony terrain between the breasts—

an early incursion of little age spots? Between the superannuated songbird and Magdalena sat a scarce-haired old man, Anglo, with cheeks and jowls that appeared inflated—*perfectly.* Scarcely a line in his face; and a pink perfect as rouge decorated it at cheekbone level. The old boy was wearing a suit and tie; and not just any suit, either. It was made of pink-striped seersucker—with a vest. Magdalena couldn't remember seeing a man actually wearing one. And the tie—it looked like a sky full of fountainhead fireworks exploding in every direction, in every color imaginable. He intimidated her from the moment she laid eyes on him. He was so old and august and formal, and yet sooner or later she would have to *talk* to him . . . But he turned out to be nothing if not *amistoso y amable.* He didn't look at her as if she were some wayward girl who had inexplicably wound up for dinner at Chez Toi.

In fact, the old man, Ulrich Strauss, turns out to be friendly, funny, very smart, and not at all condescending. The dinner begins with Sergei giving a toast of welcome and recognition of the guests of honor, the new director of the Korolyov Museum of Art, Otis Blakemore, from Stanford, sitting two seats to Sergei's right, and Blakemore's wife—Mickey they call her—who sits next to Sergei on his left. ::::::*Dios mío,* she's the pretty woman with the upswept hair Norman was hitting on in the library just now...and she's not an *americana* but a *cubana.*:::::: The waiters begin serving wine, and Magdalena, who is no drinker, is happy enough this time to have some to calm her nerves.

The table is so long—twenty-two people are seated—and comparatively narrow, and there is so much excited conversation, it's close to impossible to hear what other people are saying from more than three or four seats away or across the table. Magdalena gets into an amusing conversation with Mr. Strauss about Art Basel. Mr. Strauss is a passionate collector of antique furniture and small-scale seventeenth-, eighteenth-, and nineteenth-century representational sculpture, he says. He asks Magdalena how she happened to meet Sergei...as a side door entrance to find out who this sexy little girl wearing a corset is—i.e., what is her status? She says only that she met Sergei last week at Art Basel.

So you're interested in contemporary art.

Not really, she was just there with "some people."

What did you think of it?

Not much, to tell the truth. I thought it was ugly—on purpose! And it was so pornographic! She describes some of it in a general, decorous way. Wine at work.

Strauss tells her Tom Stoppard's mot about how "Imagination without skill gives us modern art." Then he goes on to say contemporary art would be considered a ludicrous practical joke if otherwise bright people hadn't elevated it to a higher plane... upon which a *lot* of money changes hands.

Another glass of wine and Magdalena tells about what she saw: so-called art advisers leading rich old men around by the nose and telling them, Don't *argue* with us about it. Do you want to have up-to-the-minute taste or don't you? Magdalena is at least sober enough not to mention Fleischmann or his adviser by name.

Strauss says he knows Sergei feels exactly the same way and goes to Art Basel just to enjoy the circus. The new director of the Korolyov Museum of Art has quite conservative taste and a scholarly approach. The Chagalls that Sergei donated are about as far into modern art as he feels comfortable going.

A series of general conversations occur at her and Sergei's end of the table. They talk about the beating and racist abusing of a black defendant by two white officers on YouTube. "White," not "Cuban," because nobody wants to offend the songbird or the other important Cubans at the table, so there is no reason for Magdalena to wonder if Nestor might have been involved.

They talk about the dispute between the mayor and the police chief.

They talk about the ongoing problems in Haiti.

They talk about the real estate market coming back.

Magdalena is not only too shy to join in, she has no idea what they're talking about. So she knocks back some more wine.

Then they get on the subject of Art Basel. Mr. Strauss tells of rumors of dealers and art advisers colluding to milk hedge fund bigs and others out of tens of millions.

Mr. Strauss says, "My friend Miss Otero can tell you how it works. She was there."

He turns to her, assuming that she will repeat, for the benefit of all, what she was telling him. Suddenly all these adults at this end of the table have shut up, and they're all focused on Miss Otero... upon her chest, too, but they're also dying to know what she has to say—this young thing who looks naked with her clothes on.

Magdalena feels pressure from every side. She knows she should decline, but here's Sergei, as well as Mr. Strauss and the others, looking straight at her and expecting *something*... or is she just a stray girl without a brain cell to her name? At the same time, her only real evidence comes from Fleischmann's experience... and she sure doesn't want Maurice—and Norman—to find out what she has to say on that subject. They won't hear her from way down at their end of the table... but suppose they get wind of it after dinner or something? But she can't just sit here and be a frightened child!... Not in front of Sergei like this!

So she starts off... in an appropriately modest voice... but all eleven people up at this end start leaning forward to hear her... this little *dish!*... they have been wondering what's on her mind, if anything, as she stares out from above the breastworks. She raises her voice a bit, and she feels like she's listening to somebody else talking. But her three glasses of wine have helped, and she begins to speak halfway fluently.

She touches quickly, lightly, upon all the pornography that has been injected into Miami Basel's bloodstream...

::::::I've already said too much! But all these people are staring at me! How can I just stop and turn into a dummy?! More and more of them have stopped talking to each other—so they can listen to *me!* So how can I all of a sudden... *shut up?* This is my moment to *emerge.* To command their *respect!*::::::

She doesn't realize just how many people "more and more" amounts to.

—When she gets to the part about *a certain collector* being led about by his art adviser ::::::I must stop *right now!* This is a private room, and nobody is making a sound... just me. Maurice is *right there* at the other end of the table! Norman is right there! But this is *my moment!* I can't... sacrifice it:::::: she plunges on, headlong ::::::can't help myself:::::: she makes the art advisers sound like pimps demanding a stiff price for... ecstasy—*ecstasy!*—the consummate *thrill* of being known as a player, a *playa,* in this magical market, which seems to have been concocted out of thin air. What on earth is all that so-called art they ask a fortune for at Art Basel? Imagination without skill gives us modern art. Then she turns modestly, demurely, toward her seatmate and says, "Who did you say said that?" She has the horrible realization that the entire table has gone silent. She hasn't mentioned Maurice by name nor the artist whose work he bought... nor Miss Carr, his adviser, but Maurice and Norman aren't stupid.

She cuts a glance at them. Both look stunned, like they've been punched in the nose for no reason. Yet she can't just... *stop,* can she... not in front of Sergei and her new friend, Mr. Strauss. All she can think of doing is dropping the subject of art advisers—and switching to the insane scramble of the rich on the opening day at Art Basel to get to the booths of the artists they've been advised to like. Throughout this little gossipy disquisition she keeps interjecting temporizing comments, such as, "I don't mean every collector" and "but some art advisers are completely honest—I know that," but it's too late. Fleischmann can't help but know this juicy stuff is about *him.* Norman does, too. And he'll be furious. Maurice's are the coattails Norman thinks he's going to ride to social eminence—and here is his own nurse... doing her best to ruin it all!

Sergei is beaming. He loves every point she's made! That was sensational! *She's* sensational!

She has to endure the rest of the dinner sitting there scalding in guilt and shame over what she has just said about Maurice, even though she never mentioned his name. Sister Clota's girls never commit such treachery. She feels so guilty, she can't enjoy the attention everybody at her end of the table is now eager to lavish upon her. One question after another! *What an interesting young woman!* And... *to think of what we thought when we first saw her!*

The attention only makes Magdalena feel worse. Guilt! Guilt! Guilt! Guilt! How could she have done this to Maurice? Norman will be enraged... *justifiably!*

As soon as the dinner is over, she stands up and goes directly to Sergei, smiling and extending her hand as if she's expressing her thanks... and look at her: the very picture of a polite, properly grateful guest.

Sergei is the very picture of a gracious host. He takes her proffered hand in both of his... and with a perfectly proper smile and a perfectly polite expression on his face, he says to her as if it were protocol straight out of the book:

"How can I reach you?"

14

Girls with Green Tails

The supposed habitat of Igor Drukovich's supposed sex habit, the Honey Pot was the last building in a decrepit little shopping strip down a nondescript road off Collins Avenue up in Sunny Isles, where Miami Beach merges with the mainland. The building looked like it had been built as a warehouse... big, drab, featureless, and only one story high. But out front was a blindingly bright backlit plastic sign—an enormous thing, at least twenty-five feet wide—with THE HONEY POT written across it in a lit-up blood-orange script outlined in red and yellow neon. This hot, gaudy production was mounted atop a freestanding steel column about four stories high. After dark nobody driving along Collins Avenue could keep from gawking:

THE HONEY POT

Huge huge huge brilliant brilliant brilliant lurid lurid lurid, that sign was, but it was also more than forty feet above the ground. The dozen or so men standing down here outside the club's entrance were lit by little more than the usual dim electro-gloaming that prevailed outdoors in Greater Miami's nightlife. The *little more* was an electro-tinge from above that turned all these white faces the sickly color of orangeade...

Sickly hyper-diluted orangeade was the way it struck Nestor, who had just arrived with John Smith. Sickly? It couldn't get much sicker-looking than it did right before him, on John Smith's fair white face. Too bad for John Smith...but it also did bad things to Nestor's nerves. What the hell did he know about strip clubs? There were 143 of them in the Miami area—it was a fucking *industry!*—but Nestor Camacho had never been inside even one. He had entertained John Smith all the way out here with cop stories about these funk holes. Too bad they weren't *his* stories, because they had created the impression that he knew this form of vice den inside and out. He was not unaware of that as he told the tales. *Vanity! Vanity!* ::::::A real cop who doesn't know the strip club scene? I mean, *come on!*:::::: Maybe if worse came to worst, he could *bluff* his way through...After all, John Smith had admitted from the git-go that he had never been in a dirty den like this or any other.

So the two of them stood outside the Honey Pot, discussing strategy. "We're not here to look at all the shit that goes on there," said Nestor. Mr. All Business. The leader. "We're here to find a Russian with a big mustache named Igor Drukovich." He did a quick air sculpture, putting his forefingers and the tips of his thumbs under his nose and swooping them way out as far as his ears. "Searching the place for Igor Drukovich is all we're doing. No distractions allowed. You get the picture?"

John Smith nodded yes, and then said, "You're *sure* you won't get in trouble over this? Doesn't 'relieved of duty' mean that you can't do any police work?"

At first, Nestor thought John Smith was getting squirrelly, now that he was actually here before the door to a strip club... in this disorienting orangeade gloom... If he, Nestor, pulled out at the last minute, it would save him, John Smith, from the ignominy of doing so himself.

"But I'm not here doing police work," said Nestor. "I'm not gonna flash a badge. As a matter of fact, they took my badge away from me."

"But aren't you under a form of... house arrest, I suppose it is?"

"I'm supposed to be at home from eight a.m. to six p.m. After six, I can do anything I want."

"And this is what you want?"

"I told you I'd try to help you with Korolyov, and here we are. At least we've got this much to go on." From a side pocket he withdrew a laminated copy of the picture of Igor in a car with Korolyov he had obtained from the Miami-Dade Police via the brothernet. "At least we know what the guy looks like, and we know that they know each other. That's not a bad start."

The entrance to the Honey Pot was a plain workmanlike sliding door, easily fifteen feet wide, that looked as if it had been there since long before the warehouse was converted into the Honey Pot. Immediately inside was a glass wall with a pair of glass doors leading into what resembled a movie theater vestibule.

The moment the leader and his orangeade-faced follower entered, BEAT-*unngh thung* BEAT-*unngh thung* BEAT-*unngh thung* BEAT-*unngh thung* began BEATING and *thunging* into their central nervous systems. It wasn't a fast beat and not terribly loud, but it was relentless. It never changed and never stopped going BEAT-*unngh thung* BEAT-*unngh thung.* There must have been a musical score generating it, but you couldn't hear it in this small walled-in space that served as a box office . . . a curved counter . . . behind it, a paunchy, forty-whatever white man clad in a white polo shirt with an orange Honey Pot logo embroidered on the chest pocket. He was the cashier. John Smith gave him forty dollars for the two of them. The man tried his best to be jovial. He smiled and said, "Have a good time, fellas!" The smile looked like a mean streak turned up at the corners. Nestor led the way through the door into the club itself... BEAT-*unngh thung* BEAT-*unngh thung* BEAT-*unngh thung* and sure enough, there was music behind the beat, recorded music. At the moment a girl with a teenage voice was singing, "I'm takin' you to school, fool, an' if *you* don' *get it,* I don' give it, an' if I don' give it, you don' *get it.* Get it, fool? You cool with that?" But after a few moments, the song didn't matter. It was sucked up by the BEAT-*unngh thung* BEAT-*unngh thung.*

Swivel—Nestor's and John Smith's heads turned simultaneously. Many eyes watching them! Off to the side, near the door they just went through, was a bar with a seven-to-eight-foot partition separating it from the rest of the club. Packed with women it was, young women with jacked-up white legs, pushed-up white cleavages, three-hundred-watt white eyeballs—white girls and *only* white girls, their white faces decorated with the tarty black arts of the eyeliner, eye shadow, eyelash paint, black-laden eyelids... white girls with libidos-to-let only to *white* customers... *¡Dios mío!* try mixing the white, the black, the brown, and the yellow in a place like this! It wouldn't last one hour! It would explode! Nothing left but blood and sexual debris—

"How you guys doing?" A big beefy man, close to fifty, materialized from out of the darkness... clad in the Honey Pot polo shirt with a laminated card pinned to the breast pocket bearing the orange Honey Pot script logo and the inscription ASSISTANT OPERATIONS MANAGER.

"There's plenty a seats—" He stopped right there and stared at Nestor. He frowned so hard, his eyebrows drew together like two little muscles gripping the top of his nose. "*Ayyyyy*... don't I know you?"

::::::Goddamn YouTube again! Growing this eight-day stubble of beard—*some disguise,* right!:::::: But by now Nestor was tactically ready. "Probably," he said. "How long you been working here?"

"How *long* have I been *working* here?" He seemed to find the question impudent. He closed one eye and sized up Nestor with the other. Do I swat this pest or do I let him off this time because he's so obviously clueless? The latter, he must have decided, because after the ominous pause he said, "About two years."

"Then that's it," said Nestor. "I used to come here a lot with my friend Igor." He detected a pained look on John Smith's face. "You know Igor? Russian guy? Big mustache?" With his fingers Nestor did another air sculpture of Igor's mustache. "Half the time I don't know what he's talking about. You know? But he's a great guy" . . . He smiled and shook his head in a Good Old Days way. "Know if he still comes here?"

"If it's the guy I think you mean," said the man, somewhat reassured, "yeah, he still comes here."

"No way!" said Nestor, eyes wide open . . . a happy boy. "Is he here tonight?"

"I don't know. I just come on." He gestured vaguely toward the interior. "There's plenty a seats." <<<BEAT-*unngh thung* BEAT-*unngh thung* BEAT-*unngh thung* BEAT-*unngh thung* BEAT-*unngh thung*>>>

John Smith's pale face was agitated. He kept clenching his jaws and then pressing his lips together. "I don't know if that was such a great idea, Nestor, bringing up Igor's name and telling that guy that you know him. What if he comes in half an hour from now, and the guy tells him there's somebody here asking about him?"

Nestor said, "Well, the guy—did you catch the title he has, pinned here on his chest in big letters, Assistant Some-kinda Manager? If you ask me, he's got BOUNCER written all over him."

John Smith smiled ever so slightly and said, "Did you mean that as a play on—"

But Nestor cut him off. "The guy gave me the YouTube look. You know? So I had to give him another reason why he recognizes me. Maybe I shouldn't have brought up Igor's name, but now we know he's still coming here."

John Smith said under his breath, but not very far under it, "We already *figured* that much."

Nestor said, "Come on, John! Don't be so cautious. Sometimes you gotta goose things along."

John Smith averted his gaze and didn't respond. He was not happy.

Their eyes began to adjust to the gloom. They could now see that the blaze of light on the far wall was from a stage. At this moment the show was obviously... *on.* <<<BEAT-*unngh thung* BEAT-*unngh thung* BEAT-*unngh thung* BEAT-*unngh thung*>>> Men crowded about the edge of the stage, cheering, hooting, crying out, making odd sounds. Nestor and John Smith saw them in silhouette. They looked like a single, huge colonial animal wriggling and writhing and throbbing with lust... and *blocking* their view.

Out of the darkness came a girl jacked up on six-inch-high heels, all of her, her long blond hair, her wisp of black thong *cache-sexe,* her filmy long-sleeved shirt, wide-open, revealing most of her breasts. She passed right in front of them, barely five feet away—leading a young Anglo—midtwenties?—by the hand. All he had on was a tank top—*a tank top!*—hanging outside of a pair of filthy blue jeans and a baseball cap worn backward. The notable bulge in the crotch of the jeans he obviously wasn't trying to hide. John Smith looked stunned—mesmerized. He couldn't take his eyes off them until they disappeared through a wide doorway on the far wall where a bouncer seemed to be standing guard. Over the entrance was a small but rather stately sign saying, "*Private* CHAMPAGNE ROOM *for Invited Guests.*" The couple was no longer to be seen, but John Smith's eyes remained fixed upon the doorway. It was as if it held him in its hot little Sunny Isles thrall.

Nestor shook his head. "Listen, John," he said, "this is a *strip* club? You know? There's girls with no clothes on in here. Okay? But *we* gotta go to work. We're looking for only one hot body, Igor's."

By now their eyes were getting used to the nightclub gloaming that stretched on before them all the way up to the theater lights—but there were no theater seats. The audience sat in what looked like a furniture showroom with the lights off... couches, banquettes, love seats, coffee tables arranged in no particular order. The only furniture you could really see were ten or twelve bar stools that rimmed the stage at one end.

As he threaded his way through the deep dusk of the furniturescape, Nestor was astonished at just how many barely clothed girls were leaning over the men who lounged back in all that furniture. The place was far from full. Women, any women may have been welcome at the Honey Pot, for all Nestor knew, but he saw only the kind of girl who looked primed to—*ziiiiiip*—unzip a zipper and shed every thread she had on and let it all fall into a tiny clump on the floor. More girls than he could ever have imagined were making their catches right here upon the upholstery of the Furniture Land lounge, and hauling them off toward that door, the door that so obsessed John Smith. Lots of lovely dirty girls—but no Igor.

A show had just ended. Good; several high seats on the rim of the stage had been abandoned. Once they were seated, it was like sitting at a dining room table... and the stage was the table, where you could inspect, as it were, all the juicy dirty-girls before you and smack your lips... and then *eat it... eat it all up.*

Nestor was checking out their fellow diners in the bar chairs... Not a very classy bunch. Strip club dress was casual, but these characters were down to the level of wife beaters and T-shirts with lettering on them. Half of them seemed to have dollar bills sprouting from their fingers. Nestor couldn't figure it out until he saw waitresses bringing drinks to these high-sitters. Scruffy though they were, they were tossing one-dollar bills onto the girls' trays as tips. There was a regular green blizzard. For protective coloration more than anything else, Nestor and John Smith ordered beers. The girl returned with the two beers and a bill for $17.28. The Treasury, John Smith, gave the girl a fifty-dollar bill. She brought back four fives, some coins... and *twelve* one-dollar bills, in case they hadn't figured out the protocol, which was: If it moves, tip it. John Smith gave her four of the twelve.

A disembodied Master of Ceremonies voice—they couldn't tell where it came from—announced with the jolly gravity of that calling: "And now, ladies and gentlemen, please welcome... NATASHA!"

A smattering of applause and catcalls, and BEAT *thung* BEAT *thung* BEAT *thung*s and a girl, the heralded Natasha, came swinging around the pole at the far end of the stage. Like the previous dancer, Natasha was a blonde, a pretty one, too, not gorgeous but gorgeous enough for this crowd... good enough for John Smith, too. He couldn't keep his eyes off her... Libido-lorn Nestor Camacho could... he kept scanning the men who had started coming toward the stage to get a closer look... "Natasha" wore a bright-yellow outfit that looked like a little boy's soldier suit. The jacket's military collar closed around her neck. Two rows of big white buttons ran down the front, which ended three or four inches above her navel... pierced by a tiny shiny gold ring... The pants began three or four inches below it and came down only to the top of her thighs. Her legs looked impossibly long, tiptoed atop a pair of high-heeled yellow shoes... Nestor saw all only in peripheral vision. His head was turned in a different direction... looking for a man with a waxed black Russian mustache... "Natasha" swung this way and that. She swung with the pole right up in her crotch and her legs on either side of it. *Ziiippp*—with one *zip* she opened up the entire jacket and her breasts popped out. They were not very big, but big enough for this crowd. She smiled suggestively as she BEAT *thung* THRUST *thung* HUMP *thung* SHIMMY *thung* PUMP IT *thung* and otherwise swung around the pole.

She finally swung off the pole and headed across the stage BEAT *thung* BEAT *thung* SHIMMY *thung* THRUST IT *thung* down Nestor's and John Smith's way. Nestor couldn't have cared less. He was looking into the faces of a bunch of men turned into goats by lust...Oh, Christ...some dancer, our girl... *ziiiiip!*—but the zips on the sides of the soldier boy pants that were supposed to make them fall off—"Natasha" couldn't get them to work BEAT *thung* BEAT *thung* BEAT *thung* she had to stop and struggle out of them one leg at a time BEAT *thung* BEAT *thung* the audio took no note of the problem. It got a bit awkward. But worth waiting for! This crowd didn't ask for much...Now, where the pants had been...nothing, nothing at all...a totally naked crotch denuded even of pubic hair...Brazilian-waxed away...clearing the way for the star of the show, her pudenda. That made everything quite okay with this crowd. Down to nothing but her wide-open soldier boy jacket, she thrust her pudenda and pumped her pudenda and threw her arms back and the little yellow jacket flew off and BEAT *thung* CROTCH *thung* TAIL *thung* CRACK *thung* PERI *thung* NEUM *thung* she sinks to the stage right in front of John Smith and crawls about naked and on all fours . . . in this case, her knees and elbows . . . Her tail is thrust up like a bonobo's or a chimpanzee's toward John Smith, offering a full view of the perineum and its forbidden folds, crevices, cracks, clefts, cloven melons, alluring labia, gonopores — the entire fleshy arc. BEAT *thung* BEAT *thung* BEAM *thung* STAGE *lights* HIT *spot* PORN *spot* LUST *spot* PERI *spot* NEUM *spot* BEAT *thung* BEAT*ing* POUND*ing* MEN rush FORward STUCK dollar bills INto the CRACK in her bottom . . . John Smith is transfixed, once more . . . eyes wide, mouth agape . . . Nestor searches the faces of the men packed in front of the stage . . . a waxed mustache . . . a waxed mustache . . . that's all *he's* looking for . . . A big Miami Beach municipal bus driver in uniform going "Hoot hoot hoot hoot!" in an ironic way but obviously roused to grinning pleasure by what he sees . . . reaches over John Smith's shoulder to get his not one but two one-dollar bills into the crack . . . Okay, time for more protective coloration . . . Nestor extends his arm across John Smith and puts *three* dollars in the crack . . . and finally John Smith — gingerly — reverently? — before the Devil's altar? — places a dollar bill in the CRACK in "Natasha's" ASS, and BEAT *thung thung* BEAT *thung thung* BEAT *thung thung* TODO el MUNDO has DOLlar DEStined for the CRACK in the ASS. The WAITress MAKES all CHANGE in DOLlars ADDRESSED TO the CRACK of a PRETTY girl's ASS or MY tray. Every man so BEAT privileged as to have a seat *thung* on the rim feels HONOR-bound to STICK a dollar bill *thung* into the CRACK *thung* of her ASS. In NO time the ENtire CRACK is STUFFED with DOLlar BILLS, and many more are stuck BEAT in between the *thung* ones that BEAT it into the *thung* crack itself... until the BEAT pretty girl looked as *thung* if she had some sort of great green peacock tail coming out of the CRACK in her bottom. BEAT *thung* BEAT—

The moment the music stopped, she looked John Smith in the eye, *directly*... right in the eye... still on her hands and knees right in front of him... with her bare breasts hanging down practically in his face... and *winked*. Then she got to her feet and began walking backstage, twice turning to wink at him again. Her posture was excellent. Her gait was queenly, not too fast and not too slow... She would have been the very picture of a ladylike young woman, had she not been stark naked with a promiscuous heap of dollar bills STUCK IN THE CRACK OF HER ASS. Not once did she reach back to dislodge it or otherwise note its existence. Why should she compromise her dignity? Halfway across the stage the bills began falling out of their own accord. But why should she look back at the green wake she had created? Two little men, Mexicans, if Nestor was any judge, came out immediately with brooms and dustpans to gather the dollar bills, many of which had been thrown onstage by those who, despairing of reaching the crack, settled for aiming them in her direction.

John Smith's pale face had turned red. Was he embarrassed? Was he aroused? Nestor had no idea. He had no take on pale genteel *americanos* like John Smith. As for himself, he was down too deep in his Valley of the Shadow to get cocked over whores with banners of money flying from the CRACKS of their ASSES. And that was what they were, every last one of them, WHORES.

—BEAT *thung* BEAT *thung* BEAT *thung* BEAT *thung* the BEAT *thung*

Nestor scarcely glanced at her. He was scanning the men still gathered in front of the stage. Just beyond that bunch—what is it about *that* one? Nestor's eyes were fixed upon a heavyset man wearing a black shirt unbuttoned halfway down the front, the better to see his big hairy chest. He had no grand mustache...just a scraggly one that only barely went past the corners of his mouth...but that unbuttoned black shirt and that big sloppy show of chest hair made Nestor think immediately of the photo of Igor he got from the Miami-Dade cops. He knew that picture by heart...the black shirt, the hairy chest, even the way the deep gulleys that began on either side of his nose ran down past his lips and merged with his jowls...the crooked twist of the lips that was probably meant to look *cool.*

He leaned over toward John Smith. "Maybe I'm seeing things, because the guy has only a little mustache, but I'd swear he's Igor!"

He turned back to show John Smith—*mierda!*—the man had disappeared.

Uh-ohhh. A bevy of somewhat-dressed girls descended upon the two of them. A blonde—what was it with this universe of blondes?—got to John Smith first. She wore a denim dress with a top like a bib overall's...denim suspenders over the shoulders...except that she wore nothing under the bib and her breasts bulged out on the sides, and you could see the nether curves, too, where they joined her chest. The dress looked like—*one yank!*—and it's off!...a mere puddle of cloth on the floor. She shook hands with him—by clasping the inside of his thigh and giving him a big suggestive smile and saying, "Hi! I'm Belinka. Having fun?"

Where was that guy? Nestor got a glimpse of him again...talking cozily with a bouncer. John Smith at this moment was incapable of thinking about their mission. All he could think about was what had appropriated his thigh...his *inner* thigh...not far from— The pale white face of Mr. John Smith blushed the bloodiest red Nestor had ever seen. He had no answer to her question except "Unnh hunnh." Nestor enjoyed his distress enormously but didn't dare dwell on it—*now where has that guy gone? He was right there a half-second ago!*

"I bet you wanna have *more!*" said "Belinka."

John Smith paused, at a loss for words. Finally he managed to say—his voice distraught with embarrassment—"I...guess so..."

I guess so. It was so lame, Nestor loved it, but he didn't watch. *Any second*...he scoured Furniture Land...*any second*—

In the next instant he felt a hand on the inside of his own thigh.

"Hi! I'm Ninotchka! I can see you're—"

"Hi," said Nestor, without looking at her. His eyes remained fixed upon Furniture Land. "What kind of name is Ninotchka?" he said idly.

"It's Russian," she said. "What are you looking at?"

"You're Russian? No kidding," he said. His eyes remained pinned on Furniture Land.

Long pause. Finally: "No, but my parents are... What are you looking for out there?"

"You grow up around here?" said Nestor—and he still didn't look at her.

Another pause.

"No," she said, "I grew up in Homestead."

He smiled to himself. ::::::That's the first true thing you've said! Homestead is so Low-Rent, nobody telling lies would ever have herself coming from Homestead.:::::: To her he said nothing.

The whore had had enough. He was toying with her, mocking her. Two could play that game. She slipped her hand a little bit farther up the inside of his thigh and said, "What's your name?"

"Ray," said Nestor.

"You come here a lot, Ray?" said the whore.

Nestor just kept scanning people moving about in the glamorous-damn-it nightclub gloom.

"You know, you've got a really big neck, Ray." With that she lifted her hand from his thigh and cupped it around his genitals . . . gently but completely. "A very, very big neck," she said. She gave him a mocking smile. "Your neck's getting *bigger* . . . How about a big, wet kiss on your neck?"

Out the side of his mouth, without any inflection one way or the other: "No, thanks."

"Oh, come on," she said. She began caressing his groin and said, "I can just feel it."

Nestor turned toward her for the first time—and gave her a look. "I said no thanks, which means no thanks."

The Cop Look. "Ninotchka" withdrew her hand

and didn't dare utter another sound. Nestor immediately returned to his vigil. He looked toward the far wall, where he and John Smith had entered the club . . . All at once—an electrical lurch in his heartbeat. ::::::Jesus Christ! There he is in the back, by the bar . . . the guy in the black shirt . . . I swear to God that's gotta be *him* . . . He's got a girl on his arm, literally on his arm . . . looks like a proper Sunday promenade except she's a half-dressed stripper, and right over there is *the door!*::::::

Nestor spun about on the seat of his jacked-up chair and sprang to the floor. "Ninotchka" was so frightened, she threw her body backward and hit "Belinka," who was leaning over John Smith's thigh. *Bam!* Both girls landed on their backs on the floor with their feet in the air. John Smith sat petrified upon his high chair. He stared at Nestor, with his jaw dropped.

"I see the guy!" said Nestor. "Heading for *that door!* Come on!" he said over his shoulder to John Smith and got *blip* a glimpse of him . . . sitting straight up on the bar chair—*frozen stiff.* Furniture Land. ::::::Gotta *run!*:::::: But in the sofa sea of Furniture Land . . . too much fat upholstered furniture arranged too helter-skelter . . . too many men with their legs sprawling out as they lounged back in the upholstered billows . . . too many whores with their rear ends sticking out because they were standing with their heads bent down over the customers . . . too many little coffee tables clogging up the floor space that was left . . . his only hope was to *hurdle* over men's legs . . . *veer* around the whores' tails . . . *leap* over coffee tables . . . *bango!* . . . he was off . . .

The men sunk in their plush billows—they're startled . . . they're insulted . . . they're furious—and they're not the most genteel crowd in Miami-Dade County, either!—black shirt, hairy chest! . . . Nestor turns his head for a split second—::::::It's *him!*—I'm sure! I *know* that's Igor! Igor with almost no mustache!:::::: Some almost-dressed whore has him by the arm! They're walking *around* Furniture Land to the rear where he and John Smith started out! . . . They're heading for *the door!*

Getting to the door before Igor suddenly became as urgent a problem as he had ever faced in his life. In the instant before he turned his head forward again, he sped up—*Jesus Christ!* . . . He was going to crash into them! . . . three men and two whores facing one another across a coffee table . . . no room, no way to stop in time . . . Only thing possible—he *hurdled* across the coffee table . . . brushed a whore on this side and a big tub on that side . . . "FOOKIN' EHHOLE!" It's the tub . . . ::::::Where's *he* from! . . . He's old, but he's got a hell of a voice!::::::

. . . "FAGGOT!" . . . It's one of the whores . . .

"PIECE A SHIT!"...Another man...high on lust...

...Now they're all on their feet yelling... "PUNK!"..."SHITBALL!"...

Sky-high on adrenaline, the *springing leaping* punk ::::::How could they call *me* that?!:::::: makes it to the other side of Furniture Land...*That door* is—what?—ten yards away...*Oh, shit*—a bouncer... and he's left *the door*...he's coming straight at me...he's a mile wide...big flat face like a Samoan... No way can I get around him...the Cop Look?! The brute is right in front of him, blocking his way—

"What's the big hurry, Big Boy?" Guy had *the voice* all right.

The Cop Look? Nestor had about half a second to decide—*bango!*—this one's a hard case! Not a chance! Could be an off-duty cop moonlighting... Before his decision could even take the form of words in his brain, he turned the real Nestor Camacho inside out. He twisted his body into a cringe and pointed toward the ruckus in Furniture Land...In a high-pitched voice, agonized, shaky, frightened, "They're killing each other in there! They've gone crazy! Coulda got myself killed!"

The big bouncer eyed Nestor. He didn't necessarily believe him—but the commotion in Furniture Land was a bigger problem...Cries of "NO MO'

THIS SHIT," "OH, NO, YOU DON'T!" . . . "GEDDIM!" . . . "YOU SKINNY FUCK!" . . . So many cries, they drowned out one another . . . All this commotion. "You stay *right here!*" he told Nestor. He kept jabbing his finger at the floor where Nestor stood. "You don't *move!*" And then he went rocking into the ruckus with a big gorilla stride . . . He held his arms and his hands a good gorilla foot and a half from each hip . . . *Big Man*—now he was about five King Kong steps into Furniture Land . . . basso profundo . . . he's roaring, *roaring,* "Okay! What the hell's *this* all about?!"

"That PUNK!"

"That ASSHOLE!"

"That PIECE A SHIT!" they screamed in response, pointing beyond the Big Man in the direction Nestor had gone.

Just like that Nestor started running *running* the ten or fifteen yards to the door . . . to the lair of the luscious loins . . . and look! . . . right in front of him . . . barely one step from the door . . . *the one* . . . black shirt . . . he's stopped, he and his whore, staring toward the ruckus in Furniture Land.

"—was *that* little *shithead!*"

"—cocksucker hit me right here with his elbow!"

"If I hadna jumped back, those assholes woulda—"

"—didn't come here to get pissed all over by a couple a—"

"—'s wrong with you, motherfucker? If y'all just let those little pricks run—"

Sounds of a scuffle THOOMP! THOP! EGGGGHUH!

::::::Pricks *PLURAL?*::::::

"AWRIGHT! SETTLE THE FUCK DOWN! I'M GONNA KNOCK YOUR FUCKING HEAD OFF FOR YOU AND SHIT DOWN YOUR WINDPIPE, NEXT ONE A YOU CALLS ME A—"

Igor ::::::Now I *know* this is him! I know it's *him!*:::::: *Igor!* He's got one arm around the whore's waist... They're barely two steps from *the door*. They *stop!* He's checking out the beano in Furniture Land. Whatever's going on in there, he *loves* it... so much that he keeps pulling her, hard, right up against his thigh and his chest... over and over... She just smiles and takes it and takes it and takes it and takes it and takes it MEAT BEAT MEAT BEAT MEAT BEAT MEAT BEAT What's the matter with him? He looks drunk—but that's okay! Just *stay there, don't move!* Nestor breaks into a full sprint... he's sprinting for all he's worth across the floor of a strip club. TOO LATE! Igor—if that's him—and the girl step inside *the door* and disappear... *¡Coño!* Nestor comes shuddering to a dead halt... He's stymied stymied stymied... but what's to keep him from *just going inside?* He inspects the door. There *is* no door *per se.* Three steps inside the doorway is a baffle wall. There's nothing to keep him from walking in, but he can't see in first. He looks over his shoulder . . . *¡Coño!* Here comes the bouncer, back to his station. ::::::How can I get in there?:::::: His eyes pan about the immediate vicinity . . . Not ten feet away—what's *that?* A whore's bottom! He sees her from behind as she leans over a man in a sofa seat—pink short-shorts she's wearing, so short that each of her buttocks has halfway popped out . . . *buttocks décolletage,* John Smith's term, and now Nestor *got* it. They were popping out like upside-down breasts. She had on a sleeveless shirt made of some thin lustrous material almost the same color pink . . . frilled arm openings . . . two large oval-shaped openings in the back. For what?—to show that she wore no bra? God only knew . . . Her torso was slightly turned . . . *that* way . . . But of course! She had one hand on the inside of her mark's thigh.

No time for niceties and protocol. Nestor leaned over beside her. He put on as ingratiating a smile as he could manage and said, "Hi! Don't mean to interrupt, but I need a lap dance. I *really* need a lap dance."

Maintaining her grip on the other guy's thigh, she turned her head toward Nestor and eyed him quizzically . . . then, in defense, skeptically. She was a brunette with dyed-blond streaks in her hair—at the Honey Pot, be blond no matter how you get there! We'll give you your Russian or Estonian name . . . but you've got to bring your own blond hair and sexy-ecstasy expression and lawless labial lips.

He could hear the digits clicking 0, 1, 1, 0, 0, 0, 1, 0 in her head. <<<I'm busy propositioning that guy on the sofa... he looks rich... but he hasn't come across yet... and suddenly there's this guy leaning over beside me—and he's *volunteering!*... looks like a decent sort... he's young, he's eager 0, 1, 1, 0, 0, 1, 0, 0, click click click click>>> Now she did something with her eyes and lips that made her look mischievous. She turned her head toward Nestor until they were almost cheek to cheek. In a low but actually rather sweet voice, she said, "You know what kind a men I like? *Eager* ones! I shouldn't do it—"

With that, she put her free hand inside Nestor's standing thigh—and held on as if she didn't intend to let him go—ever—and removed the other from her sofa prospect's thigh. Nestor got his first good look at the man. He looked almost distinguished... had a gray beard... meticulously trimmed... a thick head of gray hair, well groomed, a go-to-the-office shirt unbuttoned at the collar, no jacket, no tie... a pair of pale-tan pants you could tell were a *lot* more expensive than khakis... Why would a man like that come to a place like this and listen to a whore's entreaties? Even Nestor realized he was asking a naive question.

The girl looked down upon her sofa quarry and put on her most mischievous and lascivious expression and said, "Now, you stay right here! I'll be back in a minute!"—whereupon she stood up straight and let her hand slip from between Nestor's legs. The man looked at her and Nestor dumbfounded. But Nestor knew he wouldn't say a word or anything else to call attention to his real—meaning proper—self.

She took Nestor by the hand forcefully and led him the four or five yards to *the door.* The bouncer was back at his station. He looked Nestor up and down, dubiously, but being in the hands of a bona fide whore made you legitimate. She led him—still by the hand—around the baffle wall. Nestor found himself in what looked like a long, narrow, dingy, and dimly lit locker room with a row of stalls right on top of him, right in his face. He felt like he could reach out and touch them, although in fact they were about six feet away... They were an endless row of cheap partitions about five feet apart and maybe a foot higher than an airport restroom's... and instead of doors, the stalls had dark-brown-and-tan-striped curtains of Transitester that went with a wall-to-wall carpet in a jumble weave of dark brown, light brown, and tan Streptolon industrial carpet you couldn't dent with an axe... all of it rather the worse for wear but at least a stab at interior decoration at the Honey Pot. The same BEAT *thung* BEAT *thung* music that pounded the rest of the club tenderized you in this room with its congestion and low ceiling and total lack of windows. In the tiny intervals between the BEATs and the *thung*s Nestor could hear human sounds nearby, not words but sounds... from behind the curtains of the stalls... *unhh, ahhh ahhh, ooom-muh, ennngh ohhhhunh*... all of them the moans of men — not the girls... moans that sometimes did cross the border into meaningless verbiage... *ohhhyes ohhhyes, dohn*stop *dohn*stop *dohn*stop, *yes yes yes yes, diiiig* harder *diiiig* harder, bring it *home,* bring it *home* and then back to a lot of *unhhh uhnnn ahhh ahhh oooweh oooweh oooweh* sounds. Nestor listened to them all with intense interest.

The girl looked up at him with as lascivious a smile as he had ever seen in his life, and in words that slid out of her mouth as if labially, lubriciously, lubricated, "What's your name?"

"Ray," said Nestor. "What's yours?"

"Olga" slid out of her mouth.

"Olga... I've met so many Russians here tonight. You don't have any accent."

As if offering him the key to Paradise, "I'm Russian on my mother's side. I grew up here." Her lips took on the contours of unspeakable ecstasies. "You probably already know the... uhhh... guidelines. A basic lap dance is twenty-five dollars, not touching. Touching brings it up higher, depending on *what.* And, of course, cash is up front whatever it is. You still want a basic lap dance, Ray?"

"Great!" said Nestor. "Terrific!" He dug twenty-five dollars... of John Smith's money... out of his pocket, and she put it into a side pocket of her pink shorts.

"Okaaaay... thank you," said "Olga," and she took his hand and led him to a stall with the curtain pulled back. The interior was just big enough for a cot-sized bed apparently, composed of a frame, a mattress, and a self-striped tan coverlet... a modernistic lounge chair made of a fiberglass shell with a dark-brown seat cushion... with no arms... a matching stool with a brown cushion, and in the rear a Formica shelf with a basin and two taps set in... and a double-doored cabinet beneath... Just before "Olga" pulled the curtain shut, Nestor heard a man moaning far louder and more ecstatically than any other so far.

"Oh, *govno*... oh, *govno*... oh, *govno*... oh, *govno*... oh, *govno!*"

And then a woman's moans, not *that* loud but loud enough to rise above the BEAT *thung* BEAT *thung*s and the rest of it... moaning *sighs,* they were, ending in prolonged breathless sighs that went, *"Ahhhhh... ahhhhhh... ahhhhhh"*... and then they began speeding up... *"Ahhh... ahhh... ahhh"* and then faster still... *"Ahh... ahh... ahh... ahh..."*

So did the man's Oh, *govno* Oh, *govno* Oh, *govno* Oh, *govno.*

Then a convulsive sigh from the girl that went *ahh ahh ahh ahh ahh* and dived into a lake of *sobs sobs sobs* Oh, God *sob sob sob sobbbbbb ungh ungh ungh* Oh, God, oh God oh God-d-d-d...

Thereupon the man topped that with "Oh *govno* Oh *dermo* Oh *govno DERMO DERMO DERMO! BOZHE MOY! GOSPODI*..." By the end he was loud as a tenor in the opera.

"Olga" had turned away from the entrance. A single movement of her hand, and her shirt fell to the floor and then she took a deep breath and sank back toward Nestor to present her popped-out breasts.

Nestor gave her a happy smile as if to say, "Oh, good. That's nice"—no more than that, because he was already at the curtain, pulling it back just an inch or two...so he could hear more grumbling audibly inside several stalls...He could swear he heard one man complaining, "Whaddaya mean, I don't get to go all the way?" He must have been talking to his whore, because he said, "Oh, don't give me that! Don't you stand there telling me your fucking *rules*—or *no*-fucking rules!"

Another man was apparently shouting from his stall at the operatic-climax man, because Nestor heard Climax Man yelling back, "You dohn't *talk* to me like zat, you vorm!" He sounded good and drunk. His adversary yelled, "Who the fuck you think you are!" And the big voice said, "You don't eefen vant to know! You down zere, a vorm, and I up here! I am artist!"

Boos, hisses, gimme-a-breaks, and other cries of sarcastic denigration.

"You zshut ze mouzzz! You dohn't belief me? I am een ze museum!"

"Hey, can it, you guys! What the hell's going on in here?" It was the bouncer. He sounded like he was on a tear. The place quieted down.

"Olga" with the bare breasts was saying, "What are you doing, Ray, standing by the curtain? I thought you were hot for a lap dance."

"I am," said Nestor, "but I think I just heard something."

"Olga" stared at him, bare breasted and speechless.

::::::He looks exactly like Igor with a measly mustache. He speaks with a Russian accent. He says he's in a museum. That's one way to put it!::::::

John Smith was waiting outside *the door. What happened to him?* He was standing there with a big black eye. His blue blazer was smeared with dust and dirt and had a big wet splotch on a lapel.

"*¡Dios mío!* What happened?"

"I tried to catch up with you in Furniture Land—and they took it out on me."

Nestor whistled between his teeth. "I heard something going on behind me and saw a bouncer heading that way—but I had no idea it was you. "You look a little . . . messed up, I guess. Are you . . . are you okay?"

"I'll survive . . . except there are three bastards I'd like to kill. How did you make out?"

"He's our man, John."

"How do you know?"

"Let's get away from this goddamned door," said Nestor, "and I'll tell you all about it."

The Honey Pot's four-story-high backlit sign created an electric twilight out here on the street in front of the strip joint. It was an artificial twilight, but light enough for Nestor and John Smith to surveil both the club and the entrance to the parking lot behind it from inside the Camaro . . . when Nestor lifted, even a few inches, the SPTotal reflector screen that covered the windshield. SPTotal was the Apprehension Unit's brand of choice—*¡Coño!* Everything conspired to make him relive the day he and Hernandez were surveilling that crack house in Overtown.

Nestor had backed the Camaro into the driveway of a shop across the street, Buster's BoostersX, now closed, since it was going on 3:00 a.m. . . . John Smith was a soldier now, but surveillance still made him squirrelly. He was afraid Igor had somehow departed without their seeing him, or maybe there was some exit they didn't know about... or maybe Igor, being such a regular customer, could sleep over in the Honey Pot if he felt like it... maybe there were girls willing to stay and play with him... Maybe this and maybe that... but one thing Nestor knew from working the Crime Suppression Unit: You had to learn how to *wait* for the action. Without your heart trying to break out of your rib cage, you or a superior had to decide on the plan the odds favored and have the discipline to stick to it... the way Hernandez had planned the stakeout in Overtown... *¡Coño!* Why couldn't he stop thinking about it? There you had it. That was his Deep Worry.

But now it was himself and John Smith waiting in his Camaro for the quarry... and John Smith was no Sergeant Hernandez.

"Suppose he's not even going home," said John Smith. "What if he's going to a girlfriend's or something? What do we do then?"

"Maybe there's somebody who spends three or four nights a week at some strip club and then goes home at three or four in the morning to see his girlfriend, but I don't think the odds are very good. This guy strikes me as a little pathetic. His idea of a love life is *the Honey Pot?*"

"It doesn't have to be a girlfriend," said John Smith. "That was just an example. It could be a—"

"Look, John, so *anything* can happen. What does that tell you? Exactly nothing. You got to start with what's *likely* to happen and go from there. Listen, this has been a pretty good night! This is the first time we've made *any* contact with the guy. Now we know what he actually looks like."

"I still don't know how you did that," said John Smith.

"I swear, it was that black shirt he wears open down the front. He was wearing the same shirt in that picture we got from the Miami-Dade County cops. He's just spent five or six hours doing whatever the hell he likes to do in a whole building full of whores. I don't see him driving all the way back to Wynwood at three in the morning. Let's see where he *does* go."

John Smith sank back in the passenger seat and let out a sigh and closed his eyes.

About half an hour later, a heavyset guy in a black shirt open down the front, displaying the vast terrain of his hairy chest, came out of the Honey Pot by himself. Nestor nudged John Smith in the ribs and said, "Well—there's our boy."

John Smith sat low in the seat and eyed Igor Drukovich. "Jesus! He doesn't look very steady on his feet to me."

The man headed into the Honey Pot's parking lot. With the lights off, Nestor started up the Camaro.

No more than a minute had gone by when John Smith's conspiracy-muffled voice said, "What's he doing? Suppose he just walks through the lot and out the other side?"

John Smith stared at the exit from the parking lot and more minutes crawled by.

Finally, a Volvo, the big one, the Vulcan, emerged from the lot. Nestor had to look twice to see the hairy chest driving it.

Nestor took his cool sweet time folding up the reflector screen . . . all the while saying, "You wanna know my idea of the worst possible way—"

John Smith, bewildered: "He's speeding up!"

"—to die? Getting run over by a Volvo Vulcan or a Cadillac Escalade. Why I don't—"

"—Jesus!—he's almost reached that bend in the road and we haven't even—"

"—know except it would be so humiliating. I know that much."

"Nestor!"

"Cool it. I gotta let him go around the bend before I turn on the lights and start tailing him. Otherwise he's gonna wonder why he leaves the lot and some car's lights come on and start following him."

"But he's gonna disappear."

"Yeah, for about five seconds. There—he's just gone around it. Watch *this*."

Nestor turned on the Camaro's lights and drove it

onto the road slowly...then shot past the Honey Pot with a good show-off burst of Camaro acceleration and reached the bend in the road in a heartbeat... slowed down going around it...and sure enough, about 150 feet ahead there was the Volvo Vulcan... The body seemed to recede in the dark...but there was no mistaking the taillights. They were huge and rose up two feet higher than any ordinary vehicle's and wrapped around the corners in extravagant bands of light. Nestor was able to hang back this far and still keep track of it. Igor and the Vulcan were heading east...but only for half a mile...Igor turned left and headed north on A1A, the little highway that ran right along the coast. There was a fair amount of traffic, and Nestor was able to tail Igor more closely without being noticed. The green highway signs seemed to be drifting toward him. At first he was familiar with the places he was passing...Miami Gardens Drive... Northeast 192nd Street...Northeast 203rd Street... Aventura...Golden Beach...the GulfStream Park racetrack...They passed a big Russian restaurant called Tatyana's...and then Igor and the Vulcan swung left along a wide boulevard...more Russian names began turning up in the midnight gloaming... the Kirova Ballet Academy...the St. Petersburg Turkish and Russian Baths...the Ouspensky Cultural Center, which looked like just another storefront... Vladim's Paint and Body...Ivana's Nails and Spa.

Igor kept on heading west heading west. Where the hell was he going?

What they were passing now made Nestor feel like they were heading into another country. Here in the middle of the night there was something alien and ghostly about the roadsides, which were barely visible in a deep, unstable dusk created by passing headlights and highway lamps on metal stanchions so high their illumination was feeble... Every place except the 7-Eleven was dark, it seemed—Speeder Oil Change and Tuneup... Pet Pleasers Salon... IHOP, namely, the International House of Pancakes... Four Guys' Paint and Body... Spanky's Cheese Steak Factory... Tara Estates Manses for Active Adults... Supercuts... Smokey Bones BBQ and Grill... Pet Supermarket... Little Caesars Pizza... Applebee's... Wendy's... Desoto Luke's Active Adults, which seemed to consist of a pair of plain brick apartment houses with little terraces and courtyards... another 7-Eleven, lit up... Carver Toyota, with a lot full of automobiles twilit by two overhead lights... Olde Towne Bingo...

"Where are we?" said John Smith.

"Broward County," said Nestor, "but I don't know exactly where. I've never been this far west up here before."

"This is really strange!" said John Smith, an unusually animated John Smith. "And you know why? We've just entered a strange land... called

America! We're not in Miami anymore. Can't you *feel* it? Some Russian named Igor is leading us into the USA!"

Nestor analyzed this concept for traces of anti-Cuban insult, even though he had experienced the same alien feeling just a moment before... Well, John Smith was an alien himself. He was apparently a living embodiment of a creature everybody had heard of but nobody ever met in Miami, the WASP, the white Anglo-Saxon Protestant. Rationally, Nestor knew John Smith's crack about "a strange land... the USA" was harmless. Emotionally, he still resented it, harmless or not.

West west and farther west Igor kept going in his hulk with the lurid taillights. More low brick apartment buildings drifted by... "The Hampton Court... Active Adults Assisted Living Suites"...

" 'Active Adults Assisted Living,' " said John Smith. "Come on, you gotta *love* it!" He turned to get Nestor's reaction.

Nestor went to some pains not to show any reaction at all. He couldn't exactly think it through in words. Animated like this, John Smith annoyed him. The animation always came out of some feeling of superiority. John Smith could draw... concepts... out of something as ordinary as this second-rate road... "We've just entered a strange land... the USA."... That kind of thinking was a facility Nestor didn't have. Irony came always at somebody else's expense... his own, probably... Did it all come down to education? John Smith had gone to a college with an intimidating name... Yale... At that moment Nestor felt a hatred for everybody who had ever been to a college with an intimidating name... They were all pussies, when you got right down to it... but then what bothered Nestor was that maybe they weren't pussies...

West west west Igor drove the Vulcan until he reached someplace called West Park, when he turned right and headed due north up a smaller road... past Utopia... past the Deauville Abbey... more low-slung brick apartment buildings... "Active Adult Retirement Leisure Assisted Living Hospice and Coda Chateau"...

"These places—they're everywhere around here," Nestor muttered.

"It spooks you out after a while," said John Smith.

Now Igor turns left and heads *farther* west.

"Where the hell's he going?" said Nestor. "To the Everglades?"

Under the Florida's Turnpike toll road went Igor and his Volvo Vulcan, still heading west... but soon he slowed down and turned into some sort of driveway. Nestor and John Smith knew what he was heading for even before they could see the buildings themselves... Even from fifty yards away they could see the inevitable man-made lake... the Camaro's headlights were just bright enough for them to make out the fountains geysering up in the middle of the water.

Nestor barely slowed down and drove right on by the place.

"What are you doing?" said John Smith.

"I don't want to come in right behind him," said Nestor. "I'm gonna make a U-turn and come into the place from the other direction."

It took no more than a glimpse to see that here was your stone basic Active Adult housing. A metal plaque on a stanchion by the driveway bore the name Alhambra Lakes. On one side the entryway opened up onto a big parking lot... packed with cars... dimly lit by a few lamps on tall stanchions. Igor's Vulcan had just entered it. The apartment buildings were the most basic they had seen so far. At a glance they looked like two grim solid cubes of brick... each three stories high... adorned only by the inevitable tiny balconies and the sliding glass doors... no shrubbery or any other horticultural or arboricultural decoration, not even a hopeful palm tree or two.

"What do you suppose *this* is all about?" said John Smith... with a nod back toward Alhambra Lakes.

"I'm gonna drive in there," said Nestor. He pulled over onto the shoulder of the road... then made a U-turn... gunned the Camaro so suddenly, it threw John Smith's head back... but almost immediately had to slow down to turn into the Active Adults' driveway... and there was the Volvo Vulcan, nosed into a parking slot. The taillights were off, but the lights were on in its interior.

"I'm gonna drive by," said Nestor, "but don't look at him. Don't even look in his direction. I'm gonna go slow, like we're trying to find someplace to park."

Before they reached the Vulcan... there was the burly figure, Igor, opening the Vulcan's big rear door.

"Don't look," said Nestor. "Or maybe turn your head a little bit in the other direction."

Which they did. Nestor didn't even try to look with peripheral vision. When they reached the end of the row of cars, they were very close to the nearest building, and he was able to see through a wide, open entrance, which looked like a sort of tunnel. At the other end, toward the interior, more miserable overhead lighting.

"Must be a courtyard," said John Smith.

Nestor made a U-turn and drove slowly down the other side of the row. When they reached the front of the Volvo Vulcan, the interior lights were off.

"He's walking toward the building," said John Smith.

"What the hell's that he's carrying?" said Nestor. "That big flat thing."

"I don't know," said John Smith. "Looks like a portfolio. You know, an artist's portfolio."

"I'm gonna turn around again there at the end. See if you can tell where he's going."

Nestor made the turn very slowly and headed back up the other side.

"There he is," said John Smith. "He's going into that entrance, the one we just went by."

Nestor got just the barest glimpse of Igor as he disappeared into the tunnel or whatever it was called. He stopped the Camaro right there in the middle of the parking lot.

"Whattaya think he's doing here?" said Nestor. "You realize we're practically in Fort Lauderdale... and we're hell west of nowhere? I don't get it. And you say he's got a studio in Wynwood?"

"It's not just a studio, Nestor, it's a whole apartment, and it's pretty nice. I know plenty of artists, successful ones, too, who would *die* to have a setup like that."

"I do... not... get... this," said Nestor.

"Well... what do we do now?"

"There's not much we *can* do right now," said Nestor. "It's past four a.m. We can't just go wandering around the place in the middle of the night."

The Camaro's headlights were still on the building... Silence... Then John Smith said, "We'll have to come back in the morning and wait until he leaves and then see what we can do..."

Silence... the Camaro's headlights aimlessly

illuminated part of a row of cars... the lot was packed... The Camaro was almost ten years old, and Nestor thought about how now, when the engine idled, he was aware of the chassis vibrating.

"It's already early in the morning," said Nestor. "A guy like Igor—I don't see him going out to a strip club and getting drunk until three in the morning and then getting up at six. You saw all that shit he unloaded from the Vulcan. He wasn't just dropping by for a visit."

"*Ummmm*... I guess you're right," said John Smith. "Besides, we've got to go home and change. We've got to look serious when we go in there." He nodded toward the building Igor had gone into. "Do you have a jacket?"

"A jacket?... Yeah, I got *one*... It goes with a blue suit."

"Awesome!" said John Smith. "Do me a big favor. Wear the suit and some leather shoes."

"I don't know if it even fits me anymore. I got it before—well, it must a been three or four years ago." Nestor relived the whole mortifying scene then and there... Mami taking him into the men's department at Macy's... him standing there like a wooden idiot... Mami and the clerk talking—in Spanish—about how far down *this* should go and how far up *that* should go... only speaking to him twice... Mami saying, "*¿Cómo te queda de talle?*" and the clerk saying,

"Dobla los brazos y levanta los codos delante"...and him caring about only one thing...the horrible chance that somebody he knew might see him like this.

"Before you started working out at Rodriguez's?" John Smith smiled.

"Well...yeah," said Nestor.

"Awww...just do the best you can, Nestor. You can squeeze into it."

"I suppose next you're gonna want me to wear a tie," said Nestor, inflecting it with a touch of sarcasm.

John Smith's eyes lit up. "Hey, you own one?"

"Yeahhh..."

"Wear it!" said John Smith. "I will, too! We've got to look *serious!* That building's full of Active Adults. You know? They're not going to appreciate it if we show up as if we're going to the Honey Pot. Not even a twisted geek like Igor will appreciate it. We are *serious* men!"

15

The Yentas

Seven hours later, 10:30 a.m., Nestor and John Smith were driving... or, strictly speaking, John Smith was driving... into the parking lot of the Alhambra Lakes once more, this time in John Smith's brand-new gray two-door Chevrolet Assent. John Smith thought it would be rude to park Nestor's Camaro in an Active Adults' parking lot in daylight. The Camaro was a muscle car from back when muscle cars were muscle cars, and it was pimped out so ferociously, it would shove its mug into any Active Adult's face and snarl, "I'm a youthful offender. You got a problem with that?"

Of course—*hah!*—John Smith didn't say "rude" or anything close to it. He expressed it in carefully hedged, gentler words, but on this killer-bright day John Smith's good manners annoyed Nestor... his manners, among a dozen other things. Still inside the Assent's air-conditioned cocoon they trolled slowly toward the building Igor had disappeared into last night. In flagrant sunlight like this, the place looked even worse than it had in the dark. All around the base was a stretch of raggedy bare ground that no doubt at one time had been flush with lush green shrubbery. Here and there about the rim of the parking lot you saw a palm tree here... and two there... and then a gap... and three there... gap... then another lone palm tree... The whole place appeared snaggletoothed. The palms were limp and wan... the leaves bore puce-colored splotches. On the building's facade the little iron balconettes and the aluminum frames for the sliding doors looked as if they were about to fall off and die in a pile.

John Smith pointed and said, "Hey, look... Igor's Vulcan's gone."

So far, so good. Before they confronted him, they needed to know a lot more... such as what he was doing here last night... and what and where was all that stuff he hauled inside. John Smith made a U-turn at the end of the row of cars and parked in the most remote section, the one for visitors.

When they got out of the car, Nestor was really annoyed. He put on the jacket of the suit John had talked him into wearing and slid the necktie up. The jacket was too small, as he knew it would be. On top of that, John Smith insisted that Nestor carry a 9½-inches-long, 3½-inches-wide, 1½-inches-thick dosimeter—a device for measuring noise levels—in an inside jacket pocket. If anybody challenged them, Nestor was to pull out the dosimeter, and he, John Smith, would explain that they were taking noise levels. A too-tight suit *bulging* with a fifty-cubic-inch machine on one side—great. Before he had taken his first step, he could feel the inside of his shirt collar turning sodden with sweat... and sweat soaking through his jacket, creating big dark half-moons under his armpits. The suit, the tie, his black leather cop shoes... he looked like a real *guajiro*... John Smith, on the other hand, had on a light-gray suit that fit perfectly, a white shirt, a navy tie with some kind of stuffy, orderly print on it, and black leather shoes trim and narrow enough to go dancing in. He acted like it didn't bother him at all... the damned WASP... Then he had to rub it in:

"Nestor!... you look great! If you knew how good you look in a suit, you'd never wear anything else!"

Nestor had never seen the WASP in such a cheery mood before. So he shot him a finger. But John was in such a good mood, he started laughing his head off over that.

The whole sky was the pale blue dome of a heat

lamp. Nestor hadn't walked a hundred feet before he could feel the sweat pouring out for real. The parking lot was so still, he could hear their footsteps on the asphalt. Yet practically all the parking places for the tenants were occupied. Just then a hoarse, grumbling, transmission-slipping, piston-done-for bus, the small boxy kind, painted white, came groaning in off the road. The fenders flared up in big curves like the wings of a pelican in flight. It pulled up not far from Nestor and John. On the roof a foot-high sign stuck up in the air from front to back: SHOP 'N' BROWSE BUY BUS! It seemed to be a bus service that took groups of people from their Active Adult and Assisted Living homes to shopping centers and back. The driver hopped out. Look at that suntan!—a skinny young Anglo who looked as if his hide were just shipped from the tannery! He hustled around to the other side... to help a lot of old ladies get off, judging by the voices. They didn't sound tired. They sounded excited.

"... but *such*... a... *sale* I've never seen..."

"... who on earth needs four? But look in this shopping *beg*—go ahead, take a look in!..."

"... didn't even use all my coupons..."

"... thirty minutes from now? You better forget about the lemon meringue..."

"... yeah, only one kesh register open and *such*... a... *line* you..."

"...*'Attention shoppers,'* every two minutes *'Attention shoppers'*—gives me a migraine you wouldn't believe!..."

"...pushy pushy pushy, the nerve of some people the way they push..."

"...don't *keh!* Walgreens has better buys!..."

"...meringue eleven-fifteen, maybe you can get on line! Me, eleven-fifteen I gotta go up and take my pills..."

...All this to the accompaniment of music—of a *beat,* anyway—an irregular metallic beat, actually... *clink clink... clatter clatter clatter... clink... clatter... clink clink clatter...*

As Nestor and John drew closer, they could see the old ladies heading into the building, quite a few supporting themselves on aluminum walkers that *clinked* and *clattered clattered* and *clink clink clinked*...Only two old men...At least half of the old ladies, even the ones on the walkers, were carrying shopping bags... Walgreens... Walmart... CVS... Winn-Dixie... Marshalls... JCPenney... Chico's... the Gap... Macy's... Target... ShopRite... Banana Republic...Naturalizer...

Home! Back home bearing the kill they came! The élan of a party of deadeye hunters returning from the field was what they had.

"What's all this *meringue?*" said Nestor.

"Beats me," said John Smith. "We let them all go inside and get settled before *we* go in."

Okaaaaay... "the reporter"... All day John Smith had been directing this operation. He had assumed the role of captain. Maybe on this terrain "the reporter" knew best... Nestor doubted it, but he was heavily dependent upon John Smith. What other ally did he have? All right... let him run this *his* way.

So they stood outside the building. John Smith motioned for him to take out the dosimeter. Nestor, already soaked with sweat though he was, had to admit John Smith was right... the suits... the machine... nobody was likely to identify them as a pair of shady young punks loitering around an active adults apartment building and up to no good. Two properly attired young men was what they were, two young gentlemen willing to wear all these clothes while the heat lamp in the sky was heading for the max... they must have a serious mission or they wouldn't *be* here.

Once the way had cleared to John Smith's satisfaction, it was a minute or so after 11:30. The big front entrance was not an entrance in any formal architectural sense. It was nothing but a ten-foot-high, thirty-foot-long corridor where two sides of the building joined.

Thank God... no concierge desk or anything else to check who was going in or out. John Smith and Nestor walked right on in and found themselves standing on the edge of a courtyard framed by four sides of the building coming together to create a square. Like the exterior, the courtyard of the Alhambra Lakes was the fried remains of what must have been a full gardenscape of palm trees, shrubbery, and flowers once upon a time... and at dead center, a square pool with a worn-out fountain that feebly projected a single, spent spout of water up to about three feet above the surface of the pool. On the second and third floors wide slabs of concrete projected from the interior walls all the way around the square, creating a walkway, an outsized catwalk, as it were, and a back porch for every apartment on the floor. An open stairway connected all three levels in case you didn't want to take the elevator they had passed on the way in.

"We'll take the elevator up to the top," said John Smith, describing a great loop in the air with his forefinger, "and work our way down to the second floor and then down here to the courtyard, okay?"

They had the elevator to themselves on the way up. At the top, the third floor, they stepped out onto the walkway... and into a loud, noxious mechanical noise. On the far side a brown-skinned maintenance man in coveralls was cleaning the catwalk with an industrial vacuum cleaner. From somewhere below came the clinking clacking tintinnabulation of a couple of aluminum walkers. Nearby... the too-loud yawps of TV sets within the apartments...but no tenants were out in the noonday sun on this floor. John Smith went slowly past the apartments on this side, and Nestor followed, holding the "sonar audiometric monitor"... ::::::What am I—a native bearer?:::::: Somewhere within an apartment a television show was turned on so loud, you could hear every word..."But he's been her gastro-enterologist for *five years!*" says the unmistakably soapopera voice of a young woman. "And *now* he falls in *love* with her?—while spreading her cheeks for a *colonoscopy?* Oh, *men*"—she begins loading every word with sobs—"*Men—men—mennn*-uh-uh-uh-uh—they lead an entirely separate life below the beh-eh-he-ehlt!" Beside the door, on the floor of the catwalk, was a cast-iron frog, painted light green. It was only about a foot high, but it was also about a foot wide and fifteen inches long...which made it look enormous and heavy. On either side of the door was a small window. John Smith and Nestor made a point of not being nosy and looking in. The next apartment was identical, except that the program bellowing inside for all it was worth was some comedy show with the most annoying laugh track Nestor had ever heard...and beside the door was a two-foot-high cast-iron caveman with arms and shoulders like a gorilla's. It looked heavier than the frog. At the next apartment...God almighty!...a what?—Discovery

Channel show?—a bunch of lions roaring, not just one but what did they call them?—a "pride"? Must be turned up to the max, because between the lions and the industrial vacuum cleaner Nestor felt like the noise out here in this active adults pile of bricks had him paralyzed... Beside this door, a big pot of red geraniums, a regular mass of red geraniums... that turned out to be fakes.

John Smith had to get close to Nestor to make himself heard. "Keep an eye on those... *things* by the doors, whatever they are"—he pointed toward the flowerpot—"for something that says 'artist,' okay?"

Nestor nodded. He was already fed up with taking orders from John Smith. Who did he think he had become all of a sudden, the great detective?

They checked out two more apartments. Same thing... John Smith came up close to Nestor again and said, "I've never heard TV sets on that loud. What are they—deaf?"

"They're on aluminum walkers, for God's sake," said Nestor. "If they're not deaf, who is?" He didn't say it with a smile. He could tell John Smith had no idea at all where the overtone of reproof had come from. So then Nestor felt guilty.

It was so loud out here on this catwalk that neither Nestor nor John Smith realized that two figures were coming up behind them until they were almost upon them... two old ladies. One seemed terribly small. Her back was humped so far over her walker, her eyes were at about the level of Nestor's rib cage... and so rheumy, they constantly leaked tears. Her remaining hair had been dyed blond and teased up into little puffs of spun cilia meant to give the impression of thick hair, but Nestor could see right through them to the skin of her skull. All at once he felt consumed by pity and a rogue desire to protect her. The other old lady stood upright with the help of a cane. Her hair was white and thinning so badly that the part on one side looked more like a bald spot. But she had retained a lot of extra pounds and had a big round face... and she wasn't shy. She walked right up to John Smith and said, "Can I help you? You looking for something, maybe?"

The way she said it—she was a formidable presence. John Smith uttered some garbled name... "Gunnar Gerter"?... and... gestured toward Nestor and said, "This is my technician, Mr. Carbonell."

::::::*my technician*::::::

"We're taking noise-level readings," said John Smith... He gestured toward the dosimeter Nestor was holding ::::::like a flunky::::::

"Hahhh!" She let out a sardonic laugh. "At *this* place? Noise? More noise I'd like to hear. You know what you have to be to make noise? Alive."

John Smith smiled. "I don't know about that. We're getting some pretty high readings right here." Now he gestured toward the industrial vacuum cleaner and then toward the apartment they stood in front of. TV game show cheers shrieked from within. Before the woman could get onto such questions as *Why? Who sent you? From where?* John Smith said, "By the way, perhaps you can tell me something. We've been admiring your little statues by the doors. You have some artist here who does them?"

"Hughhhh"—a disdainful chortle from the little old lady bent over her walker. She had a shrill and surprisingly strong voice—*"Artists?* We got *one* artist here, or that's what he calls himself. Me, I never saw anything he ever did. Mainly he stinks the place up. The smell coming from his apartment is terrible, terrible. Are you from the Environment?"

The *environment?* Nestor couldn't imagine what she meant, but John Smith didn't skip a beat. "Yes, we *are.*"

The stout woman with the cane said, "Oh, finally already somebody comes! You could die from this stink. We been complaining about this guy for three months. We complain and complain and nobody comes. We leave messages, and nobody calls. Whatta you people got there for the messages, an answering machine or one a those trash bags, the plastic ones, the color of what I'm not gonna say."

The little old lady on the walker interrupted. "Come on, Lil. We gotta get to the dining room—to the meringy."

"*Meringy?* It's not *meringy,* Edith. Meringy is some kind a dance. It's mer*ang,* lemon meringue."

"I know, I know, but if we don't get there, it'll be gone, and today's the only day they have it."

"Edith . . . and today's the only day the Environment comes here. Besides, sometimes there's some left. Dahlia can save us some. She puts them in her bag."

"*Hughhhh!* You hear *that?*" said the stout woman. She pointed down toward the lower floors.

Sure enough, you could hear a rising percussion concert of *clink clatterclatter clink clink clatter,* even louder than the one Nestor and John Smith had heard coming out of the Shop 'n' Browse Buy Bus. A lot of people on aluminum walkers were trying to get somewhere fast.

"And that don't even count the people," said Edith, "the people who go down there and line up a half hour before the dining room opens on meringy day is what Hannah and Mr. Cutter do."

The stout one, Lil, didn't even bother correcting the *meringy.* She was busy talking to John Smith. "There is *such* . . . a . . . *stink* in this place; you can even smell it right here. Do you smell it? . . . Smell! Smell! Take a good smell!"

She was so bossy, Nestor inhaled and took a good smell. He didn't smell anything unusual. Edith, the smaller one, said: "My doctor says it's toxic . . . *toxic* . . .

Look it up, *toxic.* It's the reason I don't eat right, I don't sleep. The doctor is doubling my doses of fish oil every week. Even my hair stinks from the smell going around everywhere."

"Where is this apartment?" said John Smith.

"Right under *my* apartment," said Lil, pointing down the row of doors on the catwalk. "*Such*...a... *stink* comes up, no matter what I do."

"Me, too," said Edith, "but Lil's is worse."

John Smith said to Lil, "Have you ever tried talking to him about it?"

"Tried? I've camped outside his door. Talk about a smell! You could smell the stink coming out of his door. Neighborly he's not. I've seen him, but I never seen him go in or come out. He must do it in the dark. I've never seen him in the dining room. I hear him down in his apartment. But nobody knows his phone number or his e-mail. I go down and I ring his bell, I knock on his door, and he don't answer. I send him a letter, and he don't write back. So I call you people, and *you* don't do *bupkis.* And it's not just me and Edith. Everybody on his floor has to breathe that stink. It's like poison gas or nuclear radiation. It's a good thing nobody here's having children anymore. They'd be born with one arm or no nose or a tongue that don't reach the front teeth or with their bowels up in their chests and they'll do everything out their ears and talk with their belly buttons and think outta brains located in what they sit down on. Close your eyes and see it. *You* try it. *You* try talking to him."

John Smith and Nestor looked at each other... nonplussed. Then John Smith managed a smile and said, "I don't even know his name."

"His name is Nicolai," said Lil. "His last name starts with *K* but after that it's all *v*'s and *k*'s and *y*'s and *z*'s. A collision at an intersection they sound like they had."

John Smith and Nestor looked at each other. They didn't need to say it out loud. "Nicolai? Not Igor?"

"Do me a favor," John Smith said. "Take us there, to his apartment, so we'll know exactly which one."

"*Hahhh*—a guide you don't need!" piped up Edith. "You got maybe a *nose?*"

"Edith's right," said Lil. "But I'll take you there anyway. Too long already we been waiting for somebody from the Environment."

So all four, including *clink clatter clatter clink* Edith with her walker, got on the elevator, and Lil led them to "Nicolai's" door on the second level's catwalk. Beside the door was a two-foot-high metal statue of a tall man extending his right arm, palm-down, in a salute.

John Smith leaned toward Nestor and said, "That's Chairman Mao, except that Chairman Mao was more like five-two. Right there he's six-five. Igor is... weird."

::::::How does he know these things?::::::

The smell—it was strong, all right...but not unpleasant, if you asked Nestor. It was turpentine. He had always liked the smell of turpentine...but maybe if you had to live next door on this catwalk and smell somebody else's turpentine fumes day and night, you might get fume-whipped pretty fast.

John Smith walked past six or seven doors on the catwalk *this* way...and six or seven *that* way...and returned to "Nicolai's" apartment.

"Yeah, it's pretty strong everywhere," said John Smith. He looked at Lil. "We have to get inside there and find out exactly what the source is before we can do anything. How can we get in? Any ideas?"

"The manager's got a key to every apartment."

"Where's the manager?"

"Hahhhh!" said Edith. "The manager's never here!"

"Where is he?" said John Smith.

"*Hahhhh!* Who knows? So Phyllis fills in and covers for him. She says she likes it. Phyllis Easy to Please is what I call her."

"Who's Phyllis?"

"She's a tenant," said Lil.

"A tenant fills in for the manager?"

Lil said, "A manager here's like a super—a superintendent—in New York. A janitor with a title is what the manager is."

Nestor spoke up for the first time. "You're from New York?"

Edith, not Lil, answered the question. "*Hahhh!* Everybody *here* is from New York, or Long Island—the whole town moved down here. Who do you *think* lives in these places, people from *Florida,* maybe?"

"So does Phyllis have the key?"

"If anybody's got the key," said Lil, "Phyllis got the key. Want me to call her?" She took out her cell phone.

"By all means!" said John Smith.

"Nicolai—she don't think he's fifty-five in the first place. Phyllis don't," said Edith. "It ends up, he's got to go to the office sometimes. Phyllis knows what he looks like. He's got a big mustache goes out like this, but I haven't seen him in a long time. You got to be fifty-five and no pets and no children to buy a condo."

Lil had already turned her back for privacy. The one thing Nestor heard her say clearly was "You sitting down? You ready for this?... The Environment's here."

Lil turned toward them, closing her cell phone. She said to John, "She's coming up! She can't believe the Environment's here, either."

In no time a tall, bony old woman—Phyllis—arrived. She looked at John Smith and Nestor with a long face. Lil introduced her to them. Thank God, Lil remembered Nestor's new last name, "Carbonell," because he had already forgotten it. Phyllis's scowl changed from a scowl to a smile of withering scorn.

"Took you only three months to get here," she said. "But maybe that's what you Government people call 'rapid response.' "

John Smith closed his eyes, spread his lips into a flat grimace, and began nodding his head in the yes mode conveying the notion *Yes, yes, it hurts, but I have to admit I know exactly what you mean*. Then he opened his eyes and gave her a profoundly sincere look and said, "But when we do get here, we . . . are . . . *here*. Know what I'm saying?"

Nestor winced and said to himself, ::::::I don't *believe* this.:::::: Now he understood what it took to be a newspaper reporter: double-talk and heartfelt lies.

It must have mildly reassured stone-faced Phyllis, however, for she shot them both looks of merely mild disdain and produced a key and unlocked the apartment door.

It opened into a kitchen, a small filthy kitchen. About a week's worth of dishes and tinny-looking knives and forks and spoons with the remains not even scraped off had been stacked up helter-skelter in the sink. About a week's worth of unidentifiable spots, gobs, and spills were all over the counters on either side of the basin and on the floor. About a week's worth of garbage, fortunately desiccated by now, lay crammed into a tinny trash canister to the point where it kept the lid from closing. The place was so filthy, the pervasive smell of turpentine struck Nestor as a purifier.

Phyllis led them from the kitchen into what was no doubt designed to be a living room. Right in front of the sliding glass doors on the far wall was a big, dark, ancient-looking wooden easel. Next to it was a long industrial worktable with a stack of metal drawers at each end. The top was cluttered with tubes, rags, and God knows what else, plus a row of coffee cans with the long slender handles of paintbrushes sticking out. The easel and the table rested upon a piece of paint-spattered tarpaulin at least seven feet by seven feet. That was the only floor covering in the room. The rest was bare wood . . . that hadn't been attended to in a long time. The place looked halfway studio and halfway storeroom, thanks to the boxes and pieces of equipment piled in no discernable order against one of the side walls—rolls of canvas . . . big boxes, long, wide, but only three or four inches deep . . . Nestor guessed they were for framed pictures . . . a slide projector on top of a small metal stand about three and a half feet high . . . a dehumidifier . . . and more boxes and cans . . .

All this Nestor took in with a single glance. But Lil, Edith, Phyllis, and John Smith were absorbed in something else entirely. On the other wall were twelve paintings, six in one row and six in a row beneath it. The women were chuckling.

"You gotta look at this one, Edith," said Lil. "This one's got two eyes on the same side of his nose and look at the size a that schnozz! You see that? You see it? I got a grandson-seven-years-old's better than that. He's not so little he don't know where the eyes go!"

The three women began laughing, and Nestor had to laugh, too. The painting consisted of the thick clumsy outline of a man in profile with a childishly huge nose. Both eyes were on this side of it. The hands looked like fish. There was no attempt at shading or perspective. There was nothing but more thick, clumsy black outlines creating shapes filled in with flat colors...and no attempt to make any of them stand out from the others.

"And the one *next* to it," Lil continued. "See those four women theh? Talk about afflicted! See that? They got the eyes in the right place—but the *nose!* The poor things, they got noses that start up over one eyebrow, and then they come down as far as a normal girl's chin, and the nostrils look like a double-barrel shotgun-wants-to-blow-your-kop-off-for-you!"

More squalls of laughter.

"And take a look at that one up *theh,*" said Edith. This one was of nothing but vertical stripes of color... must have been a dozen of them...and not all that even, either. And why were they so watery? "Looks like they got soaked up by the canvas some way."

"I don't think that's suppose a be a painting," said Phyllis. "He was just getting the paint off his brushes is what I think."

She said it in an absolutely Phyllis-like way. Phyllis never joked around, but Lil and Edith and Nestor had to laugh anyway. They were all having a great time making fun of the deluded Russian who thinks he's an artist.

"*Hahhh,* you see that one?" said Edith. "That poor *zhlub,* he takes a ruler and he makes that cross *theh's*-about-to-fall-over and he looks at it and says, 'Shmuck!' "—hitting herself on the forehead with the heel of her hand—" 'I give up!' and he paints the rest of it plain white-you-gotta-give-him-credit. It's better'n 'at cockamamie cross!"

The three women laughed and laughed, and Nestor couldn't hold back a chuckle himself.

They took a look at *that* one with all the tape-worms-jumped-out-of-the-john and *that* one with the hands-look-like-two-clumps-of-asparagus and the one on the end *theh*—looks-like-a-pile-a-shucked-oysters-gone-high, and get that one!—the one below it—*Tethered at Collioure. Tethered* must mean you smear glue all over the thing and then you dump a bag full a different-colored confetti on it and you got yourself a painting!...and by the time they get to that one *theh* of the patchwork-quilt-only-he-can't-draw-a-straight-line-and-it's-all-falling-to-pieces...and that one of a pitcher of beer and a tobacco-pipe-cut-in-half...and that one *theh*—looks like two aluminum nudes-with-screw-on-nipples... and that one next to it-looks-like-three-aluminum-men-eating-playing-cards...and they're laughing until the tears come, they're shaking their heads, pulling faces, putting on sardonic smiles or intentionally retarded gapes with their mouths hanging open, rolling their eyeballs up so far they practically disappear. Edith is so swept away, she's still hunched over, leaning on her walker, but she manages to stamp her feet up and down in a paroxysm of hilarity gone wild. Not even the dead serious iron-faced Phyllis can resist. She breaks out of her iron capsule with a single burst of laughter—"Honnnkkuhhh!"

Lil says, "An *artist* he's supposed to be, and *that's* the best he can do? I'd come and go in the dark, too! My face I wouldn' wanna show people!"

Another round of uncontrollable laughter...even Nestor's professional resolve turns to jelly, and he's laughing, too. He looks over at John Smith to catch his reaction...and John Smith is oblivious of it all. He might as well be all by himself. He has his little narrow spiral notebook and his trick ballpoint out, and he's busy looking at the paintings one by one and taking notes.

Nestor sidles over and says to him, "Hey, John, whattaya doin'?" John Smith acts as if he didn't hear him and pulls a small camera out of an inside pocket of his jacket and starts taking pictures of the paintings one by one. He walks amidst the women as if he doesn't know they're there... Lil leans down to Edith's level and says in a low voice, "The big-shot."

Then he walked back past them, eyes fixed on the rear screen of the camera. Thing had him in a trance. He didn't even look up when he reached Nestor. With his back to the three women, he lowered his head, eyes fixed on his notebook, and said, "You know what you're looking at on that wall?"

"No. Somebody's day care center?"

"You're looking at two Picassos, one Morris Louis, one Malevich, one Kandinsky, a Matisse, a Soutine, a Derain, a Delaunay, a Braque, and two Légers." For the first time during this recitation, John Smith lifted his head enough to see Nestor face-to-face. "Take a good look, Nestor. You're looking at twelve of the most perfect, most subtle forgeries you or anybody else is ever going to lay eyes on. Don't worry. These aren't by 'Nicolai.' These are by a *real* artist."

With that, John Smith winked a confident, reassuring wink at Nestor.

::::::The hell with you and your reassuring me. You're trying to act like a *real* detective.::::::

* * *

To be on the safe side, Magdalena had come to the office an hour early, 7:00 a.m. She had been sitting here in her white uniform rigid as a corpse... or up to a point. This corpse's heart was going 100 b.p.m. and heading for tachycardia. The girl was braced for the worst.

Ordinarily the Worst arrived about 7:40, twenty minutes before the office opened, to brief himself on what the eight o'clock patient has been puling and mewling about... He often told Magdalena he couldn't imagine himself becoming so weak that he'd go whining to somebody like himself, to put himself up on a stage as the star of a tragedy before an audience of one... one you had to pay five hundred dollars an hour to show up*pppAHGGAHHHhahahock hock hock!*

This isn't an ordinary morning, however. This morning she's going to do it. She keeps telling herself that. *Say no now!* What possible good would it do to keep stringing it out? *Do it, do it! Say no now!*

On an ordinary morning, the two of them arrived at the office sitting next to each other in the front seat of his white Audi convertible, top down he insists, and the hell with a big girl's hair... from his apartment with two basins in the bathroom he thinks are swell...where they would have taken a shower... then gotten dressed and eaten breakfast.

She hadn't prepared exactly what to say, because there was no predicting which variety of tiresome and obnoxious he was going to be. She remembered Norman's story of "the pissing monkey." He had put the moral of that story to good use when it came time to deal with a pissing monkey named Ike Walsh of *60 Minutes*. Stripped down to its essentials, the moral was: Immobilize the monkey so he can't get on top. But was that the only strategy she had on her side, a fable about a monkey? Her heart sped up, and she despaired of *any* way to keep Norman from nailing her anytime he cared to. Norman was big and strong physically, and he had a temper...not that he ever handled her roughly...and the minutes were ticking by.

She had to calm down...and so she tried to stop thinking about Norman's volatile, ego-swollen self. She tried to focus on the immediate surroundings... the examining table, white, clean, with a fitted sheet that fit the mattress so tightly, the surface was taut... the pale beigey-gray chair the patients usually sat in for their Lust-No-Mo injections, although some of the taller ones preferred to sit on the edge of the examining table when she gave them their shots... such as Maurice Fleischmann. ::::::Come on, Magdalena!:::::: She couldn't very well put Norman out of her mind if she was going to let her thoughts stray to Maurice. Here you had one of the most powerful men in Miami. All sorts of people *jumped* when he came around... jumped to do *anything* to make him happy... jumped to make sure he had the best seat in the room... deferred to whatever he had to say... grinned all over him... laughed at anything he said that might possibly be construed as an intentional humorous affect...

...while Norman led him around like a dog. Norman had the Big Man convinced that only Norman Lewis, M.D., P.C., could do anything to lead him out of the darkness of the valley of the shadow of pornography. He even let Norman come along on his social rounds, which were among the mighty rich. Magdalena had suspected it from the beginning but by now *knew* it was true: Norman made sure that Maurice would never be free of his addiction to pornography... just think of the way he rubbed Maurice's nose in it at Art Basel... Norman *needed* Maurice to remain in his wretched condition... Maurice opened all the doors that would be closed to any run-of-the-mill pornography addiction swami. She resolved at that moment to *be strong*... and tell Maurice in so many words *exactly* what was going on... once *this*—

—the lock of the outer door was opening... Sure enough, it was 7:40. ::::::Now, remember, you texted him in plenty of time to say you would be spending the night at home... and there is no reason he shouldn't realize that "at home" means at *my own apartment,* the one I share with Amélia. What's so wrong about going over and spending some time catching up on what Amélia's been doing? I haven't heard you suggest that we get married or anything like that, have I?... No, you mustn't say that... You mustn't even hint that you've been thinking about letting yourself get entangled any further with his perverted life—no!—and don't even suggest that he's a pervert, for God's sake... Come on! Cut it out! There's no way to plan anything you're going to say to Norman... Just remember, you're not going to let him piss on you::::::—

Another latch turns, meaning he's in the office itself now. Magdalena's heart is going at a runaway pace. She never knew you could hear footfalls in this place. The floor is nothing but a concrete slab covered with synthetic carpet. Nevertheless, she could hear Norman coming nearer. His shoes made a faint *scritch* sound. Magdalena told herself to be very calm and cool. So she sat there like someone waiting to be executed...*scritch*...*scritch*...*scritch*...he was getting closer. ::::::I can't just sit here like this, like he's got my wrists strapped to the arms of the chair and I'm resigned to my fate.:::::: She stood up and went over to the pale beigey-gray cabinet—everything was pale beigey-gray in this office—where the syringes and doses of anti-libido serum were kept and pushed them around on a shelf in order to sound busy... *scritch... scritch... SCRITCH... Uhohhhh...* no more *scritch.* He must have been right in the doorway, but she wasn't going to turn around to see. A few seconds went by...and nothing. It seemed like an eternity...

"Well...good morning," said the voice, neither friendly nor unfriendly...Room temperature was all it was.

She turned about, as if surprised—and immediately regretted that. Why would she be surprised? "Good morning!" she said... ::::::Damn! That was slightly above room temperature.:::::: She didn't want to sound warm and friendly.

Norman looked huge to her. He wore a tan gabardine suit she hadn't seen before, a white shirt, and a brown necktie with an unfortunately picturesque print of goblins—must have been a dozen of them—skiing down a steep brown slope. He smiled without saying anything. It was the sort of smile in which the upper lip is lifted so that you can see the two pointed eyeteeth. She got a good eyeful of the teeth before he said, with a slight smile that she searched for irony:

"I wasn't sure whether you'd be here this morning."

"Why wouldn't I be?" She meant it to sound offhand and immediately realized it sounded combative.

"Oh, you don't remember? You stood me up last night. Rather unceremoniously."

"Unceremoniously?" said Magdalena. "What does that mean?" It was actually a relief of an odd sort to come right out and admit she didn't know what these people were talking about.

"You could have at least told me yesterday before you skipped out."

"Skipped *out!*" said Magdalena. "I *sent* you a *text!*"

"Yeah, about ten o'clock at night. You sent me one miserable little text." Norman was beginning to get a bit heated. "Why didn't you call me? Afraid I might *answer?* And when I called you, you had the phone turned off."

"Amélia went to bed early, and I didn't want to wake her up. So I shut off the phone."

"Eminently thoughtful," said Norman, "eminently thoughtful. Oh, *eminently* means the same as *highly* in this case, okay? Does *highly* help? No? Too big a word? Then make it 'very.' Okay? *'very'* thoughtful. Okay?"

"No use being... that way about it, Norman."

"What time did *you* go to bed, sweetheart? And where? Or is it no use being *that* way, either?"

"I've already told you—"

"You've already told me absolutely nothing that makes sense. So why don't you try being honest and tell me what the fuck's going on?"

"Don't use those words if you want to talk to me, okay? But since you've asked, I will mention something I haven't brought up with you before. Do you know that you have a way of filling up a room until there's no air left?"

"*Oh hohhh.* 'Filling up a room until there's no air left'! How literary we are all of a sudden. What's *that* metaphor supposed to mean?"

"What's a met—"

"What's a meta...*for,* right? I thought we were in the literary mode this morning. What's a 'mode'? Okay, let's make it 'mood' instead. You know 'mood'?"

His lip was lifted still higher to show his upper teeth. He looked like a snarling animal. It frightened Magdalena, but she was even more afraid of the pissing monkey overcoming her and subjecting her to God knew what, because now he had a whole head full of anger. She glanced about the office. It was not yet eight o'clock in the morning. Was there anybody else in this building who would hear a thing? ::::::Don't be so frightened! Just *do it*— ::::::

—and she heard herself saying, "You said to be honest and tell you what's going on. Okay, what's going on is...*you.* You fill up a room...and me, up to *here*"—she put the edge of her flat palm against her throat—"with sex, and I don't mean the joy of sex, either. I mean *perverted* sex. I can't *believe* you took poor Maurice to those pornographic art shows at Art Basel and then stood by and let him buy all these pieces of *plain, out-and-out* pornography by this Jed Whatever-his-name-is and let him spend *millions* on them. I can't *believe* you were dying to go to that orgy, the Columbus Day Regatta, in the first place, but you also wanted *me* to join in, and if I had, you would have, too. I can't *believe* I even let you persuade me to do that 'role-playing' you sprang on me as soon as we started living together, the time you had me carry that black suitcase hard as a piece a-uh-uh-uhh — fiberglass and pretend like I was knocking on your hotel door by mistake and let you *ravish* me, you called it, and tear my clothes off, and let you pull the thong of my panties out and do it to me from behind. I can't *believe* I let you do that, and I spend two days trying to persuade myself this is 'sexual freedom'! *Freedom* — ohmygod — *si ahogarme en un pozo de mierda es la libertad, encontré la libertad.*"

Norman didn't say a word. He looked at Magdalena as if she had suddenly given him a two-finger killer karate jab in the Adam's apple, and he was studying her, trying to figure out why. When he finally spoke, it was in a low voice . . . with his upper teeth bared but without a smile. "So you just neglected to mention all this before — what *is* all this bullshit?"

"I told you — "

"Oh, I know, you're too proper for talk like that.

You know what? You're about as proper as the last blow job you gave me. Do you know that!?"

"You're the one who said 'Be honest'!"

"And this is your idea of being honest? This is your idea of—*something*. I don't know *what*, but it's something clinically sick!"

" 'Clinically sick' ... is that a medical term? Is that what you tell Maurice his problem is? He's 'clinically sick'? You *want* Maurice to stay sick, don't you? You *want* him to have pus blisters—right?! Otherwise, nobody's gonna be getting you through the VIP door into Art Basel or getting you a slip for your cigarette boat on Fisher Island or getting you into Chez Toi or what's that special upper floor, the Chez Toi Club or whatever it is, with the black card?"

"God damn it—"

"It's not enough for you to be a prominent TV schloctor, is it? Noooo, you want respect, don't you! You want to—"

"Why, you *bitch!*"

"—be a socialite! Right! You wanna be invited to all the parties! So you're gonna give poor Maurice your 'clinically sick' diagnosis until—"

Norman made an animal sound and before Magdalena knew what was happening, he had grabbed her by the upper arm, just beneath the shoulder, and jerked her upward by the arm and jerked her body near his by the arm, and half-hissed, half-growled,

"Oh, I'll give you a diagnosis, bitch . . . you're a bitch, *bitch!*"

"Stop it!" said Magdalena. It was close to a scream. In that instant she was terrified. The animal sound of his voice—he called her a *bitch*—he was manhandling her—*"Bitch!"*—jerking her this way—*"Bitch!"*—and that—*"Bitch!"*—and this time she shrieked the bloodiest shriek she had ever shrieked in her life! "Stop it!" Norman swung his head about as if looking for something ::::::the bastard! He wants to make sure no one is aware of what he's doing!:::::: Norman's grip slackens for that split second . . . Magdalena breaks loose . . . more shrieking shrieking shrieking shrieking shrieking shrieking to the roar of *you bitch*—"Bitch!—you *don't*—you bitch!"—he's right behind her! . . . she *throws* herself at the crossbar latch of the door that opens out into the parking courtyard and stumbles into the sunlight, cars circling looking for parking spots, some man in a passenger seat yells, "You okay?" and doesn't pause long enough to find out but it stops Norman, anyway. Not even that sex-crazed hulk of egoplasm dares to be seen running like a madman out into a public parking lot physically overpowering a shrieking girl half his age. Nevertheless she runs through the ranks of parked cars hunched over so that he won't see her head pop above the roof of a car and go mad enough to . . . scampers hunched over . . . gasping for every next breath . . . as afraid of dying as she has ever been in her

life...her heart hammering away in her chest. ::::::Where do I go? I can't go to my apartment... *he* knows where that is!...He's turned into an animal!::::::

She reaches the car...crouches way down beside it... the door! ::::::Get in! Lock it!:::::: ...she starts to put her hand into—and a terrible heat begins rising up into her cranial cavity, burning the lining of her skull...she doesn't have her handbag! In her wild rush to escape, she left it in the examination room...her car keys and the remote and her key to the apartment...her credit cards...cash...cell phone...*driver's license!*—her only ID in this world except for her passport, but that's in the apartment, and *he has the key now!* He has it *all,* even her makeup...She doesn't dare stay here crouched beside her car...he knows the car! What if he—

—scurried hunched over until she finally saw the exit on the far side...Even then she didn't dare walk through upright...People were looking at her, a young nurse in white scurrying out of a parking lot... hunched way over like that...Look at her! So young, and she's *out to lunch* or she's having a *stroke!* That girl needs a *lot* of help...and who's going to give it to her?...Don't look at me.

Noon on yet another identical Miami day, the sky a pale-blue white-hot dome radiating ferocious heat and blinding light down upon all the shoppers on Collins Avenue and giving them stumpy shadows on the sidewalk... which they can scarcely even notice, their macular-degeneration-defying glasses are so dark... when something makes them want to open their eyes and *see*. A young man wearing some sort of white sport shirt and blue jeans has just sidled up to a building, whose shadow at noon is all of eighteen inches wide. He's carrying a big CVS shopping bag. Hurriedly, there in the stingy shade, he lifts the CVS bag and holds it upside down and starts to pull it over his head. Now the gawkers can see that there is another shopping bag stuffed inside the first... that and a white towel that wants to fall out. Hurriedly he pulls the towel out and puts it on top of his head so that it drapes his face, his ears, everything down to his shoulders, in fact, and then he pulls the shopping bags, one inside the other, down over the towel, and now the gawkers can barely see a couple of inches of the towel sticking out of the bags. They can't see his head at all. Then they see him pull a cell phone out of his blue-jeans pocket and slip it under the bags and the towel. What is this?... a nutcase—nobody can figure it out.

Under the towel and inside the bags the cell phone rings, "*¡Caliente! Caliente baby... Got plenty fuego in yo' caja china...*" and the man inside the bag says, "Camacho."

"Where are you?" says the voice of Sergeant Hernandez. "Underneath a mattress?"

"Hey, Jorge," says Nestor, "thank God it's you! Wait a second. Let me take all this shit off... This better?"

"Yeah, you sound halfway normal now. I can hear traffic. Where the hell are you?"

"Down on Collins Avenue. I put all this shit over my... my..." ::::::I'm not going to say "head." He'll think that's very weird:::::: "over the phone so they won't know I'm not at home."

"Gotcha," said Hernandez. "I do sort of the same thing—but they must know nobody has a landline anymore, just a cell phone—but never mind. Have you heard the news?"

"No... and do I even want to? I remember the last time you called me with 'the news.'"

"This time maybe you *do* want to, I don't know—anyway, they just let our crack dealers off! The grand jury wouldn't indict them!"

"You're kidding!"

"It just happened, Nestor, maybe half an hour ago. It's all over the internet."

"Wouldn't *indict* them—why not?"

"Take a wild guess, Nestor."

Nestor wanted to say, *Because of you and your jungle bunny shit,* but he caught himself. "You and me?" was all he said.

"You got it. First try. How the hell can they indict two nice young gentlemen from Overtown when the two arresting officers are racists? Right? They didn't even call us as witnesses, Nestor, and it was *our case!*"

Silence. Nestor was baffled. He couldn't figure out the consequences. Finally he said, "This means there won't be any trial. Right?"

"Right," said Hernandez. "And if you wanna know what I think, I say thank God for *that* much. I wasn't looking forward to being on the stand, and some suit is asking me, 'So, Sergeant Hernandez, how racist would you say you are? Just a little bit or a lot or somewhere in the middle?"

"But how's the Department gonna take it?"

"Oh, they're gonna say, 'Well, that makes it official. The jury has spoken. These two walking bigots cost us a case. Who needs a couple of parasites like them?' Without us they wouldna had a case in the first place. But you know about how much they're gonna take that into consideration."

"I thought grand jury proceedings are supposed to be secret."

"The are... *supposed* to be. The only opinions they're supposed to give are 'indict' and 'not indict.' But you watch TV and the radio and whoever puts this stuff on the internet—the grand jury, they're not supposed to, but they'll talk to the bastards. It sounds like they already have. If you ask me, we're fucked."

"Has anybody called you, anybody from the Department, like the zone captain or somebody?"

"Not yet, but they will . . . they will . . ."

"I don't know about you," said Nestor, "but I can't just stand around waiting for the axe to fall. We've gotta *do* something."

"Okay, tell me what. Tell me one thing we can do that won't make it worse."

Silence. "Give me a little time. I'll think of something." All he could think of at that very moment was Ghislaine. Ghislaine Ghislaine Ghislaine . . . He wasn't even thinking of what she might conceivably do for him as a witness who might back him up by testifying that whatever he had said about that big side a beef in the crack house came in the heat of a life-or-death battle. No, he was thinking solely of her lovely pale fair face.

"I'm gonna find whoever made that cell phone video and get hold of the first half of it and show what really happened."

"Yeah," Hernandez was saying, "but you've already tried that."

"Yeah, well, I'll try again, Jorge. I'm gonna pull together an entire defense."

"Bueee-no, muy bueee-no," said Hernandez in a tone that identified Nestor as a hopelessly naive kid. "But you check with me . . . okay? You gotta be careful what you pull on when you do all this pulling

together. You understand what I'm saying? Look at it this way. In a way we're better off. The fucking case is over. We don't have to sit there in some courtroom and be called every goddamned thing in the world—and *then* get thrown off the force. You see what I mean?"

"Yeah..." said Nestor in a flat tone, all the while thinking, ::::::Spoken like a true veteran bullshitter. Maybe that's a consolation for you because you're the one who actually said all that stuff. I don't feel like jumping into your grave with you.:::::: For no reason that he could have possibly explained, he thought of Ghislaine again. He could see her lovely lissome legs crossed the way they were at Starbucks... the lithe, slim, somehow *French* look of the calf of the leg whose bent knee lay atop the knee of the other... but he did not think about the mysteries of her loamy loins... He didn't think of her *that* way... Finally he said aloud, "To tell the truth, Jorge, I *don't* see what you mean. It's no consolation to me, *not* going through a trial. Me, I wish to hell there *was* going to be a trial. I'd like to lay the whole goddamn thing out on the table, and some way I'm gonna do that."

"Don't you see how little difference it's gonna make to 'lay the whole thing out on the table'?" said Hernandez. "It could just as easy make things worse."

Nestor said, "Yeah, well, you could be right... but I can't just sit here... because it's worse than that. I feel like I'm strapped into the electric chair, wondering when they're gonna throw the switch. I've gotta do something, Jorge!"

"Okaaaay, amigo, but—"

"I'll let you know," said Nestor. "Right now I gotta go." Not even so much as a goodbye.

16

Humiliation One

Amélia sat slumped back, caved in, all but submerged in the pillowy billows of the only easy chair in their apartment . . . with her legs crossed, forcing her skirt . . . which was about *this* long to begin with . . . up so far that when Magdalena came in, she wondered, at first, if it were a skirt or a shirt . . . She was disappointed to find Amélia in such a dejected state . . . disappointed to the edge of resentful. ::::::What have *you* got to be acting so self-absorbed about?:::::: Magdalena was counting on Amélia's ever-cheerful, ever-clearheaded self to listen to *her* problems. She assumed a pose of her own. She perched herself in shorts and a T-shirt on the seat of a dinner table chair with a straight back. She unconsciously dramatized her superior claim to sympathy by jackknifing one leg and lifting it high enough to put the heel on the edge of the seat and hugging the knee with both arms as if it were the only friend she had left.

"No, that's not true," said Amélia. "We're *not* in the same boat. You left *him*. *He* left *me*. You're happy. I'm not."

"I'm not *happy!*" said Magdalena. "I'm scared to death! If you had seen his face—I mean, mygod!"

Amélia shrugged with her eyebrows in a way that as much as said, "You're trying to blow nothing up into *something*."

"But his face—it was like some kind of—of—of—some kind of *fiend's!* The way he started calling me *'Bitch!—you bitch!'*—to say that's what he said doesn't *begin* to—"

Amélia broke in, "And you're so devastated, I guess you're *not* going out with your 'oligarch' friend tonight?... Give me a break... Reggie didn't even care enough to raise his voice with *me*. He was more like some boss calling in an employee and saying, 'I'm sorry, but you're just not the right fit for our organization. It's not your fault, but we're going to have to let you go.' That's the way Reggie put it. 'I'm going to have to let you go. This just isn't working out.' Those were his actual words, 'This just isn't working out.' After almost two years 'this just isn't working out.' What the hell is 'this,' I'd like to know, and what is 'working out' supposed to mean? He also said, 'It's not your fault.'

Awww...geeee... that made me feel *so much better.* You know? After two years he comes to the conclusion that 'this is not working out' and it's 'not my fault.'"

::::::Damn it! The whole world doesn't revolve around you, Amélia.::::::

Magdalena tried to put it back into orbit around herself. "And another thing, Amélia, I'm broke! He's got my credit cards, my checkbook, my cash, my driver's license—everything! I was lucky to have enough cash tucked away here to pay the locksmith. Cost a fortune!"

"What do you think he's going to do—buy thousands of dollars' worth of stuff with your credit card? Take the keys and steal your car? Break in here in the middle of the night? You already changed the lock. You think he's so wild about you he'll ruin his career just to get revenge? You're pretty hot, but I haven't noticed—" She dropped her thought. "So, anyway, who's your oligarch friend tonight?"

"His name is Sergei Korolyov."

"What's he do?"

"I think he...'invests'? Is that the word? I don't really know. But I know he collects art. He gave the Miami Museum of Art seventy million dollars' worth of paintings and they changed its name to the Korolyov Museum of Art. Do you remember that? There was a lot about it on TV."

She regretted laying it on that thick. Here's Amélia in a state of shock about Reggie—and she has to tell her about what a star *she* has a date with in a couple of hours.

"I think I remember something about it," said Amélia.

Silence...then Magdalena couldn't resist, and so she went ahead and said, "Do you remember the night I was going to Chez Toi, and you lent me your bustier? Well, that was the night I met Sergei—or that was the night he asked me for my phone number. I met him once before...you know, along with all these other people...I guess that bustier wasn't a bad idea! Don't worry. I'm not going to ask you for it again. I mean, I don't want him to think that's what I wear every night, a bustier. But I could use your advice again."

Amélia looked off in a distracted way. Obviously, she wasn't going to jump at the idea of playing couturiere for Magdalena for some dazzling date again. Finally, without looking squarely at Magdalena, she said, "Where's he taking you?"

"It's a big party on—I've heard of it, but I've never seen it—you know Star Island? At somebody's house."

Amélia smiled...sardonically..."You're too much, Magdalena. You just happen to go to dinner at a restaurant you never heard of called Chez Toi. Then you just happen to go to a big party at some place called Star Island at somebody's big house. That's only the most expensive real estate in Miami. Maybe Fisher Island—but there's not much difference."

"I didn't know that," said Magdalena.

Amélia stared at her for a moment. It was the sort of look Magdalena couldn't interpret one way or the other. It was just a... steady stare. Finally Amélia spoke:

"Do you plan to give him some papaya tonight?"

This gave Magdalena such a jolt, she let go of her loving knee and put the foot on the floor just like the other one, as if preparing for fight or flight.

"Amélia!" she said. "What kind of question is that?!"

"It's a practical question," said Amélia. "Past a certain—when guys reach a certain age they just *assume* that's part of a pleasant first date. '*Aflojate,* baby! Give it up!' When I think of all the times I just *did* things because that was what Reggie expected... That's what's called a 'relationship.' When I hear that stupid word, I want to stick my fingers down my throat."

"I've never seen you... *so down* like this before, Amélia."

"I don't know," said Amélia. "I've never had anything like this *happen* before. That bastard!—but no, he's not a bastard. Reggie, I would have gladly married him. I hope it never happens to you."

By now, tears were beginning to roll down her cheeks, and her lips were trembling. Amélia—who had always been the strong and steady one around here! Magdalena was beginning to find the whole thing embarrassing. Sure, Amélia had been hurt ::::::I wonder what actually happened with her and Reggie?:::::: but she had always had too much going for her to cave in and pity herself like this. If she started actually crying, blubbering, boo-hooing, Magdalena wasn't going to be able to take it. To just sit here and watch Amélia come to pieces—she had always admired Amélia too much for that. She was older, and better educated and more sophisticated.

Amélia snuffled back a lot of tears and pulled herself together. Her eyes were still leaking a bit, but she smiled in a perfectly natural way and said, "I'm sorry, Magdalena." Tears welled up in her eyes again. ::::::*Please* hold on to yourself, Amélia!:::::: which she did, thank God. She smiled an only slightly teary smile and said, "This hasn't been my best day, for some reason." She gave a little laugh. "Listen, *of course* I'll help you... if I can... In fact, why don't you go look in my closet. I have this new black dress with a neckline like—" With her hands she pantomimed a *V* that began on either side of her neck and plunged to her waist. "It's a little too tight for me, but it'll fit you perfectly."

* * *

Such weightlessness! Such extra-environmental vision! Such astral projection! Such bliss!

Not that Magdalena knew the terms *extra-environmental vision* and *astral projection,* but these were the two main components of the otherworldly exhilaration she felt. She had the feeling—but it was more than a feeling to her, it was very real—that she was sitting here in the creamy tan leather passenger seat of this glamorous sports car...and at the same time she was floating above the scene...having been astrally projected up here this high...and observing the incredible turn of Fate that now had Magdalena Otero, formerly of Hialeah, sitting *this close* to a man too dashing, too handsome, too rich, too much of a celebrity to have called her up and asked her out—*but he had!* He, Sergei Korolyov, the Russian oligarch who had given seventy million dollars' worth of paintings to the Miami Museum of Art, he who had given the swellest dinner party she had ever been to, at the socially swellest restaurant in all of Miami, Chez Toi...he who was driving this car, which looked so expensive, and no doubt *was* so expensive—he was right next to her, at the wheel! She could see him and herself both from up here. She could see right through the roof. She looked all around...how many people were watching this, watching Magdalena Otero sitting in this hot car that looked like it was going eighty miles an hour just parked at the curb?

Well... not many, unfortunately. Nobody knew who she was. Here, Drexel Avenue, was her official address, but how many times had she actually slept here?

Whoooooooosh—back she came from her astral cosmos just as quickly as she had beamed up to it.

And, of course, Sergei looked perfect in this setting. Quite in addition to his profile, his strong chin, the firm jawline without so much as a semblance of surplus flesh... there was also his hair. It was thick and deep brown with streaks of sun-bleached blond and swept back on the sides as if by an airstream... although in fact the two of them were inside the air-conditioned cocoon every sane driver in South Florida turned his automobile interior into. *Blip*—what about Norman and his open convertible? But Norman was *in*sane!

Sergei glanced toward her—those eyes of his!—those gleaming mischievous blue eyes! A slight smile... Since neither of them had brought up an amusing subject, a tourist from Cincinnati might have called that little smile smug. That was by no means the word that occurred to Magdalena. Oh, no. Debonair, suave, sophisticated... those were more like it. And his clothes... so *rich*-looking... his jacket—

cashmere?—so soft, she felt like burying her head in it... a lustrous white shirt—silk?—with a high, open collar made to be worn open... Of course, she was a number herself. Amélia's dress with its plunging neckline... Now and again she caught Sergei stealing a peek at the inner curves of her breasts. She felt... *hot.*

When Sergei pulled away from the curb, the car's engine barely made a sound. By now they were going north on Collins Avenue... not a lot of traffic... Condominium towers whipped past... on and on, a wall that kept any random passerby from being aware there was an ocean about two hundred yards to the east.

Magdalena kept racking her brain to come up with something... anything... *interesting* to talk to Sergei about. Thank God! Part of his sophistication was his ability to pull small talk out of thin air... no anxious silences...

Magdalena couldn't remember going this far north on Miami Beach before. They must be getting close to where Miami Beach became part of the mainland.

Sergei slowed down and gave Magdalena the merriest of smiles. "*Ahhh*... we've just entered Russia. This is Sunny Isles."

From what she could make out from the streetlights and the moonlight and the big plate glass windows lit up here and there in the tall buildings, it looked like standard Miami Beach to Magdalena... the same wall of towers east of Collins Avenue that monopolized the views of the ocean...and on the other side, west of Collins, old buildings, small buildings, huddled together for God knows how many miles.

Sergei slowed down even more and pointed toward that huddled mass and picked out a Low-Rent side street. "See that shopping strip?" he said. It wasn't very imposing, not to anybody who had ever been in Bal Harbour or Aventura. "If you cannot speak Russian, you cannot buy anyzing in zose shops. Oh, I suppose you can point at zomzing and take out zome dollars to show zat you mean, 'I buy?' Zey are real Russians. Zey speak no Engleesh, and zey haf no desire to be American! It ees like being on Calle Ocho in Miami and valking into a shop, and you cannot speak Spanish. Zey haf abzolutely no eenterest to be ze 'Americans,' eizer..."

"But what's *that?*" said Magdalena.

"What ees what?"

"That big sign. It looks like it's up in the air floating by itself."

Just beyond the shabby little shopping strip, a lurid sign blazed away in red, yellow, and orange neon: THE HONEY POT. In the darkness it didn't seem to be connected to anything below. Sergei dismissed it with a shrug. "Oh, zat. I dohn't knohw. I zink eet ees wonna zoze streep clubs."

"For Russians?"

"No, no, no, no—for zese Americans. Russians dohn't go to streep clubs. We like guuurls. Ze Americans get crazy over zeeze pornography. Nobody else goes zat crazy."

"It's all over the internet," said Magdalena. "It's something like sixty percent of all hits are for pornography. You'd be surprised how many prominent men become addicted to it. They'll spend five, six hours a day watching it on the internet; they do a lot of it at work, in their offices. It's sad! They ruin their careers."

"Een ze office? How een ze office?"

"Because at home his wife and children are there."

"How you knohw all zees?"

"I'm a nurse. I once worked for a psychiatrist." Magdalena studied Sergei's face for signs that he knew about Norman... Not even a hint, thank God. This little discourse on pornography—a triumph at last! She had proved it again... she wasn't just a little number with a beautiful face and a hot body... he would have no choice, would he... he would *have* to take her seriously... and Amélia's voice whispered into her inner ear, down the auditory canal, and set her tympanic membrane to vibrating: "Do you plan to give him some papaya tonight?"

It depended! It depended! Such decisions always depended!

Once they left Sunny Isles, heading farther north,

the scenery became less and less like Miami Beach... Hollywood... Hallandale... "Now we enter the Russian heartland." He chuckled, to show Magdalena he found that pretty amusing.

He turned off Collins Avenue onto a smaller highway that ran west. Magdalena had no idea where they were now.

"Tell me again," she said. "The restaurant we're going to is called...?"

"Gogol's."

"And it's Russian?"

"Eet eez ferry Russian," he said... with his suave smug or smug suave smile.

They headed west in the darkness... then came around a curve—and there it was, in a blazing backlit sign as lurid as the Honey Pot's: GOGOL'S!... a porte cochere out front framed by a vast riot of nude nymphs rendered in a bas-relief deep to the point of hallucinatory: GOGOL'S!

Beneath it was a regular hive of valets, young, fair-skinned. Cars were pulling in and going out at a terrific rate... a regular throng of men and women going inside...

Sergei was joking with the valets in Russian. They knew Gospodin Korolyov very well. As soon as he and Magdalena walked in, a tall, hefty man—he must have been six-feet-five or -six—in a dark suit, a white shirt, and a navy tie, his remaining black hair combed straight back over his pate—rushed up and gushed with great enthusiasm, "Sergei Andreivich!" The rest was in Russian. The man seemed to be the owner or manager at the very least. Sergei said to him in English, "This is my friend Magdalena," *Thee sees my freend*... The big man bowed slightly in a fashion Magdalena took to be "European." The place was vast... Every square inch of wall space was covered in a deep-mauve (synthetic) velvet lit only by battalions of small downlights in an otherwise black ceiling. The deep mauve was a backdrop for every form of glitter a team of Russian decorators could get their hands on. A pair of staircases leading to a second level, no more than five feet above the first, had more extravagant curves than the ones at the Paris Opera. The banisters were inlaid with striations of polished brass. Gogol's white tablecloths—a great flashing sea, thanks to the minute sequins somehow woven in... The small lamps on all the tables had mauve shades supported by flashing faux-crystal stems... At Gogol's, wherever it was possible to attach glitter rims and fringes and trims and brims—they were attached. All these things were meant to create a flashing glamour within a rich but sedate mauve gloom... but they didn't. They weren't even gaudy. They looked prissy, dinky, finicky, fussy, and gussied up. The whole cavernous dining hall looked as though it had come out of Grandmother's jewelry box.

A regular swarm of men, his age or older, gathered about Sergei. Were they loud! Were they drunk? Well, maybe it was just their way of saluting their beloved comrade, but they sure seemed drunk to Magdalena. They gave him big bear hugs. They cracked up, disintegrated, dissolved over every sentence that came out of his mouth, as if he were the greatest wit they had ever encountered in their lives. Magdalena would have given anything to have known Russian at that moment.

Sergei was no longer even trying to introduce her to these men as they came up. It was hard to introduce anybody who had you in a bear hug and was bellowing loud nothings into your ear. The only attention she got were lascivious looks of men lifting the lust in their loins all the way to their faces.

From all over the place came the deep manly laughter and the manly baritone cries of men... drunk. At the nearest table a big man, about fifty, if Magdalena was any judge, reared back into the middle of a banquette with a great grin and proceeded to down one, two, three, four shot glasses of something—vodka?—and then let out a great *ahhhhh!* His face was a blazing red, and his grin was as self-satisfied as any Magdalena had ever seen. He ground out a guttural roar of a laugh from somewhere deep in his gullet. He handed a shot glass full of whatever it was to the woman next to him...young or youngish... it was hard to tell when a woman had her hair done up in a big bun in back, like Grandmother's... she stared at the shot glass as if it were a bomb... Guttural roars all around...

Sergei managed to disengage himself from his admirers and motioned to Magdalena. The towering house hefty led them to a table. *¡Dios mío!* It was a table for ten... and Magdalena could see what was coming. Eight men and women were already seated, and two empty seats remained... for Sergei and herself. As soon as they saw Sergei, they all rose to their feet with *huzzahs* and God only knows what else. Just as Magdalena feared, Sergei was not hereby escaping his noisy worshipful cluster... He was merely substituting a new one. She was not happy. She began wondering if Sergei had brought her here to show what a hotshot he was on his home grounds. Or maybe it was worse than that. Maybe he didn't care if she was impressed or not. He just liked a nightly bath in all this adulation.

At least this time he introduced her to each Russian, Russian, Russian... a great clutter of consonants... She didn't catch a single name. She felt like she was being buried in all the *z*'s and *y*'s and *k*'s and *g*'s and *b*'s. Eight Russian strangers... all looking at her, men and women, as if she were some alien curiosity. What do we have here? Do something... Say something... Entertain us... They were all yammering away in Russian. Directly across the table sat a blocky-faced man with a bald dome and veritable thickets of black hair, obviously dyed, sticking out wildly on each side below the dome line, culminating in mutton-chops growing gloriously unkempt down to his jawbones. He seemed to be studying her face with a pathological intensity. Then he turned to a man two seats away and said something that left them both chuckling... in a way that indicated they were trying their best not to erupt into guffaws... over what?

On the menu the dishes were printed first in English, with curly Russian letters immediately below. Even in English, Magdalena scarcely recognized a single one.

A waiter materialized silently beside Sergei and handed him a folded piece of paper. Sergei read it and turned to her and said, "I must say hello to my friend Dimitri. Please excuse me. I'll be right back."

He said something to the others in Russian and rose and left the table with the waiter, who would lead him to "Dimitri." Now Magdalena found herself with eight Russians she didn't know, four men—in their forties?—and four women—in their thirties?—with fussy hot-roller-curled hairdos and "dress-up" dresses from some era gone by.

But mainly... there sat the man with all the sub-dome hair and the skin-crawling stare. Sergei had introduced him as some great chess champion.

"Number five in the world back in the time of Mikhail Tal," Sergei had confided behind his hand. None of it, including the great Mikhail Tal, meant anything to Magdalena—only the man with the explosive rim of infra-cranial hair. His name, if Magdalena had caught it correctly, was Something-or-other Zhytin. The way he stared at her unnerved her. She couldn't take her eyes—or, rather, her peripheral vision—off him. She avoided looking right at his face. He was creepy and crude to the point of sinister. ::::::Sergei, hurry up! Come back! You've left me alone with these horrible creeps—or with one, at least. He looks creepy enough to fill a whole room full of creeps.:::::: He had his elbows on the table and his forearms wrapped around either side of his plate and his back hunched over so far his head was not even six inches above his enormous cache of food. He ate everything with a spoon, which he held like a shovel. He was cramming gobs of potatoes and some sort of stringy beef into that voracious maw at a spectacular rate. Hunks of meat the spoon couldn't deal with he picked up with his fingers and gnawed at, glancing to this side and that side. He looked as if he were intent upon safeguarding his food from buzzards and dogs and thieves. Occasionally he lifted his head and flashed a knowing smile and dumped unsolicited comments—in Russian—upon the conversations around him. *Dumped* was the word. In Russian his voice sounded like a dump truck dumping a load of gravel.

Magdalena was fascinated...all too fascinated. The World's Number Five chess player lifted his head to straighten out a conversation nearby and caught her staring at him. He stopped, his head still down low over his food—a mountainous hunk of stringy beef still on his spoon—and brought her up short with a big mocking smile and said in English, with an accent but fluently, "Can I assist you in some way?" *Can I asseest you in zom vay?*

"No," said Magdalena. She was blushing terribly. "I was only—"

"What do you do?" The *you do* got buried beneath the two fingers he was sticking into his mouth in a game try to pull beef strings out from between his teeth.

"Do?"

"Do," he said, flinging a string from his mug to the rug. "What do you do to get food, to get clothes, to get someplace to sleep at night? What do you *do?*"

In some way she couldn't figure out, he was mocking her...or being just plain rude...or *some*thing. She hesitated...and finally said, "I'm a nurse."

"What kind of nurse?" said the former Number Five.

Magdalena noticed that several people at the table were motionless. They had their eyes fixed upon *her*... the man *there* with the shaved head sitting next to a woman so obese that her huge costume jewelry necklace lay flat upon her bodice as if it were a tray... and the two women *there* with pillbox hats and hair netting from way back in the last century. They wanted to hear this, too.

"A psychiatric nurse," said Magdalena. "I worked for a psychiatrist."

"What kind of psychiatrist, a logotherapist or a pill therapist?" Magdalena had no idea what he meant, but his sly little twist of the lips and the way he narrowed one eye made her feel like he was merely trying to establish how ignorant she was about her own field. She looked about quickly. If only Sergei were back! With a wary voice she said, "What is a logotherapist? I don't know that word."

"You don't know what a logotherapist is." He said it not as a question but as a statement of fact. Now his tone was like a grade school teacher's. It as much as said, "You're a psychiatric nurse—who doesn't know the most basic things about psychiatry. I guess we'd better start at the bottom."

"A logotherapist 'treats' his patients"—*treats* was soaked in irony—"with talk... the ego, the id, the superego, the Oedipal complex, and all that... mainly the patient's talk, not his. The logotherapist mainly listens... unless the patient is so boring his mind wanders, which I imagine must be very, very often. The pill psychiatrist gives his patients pills to increase the flow of dopamine and inhibit the reuptake and give them a synthetic peace of mind. *Logos* is Greek for 'word.' So which is the psychiatrist you work for?"

"*Worked* for."

"Okay, worked for. Which was he?"

These questions were making Magdalena anxious. She couldn't figure out why. The former Number Five wasn't saying anything insulting or out of bounds. So why did she feel so insulted? She just wanted to pull out of it. She wanted to say, "Look, let's talk about something else, okay?" But she didn't have the nerve. She didn't want to sound cranky in front of Sergei's friends. Once more she swept Gogol's glittering interior . . . *begging* Sergei to reappear. But there was no sign of him—and somehow she had to respond to the champion.

"Well, he did prescribe some drugs, but I suppose he was mostly the other . . . what you said." The *what you said* was like flinching before the blow she knew was bound to come next.

"Good for him!" said the great chess player. He said it without any trace of a smile, as if he really meant it. Magdalena's hopes rose—not her spirits, just her hopes. "A wise man! Logo is the way to go!" he continued. "I'm sure you'll agree—right?—the talk therapists are the slickest extortionists that ever existed." He drilled his eyebeams into her eyes and held her in place. There was no way she could get free.

"I don't know what you mean..." ::::::Please! Somebody! Get me out of this! Get him off me!::::::
"*Extortionist...¡Dios mío!* I can't really see that..."

Now it dawned on her: The entire table had stopped talking and stopped eating and even stopped drinking vodka...in order to watch the champion torment her.

"You can't really see that?" said the champion, as if that were a pathetic way to try to get out from under this. "All right, then, let's start with...tell me what an extortionist *is*." His eyes bored into hers more intently than ever. His voice insinuated that if she didn't know the answer to that, then she had no education whatsoever.

Magdalena gave up. She folded completely. "I don't know. I don't even know how to say it. You tell me."

This time he cocked his head and twisted his lips in a way that struck Magdalena and her sinking heart as openly contemptuous. "You don't know." Once more, not a question but a sad declaration of the obvious. "An extortionist is someone who says, 'You do what I say, or I will see to it that you suffer in a way you cannot stand.'" ...*I vill zee to eet zat you zuffer in a vay*... "Your logotherapist spends the first few sessions making you believe that only *he* can save you from your depression or your fear or overwhelming guilt or compulsions or self-destructive impulses or paralyzing catatonia or whatever. Once he convinces you of that, then you're *his*. You're one of his assets. He'll keep you coming until the day you're cured... a day that never comes, of course... or you run out of money... or one day you die. That's the psychiatrist you worked for, isn't it. I don't know how old your employer was, but if he's old enough to have two generations of these poor people on his hook, he'll be a very rich man for life. Of course, he'll have to sit still for a lot of whining and utterly pointless cerebration—the patients all love to go on about the meaning of their dreams and all that... but I'm sure your employer thought about other things while they driveled on—his investment portfolio, a new car, a girl with no clothes on, a delivery boy who petrifies him—anything's better than actually listening to these idiots' logorrhea. Just keeping them in his pen, that's all he has to worry about, turning them into lifers, making sure they don't start thinking for themselves and getting... *ideas*. That pretty well describes your employer, right? Maybe you were and maybe you weren't aware you were working for a learn-ed, genteel extortionist. But you were—am I not right?"

That got under Magdalena's skin! He could have been talking about Norman and his star patient, Maurice! For an instant she was tempted to mention it—but she was damned if she was going to give him the satisfaction, this horrible chess champion. ::::::What does he think he's doing? Playing with my head? He's so horribly vile! vile! vile! vile!:::::: She was on the verge of tears, but she fought them back. She mustn't give him the satisfaction of her tears, either.

"Right?" he said once more, this time in a warm, sympathetic tone.

Magdalena compressed her lips to keep *them,* this bunch of horrible Russians at the table, who were now all eyes, from seeing that her lips were trembling. Feebly, feebly, she managed to say in a low, beaten-down, vanquished voice, "I never saw anything like that . . . I don't know what you're talking about . . ." Feebler and feebler . . . overcome by defeat . . . and she couldn't figure out why he had attacked, why he could have wanted to subject her to something like this . . . or how he had done it . . . or *if* he had done it . . . since she knew she couldn't possibly have described it to another person. The great chess player never had an angry look on his face. He never expressed hostility . . . there was nothing other than the small, smug smile on his face . . . and a commanding air of intellectual superiority . . . and condescension as he tried to explain the things she didn't know in words of one syllable. How could she make somebody else understand what he was doing to her?

"Now, is it 'don't know' or 'just as soon *not*

know'?" he was saying. "Which do you honestly think it is?" He said it with the kindliest tone imaginable... with the most sympathetic and understanding of looks on his face... with the softest little smile... with the slightest of avuncular tilts of the head—

—and Magdalena was paralyzed. She lacked the power to say a word. She could reply to this vile man only by breaking into tears... but she managed to hold it down to silent convulsions... her neck, her stooped shoulders, her chest, her abdomen... convulsing. She doesn't dare try to speak. What are they thinking? Here is a ditzy, clueless little Cuban cutie-pie... and she calls herself a "psychiatric nurse"! All eight of them have their little smirks on. It isn't as if they are laughing at *her* exactly... one doesn't laugh at a helpless child... No, indeed, they wouldn't do *that*. They're just eager to see what her brainless *response* will be.

::::::I *must not!* I *will not* give them the satisfaction!::::::

She clenched her teeth; really *clenched* them. ::::::Not a single sob shall make it past my lips!—not in the presence of these blood-sucking voy—::::::

"What is going on?" Loudly—*his voice!*—but with good humor. He was coming up so directly behind her, she couldn't even see him by twisting her head about. The next moment—pressure of his hands and his weight on the frame of the back of her chair. *His voice!* came from directly above her head... but now lower, and with the faintest tinge of menace, he said in English, "Having your fun... Zhytin? I could see you playing your greasy game again from twenty feet away, and I could smell it. Quite the piece of shit, aren't you."

Then he put his hands on her shoulders and began massaging, ever so gently, the muscles between her shoulders and her neck.

She was in his very hands! With that, she gave way. Her eyes flooded with tears. They spilled down over her cheeks...

Zhytin was looking up at Sergei. He tried to cover up a sickly, guilty expression with a smile of goodwill. He said in Russian, "Sergei Andreivich, Miss Otero and I were just having an interesting discussion about psychi—"

"Molchi!" Like a fierce bark it was. Whatever it meant, Sergei had cut off Zhytin so sharply, he didn't try to utter another word. His mouth fell open in bewilderment. Sergei barks again—and the color drains out of Zhytin's blocky face. He turns white with fear. He looks at Magdalena... now he has the earnest voice of the peacemaker: "I'm very sorry... I assumed you knew we were only playing the little game of the wits."

Sergei leapt out from behind Magdalena, palms on the table, and leaned as far as he could toward the frightened face of Champion Zhytin and said something to him in Russian in a low, seething voice.

Zhytin looked at her again, this time even more frightened than before. "Miss Otero, I sincerely regret my rude behavior. I now realize that—" He halted and looked at Sergei. Sergei seethed out a few more words, and Zhytin looked at Magdalena once more and said, "I now realize that I was acting like an impudent child—" He looked at Sergei once more. Sergei said something to him brusquely in Russian... and Zhytin said to Magdalena, "I beg your forgiveness."

For an instant Magdalena was relieved by her tormentor's sudden—and total—abasement. But in the next heartbeat she began to feel uneasy. Something strange and unhealthy had been set in motion. Sergei barks out a few words, and Zhytin, the great champion, is all but prostrate before her in abject supplication. It was so strange, she felt even more deeply humiliated... to have to count on a third party to subdue her tormentor.

Sergei said to Magdalena, right in front of Zhytin, "I must apologize for our 'champion's' behavior."

These apologies were too much for Zhytin's wife, a dark-haired woman, about his age... and getting thick as a man through the shoulders and upper back. She got up from her chair as noisily as she could, stood up straight...or straight for someone with a shell back like hers...flashed a malevolent glance at Sergei, and spoke sharply to her husband, in Russian. Zhytin was the very picture of fear. He didn't look at his wife. His eyes were pinned on Sergei.

Sergei said to Zhytin in English, "It's okay. Olga is right. You should leave. In fact, I make the suggestion you do that very soon." He flicked the back of his hand within inches of Zhytin's face several times and said, *"Vaks! Vaks, vaks,"* apparently Russian for "scat."

Zhytin rose, trembling visibly. With a bent posture he took his wife's arm and skulked hurriedly toward the entrance. *He* was leaning on *her,* not the other way around.

Sergei turned back toward the other six who remained, the goon with the shaved head, the obese woman whose bosom stuck out like a table, the two women wearing pillbox hats...a very tall dour man with a too-narrow skull, sunken cheeks, and too-short shirtsleeves revealing a pair of outsized bony wrists and hands bigger than his head, and a little bull of a man whose eyes were sunk so deeply within the crevice between his overhanging brow and outcropped cheekbones, you couldn't see them. Very eerie-looking...Sergei panned a cheerful smile across all six faces, as if nothing whatsoever had just taken place. He proffered various lighthearted subjects, but they all seemed too frightened to pick up a thread of any of them.

Magdalena was mortified. She was the alien who had triggered the scene. If she had come up with something witty or smart enough—as she had at Chez Toi—the whole thing would never have developed. She wanted nothing more than to get away from this restaurant and its load of Russians. Sergei couldn't coax anything out of her, either. She was too dispirited.

After a few minutes of getting nowhere, Sergei called over the big hefty maître d' or whatever he was and had a little conversation with him in Russian. Then he smiled again at the six misshapen goons and goonygirls before him and said in Russian and then in English: "You're very lucky. Marko has a nice table for six for you. You will be very comfortable."

Sheepishly, warily, without a single word, the six got the message and got up and followed Marko, who led them to a distant destination in a far corner of Gogol's capacious floor. Sergei leaned toward Magdalena and put an arm around her shoulders. "Now, this is more like it . . . a nice table for two." He laughed out loud in the spirit of "Oh, what fun we're having!"

::::::Well . . . no and no, my dear Sergei. There are not two of us, there are three: you, me . . . and Humiliation, who occupies the other eight seats. And no, I wouldn't call this fun, particularly. All these roaring animals in this place haw-haw-haw-haw-hawing, these louts and their girlfriends, dressed, overdressed, over-the-top-dressed in musty styles and hairdos, these drunken louts with their rude animal vitality only too eager to seize the weak or unwary and have fun pulling her wings off, laughing all the while at the way she struggles... Oh, Zhytin the great Number Five—he's brilliant at it! Brilliant! A past master! What? Didn't you see it? My God, you missed a classic demonstration! But you can see the remains of her right over there... she's the little Cuban papaya at that table for ten that's nearly empty—empty in an otherwise jam-packed place like this! At a prime hour like this! Empty! She's a shamed and empty shell. Nobody wants any part of her except for our renowned papaya collector, Korolyov... He'll take her papaya and do whatever he wants with it and then throw it out like roadkill... Just feast your eyes! You can't miss her! She's alone at that huge table, except for our papaya connoisseur, and he doesn't count, of course... Yes! Take a look! What's worse than death?... *Humiliation!*... whereas her tablemate, Mr. Sergei Korolyov—he's feeling so good about himself. He thinks he can jolly her up, and why not? *He's* on top of the world! His spirits could hardly be higher! That's how a man feels when all he has to do is make an appearance... and *todo el mundo* jumps up from its chairs and comes rushing over to pour warm grins all over him and attend to his every whim. Even better, no doubt, is to see the fear on other men's faces when they cross him in any way... they're terrified, as if they fear for their lives—they actually *cringe*... the way that vile vile vile vile vile man cringed the moment Czar Sergei barked in a certain way—

—oh, Sergei is in Seventh Heaven right now... He's content to stay at this table all night... at this *huge* table for ten, just him and his little chocha with a vast white flashing sequined sea before them. You can't miss him! There he is! The mightiest man in the hall!... He can't even *begin* to understand *her* misery, can he... *Please,* my handsome savior, *please* get me out of here... out of the sight of a thousand shaming, pitying, shunning eyes... but no-o-o-o-o-o, he has to put himself on maximum display, doesn't he... Behold the Czar!... of Russia's Hallandale, Florida, heartland.::::::

Finally finally finally finally—and this *finally* felt like *finally, after five years of sheer torture—finally* Sergei suggested leaving and heading off to the big party on Star Island. His departure was like his arrival... the fawning, the bear hugs, the loud nothings in the ear, and Sergei standing up seven feet tall and expanding his chest as he watched them jump... Magdalena? She no longer existed. They looked right through her. Only the big side of beef who ran the place even said so much as goodbye . . . and that much, no doubt, only because he thought it might ingratiate him with the Czar, who had brought the little slice of papaya with him.

17

Humiliation, Too

::::::At the very beginning, as soon as he said "What do you do" and all that... "What do you do to get food, to get clothes" and whatever the rest of it was, all I had to do was say something like "Sir, do I know you?" And then, no matter what he said, I should have kept pressing him with that question, "Sir, do I know you? I'd have to get to know you *really* well before I answered questions like that" ... and if he *still* kept going, I could have added, "And something tells me I'll *never* get to know you that well, not in a thousand years, not if I can possibly avoid it" ... Well, the "not if I can possibly avoid it" might have been overdoing it, especially coming from someone my age, twenty-four, and he's in his—what?—fifties?—but that was the moment I should have cut him off, right at the very beginning, before he could get going on that vile, humiliating roll of his—::::::

And that was *all* that was on her mind as she sat here in the passenger seat barely twelve inches from Sergei, who was letting this expensive sports car out for a romp down Collins Avenue in the dark...a black hole with a regular comet of red taillights plunging into it...Sergei laughing and chuckling and chortling and saying things like, "Creenge! He creenged! He creenged like a leetle boy who knows he haf been meesbehafing!"...*whipping* past this red taillight *whipping* past the next one and *whipping* past and *whipping* past the next one and the next one *whipping* past *whipping* past *whipping* past all of them in the darkness at an unbelievable speed...totally reckless and Magdalena is aware of it all but only in her cerebellum...it doesn't even reach the pyramids of Betz, much less her thoughts...All she can *think* about is what she should have done, what she could have done to get that horrible piece of *mierda* off her..."Champion" Zhytin.

::::::You *bastardo de puta!*:::::: That kind of crude language Magdalena ordinarily didn't allow even inside her head. But she was in the throes of *Why didn't I,* that dreadful interlude when you're walking upstairs to go to bed or speeding madly down Collins Avenue—after the party is over—and *now* you think of the comebacks you should have made...to obliterate that bastard who kept scoring points off you in conversation at dinner this evening... not that Magdalena knew the term *l'esprit de l'escalier,* but she was living it right now... furiously, uselessly ransacking her brain.

Sergei was in such good spirits, he never noticed how silent and sunken in thought Magdalena was... and now he was off on the subject of Flebetnikov, the Russian who had invited them to the party they were heading for, at his mansion, estate, palace on Star Island—you really couldn't give it too grand a name... and hadn't she noticed that every Russian in Miami who lived in a big house was called an "oligarch"? What a joke that was! He himself got called an oligarch. He couldn't help but chuckle over that. An oligarchy was rule by a few... so would someone kindly tell him what it was he was ruling and with whom? In fact, he had heard that Flebetnikov's hedge fund had run into some real problems, and how many problems did a Russian have to have before he stopped being ranked as an oligarch? He chuckled again.

By now they were passing through Sunny Isles, and Sergei pointed to the left at a condominium tower on the other side of Collins Avenue. "That's where I live," he said. "I have the twenty-ninth and thirtieth floors."

That caught Magdalena's attention. "The entire floors?"

"Well... now that you say it... yes, both floors."

"How tall is the building?"

"Thirty floors."

"So that means you have the entire top two floors?" Big wide eyes.

"Ummm . . . yes."

"The *penthouse?*"

"Zey are ferry nice, zee fiews," said Sergei. "But you vill zee for yourself."

Now he had her back on his wavelength ::::::Does that mean tonight?:::::: and Amélia's question popped back into her head . . . and that hoisted her up out of her funk far enough to at least *think* about something other than the horrible scene at Gogol's . . . *You'll see for yourself* . . . and Magdalena began *feeling* the answer to that question. Could she conceivably be strong enough to go up to those *two whole floors* of a condominium tower *overlooking the ocean* and be a good girl who *no la aflojare* in his lap right then and there?—who is strong and waits for the second date? Or by that time would she be leaning so close that—why hold back now that we're practically already there?

With that, thank God, Zhytin slipped out of her mind and was gone.

Sergei took the exit off Collins Avenue onto the MacArthur Causeway. He drove slowly for a change . . .

for maybe four or five hundred yards... then pointed to the right toward Biscayne Bay... nothing but a vast black shape in the dark... "See that little bridge? That takes you onto Star Island right there."

"Star Island is that close to shore?" said Magdalena. "That's such a short bridge, I don't know how they could call it an island."

"Well," said Sergei, "it doesn't touch the mainland at any point, so I guess that's how."

They zipped across the little bridge *just like that*, but then Sergei slowed down and said, "It's the—I don't know exactly which house on the right, but is not far. It is huge."

Even in the darkness, Magdalena was aware of how lush, posh, and lavish the vegetation suddenly became the moment you arrived on Star Island... finely sculpted hedges, endless perfect allées of giant palm trees. The houses were set way back from the road. Even in this light, it was obvious that they were huge... vast... showy estates, so big that it seemed like they had been driving a very long way by the time they reached the one Sergei recognized as Flebetnikov's. He turned into the driveway... walls of shrubbery on both sides, so high and thick you couldn't see the house. The driveway came to an end between two buildings you couldn't see from the road. Each was two stories high and deep enough for a good-sized family to live in... fancy enough, too... a sort of

Bermuda-white stucco...a valet took their car... these two structures were nothing less than a double gatehouse. Beyond it...the main house. There it was. What a pile! It stretched on...and on...for a good tenth of a mile. The walkway to the house had been laid out in gigantic and conspicuously needless curves. But what was this? The beginning of the walkway was blocked by a velvet rope. To one side, barely ahead of the rope, a blonde—about thirty-five?—sat at a card table with a stack of forms before her. As Sergei and Magdalena approached the table, she flashed a bright smile and said, "You're here for the party?"

When Sergei said yes, she took two forms from the top of the pile and said, "If you'll just sign these, please."

Sergei started reading the form she handed him—and suddenly twisted his head and narrowed his eyes and stared intently, as if the thing had turned into a lizard. He shot the blonde the same look. "What is this thing?" *Vot ees dees zing?*

The blonde smiled brightly again and said, "It's a release. It's just a formality."

Now Sergei smiled. "Ah, that's good. If it's just a formality, then why we bother? Don't you agree?"

"Well," said the blonde, "we do have to have your written permission."

"Written permission? For what?"

"So we can use your likeness and your speech in the video?"

"Liiiiikeness?" said Sergei.

"Yes, so we can show you in action at the party. You'll be amazing, if you don't mind my saying so. We love European accents on these shows. You'll be wonderful... and you will, too!" she said, looking at Magdalena. "You're the best-looking couple I've seen all evening."

Magdalena loved that. She was dying to go in.

"What you mean 'these shows'?"

"Our series," said the blonde. "It's called *Masters of Disaster*. They didn't tell you? Maybe you've seen it."

"No, I have not zeen it," said Sergei, "and no, I never heard of it, and no, 'zey' did not tell me. I thought Mr. Flebetnikov is inviting me to a party. What is this *Masters of Disaster*?"

"It's a reality show. I'm surprised you haven't heard of it. Our ratings are really pretty good. Everybody's crazy about stars, but they're even crazier about seeing the stars fall and crash and burn. You know German? In German they call it *Schadenfreude*."

"So Flebetnikov, he crashed and burned?" said Sergei.

"I'm told he's a Russian oligarch, and he had a huge hedge fund and then some sort of deal went bad, and everyone's pulled out of the hedge fund, and it's a disaster for him."

Magdalena said to Sergei, "Oh, I think I *remember* him! He was in our line at the opening day of Art Basel. A big man. He kept cutting into the line ahead of people."

"Oh, also I saw him there." He chuckled. "And so now he's a master of disaster..." He turned toward the blonde. "Why do these 'masters of disaster' want to humiliate themselves this way on this show of yours?"

"Well, they seem to figure everybody already knows what happened to them, so they might as well make their comeback by showing they're bloodied but unbowed." She smiled slyly this time. "Either that... or the fee we pay them for the right to do the show."

"How much is that?"

With the same knowing smile the blonde said, "It varies, it varies. All I can tell you is that masters of disaster always cash that check."

Sergei looked at Magdalena with his eyes opened wide—which was very wide for him—and the slightest of smiles...altogether an expression that said, "This is too good to miss. How about it?"

Magdalena nodded yes with a big smile of her own. So they both signed the releases. The blonde glanced at them and said, "Oh, Mr. Korolyov, now I know who you are! Some people were talking about you just the other day! The Korolyov Museum of Art—and I can't believe I'm right here talking to you. It's an *honor*.

You're Russian, just like Mr. Flebetnikov! Am I right? I'm sure they'll want you to talk to him in Russian, and they can add subtitles. It goes over great. We did that with Yves Gaultier on Jean-Baptiste Lamarck's show. Both French." Her face turned radiant with the memory of that high point in reality show history. "The producers, the director, and the writer—they'll all be happy to see you."

Magdalena spoke up for the first time. "The writer?" she said.

"Well, yes... It's all real, of course, and he doesn't write anybody's lines for them or anything like that... but you need somebody to give the show some... *structure.* You know what I mean? I mean, you can't have sixty or seventy people in there just milling about with no focus on anything."

Sergei gave Magdalena a knowing smile of his own. He nodded toward the big house. It was an enormous spread in the 1920s Spanish Revival style.

The entrance was manned by two black doormen in tuxedos. Inside, they found themselves in a huge old-fashioned hall, an entry gallery, as they used to be called in grand houses. *¡Dios mío!* It was mobbed with merry partygoers, most of them middle-aged. What a lot of hooting and shouting! Half the men were busy getting "white-boy wasted," as Magdalena thought of it. The new sync'n'slip music was playing over the sound system.

From out of nowhere—an Anglo, a short Anglo wearing a too-big guayabera that came down almost to his knees, materialized right before them, grinning mightily, and singing out, "Mr. Korolyov! Miss Otero! Welcome! Savannah told us you were here, and are we glad! I'm Sidney Munch. I produce *Masters of Disaster*. I want you to meet Lawrence Koch."

Two men and a woman were standing together about three feet from Mr. Sidney Munch, the producer. One of them, a young man with his head completely shaved—today's fashionable solution when a young man is afflicted with baldness of the pate—stepped forward with the biggest, friendliest smile imaginable and said, "Larry Koch," and shook hands with Sergei. He was wearing a safari jacket with a countless number of pockets.

"And this is our writer, Marvin Belli, and our stylist, Maria Zitzpoppen." The writer was a young man with a round, blood-pressure-red face. His ponderous gut swelled out even worse below his belt than above it. He was the sort of bubbly, cheery soul who makes it hard for you not to smile back. The stylist, Miss Zitzpoppen, was a thin, gristly woman in a white smock whose smile looked positively dour and forced compared to Belli's. Introductions all around. Incredible smiles all around... whereupon the bald young director—unfortunately his neck was so long and so thin, his head looked like a white knob—the young director positively beamed at

Sergei. "I understand you're Russian—and you speak Russian?"

"That is true," said Sergei. *Zat ees drue.*

"Well—it would be awesome if you had a conversation with Mr. Flebetnikov. That would create some real reality and give Mr. Flebetnikov's narrative some genuine ambiance."

"That would be 'real reality'? Then what would be 'unreal reality'? I hardly know Mr. Flebetnikov." Sergei froze director Koch with a mocking grin.

"Oh, that doesn't matter," said director Koch. "All you need to get started is a couple of opening lines. And you and Ms. Otero look awesome. *Awesome!* I can tell, once you break the ice you'll do very well. You're certainly not shy, and Marvin can give you two or three good opening lines."

But Sergei had already turned toward Sidney Munch, the producer. Maintaining his look of amused disbelief, he said, "This is a reality show, I thought. And I speak lines by a writer? I think the English term for that is 'a play.' "

Without a moment's hesitation Sidney Munch said, "As I'm sure you can imagine, on television you have to create a hyper-reality before it will come across to the viewer as plain reality. Marvin and Larry here have to give all this"—he gestured toward the party in progress—"a narrative. Otherwise, it will just be confusion, and this is supposed to be Mr. Flebetnikov's own story. By the way, why do you think Mr. Flebetnikov went bankrupt like this? I hope to find out more about it, but at this point I really can't comprehend it all."

Sergei had to chuckle. "Oh, there are very few risk takers like Mr. Flebetnikov; he has—how you say it—'guts'—that is the word? He has the 'guts,' and he makes a very big bet on American natural gas production, and energy futures are never a safe bet, and the bigger you bet, the more unsafe the bet. It was a foolish mistake in the hindsight, but Flebetnikov, he has the guts. *Real* guts. That is how his hedge fund made billions of dollars in the first place. He has the real guts to take the real risks."

"That's *awesome!*" said the bald-headed young director. "We've been struggling to figure it out and make it easy for the audience to comprehend. You're *awesome,* Mr. Korolyov! Why don't you go over and have a discussion with him about all that? He's right over there. The cameras are on him." He pointed toward two of the high white camera stands. You couldn't see Flebetnikov for the crowd. But you could see video cameras aimed at him from the rear and head-on.

"So you want me to confront him and talk about his troubles," said Sergei, more amused than ever. "You will like for someone to come to you with the television cameras and start talking about *your* troubles?"

"Hah!" said Munch. "I only wish I rated that much attention! I'd love it! It's not a confrontation, not at all. It's a chance for him to give his perspective regarding this situation, and he wouldn't have agreed to come on this show if he weren't prepared to bring it all out in the open. And this time he can explain it in his own native language. Maybe he wouldn't feel comfortable going into such a complicated situation in English, but this way the entire thing can be in Russian, with English subtitles. Confrontation! *Hah!*—he'll be grateful for the opportunity to talk about it in his own native tongue and capture all the nuances. Very important, the nuances. You'll be doing him *a real favor.*"

Sergei all but laughed in his face. "So you think you instruct me to go over and talk to someone about things that interest *you,* and you film it, and that's reality?" Now he *did* laugh in Sidney Munch's face.

While Sergei was still laughing and pulling faces, Munch cast a glance at Larry, his bald-headed director in a safari jacket . . . a very quick glance, he cast . . . and resumed giving Sergei his full attention . . . but all the while keeping his arm down at thigh level and flapping the palm up and down. Without a word, Larry departed their little cluster, walking ever so slowly and casually . . . but once he was about twenty feet away, his pace sped up to the maximum. He was walking so fast, he kept having to put his hands up before him to keep from colliding with people in the crowd and continually saying something on the order of "Excuse me!... Excuse me!... Excuse me!... Excuse me!"... Magdalena caught that. Sergei hadn't seen it at all. He was having too much fun laughing at Munch and needling him with heavy sarcasm. "What a wonderful 'narrative' you have! I be an actor! My role, I go up to Flebetnikov and rub his nose in his mess, and you film it—and we call that a reality show!" What a good time he was having... showing up Sidney Munch for the fraud that he was! What a little snake!

All at once a rumble and drunken hoots and howls in the crowd off to the side... and drunken anger... "Get the fuck off my foot, you greasy tub a butter!"... Comrade Fleabittenov is more like it!"... "You don't shove *me,* you big fat piece a blubber!"... "Master of Up the Asster!" The tumult only grew louder. Whatever it was, it was heading toward Magdalena and Sergei and Sidney Munch. Following it were two mobile camera stands. You couldn't miss them, they were so tall. They rolled through the crowd like a pair of tanks.

Dios mío, the rumble! The edge of the crowd broke open—and the tumult was right on top of Magdalena. It was the great hulk of Flebetnikov himself—*enraged.* He was clad in an expensive-looking dark suit and white shirt. His neck was now bulging with veins, tendons, striations, and a pair of huge sternocleidomastoid muscles...and gorged with the blood of fury.

"Korolyov!" he bellowed.

Sidney Munch and Ms. Zitzpoppen knew enough to get out of the way. The big rabid Russian headed straight for Sergei, roaring in Russian, "You miserable little viper! You insult me, you attack me behind my back! On the TV! For three hundred million stupid Americans!"

He thrust his big red apoplectic face right in Sergei's. Barely six inches separated the two. Magdalena stared anxiously at her Sergei. He didn't move a muscle, other than to cross his arms upon his chest. He wore a smile that said *I hope you know you're crazy*. He couldn't have looked more confident or more relaxed. *Cool* was the word for it. Magdalena was so proud of her Sergei! She was dying to tell him that!

Flebetnikov continued to yell in Russian. "You dare call me a fool! A fool who did a foolish thing and lost all his money! You think I'll just take that?!"

Magdalena noticed that the two mobile cameras were right on top of them, and the cameramen had their heads practically socketed into the lenses, hungrily eating up the whole scene.

Still smiling his very cool smile, Sergei was saying in Russian, "Boris Feodorovich, you know very well that's not true. You know very well that our masters of reality here"—he motioned toward Sidney Munch and at the knob-headed director, who was right behind Flebetnikov—"will tell you any lies."

Flebetnikov went silent. Magdalena saw him flick a glance at Munch, the producer, and she saw Munch, his arms still at his side flapping his open palm upward upward upward upward. *Keep it up!* Munch seemed to be signaling, *Don't stop! Pour it on! Wipe that cynical look off his arrogant face! He's mocking you! Go get him, Big Boy! Don't stop now!*

Flebetnikov continued in Russian, "You dare stand there and mock me, Sergei Andreivich? You think I am going to put up with your arrogance! Am I going to have to wipe that smug face off for you myself?"

In Russian, Sergei responded, "Oh, come on, Boris Feodorovich, we both know this is something cooked up by these Americans. They just want to make you look foolish."

"*Foolish,* there you use that word again! You dare call me a fool in my face?! Oh, I'm sorry, Sergei Andreivich, but I can't let you go that far! Obviously, I'm bigger than you, but now you force me to do what I have to do! If you won't remove that insulting little smile from your face yourself, then you leave me no choice!"

Magdalena had no idea what they were saying—but look at Flebetnikov's face *now!* It's positively swelling up! It's gorged with blood! He's putting it even closer to Sergei's! He's close enough to bite his nose off! He's reached the boiling point! And Sergei! She is so proud of him. He is a *man!* He doesn't flinch, much less retreat. The cool look he gave Flebetnikov hasn't changed at all since this whole thing began. She sees Flebetnikov flick another glance at Munch. Munch nods a quick *yes* and flaps the open palm up and down at a furious rate. *Yes! Yes! Yes! Yes!*

In Russian, Flebetnikov said, "Remember, I don't want to do this! You *insist* that I do it!"

With that, he stepped back to give himself room to do what he "had to do." With a cross between a grunt and a roar, he swung at Sergei. It was a big ponderous right hook. Even someone not as young and fit as Sergei could have wrapped up a telephone call and said goodbye before it arrived. Sergei ducked it easily and countered by ramming his shoulder into Flebetnikov's midsection. *Grrrrooof!*—between a grunt and a deflating belly . . . and the Master of Disaster keeled over backward, him and his great gut and fat bottom. He would have hit the floor with the base of his skull had it not hit the bald-headed director's thigh on the way down. He lay on the floor with his chest and his belly heaving with shallow breaths. His eyes were open, but they focused on nothing at all and obviously saw nothing at all. Magdalena, being a nurse, knew about such things. Sergei had obviously meant only to push the big man away. But his shoulder had struck Flebetnikov squarely in the nerve bundle of the solar plexus and knocked him out.

Producer Munch wasn't the slightest bit concerned about the fallen star of his reality show. His attention was devoted entirely to his two cameramen up on their rolling camera stands. He kept hurling his fist with the forefinger rampant toward Flebetnikov and Sergei and shouting, "Get it *all!* Eat 'em *up!* Get it *all!* Eat 'em *up!*" The only ones trying to help the fat man were Magdalena and Sergei. Sergei leaned over the prostrate hulk, looking for signs of life. "Boris Feodorovich! Boris Feodorovich! Can you hear me?"

Producer Munch and Director Koch were in the throes of a dream coming true.

"Fabulous!" said Munch, who was doing an odd hula inside his guayabera.

"Awesome!" said Koch, who was a generation younger than Munch and didn't say "fabulous."

Now Sergei was kneeling beside Flebetnikov, speaking in Russian. Concern that he might have delivered a mortal blow to the fat man was written in anguish on his face. The fat man's eyes looked like two lumps of milk glass... no irises... no pupils...

"Boris Feodorovich! I swear I wasn't trying to hurt you! I was only trying to separate us from one another, so we could talk about all this like friends! And I still want to be your friend. Speak to me, Boris Feodorovich! We are proud Russians and we have let these slimy Americans make fools of us both!"

That word—*fools*—cut through the fat man's fog. All by itself it created a stimulus response bond. At last, a sign of life! Trying mightily but incapable of anything beyond a gravelly whisper, Flebetnikov kept saying something over and over.

Oddly, he didn't appear angry at all...merely sad...

Magdalena and Sergei both knelt by Flebetnikov's belly-up bulk. Sergei's head was very close to the fat man's. Then a third pair of knees appeared in their little huddle, knees in a pair of clean, smartly ironed khaki pants...flawless creases...Magdalena and Sergei looked up. It was a thin, pale young Anglo with neatly trimmed, carefully combed blond hair. He had a spiral notebook in one hand and a ballpoint pen in the other...not an ordinary ballpoint pen—no, a ballpoint pen with a digital recording microphone built into the upper part, the wider part. He wore a navy blazer and a white shirt. He looked like an Anglo college boy, the kind you saw pictures of in magazines.

He stared at Sergei and said, "Mr. Korolyov? Hi!" He sounded friendly and shy. He blushed when Sergei stared back at him. "I'm John Smith from the *Miami Herald,*" he said lightly. "I'm covering Mr. Flebetnikov's party—or reality show or whatever it is—and suddenly there was all this commotion over here." He looked down at Flebetnikov, then back to Sergei and said, "What happened to Mr. Flebetnikov?"

::::::The *Miami Herald.* John Smith . . . Why does that ring a bell?::::::

Sergei eyed the boy blankly, but not for long. Now he gave him a look that said, in no uncertain terms, "Disintegrate!" What the boy's arrival on the scene meant—it took Sergei a moment or two to size it up—Oh, *great* . . . this whole stupid business could wind up in the newspaper!

"Happen?" said Sergei. "Nothing happen. My friend Mr. Flebetnikov fell down. It was an accident. We call the doctor, for the safety. But Mr. Flebetnikov was stunned only a few seconds."

"But this gentleman over here"—John Smith looked back over his shoulder vaguely—"told me that Mr. Flebetnikov tried to hit you."

"He trip and fall," said Sergei. "It's nothing, my friend." *Eets nozzing, my fran.*

"Golly . . ." said John Smith, "I need some clarification. This gentleman back here"—another vague nod over the shoulder—"he saw the whole thing and he said Mr. Flebetnikov swung at you. But you ducked the punch—'just like a professional boxer,' he said. You ducked the punch and countered with a blow to the body that knocked Mr. Flebetnikov *out!*

He said it was *really* cool!" He put on a big awed smile, probably figuring Sergei would melt from the flattery. "Have you done much box—"

"What do I tell you? Do you hear? Nothing. I tell you nothing happen. My friend here, he trip and fall. It was an accident."

Meantime, the fat man had begun groaning, and his whisper rose to a low mutter mutter mutter.

"What did he say?" said John Smith.

"He said, 'That is true. It was an accident.'"

A voice from directly above them: "I only wish it *had* been an accident. But I'm afraid it was no-oh-oh-oh accident!"

Sergei, Magdalena, and John Smith looked up. Sidney Munch was standing over them...in his grossly outsized guayabera...so long, it looked like a dress. He peered down at them intently.

"This is *him!*" said John Smith. "The man I was telling you about!" He glanced at his spiral notebook. "Mr. Munch! He was here the whole time and told me what happened!"

"It was not a pretty sight," said Munch. He began shaking his head. He pursed his lips and turned them down glumly at the corners. He expelled a profound sigh. He addressed his words to John Smith: "I don't know why, but suddenly"—he motioned with his chin to indicate he was talking about Flebetnikov—"he started bellying his way through all these people"—he gestured at the mob of guests—"and came straight at Mr. Korolyov. They exchanged a few angry words and then"—he did the number with the chin again—"swung at Mr. Korolyov, and Mr. Korolyov ducked just like a prize-fighter and gave"—the chin again—"such a shoulder in the midsection that"—again the Flebetnikov semaphore—"went down like six sacks a fertilizer!"

Out the corner of her eye Magdalena could see one of the mobile camera units barely four feet away with its red eye on, recording it all *all all*. She nudged Sergei. He pulled out of the huddle and saw it for himself.

He was seething. He straightened himself up fully erect, looked down at Munch, and stiffened his arm and forefinger and aimed them at the camera and said in a steely voice, "You filming this, too—you *ubljúdok!*"

His steely voice rose to a shout: "This is your little play! You send your little director over to tell lies to Flebetnikov—to make him mad! Flebetnikov didn't do this! I didn't do this! *You* did this! You make up this *lie!* This is not reality—this is a lie!"

Munch put on the face of a man who has been *terribly* wounded by a cruel remark uttered for the sole purpose of hurting his feelings. "But Mr. Korolyov, how can you say this isn't reality? All of this just happened! Once something happens, it becomes real, and once it's real, it becomes part of reality. No? Mr. Flebetnikov didn't *pretend* to be angry. He was *angry!* Nobody told you that you had to *defend* yourself. *You* decided to defend yourself! And quite rightly! And quite beautifully and athletically, if I may say so. Have you ever been a prizefighter? In the ring did you—"

"THAT IS ENOUGH!" said Sergei. "You listen to me! You don't run anything that shows me, and you do not use anything I say! You do not have the right! I will sue! And that is only where we begin. You understand?!"

"But Mr. Korolyov, you signed a release!" Munch said in his same hurt voice. "You gave us permission to record whatever you did and whatever you said on our show. We proceeded on *your word.* We accepted you as a man of your word. You *signed* the release. It couldn't have made it any clearer. And certainly what we filmed will show you in a positive light. Mr."—he gave the Flebetnikov semaphore—"attacked you and you defended yourself with courage and strength and speed and athletic sureness when a man"—Flebetnikov semaphore—"double your size, double *everybody's* size, launched a surprise attack, a *physical* attack. Please think about it! You will *want* to appear on *Masters of Disaster.* Miami knows you as a noble, immensely generous benefactor of the museum, of all of South Florida. This program will show *the man* behind the great generosity. This program will show the world... a *real man!*"

Magdalena noticed that the reporter, John Smith, was recording all with his digital-recorder ballpoint pen. He was eating it all up every bit as much as Munch. And Sergei? He was deflating before Magdalena's very eyes. His big powerful blood-gorged neck was shrinking... likewise his marvelous sculpted chest—even his strong, wide shoulders were deflating rapidly. His jacket seemed, to Magdalena, to be sticking inches out beyond those once-strong, once-wide shoulders of his and drooping down. Magdalena could tell: Sergei realized that this little Sidney Munch had outsmarted him... *him,* the mighty Russian who could handle anybody, and certainly a little con man like Munch... and now Munch had tricked him into performing precisely the self-abasing, humiliating dancing-bear number he wanted him to perform—

And *he had signed the release!* He had surrendered his rights like the most pathetic mark who ever lived!

Sergei shot Munch one last malevolent stare and said in his low, seething voice, "I hope you heard me. I didn't *ask* you not to show that film. I said that you *will not* show it. Suing is not the only thing that can happen. *Other* things can happen. You will *never* see that film on television." Magdalena couldn't see Sergei's face, but she could see Mr. Munch's as he looked at Sergei. His face was frozen, except for his eyelids, which blinked blinked blinked blinked.

"Mr. Korolyov! Mr. Korolyov!" It was John Smith, coming up behind them. Sergei gave him a look that could kill, but the pale reporter, thin as an earphone wire, was relentless. "Mr. Korolyov—before you go! You were *awesome* just now! You—well, I know you're leaving, but could I give you a call? I'd like to give you a call, if that's—"

John Smith recoiled in midsentence. The look on Sergei's face seemed to take his breath away. This was not the mere look that kills. This was the look that kills and then smoke-cures the carcass and eats it.

They left the mansion and began walking back to the gatehouses. Sergei stared straight ahead—at nothing. The look on his face was as morose as any Magdalena had ever seen on a human face, even at Jackson Memorial Hospital in the moment of freefall that precedes death. He began muttering to himself in Russian. He was still walking beside her, but his mind had departed to another zone.

"Muttermirovmutterlameimutternesmayamutter-milayshmutterkhlopovmutter—"

Magdalena couldn't stand it. She broke in: "Sergei, what's wrong? What are you muttering about? Come baaaaaack!"

Sergei looked at her crossly, but at last he began speaking English. "This little midget, this bastard, this Munch—I can't believe I let that happen! That little ball of American scum—and I let him trick me! He knew exactly how to put 'me' into his stinking reality show—and I didn't see it coming! He makes me look like some idiot brawler from the streets! One minute I'm the big—what is the American word? donor?—and they honor me for giving tens of millions of dollars' worth of paintings to a museum—and now I'm a fool who sinks so low as to appear on this garbage 'reality show'! Do you know what Flebetnikov said when I leaned over him to see if he was still breathing, still had a heartbeat—I was afraid he was dead! But thank God he's still alive. He can barely talk at all, but with this pitiful voice he whispers into my ear, 'Sergei Andreivich, I did not mean it.' He didn't have to say any more. The look in his eyes—he was pleading. 'Sergei Andreivich,' he's saying, 'please forgive me. They tell me, "You got to go start a fight."' Poor Boris Feodorovich. He's broke, he's desperate. He needs the money they offer him. Then they start making hints. If he performs well on this show, maybe they give him a 'reality show' of his own. Maybe they call it *The Mad Russian*?—I don't know, but now I see how these slimy Americans work. They force Boris Feodorovich to drag me into their cesspool by attacking me—physically! Once he swings his pathetic punch, I'm in their filthy show, like it or not. I, who showed such contempt for this

Munch—he tricks me like any other poor *lokh.* I can't believe this! Some slimy little American!"

They were now at the end of the walkway, approaching the twin gatehouses. The gatehouses looked enormous in this dim electric dusk. It didn't so much illuminate them as suggest their size... an edge of slate on the roofs... the white architraves around the windows... the shadows in the deep relief of some sort of plaster medallion with fanciful figures in it.

At the very end of the walkway, the big blonde, "Savannah," was still at the card table. The light was just enough to illuminate her as she sat with her back toward them... her sleeveless dress, the whiteness of her broad, bare shoulders, the streaks of blond highlights in her hair... Sergei stopped in his tracks and said to Magdalena, "That *kvynt*... look at her. She's the one who started it all."

He didn't say it loudly. In fact, he didn't so much say it as *seethe* it. But it was loud enough for this woman, Savannah, to hear something. She rose from her chair and turned about. Magdalena's heart began racing. Sergei had the same look on his face he had just before he tore into the poor Number Five chess player at Gogol's. ::::::Dear God, spare me! I can't take another appalling scene like that one!:::::: She held her breath in absolute fear.

The woman, Savannah, broke into a smile. She sang out, "Hi! How did it go?"

A furious Sergei stared death rays at her for one beat, two beats, three beats, far too many beats... then... "It was amazing—wonderful!" It came out *Eet vas amazing—vonderful!*—but his great joy was unmistakable. "I am so glad we listen to you!"

Magdalena couldn't believe her ears. She took a half step forward and glanced ever so quickly at Sergei's face. *¡Dios mío!* Could that smile possibly be as sincere and... and... and as *heartfelt* as it looked? "Yes, we have *you* to thank, Savannah!" Oh, the comradeship, even *love,* he bathed her name in! "That was not a show," said Sergei. "It was an *experience,* a—a—a lesson in the *life itself!* Flebetnikov—Boris Feodorovich—he demonstrate us what bravery"—came out *brafery*—"is made of!"

He was giving Savannah a look of not mere happiness... but *enchantment.* He was Goodwill and Gratitude walking this earth in shiny leather shoes. So successfully did he personify these things, a remarkable smile came over Savannah's face. It was huge, and it gleamed. Her teeth sure were long... but they were also perfectly even... and so white and bright, they overwhelmed the dim electro-gloaming out here on Flebetnikov's front lawn.

"Well, thank you," she said. "But I didn't really do very much—"

"But you did! You did! You suffer my grumbles so patiently. You *encourage* me so much!" Sergei began walking toward Savannah, holding out both hands, the way one does when he offers his affection to a dear friend. The delighted, brightly luxodontic Savannah held out both hands to him, and he clasped them with his the moment he reached her.

"Suddenly he has lost everything," Sergei went on, "but he wants the world to *know*"—he gave his grip on her hands a good pump to underscore *know*—"to know that when the worst happens to a brave man, he has a strength *inside* him"—he gave *inside* a good pump—"and it is the power of the heart—the human heart!" He gave Savannah's hands two pumps, one for *the heart* and another for *the human heart.*

::::::Talk about *enchanted*. Look at the expression on her face. She's the very picture of a woman wondering if—barely able to surrender herself to the possibility that—this vision is real. This incredibly handsome celebrity with a European accent is holding both her hands in his and squeezing them—and pouring his soul into her wide eyes. Could this be true? But it *is* true! She can feel the touch of his very hands! Her eyes can't gulp down his deepest emotions fast enough!::::::

"He discover a power greater than what he live for these so many years, the power of money." A couple more pumps. "I am so sorry you were not with us"—he gestured toward the house—"to see it, but I am sure that Sidney—Mr. Munch—a man of great talent and sympathy, by the way"—*sympazy, by se vay*—"will show you the film with haste. But please, I must ask you to check one thing"—*von zing*—"I told him I am at his service any time he have a question about Boris Feodorovich and what he did these years in Russia or anything else. But I want to be certain I put all the information on this form. I was in such a rush! The e-mail, the cell phone number, the address, all these things." He gave her hands one last pump, then released them.

"All right," said Savannah, "let's check." She sat back down in her chair, reached under the table, and came up with a metal file box and put it on the tabletop. She produced a key from out of her handbag and opened it. "It should be right here on top..." With that, she withdrew a sheet of paper and said, "Here it is. Now what was it exactly you wanted me to check—e-mail, did you say?"

"Let me see it for a moment," said Sergei, who was standing beside her. She handed it to him, and he gave her the warmest and most grateful smile yet... and folded the form in two the long way and in two again and slipped it into a pocket inside his jacket... smiling smiling smiling to beat the band.

Savannah's bright luxodontic glow dimmed a bit. "What are you doing with that?"

"I must examine it in the better light." Still smiling smiling smiling, he motioned to Magdalena, took her by the arm, undid the velvet rope, and headed toward the big gatehouse. "Thank you, dear Savannah, for everything."

Savannah, honey's, glow now dimmed *a lot,* and her voice rose. "Please—Sergei—that mustn't leave here!"

::::::*Sergei,* she calls him! All that talk—he must have put her under a spell!::::::

Sergei quickened their pace and sang back over his shoulder in the cheeriest voice Magdalena could imagine, "Oh, my dear Savannah, don't worry! Everything is for the best!"

"No! Sergei!—Mr. Korolyov!—you mustn't!—you *can't!*—please!"

Sergei smiled back at her as he walked, and he was walking fast. They didn't follow the wiggly-curving walkway but cut straight across the lawn. He hailed a valet.

"Mr. Korolyov! Stop! That's not yours!" Her voice had reached a shrill, panicked level—and it seemed closer. She must be coming after them. And then, "Oh, *shit!*"

Magdalena glanced back. The woman had tripped. She sat on the grass with one shoe on and one shoe off, rubbing her ankle. The pain distorted her face. Her high heel must have sunk into the lawn. No more glow at all.

The valet pulled up in the Aston Martin. Sergei

smiled at Magdalena and chuckled and laughed and said something and laughed and chuckled some more. Any normal, unbriefed onlooker—such as the valet—would think here was half-a-drunk who must have had a cool time at the party... and got himself sloshed enough to give a valet a fifty-dollar bill. As they pulled away, Magdalena could see Savannah hurrying back to the house barefoot—with a very contemporary high-heeled kind of limp.

By the time they crossed the little bridge from Star Island to the MacArthur Causeway, Sergei was laughing so hard, he could barely catch a breath. "I wish I can stay and see the look on the face of that little toad, Munch, when the woman tell him what happen! I would give anything!"

As he drove, he put his hand on Magdalena's knee and left it there for a while. Neither of them said a word. Magdalena's heart was beating so fast and she was breathing so rapidly, she knew she couldn't have said a word without her voice quavering. Then he slipped his hand three-quarters of the way up her thigh.

Now Sergei had reached Collins Avenue. Magdalena stayed absolutely still. If he turned right, it would be toward *her* apartment. If he turned left, it would be toward his... He turned left!—and Magdalena couldn't help herself. Immediately she telepathed

Amélia over the fiber-figmental chimericoptic connection she had left on all evening, "I *told* you! It depends, it depends!" Very gently Sergei slipped his hand all the way to her crotch and began stroking it. She felt a rush of fluid rising up in her loins and telepathed Amélia again. "I swear to you, Amélia, I'm not making a decision. It's just happening."

Sergei's apartment was grander than anything she could have imagined. The living room was two stories high. The place had a very modern look but not modern in any way she had ever seen before—walls of glass so extravagantly etched with surreal swoops and swirls of women in phantasmagorical gowns, you could barely see anything through them. Sergei took her to the second floor up a curving staircase with a dark wooden banister inlaid with could-that-be-real ivory. He opened the bedroom door and bade her enter first... an enormous room lit by the sort of downlights she had seen in clubs... the bed—it was gigantic... walls of is-that-velvet—she didn't absorb another detail, for at that moment he embraced her from behind, so powerfully she could feel the overwhelming strength of his arms, not to mention his pelvic thrust. He buried his head in the crook of her neck and with a single motion *just like that* swept her dress clear off her shoulders and down as far as her waist. ::::::*Amélia's* dress—did he rip it?::::::

The *V* of the dress was so deep and so wide, it wasn't made for wearing anything under it, and there she was . . . he slid his hands up her rib cage—

The line to Amélia went down, vanished, became irrelevant from that moment on.

18

Na Zdrovia!

The very moment Sergei Korolyov picked up Magdalena in his Aston Martin to drive to Hallandale for dinner, Nestor, accompanied by John Smith, found a parking place on a block where dilapidation reigned. Nestor had never seen so many windows with sheets of metal nailed over them in his life. He and John Smith had different takes on this part of town, now called "Wynwood," which suggested lufts and wafts of zephyrs on an ancestral estate's horticultured sylvan glade, where Igor maintained his official studio, his *out-front* studio, so to speak, the one with a telephone listing. Wynwood bordered on Overtown, and Nestor, being a cop, saw it as a worn-out old industrial area full of decrepit one-, two-, and three-story warehouses that weren't worth rehabilitating... and a rat's nest of Puerto Rican petty criminals who weren't, either. John Smith, on the other hand, saw it as Miami's version of a curious new social phenomenon—and *oh, yes!* real estate phenomenon—of the late twentieth century: the "art district."

Art districts had popped up all over the place... SoHo (south of Houston Street) in New York... SoWa (south of Washington Street) in Boston... Downcity in Providence, Rhode Island... Shockoe Slip in Richmond, Virginia... and all of them were born the same way. Some enterprising real estate developer starts buying up a superannuated section of town full of dilapidated old loft buildings. Then he whistles for the artists—talent or utter lack of it makes no difference—and offers them large lofts at laughably low rents... lets it be known that this is the new artists quarter... and in three years or less... Get out of the way!... Here they come!... droves of well-educated and well-heeled people skipping and screaming with *nostalgie de la boue,* "nostalgia for the mud"... eager to inhale the emanations of Art and other Higher Things amid the squalor of it all.

In Wynwood even the palm trees were bohemian... poor raggedy strays... one over here... another one over there... and all of them mangy. The nostalgia-for-the-mudders wouldn't have had it any other way. They didn't want grand allées of stately palms. Grand allées didn't give off emanations of Art and other Higher Things amid the squalor.

At this very moment Nestor and John Smith were on a freight elevator, bound for Igor's studio on the top floor of a three-story warehouse some developer had turned into loft condominiums. All the elevators in the building were freight elevators . . . operated by sullen Mexicans who never said word one to anybody. There you had a reliable indicator of illegal-alien status. They didn't want to draw any attention to themselves whatsoever. The nostalgia-for-the-mudders loved the freight elevators, despite the fact that they were ponderous, slow, and old-fashioned. Old-fashioned freight elevators gave off some of the *nostalgie-de-la*-muddiest emanations of all—the heavy electric groan of the industrial-strength pulley machinery overcoming inertia . . . the operator's stone-sullen Mexican face . . .

Nestor had a digital camera in his hands . . . studded with dials, meters, and gauges he'd never seen or heard of before. He held it up in front of John Smith as if it were some utterly unidentifiable foreign object. "What's *this* supposed to accomplish? I don't even know what you're supposed to *look* through."

"You don't have to look *through* anything," said John Smith. "All you have to do is look *at* this image right *here* . . . and then you press *this* button. Actually—*forget* the image and just press the button. All we need is that little *whine* it makes. You only need to *sound* like a photographer."

Nestor shook his head. He couldn't stand not knowing what he was doing... and he couldn't stand it when John Smith and not himself was running the operation, despite John Smith's smooth performance at the Advanced Yentas home up in Hallandale. John Smith still insisted on this business of using outright lies as reporting devices! He had called Igor on his listed telephone number and said the *Herald* had assigned him to do a story on the recent upsurge in realistic art in Miami... and people kept mentioning him, Igor, as one of the important figures in this movement. Igor turned out to be so vain, so eager to rise up from out of obscurity... he was ready to believe it, despite the fact that his work had appeared only in two largely ignored group shows... and that there had been no such "upsurge" and no such "movement." In fact, John Smith had no such assignment, either, and wouldn't have been able to get a real *Herald* photographer to come along with him. Besides, at this point he didn't want anybody at the *Herald* to get wind of what he was doing. It was too early. He had to get the facts nailed down first. Hell, Topping the Fourth had turned severely squirrelly at the very mention of the subject.

From the moment the elevator came to a lumbering, lurching stop on the third floor... lurching because the Mexican had to swing the tiller handle this way and that to make the floor of the enormous freight cab line up just right with the level of the floor outside... the *nostalgie-de-la*-mudders loved that part, the lumbering, lurching stop... it was so *real*... Even before the doors opened, Nestor and John Smith picked up the scent of their man... *turpentine!*... Upscale *nostalgie-de-la*-mudders might or might not object to the odor. But they couldn't very well grumble, could they. *Naturally* there were working artists in these lofts, and *naturally* the painters were working with turpentine... You're in the "art district," my friend!... You'd best take the bitter with the better and consider it an emanation of Art and other Higher Things amid the squalor of it all.

As soon as Igor opened the door to his loft, it was obvious that he was *primed* for this major event in his so-far-negligible media life. His face was one great bright Rooooshian beam. If he had still had his outsized Salvador Dalí–jolly waxed mustache, it would have been really something. He had his arms stretched out. It looked like he was about to embrace them both in a Russian bear hug.

"Dobro pozalovat!" he said in Russian, and in English, "Welcome! Come in! Come in!"

Such booming bonhomie!—so much so that the two hard *C*s in a row, *Come in! Come in!*, propelled the alcohol on his breath into Nestor's and John Smith's faces. He was bigger, more heavy chested, and drunker than Nestor remembered from the

Honey Pot. And how art-district-fashionably he was dressed!...a long-sleeved black shirt with a silky sheen, rolled up to the elbows and open at the neck all the way down to the sternum...hanging outside a pair of too-tight-fitting black jeans in a game attempt to obscure his girth.

The entrance took you straight into an open kitchen at one end of a space at least forty feet long and twenty feet wide. The ceiling must have been close to fourteen feet high, making the place seem enormous...likewise, a bank of towering old-fashioned warehouse windows way down at the other end. Even now, close to 4:00 p.m., the entire work area was flooded with natural light...the easels...the metal tables...a ladder... some tarpaulins...the same sort of stuff Igor had at his hideaway studio in Hallandale. Nestor's survey of the premises came to an abrupt halt when Igor stuck his face right into *his* and exclaimed, "Ayyyyyyyyyyyy!" and took Nestor's hand and gave it a shake that felt like it had dislocated every joint in his right arm and clapped him on the shoulder in the manner that among men means, *You are my pal and we've survived a lot of good times together, haven't we!*

"This is my photographer," John Smith interjected—Nestor could tell that John Smith's facile lying mind was churning to come up with a suitable fake name. *Pop!*—"Ned," he said, probably because it started with Ne, like Nestor.

"Nade!" was the way it sounded when Igor said it. With another gush of inexplicable merriment he maintained his grip on Nade's hand and clapped him on the shoulder again. "We have a drink!" he said, reaching back to a kitchen counter and producing a bottle with a Stolichnaya vodka label but containing a pale amber liquid...He poured it into a big shot glass, which he hoisted with one hand and pointed at with the other.

"Vod*apri*ka!" he exclaimed, accenting the *apri*—and threw the entire shot-glassful down his gullet. His face turned arterial red. He emerged grinning and gasping for breath. When he finally exhaled, the air they breathed smelled like alcoholic vomitus.

"I take the vodka and I give it a little—what do you say in English?—'spitz'?—of apricot juice. You see? One little spitz—vod*apri*ka! We all have some! You come!"

With that, he led them to a big, long, stout wooden table with an odd lot of wooden chairs around it. He took the one at the head, and Nestor and John Smith flanked him. The big shot glasses awaited them. Igor brought his own shot glass and the bottle of vodaprika and a big platter of hors d'oeuvres...pickled cabbage with some kind of berries...salted cucumbers—big ones...slices of beef tongue with horseradish...salt herring...salted red salmon eggs (Low-Rent caviar)...pickled mushrooms, heaps of these briny beauties, intact or cut up and mixed with boiled potatoes, eggs, great slathers of butter and mayonnaise, great balls of them wrapped in pastry—guaranteed to keep a man warm up near the Arctic Circle and calorie-fried in Miami... all of it served in a heavy cloud of *odeur de vomi.*

"Everybody thinks the Russians, they drink only the plain vodka," said Igor. "And you know what? They are right! That's all they drink!"

Nestor could see John Smith trying to put a merry response on his baffled face.

"And you know why they drink like this?" said Igor. "I show you. *Na zdrovia!*" He grabbed a gob of salt herring with his fingers, stuffed it down the gullet, and knocked back another big shot-glassful... more blazing-red face, gasps for breath... and a veritable fog of *odeur de vomi.*

"You know why we do that? We don't like the taste of the vodka. It tastes like the chemical! This way we don't have to taste it. We only want zee alcohol. So why don't we"—he pantomimed injecting his arm with a syringe—"take it like this?"

That struck him as highly amusing. He picked up a big briny pastry ball from the platter with his fingers and stuffed it into his mouth and began chewing and talking at the same time. He picked up the bottle and refilled his glass and hoisted it once more as if to say, *This one, this the vodaprika!* He beamed at John

Smith, and then he beamed at Nestor and then at John Smith again, and—*bango!*—knocked back another shot. "And now *you* drink!"

It wasn't a question. It wasn't an order. It was a declaration. He poured each of them a glassful... and himself, too. "And now we go... when I say *'Na zdrovia.'* Okay?"

He looked at John Smith and then at Nestor... and what could you do but nod yes?

"Na zdrovia!" he exclaimed, and all three of them tilted their heads back and tossed the drink down their gullets. Even before it hit bottom, Nestor realized that this goddamned shot glass was a lot bigger than he thought it was and had no apricot taste or any other taste to lessen the shock of what was impending. The damned thing hit bottom like a fireball, and he came up gagging and coughing. His eyes were flooding with tears. John Smith's, too, and if his own face was now as red as John Smith's, then it was a fiery red.

Igor came up smiling and picking up a gob of salted herring from the platter with his fingers and shoving it into his mouth. He found Nestor's and John Smith's performance hilarious. *Hah hah hah-hah-hah haha.* Obviously he would have been disappointed if they had done any better.

"Don't worry!" he said merrily. "You must have practice! I give you two more times."

Jesus Christ! thought Nestor. This was the worst

white-boy-wasted behavior he had ever seen! It was gross! And he was taking part in it! Cubans were not big drinkers. In what was meant to be a lighthearted way, he said, "Oh, no, thanks. I think I've got—"

"No, Nade, we must have three!" said Igor. "You know? Otherwise—well, we must have three! You know?"

Nestor looked at John Smith. John Smith looked at Nestor sternly, and slowly moved his head up and down in the yes mode. *John Smith?* He was so tall and skinny. He had no normal physical courage. But he would lie, cheat...and probably steal, although he hadn't seen him do it yet...and now, it turned out, cauterize his gastrointestinal tract...to get a story.

Nestor looked at Igor and with a feeling of doom muttered, "Okay."

"That's good!" said Igor. He was very cheery about it as he refilled all three glasses.

The next thing Nestor knew—"*Na zdrovia!*"—he threw his head back and tossed the vodaprika down his open maw—*¡mierda!*—and the gagging, the doubling over, the coughing, the gasping, the flood of tears were barely under control when—

Na zdrovia! Another fireball—Ahhhhhhhu-ghh . . . eeeeeeeeuuughhh . . . *ushnayyyyyyyyyyanuck* splashed down his windpipe—burned his throat—gushed up into his nasal passages and came leaking down onto his pants—and Igor congratulated him and John Smith. "You did it! I celebrate you! Now you honorary *muzhiks!*"

Somehow *muzhiks* didn't sound all that great.

Judging by his morbid face, John Smith had suffered as much as Nestor had. But John Smith was immediately all business. Out the corner of his mouth, in a low growl, he told Nestor, "Get busy and start taking pictures."

Get busy and start taking pictures? Why, you bastard! John Smith wasn't putting on an act, either. *My photographer!* The bastard had started *believing* he was the commander! Nestor felt like throwing the damned digital camera through a window... although... *hmmmmm*... in tactical terms, he had to admit that John Smith was right. If he was supposed to be a photographer, he should start aiming the camera at something and pushing that dummy button. He felt good and humiliated when he so dutifully *started taking pictures*... dummy pictures, as instructed.

Meantime, John Smith was shaking his head in wonderment and glancing toward Igor's paintings on the walls as if he couldn't help it. "That's great, Igor... *amazing!* Is this your own personal collection?" said John Smith.

"No, no, no, no, no," said Igor, laughing in a way that says, "I forgive you for your lack of knowledge about such things." "If only that was the truth!" He gestured with a lordly sweep of his hand toward both walls. "Two months from now, half of these will go and I must paint more of them. My agent, she keeps this all the time pressure."

"Your agent?" said John Smith. "You said *she?* It's a woman?"

"Why not?" Igor said with a shrug. "She is the best in all of Russia. Ask any Russian artist. They know her: Mirima Komenensky."

"Your agent is Russian?"

"Why not?" Igor said with another shrug. "In Russia they still understand the real art. They understand the skill, the technique, the colors, the chiaroscuro, all of that."

John Smith produced a small tape recorder from his pocket and put it on the table with the sort of arching of the eyebrows that asks if this is all right. Igor answered yes with a magnanimous flip of the hand that dismissed any concerns on that score.

"And what is the reaction to realism here in the US?" said John Smith.

"Here?" said Igor. The very question made him laugh. "Here they like the fads. Here they think art begins with Picasso. Picasso left art school when he was fifteen. He said there was not anything more they could teach him. The very next semester they are teaching anatomy and perspective. If I not draw any better than Picasso, you know what I do?" He waited for an answer.

"Uhhh . . . no," said John Smith.

"I will start new movement, call it Cubism!" Waves and gales of laughter came pouring out of Igor's great lungs, alcoholizing the air still further, and Nestor felt himself swept away, struggling to avoid strangling in a vomitous stupor.

Igor filled the three glasses again. He raised his and—

"Na zdrovia!"

—Igor threw his vodaprika down his gullet. But both Nestor and John Smith brought the glasses to their lips and tilted their heads back and faked it and came up going, *Ahhhhhhhhhhh!* in mock satisfaction and wrapping their hands around their shot glasses to hide the incriminating amber liquid that remained.

Igor came up much too drunk to notice. He had knocked back five big shots of the stuff since they had been here—and only God knew how many before they arrived. Nestor felt good and drunk now, after three. It was anything but a happy intoxication, however. He felt as if he had impaired his central nervous system and could no longer think straight or use his hands deftly.

"What about abstract art," said John Smith, "like, say, ohhhh . . . Malevich, like the Maleviches in the Korolyov Museum of Art recently?"

"Malevich!" Igor sent the name rolling on the crest of his biggest wave yet. "Funny you should say *Malevich!*" He winked at John Smith, and the wave rolled on. "You know, Malevich said that the realistic art, God already give you the picture, you only have to copy it. But in the abstract art, you have to be God and create it all yourself. Believe me, I *know* Malevich!" Another wink. "He had to say that! I have seen his work when he started out. He *try* to be realistic. He haf no skill! Nozzing! If I paint like Malevich, you know what I do? I start a new movement, call it Suprematism! Like Kandinsky." He gave John Smith a significant smile... "You see Kandinsky when *he* start out. He try to paint a picture of a house... it look like a loaf of bread! So he give up and announce he start a new movement, he calls it Constructivism!" Both a wink and a smile for John Smith's benefit.

"What about Goncharova?" said John Smith. Now three artists were in play, names *le tout* Miami had been so grateful to the celebrated, the generous Sergei Korolyov for. What culture and luster he had given to the city!

Igor gave John Smith a conspiratorial smile as if to say, "Yes! Exactly! We're both thinking the same thing."

"Goncharova?!" exclaimed Igor. "She is most unskilled of all! She cannot draw, and so she makes the big mess of straight little lines, and they go here, and they go there, and they go in between, a *real* mess, and she say every line is a ray of light, and she gives it a name: 'Rayonism.' *Rayonism!* because my art is a new art, and why do *I,* the Creator, have to look behind me and think about the things already used and worn out... I don't have to think the line and the anatomy and the three dimensions and the—how you say it? modeling?—or the perspective or the color harmony, any of those things... They were *done*... years ago... centuries ago, done until they die. They are from the past. You don't bother me with the past! I am in front! All these things, they are somewhere back there!" He motioned back over his shoulder and then forward and upward. "And I am up here above all that."

John Smith said, "Could you do what these artists have done, Malevich, Kandinsky, and Goncharova?"

Igor erupted with a big belly laugh. He laughed until tears were coming out of his eyes. "It depend on how you mean that! You mean could I make Americans take this silly business serious and pay the big money for it?... No—it make me laugh too much!" He started off another laughing jag and had to force himself to stop. "No, you must not make me laugh like this. It is too funny for me! It is not good for me... not good, not good..." Finally, he seemed to have himself under control. "But if you mean, could I do painting like theirs... *Anybody* could! *I* could do it, except that makes me have to look at this *govno!*" The thought caused his belly to go rumbling again. "I haf to do it blindfolded..." Rumble bubble bubble rumble... "And I can *do* it blindfolded!"

"Whattaya mean?" said John Smith.

"I have done it already blindfolded."

"You mean that, or are you just kidding me?"

"No, I have done these things with my eyes closed... *already!*"

And I can do it blindfolded came out bubbling up and down on chuckles... but the *No, I have done these things... already* was too much for him. All the rumbles, bubbles, chuckles, bellows, and booms erupted at once—came exploding out of his lungs and his larynx and his lips. He couldn't do anything to stop the launch. He was stamping his feet up and down. His forearms and fists were pumping up and down. He was beside himself. Nestor stood over him, faking taking pictures, before he realized it was pointless. He looked at John Smith and pulled a face. But once more John Smith was all business. He looked at Nestor with the utmost seriousness. While Igor was still off on his laughing jag with his eyes shut, John Smith pantomimed pouring something into a glass. He motioned toward the kitchen with his head. The way he jerked it, with an angry ditch down the middle of his forehead, it was like a direct order. *Hop to it! Get me a big shot of vodaprika! This is a direct order!*

What did John Smith think he was doing? Did he really think that I, Nestor Camacho, was *his* photographer? Nevertheless Nestor did it—hustled over to the counter, poured a shot-glassful of Igor's *na zdrovia* apriconcoction and brought it back to John Smith. He couldn't constrain a scowl, but John Smith didn't even seem to notice.

When Igor finally descended from his jag and opened his eyes, John Smith held out the vodka toward him and said, "Here, have this." Igor was still heaving his chest, trying to reinflate his lungs, but didn't say no to the drink. As soon as he was able, he took the shot glass and tossed it back and went *ahhhhhhh!*...*ahhhhhhhhh*...*ahhhhhhhh*...

"You okay?" John Smith said.

"Yes, yes, yes, yes"...still breathing hard... "Could do nothing about it...You ask me something so funny...you know?"

"Well, where are those paintings now, the ones you did with your eyes closed?"

Igor smiled and started to say something—but then the smile vanished. Drunk as he was, he seemed to realize that he had gotten himself into treacherous territory.

"Ohhhh, I don't know." He gave a shrug to show it was of no importance. "Maybe I threw them away, maybe I lost them...I only amuse myself with them...I give them away—but who is want them?...

I put them in someplace I do not remember... I lose them"—he shrugged once more—"I don't know where they are."

John Smith said, "Let's say you *gave* them away. Who would you give them to?"

Igor responded not with a smile but with a canny look and all but closed one eye. "Who would want them?—even if those... 'artists'... themselves painted them? I will not want them if they give them away across the street."

"The Miami Museum of Art certainly seemed happy to get the real things. They valued them at seventy million dollars."

Igor said, "Here they like the fads, I was telling you. That is their... that is their—I cannot tell them what they like. *De gustibus non est disputandum.*" Another shrug... "You do what you can, but there is not much you can do with some people..."

Nestor saw John Smith take a deep breath, and somehow he could tell he had worked up the courage to ask the big one. He had bitten the bullet.

"You know," said John Smith, taking another deep breath, "there are people who say you actually *did* do those paintings in the museum."

A sharp intake of breath—and no words. Igor just stared at John Smith. He shut one eye nearly all the way, as before, but now there was no mirth in his expression.

"*Who* says that!?" Uh-oh. Nestor could tell that one last redoubt of sound judgment in Igor's voda-prikized mind had come alive in the eleventh hour. "I want to know *who!*—what *persons!*"

"I don't know," said John Smith. "It's one of those things you just *uh*... *uh* that's in the air. You know how it is."

"Yes, I know how it is," said Igor. "It's a *lie!* That is how it is, a *lie!*" Then, as if realizing he was protesting too much, he forced out a *huhhh* that was supposed to make it lighter. "That is the most silly thing I have ever heard. You know the word *provenance?* Museums, they have a whole system. Nobody could get away with something like that. That is the more craziest idea! Why is anyone want to even try something like that?"

"I could think of a reason," said John Smith. "If somebody paid him enough money."

Igor just stared at John Smith. Not a trace of mirth or even irony in his face, not even a proto-wink. He couldn't have looked more stone-cold serious. "I give you advice," he said finally. "You don't even mention such a thing to Mr. Korolyov. You don't even tell anybody who ever *see* Mr. Korolyov. You understand?"

"Why do you mention Sergei Korolyov?" said John Smith.

"He is the one who gave the paintings to the museum. There was a big celebration for him."

"Oh... Do you *know* Korolyov?"

"NO!" said Igor. He froze as if someone had just put a knifepoint against his neck. "I don't even know what he looks like. But everybody knows about him, every Russian. You don't play around with him the way you play around with me."

"I'm not playing around—"

"Good! You don't even let him know you think about these things, these gossips!"

Have a seat. Have a seat, my ass! What was *that* supposed to mean? The Chief *never* had to *have a seat* before he could go into Dio's office. It was always him walking down the hall past all those dismal little used-to-be Pan Am seaplane offices with his shoulders back and his chest out. He wanted to make sure even the City Hall lifers got a good look at Chief Booker's black mightiness... and if the door was open, there would always be some white or Cuban lifer standing just inside an open door who would sing out with an ingratiating, worshipful "Hi, Chief!" and His Mightiness would turn toward him and say, "Hey, Big Guy."

But just now when he came down the hall, there were no lifers singing out "Hi, Chief" or anything else. They couldn't have contained their worshipfulness more completely. They had no reaction to his mightiness whatsoever.

Could it be that Dio's chilliness had seeped out into the whole place? Things hadn't been comradely between him and Dio ever since the day the two of them had it out over Hernandez and Camacho and the crack house bust... before an audience of five, but those five, given their position and their big Cuban mouths, were quite enough. They were witnesses to him caving in to Dio over his mortgage payments and his status as the big black Chief. Of course, they probably didn't know about the mortgage payments, but the other part—they'd have to be off musing in another world not to get it immediately. The Chief had felt humiliated ever since... more than the witnesses in that room could have imagined. He had buckled under to that pretentious Cuban hack, Dionisio Cruz, him and his purely, blatantly, political concerns...

Have a seat... Dio's keeper of the gate, a horse of a woman named Cecelia... who wore the false eyelashes of a nine-year-old playing Makeup in the mirror... above jaws the size of a Neanderthal's... she had said, "Have a seat." No excuse, no explanation, not even a smile or a wink to show she realized how bizarre this was... just "Have a seat." A "seat," in point of fact, was a wooden armchair, along with four or five other wooden armchairs, in a mean little space created by removing the front wall of a mean little office. The Chief had just passed this so-called waiting room in City Hall, and wouldn't you know the kind of people you'd find in there? Anthony Biaggi, a sleazeball developer who had his eyes on some derelict school building and school yard up in Pembroke Pines... José Hinchazón, an ex-cop fired years ago during a corruption scandal who now ran a shady "security" service... an Anglo who looked to the Chief like Adam Hirsch, of the failing-tour-boat-and-bus Hirsches... Have a seat in a room with that bunch?

So the Chief, looking down, gave the horse face of Cecelia an ambiguous, unsettling grin he had used to good effect many times before. He narrowed his eyes and curled back his upper lip, revealing his top row of big white upper teeth, which looked even bigger against the background of his dark skin. It was meant to indicate that he was about to broaden it even more... into a grin of pure happiness... or chew her up.

"I'll be down the hall"—he nodded his head in that direction—"when Dio is ready to see me."

Cecelia wasn't the kind who was likely to flinch. "You mean the waiting room," she said.

"Down the hall," he said, looking more and more like he was going to chew her up—and spit her out. He took one of his cards out and turned it over and wrote a telephone number on the back. He handed it to her and turned his ambiguous grin into a happy grin, which he hoped she would perceive as ironic and become even more unsettled or at least more confused.

When he walked back down the hall and passed the pathetic waiting room, he could tell out of the corner of his eye that all three of them were looking up at him. He turned toward them but acknowledged only one, Hirsch—and he didn't really know which Hirsch this was, Adam or his brother Jacob.

As before, nobody was paying "Hi, Chief" homage from the mouth of an open door, which meant he couldn't slip into anybody's office and start up a conversation to kill time while he waited for a summoning... a *summoning* from his Cuban master.

Hell, he couldn't just loiter in the hallway could he... *Goddamned Dio!* All of a sudden he had the gall to treat him like any other humble petitioner who turns up at the court pleading for something from the king.

There was no other solution but to go down to the lobby of this Pan Am city hall and make make-believe phone calls. People going in and out of City Hall saw him standing off to the side, tapping on the glass face of his iPhone. They were unaware of his fall from grace... so far, anyway... they clustered about him almost like rap fans... "Hi, Chief!"... "Hey, Chief!"... "What's going down, Chief?"... "You da man, Chief!"... and he was kept busy parceling out the *Hi, Big Guys* and *Hey, Big Guys* incessantly...

How ironic... Him! Cyrus Booker, Chief of Police, mighty black presence at the heart of Miami city government... Him! Chief Booker, reduced to this insulting insignificance, lurking in a lobby... playing a stupid defensive game... trying not to lose instead of risking whatever it took to win... *Him!* Why should *he* be cringing before *any*body? He was born to lead... and he was young enough, only forty-four, to fight his way back to the top... if not in this role then another one where the top was even higher, although he couldn't think at this very moment what that might be... if necessary, he'd *build* it!... and what was all this pants-twisting fear about the house and the mortgage? What difference would a house in Kendall make in history's verdict?... but then he thought of another verdict... his wife's... She would be anguished, for maybe twenty-four hours... and then furious!... *ooounnnghhh* Jesus God!... but a man couldn't flinch at a wife's fury if he was going to risk all... to achieve all, could he? *Shiiiiiiiit!* She'd be on the warpath... "Nice going, Big Shot! No job, no house, no income, but *noooohhh*... you're not gonna let that—"

His phone rang. He answered it as he always did: "Chief Booker."

"This is Cecelia at Mayor Cruz's office"... "at Mayor Cruz's office," as if he wouldn't have any idea which Cecelia, out of the thousands in this city, in this world, this *particular* Cecelia might be. "The Mayor can see you now. I went to the waiting room... and I couldn't find you. The Mayor has a very busy schedule this afternoon."

Frosty? Goddamn *freezing over!*... Well, up yours, Horse Head! But all he said was "I'll be right there." Damn! Why had he stuck in the "right"? Made it sound like he was going to hustle... obediently.

For security reasons, you could only reach the second floor by elevator. Damn and damn again! On the elevator he was trapped with two more *Hi, Chiefs*, and one of them was a nice kid who wrote bulletins for the Bureau of Environmental Management, a black kid named Mike. He gave Mike a *Hey, Big Guy*... but he was unable to smile! He could only show his teeth!

He practiced smiling as he walked down the narrow hallway. He had to have one ready for Cecelia. When he reached her desk, she pretended for a moment not to see him. Then she looked up at him. How big and horsey that *bitch's* teeth were! She said, "Ah, there you are," and even had the nerve to flick a glance at the watch on her wrist. "Please go right in." The Chief spread the smile he had been practicing from cheek to cheek. He hoped it read, "Yes, I understand the petty little game you're playing, and no, I'm not going to get down to your level and play it."

When he walked into the Mayor's office, old

Dionisio was seated in a big mahogany swivel chair upholstered in oxblood leather. The swivel chair was so big, it looked like a Mahogany Monster, and the oxblood leather looked like the inside of its mouth about to swallow Old Dionisius whole. He was leaning back into it with a gloriously bored self-satisfaction at a desk with a surface you could land a Piper Cub on. He didn't get up to welcome the Chief the way he usually did. He didn't even straighten up in the chair. If anything, he leaned back still further, to the limit of the chair's joint springs.

"Come in, Chief, and have a seat." There was a confident note of summons in his voice, and a nonchalant flip of the wrist indicated the other side of the desk. The *seat* was a straight chair immediately opposite Old Dio. The Chief sat down, making sure his posture was perfect. Then Old Dio said, "How goes the tranquility of the citizenry this afternoon, Chief?"

The Chief smiled slightly and indicated the small police radio clipped to the belt of his uniform. "Haven't had one call in the thirty minutes I've been here waiting."

"That's good," said the Mayor. His dubious look of mockery remained on his face. "So what can I do for you, Chief?"

"Well, you probably remember that incident at Lee de Forest High? A teacher was arrested for assaulting a student and spent two nights in jail? Well, now he has a trial coming up, and the courts consider a teacher assaulting a student on par with some lowlife assaulting an eighty-five-year-old man leaning on an aluminum walker in the park."

"All right," said the Mayor, "I'll accept that. And therefore...?"

"We now know it was the other way around. The student assaulted the teacher. The student is a Haitian gang leader with a juvenile record for violence, and the other students are afraid of him. As a matter of fact, they're scared shitless, if you want to know the truth. He ordered five of his hangers-on to lie to the officers and say the teacher assaulted *him*."

"Okay, what about the other students?"

"Everyone else the officers interviewed said they didn't know. Said they couldn't *see* what happened, or they were distracted by something else, or—the long and short of it was, this punk and his gang would do something to them if they came even close to telling what happened."

"And now...?"

"And now we have confessions from all five of the 'witnesses.' They all admit they lied to the officers. What this means is, the DA has no case. Mr. Estevez—that's the teacher—will be spared what could have been a *very* stiff sentence."

"That's good work, Chief, but I thought this was a School Police case."

"It was, but now it's under the jurisdiction of the court and the District Attorney's office."

"Well, then, we have a happy ending, don't we, Chief," said the Mayor, putting his elbows up and clasping his hands behind his neck and lying back to about as laid-back as a man could get in a swivel chair. "Thank you for going to the trouble to bring me this happy news of justice served, Chief. And that's why you had to see me in person and make this appointment at the busiest time of my day?"

The irony, the snottiness, the belittling and disdainful way he wrote him off as a pest—eating up his precious time—the full-bore contempt and blatant disrespect . . . that did it. That pulled the trigger . . . No more holding back . . . He was *doing* it . . . risking all . . . even the house in Kendall so beloved by his beloved wife, whose beautiful face blipped through his corpus callosum at the very moment he said, "Actually . . . there's one other element to it."

"Oh?"

"Yeah. It's the officer who broke the case. He prevented a terrible miscarriage of justice. Mr. Estevez's career, maybe his life, would have been destroyed. He owes a lot to this officer. We all do. I'm sure you'll recall his name . . . Nestor Camacho."

That name did terrible things to the Mayor's ultra-supine posture. His hands descended from behind his neck, his elbows hit the top of the desk, and his head tilted forward. "What are you talking about?" he said. "I thought he was relieved of duty!"

"He was. He still is. But right after he handed over his badge and his gun—must not have been sixty minutes—he gave me the names of all five boys. He had done this all on his own. One of them he had already had a long talk with, and the kid had recanted what he had told the School Police. By now, Camacho was relieved of duty, and so I told the Detective Bureau to interrogate the other four. They didn't stick to their story very long. As soon as they knew there'd been a break in their ranks and they might be arrested and prosecuted for perjury, that was it. They all folded. They're only kids, after all. Tomorrow the DA's gonna announce they're dropping the case."

"And they're gonna release Camacho's name?"

"Oh yes, of course," said the Chief. "I've given this a lot of thought, Dio...I'm restoring him to duty... the badge, the gun, the whole thing."

With that, the Mayor bolted forward in his chair as if the springs themselves had launched him.

"You can't do that, Cy! Camacho just got relieved of duty—for being a goddamned racial bigot! We'll lose all the credibility we gained with the African American community when we put that little sonofabitch on ice. I should have made you fire him outright. All of a sudden—what's it been, three weeks?—all of a sudden, he's back in the picture, bigger than ever, and he's a fucking hero. Every African American in Miami's gonna be up in arms all over again—except for one, the goddamn Chief of Police! It seems like yesterday, they all saw your little bigot in action and heard him spew out all that racist shit of his, live, in the raw, on YouTube. And now he'll have the fucking Haitian community in a fucking uproar. They were out in the streets for two days raising holy hell before. Now they'll really be out in the streets, soon as they find out this known racist, this Ku Klux Camacho of yours, has managed to switch the blame onto one of their own. I told you this kid is a one-man race riot, didn't I? And now you're gonna restore him to duty and not only that, glorify him! I don't get you, Cy. I really don't. You know very well that one of the main reasons you were made chief was that we thought you were the man to keep the peace with all these—*uh uhhh*—communities. So you think I'm gonna stand by and let you turn racial friction into a goddamn conflagration on *my watch?* Noooooooo, hoooooooh, my friend, you're not gonna do that! Otherwise you're gonna make me do something I'd rather not have to do."

"Which is what?" said the Chief.

The Mayor snapped his fingers. "You'll be gone like *that!* That I can promise you!"

"You can't promise me a goddamned thing, Dionisio. Remember? I don't work for you. I work for the City Manager."

"That's a distinction without a difference. The City Manager works for *me*."

"Oh, you may have gotten him the job, and you're the one who pushes his buttons, but the City Charter thinks he works for the City Council. You hand him this goddamned thing, and the press is all over him, and he'll panic. He'll be shitting bricks! I know some Councilmen—I *know* them—exactly the same way you *know* your so-called City Manager—and they're ready to give your dicky-boy such holy hell, they're so stoked to call him your personal tool... in utter violation of the Charter's mandate... your little boy will turn into a gibbering dwarf. He'll call for a goddamned committee to study the problem for ten months or until it goes away."

"All you can do is delay me, Cy... maybe. But you're already dead meat. The difference between you and me is, I have to think about the whole city."

"No, Dio, the difference between you and me is that you are incapable of thinking about anything other than what the whole city thinks of Dio. Why don't you try going into a small quiet room and thinking about right and wrong... I bet some of it will come back to you."

The Mayor twisted his lips into a smirk. "Dead meat, Cy, dead meat."

The Chief said, "You do what you have to do, and I'll do what I have to do... and we'll see, won't we."

He stood up and stared at Mayor Dionisio Cruz as belligerently as he had ever confronted anybody in his life... and never blinked once. But neither did Dio, who remained seated in the luxurious oxblood-leather-and-mahogany maw of his mammoth swivel chair and—coolly—stared back. The Chief wanted to laser Dio's eyeballs out of his skull. But Dio didn't flinch. Neither of them moved a muscle or said a word. It was a classic Mexican standoff, and it seemed to go on for ten minutes. In fact, it was closer to ten seconds. Then the Chief wheeled about and showed Dio his big powerful back and stormed out of the room.

On the way down in the elevator he could feel his heart beating as fast as it had when he was a young athlete. In the lobby there were citizens who had no idea he had been frozen out, cryogenized, two flights up. Down here, among these innocent souls, the *Hi, Chief!*s rang out as they always had. Uncharacteristically he ignored them, these good souls, his fans. He was completely focused upon something else.

The moment he stepped out of this ridiculous stucco Pan American Air-head city hall, Sergeant Sanchez pulled up in the big black Escalade, and the Chief got into the seat beside him. He realized he must have looked more morose and upwrought than Sanchez had ever seen him.

Not knowing quite what to say—but curious

about what had happened—Sanchez said, "Well, Chief... *uhhh*... how'd it go?"

Staring straight out through the windshield, the Chief said two words: "It didn't."

No doubt Sanchez was dying to say, "*What* didn't?"... but he was afraid to ask anything so direct. So he screwed up his courage and said, "It didn't? It didn't what, Chief?"

"It didn't *go,*" said the Chief, still looking straight ahead. After a few beats he said to the windshield, "But it *will.*"

Sanchez realized he wasn't talking to *him*. This was a conversation with his high and mighty Self.

The Chief took his iPhone out of his breast pocket and tapped its glass face with his fingertip twice and held the thing to his ear and said, "Cat." It was a command, not telephone manners. "Call Camacho—right now. I want him in my office ASAP."

19

The Whore

Magdalena woke up in a hypnopompic state. Something was stroking her. It caused no alarm, however, just a semiconscious bewilderment amidst her struggle to turn her lights on. By the time it slid up her mons pubis and her abdomen and began dwelling upon the nipple of her left breast, she had put it all together in a picture, even though her eyes remained closed. She and Sergei lay naked in his outsized bed in his great duplex in Sunny Isles—and she couldn't believe it. She couldn't believe a man his age could regenerate over and over, before they had finally gone to sleep. Now she opened her eyes, and with a single glance at the gap where a set of almost comically magnificent curtains came together, she could tell it was still black out. They couldn't have been asleep more than a couple of hours—and obviously he was ready to go at it again. The Korolyov Museum of Art . . . She was in bed with a famous Russian oligarch. *Todo el mundo* knew who he was and how handsome he was. His body impinged upon hers, and his hand was stroking her here . . . and there . . . and there and there and there, and she despaired. She was a whore for the Korolyov Museum of Art in the body of an oligarch, an alien who spoke English with a heavy accent. But then the tips of her breasts became erect on their own, and the flood in her loins washed morals, despair, and all other abstract assessments away in a cloud of some sort of divine cologne of his. Now his big generative jockey was inside her pelvic saddle, riding, riding, riding, and she was eagerly swallowing it swallowing it swallowing it with the saddle's own lips and maw—all this without a word. But then he began moaning and punctuating the moans with an occasional faux-agonized exclamation in Russian. It sounded like "Zhyss katineee!" He was amazing. He seemed to be able to last forever, so long that sounds finally came from her lips involuntarily . . . *"Ah . . . ah . . . ahh . . . ahhh . . . Ahhhhhhh"* as she climaxed over and over . . . When at last he was just lying next to her, she was able to think again. The clock on his bedside table said 5:05 a.m. Was she a whore? No! This was the modern sequence of love!—of romance! If anything, he was crazy about her. He was ready to love her to death. He couldn't get enough of her, which meant her*self,* too, her spirit, her uniqueness as a person, her *soul.* Just looking at her, wanting her, yielding himself totally to her, wanting to have her every waking moment—and *unwaking* moment, too, obviously—*Dios mío,* she was so tired, so exhausted, she wanted to submerge herself in sleep—but then she had a vision of breakfast with him. Maybe they would be in terry cloth robes. He had some luxurious terry cloth robes hanging in the bathroom... the two of them having breakfast at a little table, looking out at the ocean, looking at each other, talking languorously, laughing at little things, their entire beings suffused with the sweetness, the dreaminess made possibly by, yes, carnal divine feelings that are the... the... the *distillation* of things that cannot be expressed in mere words, this perfect yielding to—*¡Dios mío!* what was *that?!*—Pling pling pling plingplingpling pling pling plingplingpling pling pling plingpling pling pling plingpling—Sergei rolled over and reached toward his bedside table—toward his iPhone. The music was his phone's soft and soothing ring Pling pling pling plingplingplingpling pling pling—and she *knew* that music... but from where?... *Ahh!* from many years ago! Twice her mother had taken her at Christmastime to a ballet for children. What was it called? All she could think of was "The Dance of the Sugar Thumbs"... but that couldn't be it—"The Dance of the Sugar Plum Fairy"! That's what it was! Yes, and the name of the whole thing was... *The*

Nutcracker!... It came back to her! And it was by a great composer... What was his name?... *Chaivovsky!... that was it!... Chaivovsky!*... He was a really *great* composer, a *famous* composer of beautiful music. *Nestor* blipped through her head. To think that Nestor had one thing in common with Sergei—playing around with phone rings. Funny. Even in this little detail, come to think of it, Sergei was the aristocrat. *Chaivovsky*—a great classical composer!... whereas Nestor reveals his true Hialeah self... He has to choose a Low-Rent song by Bulldog, and Bulldog is like Dogbite and Rabies—an imitation of Pitbull. In a silly little thing like this, playing around with a phone ring, Sergei was part of a higher order of things. Sergei p l i n g pling pling propped himself up onto an elbow. She looked at the curve of his bare back. He had such a great body. He picked up the telephone with his other hand. That was the end of *The Nutcracker.* This call was so *early*... It was still dark out.

"Hello?" said Sergei. But the rest was in Russian. His voice began rising. He asked the caller something... a lag while the caller responded... Louder, Sergei asked another question. A lag... and Sergei asked another question, this time angrily. In all of it Magdalena could make out only one word, a name—"Hallandale"—the name of a town just north of Sunny Isles. The lag... and this time Sergei became furious. He was yelling.

He threw the phone on the bed. He swung his legs over the side of the bed, raising his body upright and steadying himself on the heels of his hands... He just sat there... with his spine straight as a string, and his head, too.

Under his breath he said something just as furiously. He shook his head from side to side in the semaphore that says, "A hopeless case... hopeless... hopeless..."

"What's wrong, Sergei?" said Magdalena.

He didn't even turn his head toward her. He said one word, "Nothing." And he didn't really *say* that. He *breathed* it.

He stood up and walked stark naked... muttering and shaking his head the whole time... to the closet where he kept his dressing robes... and pulled one out from off a big mahogany hanger... a real production, this robe, heavy silk in a pattern of navy blue, medium blue, and red, with white dots no bigger than grains swooping up and down like comets... huge red quilted lapels and cuffs... He flailed his arms into the sleeves. He stood facing her... without seeing her...

...Ah!—a note of hope! Even though he was five or six steps away, his *polla* was practically hanging in front of her face... and it was tumescent!—definitely tumescent! ::::::a sign that I still exist!:::::: but his eyes didn't show it... Inside his head all seven types of neurons were banging into synapses to the nth degree... She was dying to ask him what about. She propped *herself* up on one elbow... wondering if the sight of her breasts with suddenly erect nipples might not make him seriously tumescent... mad for *coño*... but he successfully contained his lust, if any... apparently she no longer existed at this point, and obviously no curiosity on her part would be welcome.

He had scarcely stepped into his slippers... which were velvet and embroidered with what?—an ornate monogram in Russian characters?... and must have cost more than all the clothes he had so rutrutruttingly removed from her body last night put together... Last night... That must not have been all that long ago, because she felt so tired, even a bit groggy... The light that seeped out of the edges of the curtains looked awfully dim... had the sun even come up?... which made the telephone call even harder to figure out... *Something* had happened... He had scarcely stepped into his slippers when a doorbell chimed... didn't ring, didn't buzz... chimed like the middle key on a xylophone... Nobody was going to set off an explosion or any other alarming sound by pressing a button outside Sergei Korolyov's bedroom...

Sergei ran his fingers through his hair and headed for the door... and Magdalena slid back under the covers to hide her bare body and considered sinking as far into the pillows as she possibly could and turning her back toward whatever was about to happen . . . but her curiosity got the better of her and she lay there under covers that hid all of her up to her cheekbones—but not her eyes. She didn't want to miss a thing. Sergei said something in Russian at the door . . . a low voice responded outside. Two men entered, both about thirty-five . . . wearing identical tan—gabardine?—suits and navy—black?—polo shirts . . . one tall and slope shouldered with his balding head shaved down to an unfortunately misshapen knob . . . the other shorter, heavier . . . showing the world a head of wavy dark-brown hair he obviously worked on *a lot* . . . Both had deep-set eyes and struck Magdalena as hard cases. The taller one, from the servile way he shook his head, seemed to be apologizing for having awakened Sergei so early and then handed him a newspaper opened to a certain page . . . Still standing there, Sergei pored over it for about a minute that seemed to stretch out for an hour, since all of them, Magdalena included, wanted to get the godfather's reaction. He scowled at the two men as if they had done something not only wrong but stupid. He didn't say a word. He ordered them through a pair of old-fashioned doors with panes of glass and heavy wooden muntins—by pointing at them with a stiff arm and a forefinger that suddenly seemed a foot long. The doors led into a small study. En route they had to pass within five or six feet of the bed. Each of them took a single glance at Magdalena, each nodded his head all of two inches, each uttered, "Miss," without so much as a micro-second slowing of their obedient march to the study. A micro-nod... a micro–word of greeting—no, not greeting; rather, a bare minimal acknowledgment of her existence. A hot wave of humiliation ran through her brain. Their "hospitality" was automatic. She was no doubt one in a sequence of naked young things to be found in the master bed in the morning.

Inside the study, she could see the smaller one, the one who loved his own wavy hair, fetching a wireless telephone receiver and handing it to Sergei where he sat. Sergei was growling into the telephone... in Russian. The only things Magdalena could understand were "Hallandale" and the expression "active adults"... which meant nothing to her but stood out simply because it was in English. When he finally concluded this Russian barrage of his, he handed the telephone back to the bodyguard with the wavy locks... and made note of Magdalena for the first time since the two men had arrived.

He emerged from the study and said, "A situation has developed." He said it in a grave voice. He hesitated, as if he were going to say more... and he did: "Vladimir will take you home."

He marched straight into his dressing room. He didn't even give her another glance. That left Magdalena trapped under the bedcovers—naked. The two bodyguards stood inside the study... It hit her like a physical pressure... wave after wave of humiliation... abandoned with no clothes on in a big over-the-top bedroom with a pair of hard-looking Russians who could see her through the glass doors any time they cared to. At first she felt fear. But fear gave way to a scalding shame that she had let herself be used this way... a used *coño* waiting to be swept out like the rest of the filth of this place... *Vladimir will take you home*... After an interminable few minutes she was suffocating from the shame and humiliation of it all... and finally Sergei reappeared... hastily clad in an expensive-looking pale-blue shirt stuffed into a pair of blue jeans... she didn't know he possessed anything so common as blue jeans... He was shod in a pair of ochre-color pigskin moccasins that must have cost a thousand dollars... and no socks... and no smile... just the worst, the curtest expression of hospitality she had ever heard: "Vladimir will take care of everything. If you want breakfast, the cook will prepare it. I'm sorry, but this is an emergency. Vladimir will look after you." He walked out of the room with the other bodyguard, the shorter one who worked hard on his hair.

Magdalena was furious but too stunned to show it.

Like a zombie with a heavy Russian accent, the one called Vladimir said, "When you are ready, I take you. I wait for you outside." He walked out the door and shut it carefully behind him.

His matter-of-fact manner made Magdalena feel as if he were used to hauling one naked girl or another out of here every morning.

"You bastard!" she said under her breath as she crawled out from under the covers and stood up. Her heart was hammering away. She had never felt more humiliated in her life. Sergei's sadistic chess master at Gogol's was nothing compared to the Master himself. For a moment she stood stock-still. In a wall mirror she could see a beautiful girl standing there stark naked in a huge over-elegant bedroom decorated in what was meant to be a grand manner but wound up looking more fussy and finicky than anything else... with its swags and antique chairs and chests and a fleet of deep-purple draperies pulled back by ridiculous gold-embroidered pulls into velvet folds as deep as a creek. That naked girl in the mirror looked more like a little whore than any girl she had ever beheld, and now the slut was supposed to gather up her cheap, trashy, *puta*-cutie clothes and get the hell out of here... now that she's been consumed like a soufflé or cigar, and Vladimir... has instructions to throw the trash out.

In the bathroom there were so many mirrors the little bitch could see her bare whore's *ass* and *boobs* from every conceivable angle. Fortunately, she had worn Amélia's simple black dress for last night... yeah, so simple it was open in front down *to here* in a wide *V*... and sure, she could make her exit by daylight inconspicuously, since people could only see the inner halves of her boobs, and each nipple would be covered by a ribbon's width of the dress's black *faux*-silk cloth.

The pumps on her feet were scooped low and made of black satin with heels as high as they came, and they came *very* high this year. She looked like a tower of sex on tiptoes. Oh, well, no reason not to top it all off with some rake-a-cheek raspberry lipstick... and enough black eyeshadow to make her eyes look like a pair of glistening orbs floating upon a pair of concupiscent mascara pools.

She put her Big handbag over her shoulder, this year's Big, of course, made of the very best black faux-python. She was about to walk out of the room, concentrating on how to contain her resentment of that robot with the shaved head, Vladimir, and enervated and humiliated by what he knew about her night and this morning... ::::::Sergei! You really are a bastard! You know that?:::::: She swore she would *let him know that* if she were ever so unfortunate as to run into him again. ::::::How could you possibly let those two Russian aborigines into the room?:::::: Was that perversity? No, it was worse than that. He had gotten what he wanted. He had fucked her. So now she was just a piece of equipment lying around. And what does a piece of equipment care about how things look? Since when have pieces of equipment started having a moral sense that picks up feelings such as modesty?... Or, to put it another way, since when have whores started to feel like anything more than whores?

Now Magdalena was *really* angry. She noticed the newspaper lying on the floor by the chair where Sergei had sat down to read it. She picked it up and scanned the lower half-a-page he had been reading... in the *Herald's* Section C, "Arts and Entertainment."

Most of it was taken up by an article with a headline topped by a small, dense line of type in all-capital letters: REALIST SPEAKS OUT.

It began, "If laughs could kill, every prominent modern artist from Picasso to Peter Doig would have died in a pile this week on the floor of the Wynwood studio of a member of the most endangered species in the entire art world: a realist painter.

"Big, hearty, belly-laughing Russian-born Igor Drukovich is not the best-known artist in Miami, but he might be the most colorful."

Magdalena wondered ::::::*"Belly-laughing?"* What does it mean, *"belly-laughing"*?:::::: buzz... buzz... buzz... she read on. This Drukovich keeps tossing down shots of some vodka concoction he's dreamed up. Now he's saying, "Picasso can't draw"... If he,

Drukovich couldn't draw any better than Picasso, he'd start a new movement and call it Cubism...And what was *that* supposed to mean? She didn't pause to figure it out...buzz...buzz...buzz...three Russian artists she'd never heard of...Mal-a-*who?*...At least she'd *heard* of Picasso...Whoever wrote this thing obviously thinks all this art and culture stuff is just *fascinating*...Magdalena glanced at the byline...John Smith...*Dios mío*...that same name again!...but it's all so boring, she can't imagine what set Sergei off like that...she can feel herself dozing off...falling asleep like a horse...standing up—*pop!*—up *pops* Sergei's name from out of nowhere: "Twenty paintings, valued at $70 million, were donated to the Miami Museum of Art by the recently arrived Russian collector Sergei Korolyov."

Now she's alert...*What about Sergei?*...Sergei?...But there is nothing more about Sergei...buzz...buzz...buzz...just more about the Russian painters, Malevich, Goncharova, and Kandinsky...The "big, hearty, belly-laughing" Russian painter, this Drukovich, has another shot of vodka and starts making fun of all three of them...buzz...buzz...buzz...Does Drukovich think he could do what they've done? "*Anybody* could!" he says. "*I* could do it, except that makes me have to look at this [s--t]." He says he'd have to do it blindfolded, and as a matter of fact he has actually done it blindfolded...buzz buzz...

another shot of vodka... Somebody asks him where these paintings are... He says he doesn't know... Maybe he threw them away or lost them or gave them to somebody... If he gave them away, who would he give them to?... "Who would want them?" says the Russian. Somebody says, "The Miami Museum of Art certainly seemed happy to get the real things. They valued them at $70 million... Maybe you gave them to the museum."... *laugh laugh laugh*... The Russian says, "That is the most silly thing I ever heard"... more vodka... buzz buzz buzz buzz... The guy must be drunk as a monkey by now... Magdalena reads the whole thing to the end... no more mention of Sergei... Then what freaked Sergei out? Would he get that mad because somebody nobody has ever heard of said he didn't like what Sergei had given the museum?... That must be it... He must be very proud and very touchy about that... buzz... buzz... buzz... and to think she just forced herself to read all that stuff...

As ordered, Vladimir was waiting when Magdalena left Sergei's suite. He bore the absolutely blank expression of the efficient automaton that he was. He didn't move a muscle in his face when he saw her. But his very presence was enough to turn her head hot with shame. What would she look like to the rest of the world this morning? That was easy: like a cheap slut the morning after the orgy, wearing the same boobs-rampant almost-a-dress she arrived in last night . . . still dripping with diseased papaya ooze.

Thank God there was an elevator that took you straight down to the underground parking garage. Without a word, Vladimir led her to what turned out to be Sergei's limousine, a tan Mercedes Maybach. She got into the capacious backseat and scrunched down into a corner, seeking invisibility. The only scenery she could see, as they went up a ramp and out onto Collins Avenue, was the back of the hairless white knob that was Vladimir's head behind the wheel.

::::::Vladimir, don't you say so much as one word to me.::::::

It turned out that she had nothing to fear on that score. So then she became paranoid.

::::::Sergei treated me like a cheap whore. What if this sinister automaton of his is not taking me home—but kidnapping me and holding me captive in some place I've never heard of where they'll force me to commit unspeakable acts?::::::

Now her eyes were fixed upon the landscape as it rolled by. Desperately she looked for reassuring landmarks. But she knew so little about the geography up here north of Miami Beach—

Thank God! The Fontainebleau came drifting past . . . they were on the right route . . . She stared again at Vladimir's noggin . . . A whole new rush of possible disasters began romping through her head... How was she going to live now?... Had she assumed somewhere in her head that Sergei was going to keep her the way Norman had?... It had never come to her before in just so many words. ::::::I was a kept woman all that time! It's true! I turned my back on my family and Nestor and everybody else because Norman was a television celebrity... *Some celebrity*... he let himself be used anytime TV pimps were looking for some egotist with a medical degree to turn on the pervert in every viewer with the hottest news about pornography addiction... while the rest of the fraternity of psychiatrists looks upon him as a publicity addict and social climber who would do anything to call attention to himself... including cheapening the profession... *¡Dios mío!* How do I let myself fall for these corrupt creeps?::::::

She was so ashamed, she had Vladimir let her out a block from her apartment. She didn't want anyone to see her coming home in this car. Why is that girl wearing last night's party clothes being returned to this Low-Rent (for Miami Beach) neighborhood this early in the morning in some rich man's limousine driven by some rich man's lumpy-bonehead automaton? Do we have to spell it out for you?

It was one of those miserable laundry-ironing-room Miami days. She walks one block and she already feels hot and sweaty and sorry for herself. She tries but can't hold the tears back. The mascara supposedly adding drama to her eye sockets is running down her cheekbones, which is no more than she deserves, the little whore.

::::::Please, God, don't let Amélia be home... Don't let her see me like this!:::::: She can't even *try* to fool Amélia... not on *this* subject. Magdalena barely has the door open and... Amélia is standing right there with her hands on her hips. She takes one look at Magdalena in the night-before black dress she lent her, and a what-have-we-here grin comes sneaking across her lips.

"And where have *we* been?" she said.

"Oh, you know where I've been—" And with that, Magdalena's leaky eyes opened wide, and her mouth fell ajar... and she *burst* into tears. Her sobs came out in regular paroxysms. She knew she had to tell Amélia the whole story, down to the most humiliating details... but at this moment that was the least of her concerns. What gripped her was fear.

"Come *on*," said Amélia. "Hey!—what's wrong?" She put her arms around Magdalena—and would never know how grateful her morose roommate was for that little embrace. Even if she were calm and composed, Magdalena would never find the words to express what Amélia's show of *protection* meant to her at that moment.

"Oh, my God, I feel so disgusting. That was the

worst *sob* night *sob* of *sob* my whole life! *sob sob sob sob.*" Her words were swimming against waves and waves of sobs.

"Tell me what happened," said Amélia.

sobbing sobbing sobbing "And I thought he was so *sob* cool *sob* and everything...and cultured *sob*... and like *sob* European *sob* and all and *sob* knew all these things about art *sob* and had all these good manners...and you wanna know what he really is?...He's the nastiest *pig* that ever lived! He sticks his dirty snout here *sob* and there *sob* and wherever he likes and then he treats me like *mierda!*"—a regular bucket of *sobs*—"I *feel* so filthy!" *sob sob sob sob*...

"But what *happened?*"

"He brings these two...*goons* of his into the bedroom, right into the bedroom, and I'm still in bed, and he's mad and yelling at them in Russian about something...and I'm thinking, 'Like I don't even exist'—but I exist, all right! *sob* I'm that piece of used *coño sob* over there *sob* in the bed *sob sob sob* and he's ordering them to throw the used *coño* out like the rest of the trash *sob* before it starts smelling *sob sob sob sob.* He freaked me out, Amélia...*totally freaked* me out...but it's worse than that. He's scary. All he says to me is 'Something's come up. Vladimir will drive you home.' That's it!—and we have just spent all night—'Vladimir will drive you home'! Vladimir is one of those goons...this big tall Russian with a shaved head . . . shaved right down to the bone . . . and that bald bone—it has all these lumps and bumps in it and no brains, just video game circuits . . . He's a robot, and whatever Sergei tells him to do, he does. He drove me back here without saying one word. He has his orders. Take this piece of used *coño* out and dump it. So he drives it here and dumps it . . . There's something—very wrong—there's something *evil* about that whole setup. It's scary, Amélia!"

She could tell Amélia was already bored by this recitation and couldn't think of anything cogent to say. Finally she came up with "Well, I don't really know anything about your Sergei other than—"

Magdalena laughed sourly and muttered, "*My* Sergei . . ."

"—what you've told me, but it sounds to me that for such a handsome, sophisticated oligarch-I-guess-he-is, he's got the heart of one of those Russian Cossacks who used to go around cutting off the hands of little children caught stealing bread."

Magdalena, genuinely startled: "Russian *Cossacks?*"

"Now, don't start panicking all over again! I swear there *aren't* any more Russian Cossacks," said Amélia. "Not even in Sunny Isles. I don't know why they suddenly popped into my head."

"Cutting off the hands of little children caught stealing bread . . ."

"Okay, okay," said Amélia. "I didn't mean to come up with such an extreme comparison... but you know what I mean..."

Just as Magdalena was about to say something, a chill ran through her body. She wondered if Amélia could tell she was trembling.

Toward evening, Nestor and Ghislaine were in the Korolyov Museum of Art studiously inspecting a painting about three feet high and two feet wide... A caption on the wall said, "Wassily Kandinsky, *Suprematist Composition XXIII,* 1919."

::::::What the hell is *that* supposed to be?:::::: Nestor wondered.

There was a big aquamarine brushstroke down *here* near the bottom and a smaller brushstroke up *there* in red... but a red dull as a brick. The two had nothing to do with each other, and in between them... a huge batch of narrow black lines, long, short, straight, bent, sickly, crippled, running over one another in promiscuous tangles but veering away from the occasional congestion of dots and dabs of every color you could imagine, so long as it clashed. ::::::Is this supposed to be *a joke* on a lot of serious people who think this is a great thing the public-spirited oligarch Sergei Korolyov has done for Miami?:::::: It was so crazy, Nestor couldn't help but lean close to Ghislaine and say... in the kind of hushed house voice:

"That's great, huh? Looks like an explosion in a sanitation dumpster!"

Ghislaine said nothing at first. Then she leaned close to Nestor and said in a pious tone, "Well, I don't think it's here because they hope you'll like it or you won't like it. It's more because it's a sort of milestone."

"A *milestone?*" said Nestor. "What kind of *milestone?*"

"A milestone in art history," she said. "I took a class last semester in early-twentieth-century art. Kandinsky and Malevich were the first two artists to do abstract paintings and nothing but abstract paintings."

That was a jolt. Nestor could tell that in her own mild, sweet way, without wanting to hurt his feelings, Ghislaine had rebuked him. Yeah! He hadn't figured out exactly how, in so many words, but she had rebuked him... in a hushed tone. What was it with all these reverent voices?... as if the Korolyov Museum were a church or a chapel. There must have been sixty or seventy people in the two rooms. They huddled reverently before this painting and that painting, the faithful did, and they communed... communed with what?... Wassily Kadinsky's ascendant soul?... or with Art itself, Art the All-in-One?...

It beat Nestor... These people treated art like a religion. The difference was that you could get away with joking about religion... You only had to think of all the ways people played with the Lord, the Savior, Heaven, Hell, the Outer Darkness, Satan, the Choir of Angels, Purgatory, the Messiah, Creeping Jesus... for humorous effect... In fact, there were plenty of people who wouldn't feel comfortable using them seriously... whereas with Art you didn't dare make fun of it... it was serious stuff... if you went around making would-be funny remarks... obviously you were a *palurdo*... a simpleton... a meathead unable to detect the self-demeaning clumsiness of your sacrilege... So *that* was it! *That* was why treating Kandinsky's *Suprematist Composition XXIII* as a big solemn joke was so unfunny, puerile, excruciatingly embarrassing... that was why Ghislaine couldn't just go along with it and emit a harmless little chuckle to lighten the load of his insensitivity and move on to some other subject... That, in turn, made him terribly aware of his lack of education.

It wasn't that people with college degrees were any smarter than other people. He knew so many retards with BAs after their names, he could publish a reference book called *Who's a Loser.* But along the way they picked up all this... *stuff* you needed for conversations. Magdalena used to call it "all that museum stuff," and that was his problem now. He didn't have—but he broke off that train of thought because he just couldn't have Magdalena on his mind. All he could think of now was that Ghislaine had rebuked him . . . in the mildest way she could think of, but she had *rebuked* him, and he was damned if he was just going to stand here in front of this piece-a-shit painting as the penitent rebuked little boy.

All at once he heard himself saying, "Well, I'm not here to love art. I'm here working on a case."

"You're—did you say *case?*" Ghislaine didn't know quite how to put it. "I mean, I thought you were . . ."

"You thought I'd been 'relieved of duty'? Right? I'm still relieved of duty, but what I'm doing here is a private investigation. It's about these paintings." He swept his hand in an arc, as if to take in every painting in the place. He knew he shouldn't say it, but this was a way to bury Ghislaine's *milestone* loftiness and all the rest of it. He leaned next to her ear and said, "These are all fakes, everything in both rooms."

"What?" said Ghislaine. "What do you mean, *fakes?*"

"I mean they're forgeries. Pretty good ones, I hear, but *forgeries,* every last one of them."

Nestor loved the startled look on her face. He had rocked her with that one. Whether or not he was a *palurdo* suddenly became irrelevant. He had hoisted the whole subject up to an infinitely more important plane...where art historians were little butterflies or insects.

"Yeah," he said, "I'm afraid that's true. They're forgeries, all right, and I know who Korolyov went to, to get them done, and I've been in the secret studio where he did them. What I've got to do is prove it. If they're fakes—" He shrugged, as if to say, "Then we won't have to waste time on that milestone stuff."

There you had it! His work, his expertise as a private investigator, made her rebuke seem silly and girlish—and only then did he realize he shouldn't have divulged *anything* about what he was doing. Now, on behalf of nothing but his wounded vanity, he had entrusted all this to a college girl he barely knew.

No! He *did* know her. She was transparent, and she was honest. He could *trust* her. He could tell that from the very start. Nevertheless...now that he had gone and done something foolish, it was time to get absolutely serious.

He gave her something just short of a Cop Look. "That's just between us, you and me, okay? You understand?"

He Cop-Looked at her until he got that pledge out of her. "Yes," she said in a tiny voice, almost a whimper, "I understand."

Now he felt guilty. The quickest way to alienate her—and lose her trust—would be to continue in this tough-guy mode. So he broke into the softest and most loving smile he could come up with. "Oh, I'm sorry," he said. "I didn't mean to sound so... so... serious and everything. If there's anyone I can trust, it's you. I absolutely—I just *know* that. I've known that from the start, and—"

He caught himself. From the start of *what* exactly? Now he was going overboard in the other direction.

"Anyway, you know what I mean... So that's the main reason I'm here. I figured I should actually *see* all this—and I figured it was a chance to see *you*. I can't begin to tell you how much it means to me that you're here."

Now the loving look he gave her was completely sincere. Having her by his side was a little bit of Heaven. For the first time, the words actually formed in his mind: "I'm in love with her."

¡Mierda!—his iPhone! He had turned off the ring and put it on vibrate and now it was hopping around in his pocket. The caller ID told him it was John Smith. So he shot a quick *Dios mío* look at Ghislaine and bolted out of the gallery and into the lobby and put both hands around the offending instrument and answered in an exceedingly hushed voice:

"Camacho."

"Nestor, where are you?" said the voice of John Smith. "You sound like you're underneath a load of sand."

"I'm in the museum. I thought I'd actually take a look at these—what we're talking about. I'm—"

John Smith trampled right over Nestor's voice: "Listen, Nestor, I just heard from Igor. He's in a bad way. He just read the article—or somebody read it to him."

"This late?"

"Somebody called him. I doubt Igor even *reads* English, and probably the same goes for his friends, whoever they might be. Anyway, he's really agitated. I thought at first he was mad at *me*. He probably *is,* but that wasn't what he was all worked up over. He's terrified. He thinks Korolyov's going to come get him. He really believes that. He's afraid they'll *ambush* him, ambush, as in *kill,* assassinate. He thinks they've already got the place staked out. He hasn't seen them, they haven't threatened him—he's paranoid in the extreme. I said, 'You think he'd come get you just because you made fun of his paintings?' He doesn't say anything for a minute. Then he says, 'No'—ready for this?—'because I'm the one who painted the pictures. Why did you have to print all that about me doing those pictures with my eyes closed? You've done this to me! You practically drew them a map,' and on and on. He's half crazed, Nestor... but he's admitted it!"

"He came right out and said he forged them? Was

anybody else listening to this conversation—or is it your word against his?"

"It's better than that," said John Smith. "I've got it all on tape—and he agreed to it. I told him he ought to have a record of every step of the way."

"But isn't he confessing to being a forger?"

"That's the least of his worries right now. He thinks they're coming after him. Besides, if you ask me, he's dying to have his great talent 'revealed.'"

::::::Jesús Cristo.:::::: Something about John Smith's enthusiasm, his joy in the hunt, his anticipation of a great journalistic coup, spooked Nestor. ::::::"dying"::::::"

20

The Witness

¡Caliente! Caliente baby... Got plenty fuego in yo' caja china... Means you needs a length a Hose put in it. ::::::*Jesus!* What time is it?:::::: Nestor rolled over to his iPhone and picked it up ::::::5:33 a.m.—*mierda*:::::: and growled as truculently as he had ever growled in his life: "Camacho."

The woman on the line said, "Nestor?" with a big question mark... She wasn't at all sure that this inhospitable animal voice was Nestor Camacho's.

"Yes," he said, in the tone of voice that conveys the message "Kindly disintegrate."

Feebly, almost tearfully, the woman said, "I'm sorry, Nestor, but I wouldn't call you like this unless I absolutely had to. It's me... Magdalena." Her voice began breaking. "You're the... only... person who... can *help me!*"

::::::*It's me... Magdalena!*::::::

A single memory swept in under the radar, which is to say subliminally, and suffused Nestor's nervous system without ever becoming a thought... *blip* Magdalena is dumping him on the street in Hialeah and speeding off so fast in her mysteriously acquired BMW that the tires are squealing and two wheels actually lift off the ground as she turns at the intersection to get away from him. It came in under the radar, but it did a good job of finishing off love, lust, libido, even sympathy... at 5:30 a.m.

"Nestor?... Are you there?"

"Yeah, I'm here," he said. "You have to admit this is pretty weird."

"What is?"

"Getting a call from you. Anyway, *¿qué pasa?*"

"I don't know if I can explain all this over the telephone, Nestor. Can't we meet—for coffee, breakfast... *anything?*"

"When?"

"Now!"

"Does it have to be right now? It's five-thirty in the morning. I went to bed at two."

"Oh, Nestor... if you never do an*uh-uh-uh-uh-uh-uh*ther thi-ing for me! I ne-e-ee-eed you now-ow-ow." Her words were breaking up into tears, even little words like *now* and *thing.* "I ca-a-n-n't sleep. I haven't slept all night. I'm so scared. Nestor! Please hel-l-lp me-ee-ee!"

As has been true throughout recorded history, rare is the strong man strong enough to shrug off a woman's tears... To that add Nestor's pride in his strength and—dare he even *think* it?—*valor* as a protector—the man on the mast about to plunge to his death... Hernandez about to be strangled by the giant in the crack house... the tears of a woman pleading for the Protector... He caved.

"Well... where?" he said. Both of them had roommates in apartments so small there would be no privacy. Okay; they should meet for coffee, but what was open this early? "Well, there's always Ricky's," said Nestor.

Magdalena was astounded. "You don't mean Ricky's in *Hialeah!*"

::::::Oh, but I do:::::: Nestor said to himself. The simple truth was the moment he said "Ricky's," the ambrosial smell of the pastelitos came back to him... and made him intensely hungry... which in turn convinced him that he couldn't possibly stay awake without Ricky's. All he said out loud was "I don't know any other place that opens at five-thirty a.m., and if I don't have something to eat, you're gonna have a zombie on your hands."

So they settled on Ricky's forty-five minutes from

now, which would be 6:15 a.m. Nestor couldn't hold back a profound sigh... followed by a profound groan... What was he doing?

Nestor had to park the Camaro two blocks away from Ricky's, and walking those two blocks reignited his many Hialeah resentments. In his mind not only his parents but his neighbors—he could see Mr. Ruiz snapping his fingers as if he had forgotten something and slipping back into his house so he wouldn't have to pass by El Traidor Nestor Camacho on the street—*all of Hialeah* had treated him like an embarrassment, or maybe a plain rat, after he rescued ::::::yes, I *saved* the man! I never even thought of arresting the man on the mast!... The only ones who gave me an even break were Cristy and Nicky at Ricky's::::::... and with that, the free-floating *lust* he had always had for Cristy *blipped* through his loins and gave him a mild lift.

Now he was on the sidewalk of that mean little row of rickety shops he'd have to pass on the way to Ricky's. Oh, yeah... there it all was... the stupid Santería shop where Magdalena's mother went to get all that voodoo rigmarole... Wouldn't you know it! Right there in the window was a three-foot-high ceramic Saint Lazarus, in the sickly, sallow shade of yellow that brought out the sickly brown-black leprosy lesions that covered his body.... Magdalena's mami... my *own* mami... Why does that woebegone leper make me think of *my* mami?... a woebegone soul living on the sufferance of others... She has to believe her *caudillo,* of course... but she *must* keep her son the traitor's love... and offers him, despite his transgressions, a nice soft pallet of pity... "I forgive you, my prodigal son, I forgive you"... *Disgusting* was what it was!

But now he gets his first whiff of the pastelitos, meaning Ricky's is just ahead. *Ambrosia!* He's at the door... he can *feel* his teeth cutting through the filo dough, he can *see* the filo dough shedding flakes as beautiful as tiny flowers, he can *taste* the ground beef and minced ham his teeth are delivering onto his very tongue upon a bed of filo petals. Now he goes inside... It seems like an eternity since he stood in this doorway, but nothing has changed. There's the big glass counter with its bulb-lit shelves of baked bread, muffins, cakes, and other sweet things. The little round tables and their old-fashioned bentwood chairs are still there—unoccupied, here at 6:15 in the morning. Okay, he'll sit there with Magdalena when she arrives... Above all, the rich aroma of the pastelitos! That's what Heaven will be like. Four men are at the counter waiting for their orders—construction workers, if Nestor has to guess. Two of them have on hard hats, and all four are wearing T-shirts, jeans, and work boots. Waiting... there's no sign of Cristy or Nicky—

—at that moment a coloratura cry from somewhere behind the counter: "Nestor!"

He can't see her yet, the counter is so high, but there's no mistaking that voice, soaring through some high-flying register. Mygod!—the way it fills Nestor with joy! He doesn't completely understand why at first. She stuck by him throughout all this, treating him as *him* and not some counter in a political game. True, true, but don't try to fool yourself, Nestor! You *want* her, don't you! So cute, so lively, so nicely put together in her small way, such a *gringa* among *gringas* with her spinning *gringa* hair, such a sweet, promising *socket,* my heavenly *gringa* socket, my Cristy!

"Cristy!" he sings out, *"mía gringa enamorada!"*

He's aroused by the very thought! He goes straight to the counter, pushes past the four construction workers as if they're air, sings out a happy greeting, a loud one—at the same time making sure it can be interpreted as a jocular voice: "Cristy, the one and only! You got any idea how much I miss you all the time?!"

Now he can see the very top of her *gringa* locks and her joking eyes—she knows how to play the game, too—*"Mío querido pobrecito,"* she says in a teasing voice, "you *missed* me? *Awwww,* just didn't know how to find me, did you? I'm only here every morning from five-thirty on."

She has stopped two steps from the counter—and her waiting construction worker customers—holding up a tray with two orders of pastelitos and coffee with her left hand and giving him a look of—if not love, something close to it. Nestor leans into the counter until his body is practically draped over it, so he can reach out near her with his right hand. She slides the tray up onto the counter without so much as a glance at the construction workers in order to take Nestor's hand into the grasp of both of hers. She gives it a playful squeeze and releases it. She's totally committed to him with her eyes.

"Yeah, *mía gringa,*" Nestor says, "the Department don't make it easy for me to get around anymore."

"Oh, people have told me about it."

"I don't doubt that, but whatta they *say* about it?" said Nestor.

A deep voice: "They say, 'Whyn'tchoo stop sniffing the girl and let her bring us our damned food.' "

It was one of the construction workers Nestor had just pushed past...without so much as a *por favor.* A good five inches taller than Nestor, this tub was, and God knows how much heavier...*americano* construction worker from top to bottom—the hard hat, the forehead slick with sweat, the full mustache worn with the accoutrement of an eight-day growth of beard that gave a grizzly look to his sweating jowls, the white T-shirt, now sweat stained the color of broth and stretched over a long expanse of flesh that rated the term "wrestler's gut," a pair of fleshy but thick arms, one with a so-called half-sleeve tattoo featuring a huge eagle surrounded by crows wrapped around his biceps and triceps, a pair of gray Gorilla-brand twill working stiff's pants, scuffed brown steel-toed boots, soles thick as a slice of roast beef—

Nestor was in such a good mood, thanks to Cristy, he would have been glad to laugh at the big lug's crack—which did have a valid point, after all—and let it pass...except for one word: *sniffing.* Especially coming from the working-stiff lips of a hulk like this one, it meant sniffing Cristy in a sexual way. Nestor ransacked his brain to find a reason why even that might be okay. He tried and he tried, but it wasn't okay. It was an insult...an insult he had to stomp to death on the spot. It was disrespectful to Cristy, too. As every cop on patrol knew, you couldn't wait. You had to shut big mouths *now.*

He stepped away from the counter and gave the *americano* a friendly smile, one you could easily interpret as a weak smile, and said, "We're old friends, Cristy and me, and we haven't seen each other for a long time." Then he broadened the smile until his upper lip curled up and bared his front teeth...and kept stretching that grin until his long canines—i.e., eyeteeth—made him look like a grinning dog on the verge of ripping open human flesh, as he added, "You got a sniffing *problem* with that?"

The two men locked eyes for what seemed like an eternity... Triceratops and allosaurus confronted each other on a cliff overlooking the Halusian Gulp... until the big *americano* looked down at his wristwatch and said, "Yeah, and I gotta be outta here and back on the site in ten minutes. You got a problem with *that?*"

Nestor nearly burst out laughing. "Not at all!" he said, chuckling. "Not at all!" The contest was over the moment the *americano* averted his eyes, supposedly to look down at his watch. The rest of it was double-talk... trying to save face.

Suddenly Cristy was looking right past Nestor in a significant way but not a happy way. "You have a visitor, Nestor."

Nestor turned around. It was Magdalena. He never dreamed that Cristy knew about him and Magdalena. Magdalena was dressed plainly, modestly, in jeans and a mannish long-sleeved, loose-fitting light-blue shirt buttoned at the wrists and not far from all the way up in front, simply, sensibly. Her face—what was it about her face? A big pair of dark glasses covered a lot of it. Even so, she looked so... pale. "Pale" was about as far as his analytical powers could take him. Men don't notice a girl's makeup until it's missing and even then have no idea what's missing. The Magdalena he knew always turned her eye sockets into dark shadowy backdrops that brought out her flashing big brown eyes. On her cheekbones she always wore blush. Nestor was innocent of any such sophisticated knowledge. She looked pale, that was all, pale and haggard—was that the word? She wasn't herself. Plainly, modestly, simply, and sensibly—they were not her, either. He walked right up to her and stared into—or rather, upon—a pair of impenetrable dark lenses. He saw his own dim, small reflection . . . and no sign of her at all.

"Well, it *is* you, isn't it." Amiably he said it, amiably but without emotion.

"Nestor," she said, "you're so kind to *do-oo thi-is.*" The *do* and the *this* nearly broke apart in sobs.

What should he do now? Console her with a hug? But God knew what teary outcome that would have. He also didn't want to greet her with an embrace right in front of Cristy. Shake hands? To greet Magdalena with a handshake, after all the time they had lain side by side over the past four years, was too wooden to contemplate. So he just said, "Here . . . why don't we sit down."

It was the little round table farthest from the counter. They sat down on the old bentwood chairs. He felt more awkward by the moment. She was as gorgeous as ever. But that didn't convert from an observation to an emotion. All he could think up to say was "What would you like? Coffee? A pastelito?"

"Just a *café cubana* for me."

She began to slide her chair back, as if to go to the counter herself, but Nestor stood up and motioned to her to stay seated. "I'll get it," he said. "It's my treat." The truth was, he *longed* to escape from the table. He was embarrassed. She was *so beautiful!* He wasn't swept away by lust but by awe. He had forgotten. Everyone would be staring at her. He flicked a glance toward the counter... and, yes, they were... the four construction workers, Cristy, even Ricky... Ricky *himself* had left the kitchen area long enough to gawk. Nestor began to get ideas of his own, but he wasn't going to dwell on any such ideas, was he? The fact that she had come back to him because she needed him now... the completely vulnerable look she gave him... these had nothing to do with lust, did they? But he could see—*see!*—as if it were all happening right now—he could *see* her the time he was lying in bed, and she was standing a couple of feet from him naked, except for a wisp of lace panties, and she gave him that teasing look she had at such moments, slowly slipping her fingers inside the elastic band—*that teasing look!*—and lowering them... *slowly* lowering them... until—

::::::But she's already betrayed you once, you imbecile! What makes you think she's changed? Just because she's boo-hooing for your help? What about Ghislaine? You haven't *done* anything... but you're just outside the door. How is *she* supposed to feel? But she wouldn't have to know, would she... Oh, some game that would be... there's not enough testosterone in your body to turn you into that much of a fool. Well... why not just go with the flow for a while? Great, Nestor! There you have the very battle cry of the fool!::::::

At the counter, Nicky brought him the two *cafés cubanas* he ordered. He didn't know Nicky nearly as well as Cristy, but she leaned her chin over the counter and cast her eyes at his table, then turned back to him and said, "So, that's Magdalena?"

He nodded yes, and she arched her eyebrows in an exaggerated and very knowing way. Did that mean that *everybody* knew about the two of them?

He returned to the table with the two coffees... and his first friendly smile. "Magdalena, you look terrific. You know that? You don't look like somebody worried to death." He continued smiling.

That didn't change her mood in the slightest. She hung her head. " 'Worried to death...' " she muttered... then she lifted her head and faced him. "Nestor... I'm *scared* to death! *Pleeease!*... I don't know of anybody, not a single soul, to tell me what to do, except you. You'll know because you used to be a policeman."

"I still am," he said, a bit more curtly than he meant to.

"But I thought—" She didn't know how to put it.

"You thought I had been thrown off the force. Right?"

"I guess I got confused. There are so many things written about you in the newspapers. Do you realize how many big stories they've written about you?"

Nestor shrugged. That was his outward response. Inside he tingled with vanity. ::::::I never thought about it that way before.::::::

"I was what's called 'relieved of duty.' I'm still a cop, but 'relieved of duty' is bad enough."

Magdalena obviously didn't understand. "Well... whatever it is, I trust you-oo-ooo"—her words rolled out on mere sobs—"Nes-tor-or-or-or."

"Thank you." Nestor tried to sound sincerely moved. "Why don't you go ahead and tell me what you're worried about."

She took off the dark glasses to wipe the tears from her eyes. ::::::*¡Dios mío!* They're all red and puffy... and she's so pale!:::::: She quickly put the glasses back on. She knew what she looked like. "This whole thing is driving me crazy." She snuffled back more tears.

"Look, you're gonna be all right! But first you gotta tell me what it *is*."

"All right, I'm sorry," she said. "Well, so yesterday I was in Sunny Isles visiting a friend of mine. He's always been so cool and aw-aw-aw-all tha-at—" She broke down again and began sobbing silently, lowering her head and muffling her nose and mouth with a napkin.

"Magdalena—come on now," said Nestor.

"I'm sorry, Nestor. I know I sound... paranoid or something. Anyway, I was visiting this friend of mine... he's very successful. He has this two-story apartment, like a penthouse, in a condo on the ocean. So I'm there in Sunny Isles, and we're just talking about one thing and another, and his phone ri-i-i-iings..."—she sobbed silently—"and from that moment on, my friend, who is always so cool and elegant and confident, becomes very nervous and all tensed up and angry—I mean, he's a different person... you know? He's yelling into the telephone in Russian. He's Russian himself. And pretty soon these two men show up. They looked like out-and-out thugs to me. One of them was really scary. He was a big tall guy with a completely shaved head, and his head was—it looked too small for a man as big as he was. It had these odd *shapes* to it, these sort of hills, like the mountains on the moon or something. It's hard to describe. Anyway, this big tall guy gives my friend a newspaper, yesterday's *Herald,* and it's turned to a particular page. I saw it later on. It was a long article about some Russian artist I never heard of who lives in Miami and does—"

::::::*Igor!*::::::

Nestor interrupted a little too excitedly. "What was his name, the artist?"

"I don't remember," said Magdalena. "Igor Something-or-other—I don't remember the last name—and now my friend is really mad and starts rushing around and giving orders and being abrupt with everybody, including me. He tells me I'm going home. He doesn't *ask* me or say *why*. He just orders one of the thugs to drive me home. All he says to me is 'Something's come up.' He doesn't offer me one clue what this is about. Then he goes into this little library in the next room and takes the two thugs in there with him, and he starts yelling at them—not actually yelling, but he's obviously mad—and then he starts sort of barking orders into the telephone. It's all in Russian, but this library has double doors, and they don't close them completely, and I can hear what they're saying even though I don't understand any of it, except for one thing, Hallandale. And then he and one of the thugs rush out, without any explanation. The other thug, the tall one with the shaved head—he's like a... a... a *robot*. He drives me home and doesn't say one word the whole time. It's all beginning to be... you know, weird and sort of spooky, the way he orders them around and they just take it. But... What's that look you're giving me, Nestor?"

"I'm just surprised, I guess," said Nestor. He was

conscious of breathing too fast. "And what's your friend's name?"

"Sergei Korolyov. You may have heard of him? He gave the Miami Museum of Art about a hundred million dollars' worth of paintings by famous Russian artists, and they named the whole museum after him."

Had he ever heard of Sergei Korolyov?!

In the throes of astonishment a wave of information compulsion—the compulsion to impress people with information you have and they would love to have but don't—the police investigator's best friend, in fact—the wave hit Nestor head-on.

Have I ever heard of Sergei Korolyov!

::::::You're gonna be *bowled over* by what I'm about to tell you:::::: but at the last moment another compulsion—a cop caution to guard information—brought him back from the edge.

"How did you meet this guy Korolyov?"

"At an art show. Anyway, he invited me to dinner."

"Where?"

"Some restaurant up in Hallandale," said Magdalena.

"And what was that like?"

"All that was fine. But being there with Sergei—" She hesitated, then added, "Korolyov . . . gave me a strange feeling." Nestor wondered if she had added the "Korolyov" so he wouldn't get the idea she had an intimate thing with the guy. "From the minute we got there, starting with the parking valets, everybody treated Sergei"—she paused again but must have decided that the "Korolyov" was too heavy to keep hauling into the conversation—"treated Sergei like a king, or maybe czar is the word, only not a czar even... more like a dictator...or a godfather. That was what started making me nervous, all this godfather stuff, not that I thought 'godfather' at the time. Everywhere we went in that place, as soon as he came close, everybody stopped whatever they were doing and—well, they might as well have been bowing to him. If he didn't like what somebody was saying, they'd turn around and say the opposite of what they'd just said—right away! I've never seen anything like it. There was some kind of famous Russian chess player there who was giving me a hard time—I still don't know why—and so Sergei ordered him to leave, and believe me, he *left!* Right away! Then he ordered the other six people at the table to move to another table—and they did—right away! A lot of it was embarrassing, but I have to admit it was sort of exciting to be with someone with so much power. But what I saw there was nothing compared to what happened yesterday."

Poof! the aura of his Manena and his Manena's good looks, and memories of life below the waist, vanished—*just like that.* Now all Nestor saw before him was . . . a *witness,* a woman who had seen Korolyov read John Smith's article about Igor and turn into a homicidal maniac right then and there, before her very eyes, and start ordering people around like World War III just broke out and start screaming into the phone about Hallandale and rush off with one of his goons . . . He looked at his watch: 6:40 a.m. Should he call John Smith or text him? Probably text him. But writing was not his greatest strength. The idea of tapping all this out with fingers on the glass face of an iPhone—

"Magdalena"—no longer Manena—"I'll be right back." He headed for the men's room, which was no bigger than a closet. Inside, he locked the door and made the call.

"Hel-lohhhh . . ."

"John, this is Nestor. I'm sorry to call you this early, but I just ran into an old friend—I'm in Hialeah, having breakfast—and she told me something you ought to know before you go in there for your meeting at the newspaper. They want an eyewitness? Well, here's an eyewitness." He proceeded to tell him what Magdalena had seen . . . the panic that rattled Korolyov "as soon as he read your story yesterday" . . . and the one word she had understood in a regular hurricane of Russian: *Hallandale.*

"All this may mean nothing," said Nestor, "but

I'm gonna drive up there to the condo and check on Igor."

"Nestor, that's awesome! Truly awesome. You know what you are, Nestor, you're a great man! I'm not kidding!"... John Smith gushed in that fashion for a while. "I worry about your being out in public" ::::::*your*:::::: "so much in broad daylight during the curfew hours—eight to six, right?"

"Yeah," said Nestor. "I guess I should play it a little safer."

"What'll they do if they catch you?"

Nestor went silent. He didn't like to think about it, much less talk about it... "I guess they'd... throw me off the force."

"Then is it all that important to go check on Igor *now?*"

"You're right, John... but I just gotta do it."

"I don't know... well, be careful, for godsake, will you?"

On the way back to the table, he started thinking it over... the Honey Pot and tailing Igor to the Alhambra Lakes Active Adults condo?... That was late at night, long after 6:00 p.m. So that was okay... But returning the next day, posing with John Smith as an inspector from "the Environment"? That was *insanity*. Maybe what saved him was the suit and tie. If he looked as weird in that outfit as he felt in it, then he was in no danger. In any case, taking that chance had paid off. They had discovered a whole wall of new Igor forgeries and had taken some great pictures...and here he was, returning to the Active Adults condo in blindingly bright Miami sunlight. Lil was no genius, but she was no dummy, either. What if by now she had figured it out...seen him on YouTube or on the network news...and wondered what a cop was doing there making out like he was from the Environment?

But something was propelling him to go back there anyway.

When he returned to the table, he managed to put on a cool face. The Witness's face was not cool at all. She kept looking here...looking there...all the while gnawing at the knuckle of her index finger...or that was what it looked like.

"Magdalena, don't keep thinking about the worst that can happen. Nothing at all has happened so far...but if you're really worried, why don't you move in with someone else for a few days?"

The look she gave him made him think she was waiting for him to say, "Why don't you move in with me?"...He had no urge at all...He couldn't see her lowering her panties anymore...He didn't *need* a witness in his tiny apartment...He looked at his watch..."Seven-fifteen." He said it aloud. "I've got forty-five minutes to get home before the curfew begins."

* * *

Nestor didn't actually think of driving home for a second. He was just keeping a Witness on an even keel. In fact, he headed straight for I-95 up to Hallandale.

He braked the Camaro down from sixty miles an hour to forty-five and not one m.p.h. faster—now that it was a couple of minutes past 8:00 a.m.... and all he needed was to do something stupid like getting himself pulled over by a state trooper for speeding and have his violation of the curfew come out that way. He was down closer to forty as he swung around that last big curve on Hallandale Beach Boulevard—

—and there it was, the Alhambra Lakes Home for Active Adults, baking a little harder beneath the great Miami heat lamp... crumbling a little more... the "terraces" sagging a little more and that much closer to giving up and plunging upon the concrete below in a pile. The place was silent as a tomb... Like 99-plus percent of the citizens of South Florida, Nestor had never seen a tomb... and "silent"—how would *he* know? From here inside the Camaro with the windows up and the air-conditioning struggling to push a gale through the vents, Nestor could hear nothing from outside. He just assumed it was silent. He thought of everybody in the Alhambra Lakes Home for Active Adults as—well, not as *dead* exactly, but they weren't what he would call alive, either. They were in Purgatory. In Nestor's take on how the nuns had explained Purgatory, it was a huge space... a space too big to be called a room... like those huge spaces in the Miami Convention Center... and all the newly dead souls milled about anxiously in that space, wondering what region of life after death God was going to dispatch them to... for eternity, which of course never ends.

Once more he parked in the visitors' parking zone nearest the highway and farthest from the building's main entrance. He was already wearing his darker-than-dark CVS wire-rim sunglasses... in the name of vanity, not subterfuge... but now he reached under the front seat and pulled out his white looks-like-woven-straw plastic porkpie hat with its big brim... in the name of disguise.

How long? Maybe five seconds?—after the air-conditioning turned off, a suffocating heat took over the Camaro's interior. When he got out, there was no fresh air... just stultifying heat from the great heat lamp. His clothes felt like they were made of blanket wool and leather, even his mock-gingham polyester shirt. He had picked it out to meet Magdalena because it had long sleeves. He didn't want to flex so much as an inch of Camacho muscles. His chino pants might as well have been leather. They were tailored so tight in the seat, every step he took seemed to squeeze more sweat out of the flesh of his crotch. A couple of times he looked down to see if it showed. The vast parking lot was a dazzle of sunlight flashing off metal trim, so much so that the cars became mere shapes and shadows—even when peered upon through darker-than-dark cop shades. By squinting he was able to make out Igor's Vulcan SUV. Well, he hadn't gone off somewhere, in any case—not that he was in any mood to venture out into public, from the way John Smith described his paranoia. Uh-oh, up at the curb near the entrance there were two police cruisers from the Broward County Sheriff's Office. That was all he needed... some cops standing around who could easily recognize, cop shades and all, the curfew-coshing, relieved-of-duty Miami cop who had insisted on getting himself a lot of publicity—most recently bad.

As he approached the police cars, he turned his head and his big-brimmed hat away from them, as if for some inconceivable reason he were inspecting the cheap painted bricks of the facade. He could hear such a clatter of aluminum walkers, he wondered if a crowd of them was heading to breakfast... but that couldn't be... the active adults always amassed for meals at the earliest possible hour. There certainly wouldn't be so many of them heading for breakfast after 8:00 a.m. When he went inside, quite a lot of them were standing or clattering about the lobby, talking to one another... or whispering to one another as closely as they could get to one another's ears. *¡Santa Barranza!* Not twenty feet away from him was Phyllis, the fill-in superintendent. She might recognize him. The last thing he needed was to get entangled with someone like her... absolutely humorless and by nature a hard case... More aluminum walkers, clattering from one side to the other, were crowded into the opening that led into the courtyard. But nobody seemed to be going in. It was as if all the walkers had become entangled and choked the opening. Quite a buzz of conversation, too... a mass of old women clanking and buzzing and buzzing and clanking. No use trying to go in that way. Nestor ducked into the elevator and went up to Igor's floor, the second... He emerged onto the catwalk... there was more buzzing and clanking and clanking and buzzing. He couldn't remember seeing this much activity on a catwalk the first time he was here during the day... He began walking toward Igor's apartment... slowly and gingerly.

"Look, Edith—right there—it's one a them from the Environment... You don't believe me, then who is that?!"

It was from slightly up ahead. He immediately recognized the voice as big Lil's and now he spotted them... Warily he started walking toward them... and they came walking and clattering toward *him*.

Lil looked as hearty as ever. As usual Edith was hunched over her walker, but now she was clanking and clattering along at quite a pace.

Even from this far away Nestor could hear Edith saying, "*Now* he comes . . . *after* the smell goes away."

"So where's the tall one?" said Lil. "He's the one with all the—" She broke it off and tapped her forehead with her forefinger.

::::::Thanks:::::: Nestor said to himself. ::::::Why did she say "all"?:::::: He couldn't remember what he'd said last time or if he'd said anything.

Lil came straight up to him. Without so much as a hello she said, "So *now* they send you back—we have to drop dead first, and then maybe you show up."

Nestor stood there and shrugged and started to say, "That's not necessary"—but he got no further than the—"*ne*—"

"Can you believe this?" said Lil. "This I never heard of in my life. We get heart attacks here. We get strokes. People fall. They break their hips. They break an arm. But a neck?! Who ever heard of such a thing? And falling all the way down to the bottom. Mygod, mygod, what a terrible thing. Such a thing to happen here. Such a shock. I don't know what to tell you."

"I don't—who broke a neck?" said Nestor.

Edith piped up from about Nestor's waist level, "*Who?* . . . Am I hearing right? Over at the Environment they send you all the way over here, but *why* they forget to tell you?" She looked up at Lil and tapped her own forehead.

"But *who!?*" said Nestor.

"The *artist,*" she said in the slow, emphatic pronunciation one puts on for dense people who just don't get it. "The one with the turpentine and he couldn't draw, the poor man."

Nestor was so shocked, he heard a sound like a rush of steam in his ears. He couldn't shut it off. The feeling in his brain—a wave of guilt he was too shocked to analyze. He looked at Lil. Why Lil and not Edith he couldn't explain, either. He could only *feel* that Edith was too small and twisted to be trusted.

"When was this?" he said to Lil. "What happened?"

"During the night sometime, it hadda be, the poor soul. Exactly when? Exactly when I don't know. Everybody they talk to, nobody knows. But a broken neck—he's right down there on the concrete. If you could see through this floor, he's right underneath your feet, if—"

Nestor recognized it, the same feeling he almost gave way to when he was talking to Magdalena earlier and was *dying* to tell her what she didn't know about Korolyov. Information compulsion. Lil was now in its thrall. It seemed that someone had found Igor's body at the bottom of the stairs just before dawn. He had tumbled down headfirst. Anybody could see his neck was broken. The rest of his body lay twisted about on the steps just above it. Rigor mortis had begun to set in by the time they found him. He still reeked with alcohol. Wasn't hard to add up two and two, was it. By the time Lil woke up, the police were already here... and tenants were already out on the catwalks, chattering and clattering and pointing... a regular percussion concert for aluminum walkers. At first they all clattered to the courtyard, where you could get the best view. Igor's body—or "Nicolai's," as Lil put it—was at the bottom of the stairway from the second level to the courtyard level. Right away, the police put a blanket over the body but left it the way it was, all twisted and broken. Why didn't they take the poor man's body away and stretch it out horizontal and give what was left of him a little dignity? But he was still there, and the police were standing around doing nothing but putting up yellow crime-scene tape that you see in the movies. Same thing. They taped off the stairway, so nobody could go up or down. Then they built a whole fence of yellow tape in the courtyard to keep people from getting too close to the body, there were so many nosy people in the courtyard. Then they shooed them all out and began putting tape across every opening to the courtyard.

"Take a look. You see right there?" said Lil. "The

tops of the stairway?...That's the tape. And over *there?*"

She was pointing past the stairway. For the first time Nestor could see a fence of yellow tape around the entrance to an apartment...Igor's. Two bored cops stood nearby. "You should take a look!" Lil said with enthusiasm. "A good look. Things like that you don't see around here. A big piece a tape, *this wide*"—about six inches—"they glued it over the handle to the door and the keyhole. And on the piece a tape? The writing you can't see from here. It's a warning about how the tape—don't mess with it. You ever see such a thing? A good look you should get. I got here before they put that big piece a tape, and the door was still open. They had a whole bunch a cops in there. Looked the same as it was when we saw it, except all those pictures were gone from that wall."

"They were *gone?!*" said Nestor. He hadn't meant to reveal such surprise. "You're sure?"

"Of *course* I'm sure. The ones in a line on that long wall. *Them* I woulda noticed, they were so bad. Maybe the poor man couldn't stand them. Maybe he threw them out. Pictures like that, I had them on *my* wall, I woulda started drinking, too... the poor soul," she added, so as not to speak ill of the dead.

"They're *gone*..." said Nestor, as much to himself as to her.

Just then one of the cops turned, and Nestor

thought he was looking right at him. *¡Mierda!* Maybe it was because he was so much younger than anybody else up here on the catwalk. Or maybe—the first one must have said something to the other one, because now they were both looking right at him. He wanted to pull his plastic straw hat down over his face, but that would only make it worse.

"I wanna see it from over there," Nestor said to Lil. He indicated the opposite side of the catwalk.

"Over *there?* Straight *there* you should go for a good look," said Lil, indicating the yellow tape around Igor's doorway.

"No... first I go over *there,*" said Nestor. He hoped he didn't sound as frightened as he really was. He wheeled about to leave, but not before Lil glanced sideways at Edith. He could see the striations in her neck as she lowered her lips on one side, as if to say, "The boy's a nut job."

He tried to walk nonchalantly in a crouch that would keep him below the eye level of the aluminum walker gawkers and the rest of the spectators up here. Walking nonchalantly in a crouch—it couldn't be done. The active adults were staring at him. He must have looked like a prowler or something. So he stood up... and now he could see all too well the hulk down there, shrouded, misshapen... Igor?... the living person he had tailed back to this "secret" place of his?... He felt himself sinking helplessly—*too late* to do anything about it!—into a sump of sheer guilt... He had *"tailed"* him, and that was the first step, wasn't it! ::::::Please, Dios, let it be that he got drunk and fell down the stairs of his own accord... He was just a forger! He didn't deserve to be struck dead! And *I* started it, and—wait a minute... what am I talking about? I didn't tell Igor to start forging pictures... I didn't tell him to aid and abet some outrageous Russian con man... I didn't tell him to set up a secret studio in some Active Adults condo in Hallandale... I didn't tell him to become an alcoholic and drink his vodaprikas all day long... I didn't tell him to go to the Honey Pot and pay for whores.:::::: By and by, staring at the crumpled dead hulk of Igor, Nestor worked it out in his mind... He hadn't created Igor and turned him over to a bunch of homicidal thugs... By and by he had absolved himself... without divine intervention, but *Dios mío, all—*

—all four cops in the courtyard were staring up at him as he had been staring down at the remains of Igor... a bunch of Anglos these Broward County cops were, too!... They'd be happy to turn him in. ::::::Am I getting paranoid?... But they *are* looking at me, just like the two at Igor's door, right? I'm bailing!::::::

Nestor crouched again, but this time he made no pretense of being nonchalant. He scuttled to the elevator and went to the ground floor—halfway expecting Broward County cops to be waiting for him at the elevator door...He *was* getting jumpy, wasn't he?!...He tried not to walk *too* fast toward the lot near the highway, where he had left the Camaro... and practically laid down rubber getting out of there. ::::::I don't believe this! This is what it feels like to be a hunted man!::::::

Driving east on Hallandale Beach Boulevard toward Sunny Isles he began to pull himself together. ::::::Get home! That's the main thing. Actually *be there,* in case they send somebody around to check.:::::: Nevertheless, he had to find a pay phone and make one call...now. If he used his iPhone, they'd know who he was and where he was in half a second...but where innanamea*dios* was there a pay phone? It was as if pay phones had disappeared from the face of the earth...or Hallandale, whichever...Miles drifted by...His eyes searched every gasoline station, every shopping strip, every motel parking apron, every drive-through restaurant, the Broward County water authority grounds, even utterly hopeless cases...a little one-story store with cheap garden statuary all over the lawns, unicorns, bears—big ones—cherubs, elves, Abraham Lincoln, two Virgin Marys, a plaster flying fish, a plaster Indian with a plaster headdress—

Finally, some sort of nightclub by the side of the road...called Gogol's...The parking lot was empty, but in the corner nearest the club—a pay phone.

Thank God he had change. He had to call Information for the number of the Broward County Sheriff's Office... and after more coins, they threw him in voice mail jail. The recorded voice of a woman said: "You have reached the Broward County Sheriff's Office. Please listen carefully. For emergencies, press zero-zero... to report non-emergency incidents, press two... for billing and accounting, press three... for human resources, press four"... until at last... a human voice: "Homicide. Lieutenant Canter."

"Lieutenant," said Nestor, "I have some good information for you. You have something to record this with?"

"Who's calling?"

"I'm sorry, Lieutenant, all I can give you is the information, but it's good information."

A pause. "Okay... go ahead."

"As soon as the ME gets there—" Uh-oh, "ME" sounded too cop-like. He rephrased it, "The medical examiner"—but that didn't help much... still too much cop knowledge. By now the lieutenant must have pushed the rocker switch to the tape recorder—"After the medical examiner arrives and gets finished, you'll be getting an ambulance with a corpse tagged"—he spoke very slowly—"Ni-co-lai Ko-pin-sky... Okay?... from the Alhambra Lakes Home for Active Adults. His real name is I-gor Dru-ko-vich... Okay? He's an artist with a telephone listing in Miami. He apparently broke his neck in a fall down a stairway. But the ME... uhh..."—oh, the hell with it... he just left it at ME—"shouldn't take that at face value. He should do an autopsy to determine if it was an accident... or something else... Okay? The paintings he did... *uhhh*... he did them in the exact style of famous artists—and we're talking *exact* here, Lieutenant—twelve of 'em are missing from his apartment at the condo—"

With that, Nestor hung up abruptly. He jumped into the Camaro and gunned it, heading back to Miami. ::::::Am I crazy? I can't go "gunning it" anywhere. *I'm a wanted man!* a *hunted* man, for all I know. All I need is some Broward County trooper to haul me in for speeding... *speeding!*::::::

He slowed the Camaro to the wanted-man speed of just a shade below the speed limit. He let his breath out and became conscious of his heart beating too fast.

Mierda! The clock on the dashboard... way after 8:00 a.m.! The *curfew*—but also John Smith!... must be in his big meeting at the *Herald* by now—

This one Nestor could make on his iPhone while he drove... He had John Smith's number in his contacts list... *¡Dios mío!* All he needed *now* was for some Broward County cop *palurdo americano* to pull him over for driving while using a handheld device... He looked into the rearview mirror... and then the two side wing mirrors . . . then scanned the road ahead . . . the road and the shoulders . . . a chance he had to take. The wanted man tapped out the number on the glass face of the iPhone—

It was just a figure of speech, of course—"they've really got the noose around my neck now"—but Ed Topping could actually feel a constriction in his neck . . . or his throat, in any event. Things had progressed to where he couldn't very well expect John Smith to discuss all this standing up. Oh no, this time, the three of them—John Smith, Stan Friedman, and himself—were seated at a round table near his desk. And there was a fourth: the *Herald*'s number one libel lawyer, Ira Cutler. He was a man in his early fifties, probably, one of those late-middle-aged men who still had smooth jowls, big ones, and smooth bellies that looked inflated not by age but by the vitality, the ambition and ravenous appetites of youth. He reminded Ed of the portraits of great men in the eighteenth century by the Peale brothers, who always gave their subjects smooth, stout stomachs as a sign of success and vigor. Belly, jowls, shiny fingernails, ironed white shirt, and all, Ira Cutler was a well-dressed, well-fed, highly buffed pit bull when it came to legal questions, and he loved litigation, especially in the courtroom, where he could insult people to their faces, humiliate them, break their spirits, ruin their reputations, make them cry, sob, blubber, boohoo... and it was all sanctioned. He had it in him to stop this six-foot-two baby, John Smith, in his tracks. There was something really crude about Cutler. Edward T. Topping IV would not like to have him to dinner or anywhere else his drooling-pit-bull persona might reflect badly upon the House of Topping... but he was welcome to be on his worst behavior at this table.

"Well, gentlemen... let's get things under way," said Ed. He looked at each of the other three, supposedly to see if they were "on board," as the phrase goes, but actually to make them recognize his authority, which was in fact wilting in the presence of this tough guy. His T-4 gaze settled, as best he could make it settle, upon John Smith. "Why don't you tell us about this latest piece of information you have." Report in, soldier—that was the aura Ed wanted his leadership to establish.

"As I told you, sir, I think we have the sort of eyewitness information our case lacked. The off-duty policeman who's been helping me in this, Nestor Camacho, ran into an old girlfriend who happened to be visiting Sergei Korolyov when he read our story yesterday about the painter, Igor Drukovich, who we think forged the paintings Korolyov gave to the museum. She described Korolyov's reaction—"

Ira Cutler broke in. He spoke in a curiously high-pitched voice. "Wait a minute... Camacho... Isn't that the name of the cop who got fired recently for making racial remarks?"

"He wasn't *fired,* sir, he was 'relieved of duty.' That means they take the cop's badge and service revolver away until they investigate the case."

"Ummm... I see," said Cutler... in the tone that says, "I *don't* see, but go ahead. We can come back to this bigot later."

"Anyway," said John Smith, "this woman, a friend of his"—and he went on to describe the scene, Korolyov's panic and the rest of it, as relayed by Nestor.

Ed looked at Cutler. Cutler said, "First of all, that's not an eyewitness's account. It's corroborating evidence, but an eyewitness is somebody who actually saw the crime while it was taking place. It's information you can use in making a case, but it's not eyewitness evidence."

Ed said to himself, ::::::Thank God for you, Cutler! Nobody's throwing any knuckleballs past *you,* baby!:::::: It was all he could do to suppress a smile. He lifted his chin and looked at John Smith. What a look it was! It came with the bearing of a tolerant-up-to-a-point leader. "Tell Mr. Cutler what else you have." ::::::Now that he's blown your big one out of the sky.::::::

John Smith turned to Igor's outright confession that he had forged the paintings. He told of the photographs he had of Igor's forgeries-in-the-making... and his revealing all the steps Korolyov had taken to give the paintings a lock-tight authentic provenance, including the name of the German expert and the trip to Stuttgart to pay him off. He told him about the sub-forgery, so to speak, of a catalogue from a hundred years ago, printed on paper from the period... the catalogue was a work of art in its own corrupt way. John Smith paid an un–John Smithly lyrical tribute to the skill it took to fabricate it... finding paper from a hundred years ago, duplicating binding eccentricities, out-of-date photo-reproduction processes, even rhetorical quirks from the period... In fact, it was all so un–John Smithly lyrical, the catalogue seemed to rise up from out of its ankle-sucking sleaze into some Dionysian eminence far above the scales of right and wrong...

When John Smith finished, Ed looked at his salvation, a man immune to childish ambitions and emotions... Lawyer Cutler. Stan Friedman and John Smith himself fixed their eyes, too, upon the pit bull with the law degree.

The unassailable arbiter leaned forward and thrust his elbows and forearms on the top of the table and looked at each of them in turn with an expression of absolute canine dominance... canine, insofar as a middle-aged man with jowls, a belly, a newly laundered and crisply ironed white shirt, and a fine Italian silk necktie could actually look like a pit bull. Then he spoke:

"Based on what you've told me . . . there is no way you can run a story saying that Korolyov has done this or done that, other than give these paintings to the museum, not even on the basis of the forger's admissions. Your man, Drukovich, seems *eager* to take credit for his own talent and audaciousness. That's typical of hoaxers of any sort. Besides that, he's an out-and-out drunk and obnoxiously proud of what he's done."

::::::Yes! I *knew* I could count on you! You're a realist in the midst of these juveniles who have virtually nothing to lose, no matter what we run . . . whereas I—I have everything to lose . . . such as my career, my livelihood . . . all to the music of my wife's unending scorn. I can just hear her, "You've always had your shiftless and trifling tendencies—but my God! do you have to take it up to this level? Do you have to libel a leading citizen, a man so generous they rename a museum for him and carve his name in marble letters *this big* and *this deep* on the face of the museum, and the Mayor and half of the other eminent citizens of Greater Miami—including my shiftless, trifling, used-to-be-eminent, self-destroyed husband—all these eminent people come to a banquet in his honor, and now you're intent upon making them look like dupes, fools, marks, hooples, hicks—all because of some newborn post-puppy's ideals of a free press with a mission to fearlessly inform . . . and make a name for his Yale-educated self and his self-educated ego—well, I hope your own trifling, shiftless ego is happy now! Your *freedom of the press,* your *mission* of the press, oh, you sentinel of the citizenry, you, who keeps watch while they sleep—*yaghhhhhn!* you incompetent dope, who was about to take his first big step as a big-time newspaper editor—first big step . . . oh, yes! . . . into the worst car wreck imaginable *yaghhhhhhhh!*" God bless you, Ira Cutler! You saved me from the weakest side of myself! On this subject there is no higher power than—::::::

Ira Cutler's voice broke in. "You can't afford to *accuse* Korolyov of anything—"

::::::Yes! Tell 'em, brother! Tell 'em where it's at!::::::

"—because you lack sufficient objective evidence and have no eyewitness. You can't even indicate that Korolyov is to *blame* for any of it—"

::::::Oh, testify, brother! Draw 'em a map of the straight and narrow!::::::

An enormous weight slid from his shoulders . . . The monkey jumped off his back. Finally he could let his breath out! ::::::There *is* a God in Heaven! I'm freed from the—::::::

The high-pitched voice of the pit bull sounded again: "On the other hand, you've got some strong material there, and you've nailed down the facts you have pretty well, it seems to me. Whatshisname—Igor?—says he forged the paintings, and you've got that on tape. That's what he said. You've established the fact that the same Russian painter goes by two names, Igor in the city and Nicolai in the country—"

::::::But what's going on? What is this "on the other hand" business all of a sudden?...and this "strong material" stuff? My pit bull is cutting the ground out from under me with his hind legs? Stick to your guns! Stick to your guns, you miserable hound!::::::

"—and he has a secret studio in an old-age condominium in Hallandale, which is north of nowhere," Cutler was saying, "and you can use that material, so long as (a) this guy was aware you were taping it, and (b) you don't write it so that it looks like your sole purpose in going to all this trouble has been to expose Korolyov as a fraud." He looked at John Smith and said, "I understand you've tried to get in touch with Korolyov, John."

::::::"John" he calls him, and I know he's never laid eyes on him before. But he sees him for what he is—a kid! A kid playing with fire! Just a kid!::::::

"Yes, sir," said John Smith. "I've left—"

He broke it off because a cell phone began ringing somewhere in his clothes. He dug it out of the inside jacket pocket and looked at the caller ID. Before answering he bolted upright and—looked at Counselor Cutler and said, "I'm sorry . . . sir . . . but I have to take this." He went to a corner of the office and nestled his face so closely into it that one cheek was mashed against the interior wall and the other against the exterior glass wall, even with the BlackBerry squeezed in between.

The first thing they heard after "Hello" was John Smith saying, "Jesus!" in something close to a moan, a very much un–John Smithly "Jesus" and even more un–John Smithly moan. Then he went, "Ooooo-ouh!" as if he had just been punched in the pit of his stomach. Nobody could imagine such sounds coming out of John Smith's body. He stayed in the corner for what seemed like forever but was more likely twenty or thirty seconds. Then in a soft, polite tone, he said, "Thank you, Nestor."

John Smith had a pale complexion, but when he turned around, he was as white as a corpse. All the blood had drained from his face. He stood stock-still and said in a hopelessly defeated voice, "That was my best source. He's in Hallandale. They just found Igor Drukovich dead at the bottom of a stairway. His neck was broken."

::::::Damn!:::::: said Ed to himself. He knew what

that meant . . . There was no way he could *not* run the story now . . . and Sergei Korolyov's name was cut in stone on the front of the museum . . . and he had sat just two seats from him at dinner! ::::::And now there's no way I can get out of risking *my* neck. Fearless Journalist Ed Topping . . . Damn! and damn again!::::::

21

The Knight of Hialeah

Barely 6:45 a.m.—and all was uproar in the office of Edward T. Topping IV. Too many people in here! Too much noise! He hadn't had time to take so much as a glance at that great symbol of his eminence, his glass-wall view of Biscayne Bay, Miami Beach, the Atlantic Ocean, 180 degrees of blue horizon, and a billion tiny glints flashing off the water as the great Heat Lamp above began to amp up the juice. He hadn't even been able to sit down at his desk, not once, unless you counted leaning his long bony haunches against the edge of it from time to time.

He had a telephone receiver at his ear and his eyes fixed upon the screen of his Apple ZBe3 computer. Impatient, frantic, even panicked calls, texts, tweets, twits, and e-screams were hurricaning in from all over the country... all over the world, in fact... from an anguished art dealer in Vancouver, where it was 3:45 a.m., some art fair impresario from Art Basel in Switzerland, where it was 12:45 p.m., an auction house in Tokyo, where it was a quarter of eight at night, and an anguished—no, panicked-to-the-point-of-screaming—private collector in Wellington, New Zealand, where it was just a few minutes from tomorrow, and every sort of news organization, including British, French, German, Italian, and Japanese television, quite in addition to every sort of old, cable, and inter network in America. CBS had a camera crew waiting in the lobby downstairs—at 6:45 a.m.!

John Smith's story had just broken. The *Herald* had published it online at six o'clock last night to establish priority—i.e., a scoop. Six hours later it came out in the newspaper's first edition beneath two words in capital letters, two inches high and bold and black as a tabloid's and stretching all the way across the front page:

DEADLY COINCIDENCE

Every hotshot in the Chicago Loop Syndicate who was desperate to be "where things are happening" had boarded one of the Loop's three Falcon jets as soon as the story broke online and had taken off for Miami. Where things were happening was in the office of the *Herald*'s editor in chief, Edward T. Topping IV. In there right now were eight—or was it nine!—Loop executives, including the CEO, Puggy Knobloch, plus Ed himself, Ira Cutler, and Adlai desPortes, the *Herald*'s new publisher. For some reason the city editor, Stan Friedman, and John Smith, the man of the hour, had stepped out for a moment. The most intoxicating chemical known to man—adrenaline—was pumping through the room in waves waves waves waves, making the Loop troupe feel they had inside-the-belly box seats for one of the biggest stories of the twenty-first century: A new $220 million art museum, the anchor of a huge metropolitan cultural complex, is named for a Russian "oligarch" following his extraordinary gift of "seventy million dollars'" worth of paintings. Master masons have long since carved his name in marble over the entrance—THE KOROLYOV MUSEUM OF ART—and now, look at us at this moment, here in this office. We are the maximum leaders. It is our journalists who have just exposed this great "donor" as a fraud.

Decibels above the hubbub and the buzz of any place where things are happening, Ed could hear Puggy Knobloch's loud, ripe honk honking out, "*Haaaghh*—the old lady thinks 'the Environment' is the name of a government agency!?" *Haaaghh!* was Puggy's laugh. It was like a bark. It drowned out every other sound—for about half a second—as if to say, "You think that's funny? Okay, here's your reward: *Haaaghh!*"

Oh, the adrenaline pumped pumped pumped!

Another voice rose above the rumble and the roar. Attorney Ira Cutler's. You couldn't miss it, not that voice. It was like the whine of a metal lathe. He was holding up the newspaper, with its gigantic DEADLY COINCIDENCE, before the eyeballs of Puggy Knobloch.

"Here! Read the lead!" said Ira Cutler. "Read the first two paragraphs."

He tried to hand the newspaper to Knobloch, but Knobloch raised his big meaty hands, palms outward, to reject it. He looked offended. "You think I haven't read it?"—in a tone that said, <<<Good God, man, you *really* don't know who you're talking to in such an impudent way?>>>

But that didn't stop Cutler for a second. He had immobilized the maximum leader with his laser stare and his ceaseless, insistent, rat-tat-tat-tat-tat of words. He jerked the newspaper back and said, "Here! I'll read it for you.

" 'Deadly Coincidence,' it says, and right below that, 'By Dusk, He Claims He Forged Museum's Treasures. By Dawn—He's Dead'...and then the byline, 'By John Smith.' And then it says,

" 'Just hours after Wynwood artist Igor Drukovich called the *Herald* claiming he forged the estimated

$70 million in Russian Modernist paintings now in the Korolyov Museum of Art—the core of its collection—he was found dead this morning at dawn. His neck was broken.

"'His body lay sprawled headfirst at the bottom of a flight of stairs in a senior citizens condominium in Hallandale—where he maintained, the *Herald* has learned, a secret studio, under the name Nicolai Kopinsky.'"

The pit bull lowered the newspaper, gleaming with self-commendation. "You get it, Puggy?" he crowed to Knobloch. "Got the picture now? You follow the strategy? We don't *accuse* Sergei Korolyov of *anything*. The museum that owns the pictures just happens to bear his name, that's all." Cutler gave a mock shrug. "Not much we could do about that, was there. You get the key word: *claim?* I had a hard time getting it across to John Smith. He wanted to use words like Drukovich *revealed* the forgery or *confessed* or *described how* or other words that might indicate we *assume* Drukovich is telling the truth. No, I saw to it we used a word that can more easily be taken to mean we're skeptical: He *claims* he forged them...that's what he *claims*...It took me an hour to knock some sense into the kid."

Oh, Ed remembered all that. ::::::We—me included—put poor John Smith through a real nosebleeder.:::::: A nosebleeder was what you called it when everybody is leaning over the shoulder of the reporter as he writes. If he should suddenly lift his head up straight, he would give somebody a bloody nose.

Ah, but the adrenaline pumps pumps pumps pumps for the unknown as well—combat! How will the con man respond? How will he fight? Who will he attack—and with what?

Shortly before 8:00 a.m. the intoxication of being *where things are happening* was pumping up to the max, when Stan Friedman popped back into the room. This time he was not thrilled. He was carrying a white envelope...and his face had turned very glum. He brought that grim visage and the envelope straight to the *Herald*'s publisher, Adlai desPortes, who until that moment had been enjoying the greatest adrenaline high of his life. Friedman immediately ducked out of the room again. Publisher desPortes read the letter, which was apparently not long, and very soon he brought the letter and his own glum face straight to Ed. Ed read it and ::::::Jesus Christ! Exactly what does *this* mean?:::::: he took the letter and his glum—no, not glum, *petrified*—face straight to Ira Cutler, and the room began to grow quiet. Everyone realized that Gloom had entered the room, and it grew quieter still.

Ed realized how weak and confused this made him look. *Owww*. It was time for him to step forward and show leadership. He raised his voice and said in what he intended to be the key of casual and lighthearted: "Hey, everybody, Ira here has some late-breaking news." He waited for and never got a reaction to the casual and lighthearted *mot—late-breaking*—left over from the twentieth century. "We have word by messenger from the other side!" No sign of casual, light hearts in the room. "Ira, why don't you read that letter out loud for us."

The room didn't seem anywhere near as blasé as Ed meant that to sound.

"Oh, kaaay," said Cutler. "What have we here?" It was always a surprise to hear the high pitch of the pit bull's voice, especially in front of this many people. "Let's see...let's see...let's see...what we have here is...This communication seems to be from...the law firm of Solipsky, Gudder, Kramer, Mangelmann, and Pizzonia. It is addressed to Mr. Adlai desPortes, Publisher, the *Miami Herald,* One Herald Plaza et cetera, et cetera...hmmmm...hmm...and so forth.

"'Dear Mr. desPortes, We represent Mr. Sergei Korolyov, subject of a front-page article in today's edition of the *Miami Herald*. Your scurrilous and highly libelous depiction of Mr. Korolyov has already been repeated worldwide in print and electronic media. With patently false data and unconscionable insinuations, you have maligned the reputation of one of Greater Miami's most civic-minded, generous, and highly respected citizens. You have relied heavily upon the fabrications, and, quite possibly, hallucinations, of an individual known to be suffering from an advanced stage of alcoholism. You have used your high position in a reckless, malicious, totally irresponsible way, and, depending upon the validity, if any, of certain assertions, felonious, as well. If you will publish an immediate retraction of this calumny-laden "story" and an apology for it, Mr. Korolyov will regard that as an ameliorating factor. Yours very truly, Julius M. Gudder, of counsel, Solipsky, Gudder, Kramer, Mangelmann, and Pizzonia.' "

Cutler narrowed his eyes and surveyed the room with a poisonous little smile on his lips. He was in his element. Let's you and him fight! I'll provide all the slurs you'll need to bite him in the ass with . . . His eyes settled upon the official recipient of this slap across the face, Publisher Adlai desPortes. Publisher desPortes did not seem to be in any rush to avenge the honor of the *Miami Herald*. In fact, as his presumed French ancestors might have put it, he seemed decidedly *hors de combat*. He seemed dumbfounded, very much including the word's literal meaning: speechless. My God, being publisher of the *Miami Herald* wasn't supposed to involve such shit as *felonious!* It was supposed to involve going out to three-hour lunches with advertisers, politicians, CEOs, CFOs, college and foundation presidents, patrons of the arts, long-term celebrities, but also fifteen-minute stars hot off national TV dance shows, music shows, quiz shows, reality shows, and body shows, and TV dance-show, music-show, and game-show winners, all of whose presence demanded a suave, perpetually tanned, perpetually gregarious host, whose small talk never clicked and clacked because too many marbles got in the way, and whose very face brought out the most obsequious welcomes by name and aims to please by maître d's and owners of all the best restaurants. There was nothing suave about him at this moment, however. His mouth hung slightly open. Ed knew precisely what desPortes was asking himself... Have we committed a terrible blunder? Have we done what scientists call hopey-dopey research, in which the hope for a particular outcome skews the actual findings? Have we relied on the word of a man who we ourselves know to be a pathetic drunk? Was Drukovich's wall-full of forgeries missing for no other reason than that he had stored them somewhere else—if, in fact, they were forgeries at all? Have we hopey-doped Korolyov's every move... when, in fact, he was innocent of any duplicitous intent? Did he, Ed, know precisely what was running through the mind of the grandly named Adlai desPortes because that was precisely what was running through Edward T. Topping IV's mind, too?

Like a good pit bull, always spoiling for a fight,

Cutler seemed to look through the hides of all the Eds and Adlais before him and see all the limp spines. So it fell to him, the task of stiffening them and making them stand up straight.

"Beautiful!" he said, grinning as if the most jolly game in the world had just begun. "You gotta love it! Have you ever heard a bigger bagful of hot air in your life?... masquerading as a missile? Try to find one fact in our story that they deny... You won't find it, because they can't, either! They can't deny specifically what we have accused Korolyov of doing—because we haven't accused him of *anything!* I hope you know," he said, "that the moment they file a libel suit, they're inviting a real strip search."

Cutler not only smiled, he began rubbing his hands together as if he couldn't imagine any prospect more delightful. "This is all bluster. Why are they sending this thing—by hand—so early in the morning?" He scanned all the faces again, as if someone might get it immediately... Silence... Stone... "It's pure PR!" he said. "They wanna get on the record about how 'scurrilous' this all is, so that no more news stories will go out without their all-threatening denial included. That's all we've got here."

Ed felt the need to demonstrate his leadership by commenting in some trenchant way. But he couldn't think of anything to say in any way, trenchantly or otherwise. Besides, the letter was addressed to des-

Portes, wasn't it? It was up to him, right? Ed stared at Adlai desPortes. The man looked as if he had just been poleaxed at the base of the skull. He was a blank, out on his feet. Ed knew what he, the publisher, was thinking, because he, Ed, was thinking the same thing. Why had they let this ambitious juvenile, John Smith, have his way? He was a *boy!* He looked like he never had to shave! His whole case was based on a sudden burst of "truth" from the breast of a hopeless drunk—who was now dead. With this lawyer Julius Gudder brandishing the scalpel, Korolyov and Company would reduce Igor Drukovich's reputation and veracity to a stain on a bath mat.

Publisher desPortes came to life and, so to speak, took the words right out of Ed's mouth: "But Ira, aren't we relying awfully heavily on the testimony of a man with a couple of serious handicaps? One, he's dead and, two, he was dead drunk when he was alive?"

That drew some laughs, and thank God for that! Signs of life among the undead!

The pit bull, however, wasn't having any of it. His voice hit only higher, harsher, more haranguing tones as he said, "Not at all! Not at all! The man's sobriety or lack of it has nothing to do with it. This is a story about a man who led a double life, one open, one completely secret, and he's found dead—conceivably murdered—under mysterious circumstances. Whatever he says on the eve of his puzzling death becomes highly relevant, even if the facts cast a shadow on others."

Well put, Counselor! But it did nothing to slow Topping's tachycardia. Just then Stan Friedman came into the room with a very sad-looking John Smith in tow. Ed felt like addressing the whole group and saying, "Why, hello, Stan. Managed to get your ace investigative boy reporter back into the room, have you? But why? He's such a child, he can't even stand to *listen* to what he's done to us all for the sake of his own childish ambition. Couldn't even show enough backbone to stay in the room and listen to how it's turned out, could you? Short Hills, St. Paul's, Yale—*yaaaaaagggh!*... So this is what the paneled mahogany life turns out these days—weaklings who nevertheless think they have the birthright to do what they please, no matter how much it hurts mere commoners. No wonder you're hanging your head like that. No wonder you're afraid to look at anybody."

The little bastard, led, practically by the hand, by Stan, was heading straight for Ira Cutler. The entire room was quiet. Everybody, every shaken body, wanted to know what this was supposed to be about. Even Ira Cutler looked bemused, something he tried never to look. Stan left John's side and went to the pit bull's and said something, quite a bit, in fact, in a very low voice. After a while both glanced at John

Smith, whose head was hanging down so low, he probably couldn't see them.

Stan said, "John—"

John Smith walked toward the two of them, hangdog all the way. He nodded feebly at Cutler and said something to him in not much more than a whisper. From a pocket inside his blazer he pulled several sheets of paper and handed them to Cutler. They seemed to be handwritten. Cutler studied them for what seemed like ten minutes—then the whine of the metal lathe and Cutler said, "I think John wants me to apologize for him for ducking out of the room so much. He had his phone on vibrate and had to keep stepping outside to take these calls. Gloria, at Stan's desk, had his phone number so she could reach him. So far he's had queries"— Cutler raised the sheets of paper as evidence—"queries from literally all over the world, and they're all panicked about the same thing. In the relatively short time since the Korolyov Museum of Art opened, they have bought tens of *millions* of dollars' worth of paintings—or maybe not worth—from dealers representing Korolyov. And that's just the ones who have called the *Herald*. God knows what the total will be. I never knew he was selling pictures on the side." Cutler looked about the room... Nobody else had, either.

Cutler broke into a pit bull grin. "Hmmmm... I

wonder if he's taking a seventy-million-dollar tax deduction from forgeries he gave the museum to wipe out whatever he's making from forgeries on the side... On this list John has all the names, all the contact information, and he has taped recordings of the calls he made from Gloria's desk. He's had calls from galleries, dealers, other museums—well, you can imagine. But the one that intrigues me is the one from a guy who owns a small printing press in Stuttgart. He's worried because he thinks he'll be blamed for something he did in all innocence. For some Russian company he manufactured a catalogue of a Malevich show, in French, from the early nineteen twenties. He says the company provided paper from at least as far back as the twenties, old typefaces, layouts, designs, binding thread, the works. The guy thought this was for some kind of Malevich centennial, and hey, what good fun! Clever, too. Then he saw some Maleviches on the wire and internet coverage of John's story and the possibility of forgery by some Russians and put two and two together. Gentlemen, I think what we're looking at is maybe the biggest scam in art history unraveling right before our eyes."

Ed and everybody else had their eyes pinned on John Smith. ::::::My God, this kid's the one who has broken this case wide open! So why is he still there with his eyes all downcast, shaking his head?:::::: He heard Stan explaining to Ira Cutler that John Smith had been terribly stricken with guilt ever since Igor Drukovich was found dead, and he's still stricken. "He's convinced that if he hadn't written that original story on Drukovich — to provoke the very revelations that came to light this morning — Drukovich would still be alive. I'm telling you he's in a bad way."

Suddenly Ed burst forth with a loud voice and vehemence, in short, a roar, which nobody, including himself, knew he was capable of: "SMITH, COME HERE!" Now more frightened than forlorn, John Smith stared at his maximum editor, who said, "FEEL GUILTY ON YOUR OWN GODDAMNED TIME! YOU'RE WORKING FOR ME NOW, AND YOU'VE GOT A BIG STORY TO WRITE FOR TOMORROW!"

Nobody knew Edward T. Topping IV had it in him! All the Loop Syndicate and *Herald* brass saw and heard it happen! It was in that moment, they all decided, that Ed Topping — old "T-4" — had become a new man, a strong man, a real man, and a credit to the newspaper game.

Ed was surprised, too. Actually — and he knew it — he had thundered at John Smith out of fear, fear that the kid might mope off without writing the story that would get him, Ed Topping, and lots of others, out of a real jam.

* * *

Her talk with Nestor had reduced Magdalena's fear level from terrified to scared witless. There *is* a difference, and she could feel it; but she still got almost no sleep that night. She couldn't find a single position lying in bed in which she wasn't unpleasantly aware of her heartbeat. It wasn't all that fast, but it was primed to gallop at any moment. After a few hours... or that's what it felt like... she heard the latch on the front door turning, and that almost set her off. Her heart bolted, as if it wanted to attain insane levels of atrial fibrillation. She prayed to God to make it so—

—and it was so: only Amélia coming home. "Thank you, God!" She actually said it aloud, although under her breath.

The last two nights, Monday and Tuesday, Amélia had been at his place near the hospital, he being the thirty-two-year-old resident neurosurgeon suddenly in her life. Neurosurgeon! Surgeons were at the top of the status hierarchy at all hospitals, because they were men of action—surgeons were usually men—men of action who routinely held human life in their hands—literally, tactilely—and currently neurosurgeons were the most romantic of all. They faced the greatest risks of all surgeons. By the time someone had reached the point of needing brain surgery, he was already in a very bad way, and the rate of deaths in their field was the highest of all. (At the bottom of the ladder were dermatologists, pathologists, radiologists, and psychiatrists; no crises to go through, no emergency calls at night at home or, on days off, or over the hospital speaker system, no mortifying treks to waiting rooms in your scrubs, trying to think up the right rhetoric for telling the praying wrecks that their loved one just died on the table and why.) It occurred to Magdalena that Amélia's and her love lives were now reversed. It seemed like only yesterday that Amélia was Reggie-less and forlorn, while she was about to go out with a young, famous, rich, handsome, dashing Russian named Sergei. Now there was no more Sergei, she devoutly hoped. She was forlorn, and on top of that frightened half to death, while Amélia was busy getting it on with a young second-generation Cuban neurosurgeon who was romantic per se.

Magdalena must have finally fallen asleep for a couple of hours sometime after six, because she had glanced at the luminous hands on her alarm clock and *blip* she was waking up, and the same clock now said 9:30. Not a sound in the apartment; Amélia must still be sleeping, because she came home late, and this was one of her days off. Magdalena could have happily remained lying there, but all the circumstances of her miseries and fears came plunging back from out of the hypnopompic fog and made her too *wary* to stay lying there in supine vulnerability. So she got up and put a cotton bathrobe over the T-shirt she slept in and went into the bathroom and brought two cupped hands full of cold water up to her face and felt no better. Her heart was again drumming away a little too fast, and she had a dull headache and a great weariness such as she never had in the morning. She went to the kitchen and made herself a cup of Cuban coffee, and that better pull her out of this, the coffee, or—the main thing was to be *wary* and scream to Amélia and call 911 the *moment* she heard anything, *not* after she went to the door and listened more closely. She went into their tiny living room and sat down in one of the armchairs, but even holding the cup made her tired. So she got up to put it on the little makeshift coffee table and, being on her feet, turned on the TV, digiting the sound down very low, so as not to wake up Amélia. A Spanish channel was on, and she found herself watching a talk show. The host was a comedian who went by the name Hernán Loboloco. He preferred to be called Loboloco, not Hernán, because Loboloco meant Crazywolf and he was a comedian. His specialty was asking his guests serious questions in the voices of other people, famous people, such as asking a champion skateboarder about half-pipe stunts in the angry, hortatory voice of Cesar Chavez warning the Americans about encroachments. He was very good at it—he could also make extremely funny animal sounds, which he was likely to do at any moment—and Magdalena usually enjoyed Loboloco on the rare occasions she watched TV. But being so depressed and wary, she wasn't in shape to find anything funny, and the canned laughter irritated her enormously, even at low volume. Why would a comedian as good as Loboloco feel like he needed canned laughter? It didn't help the show, it made it sound cheesy and—

Her heart nearly jumped out of her rib cage. The lock on the door was turning and the door *burst open!* Magdalena jumped to her feet. Her new iPhone was *back in the bedroom—no time!*—no 911!—no Nestor! She wheeled about—and it was Amélia... with a big thirty-two-ounce Nalgene bottle of water she was tilting back and gulping down. Her skin was glowing with sweat. She was wearing black Lycra tights that came down to just below the knees and a black racer-back halter top with some crisscross cutouts. She wore no makeup and had her hair pulled back in a ponytail. Add it all together and it said spinning, the new fad. Everybody in the class—and rare was the Xersoul older than thirty-five—sat astride a stationary bicycle, one amid rank after rank after rank of them, and took orders from a teacher, male or female, who bellowed out commands and denunciations like a sadistic drill sergeant until everybody was pedaling away to the very limits of her lung capacity and leg strength and endurance. Three out of every four of these volunteer masochists were women so eager—to the point of desperation—to *get in shape,* they would subject themselves to . . . even this. Well . . . Magdalena would subject herself to this torture, too, except that classes cost thirty-five dollars a pop, and she had barely that much to keep herself fed—never mind fit—for a week, and even at that rate what little money she had left in the bank would run out in a month . . . and what was she going to do *then?*

Between gulps from the Nalgene container—she had progressed no farther than just inside the door—Amélia caught sight of Magdalena standing stock-still in front of the armchair on the balls of her feet, knees bent, as if she were about to leap or flee.

Amélia stopped gulping long enough to say, "Magdalena, what's that look on your face?"

"Well, I . . . *uhh* . . . I guess I'm just surprised. I thought you were still sleeping. I heard you come in last night, and it seemed pretty late."

Amélia took a few more gulps from the Nalgene bottle, whose volume must have been nearly as great as her head's.

"Since when are you into spinning?" said Magdalena.

"How do you know I've been spinning?"

"It's not hard . . . that outfit, the size of that water

bottle, your face is red—I don't mean red *sick,* I mean red *workout,* a really *hard* workout."

"To be honest, this is the first time I ever tried it," said Amélia.

"Well," said Magdalena, "what do you think?"

"Oh, it's great...I think...I mean, if you live through it! I never voluntarily worked that hard in my life! I mean, I...am...really wiped."

Magdalena said, "Why don't you sit down?"

"But I feel so—I have to take a shower."

"Oh, come on, sit down for a minute."

So Amélia sprawled in the easy chair and sighed and let her head tilt so far back she was looking straight up at the ceiling.

Magdalena smiled, and it occurred to her, in so many words, that this was the first time she had smiled even once over the past forty-eight hours, and she said, "This new interest in working out, I mean *really* working out, it wouldn't have anything to do with neurosurgery, would it?"

Amélia chuckled faintly and lifted her head and sat up straight. For the first time she noticed the television was on. The Loboloco show was still going, displaying a lot of grins and orthodontically perfect white teeth and gestures and moving lips...giving way to what were no doubt convulsions of laughter that made almost no sound at all, since Magdalena had turned the volume down... "What's that you're watching?" said Amélia.

"Ohhh... nothing," said Magdalena.

"Isn't that Loboloco?" said Amélia.

Immediately on the defensive, Magdalena said, "I wasn't really *watching* it, and I had the sound down really low, thinking you might still be asleep. I know Loboloco is stupid, but there are shows that are *stupid* stupid and some that are stupid *funny*... like *The Simpsons* and anything Will Ferrell is in, and I think Loboloco's kind of like that, stupid *funny,* or sometimes he is—" ::::::Let's get off Loboloco!:::::: "Wait, what were you *saying?*"

"*Saying?* Gosh, I already forgot," said Amélia.

"We were talking about spinning," said Magdalena, "and how you got into it..."

"I don't remember *what* I was saying," said Amélia. "Well... whatever... I found out today you can't exercise really hard and think about anything but *ohmygod can I make it through this!* You can't think about your problems at the same time. You should try it, Magdalena. I can *guarantee* you can't spin really hard and think about... all this other stuff, too. You have to give yourself a break! You know what I mean? But how *are* you feeling? You sound a little better."

Magdalena said, "A little... did I tell you I saw Nestor yesterday?"

"What?! Umm . . . no! You somehow failed to mention that one . . . Why?"

"Well, I just . . . I guess I just . . ."

"You just what?" said Amélia. "Come on, spit it out, girl!"

Sheepishly Magdalena said, "I called him."

"You *called* him? You probably made his decade *hahahah!* Oh boy, a few dozen Hail Marys have hit the jackpot."

"Well, I don't know. I called him because he's a cop. And I guess I just thought he could help me, you know, with what happened with Sergei."

"You *told* him about *that?*" said Amélia.

"Well, I mean, not about me being left naked in Sergei's bed. Nothing about Sergei's bed at all, or anything at all about how I know Sergei except that I was visiting him, me and some other people—and, you know, I didn't even tell him what time of day this all was. I just said the whole setup freaked me out, Sergei giving people orders like he's Mafia, the head of the Pizzo crime family or something, and he orders this huge bald-headed robot *goon* to drive me home—and maybe Nestor could tell me what to do besides go to the police, because if I did, it might get out, and then Sergei would send the goons after me for real."

"Isn't he on the outs, though?" said Amélia. "Like, is he even still a cop?"

"Well, I don't really know. I mean, we know he's been in the papers and everything, and even though some of it seemed pretty bad, it's like he's almost famous or something."

"The boy from Hialeah you couldn't wait to get rid of?"

Amélia had begun to smile, and it was pretty obvious that she found all this amusing, but Magdalena didn't hold it against her. Just having somebody to talk to helped her see things in a more organized way and, come to think of it, assess Nestor's place in the world.

"Yeah, I was kind of surprised myself," she said. "It was like he was different, though—you know? When I saw him the other day, it was like he was bigger or something or—"

"Maybe now he just has more time to go to the gym..."

"It's not *that*. I mean like if he got any *more* muscles, I don't know where he'd put them," said Magdalena. "But I don't mean physically bigger. I didn't really know who else to turn to, and when I first saw him again, I was like, 'Oh, that's the same old Nestor,' but then after I started telling him the story he just got like...so mature, *concerned,* like he was really listening to me, like he really wanted to *know,* you know?"

"Yeah," said Amélia, "because he's still madly in love with you."

"It wasn't that. It was like he was being all manly and taking charge. He wasn't listening just to make me feel better; he started firing questions at me, like really detailed cop questions, like he knew something about it and knew what to do. He was kind of...I don't know..." She laughed, to take the edge off the word she was about to use—"hot."

"Oh, my God, I thought I'd never see the day come when you called Nestor Camacho hot."

"I don't mean it like holy-shit, head-swivel hot... just like strong. You know what I mean? It made me wonder if maybe—" She cut it off there.

"You think you should have stayed with Nestor?"

"Well, I feel like maybe I took him for granted," said Magdalena. "I mean, no one else has really been there for me like he has. And when something happens, he's the one I think of first. That has to mean something, doesn't it?"

"Well, I can't really say you've gone *up* from there."

"Yeah, seriously, a perv, then a criminal," said Magdalena. "I was really going places, wasn't I."

"Don't be too hard on yourself," said Amélia. "I guess you could do worse than Nestor. He was really good for you. How did you guys leave it?"

"We didn't really," said Magdalena. "That's the weird thing. Just as I really started to feel something for him again, he was practically out of his chair."

"Typical guy."

"No, I mean literally. He was like, 'I gotta go call my partner' and ran out of there. It was so—what's the word? Valiant? Like he was going off to fight—oh, I don't know."

"Your knight from Hialeah!" said Amélia.

Suddenly they both were looking at the television screen. The pattern of light and shadows had changed abruptly. The Loboloco show had obviously been indoors, in some studio, and the contrast between bright parts of the screen and dark parts was minimal. But now you were outside in a punishing noonday sunlight that made the shadows of a building look like India ink in contrast. It was a courtyard of some three- or four-story building with wraparound terraces—no, interior walkways they were—that projected over the courtyard. Between the floors were big outdoor stairways, and at the foot of one of them what was obviously a person's body lay sprawled upon the last few stairs at a downward angle, headfirst, beneath some sort of white cloth, the head, too, meaning the person was dead. There were cops standing near it and a barrier, more or less, of yellow crime-scene tape holding back a bunch of mainly old people, quite a few of them leaning on aluminum walkers.

"Hey, turn that up for a second," said Amélia.

So Magdalena digited the volume up, and the face of a reporter appeared on the screen, a young woman with blond hair. "You ever notice they're always blondes, even on the Spanish channels?" Amélia said with some irritation. The blonde was holding a microphone and saying, "—and one of the mysteries is that the artist was known in this senior citizens condominium in Hallandale—although he seldom had anything to do with his neighbors—as Mr. Nicolai Kopinsky, and his apartment was apparently some sort of clandestine studio, which he never allowed anyone to enter."

"Oh, my God!" said Magdalena. "Did she say Hallandale?"

"Yeah, Hallandale."

"Oh, my God-d-d-d-d-d," said Magdalena, turning it into a cross between an exclamation and a moan and covering her face with her hands. "That's what Sergei said on the telephone, 'Hallandale.' All the rest of it was in Russian! Oh, my God-d-d-d in Heaven! I've gotta call Nestor! I gotta find out what's going on! Hallandale! Oh, dear God!"

She managed to collect herself long enough to run the few steps to her bedroom and pick up her phone and come back to the living room, where she wouldn't be alone, and scroll down her contact list to "Nestor." It began ringing almost immediately, and almost immediately a mechanical voice answered, "—is not available. If you would like to leave a—"

Magdalena looked at Amélia with absolute despair upon her face and said in a tone that suggested the end of the world, "He doesn't answer."

* * *

As soon as the elevator door opened on the second floor, Cat Posada was right there, waiting for him.

"Officer Camacho?" she said, as if she wasn't sure exactly who he was. "Follow me. I'll take you to the Chief's office."

Nestor studied her pretty face to detect . . . *anything*. It was about as easy to read as a brick. He couldn't stand it. This was the very girl he had lusted for on this very same spot . . . even in the middle of a crisis that had rendered him speechless at the time. Was it possible that she really *didn't* remember? All at once, without planning it, he heard himself saying, "Well, here we go again. The long march."

She was already walking when she glanced back and said, "Long march? It's just down the hall."

It was the tone that says, "I have no idea what you're talking about and it's not worth my time to find out." As before, she led him to just outside the Chief's office and stopped. "I'll let him know you're here." Then she disappeared inside.

In no time she came out of the office. "You can go in."

Nestor tried one last time to get a sign . . . from her lips, her eyes, her eyebrows, a tilt of the head—just a sign, *any* sign, goddamn it! Her loins weren't even a part of the anatomy at this moment. But all he got was the brick.

With a sigh Nestor went inside. The Chief didn't even look up at first. ::::::Christ!—*he's big*.:::::: He knew that, but now it was as if he were taking it in all over again. Not even his long-sleeved navy shirt with all the stars across the collars could hide the sheer physical might of the man. He had a ballpoint pen in his hand. He seemed to be absorbed in some computer-generated material on his desk. Then he looked up at Nestor. He didn't stand or offer his hand. He just said, "Office Camacho..." It wasn't a greeting. It was a statement of fact.

::::::*Hello, Chief?... It's good to see you, Chief?*:::::: None of it was going to sound right. He settled for the one word, "Chief." It was a plain acknowledgment.

"Have a seat, Officer." The Chief pointed to a straight-backed chair, armless, directly across from the desk. It was all such a replay of the first meeting, Nestor's heart sank. Once he sat down opposite the Chief, the Chief looked at him with a long, level gaze and said, "I have some things—"

He stopped and looked toward the open door. Cat was peeking through it. "Chief?" she said in a tentative voice. Then she beckoned, and the Chief got up, and they stood *tête-à-tête* in the doorway. Nestor could hear her first words, "Chief, I'm sorry to interrupt, but I thought you should know."

Then she lowered her voice until he could hear nothing but a low buzz. He thought he picked up the name Korolyov, but he also knew it could be sheer paranoia. Korolyov was the reason he had been disobeying the curfew, and that was no doubt the reason the Chief had ordered him to come in. ::::::*Oh, Dios Dios Dios*:::::: but he was too discouraged to pray to God. And why would God stoop to help him in the first place? ::::::"Oh, Lord, thou who hath forgiven even Judas, I have committed the sin of deceit, which involves cheating as well as lying"...Oh, the hell with it. It's hopeless! Judas at least did a lot to help Jesus before he sinned against him. And me? Why should God even bother to notice me? I don't deserve it...I'm truly fucked.::::::

The Chief and Cat kept buzzing at a very low volume. Occasionally he would cut loose out loud with a profane oath. "Oh, for Christ's sake"..."Jesus Christ"...and one "Holy freaking Jesus"...Fortunately, he actually said "freaking."

Finally he ended his little parley with Cat and started back toward his desk—but then wheeled about and said out loud as she headed back to *her* desk, "Tell 'em they can say whatever they want, but there's no way I would have turned that plane back, even if I'd known about it. The man's got a Russian passport, he hasn't been charged with anything, he hasn't been singled out as 'a person of interest,' nobody has even directly *accused* him of anything, not even the freaking *Herald*. So how do you turn the plane around? You've got a *notion?* Those newspaper execs have never run a damn thing in their lives. They just sit on committees and try to think up ways to justify their existence."

Nestor was dying to know what the Chief and Cat had been talking about. It had *Korolyov* written all over it. But Nestor was not going to risk so much as one question. ::::::"Oh, excuse me, Chief, but did you and Cat happen to be talking about—" I'm not going to open my mouth about that—especially not that—or anything else unless the Chief asks me a direct question.::::::

The Chief sat down at his desk, and ::::::I knew it! I knew it! He still has on his angry scowl from thinking about everyone who gave him so much outrageous grief. . . :::::: The Chief cast his eyes down and shook his head in a semaphore that said, "Clueless fucking assholes," then looked up at Nestor with *clueless fucking assholes* still written all over his face and said, "Okay, where were we?"

::::::Damn! That scowl! He thinks that I must be one of them, the one who caused him to forget.::::::

"Oh, yeah, I remember," said the Chief. "I have some things of yours here."

With that, he leaned so far over to one side of his desk that even his great hulk almost disappeared. Nestor could hear him opening a lower drawer. When he brought himself up again, he had something unwieldy in his hands . . . turned out to be a pair of pale-gray boxlike containers, one small and one considerably bigger. Cops called them "malcontainers." They were for storing evidence in criminal cases. The Chief put them in front of him on the desk. He opened the smaller one—

—and the first sign from On High that Nestor got was a flash of gold as the Chief withdrew it from the container. Now he could see the whole thing as the Chief extended his arm across the desk and handed it to him.

"Your badge" was all he said.

Nestor stared at it in the palm of his hand as if he had never seen such a wondrous object before. Meantime, the Chief was opening the other container . . . and extending a large ungainly cincture of leather and metal across the desk. It was a Glock 9 in a leather holster attached to a gun belt.

"Your service revolver," said the Chief—tonelessly.

Nestor now had the badge in one hand and was supporting the Glock and its rig with the other. He stared at them . . . probably longer than he should have . . . before turning his eyes up toward the

Chief... and managing to say in a shaky voice, "Does this mean..."

"Yeah," said the Chief, "that's what it means. You're restored to active duty. Your next shift with the Crime Suppression Unit will begin at four p.m. tomorrow."

Nestor was so overcome by this miracle, he didn't know how to respond. So he tried, "Thank you—*uhhh*—"

The Chief spared him the struggle. "Now, I have a word of advice—no, I take that back. This is an order. What I'm doing is going to create a certain amount of static. But I don't want to hear about you talking to the press in any way, shape, or form. You got that?"

Nestor nodded yes.

"You can be sure you're going to be *in the press* tomorrow. You understand? The DA is going to announce that he is dropping the charges against the teacher at Lee de Forest—José Estevez—due to lack of evidence... They'll mention you. You were the one who exposed the 'evidence' for what it was, a plot by a bunch of frightened boys to protect that punk so-called gang leader Dubois. I *want* you in the press in that regard. But what I said still goes. You don't *talk* to the press. You don't *confirm* information. You don't *respond* to the press in any way. And I'll say it again: That's... an... *order.*"

"I understand, Chief." Somehow the way he said

it—*I understand, Chief*—made him *feel* that he was back on the force again.

The Chief put his forearms on the desk and leaned as far toward Nestor as he possibly could...and for the first time betrayed an emotion other than his note of stern do-not-defy-me authority. He let his lips widen all the way across his face...and his eyes came alive...and the flesh over his cheekbones welled up into two soft pillows of warmth...and he said... "Welcome back, Camacho."

He said it softly...and it was only a smile from a policeman in the decrepit downtown of Miami, Florida, in the first place...but did any light ever come from any more radiant place On High...or render a man's soul calmer or more blessed...or lift him more completely clear of this trough of mortal error we are fated to live out our lives in?

Outside, on the street, Nestor didn't feel vindicated or redeemed or triumphant or anything like that. He felt lightheaded, disoriented, as if a staggering load he had been carrying for a very long time had been removed from his back by magic, and the Big Heat Lamp was up there roasting his coconut as usual, and he didn't even know in what direction he was walking. He had no idea what street it was. He felt completely, totally out of it... but wait a minute, he really should call her anyway.

He scrolled down his contact list until he found her name and tapped the iPhone's glass face.

In practically no time she answered, "Nestor!"

"Well, I have some good news. The Chief gave me my badge and my revolver back. I'm reinstated; I'm a real cop again."

"Oh, my God, Nestor! That's... *so... wonderful!*" said Ghislaine.

About the Author

Tom Wolfe is the author of more than a dozen books, among them *The Electric Kool-Aid Acid Test, The Right Stuff, The Bonfire of the Vanities, A Man in Full,* and *I Am Charlotte Simmons*. A native of Richmond, Virginia, he earned his BA at Washington and Lee University and a PhD in American Studies at Yale. He received the National Book Foundation's 2010 Medal for Distinguished Contribution to American Letters. He lives in New York City.